BY DORIS LESSING

The Grass Is Singing
This Was the Old Chief's Country (short stories)
Five (short novels)
Retreat to Innocence
The Habit of Loving (short stories)
In Pursuit of the English
Going Home
Fourteen Poems
The Golden Notebook
A Man and Two Women (short stories)

Children of Violence:
  Martha Quest
  A Proper Marriage
  A Ripple from the Storm
  Landlocked
  Final volume

CHILDREN
of VIOLENCE

volume one
MARTHA QUEST
volume two
A PROPER
MARRIAGE

Doris Lessing

Simon and Schuster, New York, 1964

First Printing

Library of Congress Catalog Card Number: 64-22409
Design by Betty Crumley
Manufactured in the United States of America
Printed by The Murray Printing Company, Forge Village, Mass.
Bound by Book Press, Brattleboro, Vermont

12|66

Publisher's Note
Martha Quest and *A Proper Marriage* are the first two of what will be a series of five novels by Doris Lessing. The overall title of this series is *Children of Violence*.

ONE

MARTHA QUEST

part one

*I am so tired of it, and also tired of the future
before it comes.*

OLIVE SCHREINER

1

Two elderly women sat knitting on that part of the verandah which
was screened from the sun by a golden shower creeper; the tough
stems were so thick with flower it was as if the glaring afternoon was
dammed against them in a surf of its own light made visible in the
dripping, orange-coloured clusters. Inside this coloured barrier was
a darkened recess, rough mud walls (the outer walls of the house
itself) forming two sides, the third consisting of a bench loaded with
painted petrol tins which held pink and white geraniums. The sun
splashed liberal gold through the foliage, over the red cement floor,
and over the ladies. They had been here since lunchtime, and would
remain until sunset, talking, talking incessantly, their tongues merci-
fully let off the leash. They were Mrs. Quest and Mrs. Van Rensberg;
and Martha Quest, a girl of fifteen, sat on the steps in full sunshine,
clumsily twisting herself to keep the glare from her book with her
own shadow.

She frowned, and from time to time glanced up irritably at the
women, indicating that their gossip made it difficult to concentrate.
But then, there was nothing to prevent her moving somewhere else;

and her spasms of resentment when she was asked a question, or her name was used in the family chronicling, were therefore unreasonable. As for the ladies, they sometimes allowed their eyes to rest on the girl with that glazed look which excludes a third person, or even dropped their voices; and at these moments she lifted her head to give them a glare of positive contempt; for they were seasoning the dull staple of their lives—servants, children, cooking—with a confinement or scandal of some kind; and since she was reading Havelock Ellis on sex, and had taken good care they should know it, the dropped voices had the quality of an anomaly. Or rather, she was not actually reading it: she read a book that had been lent to her by the Cohen boys at the station, while Ellis lay, like an irritant, on the top step, with its title well in view. However, there are certain rites in the talk of matrons, and Martha, having listened to such talk for a large part of her life, should have learned that there was nothing insulting, or even personal, intended. She was merely expected to play the part "young girl" against their own familiar roles.

At the other end of the verandah, on two deck chairs planted side by side and looking away over the bush and the mealie fields, were Mr. Quest and Mr. Van Rensberg; and they were talking about crops and the weather and the native problem. But their backs were turned on the women with a firmness which said how welcome was this impersonal talk to men who lived shut into the heated atmosphere of the family for weeks at a time, with no refuge but the farmwork. Their talk was as familiar to Martha as the women's talk; the two currents ran sleepily on inside her, like the movements of her own blood, of which she was not conscious except as an ache of irritation when her cramped position made her shift her long, bare and sunburnt legs. Then, when she heard the nagging phrases "The Government expects the farmers to . . ." and "The kaffirs are losing all respect because . . . ," she sat up sharply; and the irritation overflowed into a flood of dislike for both her parents. Everything was the same; intolerable that they should have been saying the same things ever since she could remember; and she looked away from them, over the veld.

In the literature that was her tradition, the word *farm* evokes an image of something orderly, compact, cultivated; a neat farmhouse in a pattern of fields. Martha looked over a mile or so of bush to a strip of pink ploughed land; and then the bush, dark green and sombre, climbed a ridge to another patch of exposed earth, this time a clayish yellow; and then, ridge after ridge, fold after fold, the bush stretched to a line of blue kopjes. The fields were a timid intrusion on a landscape hardly marked by man; and the hawk which circled in mile-wide sweeps over her head saw the house, crouched on its long hill, the cluster of grass huts which was the native compound huddled on a lower rise half a mile away; perhaps a dozen patches of naked soil—and then nothing to disturb that ancient, down-peering eye, nothing that a thousand generations of his hawk ancestors had not seen.

The house, raised high on its eminence into the blue and sweeping currents of air, was in the centre of a vast basin, which was bounded by mountains. In front, there were seven miles to the Dumfries Hills; west, seven miles of rising ground to the Oxford Range; seven miles east, a long swelling mountain which was named Jacob's Burg. Behind, there was no defining chain of kopjes, but the land travelled endlessly, without limit, and faded into a bluish haze, like that hinterland to the imagination we cannot do without—the great declivity was open to the north.

Over it all curved the cloudless African sky, but Martha could not look at it, for it pulsed with light; she must lower her eyes to the bush; and that was so familiar the vast landscape caused her only the prickling feeling of claustrophobia.

She looked down at her book. She did not want to read it; it was a book on popular science, and even the title stiffened her into a faint but unmistakable resentment. Perhaps, if she could have expressed what she felt, she would have said that the calm factual air of the writing was too distant from the uncomfortable emotions that filled her; perhaps she was so resentful of her surroundings and her parents that the resentment overflowed into everything near her. She put that book down and picked up Ellis. Now, it is hardly possible to be bored by a book on sex when one is fifteen, but she was restless because this collection of interesting facts seemed to have so little to do with her own problems. She lifted her eyes and gazed speculatively at Mrs. Van Rensberg, who had had eleven children.

She was a fat, good-natured, altogether pleasant woman in a neat flowered cotton dress, which was rather full and long, and, with the white kerchief folded at the neck, gave her the appearance of a picture of one of her own grandmothers. It was fashionable to wear long skirts and tie a scarf loosely at the neck, but in Mrs. Van Rensberg the fashion arranged itself obstinately into that other pattern. Martha saw this, and was charmed by it; but she was looking at the older woman's legs. They were large and shapeless, veined purple under the mask of sunburn, and ended in green sandals, through which her calloused feet unashamedly splayed for comfort. Martha was thinking with repugnance, Her legs are like that because she has had so many children.

Mrs. Van Rensberg was what is described as uneducated; and for this she might apologize, without seeming or feeling in the slightest apologetic, when a social occasion demanded it—for instance, when Mrs. Quest aggressively stated that Martha was clever and would have a career. That the Dutchwoman could remain calm and good-natured on such occasions was proof of considerable inner strength, for Mrs. Quest used the word "career" not in terms of something that Martha might actually do, such as doctoring, or the law, but as a kind of stick to beat the world with, as if she were saying, "My daughter will be somebody, whereas yours will only be married." Mrs. Quest had been a pretty and athletic-looking English girl with light-brown hair and blue eyes as candid as spring sunshine; and she was now exactly as she would have been had she remained in England: a rather tired and disappointed but decided matron, with ambitious plans for her children.

Both ladies had been living in this farming district for many years, seventy miles from the nearest town, which was itself a backwater; but no part of the world can be considered remote these days; their homes had the radio, and newspapers coming regularly from what they respectively considered as Home—Tory newspapers from England for the Quests, nationalist journals from the Union of South Africa for the Van Rensbergs. They had absorbed sufficient of the spirit of the times to know that their children might behave in a way which they instinctively thought shocking, and as for the book Martha now held, its title had a clinical sound quite outside their own experience. In fact, Martha would have earned nothing but a good-natured and traditional sigh of protest, had not her remaining on the steps been in itself something of a challenge. Just as Mrs. Quest found it necessary to protest, at half-hourly intervals, that Martha would get sunstroke if she did not come into the shade, so she eventually remarked that she supposed it did no harm for girls to read that sort of book; and once again Martha directed towards them a profoundly scornful glare, which was also unhappy and exasperated; for she felt that in some contradictory way she had been driven to use this book as a means of asserting herself, and now found the weapon had gone limp and useless in her hands.

Three months before, her mother had said angrily that Epstein and Havelock Ellis were disgusting. "If people dug up the remains of this civilization a thousand years hence, and found Epstein's statues and that man Ellis, they would think we were just savages." This was at the time when the inhabitants of the colony, introduced unwillingly through the chances of diplomacy and finance to what they referred to as "modern art," were behaving as if they had been severally and collectively insulted. Epstein's statues were not fit, they averred, to represent them even indirectly. Mrs. Quest took that remark from a leader in the *Zambesia News;* it was probably the first time she had made any comment on art or literature for twenty years. Martha then had borrowed a book on Epstein from the Cohen boys at the station. Now, one of the advantages of not having one's taste formed in a particular school is that one may look at the work of an Epstein with the same excited interest as at a Michelangelo. And this is what Martha did. She felt puzzled, and took the book of reproductions to her mother. Mrs. Quest was busy at the time, and had never found an opportunity since to tell Martha what was so shocking and disgusting in these works of art. And so with Havelock Ellis.

Now Martha was feeling foolish, even let down. She knew, too, that she was bad-tempered and boorish. She made resolutions day after day that from now on she would be quite different. And yet a fatal demon always took possession of her, so that at the slightest remark from her mother she was impelled to take it up, examine it, and hand it back, like a challenge—and by then the antagonist was no longer there; Mrs. Quest was simply not interested.

"Ach," said Mrs. Van Rensberg, after a pause, "it's not what you read that matters, but how you behave." And she looked with good-natured affection towards Martha, who was flushed with anger and with sunshine. "You'll have a headache, my girl," she added automatically; and Martha bent stubbornly to her book, without moving, and her eyes filled with tears.

The two women began discussing, as was natural, how they had behaved when young, but with reservations, for Mrs. Van Rensberg sensed that her own experience included a good deal that might shock the English lady; so what they exchanged were not the memories of their behaviour, but the phrases of their respective traditions, which sounded very similar—Mrs. Van Rensberg was a member of the Dutch Reformed Church; the Quests, Church of England. Just as they never discussed politics, so they never discussed—but what did they discuss? Martha often reflected that their years-old friendship had survived just because of what had been left out, everything of importance, that is; and the thought caused the girl the swelling dislike of her surroundings which was her driving emotion. On the other hand, since one lady was conservative British and the other conservative Afrikaans, this friendship could be considered as a triumph of tact and good feeling over almost insuperable obstacles, since they were bound, by those same traditions, to dislike each other. This view naturally did not recommend itself to Martha, whose standards of friendship were so high she was still waiting for that real, that ideal friend to present himself.

"*The Friend,*" she had copied in her diary, "*is some fair floating isle of palms eluding the mariner in Pacific seas . . .*" And so down the page to the next underlined sentence: "*There goes a rumour that the earth is inhabited, but the shipwrecked mariner has not seen a footprint on the shore.*" And the next: "*Our actual friends are but distant relations of those to whom we pledged.*"

And could Mrs. Van Rensberg be considered even as a *distant* relation? Clearly not. It would be a betrayal of the sacred name of friendship.

Martha listened (not for the first time) to Mrs. Van Rensberg's long account of how she had been courted by Mr. Van Rensberg, given with a humorous deprecation of everything that might be described (though not by Martha, instinctively obedient to the taboos of the time) as Romance. Mrs. Quest then offered an equally humorous though rather drier account of her own engagement. These two heavily, though unconsciously, censored tales at an end, they looked towards Martha, and sighed, resignedly, at the same moment. Tradition demanded from them a cautionary moral, helpful to the young, the fruit of their sensible and respectable lives; and the look on Martha's face inhibited them both.

Mrs. Van Rensberg hesitated, and then said firmly (the firmness was directed against her own hesitation), "A girl must make men respect her." She was startled at the hatred and contempt in Martha's suddenly raised eyes, and looked for support towards Mrs. Quest.

"That's right," said Mrs. Quest, rather uncertainly. "A man will never marry a girl he does not respect."

Martha slowly sat up, closing her book as if it were of no more use to her, and stared composedly at them. She was now quite white with the effort of controlling that hatred. She got up, and said in a low tight voice, "You are loathsome, bargaining and calculating and . . ." She was unable to continue. "You are *disgusting,*" she ended lamely, with trembling lips. Then she marched off down the garden, and ran into the bush.

The two ladies watched her in silence. Mrs. Quest was upset, for she did not know why her daughter thought her disgusting, while Mrs. Van Rensberg was trying to find a sympathetic remark likely to be acceptable to her friend.

"She's so difficult," murmured Mrs. Quest apologetically; and Mrs. Van Rensberg said, "It's the age, my Marnie's just as bad." She did not know she had failed to find the right remark: Mrs. Quest did not consider her daughter to be on a level with Marnie, whom she found in altogether bad taste, wearing grown-up clothes and lipstick at fifteen, and talking about "boys." Mrs. Van Rensberg was quite unconscious of the force of her friend's feeling. She dismissed her strictness with Martha as one of those English foibles; and besides, she knew Marnie to be potentially a sensible woman, a good wife and mother. She continued to talk about Marnie, while Mrs. Quest listened with the embarrassment due to a social *gaffe,* saying "Quite" or "Exactly," thinking that her daughter's difficulty was caused by having to associate with the wrong type of child, meaning Marnie herself. But the Dutchwoman was unsnubbable, since her national pride was as deep as the Englishwoman's snobbishness, and soon their conversation drifted back to servants and cooking. That evening, each would complain to her husband—one, with the English inarticulateness over matters of class, that Mrs. Van Rensberg was "really so trying," while the other, quite frankly, said that these rooineks got her down, they were all the same, they thought they owned the earth they walked on. Then, from unacknowledged guilt, they would ring each other up on the district telephone, and talk for half an hour or so about cooking and servants. Everything would continue as usual, in fact.

In the meantime, Martha, in an agony of adolescent misery, was lying among the long grass under a tree, repeating to herself that her mother was hateful, all these old women hateful, every one of these relationships, with their lies, evasions, compromises, wholly disgusting. For she was suffering that misery peculiar to the young, that they are going to be cheated by circumstances out of the full life every nerve and instinct is clamouring for.

After a short time, she grew more composed. A self-preserving nerve had tightened in her brain, and with it her limbs and even the muscles of her face became set and hardened. It was with a bleak and puzzled look that she stared at a sunlit and glittering bush which stood at her feet; for she did not see it, she was seeing herself, and in the only way she was equipped to do this—through literature. For if one reads novels from earlier times, and if novels accurately reflect, as we hope and trust they do, the life of their era, then one is forced to conclude that being young was much easier then than it is now. Did X and Y and Z, those blithe heroes and heroines, loathe school, despise their parents and teachers who never understood them, spend years of their lives fighting to free themselves from an environment they considered altogether beneath them? No, they did not; while in a hundred years' time people will read the novels of this century and conclude that everyone (no less) suffered adolescence like a disease, for they will hardly be able to lay hands on a novel which does not describe the condition. What then? For Martha was tormented, and there was no escaping it.

Perhaps, she thought (retreating into the sour humour that was her refuge at such moments), one should simply take the years from, let us say, fourteen to twenty as read, until those happier times arrive when adolescents may, and with a perfectly clear conscience, again enjoy themselves? How lucky, she thought, those coming novelists, who would be able to write cheerfully, and without the feeling that they were evading a problem: "Martha went to school in the usual way, liked the teachers, was amiable with her parents, and looked forward with confidence to a happy and well-spent life"! But then (and here she suffered a twisting spasm of spite against those cold-minded mentors who so persistently analyzed her state, and in so many volumes), what would they have to write about?

That defensive spite released her, and it was almost with confidence that she again lay back, and began to consider herself. For if she was often resentfully conscious that she was expected to carry a burden that young people of earlier times knew nothing about, then she was no less conscious that she was developing a weapon which would enable her to carry it. She was not only miserable, she could focus a dispassionate eye on that misery. This detached observer, felt perhaps as a clear-lit space situated just behind the forehead, was the gift of the Cohen boys at the station, who had been lending her books for the last two years. Joss Cohen tended towards economics and sociology, which she read without feeling personally implicated. Solly Cohen was in love (there is no other word for it) with psychology; he passionately defended everything to do with it, even when his heroes contradicted each other. And from these books Martha had gained a clear picture of herself, from the outside. She was adolescent, and therefore bound to be unhappy; British, and therefore uneasy and defensive; in the fourth decade of the twentieth century, and therefore inescapably beset with problems of race and class; female, and obliged to repudiate the shackled women of the past. She was tormented with guilt and responsibility and self-consciousness; and she did not regret the torment, though there were moments when she saw quite clearly that in making her see herself thus the Cohen boys took a malicious delight which was only too natural. There were moments, in fact, when she hated them.

But what they perhaps had not foreseen was that this sternly objective picture of herself merely made her think, no doubt unreasonably, Well, if all this has been said, why do I have to go through with it? If we *know* it, why do we have to go through the painful business of living it? She felt, though dimly, that now it was time to move on to something new, the act of giving names to things should be enough.

Besides, the experts themselves seemed to be in doubt as to how she should see herself. There was the group which stated that her life was already determined when she still crouched sightless in the womb of Mrs. Quest. She grew through phases of fish and lizard and monkey, rocked in the waters of ancient seas, her ears lulled by the rhythm of the tides. But these tides, the pulsing blood of Mrs. Quest, sang no uncertain messages to Martha, but songs of anger, or love, or fear or resentment, which sank into the passive brain of the infant, like a doom.

Then there were those who said it was the birth itself which set Martha on a fated road. It was during the long night of terror, the night of the difficult birth, when the womb of Mrs. Quest convulsed and fought to expel its burden through the unwilling gates of bone (for Mrs. Quest was rather old to bear a first child), it was during that birth, from which Martha emerged shocked and weary, her face temporarily scarred purple from the forceps, that her character and therefore her life were determined for her.

And what of the numerous sects who agreed on only one thing, that it was the first five years of life which laid an unalterable basis for everything that followed? During those years (though she could not remember them), events had occurred which had marked her fatally forever. For the feeling of fate, of doom, was the one message they all had in common. Martha, in violent opposition to her parents, was continually being informed that their influence on her was unalterable, and that it was much too late to change herself. She had reached the point where she could not read one of these books without feeling as exhausted as if she had just concluded one of her arguments with her mother. When a native bearer came hastening over the veld with yet another parcel of books from the Cohen boys, she felt angry at the mere sight of them, and had to fight against a tired reluctance before she could bring herself to read them. There were, at this very moment, half a dozen books lying neglected in her bedroom, for she knew quite well that if she read them she would only be in possession of yet more information about herself, and with even less idea of how to use it.

But if to read their books made her unhappy, those occasions when she could visit them at the store were the happiest of her life. Talking to them exhilarated her, everything seemed easy. She walked over to the kaffir store when her parents made the trip into the station; sometimes she got a lift from a passing car. Sometimes, though secretly, since this was forbidden, she rode in on her bicycle. But there was always an uneasiness about this friendship, because of Mrs. Quest; only last week, she had challenged Martha. Being what she was, she could not say outright, "I don't want you to know Jewish shopkeepers." She launched into a tirade about how Jews and Greeks exploited the natives worse than anyone, and ended by saying that she did not know what to do with Martha, who seemed bent on behaving so as to make her mother as unhappy as possible. And for the first time that Martha could remember, she wept; and though her words were dishonest, her emotion was not. Martha had been deeply disturbed by those tears.

Yesterday, Martha had been on the point of getting out her bicycle in order to ride in to the station, so badly did she need to see the Cohen boys, when the thought of another scene with her mother checked her. Guiltily, she left the bicycle where it was. And now, although she wanted more than anything else to tell them about her silly and exaggerated behaviour in front of Mrs. Van Rensberg, so that they might laugh good-naturedly at it, and restore it to proportion, she could not make the effort to rise from under the big tree, let alone get out the bicycle and go secretly into the station, hoping she would not be missed. And so she remained under the tree, whose roots were hard under her back, like a second spine, and looked up through the leaves to the sky, which shone in a bronze clamour of light. She ripped the fleshy leaves between her fingers, and thought again of her mother and Mrs. Van Rensberg. She would *not* be like Mrs. Van Rensberg, a fat and earthy housekeeping woman; she would *not* be bitter and nagging and dissatisfied, like her mother. But then, who was she to be like? Her mind turned towards the heroines she had been offered, and discarded them. There seemed to be a gap between herself and the past, and so her thoughts swam in a mazed and unfed way through her mind, and she sat up, rubbing her stiffened back, and looked down the aisles of stunted trees, over a wash of pink feathery grass, to the red clods of a field which was invisible from the house.

There moved a team of oxen, a plough, a native driver with his long whip, and at the head of the team a small black child, naked except for a loincloth, tugging at the strings which passed through the nostrils of the leaders of the team. The driver she did not like— he was a harsh and violent man who used that whip with too much zest; but the pity she refused herself flooded out and surrounded the black child like a protective blanket. And again her mind swam and shook, like clearing water, and now, instead of one black child, she saw a multitude, and so lapsed easily into her familiar daydream.

She looked away over the ploughed land, across the veld to the Dumfries Hills, and refashioned that unused country to the scale of her imagination. There arose, glimmering whitely over the harsh scrub and the stunted trees, a noble city, set foursquare and colonnaded along its falling, flower-bordered terraces. There were splashing fountains, and the sound of flutes; and its citizens moved, grave and beautiful, black and white and brown together; and these groups of elders paused, and smiled with pleasure at the sight of the children—the blue-eyed, fair-skinned children of the North playing hand in hand with the bronze-skinned, dark-eyed children of the South. Yes, they smiled and approved these many-fathered children, running and playing among the flowers and the terraces, through the white pillars and tall trees of this fabulous and ancient city . . .

It was about a year later. Martha was seated beneath the same tree, and in rather the same position, her hands full of leaves which she was unconsciously rubbing to a green and sticky mess. Her head was filled with the same vision, only more detailed. She could have drawn a plan of that city, from the central market place to the four gates. Outside one of the gates stood her parents, the Van Rensbergs, in fact most of the people of the district, forever excluded from the golden city because of their pettiness of vision and small understanding; they stood grieving, longing to enter, but barred by a stern and remorseless Martha—for unfortunately one gets nothing, not even a dream, without paying heavily for it, and in Martha's version of the golden age there must always be at least one person standing at the gate to exclude the unworthy. She heard footsteps, and turned her head to find Marnie picking her way down the native path, her high heels rocking over the stones.

"Hey," said Marnie excitedly, "heard the news?"

Martha blinked her eyes clear of the dream, and said, rather stiffly, "Oh, hullo." She was immediately conscious of the difference between herself and Marnie, whose hair was waved, who wore lipstick and nail varnish, and whose face was forced into an effect of simpering maturity, which continually vanished under pressure from her innate good sense. Now she was excited she was like a healthy schoolgirl who had been dressing up for fun; but at the sight of the sprawling and undignified Martha, who looked rather like an overgrown child of eleven, with a ribbon tying her lanky blond hair, and a yoked dress in flowered print, she remembered her own fashionable dress, and sat primly on the grass, placed her black heels together, and looked down at her silk-stockinged legs with satisfaction.

"My sister's getting married," she announced.

There were five sisters, two already married, and Martha asked, "Who, Marie?" For Marie was next, according to age.

"No, not Marie," said Marnie with impatient disparagement. "Marie'll never get herself a man, she hasn't got what it takes."

At the phrase "get herself a man," Martha flushed, and looked away, frowning. Marnie glanced doubtfully at her, and met a glance of such scorn that she blushed in her turn, though she did not know what for.

"You haven't even asked who," she said accusingly, though with a timid note; and then burst out: "Man, believe it or not, but it's Stephanie."

Stephanie was seventeen, but Martha merely nodded.

Damped, Marnie said, "She's doing well for herself, too, say what you like. He's got a V-8, and he's got a bigger farm than Pop."

"Doing well for herself" caused Martha yet another internal shudder. Then the thought flashed across her mind: I criticize my mother for being a snob, but despise the Van Rensbergs with a clear conscience, because my snobbishness is intellectual. She could not afford to keep this thought clear in her mind; the difficult, painful process of educating herself was all she had to sustain her. But she managed to say after a pause, though with genuine difficulty, "I'm glad, it will be nice to have another wedding." It sounded flat.

Marnie sighed, and glanced down at her pretty fingernails for comfort. She would have so much liked an intimate talk with a girl her own age. Or rather, though there were girls of her own age among the Afrikaans community growing up around her father's farm, she would have liked to be friends with Martha, whom she admired. She would have liked to say, with a giggle, that she was sixteen herself and could get a man, with luck, next year, like Stephanie. Finding herself confronted by Martha's frowning eyes, she wished she might return to the verandah, where the two mothers would be discussing the fascinating details of the courtship and wedding. But it was a tradition that the men should talk to the men, women with the women, and the children should play together. Marnie did not consider herself a child, though Martha, it seemed, did. She thought that if she could return by herself to the verandah, she might join the women's talk, whereas if Martha came with her they would be excluded. She said, "My mom's telling your mom."

Martha said, with that unaccountable resentment, "Oh, she'll have a wonderful time gossiping about it." Then she added quickly, trying to make amends for her ungraciousness, "She'll be awfully pleased."

"Oh, I know your mom doesn't want you to marry young, she wants you to make a career," said Marnie generously.

But again Martha winced, saying angrily, "Oh she'd love it if I married young."

"Would you like it, hey?" suggested Marnie, trying to create an atmosphere where they might "have a good talk."

Martha laughed satirically and said, "Marry young? Me? I'd die first. Tie myself down to babies and housekeeping . . ."

Marnie looked startled, and then abashed. She remarked defiantly, "Mom says you're sweet on Joss Cohen." At the sight of Martha's face she giggled with fright. "Well, he's sweet on you, isn't he?"

Martha gritted her teeth, and ground out, "*Sweet* on!"

"Hell, he likes you, then."

"Joss Cohen," said Martha angrily.

"He's a nice boy. Jews can be nice, and he's clever, like you."

"You make me sick," said Martha, reacting, or so she thought, to this racial prejudice.

Again Marnie's good-natured face drooped with puzzled hurt, and she gave Martha an appealing look. She stood up, wanting to escape.

But Martha slid down a flattened swathe of long grass, and scrambled to her feet. She rubbed the back of her thighs under the cotton dress, saying, "Ooh, taken all the skin off."

Her way of laughing at herself, almost clowning, at these graceless movements, made Marnie uncomfortable in a new way. She thought it extraordinary that Martha should wear such clothes, behave like a clumsy schoolboy, at sixteen, and apparently not mind. But she accepted what was in intention an apology, and looked at the title of the book Martha held—it was a life of Cecil Rhodes—and asked, was it interesting? Then the two girls went together up the native path, which wound under the low scrubby trees, through yellow grass that reached to their shoulders, to the clearing where the house stood.

It was built native style, with mud walls and thatched roof, and had been meant to last two seasons, for the Quests had come to the colony after seeing an exhibition in London which promised new settlers that they might become rich on maize-growing almost from one year to the next. This had not happened, and the temporary house was still in use. It was a long oval, divided across to make rooms, and around it had been flung out projecting verandahs of grass. A square, tin-roofed kitchen stood beside it. This kitchen was now rather tumble-down, and the roof was stained and rusted. The roof of the house too had sagged, and the walls had been patched so often with fresh mud that they were all colours, from dark rich red through dulling yellow to elephant grey. There were many different kinds of houses in the district, but the Quests' was original because a plan which was really suitable for bricks and proper roofing had been carried out in grass and mud and stamped dung.

The girls could see their mothers sitting behind the screen of golden shower; and at the point where they should turn to climb the verandah steps, Martha said hastily, "You go," and went off into the house, while Marnie thankfully joined the women.

Martha slipped into the front room like a guilty person, for the people on the verandah could see her by turning their heads. When the house was first built, there had been no verandahs. Mrs. Quest had planned the front of the house to open over the veld "like the prow of a ship," as she herself gaily explained. There were windows all around it, so that there had been a continuous view of mountains and veld, lightly intersected by strips of wall, like a series of framed "views." Now the verandah dipped over them, and the room was rather dark. There were chairs and settees, and a piano on one side, and a dining table on the other. Years ago, when the rugs and chintzes were fresh, this had been a pretty room, with cream-washed walls and smooth black linoleum under the rugs. Now it was not merely faded, but dingy and overcrowded. No one played the piano. The silver teatray that had been presented to Mrs. Quest's grandfather on retirement from his bank stood on the sideboard among bits of rock, nuts and bolts from the ploughs, and bottles of medicine.

When Mrs. Quest first arrived, she was laughed at, because of the piano and the expensive rugs, because of her clothes, because she had left visiting cards on her neighbours. She laughed herself now, ruefully, remembering her mistakes.

In the middle of the floor was a pole of tough thornwood, to hold the end of the ridgepole. It had lain for weeks in a bath of strong chemical, to protect it from ants and insects; but now it was riddled with tiny holes, and if one put one's ear to it there could be heard a myriad tiny jaws at work, and from the holes slid a perpetual trickle of faint white dust. Martha stood beside it, waiting for the moment when everyone on the verandah would be safely looking the other way, and felt it move rockingly on its base under the floor. She thought it typical of her parents that for years they had been reminding each other how essential it was to replace the pole in good time, and, now that the secretly working insects had hollowed it so that it sounded like a drum when tapped, remarked comfortingly, "Well, it doesn't matter, the ridgepole never really rested in the fork, anyway." And indeed, looking up at the thatch, one could see a clear two inches between the main spine of the roof and its intended support. The roof seemed to be held well enough on the web of light poles which lay under the thatch. The whole house was like this— precarious and shambling, but faithful, for it continued to remain upright against all probability. "One day it'll fall on our heads," Mrs. Quest would grumble when her husband said, as usual, that they could not afford to rebuild. But it did not fall.

At a suitable moment, Martha slipped into the second room. It was her parents' bedroom. It was a large square, and rather dark, for there were only two windows. The furniture was of petrol and paraffin boxes, nailed together and painted and screened by cretonne. The curtains, originally bought in London, had faded to a yellowish grey. On the thin web of the stuff, which hung limp against the glare, showed a tenacious dark outline of strutting peacocks. There were two large iron beds standing side by side on one wall, a dressing table facing them on the other. Habit had not dulled Martha into blindness of these things, of the shabby neglect of the place. But the family lived here without *really* living here. The house had been built as temporary, and was still temporary. Next year they would go back to England, or go into town. The crops might be good; they would have a stroke of luck and win the sweepstake; they would find a gold mine. For years Mr. and Mrs. Quest had been discussing these things; and to such conversations Martha no longer listened, for they made her so irritable she could not stand them. She had seen clearly, when she was about eleven or twelve, that her parents were deluding themselves; she had even reached the stage where she could say, If they really wanted to move, they would. But this cold, exasperated thought had never been worked out, and she still shared her parents' unconscious attitude, although she repudiated their day-dreaming and foolishness, that this was not really her home. She knew that to Marnie, to others of their neighbours, this house seemed disgracefully shabby, even sordid; but why be ashamed of something that one has never, not for a moment, considered as home?

When Martha was alone in this room, and had made sure the doors were closed, she moved carefully to the small square mirror that was nailed to the centre of the window, over the dressing table. She did not look at the things on the dressing table, because she disliked them. For many years, Mrs. Quest had been describing women who used cosmetics as fast; then she saw that everyone else did, and bought herself lipstick and nail varnish. She had no instinct for them, and they were the wrong colour. Her powder had a musty, floury smell, like a sweet, rather stale cake. Martha hastily put the lid on the box and slipped it into a drawer, so as to remove the smell. Then she examined herself in the mirror, leaning up on her toes, for it was too high: Mrs. Quest was a tall woman. She was by no means resigned to the appearance her mother thought suitable. She spent much time, at night, examining herself with a hand mirror; she sometimes propped the mirror by her pillow, and, lying beside it, would murmur like a lover, "Beautiful, you are so beautiful." This happened when Mrs. Quest had made one of her joking remarks about Martha's clumsiness, or Mr. Quest complained that girls in this country matured so early.

She had a broad but shapely face, with a pointed chin, severe hazel eyes, a full mouth, clear straight dark brows. Sometimes she would take the mirror to her parents' bedroom, and hold it at an angle to the one at the window, and examine herself, at this double remove, in profile; for this view of herself had a delicacy her full face lacked. With her chin tilted up, her loose blond hair falling back, her lips carefully parted in an eager, expectant look, she possessed a certain beauty. But it seemed to her that her face, her head, were something quite apart from her body; she could see herself only in sections, because of the smallness of the mirror. The dresses her mother made looked ugly, even obscene, for her breasts were well grown, and the yokes emphasized them, showing flattened bulges under the tight band of material; and the straight falling line of the skirt was spoiled by her full hips. Her mother said that girls in England did not come out until at the earliest sixteen, but better still eighteen, and girls of a nice family wore dresses of this type until coming out. That she herself had not "come out," and that her family had not by many degrees reached that stage of *niceness* necessary to coming out, was not enough to deflect her. For on such considerations is the social life of England based, and she was after all quite right in thinking that if only she had married better, of if *only* their farming had been successful, it would have been possible to arrange with the prosperous branch of family that Martha should come out. So Martha's sullen criticisms of her snobbishness had no effect at all; and she would smooth the childish dresses down over Martha's body, so that the girl stood hunched with resentment, and say with an embarrassed coyness, "Dear me, you are getting a pouter pigeon, aren't you?"

Once, Mrs. Van Rensberg, watching this scene, remarked soothingly, "But, Mrs. Quest, Martha has a nice little figure, why shouldn't she show it?" But outwardly the issue was social convention, and not Martha's figure; and if Mrs. Van Rensberg said to her husband that Mrs. Quest was going the right way to make Martha "difficult" she could not say so to Mrs. Quest herself.

This afternoon was a sudden climax after a long brooding underground rebellion. Standing before the mirror, she took a pair of scissors and severed the bodice from the skirt of her dress. She was trying to make the folds lie like Marnie's, when the door suddenly opened, and her father came in. He stopped, with an embarrassed look at his daughter, who was naked, save for a tiny pair of pink drawers; but that embarrassment was having it both ways, for if Martha was still a child, then one could look at her naked.

He said gruffly, "What are you doing?" and went to a long cupboard beside his bed, formed of seven petrol boxes, one above another, painted dark green, and covered by a faded print curtain. It was packed with medicine bottles, crammed on top of each other so that a touch might dislodge them into an avalanche. He said moodily, "I think I'll try that new stuff, I've a touch of indigestion," and tried to find the appropriate bottle. As he held them up to the light of the window, one after another, his eyes fell on Martha, and he remarked, "Your mother won't like you cutting her dresses to pieces."

She said defiantly, "Daddy, why should I wear dresses like a kid of ten?"

He said resentfully, "Well, you are a kid. Must you quarrel all the time with your mother?"

Again the door swung in, banging against the wall, and Mrs. Quest entered, saying, "Why did you run off, Martha, they wanted to tell you about Stephanie, it really is rude of you—" She stopped, stared, and demanded, "Whatever are you doing?"

"I'm not wearing this kind of dress any more," said Martha, trying to sound calm, but succeeding only in her usual sullen defiance.

"But, my dear, you've ruined it, and you know how badly off we are," said Mrs. Quest, in alarm at the mature appearance of her daughter's breasts and hips. She glanced at her husband, then came quickly across the room, and laid her hands on either side of the girl's waist, as if trying to press her back into childhood. Suddenly Martha moved backwards, and involuntarily lifted her hand; she was shuddering with disgust at the touch of her own mother, and had been going to slap her across the face. She dropped her hand, amazed at her own violence; and Mrs. Quest coloured and said ineffectually, "My dear . . ."

"I'm sixteen," said Martha, between set teeth, in a stifled voice; and she looked towards her father, for help. But he quickly turned away, and measured medicine into a glass.

"My dear, nice girls wear clothes like this until—"

"I'm not a nice girl," broke in Martha, and suddenly burst into laughter.

Mrs. Quest joined her in a relieved peal, and said, "Really my dear, you are ridiculous." And then, on a more familiar note, "You've spoiled that dress, and it is not fair to Daddy, you know how difficult it is to find money . . ." She stopped again, and followed the direction of Martha's eyes. Martha was looking at the medicine cupboard. Mrs. Quest was afraid that Martha might say, as she had said to her, that there must be hundreds of pounds' worth of medicines in that cupboard, and they had spent more on Mr. Quest's imaginary diseases than they had spent on educating her.

This was, of course, an exaggeration. But it was strange that when Martha made these comments Mrs. Quest began arguing about the worth of the medicines: "Nonsense, dear, you know quite well it can't be hundreds of pounds." She did not say, "Your father is very ill." For Mr. Quest was really ill, he had contracted diabetes three or four years before. And there was an episode connected with this that neither Martha nor Mrs. Quest liked to remember. One day, Martha was summoned from her classroom at school in the city, to find Mrs. Quest waiting for her in the passage. "Your father's ill," she exclaimed, and then, seeing that Martha's face expressed only: Well, there's nothing new in that, is there?, added hastily, "Yes, really, he's got diabetes, he must go to the hospital and have tests." There was a long silence from Martha, who at length muttered, like a sleep-walker, "*I knew it.*" Almost the moment these words were out, she flushed with guilt; and at once she hastened to the car, where her father sat, and both women fussed over him, while Mr. Quest, who was very frightened, listened to their reassurances.

When Martha remembered that phrase, which had emerged from her depths, as if it had been waiting for the occasion, she felt uneasy and guilty. Secretly, she could not help thinking, He wanted to be ill, he likes being ill, now he's got an excuse for being a failure. Worse than this, she accused her mother, in her private thoughts, of being responsible.

The whole business of Mr. Quest's illness aroused such unpleasant depths of emotion between mother and daughter that the subject was left alone, for the most part; and now Mrs. Quest said hastily, moving away to the window, "You're upsetting your father, he worries about you." Her voice was low and nagging.

"You mean *you* worry about me," said Martha coldly, unconsciously dropping her voice, with a glance at her father. In a half-whisper she said, "He doesn't even notice we're here. He hasn't *seen* us for years . . ." She was astounded to find that her voice shook, she was going to cry.

Mr. Quest hastily left the room, persuading himself that his wife and daughter were not quarrelling, and at once Mrs. Quest said in a normal voice, "You're a worry to us. You don't realize. The way you waste money and—"

Martha cut it short, by walking out of the room and into her own. The door did not lock, or even fasten properly, for it hung crooked. It had been formed of planks, by a native carpenter, and had warped in the rainy seasons, so that to shut it meant a grinding push across a lumpy and swelling lintel. But though it did not lock, there were moments when it was invisibly locked, and this was one of them. Martha knew her mother would not come in. She sat on the edge of her bed and cried with anger.

This was the pleasantest room of the house, a big square room, freshly whitewashed, and uncrowded. The walls rose clear to the roof, which slanted down on either side of the ridgepole in a gentle sweep of softly glistening thatch, which had turned a greyish gold with the years. There was a wide, low window that looked directly over a descent of trees to an enormous red field, and a rise on the other side, of fresh parklike bush—for it had never been cut to feed mine furnaces, as had most of the trees on the farm—and beyond this slope rose the big mountain, Jacob's Burg. It was all flooded with evening sunlight. Sunset: the birds were singing to the day's end, and the crickets were chirping the approach of night. Martha felt tired, and lay on her low iron bedstead, whose lumpy mattress and pillows had conformed comfortably to the shape of her body. She looked out past the orange-tinted curtains to the sky, which was flooded with wild colour. She was facing, with dubious confidence, what she knew would be a long fight. She was saying to herself, I won't give in, I won't; though it would have been hard for her to define what it was she fought.

And in fact the battle of the clothes had begun. It raged for months, until poor Mr. Quest groaned and went out of the room whenever the subject was raised, which was continuously, since it had become a focus for the silent struggle between the women, which had nothing to do with clothes, or even with "niceness."

Mr. Quest thought of himself as a peace-loving man. He was tall and lean and dark, of slow speech and movement; he was handsome too, and even now women warmed to him, and to the unconscious look of understanding and complicity in his fine dark eyes. For in that look was a touch of the rake; and at these moments when he flirted a little with Mrs. Van Rensberg, he came alive; and Mrs. Quest was uneasy, and Martha unaccountably rather sad, seeing her father as he must have been when he was young. His good looks were conventional, even dull, save for his moments of animation. And they were rare, for if Mr. Quest was a rake, he did not know it.

When Mrs. Quest said teasingly, but with an uneasy undertone, "Mrs. Van Rensberg, poor soul, got quite flustered this afternoon, the way you flirted with her," Mr. Quest said, rather irritated, "What do you mean, I flirted? I was only talking for politeness' sake." And he really believed it.

What he liked best was to sit for hours on end in his deck chair on the verandah, and watch the lights and shadows move over the hills, watch the clouds deploying overhead, watch the lightning at night, listen to the thunder. He would emerge after hours of silence, remarking, "Well, I don't know, I suppose it all means something"; or "Life is a strange business, say what you like." He was calm, even cheerful, in his absent-minded way, as long as he was not disturbed, which meant, these days, as long as he was not spoken to. At these moments he became suffused with angry irritation; and now both women were continually appealing for his support, and he would reply helplessly, "For heaven's sake, what is there to quarrel *for?* There isn't anything to quarrel *about.*" When his wife came to him secretly, talking insistently until he had to hear her, he shouted in exasperation, "Well, if the child wants to make herself ridiculous, then let her, don't waste your time arguing." And when Martha said helplessly, "Do talk to her, do tell her I'm not ten years old any longer," he said, "Oh, Lord, do leave me alone, and anyway, she's quite right, you're much too young, look at Marnie, she makes me blush wriggling around the farm in shorts and high heels." But this naturally infuriated Martha, who did not envisage herself in the style of a Marnie. But the women could not leave him alone, several times a day they came to him, flushed, angry, their voices querulous, demanding his attention. They would not leave him in peace to think about the war, in which he had lost his health, and perhaps something more important than health; they would not leave him to dream tranquilly about the future, when some miracle would transport them all into town, or to England; they nagged at him, as he said himself, like a couple of darned fishwives! Both felt that he let them down, and became irritable against him, so that at such times it was as if this very irritation cemented them together, and against him. But such is the lot of the peacemakers.

2

Early in her sixteenth year, Martha was expected to pass the matric —it goes without saying, quite brilliantly. She did not even sit the examination; and it was not the first time she had withdrawn from a situation through circumstances which it occurred to no one, particularly Martha herself, to call anything but bad luck. At eleven, for instance, there had been just such a vital examination, and she had become ill the week before. She was supposed to be exceptionally musical, but by some fatality was always prevented from proving it by gaining the right number of marks. She was prepared for confirmation three times, and in the end the whole thing was allowed to drop, for it appeared that in the meantime she had become an agnostic. And now here was this important examination. For months Mrs. Quest was talking about university and scholarships, while Martha listened, sometimes eagerly, but more often writhing with embarrassment. A week before the vital date, Martha got pink eye, which happened to be raging through the school. Not a very serious affliction, but in this case it appeared Martha's eyes were weakened.

It was October, the month of heat and flowers, and dust and tension. October: the little town where Martha was at school was hung with flowers, as for a festival. Every street was banked with purple-blooming trees, the jacarandas held their airy clouds of blossom over every sidewalk and garden; and beneath them blew, like a descant, the pale pink-and-white bauhinias; and behind, like a deep note from the trumpet, the occasional splash of screaming magenta where a bougainvillea unloaded its weight of colour down a wall. Colour and light: the town was bombarded by light, the heat beat down from a whitish sky, beat up from the grey and glittering streets, hung over the roofs in shimmering waves. The greens of the foliage were deep and solid and shining, but filmed with dust; like neglected water where debris gathers. As one walked past a tree, the light shifted glittering from facet to facet of a branch or leaf. How terrible October is! Terrible because so beautiful, and the beauty springs from the loaded heat, the dust, the tension; for everyone watches the sky, and the heavy trees along the avenues, and the sullen clouds, while for weeks nothing happens; the wind lifts an eddy of dust at a street corner, and subsides, exhausted. One cannot remember the smell of the flowers without the smell of dust and petrol; one cannot remember that triumphant orchestra of colour without the angry, white-hot sky. One cannot remember . . . Afterwards Martha remembered that her eyes had ached badly, then they closed and festered, and she lay in half-darkness making jokes about her condition because she was so afraid of going blind. She was even more afraid of her fear, because nothing could have been more absurd, since half the girls in the school were similarly afflicted. It was merely a question of waiting until her eyes grew better. She could not bear to lie in bed and wait, so she pestered the nurse until she could sit on a verandah, screened by a thick curtain of golden shower from the street, because she could assure herself she was not blind by looking through her glowing eyelids at the light from the sky. She sat there all day, and felt the waves of heat and perfume break across her in shock after shock of shuddering nostalgia. But nostalgia for what? She sat and sniffed painfully at the weighted air, as if it were dealing her blows like an invisible enemy. Also, there was the examination to be taken; she always relied on intensive study during the last fortnight before an examination, for she was the kind of person with a memory that holds anything, almost photographically, for about a month; afterwards what she had learned disappeared as if she had never known it. Therefore, if she took the examination, she would probably pass, but in a mediocre way.

Mrs. Quest was told that her daughter had pink eye. Then she got a letter from Martha, a very hysterical letter; then another, this time flat and laconic. Mrs. Quest went into town, and took her daughter to an oculist, who tested her and said there was nothing wrong with the eyes. Mrs. Quest was very angry, and took her to another oculist; the anger was the same as that she directed towards those doctors who did not immediately accept her diagnoses of her husband's condition. The second oculist was patient and ironical and agreed to everything Mrs. Quest said.

Curious that Mrs. Quest, whose will for years had been directed towards Martha distinguishing herself—curious that she should accept those damaged eyes so easily, even insist that they were permanently injured when Martha began to vacillate. For as soon as Mrs. Quest arrived in town and took the situation in hand, Martha found herself swept along in a way she had not foreseen. If one can use the word "see" in connection with anything so confused and contradictory. The end of it was that Martha went back to the farm—"to rest her eyes," as Mrs. Quest explained to the neighbours, with a queer pride in the thing which made Martha uneasy.

So here was Martha at home, "resting her eyes" but reading as much as ever. And how curious were the arguments between the two women over this illogical behaviour. For Mrs. Quest did not say, "You are supposed to have strained your eyes, why are you reading?" She made remarks such as "You do it on purpose to upset me!" Or "Why do you have to read that kind of book?" Or "You are ruining your whole life, and you won't take my advice." Martha maintained a stubborn but ironical silence, and continued to read.

So here was Martha, at sixteen, idle and bored, and sometimes secretly wondering (though only for a moment, the thought always vanished at once) why she had not sat that examination, which she could have passed with such ease. For she had gone up the school head of her class, without even having to work. But these thoughts could not be clearly faced, so she shut them out. But why was she condemning herself to live on this farm, which more than anything in the world she wanted to leave? The matric was a simple passport to the outside world, while without it escape seemed so difficult she was having terrible nightmares of being tied hand and foot under the wheels of a locomotive, or struggling waist-deep in quicksands, or eternally climbing a staircase that moved backwards under her. She felt as if some kind of spell had been put on her.

Then Mrs. Quest began saying that Marnie had just passed the matric, and she said it unpleasantly: Look, if she can pass it, why not you?

Martha did not want to see Marnie, and it was easy to avoid doing so, for the Van Rensbergs and the Quests were drifting apart. It was more than one of the inexplicable changes of feeling between neighbours; there was a good reason for it. Mr. Van Rensberg was becoming violently nationalist, and Mrs. Van Rensberg had an apologetic look on her face when she saw Mrs. Quest at the station. And so, by a natural reaction, the Quests began saying, "These damned Afrikaners," although the two families had been friends, shelving the question of nationality for so many years.

Martha did not want to think of these things, she was turned in on herself, in a heavy trancelike state. Afterwards she was to think of this time as the worst in her life. What was so frightening was this feeling of being dragged, being weighted. She did not understand why she was acting against her will, her intellect, everything she believed. It was as if her body and brain were numbed.

There was nothing to do. The farm lay about her like a loved country which refused her citizenship. She repeated the incantatory names of childhood like a spell which had lost its force. The Twenty Acres, the Big Tobacco Land, The Field on the Ridge, the Hundred Acres, the Kaffir Patch, the Bush by the Fence, the Pumpkin Patch— these words became words; and, walking by herself across the Twenty Acres, which was bounded on three sides by a straggle of gum trees (a memory of her father's afforestation phase), a patch of sloping land tinted pink and yellow, full of quartz reefs and loose white pebbles, she said to herself scornfully, Why Twenty Acres? It's about twelve acres. Why the Hundred Acres, when it is only seventy-six? Why has this family always given large-sounding names to things ordinary and even shabby? For everything had shrunk for her. The house showed as if an unkind light had been shone on it. It was not only shabby, it was sordid. Everything decayed and declined, and leaned inwards.

And, worse, far worse, she was watching her father with horror, for he was coming to have, for her, the fatal lethargy of a dream-locked figure. He had the look of a person half claimed by sleep. He was middle-aged, she told herself, neither young nor old; he was in the long middle period of life when people do not change, but his changelessness was imposed, not by a resisting vigour but by—what? He was rising late in the morning, he dreamed over breakfast, wandered off into the bedroom to test himself for his real disease and for various imaginary ones; returned early from the farmwork to lunch, slept after it, and for a longer time every day, and then sat immobile in his deck chair, waiting for the sunset. After it, supper—a calculatedly healthy meal—and an early bed. Sleep, sleep, the house was saturated by it; and Mrs. Quest's voice murmured like the spells of a witch, "You must be tired, darling; don't overtire yourself, dear." And when these remarks were directed at Martha, she felt herself claimed by the nightmare, as if she were standing beside her father; and, in fact, at the word "tired" she felt herself tired, and had to shake herself.

"I will *not* be tired," she snapped to her mother, "it's no good trying to make me tired": extraordinary words; and even more extraordinary that Mrs. Quest did not question them. Her face fell in patient and sorrowful lines, the eternal mother, holding sleep and death in her twin hands like a sweet and poisonous cloud of forgetfulness—that was how Martha saw her, like a baneful figure in the nightmare in which she herself was caught.

But sometimes their arguments were more sensible. "You are terribly unfair to your father," Mrs. Quest complained. "He's ill, he's really ill."

"I know he's ill," said Martha, miserably, feeling guilty. Then she roused herself to say, "Look at Mr. Blank, he's got it, too, he's quite different." Mr. Blank, over the other side of the district, had the same disease, and much more seriously than Mr. Quest, and led an active life, as if this business of injecting oneself with substitute gland juices once a day was on the same level as cleaning one's teeth or making a point of eating fruit for breakfast. But Mr. Quest was completely absorbed in the ritual of being ill, he talked of nothing else—his illness and the war, the war and illness; it was as if a twin channel drove across his brain, and if his thoughts switched from one subject, they must enter the other, like a double track leading to the same destination.

It even seemed to Martha that her father was pleased that the Van Rensbergs no longer visited them, because with Mr. Van Rensberg he talked about the farm, while with Mr. McDougall, who took his place, he shared memories of the trenches.

Martha, coming down the verandah, a silent and critical figure, would see her father at one end, leaning back in his deck chair like a contemplative philosopher, and hear his voice: "We were out in no man's land, six of us, when the star shells went up, and we saw we weren't three paces from the Boche trenches and . . ."

At the other end of the verandah, Mrs. Quest was talking to Mrs. McDougall: "That's when we got the wounded in from Gallipoli and . . ."

Martha listened, absorbed in these twin litanies of suffering in spite of herself, for they had been murmuring down her childhood as far back as she could remember, and were twined with her deepest self. She was watching, fearfully, the effect on herself of the poetry of suffering; the words "no man's land," "star shells," "Boche," touched off in her images like those of poetry; no man's land was the black and wasted desert between the living forces; star shells exploded in coloured lights, like fireworks, across her brain, drenched in reminiscence; Boche was fearful and gigantic, nothing human, a night figure; the tripping word "Gallipoli" was like a heroic dance. She was afraid because of the power of these words, which affected her so strongly, who had nothing to do with what they stood for.

On one such afternoon, when she was standing on the steps, listening, her father called out to her, "Matty, did I ever tell you about—" and she said ungraciously, but with discomfort, "Quite a thousand times, I should think."

He jerked up his head and stared at her, and onto his face came that look of baffled anger. "It's all very well for you," he said. "We came out of the trenches, and then suddenly the war was bad form. The Great Unmentionable, that's what you called it."

"*I* didn't call it anything," she remarked at last, sullenly humorous.

She moved away, but he called after her, "All you pacifists, there were pacifists before the last war, but when it started, you all fought. You'll fight, too, you'll see."

Martha had never thought of herself as a pacifist, but it seemed she was one; she played this part against her father's need, just as, for him, she was that group of people in the 'Twenties who refused to honour the war, although the 'Twenties were the first decade of her life, and she could hardly remember them. She was creating them, however, for herself, through reading, and because of this, the mere sound of the word *young*, which had apparently been some sort of symbol or talisman during that decade, sprung in her a feeling of defiance and recklessness.

Similarly, when Mr. Quest complained about the international ring of Jews who controlled the world (which he had taken to doing lately, after reading some pamphlet sent to him through the post), Martha argued against him, in the most reasonable and logical manner; for one does not learn so young that against some things reason is powerless. And when Mrs. Quest said that all the kaffirs were dirty and lazy and inherently stupid, she defended them. And when both parents said that Hitler was no gentleman, an upstart without principles, Martha found herself defending Hitler too; it was this which made her think a little and question her feeling of being used, her conviction that when her parents raised their voices and argued at her, on a complaining and irritable note, insisting that there was going to be another war with Germany and Russia soon (this was at a time when everyone was saying another war was impossible, because whom would it benefit?), this new war was in some way necessary to punish her, Martha, who talked of the last one so critically.

Jonathan Quest, the younger brother, came home for the holidays from his expensive school, like a visitor from a more prosperous world. For the first time, Martha found herself consciously resenting him. Why, she asked herself, was it that he, with half her brains, should be sent to a "good school," why was it he should inevitably be given the advantages? There was something uneasy in this criticism, for she had been telling her mother fiercely that nothing would induce her to go to a snob school, even if her eyes did get better. She was becoming aware of several disconnected strands of her thinking. And this was brought to a climax by Jonathan himself. He was a simple, good-natured boy, very like his father to look at, who spent his holidays visiting the neighbouring farmers, riding in to the station to visit Socrates the Greek, and the Cohen family at the little kaffir store. He was on the best of terms with everyone. But it struck Martha as unjust that this brother of hers who despised the Afrikaners (or rather, who took up the orthodox British attitude towards them, which was the same thing) should spend the day at the Van Rensbergs' house like a second son, and drop in for a chat with the Cohen brothers as if it was the most natural thing in the world.

Martha asked him sarcastically, "How do you reconcile the Jews ruining the world with going to see Solly and Joss?"

Jonathan looked uncomfortable and said, "But we've known them all our lives."

When she looked pointedly quizzical, he said, "But you never go and see them at all."

"That's not because I feel the way you do."

Jonathan was embarrassed, because he would not have said he felt any way rather than another; he merely repeated what his parents said, and what he had heard at school. "Well, if you think Hitler is all right, how do you reconcile that?"

"But I never said he was all right, all I said was—" She stopped and blushed; and it was his turn to look quizzical. It was true that all she had said was that Hitler's being an upstart was no criticism of his capabilities, but in this household it was as good as a defence.

She began a long rational argument; he refused to argue, merely teasing her, "Matty's lost her temper, Matty's lost her temper," singing it like a child.

"You're nothing but a baby," she concluded scornfully, which was how their arguments always ended, and she turned away. Now, that act of turning away implies something one turns towards—and she picked up a book, at random, from the bookcase. This was also a familiar act. How many times had she not simply reached for the nearest book, as if to remark, "I have authority for what I say"?

It occurred to her that the phrase "Martha is a great reader" was being used by herself exactly as her mother used it, and with as little reason. For what was she reading? She read the same books over and over again, in between intervals of distracted daydreaming, in a trance of recognition, and in always the same place, under the big tree that was her refuge, through which the heat pumped like a narcotic. She read poetry, not for the sense of the words, but for the melodies which confirmed the rhythm of the moving grasses and the swaying of the leaves over her head, or that ideal landscape of white cities and noble people which lay over the actual vistas of harsh grass and stunted trees like a golden mirage.

She went through the house searching for something different. It was full of books. Her own room had shelves packed with fairy stories from her childhood, and with poetry. In the living room, her parents' bookcases were filled with the classics, Dickens and Scott and Thackeray and the rest, inherited from prosperous Victorian households. These she had read years before, and she now read them again, and with a feeling of being starved. One might equate the small black child with Oliver Twist—but what then? There were also, lying everywhere, books on "politics" in her parents' sense of the word, such as the memoirs of Lloyd George, or histories of the Great War. None of these seemed to have any reference to the farm, to the gangs of native labour, to what was described in the newspapers, or even to *Mein Kampf*, which had started this restless condition of mind.

But one day, slipped behind the rows of dusty books, she found a volume of H. G. Wells, and, as she held it in her hand, was very conscious of a dull feeling of resistance, a disinclination. It was so strong that she nearly put it down and reached as usual for Shelley or for Whitman; then she became conscious of what she was doing, and stood wondering at herself. For she had felt this before. She looked at the book again. It was the *Concise History of the World,* and the name on the flyleaf was "Joshua Cohen." Now, she had dropped her childish friendship with the Cohen boys from the moment Marnie had said, "Joss Cohen is sweet on you." She missed them. And yet she could not face them. At first it was because the relief of escaping the barrage of criticism was so great: there was no longer any necessity to read their books, examine her own ideas. Recently it had been because of some obscure and unadmitted shame about her strained eyes. She took the book to her refuge, the tree, and read it through; and wondered why it was that she could read the most obscure and complicated poetry with ease, while she could not read the simplest sort of book on what she called "facts" without the greatest effort of concentration. She brought herself to decide she would make an effort to renew that friendship with the Cohens, for there was no one else who could help her. She wanted them to tell her what she must read. For there are two ways of reading: one of them deepens and intensifies what one already knows; from the other, one takes new facts, new views to weave into one's life. She was saturated with the first, and needed the second. All those books she had borrowed, two years before—she had read them, oh, yes; but she had not been ready to receive them.

And now what was she to do? For she had behaved very badly to the Cohen boys. She saw them at the station sometimes. Now, to avoid *seeing* people one has known for years is something of a feat, and Martha achieved it by the simple device of saying to herself, They wouldn't think *that* of me—"*that*" being anti-Semitism—and smiling at them constrainedly, like an acquaintance. They nodded back, and left her alone, as she apparently desired.

The village held about fifty souls, and had sprung up untidily around the first store, owned by Socrates the Greek, who was known to the farmers as Sock. There was a garage, run by a Welshman; a farmers' hall; the station beside the railway, a long tin-roofed shack on wooden piles; a ganger's cottage; and a hotel, also owned by Socrates, in which there was a bar, which was the real social centre of the district. These buildings were scattered over a few acres of red dust; and along the railway line was a stretch of brownish water, where ducks swam until Mrs. Socrates came out to catch one for the hotel dinner, and where the oxen from the farmers' waggons were unyoked while the waggons were loaded, and stood knee-deep in green scum, raising their eyes tranquilly as the train thundered past over their heads. There were two trains a week, and twenty miles away was the end of the line, for beyond was the long ascent to the great escarpment at the verge of the Zambesi Valley. But there was a great deal of road traffic, and all day the cars stood in the dust outside the bar.

Years before, the Quests used to make the trip in to the station twice a week, for Mrs. Quest was sociable; but Mr. Quest disliked being disturbed so much that now they went once a month, and Mrs. Quest must begin fighting with her husband at least a week before.

"Alfred," she would say, with a sort of offhand defiance, "remember, we are going in to the station tomorrow."

He did not hear. Or rather, he raised vaguely irritable eyes towards her, and dropped them again, hunching his shoulders against her voice.

"Do listen, dear. I told you, we are out of flour, and the boys need new aprons, and the sugar's practically finished."

He kept his eyes lowered, and his face was stubborn.

"Alfred!" she shouted.

"What *is* it?" he demanded, and glared at her.

Startled by the glare, which nevertheless she had been provoking and facing with obdurate strength for years, she murmured, abashed but determined, "We must go to the station."

"We can send the waggon," he said hastily, getting up to escape.

"No, Alfred, you know you always say you can't spare the waggon, and it's silly to send the waggon for two sacks of . . ." He was at the door, on his way out; but she raised her voice after him: "Besides, I want to see if they've any nice materials, I'm really down to my last rag."

And now he stopped, and gave her another glare, in which there was guilt and reproach, for she was using the weapon he dreaded most: she was saying, The very least you can do is to let me have a little trip once a month, when you've made me live on this awful farm, and we're so poor, and my children have been dragged down to the level of the Van Rensbergs and . . .

"Oh, all right, all right, have it your own way," he said, and sat down, reached for the newspaper, and covered himself with it.

"Tomorrow," she said. "We will go in after lunch, and Martha can help me get ready."

Her husband's defiant eyes were hidden by the newspaper, which nevertheless gave a small protesting shake; but Martha's eyes were lifted towards her, with the sullen enquiry, "Why do we have to *get ready* for half an hour's trip?"

"Oh, well—you know—with everything . . ." Mrs. Quest lapsed into confusion.

"Good Lord," said Martha irritably, "to hear us talk, you'd think we were off to England or something."

This was a familiar joke, and allowed Mrs. Quest to give her girlish and rather charming laugh; though no one else laughed. "Well, with this family I've got, and no one lifts a finger but me . . ." This was not a grumble, but an appeal that please, please, for pity's sake, they should laugh, this irritable, resisting couple, and make things easier. She sighed, as Martha's face remained glum and the newspaper was held firmly upright against her.

Next morning at breakfast she said, "Don't forget we're going to the station."

Now he was resigned. "*Must* we?"

"Yes, we must. Besides, you know you'll enjoy it once we get there."

This was a mistake. "I do not enjoy it. I loathe it. Besides, we haven't any petrol."

"There's a spare tin in the storeroom," said Mrs. Quest firmly. And now there was no help for it; Mr. Quest groaned, and accepted his fate; and as he went off to the garage he even looked interested; the cloud of introspection was lifting, and his eyes intently followed what his hands did. It always worried Martha, made her uneasy, to see how those brooding eyes must concentrate, force themselves outwards, watching his hands as if they were clumsy creatures that were separate from himself.

The garage was a roof of tin over two walls of plastered logs, open at each end; and he reversed the car slowly out into the bush, so that it bounced and jerked over the rough ground, and then forwards into an empty space. Then he got out, and stood frowning at the car. It was a very old Ford; the paint had gone; there were no side curtains —they had been lost somewhere; one door was tied with rope; and a part of the canvas hood, which had decayed into holes, was thatched over. He had bought it for thirty pounds ten years before.

"The engine's as good as ever," he murmured proudly. And he called Martha to say, "It isn't the body of a car that matters. Only fools pay good money for paint and varnish. What matters is the engine." He liked to have Martha there when he attended to the car; he would even send the servant to fetch her. Now, Martha did not mind about how cars looked; but she was irritated because of this one's extreme slowness; so her face was as absent and dreamy as his own while he fetched water in a watering can, and fed the radiator, and took off the rope from the useless handle and retied it. Slowly, because he got no response to his remarks, he began glaring at her. "It's all very well," he would begin, "it's all very well for *you* . . ." More often than not, the sentence was never finished, for a humorous look would come over her face, and their eyes met.

"Oh, Daddy," she protested, grumbling, "why is it all very well, I haven't said a word!" Here she might begin edging away, with longing glances at the house. It was so hot; the heat and light glittered into her eyes from the battered old car.

"Where are you going?" he demanded, sounding offended; and she returned to sit on the running board, opening the book she had held in her hand. Now he was mollified, and he sounded cheerful, as he stroked the warm thatch on the roof, and said, "I always did like thatching, there's something about the look of a nice piece of thatch. I remember my cousin George—he was an expert thatcher, back Home. Of course, he knew his job, not like these damned niggers, they slam it on any old how. When you go back to England, Matty, the first thing you must do is go to Colchester and see if George's kids are half the man their father was—if so, you'll see a piece of thatching you'll find nowhere else in the world. *Matty!*" he shouted at her bent and absorbed head.

"*What?*" she asked, exasperated, lifting her eyes from the book.

"You're not listening."

"I am listening."

"It's all very well for *you*," came the grumbling voice.

When he had fiddled with the car for an hour or so, he came back to the house, followed by Martha, and demanded tea. He would not go down the farm that day. And then, about twelve o'clock, he began worrying that the lunch was late and they would never get off that afternoon.

"But Alfred," said poor Mrs. Quest, "first you won't go at all, and then you start fussing hours before—"

"It's all very well, you haven't got to nurse a twenty-year-old car over these roads."

Martha gritted her teeth in anger. Standing on the hill, one could see the other farmers' cars racing through the trees, like tiny black beetles, the red dust spurting up behind them. Other people made the journey to the station in a few minutes.

After lunch, the anxious Mr. Quest went to the car and again tested the radiator. It was likely to be empty; and then he would call for half a dozen eggs, and break them one after another into the cavity. The eggs would form a sticky sediment over the leaky bottom of the radiator. Once someone had suggested mealie meal, which he tried immediately, with all the cautious enthusiasm of a scientific experimenter. "There must be something in it," he murmured as he poured handfuls of the white floury stuff into the car. But halfway along the track, the cap shot off with an explosion, and lumps of porridge flew all over the windscreen, so that the car came to a blind and sliding stop against a large tree. "Well," said Mr. Quest thoughtfully, "that's interesting. Perhaps if one used a finer grain it might . . ."

On the whole, eggs were more predictable; though it was important not to drive too fast, and to stop frequently, so that the engine might cool, as otherwise the water might boil the clotted egg off the bottom of the radiator, and then . . .

After lunch Mr. Quest called peremptorily, "May! Matty! Come on, the engine's started, we must go." And Mrs. Quest, half laughing, half grumbling, ran to the car, adjusting her hat, while Martha followed unhurriedly, with a look of exhausted resignation.

The car was poised at the edge of a flattish space, on the brow of the hill. Mr. Quest sat urgently forward, clasping the brake with one hand, hugging the steering wheel with the other.

"Now!" he exclaimed, letting go the brake. Nothing happened. "Oh, damn it all," he groaned, as if this were the last straw. "Come on, then." And he and Mrs. Quest began swinging back and forth in their seats, so the car was joggled inch by inch over the edge, and slid precariously down the rutted pebbly road to the foot of the hill, where there was a great ditch. Into this it slid, and stopped. "Oh, damn it *all*," Mr. Quest said again, on a final note, and looked around at his women in an aggrieved way.

He tried the starter, without much hope. It worked at once, and the car flew up over the edge of the ditch in a screeching bounce, and down the track between the mealie fields. The maize stood now in its final colouring, a dead silvery gold, dry as paper, and its whispering against the wind was the sound of a myriad fluttering leaves. Below this Hundred Acres Field lay the track, the old railroad track, and now Mr. Quest stopped the car, got out, took off the radiator cap, and peered in. There was a squelchy bubbling noise, and a faintly rotten smell. "It's all right so far," he said, with satisfaction, and off they went.

Halfway, they stopped again. "At three and a half miles, the petrol ought to show . . ." murmured Mr. Quest, looking at the petrol gauge. For it was seven miles to the station. Or rather, it was five and three-quarters; but just as it was seven miles to the Dumfries Hills (in fact, six) and seven to Jacob's Burg (at least nine), so the distance to the station must be seven miles, for to have a house in the dead centre of a magically determined circle offers satisfaction beyond all riches, and even power. But a poetical seven miles is one thing, and to check one's petrol gauge by it another; and Mr. Quest frowned and said, "I'd better take the thing to the garage. I cannot understand—if these people can make an engine to last a lifetime, why is everything else so shoddy?"

At the station, Mrs. Quest descended at Socrates' with her shopping lists, and Mr. Quest drove off to the garage. Martha lagged on the verandah until her mother had forgotten her in her eager talk with the other women at the counter, and then walked quickly to the belt of trees which hid the kaffir store. It was a large square brick erection, with a simple pillared verandah. Martha went through the usual crowd of native women with their babies on their backs, pushed aside the coloured bead curtain at the door, and was inside the store. It had a counter down the centre, and on it were jars of bright sweets, and rolls of cotton goods. There were sacks of grain and sugar around the walls, bicycles, cans of paraffin, monkey nuts. Over the counter, cheap beads, strips of biltong, mouth organs and glass bangles dangled and swung together. The smell was of sweat and cheap dyes and dust, and Martha sniffed it with pleasure.

Old Mr. Cohen nodded at her, with a distance in his manner, and, having asked politely after her parents, who owed him fifty pounds, waited for an order.

"Is Solly in?" she asked, rather too politely.

The old man allowed his eyebrows to lift, before replying, "He's in, for anyone who wants to see him."

"I would like to see him," she said, almost stammering.

"You used to know the way," he said laconically, and nodded at the closed flap of the counter, under which she had ducked as a child. She had expected him to lift it for her now; clumsily, she tried to move it, while he watched her. Then, taking his time, he lifted it, and moved aside so that she might go through.

She found herself saying, "You're mistaken, I didn't mean . . ."

His eyes snapped around at her, and he said sarcastically, "Didn't mean what?" He at once turned away to serve a native child, who was so red with dust from the road that his black skin had a rusty look, some acid-green sweets from a jar.

Martha walked into the back room, and found the Cohen boys reading, one in each of the two big easy chairs, which she privately thought in unpleasant taste, as was the whole room, which was very small, and crowded with glossy furniture and bright china ornaments; there was an effect of expensive ostentation, like the display window of a furniture store. And in this ugly and tasteless room sat Solly and Joss, the intellectuals, reading (as she took care to see) Plato and Balzac, in expensive editions.

After a startled look at her, they looked at each other, and after a long pause Solly remarked, "Look who's here!" while Joss returned, "Well, well!" and they both waited, with blandly sarcastic faces, for her to speak.

She said, "I've brought back a book of yours," and held it out.

Solly said, "My grateful thanks," extended a hand, and took it.

Joss was pretending to read, and this annoyed her; for, as Mrs. Van Rensberg had suggested, he had once been her particular friend. But it was also a relief, and she said, rather flirtatiously, to Solly, "May I sit down?" and sat forthwith.

"She's got to be quite a smart girl, h'm?" said Solly to Joss, and the boys openly and rudely examined her.

As a result of her quarrels with Mrs. Quest, she was now making her own clothes. Also, she had starved herself into a fashionable thinness which, since she was plump by nature, was not to everyone's taste. Apparently not to the Cohen boys', for they continued, as if she were not present:

"Yellow suits her, doesn't it, Solly?"

"Yes, Joss and that cute little slit down the front of the dress, too."

"But too thin, too thin, Solly, it comes of giving up that rich and unhealthy Jewish food."

"But better thin and pure, Joss, than fat and gross and contaminated by—"

"Oh, shut up," she said, in discomfort; and they raised their eyebrows and shook their heads and sighed. "I know you think . . ." she began, and once again found it hard to continue.

"Think what?" they demanded, almost together, and with precisely the keen, sarcastic intonation their father had used.

"It isn't so," she stammered, sincerely, looking at them in appeal; and for a moment thought she was forgiven, for Joss's tone was quite gentle as he began: "Poor Matty, did your mummy forbid you to come and see us, then?"

The shock of the words, after the deceptively gentle tone, which reached her nerves before the sense of them, caused her eyes to fill with tears. She said, "No, of course she didn't."

"Mystery," said Joss, beginning the game again, nodding at Solly; who sighed exaggeratedly and said, "We're not to know, dear, dear."

Suddenly Martha said, not at all as she had intended, but with a mixture of embarrassment and coyness, "Mrs. Van Rensberg was gossiping." She glanced at Joss, whose dark face slowly coloured; and he looked at her with a dislike that cut her.

"Mrs. Van Rensberg was gossiping," said Solly to Joss; and before the exchange could continue, she cut in: "Yes, and I suppose it was silly, but I couldn't—take it." The defiant conclusion ended on a shortened breath; this interview was not as she had imagined.

"She couldn't take it," sighed Joss to Solly.

"She couldn't take it," Solly sighed back; and with the same movement, they picked up their books, and began to read.

She remained where she was, her eyes pleading with their averted faces, trying to subdue the flood of colour she could feel tingling to the roots of her hair, and when, after a long silence, Solly remarked in a detached voice, "She couldn't take us, but she's still here," Martha got up, saying angrily, "I've apologized, you're making a mistake. Why do you have to be so thin-skinned?" She went to the door.

Behind her back, they began laughing, a loud and unpleasant laughter. "She's cut us dead for two years, and she says we're thin-skinned."

"I *didn't* cut you—why must you talk about me as if I weren't here?" she said, and stumbled out, past Mr. Cohen. She found the flap of the counter down, and had to wait, speechless, for him to lift it, for she was on the verge of crying.

He looked at her with what she thought was a tinge of kindliness; but he opened the flap, nodded quietly, and said, "Good afternoon, Miss Quest."

"Thank you," she said, with the effect of pleading; and walked back up the dusty path to the village, as the bead curtain swung and rattled into stillness behind her.

She walked over the railway tracks, which gleamed brightly in the hot sunlight, to the garage, where Mr. Quest was in absorbed conversation with Mr. Parry. He was repeating urgently, "Yes, there's going to be a war, it's all very well for you people . . ."

Mr. Parry was saying, "Yes, Captain Quest. No, Captain Quest." In the village, the war title was used, though Mr. Quest refused it, saying it was not fair to the regular soldier. Martha used to argue with him reasonably, thus: "Are you suggesting that it is only the peacetime soldier who deserves his title? Do you mean that if civilians get conscripted and killed it's on a different level from . . ." and so on and so on—ah, how exasperating are the rational adolescents! For

Mr. Quest gave his irritable shrug of aversion and repeated, "I don't like being Captain, it's not fair when I haven't been in the Army for so long. What Martha thought privately was, How odd that a man who thinks about nothing but war should dislike being Captain; and this point, the real one, was of course never mentioned during those *reasonable* discussions

Mr. Parry was listening nervously to Mr. Quest, while his eyes anxiously followed his native assistant, who was dragging an inner tube through the hot dust. At last he could not bear it, and, saying, "Excusing me, but . . . " he darted forward and shouted at the native, "Look you, Gideon, how many times have I told you . . ." He grabbed the tyre from the man's hand, and took it over to a tub of water. Gideon shrugged, and went off to the cool interior of the garage, where he sat on a heap of outer tyres, and began making patterns on the dust with a twig. "Look you, Gideon . . . ." shouted Mr. Parry; but Gideon wrinkled his brows and pretended not to hear. Mr. Parry's Welsh speech had lost nothing of its lilt and charm; but the phrases had worn slack; his "Look you" sounded more like "Look ye"; and when he used the Welsh "whatever," it came haphazard in his speech, with a surprised, uncertain note.

Mr. Quest, disappointed of a listener, came to the car, climbed in, and said, "They don't listen. I was telling him the Russians are going to join with the Germans and attack us. I know they are. Just after the war—*my* war—I met a man in a train who said he had seen with his own eyes the way the Russians were kidnapping German scientists and forcing them to work in their factories so they could learn to make tanks to smash the British Empire. I said to Parry . . ."

Martha heard these words somewhere underneath her attention, which was given to her own problems. Mr. Quest looked over his shoulder at her, and said sarcastically, "But don't let me bore you with the Great Unmentionable. Your time'll come, and then I can say I told you so."

Martha turned her face away; her lids stung with tears; she felt the most rejected and desolate creature in the world. It occurred to her that the Cohen boys might have felt like this when she (or so it had appeared) rejected them; but she dismissed the thought at once. The possessors of this particular form of arrogance may know its underside is timidity; but they seldom go on to reflect that the timidity is based on the danger of thinking oneself important to others, which necessitates a return of feeling. She was saying to herself that she could not imagine the clever and self-sufficient Cohen brothers caring about her one way or the other. But we were friends all our childhood, a voice said inside her; and that other voice answered coldly, Friends are whom you choose, not the people forced on you by circumstances. And yet she was nearly crying with misery and humiliation and friendlessness, in the hot back seat of the car, while grains of sunlight danced through the fractured roof, and stung her flesh like needles. For the first time, she said to herself that the Cohens were almost completely isolated in the district. The farmers nodded to them, offered remarks about the weather, but never friendship. The Greek family maintained a complicated system of friendship with the other Greeks from stores all along the railway line. The Cohens had relations in the city, no one nearer.

At last Mr. Parry found a trail of bubbles sizzling up through the dirty water from the tube, and shouted to Gideon, "Come ye, now, you lazy black loafer, and do it quick whateffer you do, and listen well, now."

Gideon indolently lifted himself and went to mend the puncture, while Mr. Parry came back to the car in order to resume his conversation with Mr. Quest.

"Sorry, Captain, but if you want a good job, you do it yourself, whateffer else, it's no good trusting the blacks, they've no pride in their work."

"As I was saying, you people have your heads buried in the sand Anyone can see war is coming. If it's not this year, it'll be the next, as soon as they're strong enough."

"You think the Jerries'll have another shot at us?" asked Mr. Parry, polite but doubtful, and turned so that he might keep an eye on Gideon.

Another native came loping across the railway tracks and stopped by the car. "Baas Quest?" he asked.

Mr. Quest, once again interrupted, turned his darkly irritable eyes on him. But Martha recognized him: he was the Cohen's cook; and she reached for the parcel he held.

"For me," she said, and asked the man to wait. He went off to help Gideon with the tyre.

The parcel was a book from Joss, entitled *The Social Aspect of the Jewish Question,* and inside was a note: "Dear Matty Quest, This will be good for your soul, so do, *do* read it. Yours thin-skinnedly, Joss."

She was filled with outrageous delight. It was forgiveness. She interrupted her father once again to borrow a pencil, and wrote: "Thanks for the book. As it happened, I borrowed it from you and of course agreed with it, three years ago. But I shall read it again and return it next time we come to the station." She was determined that would be very soon.

Next mail day she suggested that they should make the trip, but her father refused, with an air of being exploited.

"Why do you want to go?" asked Mrs. Quest curiously; and Martha said, "I want to see the Cohen boys."

"You're making friends with them?" demurred Mrs. Quest.

"I thought we always were friends with them," said Martha scornfully; and since this put the argument on that hypocritical level where it was maintained that of course the Quests did not think Jews, or even shopkeepers, beneath them, and the only reason they did not continually meet was an inconvenience of some sort, Mrs. Quest could not easily reply.

Martha telephoned the McDougalls to ask if they were going to the station. They were not. She asked the Van Rensbergs; Marnie said awkwardly that Pop didn't often go to the station these days. Finally she telephoned Mr. McFarline, the old miner from the small working in the Dumfries Hills; and he said yes, he was going to town tomorrow. She told her mother she would get a lift back (for "town" in this case meant the city, not the station, as it sometimes did), and added, with the apparently deliberate exaggeration which was so infuriating, "If I don't get a lift, I'll walk." Which of course was absurd, infringed one of the taboos—"a young white girl walking alone," etc.—and was calculated to provoke an argument. The argument immediately followed; and both women appealed to Mr. Quest.

"Why shouldn't she walk?" demanded Mr. Quest vaguely. "When I was a young man in England, I used to walk thirty miles an afternoon and think nothing of it."

"This isn't England," said Mrs. Quest tremulously, filled with horrid visions of what might happen to Martha if she encountered an evil native.

Martha came back with "I walk miles and miles all over the farm, but that doesn't matter, for some reason. How can you be so illogical?"

"Well, I don't like it, and you promised not to go more than half a mile from the house."

Martha laughed angrily, and chose this moment to say what until now she had been careful to keep dark: "Why, I often walk over to the Dumfries Hills, or even to Jacob's Burg, I've been doing it for years."

"Oh, my dear," said Mrs. Quest helplessly. She had known quite well that Martha was doing this, but to be told so now was another thing. "What would happen if a native attacked you?"

"I should scream for help," said Martha flippantly.

"Oh, my dear . . ."

"Oh, don't be ridiculous," said Martha angrily. "If a native raped me, then he'd be hung and I'd be a national heroine, so he wouldn't do it, even if he wanted to, and why should he?"

"My dear, read the newspapers, white girls are always being ra— attacked."

Now, Martha could not remember any case of this happening; it was one of the things people said. She remarked, "Last week a white man raped a black girl, and was fined five pounds."

Mrs. Quest said hastily, "That's not the point, the point is girls get raped."

"Then I expect they want to be," said Martha sullenly; and caught her breath, not because she did not believe the truth of what she said, but because of her parents' faces: she could not help being frightened. For they were united for once, in genuine emotion, and began lecturing her on the consequences of her attitude. It ended with "And so they'll drive us into the sea, and then the country will be ruined, what would these ignorant blacks do without us." And the usual inconsequent conclusion: "They have no sense of gratitude at all for what we do for them." It had all been said so often that it rang stale and false for both sides; and Martha remained silent in a way which they could take as an agreement, for comfort's sake.

Next morning she was waiting down on the track, by the signpost in the long grass, for Mr. McFarline; and they made the journey to the station in just over ten minutes.

Mr. McFarline was a charming and wicked old Scotsman who lived alone on his mine, which he worked in a way which cost him the very minimum in money, but a good deal in human life. There were always accidents on his mine. Also, his native compound was full of half-caste children, his own. He was extremely wealthy, and very popular. He gave generously to charity, and was about to stand for Parliament for one of the town constituencies. Because of the work in connection with getting himself elected, he often went into town.

As the car raced dangerously through the trees, he squeezed Martha's knee in an experimental way and tried to put his hand up her skirt. She held the skirt down, and moved coolly away to the other side of the car, as if she had not noticed the action. So he took his hand away, and concentrated on showing her how nearly it was possible to escape death, with perfect sangfroid, at every bend of the road. He took the paint off his back mudguard at the last raking turn; and they stopped before Sock's store in a billowing cloud of

dust. Martha's heart was beating wildly for several reasons. No one
had ever tried to put his hand up her skirt before, and she was petri-
fied at the wild driving. She looked confused and alarmed; and the
old Scotsman decided to see her as the little girl he had known for
years. He took a ten-shilling note from his stuffed wallet, and gave it
to her.

"For when you go back to school," he said bluffly.

Martha almost handed it back; but was unable to, partly because
ten shillings was such a large sum for her, and partly because of a
feeling which she described to herself as: If I refuse it, he will think
it's because of the way he tried to touch me. She thanked him politely
for the lift, and he roared away over the railway track on the road
to the city, singing, "You're a bonny lassie . . ."

She had the book on the Jewish question (which she had not reread, thinking it unnecessary to gild the already sound coinage of
her opinions) under her arm. She went over to the kaffir store. Mr.
Cohen greeted her, and lifted the counter for her. He was a short,
squat man; his hair was a close-growing, crinkling cap of black; his
skin was pallid and unhealthy. He had, she thought secretly, the look
of a toad, or something confined and light-shunning; and in fact he
was hardly ever away from his counter; but the commercial look of
the small shopkeeper was tempered in him by purpose and dignity,
which was not only because of his ancient culture, but because this
penniless immigrant from Central Europe had chosen such a barren
place, such exile, for the sake of his brilliant sons. His eyes were
black and wise and shrewd, and it was impossible not to like him.
And yet Martha found him repulsive, and was guilty; it was strange
that she could find the oily fatness of the Greek Socrates repulsive
without any sense of guilt at all, but this question of anti-Semitism,
this shrinking nerve, put her on guard against herself, so that her
manner with Mr. Cohen was always strained.

In the back room Martha found Solly, alone; and was pleased that
the brotherly solid act could not be repeated. Besides, there was
something uneasy and false in it, for there was a strong current of
antagonism between the two brothers, a temperamental difficulty
which expressed itself politically—Solly being a Zionist, while Joss
was a Socialist. Solly was a lanky, tall youth, with a big head on a
long thin neck, and big bony hands at the end of long arms; he was
altogether knobbly and unintegrated, and his enormous, sombre
black eyes brooded abstractedly on the world around him in a way
that gave Martha a feeling of kinship to him; but this was perhaps
not an altogether welcome relationship, reminding her, as it did, of
her father. If she was to fight the morbid strain in herself, which was

her father's gift, then how could she admire Solly wholeheartedly, as she wished to do? On the whole, she was easier with Joss, who was short and compact and robust, with humorous direct eyes and a sarcastic practicality, as if he were always saying, "Well, and what's the fuss about, it's all quite easy!"

Solly took the book, without any sign of the hostility of the previous meeting; and no sooner had she sat down than Mrs. Cohen came in with a tray. The older Cohens were strictly kosher, and the sons were lax. For years Mrs. Cohen had been scrupulously sorting her crockery and cutlery, washing them herself, forbidding the native servants even to touch them; but at the table, Joss and Solly, usually deep in bitter argument, would reach for the wrong knives, and stack the plates carelessly about them, while Mrs. Cohen scolded and pleaded. By now she had learned to say, "I'm too old to learn new ways," and with a sorrowful tolerance. She continued to wash and sort her things, but made no comment if her sons misused them. It was a compromise in which Martha could see no sense at all; if her own parents had been guilty of such *unreasonable* behaviour, how irritably would she have argued with them! In Mrs. Cohen, however, it merely struck her as charming. The mere sight of the plump old Jewish woman, with her fine, dark, sad eyes, made her feel welcomed; and she at once accepted, enthusiastically, when she was bidden, "You'll stay eat with us?" In a few moments they were talking as if she had never absented herself from the family for two years.

Solly was leaving shortly to study medicine in Cape Town, and Mrs. Cohen was urging him to live with her cousin there. But Solly wanted independence, a life of his own; and since this vital point was never mentioned, the argument went on endlessly about buses and transport and inconvenience; and it reminded Martha of her own home, where this kind of surface bickering was equally futile.

Joss came in, gave Martha an ambiguous look, and forbore to comment, in a way which made her voice rise to a jaunty brightness. He was intending to study law, but was staying at home with his parents until they could move into town, which they planned to do. The store was to be sold. This solicitude for his father and mother only struck Martha as a kind of betrayal to the older generation; she found it extraordinary; even more strange that he sided with his parents against Solly's desire to fend for himself. He sounded more like an uncle than a brother.

They sat down to table, and Mrs. Cohen asked, "And when are you going back to your studies, Matty? Your mother must be worrying herself."

Martha replied awkwardly, "My eyes aren't better yet," and lowered them towards her plate. When she raised them, she found Joss critically studying her in the way she had feared.

"What's wrong with them?" he enquired bluntly. She gave an uncomfortable movement with her shoulders, as if to say, "Leave me alone." But in this family everything was discussed; and Joss said to Solly, "Her eyes are strained, well, well!"

Solly refused, this time, to make the alliance against her, and asked, "What's it got to do with you?"

Joss raised his brows, and said, "Me? Nothing. She used to be such a bright girl. Pity."

"Leave her alone," said Mr. Cohen unexpectedly, "she's all right." Martha felt a rush of warmth towards him, which as usual she could not express, but dropped her eyes, and even looked sullen.

"Of course she's all right," said Joss carelessly; but there was a note in his voice . . .

Martha looked quickly at him, and at once interpreted his agreement as a reference to her own appearance; and this she half resented, and half welcomed. Since her incarnation as a fairly successful imitation of a magazine beauty, the Cohen boys were the first males she had tried herself against. But she had never said to herself that her careful make-up and the new green linen had been put on to impress them, and therefore she felt it as a false note that either should mention or even react to her appearance—a confusion of feeling which left her silent, and rather sulky. After the meal, Mr. Cohen went back to the shop, and Mrs. Cohen to her kitchen, with the mishandled crockery; and the three young people were left together. Conversation was difficult, and soon Martha felt she should leave. But she lingered; and it was Solly who at last went out; and at once she and Joss were at ease, as she and Solly were, by themselves: it was three of them together that set up the jarring currents.

At once Joss enquired, "And now what's all this about not going to university?"

The direct question, which she had never put to herself, left her silent; but he persisted. "You can't hang about this dorp doing nothing."

She said, "But you are at home, too."

His look said that she must see this was no analogy; he tried not to sound bitter as he remarked, "My parents have no friends in the village. It'll be different when they're in town."

Again she was silent, feeling apologetic for herself and for her parents. She got up and went to the bookcase, to see what was new in it; but this represented the family: the Jewish classics, books on

Palestine, on Poland and Russia; this was the source of the rapidly diverging streams which were Solly and Joss; and these new books would be in their shared bedroom. Into this room it was impossible to go, since she was now Miss Quest; and the glance she directed towards Joss was troubled.

He had been watching her, and, at the glance, he lifted from a table beside him a large pile of books and handed them to her. Again she felt that flush of delight; for he must have prepared them for her. He remarked calmly, "Take these, good for your soul."

She looked at the titles, and was at once indignant, as a child might be if a teacher urged her to study subjects she had mastered the year before.

"What's the matter?" he asked sardonically. "Not up your street?"

She said, "But I know all this." At once she wished the words unsaid, for they sounded conceited. What she meant was, "I agree with all the things these books represent."

He studied her, gave an incredulous grimace, and then fired the following questions at her, in the offhand indifferent manner of the initiate to a breed utterly without the law:

"You repudiate the colour bar?"

"But of course."

"Of course," he said sardonically. And then: "You dislike racial prejudice in all its forms, including anti-Semitism?"

"Naturally"—this with a touch of impatience.

"You are an atheist?"

"You know quite well that I am."

"You believe in socialism?"

"That goes without saying," she concluded fervently; and suddenly began to laugh, from that sense of the absurd which it seemed must be her downfall as a serious person. For Joss was frowning at the laugh, and apparently could see nothing ridiculous in a nineteen-year-old Jewish boy, sprung from an orthodox Jewish family, and an adolescent British girl, if possible even more conventionally bred, agreeing to these simple axioms in the back room of a veld store in a village filled with people to whom every word of this conversation would have the force of dangerous heresy.

"You sound as if you were asking a catechism," she explained, giggling irrepressibly.

He frowned again; and at once she felt indignant that he might be surprised because she had made the same intellectual journey he had. "So what are you going to do about it?" he demanded practically. Also, he sounded aggressive; she was beginning to feel childish and wrong for having laughed; she felt she had hurt him.

"I don't know," she said, and there was an appeal in it. She raised her eyes to his and waited. Because of the look on his face, she at once became conscious of the picture she presented, standing there in front of him, a young girl in a green linen frock that emphasized every line in her body.

"I suppose you are all right," he conceded slowly, looking at her with approval; and she felt the unfairness of it. This was an intellectual discussion, wasn't it? Why, then, that note in his voice?

Her look at him was now as aggressive as his had been. "It's all very well for you, you're a man," she said bitterly, and entirely without coquetry; but he said flippantly, even suggestively, "It will be all quite well for you too!"

He laughed, hoping she might laugh with him. But she stared at him in dismayed outrage, then muttered, "Oh, go to hell," and for the second time left that room, and went out into the glaring sunlight. No sooner had she gone than she understood she had been as touchy and thin-skinned as she had said he was, and almost went back. Pride forbade it; and she went on into the village.

The place had a deserted look. Four in the afternoon: the sky was huge and cloudless, the sun loomed swollen through a reddish haze, and the tin roofs reflected a dulled and sombre light. It was likely to rain soon; but now the long brown pond had shrunk within lips of cracked mud to a narrow scummy puddle. Outside the bar stood half a dozen big cars, outside the station about twenty shabbier cars. Among them was the Van Rensbergs'; and they were packed with children of all ages.

What the British referred to as "the Afrikaans element" had come in for their mail.

Now, it is quite easy to remark the absurdities and contradictions of a country's social system from outside its borders, but very difficult if one has been brought up in it; and for Martha, who must have seen that very sight dozens of times before, it was a moment of illumination, perhaps because she was feeling sore and rejected under Joss's treatment of her; and there was something in the bearing and character of those people kin to what she felt.

On mail days there were cars of every degree of wealth, from the enormous American cars of the tobacco farmers down to eccentric creations like the Quests', but the owners of these cars met together without any consciousness of degree. English and Scotch, Welsh and Irish, rich and poor, it was all backslapping and Christian names, a happy family atmosphere which had a touch of hysterical necessity in it, since the mail days, gymkhanas and dances were false tokens of community—for what is a community if not people who share their experience? The fact was, this district was divided into several separate communities, who shared nothing but Christian names, cards at Christmas, and a member of Parliament. The eastern part of the district, all along the flanks and slopes of Jacob's Burg, was where the tobacco families lived, and here the common denominator was wealth; they were regarded by the rest with tolerance, for they went in for bottle parties, divorces, and modern restlessness. North and west of the Quests' farm Scots families were settled, mostly related, hard-working, modest, sociable people who visited a great deal among themselves. Half a dozen Irish inhabited the slopes of the Oxford Range; but this was not a group; one cannot think of the Irish except as picturesque individualists. Near them were five farms where lived a collection of the English eccentrics who reach their richest bloom only in the colonies. Colonel Castairs, for instance, who lived by himself in a ranging stone mansion, sleeping all day and reading all night, preparing himself to write that history of melancholia through the ages which he would one day begin; he was now over seventy. There was Lord Jamie, who walked naked around his farm, and ate only fruit and nuts; and quarrelled bitterly with his wife because she clothed their children, for he held the view that even so much as a diaper on a baby was an insult to the God who created Adam and Eve. There was a story that once he had come raking into the village on a great black horse, quite naked, with his wild red beard and his mane of red hair sparking fire in the sunlight, a great rough-cast man, whose fiercely innocent blue eyes stared out from the waving locks of his hair like the eyes of an enquiring savage. He dismounted from his horse, and went into the store to buy a pound of tobacco, a bottle of whisky, and the weekly newspaper; and it seemed that everyone in the store greeted him as casually as if he were as decently covered as they. Then they began talking about the weather; and so it had never happened again; and the incident retreated into the fabulous past of kaffir wars, and pioneers, and violence. How exciting life must have been then, sighed the people in the district, remembering their distant origins—and yet the district had not been settled much more than thirty years. How wonderful if the wild man on the black horse appeared again in his scandalous glory! How wonderful if Commander Day walked into the store (as he had once, in the golden age) flanked by his two half-tamed leopards, with his three native concubines behind him—but alas, alas, he did not, they did not; the time for the creation of legends was past.

For many years, between this essential group of gentle maniacs and the Quests' farm there had been hundreds of acres of empty

ground, considered too poor to farm. On its verge, sharing a boundary with the Quests, were the Van Rensbergs, like the solitary swal-
low which would one day make a summer; for five years before another Afrikaans family arrived, rocking along the track in a hooded
waggon, a vehicle which had, to this district, only literary associa-
tions from the Great Trek. Soon there came another family, and then
another . . . And now, inside this district whose pattern of living
was a large farm and two or three children, with a governess and
maybe an assistant, grew up a close-knit, isolated community of
Dutch people, who worked fifty and a hundred acres where the British used thousands, and made their farming pay; who bred healthy
children, eight and ten to a family; who built their own hall, and a
thatched church where they worshipped their angry God. And their
speech had the rich cadences of a living religion.

They came to fetch their mail on a day when the village would be
empty. Their cars drew up together outside Socrates' store; moved
away together to the garage across the railway track; returned together to the station building, one after another in a file, with the
slow deliberation that suggested a team of covered waggons.

So it was today. There were eleven cars, standing behind each
other; and from them had come enough people to populate a small
village, men, women and children, talking, reading mail, playing in
groups.

Martha stood on Socrates' verandah among the grain sacks and
looked at them, and tried to find what it was which gave these people their look of cohesion. Physically they were strong and broadly
built, with the blunt open features of their Dutch ancestry; but the
word "Dutch" surely suggests a picture of fair skin and hair, blue
eyes, an easy health? These people tended to be dark, as if the sun
had fed a strain of resistance into defenceless light skin and the light
hair that becomes dry and limp in the south. The older women wore
black—here the colour of respectability, though in other cultures,
other contexts, it may be the colour of mourning or sophistication.
The younger women wore print frocks that were pretty rather than
smart; some of the children wore the flapping sunbonnets of the
tradition; the men were in the male uniform of the country, khaki
shorts and open-necked shirts. No, the clothing here expressed only
a restlessness, a movement, even uncertainty; for if it was true that
the pretty sunbonnets could have been seen nowhere else, the little
girls' frocks were likely to have been made by a pattern from an
English magazine; and if no one but a certain type of Dutchwoman
would wear those black lace hats (so that, catching sight of one a

hundred yards away, one might imagine the face under it, broad, practical, humorous, earthy), then the black dress she wore with it was probably mass-produced in America.

The closeness of this group expressed itself somewhere else, perhaps in the look of dogged self-sufficiency, the look of the inveterate colonizer; but in that case, they were colonizers in a country which considered itself past the colonizing stage. Not so easy to put flesh and blood on the bones of an intellectual conviction; Martha was remembering with shame the brash and easy way she had said to Joss that she repudiated race prejudice; for the fact was, she could not remember a time when she had not thought of people in terms of groups, nations, or colour of skin first, and as people afterwards. She stood on the verandah of Socrates' store, and looked over the empty dusty space to the railway line, and thought of the different people who passed there: the natives, the nameless and swarming; the Afrikaans, whose very name held the racy, poetic quality of their vigorous origins; the British, with their innumerable subgroupings, held together only because they could say, "This is a British country"—held together by the knowledge of ownership. And each group, community, clan, colour, strove and fought away from the other, in a sickness of dissolution; it was as if the principle of separateness was bred from the very soil, the sky, the driving sun; as if the inchoate vastness of the universe, always insistent in the enormous unshrouded skies, the enormous mountain-girt horizons, so that one might never, not for a moment, forget the inhuman, relentless struggle of soil and water and light, bred a fever of self-assertion in its children, like a band of explorers lost in a desert, quarrelling in an ecstasy of fear over their direction, when nothing but a sober mutual trust could save them. Martha could feel the striving forces in her own substance; the effort of imagination needed to destroy the words *black, white, nation, race,* exhausted her, her head ached, and her flesh was heavy on her bones. She looked at the Van Rensbergs' car, and thought that she had known them for years, and yet she was reluctant even to cross the dust and greet them. She walked off the verandah and towards the car, smiling rather queerly, for when it was too late to retreat it occurred to her that they might not wish to have their friendship with the Quests so publicly emphasized.

She came to a standstill at the car door, and said good afternoon to Mr. Van Rensberg. He nodded at her, and went on reading the newspaper, having made a hunching movement with his shoulder towards the back of the car, where Marnie was sitting with two married sisters who held small babies. There was a young man beside Mr. Van Rensberg, who greeted Martha, and she smiled at him hastily, thinking, This must be a cousin; for his face was the family face.

Marnie was smiling with constrained pleasure, and looked uncomfortably at her father's back; and this made Martha wish she had not come. Over his shoulder, she could see the name of the most rabid nationalist journal from the south; while she did not know the language, there was hardly any need to, for the words and phrases of nationalism are the same in any tongue, but the knowledge that the brain behind the close-cropped black head beside her was agreeing with what was bound to be a violent complaint about the very existence of the British made her drop her voice like a guilty person as she said to Marnie, "Why don't you come over and see me soon?"

"I'd like to, man, I'd like to," agreed Marnie, in the same low tone, and with another glance at her father. "Your dress is the tops, Martha," she added. "May I have the pattern?"

"Of course," said Martha, with an involuntary glance at Marnie's matronly body. "Come over for the day . . ." She had lowered her voice almost to a whisper; the absurdity of it made her angry. She and Marnie quickly said goodbye, smiling at each other like conspirators; she dropped another smile in the direction of the attentive young man in the front seat, and hastily retreated back to the store.

She had no lift home. She would have liked to walk; she intended to, but . . . She imagined that eyes would follow her, queerly, as she set off, on foot, along a road where a dozen cars might be expected to pass that afternoon. *White girls do not . . .* As she was hesitating on the verandah, she saw Joss approaching, and smiled with what was, had she known it, a tenderly amused appreciation of the figure he cut. He wore a respectable dark suit, he carried books under his arm, he moved in a careful, constrained way, eyes watching the direction of his feet, his shoulders a little hunched. He seemed, in fact, already the sober professional man he intended to become; he was altogether out of place among these khaki-clad, open-air people; and knew it, and approved. For these farmers, these men of the soil: when they approached, one saw first the exposed developed limbs, the body; one marked the hard muscled forearm perhaps, or the bronze knotted pillar of the thigh, or the stride, or the swing of the arms; they moved magnificently, at ease, slowly, to match the space and emptiness of the country—no suggestion here of limbs grown cautious and self-contained, against possible undesired contact. Yes, here one stands at a distance from a man, a woman, and sees them whole. First the way of walking, the stance of the body. Then lift your eyes to the face, and the first impression is confirmed: what fine, exposed, frank faces, wholesomely weathered, unafraid, open to every glance. And then (but lastly) the eyes, look straight at the eyes—which of course meet yours with the completest frankness. Nothing to hide here, they say; everything aboveboard, take it or leave it. But always, behind the friendly brown eyes, the welcoming blue ones, is the uneasiness; something not easily defined, but expressed best, perhaps, in a moment of laughter. The man laughs, out loud, an infectious wholehearted laugh; but there is a faint sideways flickering movement of the eyes, the eyes are not altogether there, there is an absence, something blank and empty. Take, for instance, that contingent of fine young colonials marching down the Strand with their English cousins. What fine young men, what physique; a head taller than the rest, bronzed, muscled, strong as horses. Then look at the eyes. But the eyes seem to say, "What do you want with us? Aren't our bodies enough for you?" There is a pale and fretful look; the soft and luminous darkness that should lie behind the iris is simply not there. Something is missing.

And so it seems that one cannot have it both ways, one has to choose; and Joss chose, without any hesitation.

Martha, watching him approach, was conscious of the most perverse but definite feeling of pity. Why pity? She envied him almost to the point of bitterness, knowing exactly what he wanted, and how to get it. She saw how the compact, neat body, hidden under dark-grey flannel, moved carefully across the sunlit, filthy dust, as if every nerve and muscle were connected direct to his will; she saw how his eyes were focused, steady and direct, the whole of himself behind them, so that it was only when one looked into his eyes that one saw him; she saw the great difference there was between Joss and these farmers, and she half envied, half pitied him. Pity? What for? One does not pity a person who knows what it is he chooses, and why.

Martha was watching him in a way which would allow her to pretend, to herself at least, that she was not; she was afraid he might go past her with another of his formal nods. He came straight towards her, however, extended the books, and said brusquely, "I thought you'd like these."

"How did you know I was still here?"—with feminine obliquity.

"I can see the store through the trees."

For a moment Martha was irrationally angry, as if she had been spied upon; then he asked, "How are you getting home?" and she replied defiantly, "I'm walking." It seemed, however, that Joss could see no reason why she should not walk; and after a hesitation he merely said, "So long!" and walked back across the dust. Martha was disappointed—he might have asked her back to his home, she thought. Then she understood that he was waiting for her to invite herself; and this confused her. She shrugged away the thought of Joss, who always made her feel deficient in proper feeling; and with the parcel of books under her arm, which gave her confidence, she walked away off Socrates' verandah, and along the road home.

She had never made this journey on foot; always by car, or, as a child, perched on top of the hot hairy grain sacks on the waggon. During the first mile she was remembering the creaking sway of the old waggon, which seemed always as if it might spring apart between the dragging weight of the sacks and the forward-heaving oxen; there was a place towards the front of the waggon where it seemed that the tension was localized, and here she had liked to sit, shuddering with excitement, because of the groaning timbers under her, which always were on the point of flying asunder, but never did, carrying their burden mile after slow and labouring mile. She was remembering the alarming way the sacks shifted under her; heavy sacks they were, but sliding and subsiding easily with the sway of the vehicle. She remembered the pleasurable warm smell of the cow droppings falling plop, plop into the red dust, and releasing, deliciously, the odours of fresh grass; so that, although the waggon wheels perpetually flung up rivers of red sand, and she travelled in a column of whirling ruddy dust, the sweet perfumes of newly cudded grass mingled with it, mile after mile, as if the four-divided stomachs of the great oxen were filled with nothing but concentrated memories of hours of grazing along the water-heavy vleis.

Later, she hesitated outside the McDougalls' farm; for if she went in she would be given a wonderful Scotch tea of bannocks and grid-dle cakes and newly churned butter. But she did not go in, for the McDougalls had not yet noticed that she was now Miss Quest; they still treated her like a child, and this she could not bear.

She walked more slowly now, not wanting the journey to end; she was savouring freedom: the station far behind, where she was convinced everyone remarked her, commented on her; the house not yet in sight, where the mere existence of her parents was like a re-minder that she must be wary, ready to resist. Now there was no one to mark her, not a soul in sight; and she dawdled along the track, skipping from one rut to another, and pulling from their delicate green sheaths the long sweet-tasting grass stems that are as pleasant to chew along a dusty road as sticks of sugar cane. She was happy because she was, for the moment, quite free; she was sad because before long she would reach home; these two emotions deepened to-gether, and it flashed across her mind that this intense, joyful melancholy was a state of mind she had known in the past and— But at once she dismissed the thought; it passed as lightly as the shadow of a wing of a bird, for she knew that the experience associated with that emotion was not to be courted. One did not lie in wait for it; it was a visitor who came without warning. On the other hand, even the fact that the delicious but fearful expectation had crossed her mind at all was enough to warn it away; the visitor liked darkness, this Martha knew, and she hastened to think of something else. At the same time, she was thinking that she had associated the experience with what she now, rather scornfully, called her "religious phase"; and becoming an atheist, which she had done from one day to the next, as easily as dropping a glove, had been painful only because she imagined she must pay the price for intellectual honesty by bidding farewell to this other emotion, this fabulous visitor. It seemed, then, that no such price had been asked of her, it seemed that—

Martha caught herself up, already bad-tempered and irritable: she must *not* analyze, she must not be conscious; and here she was, watching the movements of her own mind as if she were observing a machine. She noted, too, that she was walking very fast, quite blind to the beauties of the trees and grass. For it was evening, and very beautiful; a rich watery gold was lighting the dark greens of the foliage, the dark red of the soil, the pale blond of the grass, to the solemn intensity of the sunset hour. She noted a single white-stemmed tree with its light cloud of glinting leaf rising abruptly from the solid-packed red earth of an anthill, all bathed in a magical sky-reflecting light, and her heart moved painfully, in exquisite sadness. She consciously walked more slowly, consciously enjoyed the melancholy; and all at once found herself on a slight rise, where the trees opened across a wide reach of country; and the sight, a new one, caused her to forget everything else. She could see their house, crouched low on the green-shrouded hill, and between was an unbroken stretch of silver-gold mealies; it was perhaps five miles from where she stood to the Van Rensbergs' boundary, a dark belt of trees behind which solemn blue sky rose like a wall. The mealies swayed and whispered, and the light moved over them; a hawk lay motionless on a current of blue air; and the confused and painful delirium stirred in her again, and this time so powerfully she did not fear its passing. The bush lay quiet about her, a bare slope of sunset-tinted grass moving gently with a tiny rustling sound; an invisible violet tree shed gusts of perfume, like a benediction; and she stood quite still, waiting for the moment, which was now inevitable. There was a movement at the corner of her eye, and she turned her head, cautiously, so as not to disturb what was swelling along her nerves, and saw a small buck, which had come from the trees and stood quietly, flicking its tail, a few paces away. She hardly dared to blink. The buck gazed at her, and then turned its head to look into the bush, laying its ears forward. A second buck tripped out from the trees, and they both stood watching her; then they walked daintily across the ground, their hooves clicking sharp on the stones, the sun warm on their soft brown hides. They dropped their heads to graze, while their little tails shook from side to side impatiently, with flashes of white.

Suddenly the feeling in Martha deepened, and as it did so she knew she had forgotten, as always, that what she had been waiting for like a revelation was a pain, not a happiness; what she remembered, always, was the exultation and the achievement, what she forgot was this difficult birth into a state of mind which words like *ecstasy, illumination,* and so on could not describe, because they suggest joy. Her mind having been formed by poetic literature (and little else), she of course knew that such experiences were common among the religious. But the fact was, so different was "the moment" from what descriptions of other people's "moments" led her to believe was common, that it was not until she had come to accept the experience as ordinary and "incidental to the condition of adolescence" as she put it, sourly, and with positive resentment, that it occurred to her, Why, perhaps it is the same thing, after all? But if so, they were liars, liars one and all; and that she could understand, for was it not impossible for her to remember, in between, how terrible an illumination it was?

There was certainly a definite point at which the thing began. It was not; then it was suddenly inescapable, and nothing could have frightened it away. There was a slow integration, during which she, and the little animals, and the moving grasses, and the sun-warmed trees, and the slopes of shivering silvery mealies, and the great dome of blue light overhead, and the stones of earth under her feet, became one, shuddering together in a dissolution of dancing atoms. She felt the rivers under the ground forcing themselves painfully along her veins, swelling them out in an unbearable pressure; her flesh was the earth, and suffered growth like a ferment; and her eyes stared, fixed like the eye of the sun. Not for one second longer (if the terms for time apply) could she have borne it; but then, with a sudden movement forwards and out, the whole process stopped; and *that* was "the moment" which it was impossible to remember afterwards. For during that space of time (which was timeless) she understood quite finally her smallness, the unimportance of human-

ity. In her ears was an inchoate grinding, the great wheels of movement, and it was inhuman, like the blundering rocking movement
of a bullock cart; and no part of that sound was Martha's voice. Yet
she was part of it, reluctantly allowed to participate, though on
terms—but what terms? For that moment, while space and time (but
these are words, and if she understood anything it was that words,
here, were like the sound of a baby crying in a whirlwind) kneaded
her flesh, she knew futility; that is, what was futile was her own
idea of herself and her place in the chaos of matter. What was demanded of her was that she should accept something quite different;
it was as if something new was demanding conception, with her flesh
as host; as if there were a necessity, which she must bring herself to accept, that she should allow herself to dissolve and be formed by that
necessity. But it did not last; the force desisted, and left her standing
on the road, already trying to reach out after "the moment" so that she
might retain its message from the wasting and creating chaos of darkness. Already the thing was sliding backwards, becoming a whole in
her mind, instead of a process; the memory was changing, so that it
was with nostalgia that she longed "to try again."

There had been a challenge that she had refused. But the wave
of nostalgia made her angry. She knew it to be a falsity; for it was
a longing for something that had never existed, an "ecstasy," in short.
There had been no ecstasy, only difficult knowledge. It was as if a
beetle had sung. There should be a new word for *illumination*.

She saw that she was standing off the road, in the grass, staring
at the two little buck, who indifferently flicked their tails and grazed
their way off into the bush. Martha thought that she had often shot
these little creatures, and that she would never do so again, since they
had shared the experience with her. And even as she made the decision, she was as helplessly irritable as if she had caught herself
out in a lie which was pointless. She felt, above all, irritable; not
sad, merely flat and stale; the more because not five minutes after
"the moment" it had arranged itself in her mind as a blissful joy;
it was necessary, apparently, to remember the thing as an extremity
of happiness.

She walked slowly homewards, taking a short cut along the fence
through the mealies. The ground was hard and packed, cracked
across with drought under her feet, which ached, for her sandals
were meant for show and not use. She climbed the hill draggingly,
and went to her room, so as to compose herself before meeting her
parents, or rather, her mother, for to *meet* her father was rather like
trying to attract the attention of an irritable spectre.

Alas for visions and decisions. In her bedroom she felt nothing but angry resentment: against the people in the district, against Mr. McFarline, against Marnie, who would now "drop over" and borrow patterns.

Her mother entered with the oil lamp, for it was dusk, and exclaimed, "My dear, I was worrying, and you don't even tell me you're home."

"Well, there's no harm done, safe and sound and still a virgin."

"My *dear—*" Mrs. Quest checked herself, and hung the lamp on the wall. The flame vibrated bluely, then sent a pleasant yellow glow over the uneven plaster, and up to the thatch, where a strand of tarnished silver glistened among shadow. "How did you get back?" asked Mrs. Quest cautiously.

"Walked," Martha said aggressively; and even felt disappointed because Mrs. Quest did not protest.

"Well, come on, we're going to have supper now."

Martha followed her mother obediently, and suddenly found herself saying, in a bright flippant voice, "That dirty old man, Mr. McFarline, he tried to make love to me." She looked at her father, but he was slowly crumbling his bread in time with his thoughts.

Mrs. Quest said hastily, "Nonsense, you're imagining it, he couldn't have done."

The suggestion that she was too young for such attentions made Martha say, "And then he had an attack of conscience, and offered me ten shillings." She giggled uncomfortably, with another glance at her abstracted father; and Mrs. Quest said, "He knows better, he's too nice."

"Nice," said Martha acidly, "with a compound full of his children."

Mrs. Quest said hastily, with a glance at the servant who was handing vegetables, "You shouldn't listen to gossip."

"Everybody knows it, and besides, I heard you saying so to Mrs. McDougall."

"Well, but that doesn't mean—I don't think . . ."

"Damned hypocrisy," said Martha, "all this colour-bar nonsense, and Mr. McFarline can sleep with whoever he likes and—"

"My dear," said Mrs. Quest, with a desperate look towards the impassive servant, "do think of what you're saying."

"Yes, that's all you think of, provided all the lies and ugliness are covered up."

Mrs. Quest raised her voice in anger, and the battle was on; mother and daughter said the things both had said so often before; not even waiting for the other to finish a sentence, until the noise caused Mr. Quest to snap out, "Shut up, both of you."

They looked at him immediately, and with relief; one might have supposed this was the result they intended. But Mr. Quest said no more; after a baffled and exasperated glare, he dropped his eyes and continued to eat.

"You hear what your father says?" demanded Mrs. Quest unfairly.

Martha was filled with frightened pain, at this alliance against her; and she exclaimed loudly, "Anything for peace, you and your Christianity, and then what you do in practice . . ." But almost at once she became ashamed, because of the childishness of what she was saying. But the things we say are usually on a far lower level than what we think; it seemed to Martha that perhaps her chief grievance against her parents was this: that in her exchange with them she was held down at a level she had long since outgrown, even on this subject, which, to her parents, was the terrifyingly extreme outpost of her development.

But her remark at least had had the power to pierce her father's defences, for he raised his head and said angrily, "Well, if we're so rotten, and you haven't any time for us, you can leave. Go on," he shouted, carried away by the emotions his words generated, "go on, then, get out and leave us in peace."

Martha caught her breath in horror; on the surface of her mind she was pointing out to herself that her own father was throwing her out of her home—she, a girl of seventeen. Deeper down, however, she recognized this for what it was, an emotional release, which she should ignore. "Very well," she said angrily, "I will leave." She and her father looked at each other across the breadth of the table—her mother sat in her usual place at the head; and those two pairs of dark and angry eyes stared each other out.

It was Mr. Quest who dropped his head and muttered, half guiltily, "I simply cannot stand this damned fight, fight, fight!" And he pettishly threw down his napkin. Immediately the servant bent and picked it up, and handed it to his master. "Thanks," said Mr. Quest automatically, arranging it again across his lap.

"My *dear*," said Mrs. Quest, in a small appealing voice to her husband.

He replied grumblingly, "Well, fight if you like, but not when I'm around, for God's sake."

Now they all remained silent; and immediately after the meal Martha went to her bedroom, saying to herself that she would leave home at once, imagining various delightful rescues. The parcel of books lay unopened on her bed. She cut the string and looked at the titles, and her feeling of being let down deepened. They were all on economics. She had wished for books which might explain this confusion of violent feeling she found herself in.

Next day she rose early, and went out with the gun and killed a duiker on the edge of the Big Tobacco Land (where her father had grown tobacco during his season's phase of believing in it). She called a passing native to carry the carcase home to the kitchen, which, as it happened, was already full of meat.

But put this way it implies too much purpose. Martha woke early, and could not sleep; she decided to go for a walk because the sunrise was spread so exquisitely across the sky; she took the gun because it was her habit to carry it, though she hardly ever used it; she shot at the buck almost half-heartedly, because it happened to present itself; she was surprised when it fell dead; and when it was dead, it was a pity to waste the meat. The incident was quite different from actually planning the thing, or so she felt; and she thought half guiltily, Oh, well, what does it matter, anyway?

After breakfast she again looked at Joss's books, skimming through them rapidly. They were written by clearly well-meaning people who disliked poverty. Her feeling was, I know this already; which did not only mean that she agreed with any conclusion which proved hopelessly unfair a system which condemned her, Martha Quest, to live on the farm, instead of in London with people she could talk to. She made this joke against herself rather irritably, for she knew it to be half true. What she felt was, Yes, of course poverty is stupid, so why say it again? How do you propose to alter all this? And "all this" meant the farm, the hordes of deprived natives who worked it, the people in the district, who assumed they had every right to live as they did and use the natives as they pleased. The reasonable persuasiveness of the books seemed merely absurd, when one thought of the violent passions ranged against them. She imagined the author of books like these as a clean, plump, suave gentleman, shut in a firelit study behind drawn curtains, with no sound in his ears but the movement of his own thoughts.

She kept the books a week, and then returned them on a mail day with the postboy. She also sent a note saying: "I wish you would let me have some books about the emancipation of women." It was only after the man had left that the request struck her as naïve, a hopeless self-exposure; and she could hardly bear to open the parcel which was sent to her. Inside was the note she had expected: "I'm glad you have absorbed so much knowledge of economics in three days. What a clever girl you are. I enclose helpful handbook on sexual problems. I could ask Solly, who has a fine collection of psychology, etc., but alas, he has gone off to "live his own life," and our relations are not such that I could handle his books without asking him." The enclosed book was Engels' *Origin of the Family*. Martha read it, and agreed with every word of it—or rather, with what she gained from it, which was a confirmation of her belief that the marriages of the district were ridiculous and even sordid, and most of all old-fashioned.

She sat under her tree, hugging her sun-warmed arms, feeling the firm soft flesh with approval, and the sight of her long and shapely legs made her remember the swollen bodies of the pregnant women she had seen, with shuddering anger, as at the sight of a cage designed for herself. Never, never, never, she swore to herself, but with a creeping premonition; and she thought of Solly's books, now out of bounds, because he and Joss so unreasonably insisted on quarrelling; and she thought of Joss, for whom she was feeling a most irrational dislike. At one moment she scorned him because he had dared to treat her like an attractive young female; and the next because he had taken her at her word, and simply offered books; and this confusion hardened into a nervous repulsion: Well, she could do without Joss!

She returned Engels, with such a formal note that no further word came from him, though she was waiting for one; and then melancholy settled over her, and she wandered around the farm like a girl under a spell of silence.

One morning she came on her father, seated on a log of wood at the edge of a field, watching the natives dig a furrow for storm water. Mr. Quest held his pipe between his teeth, and slowly rolled plugs of rich dark tobacco between his palms, while his eyes rested distantly on his labourers.

"Well, old son?" he enquired, as Martha sat beside him; for he might call either his male or his female child "old son."

Martha rested the rifle across her knees, pulled herself some chewing grass, and lapsed into his silence; for these two, away from Mrs. Quest, were quite easy together.

But she could not maintain it; she had to worry at him for his attention; and soon she began to complain about her mother, while Mr. Quest uneasily listened. "Yes, I daresay," he agreed, and "Yes, I suppose you are right"; and with every agreement his face expressed only the wish that she might remove this pressure on him to consider not only her position but his own. But Martha did not desist; and at last the usual irritability crept into his voice, and he said, "Your mother's a good woman," and he gave her a look which meant "Now, that's enough."

"Good?" said Martha, inviting him to define the word.

"That's all very well," he said, shifting himself slightly away.

"What do you mean by 'good'?" she persisted. "You know quite well she's— I mean, if goodness is just doing what you want to do, behaving in a conventional way, without thinking, then goodness is easy enough to come by!" Here she flung a stone crossly at the trunk of a tree.

"I don't see where you end, when you start like this," said Mr. Quest, complainingly. For this was by no means the first time this conversation had taken place, and he dreaded it. They were both remembering that first occasion, when he had demanded angrily, "Well, don't you love your mother, then?" and Martha had burst into peals of angry laughter, saying, "Love? What's love got to do with it? She does exactly as she wants, and says, 'Look how I sacrificed myself,' she never stops trying to get her own way, and then you talk about love."

After a long silence, during which Mr. Quest slowly slid away into his private thoughts, Martha said defiantly, "Well, I don't see it. You just use words and—it's got nothing to do with what actually goes on . . ." She stopped, confused; though what she felt was clear enough: not only that people's motives were not what they imagined them to be, but that they should be made to see the truth.

"Oh, Lord, Matty," said Mr. Quest, suddenly bursting into that helpless anger. "What do you want me to do? The last year has been hell on earth, you never stop bickering."

"So you want me to go away?" asked Martha pathetically; and her heart sang at the idea of it.

"I never said anything of the sort," said poor Mr. Quest, "you're always so extreme." Then, after a pause, hopefully: "It wouldn't be a bad idea, would it? You always say you've outgrown your mother, and I daresay you have."

Martha waited, and it was with the same hopeful enquiry she had felt with Joss: she was wanting someone to take the responsibility for her; she needed a rescue. Mr. Quest should have suggested some practical plan, and at once, very much to his surprise, he would have found an amenable and grateful daughter. Instead, the silence prolonged itself into minutes. He sighed with pleasure, as he looked over the sunlit field, the silent, heat-slowed bush; then he lowered his eyes to his feet, where there were some ants at work in an old piece of wood.

Suddenly he remarked, in a dreamy voice, "Makes you think, doesn't it, seeing these ants? I wonder how they see us, like God, I shouldn't be surprised? When that soil specialist was out last year, he said ants have a language, and a police force—that sort of thing."

There was no reply from Martha. At last he shot her an apprehensive glance sideways, and met eyes that were half angry, half amused, but with a persistent criticism that caused him to rise to his feet, saying, "How about going up to the house and asking for some tea? Weather makes you thirsty."

And in silence the father and daughter returned to the house on the hill.

3

Mrs. Quest watched her daughter and husband returning from the fields, with nervous anticipation. The night before, in the dark bedroom, she had demanded that he must speak to Martha, who wouldn't listen to her own mother, she was ruining her future. Mr. Quest's cigarette glowed exasperatedly, illuminating his bent and troubled face; and at the sight of that face, Mrs. Quest leaned over the side of the bed towards him, and her voice rose into peevish insistence; for as long as the darkness allowed her to forget her husband's real nature, she spoke with confidence. And what was he expected to say? he demanded. "Yes, yes, I daresay," and "I am quite sure you're right," and "Yes, but, May, old girl, surely that's putting it a bit strongly?"

Mrs. Quest had lain awake most of the night, framing those angry complaints against him in her mind that she could not say aloud. Since it had always been understood that only bad luck and ill-health had brought the family to such irremediable if picturesque poverty, how could she say now what she thought: For heaven's sake, pull yourself together, and run the farm properly, and then we can send Martha to a good school, which will undo the bad effects caused by the Van Rensbergs and the Cohen boys?

She thought of writing to her brother; she even made this decision; then the picture of Martha in a well-regulated suburban London household, attending a school for nice English girls, entered her mind with uncomfortable force. She remembered, too, that Martha was seventeen; and her anger was switched against the girl herself; it was too late, it was much too late, and she knew it. Thoughts of Martha always filled her with such violent and supplicating and angry emotions that she could not sustain them; she began to pray for Martha: Please help me to save her, please let her forget her silly ideas, *please let her be like her brother*. Mrs. Quest fell asleep, soothed by tender thoughts of her son.

But it seemed that half an hour's angry and urgent pleading last night had after all pricked Alfred into action. There was something in the faces of these two (they were both uncomfortable, and rather flushed) that made her hopeful. She called for tea, and arranged herself by the tea table on the verandah, while Martha and Mr. Quest fell into chairs, and each reached for a book.

"Well, dear?" asked Mrs. Quest at last, looking at them both. Neither heard her. Martha turned a page; Mr. Quest was filling his pipe, while his eyes frowningly followed the print on the pages balanced against his knee. The servant brought tea, and Mrs. Quest filled the cups.

She handed one to Mr. Quest, and asked again, "Well, dear?"

"Very nice, thank you," said Mr. Quest, without looking up.

Her lips tightened, and as she gave Martha her cup she demanded jealously, "Had a nice talk?"

"Very nice, thank you," said Martha vaguely.

Mrs. Quest regarded them both, and with a look of conscious but forgiving bitterness. Her husband was half hidden in a cloud of lazy blue smoke. He was the very picture of a hard-working farmer taking his repose. Martha, at first sight, might pass for that marriageable and accomplished daughter it seemed that Mrs. Quest, after all, desired. In her bright-yellow linen dress, her face tinted carefully with cosmetics, she appeared twenty. But the dress had grass stains on it, was crumpled, she was smoking hungrily, and her fingers were already stained with nicotine, her rifle was lying carelessly across her lap, and on it was balanced a book which, as Mrs. Quest could see, was called *The Decay of the British Empire*. That Martha should be reading this book struck her mother as a criticism of herself; she began to think of the hard and disappointing life she had led since she came to the colony; and she lay back in her chair, and onto her broad, square, rather masculine face came a look of patient regret; her small blue eyes clouded, and she sighed deeply.

The sigh, it appeared, had the power to reach where her words could not. Both Martha and Mr. Quest glanced up, guiltily. Mrs. Quest had forgotten them; she was looking through them at some picture of her own; she was leaning her untidy grey head against the mud wall of the house; she was twiddling a lock of that limp grey hair round and round one finger—a mannerism which always stung Mr. Quest—while with the other hand she stroked her skirt, in a tired, hard, nervous movement which affected Martha like a direct criticism of ingratitude.

"Well, old girl?" demanded Mr. Quest, with guilty affection.

She withdrew her eyes from her private vision, and rested them on her husband. "Well?" she returned, and with a different intonation, dry, and ironic, and patient.

Martha saw her parents exchange a look which caused her to rise from her chair, in order to escape. It was a look of such sardonic understanding that she could not bear it, for it filled her with a violent and intolerable pity for them. Also, she thought, How *can* you be so resigned about it? and became fearful for her own future, which she was determined would never include a marriage whose only basis was that ironic mutual pity. Never, never, she vowed; and as she picked up her rifle and was moving towards the steps she heard a car approaching.

"Visitors," she said warningly; and her parents sighed at the same moment, "Oh, *Lord!*"

But it was Marnie, sitting beside one of her sisters' husbands.

"Oh, Lord," said Mr. Quest again. "If she's wearing those damned indecent shorts, then . . ." He got up, and hastily escaped.

The car did not come close to the house, but remained waiting on the edge of the small plateau in front. Marnie approached. She was not wearing shorts, but a bright floral dress, with a bunch of flowers and lace at the neck. She was now very fat, almost as large as her mother; and her heavy browned arms and legs came out of the tight dyed crepe like the limbs of an imprisoned Brunhilde. Her hair was crimped into tight ridges around the good-natured housewife's face.

"I haven't come to stay," she called from a distance, and quickened her steps. Martha waited for her, wishing that her mother also would go away; but Mrs. Quest remained, watchful above the teacups. So she walked down to meet Marnie, where they might both be out of earshot.

Marnie said hastily, "Listen, Matty, man, we're having a dance, well, just friends, sort of, and would you like to come? Next Saturday?" She looked apprehensively at Mrs. Quest, past Martha's shoulder.

Martha hesitated, and found herself framing excuses; then she agreed, rather stiffly, so that Marnie coloured, as if she had been snubbed. Seeing this, Martha, with a pang of self-dislike, said how much she had been longing to dance, that in this district there was nothing to do—even that she was lonely. Her voice, to her own surprise, was emotional; so that she too coloured, as at a self-betrayal.

Marnie's good heart responded at once to what must be an appeal, even a reproach, and she said, "But Matty, man, I've been wanting to ask you for ages, really, but I thought that . . ." She stumbled over the unsayable truth, which was half a complaint against the snobbish English and half an explanation of her father's attitude. She went on in a rush, falling back into the easy, suggestive raillery: "If you knew what my brother Billy thinks of you, oh, man! He thinks you're the tops." She giggled, but Martha's face stopped her.

The two girls, scarlet as poinsettias, were standing in silence, in the most confusing state of goodwill and hostility, when Mrs. Quest came down the path. From a distance, they might have been on the point of either striking each other or falling into each other's arms; but as she arrived beside them, Martha turned and exclaimed vivaciously, "I'm going to dance at Marnie's place on Saturday night!"

"That's nice, dear," she said doubtfully, after a pause.

"It's only just informal, Mrs. Quest, nothing grand," and Marnie squeezed Martha's arm. "Well, be seeing you, we'll come and fetch you about eight." She ran off, calling back, "My mom says Matty can stay the night, if that's all right." She climbed heavily into the car, sending back beaming smiles and large waves of the hand; and in a moment the car had slid down off the hill into the trees.

"So you're making friends with the Van Rensbergs," said Mrs. Quest reproachfully, as if this confirmed all her worst fears; and a familiar note was struck for both of them when Martha said coldly, "I thought you and the Van Rensbergs had been *friends* for years?"

"What's all this about Billy?" asked Mrs. Quest, trying to disinfect sex, as always, with a humorous, teasing voice.

"What about him?" asked Martha, and added, "He's a very nice boy." She walked off towards her bedroom, in such a state of exaltation that a voice within her was already enquiring, Why are you so happy? For this condition could be maintained only as long as she forgot Billy himself. She had not seen him for two or three years, but it occurred to her that he might have caught sight of her somewhere; for surely he could not have tender memories of their last encounter? Martha, on a hot, wet, steamy afternoon, had spent two hours wriggling on her stomach through the undergrowth to reach a point where she might shoot a big koodoo that was grazing in a corner of the Hundred Acres. Just as she rested the rifle to fire, a shot rang out, the koodoo fell, and Billy Van Rensberg walked out from the trees a few paces away, to stand over the carcase like a conqueror. "That's my koodoo!" said Martha shrilly. She was covered with red mud, her hair hung lank to her shoulders, her eyes trickled dirty tears. Billy was apologetic but firm, and made things worse by offering her half; for it was not the meat she cared about. He bestrode the carcase, and began stripping off the hide: a brown, shockheaded lad, who occasionally lifted puzzled blue eyes towards this girl who walked around and around him, crying with rage, and insisting, "It's not fair, it's not fair!" Finally she said, as the hot smell of blood reeked across the sunlight, "You're no better than a butcher!" With this, she marched away across the big red clods of the field, trying to look indifferent. Martha had long since decided that this incident belonged to her childhood, and therefore no longer concerned her; and it made her uncomfortable that Billy might still be remembering it. Altogether, the mere idea of Billy aroused in her an altogether remarkable resentment; and she chose not to think of him.

This was on a Wednesday. During the next day or two she could scarcely eat or sleep; she was in a condition of restless expectation that was almost unbearable. The Saturday dance seemed like an entrance into another sort of life, for she was seeing the Van Rensbergs' house magnified, and peopled with youthful beings who had less to do with what was likely than with that vision of legendary cities which occupied so much of her imagination. The Quests were watching, with fearful amazement, a daughter who was no longer silent and critical, but bright-eyed and chattering and nervous: a proper condition for a girl going to her first dance.

Martha was agonized over what to wear, for Marnie, who had been wearing grown-up clothes since she was about thirteen, would of course have evening dresses. Mrs. Quest hopefully offered a frilly pink affair which had belonged to a ten-year-old cousin, saying that it came from Harrods, which was a guarantee of good taste. Martha merely laughed, which was what Mrs. Quest deserved, for she was seeing her daughter as about twelve, with a ribbon in her hair, an Alice-in-Wonderland child, for this vision made the idea of Billy less dangerous. There was a quarrel: Martha began sarcastically to explain why it was that even if she had been twelve she could not have worn this pink frilled georgette to the Van Rensbergs' house, since nice little English girls were not for export. At length, Mrs. Quest withdrew, saying bitterly that Martha was only trying to be difficult, that she needn't think they could afford to buy her a new one. She had the pink dress ironed and put on Martha's bed; Martha quickly hid it, for she was really terrified at what the Van Rensbergs might say if they ever caught sight of that charming, coy, childish frock.

On the Friday morning she telephoned Mr. McFarline, and was down at the turn-off waiting for him before nine in the morning.

Mr. McFarline drove more slowly than usual to the station. He was nervous of Martha, who had accepted ten shillings from him, like a child, but who was now using him with the calm unscrupulousness of a good-looking young woman who takes it for granted that men enjoy being used. She was looking, not at him, but out of the window at the veld; and he asked at last, "And what's the great attraction at the station?"

"I'm going to buy material for a dress," she announced.

He could think of no approach after that impersonal statement that might make it possible to joke with her, or even ask her for a kiss; and it occurred to him that the stern young profile, averted from him as if he were not there, was not that of a girl one might kiss. Mr. McFarline was made to think, in fact, of his age, which was not usual for him. Two years before, this girl and her brother had come riding on their bicycles over to his mine, eating chocolate biscuits, and listening to his tales of adventurous living, accepting his generous tips with an equally generous embarrassment. No more than two years ago, he had slapped Martha across the bottom, pulled her hair, and called her his lassie.

He said sentimentally, "Your father has no luck, but he's got something better than money."

"What's that?" asked Martha politely.

He was driving along a piece of road that was dust between ruts, on a dangerous slant, and it was not for several seconds that he could turn his eyes to her face. She was looking at him direct, with a slow quizzical gleam that made him redden. An outrageous idea occurred to him, but he dismissed it at once, not because he was afraid of his neighbours knowing about his life, but because Martha was too young to acknowledge that she knew: there was something in her face which made him think of his children in the compound, and even more of their mothers.

With a short, amused laugh, Martha again turned to the window.

He said gruffly, "It's a fine thing for your father, a daughter like you. When I look at you, lassie, I wish I had married."

Once again Martha turned to look at him, her eyebrows raised, her mouth most comically twisted. "Well," she said, "you couldn't marry them all, one can see that."

They had reached the station, and he dragged at the brakes. His heavy, handsome face, with its network of tiny red veins, was now a uniform purple. Martha opened the door, got out, and said, very politely, "Thanks for the lift." She turned away, then over her shoulder gave him a delightful amused smile, which at once infuriated Mr. McFarline and absolved him of guilt. He watched her walk away, in her rather stiff awkward manner, to Socrates' store; and he was swearing, Damn little . . . Then he, too, laughed, and went off to town in the best of good spirits, though at bottom he was very shocked; for when he was drunk he enjoyed thinking of himself as a sinner, and it was in these moods that the local charities were sent such generous cheques.

Martha went into the Greek store. It was empty. Socrates was behind the counter, as usual, reading a murder story. He greeted her as "Miss Quest," and showed her what materials he had, apologizing for not having anything good enough for such a fine young lady. He was a short, plump man, with black eyes like raisins, and a pale, smooth skin, and a manner of serving that was adjusted to the customer. In this case, he was suggesting that Mr. Quest owed him a hundred pounds; and Martha said coldly, "No, I'm afraid you're quite right, you have nothing very attractive, have you?" She walked out, reluctantly, for there was a piece of green figured silk she would have liked to buy.

On the verandah she stood hesitating, before plunging into the glare of that dusty space, where the sunlight lashed up from tin roofs and from the shrinking pond. A dark greasy cloud held light like a vast sponge, for the sun rayed out whitely from behind it, like incandescent swords across the sky. She was thinking apprehensively, I hope he doesn't get angry and send Daddy a bill. She was also thinking, Damned little dago; and checked herself, with guilt, for "dago" was a word she had outlawed.

She narrowed her eyes to a slit of light, and walked out towards the Cohens' store. She parted the bead curtain with relief, though blindly, and expected her eyes to clear on the sight of Mr. Cohen; but it was Joss who stood there, palms down on the counter, like a veritable salesman, waiting for a native to make up his mind over a banjo. This man, seeing a white person enter, moved aside for her, but she saw Joss's eyes on her, and said in kitchen Kaffir, "No, when you've finished." Joss gave a small approving nod; and she watched the man finger the instrument, and then another, until at last he began counting sixpences and shillings from a piece of dirty cloth that was suspended from his neck. The banjo cost thirty shillings, which was two months' wages to this farm worker, and when he left, clutching the instrument with a childlike pleasure, she and Joss exchanged looks which left nothing to say. She even felt guilty that she was coming to buy anything so frivolous as an evening frock; and with this feeling was another, an older one: a helpless anger that her father's debt of a hundred pounds at Sock's store was more than the farmworker might earn in the whole of his short life.

Joss said, "And what can I do you for?" and she watched him pull out the heavy rolls of stuff and stack them along the counter.

"Why are you still here?" she asked, acknowledging to herself that she had come to get some news of him.

"Delay over the sale. Sock's working a pretty point. He knows we're keen to sell out."

"And so you can't start university. I don't see why you should sacrifice yourself," she said indignantly.

"My, my, listen to the rebel who never leaves home," he remarked, raising his eyes to the fly-covered ceiling, while he competently slipped yards of pink cotton from hand to hand.

"That isn't why I don't leave home," said Martha stiffly, as if he had been accusing her of wrong feeling.

"You don't say," he said sarcastically; and then, more gently, when she lifted troubled eyes to his face: "Why don't you be a brave girl and get into town, and learn a thing or two?"

She hesitated, and her look was appealing; and he said, "I know you're very young, but you could get into a girls' hostel, or share a flat with someone, couldn't you?"

The idea of a girls' hostel struck Martha before the kindness of his intention, and her eyebrows swiftly rose in derision.

He gave her a look which said plainly, "What the hell do you want, then?" and became impersonal. "I don't think we have anything suitable, you'd better try Sock, he's got a consignment of new materials."

"I've been to Sock," she said plaintively, feeling abandoned.

"Then if he hasn't, we certainly haven't." He laid his palms downwards again, in the salesman's gesture which annoyed her, like an affectation. But she still waited. Soon he let his hands fall from the counter, and looked at her seriously. He was relenting. "I'll choose something for you," he said at last, and looked along the shelves. Martha, thinking of their tasteless back room, was momentarily alarmed, and ashamed of herself for the feeling; but he reached down a roll of white cotton, and said with a rough, unwilling tenderness, which touched her deeply, "White. Suitable for a young girl."

She saw at once it would make an attractive dress, and said, "I'll have six yards." And now his look seemed to say that she had agreed too quickly; and she fingered the crisp material to please him, while her mind already held a picture of how it would look made up. "I'm going to dance at the Van Rensbergs'," she remarked, with a confused intention; and his face stiffened, after a quick glance, and he cut the material without speaking.

"Why don't you come and dance with me?" he asked like a challenge.

"Why don't you ask me?" she replied quickly. But there was no response. He was folding the material, smoothing it in a way which kept her looking at his hands; and at last he tied it and handed it to her with a slightly sardonic bow. "On the account?" he enquired.

"No, I'm paying." She handed over the money, and waited for at least a look from him; but he said, "So long!" and went quickly into the back part of the building, leaving the store quite empty. So she began the hot, wearying walk home, but this time was overtaken by the McDougalls before she had gone more than a few hundred yards.

As soon as she had reached her room, and spread the material on her bed, Mrs. Quest entered, saying virtuously, "Oh, my dear, we've been so worried . . ." Then she saw the material, and reddened with anger. "How dare you waste your father's money when you know we haven't got it and we owe Sock so much money as it is?"

"I paid for it myself," said Martha sullenly.

"How could you pay for it yourself?"

"There was the money from last Christmas, and the ten shillings Mr. McFarline gave me."

Mrs. Quest hesitated, then chose a course and insisted, "The money wasn't given to you to waste, and in any case . . ."

"In any case, what?" asked Martha coldly.

Again Mrs. Quest hesitated; and at last her feelings expressed themselves in a voice that was uncertain with the monstrousness of what she was saying: "Until you're twenty-one, you've no right to own money, and if we took it to court, the judge would . . . I mean, I mean to say . . ." Martha was quite white, and unable to speak; it was her silence, the bitter condemnation in her eyes, which caused her mother to walk out of the room, saying unhappily: "Well, at least, I mean, I must speak to your father."

Martha was exhausted with the violence of what she felt, and it was only the thought that this was midday Friday, and the dress must be ready tomorrow, that enabled her to go on sewing.

At suppertime Mrs. Quest was bright and humorous, and there was an apology in her manner which Martha might have answered; but she was repeating to herself that the incident over the money was something she would never, never forget—it was to join the other incidents chalked up in her memory. Mr. Quest ate his meal in peace, gratefully persuading himself that this unusual silence between his womenfolk was one induced by harmony and goodwill.

Immediately after supper Martha went to her room, and soon they heard the whirr of the sewing machine. Mrs. Quest, in an agony of curiosity, timidly entered her daughter's room towards midnight, saying, "You must go to bed, Matty, I order you."

Martha did not reply. She was sitting on the bed, surrounded by billowing folds of white. She did not even lift her head. Mrs. Quest tugged the curtains across invading moonlight that flung a colder greener light over the warm dull lampshine, and said, "You'll spoil your eyes."

"I thought my eyes were already spoiled," said Martha coldly; and for some reason Mrs. Quest was unable to answer what seemed to be an accusation. She left the room, saying ineffectually, "You must go to bed at once, do you hear me?"

The machine whirred until nearly morning, an unusual undercurrent to the chirping crickets, the call of the owl. Mrs. Quest woke her husband to complain that Martha would not obey her; but he said, "Well, if she wants to make a fool of herself, let her," and turned over in bed with a clanging of the ancient springs. Martha heard both these voices, as she was meant to; and though she had been on the point of going to bed, since the sky was greying in the square of the window and she was really very tired, she made a point of working on for another half hour.

She woke late, from a dream that she was wearing her white frock in a vast ballroom hung with glittering chandeliers, the walls draped with thick rich crimson; and as she walked towards a group of people who stood rather above the floor, in long fluted gowns, like living statues, she noticed a patch of mud on her skirt and, looking down, saw that all her dress was covered with filth. She turned helplessly for flight, when Marnie and her brother came towards her, bent with laughter, their hands pressed over their mouths, gesturing to her that she must escape before the others, those beautiful and legendary beings at the end of the long hall, should catch sight of her.

She sat up in bed, and saw that the room was filled, not with sunlight, but with a baleful subdued glare reflected from clouds like steel mountains. It was nearly midday, and if she was to finish her dress she must hurry. But the thought of it was no longer a pleasure; all the delight had gone from it while she slept. She decided, tiredly, that she would wear an ordinary dress; and it was only because Mrs. Quest put her head around the door to say that lunch was ready, and Martha must come at once, that she replied she would not take lunch, she had to finish the dress.

Work on it restored the mood she had lost; and when it began to rain, her exultation was too great to be deepened—these were the first rains of the season; and she sat on the bed, clicking her needle through the stiff material, while overhead the old thatch rustled as the wet soaked in, as if it remembered still, after so many years, how it had swelled and lifted to the rain when it stood rooted and uncut. Soon it was soaked, and the wet poured off the edge of thatch in glittering stalactites, while the grey curtain of rain stood solid behind, so dense that the trees barely twenty paces away glimmered like faint green spectres. It was dark in the room, so Martha lit a candle, which made a small yellow space under the all-drenching blackness; but soon a fresh coloured light grew at the window, and, going to it, Martha saw the grey back of the storm already retreating. The trees were half emerged from the driving mists, and stood clear and full and green, dripping wet from every leaf; the sky immediately overhead was blue and sunlit, while only a few degrees away it was still black and impenetrable. Martha blew out the candle, and put the last stitches in her dress. It was only four in the afternoon, and the hours before she would be fetched seemed unbearable. At last, she went in to supper in her dressing gown; and Mrs. Quest said nothing, for there was a dreamy, exalted look on her daughter's face which put her beyond the usual criticisms.

Five minutes before eight o'clock, Martha came from her room, a candle in each hand, with her white dress rustling about her. To say she was composed would be untrue. She was triumphant; and that triumph was directed against her mother, as if she said, You can't do anything about it now, can you? She did not look at Mrs. Quest at all, but passed her steadily, her naked brown shoulders slightly tensed. Nor did her pose loosen, or she stand naturally, until she was before her father, where she waited, her eyes fixed on his face, in a look of painful enquiry. Mr. Quest was reading a book printed by a certain society which held that God had personally appointed the British nation to rule the world in His Name, a theory which comforted his sense of justice; and he did not immediately raise his eyes, but contracted his brows in protest as the shadow fell over his book. When he did, he looked startled, and then gazed, in a long silence, at Martha's shoulders, after a quick evasive glance at her demanding, hopeful eyes.

"Well?" she asked breathlessly at last.

"It's very nice," he remarked flatly, at length.

"Do I look nice, Daddy?" she asked again.

He gave a queer, irritable hunch to his shoulders, as if he disliked a pressure, or distrusted himself. "Very nice," he said slowly. And then, suddenly, in an exasperated shout: "Too damned nice, go away!"

Martha still waited. There was that most familiar division in her: triumph, since this irritation was an acknowledgment that she did in fact look "nice"; but also alarm, since she was now abandoned to her mother. And Mrs. Quest at once came forward and began, "There you are, Matty, your father knows what is best, you really cannot wear that frock and . . ."

The sound of a car grew on their ears; and Martha said, "Well, I'm going." With a last look at her parents, which was mingled scorn and appeal, she went to the door, carefully holding her skirts. She wanted to weep, an impulse she indignantly denied to herself. For at that moment when she had stood before them, it was in a role which went far beyond her, Martha Quest: it was timeless, and she felt that her mother, as well as her father, must hold in her mind (as she certainly cherished a vision of Martha in bridal gown and veil) another picture of an expectant maiden in dedicated white; it should have been a moment of abnegation, when she must be kissed, approved, and set free. Nothing of this could Martha have put into words, or even allowed herself to feel; but now, in order to regain that freedom where she was not so much herself as a creature buoyed on something that flooded into her as a knowledge that she was moving inescapably through an ancient role, she must leave her parents who destroyed her; so she went out of the door, feeling the mud sink around her slight shoes, and down the path towards a man who came darkly against stars which had been washed by rain into a profusely glittering background to her mood. Martha, who had known Billy Van Rensberg all her childhood, who had been thinking of him during the last half hour with suppressed resentment, as of something she must bypass, an insistent obstacle, found herself now going towards him half fainting with excitement. For she at once told herself this was not Billy; this man, whose face she could clearly see in the bright glow, might be a cousin of some kind, for he had a family likeness.

Martha found herself on the back seat of the car, on his knee, together with five other people, who were so closely packed together it was hard to know whose limbs were whose. Marnie's half-smothered voice greeted her from the front seat. "Matty, meet—Oh, Georgie, stop it, I've got to do the intros, oh, do stop it. Well, Matty, you'll have to find out who everybody is." And she stopped in a smother of giggles.

While the car slid greasily down the steep road, and then skidded on its brakes through the mealie-fields, Martha lay stiffly on the strange man's knee, trying to will her heart, which was immediately beneath his hand, to stop beating. His close hold of her seemed to lift her away from the others into an exquisite intimacy that was the natural end of days of waiting; and the others began to sing, "Horsie, keep your tail up, keep your tail up, keep your tail up"; and she was hurt that he at once joined in, as if this close contact which was so sweet to her was matter-of-fact to him. Martha also began to sing, since it appeared this was expected of her, and heard her uncertain voice slide off key; and at once Marnie said, with satisfaction, "Matty's shocked!"

"Oh, Matty's all right," said the strange man, slightly increasing the pressure of his hand, and he laughed. But it was a cautious laugh, and he was holding her carefully, with an exact amount of pressure; and Martha slowly understood that if the intimacy of the young people in this car would have been shocking to Marnie's mother, or at least to her own, it was governed by a set of rigid conventions, one of which was that the girls should giggle and protest. But she had been lifted away into a state of feeling where the singing and the giggles seemed banal; and could only remain silent, with the strange man's cheek against hers, watching the soft bright trees rush past in the moonlight. The others continued to sing, and to call out, "Georgie, what are you doing to Marnie?" or "Maggie, don't let Dirk get you down," and when this attention was turned to Martha and her partner, she understood he was replying for her when he said again, "Oh, Matty's all right, leave her alone." She could not have spoken; it seemed the car was rocking her away from everything known into unimaginable experience; and as the lights of her own home sank behind the trees, she watched for the lights of the Van Rensbergs' house as for the beacons on a strange coast. The singing and shouting were now a discordant din beneath the low roof of the car; and in their pocket of silence, the man was murmuring into Martha's ear, "Why didn't you look at me then, why?" With each "why" he modified his hold of her in a way which she understood must be a divergence from his own code; for his grip became compelling, and his breathing changed; but to Martha the question was expected and delightful, for if he had been looking for her, had she not for him? A glare of light swept across the inside of the car, the man swiftly released her, and they all sat up. The Van Rensbergs' house was in front of them, transfigured by a string of coloured lights across the front of the verandah, and by the moonlit trees that stood about it.

They tumbled out of the car, and nine pairs of eyes stroked Martha up and down. She saw she was the only person in evening dress; but at once Marnie said, in breathless approval, "You look fine, Matty, can I have the pattern?" She took Martha's arm, and led her away from the others, ignoring the lad with whom she had been in the car. Martha could not help glancing back to see how he took what she felt as a betrayal, for she was dizzy and shocked; but George had already slipped his arm around another girl, and was leading her to the verandah. She looked around for her own partner, feeling that surely he must come forward and claim her from Marnie, but the young man, in a tight uncomfortable suit whose thick texture her fingers knew, and whose appearance had the strangest look of alienation, was bending, with his back to her, over the open engine of the car, reaching down into it with a spanner.

So she went forward with Marnie, onto the wide verandah, which was cleared for dancing. There were about a dozen people waiting. She knew them vaguely by sight, having seen them at the station, and she smiled in the manner of one who has been prevented from achieving friendship by all manner of obstacles. Marnie took her through the verandah and into the room behind, where Mr. Van Rensberg was sitting in his shirt sleeves, reading a newspaper beside an oil lamp. He nodded, then raised his head again and stared rudely; and Martha began to feel ashamed, for of course her dress was too elaborate for the occasion; and it was only Marnie's exclamations of delight and admiration that kept her mood from collapsing entirely.

Martha watched her friend rub lipstick onto protruding, smiling lips before the mirror, and waited on one side, for she did not want to see herself in the glass; but as they returned to the verandah she caught sight of herself in a windowpane; she did not know this aloof, dream-logged girl who turned a brooding face under the curve of loose blond hair; so strange did it seem that she even glanced behind her to see if some other girl stood there in just such another white dress, and noticed her escort standing just outside the door to the verandah.

"You're all right," he said, impatiently, as if he had been kept waiting; and an old gramophone began to play from behind a window.

At once the space filled with couples; and Martha, lagging back to watch, to adjust herself, was dismayed by a savage discrepancy between what she had imagined and what was happening; for dancing may mean different things to different people, but surely (or so she felt) it could not mean this? Male and female, belly to belly, they jigged and bounced, in that shallow space between roof and floor of the verandah which projected out into the enormous night, in a good-natured slapdash acceptance of movement, one foot after another, across the floor, as if their minds owned no connection with what their bodies and limbs were doing, while the small tinny music came from the neat black box. It was a very mixed group—that is, it must appear so to an outsider, though Martha felt the partners were chosen according to certain invisible obligations. The one link missing was joy of any kind. The married couples walked themselves cheerfully around; partners of marked family resemblance stuck together as if their very features bound them; the only members of the party who seemed unbound by these invisible fetters were several small girls between nine or ten and fifteen, who danced together, politely adjusting their movements, while their eyes watched the older members of their society with patient envy, as if anticipating what must seem to them a delicious freedom. The women wore ordinary dresses, the young men stiff suits, in which they looked ugly, or the easy khaki of their farmwear, which made them into handsome peasants. Martha was again humiliated because of her dress, though there was no criticism, only detached curiosity, in the glances she received.

She looked instinctively towards her partner for support, feeling that his appreciation would sustain her. And this time she really looked at him, and not at the mental image created by the idea of dancing, of one's "first dance." He was a half-grown, lanky youth, with light hair plastered wetly across a low forehead, and the heavy muscles of shoulders and arms—too heavy for the still boyish frame —distorted the neat clerkly suit. He was regarding her with embarrassed pride, while he jerked her loosely around the dancing space, one stride after another, his arms pumping, with a check at each corner so that they might achieve a change of direction. The truth came into her mind, and at the same moment she stammered out, "I don't know your name"; and he at first stretched his mouth into a polite laugh, as at a jest, and then stopped dead, and dropped his arms, and stood staring at her, while his blunt and honest face went crimson.

"What's my name?" he asked; and then, to save them both: "You've got a funny sense of humour." Again he held her in a dancing position, while his limbs laboured through the movements dictated by his mind, and they continued self-consciously around the verandah.

"Well, I haven't seen you for so long," she apologized, and again, even as she spoke, understood that it was he who had sat beside his father at the station; she could not imagine how she had failed to see Billy in this young man.

"Oh, all right, all right," he half muttered; and then suddenly burst out singing, in Afrikaans, which was as good as saying, "We have nothing to say to each other."

Others joined in; it was a folk tune, and the small jazzy tune stopped, and someone put on another record. Now all the people on the verandah had arranged themselves quickly into two long lines, facing each other, while they clapped their hands. Martha, who had never seen the old dances, shook her head and fell out, and, as soon as the dancing began, found the spontaneous joy of movement that had been lacking in the other. Everyone enjoyed himself, everyone smiled, and sang; for the few minutes the music lasted, every person on the verandah lost self-consciousness and became part of the larger whole, the group; their faces were relaxed, mindless, their

eyes met those of the men and the women they must meet and greet
in the dance with an easy exchange. It was no longer their responsibility; the responsibility of being one person, alone, was taken off
them. And soon the music stopped, and the other, newer music, with
its wailing complaint, took its place. But Martha had fled, to collect
herself, into the kitchen, where Mrs. Van Rensberg was arranging
the supper.

Marnie ran after her, pulled her aside and said, "It's all right. I've
told him you didn't mean it, you're not stuck-up, you're just shy."

Martha was resentful that she had been thus discussed, but found
herself being pushed forward into Billy's arms, while Marnie patted
them both encouragingly, saying, "That's right, that's the idea, don't
take offence, man, the night is yet young."

Billy held her at arm's length, and gave her troubled but pleading
glances; and she chattered brightly, on a note she knew was false.
But she felt cold, and nervous. She wished bitterly she had not come;
and then that she was better able to adjust herself, and the small
tight critical knot in her could dissolve, and she become one with
this friendly noisy crowd of people. She set herself to be nice to
Billy, and for this he was half grateful, or at least took it as better
than nothing. As the night slowly went by, and they made repeated
trips to the buffet inside, where there were ranks of bottles of Cape
brandy, and ginger beer, another illusory haze formed itself, within
which she was able to persuade herself that Billy was the culmination of the last few days of helpless waiting: even, indeed, that the
white frock had been made for him.

By midnight the house was filled with singing and laughter and
the thin churning gramophone music could be heard only in
snatches. The crowd had a confined look; the rooms were too full,
and couples continually moved to the verandah steps, laughing and
hesitating, because outside the ground was churned to a thick red
mud, and the moon shone on the puddles left by the storm. Some
made a tentative step down, while the others shouted encouragement; then owned themselves beaten, and went to find a private
corner in one of the busy rooms, or in the kitchen, where Mrs. Van
Rensberg stood, hour after hour, slicing the bread, piling cream and
fruit on the cakes. Martha saw Marnie seated on the knee of a
strange youth while both talked to Mrs. Van Rensberg; and she
wished enviously that her own mother might be as tolerant and
generous. For while she watched Marnie, as a guide to how she
might behave herself, she knew it was impossible for her to do the
same: she was not so much shocked as dismayed at the way Marnie
was with one young man after another, as if they were interchange-

able. She saw, too, that it was not her formal dress but the fact that she was dancing only with Billy that set her apart from the others. Yet she could not have gone with anyone else; it would have driven across the current of feeling which said that Billy—or rather, what he represented—had claimed her for the evening; for alcohol had strengthened the power of that outside force which had first claimed her four days before, at the moment she agreed to go to the dance. She was not herself, she was obedient to that force, which wore Billy's form and features; and to the others it seemed as if she was as helpless to move away from him as he was reluctant to let her go. This absorbed couple who moved in a private dream were felt to be upsetting; whichever room they entered was disturbed by them; and at length Mr. Van Rensberg broke the spell by arresting Martha as she trailed past him on Billy's arm, by pointing his pipestem at her and saying, "Hey, Matty, come here a minute." She faced him, blinking and visibly collecting herself. The soft look on her face disappeared, and she became watchful, gazing straight at him.

Mr. Van Rensberg was a short, strong, thickset man of about sixty, though his round bristling black head showed not a trace of grey and his weathered face was hardly lined. He wore a dark-red scarf twisted thick around his bull neck, though it was swelteringly hot; and over it the small black, mordant eyes were as watchful as hers.

"So your father lets you come visiting us, hey?" he demanded.

Martha coloured; and half laughed, because of this picture of her father; and after a hesitation she said, consciously winsome and deferential, "You used to come visiting us, not so long ago." She checked herself, with a quick glance at the others—for there were several people listening; she feared he might resent this reminder of his long friendship with the Quests.

But he did not take her up on this point. With a kind of deliberate brutality, he lifted his pipestem at her again, and demanded, Did she admit that the English behaved like brutes in the Boer War?

At this, she could not help laughing, it was (to her) such an irrelevance.

"It's not a funny matter to us," he said roughly.

"Nor to me," said Martha, and then, diffidently: "It was rather a long time ago, wasn't it?"

"No!" he shouted. Then he quietened, and insisted, "Nothing has changed. The English are arrogant. They are all rude and arrogant."

"Yes, I think that's true," said Martha, knowing it was often true; and then could not prevent herself asking that fatally reasonable question, "If you dislike us so much, why do you come to a British colony?"

There was a murmur from the listening people. There seemed to be many more people in the room than before, they had been crowding in, and Martha found herself thinking how different was this man's position in his household to her father's: the silence was due to him as a spokesman, he was a patriarch in a culture where the feared and dominating father is still key to the family group; and Martha felt a twinge of fear, because she understood this was not to be taken as a personal conversation, she was being questioned as a representative. And she did not feel herself to be representative.

Mr. Van Rensberg dropped his pipe in dramatic comment, with a nod at the others, and remarked heavily, "So! So!"

Martha said quickly, with the defensive humour which she could not prevent, though she knew he found it insulting, "I don't see why you shouldn't come, why shouldn't you? As far as I am concerned, you're welcome."

There was a silence, he seemed to be waiting for more; then he said, "There should be equal rights, there should be rights for both languages."

Martha was remembering, very ruefully, that other conversation, with Joss. She smiled and said firmly, with considerable courage, considering the nature of her audience, that she believed in equal rights for all people, regardless of race and—

Billy tugged at her from behind, and said in an urgent voice, "Hey, Matty, come and dance."

Mr. Van Rensberg, who had dismissed the improbable suspicion from his mind as soon as it appeared said, rather taken aback, "Well, that's all right, then, that's all right." Afterwards, he would call Martha a hypocrite, like all the English.

On the verandah, Billy called her one to her face, without knowing he was doing so. "Why don't you learn to speak Afrikaans?" he asked, as if this followed naturally from what he had heard her say.

But to Martha this was narrowing the problem away from its principles, and she said, half flippantly, "Well, if it's a question of doing justice to majorities, one'd have to learn at least a dozen native languages as well."

His hand tightened across her back. To him it was as if she put the Afrikaans language on a level with those of the despised kaffirs. It was a moment of hatred; but at last he gave a short, uncomfortable laugh, and bent his head beside hers, closing his eyes to the facts of her personality, wishing to restore their illusory unity. It was late, some of the people had already left, and Martha was dancing in his arms stiffly and unwillingly, frowning over the incident that had just occurred. He felt that dancing would no longer be enough—

or rather, that it was too late to wait for the spell to settle over them again. He drew her to the verandah steps. The moon was now standing level with the tops of the trees, the mud of the clearing was glimmering with light. "Let's go down for a minute," he said.

"But it's all muddy," she protested.

"Never mind," he said hastily, and pulled her down.

Once again the wet squelched around her shoes, and she picked her way from ridge to ridge of hardening mud, hanging on Billy's arm, while he steered them both to the side of the house, out of sight. She tried to hold her skirts clear of the mud, while he pinned her arms down with his, and kissed her. His mouth was hard, and ground her head back. She resented this hard intrusive mouth, even while from outside—always from outside—came the other pressure, which demanded that he should simply lift her and carry her off like booty—but to where? The red mud under the bushes? She pushed aside this practical and desecrating thought, and softened to the kiss; then she felt a clumsy and unpracticed hand creeping down her thigh, and she jerked away, saying in a voice that annoyed her, because of its indignant coldness: "Stop it!"

"Sorry," he said at once, and let her go, with a humility that made her loathe him.

She walked away in front of him, leaving him to follow as he wished, and walked confusedly up the steps, because the few couples that were left were watching them with derisive smiles, and none of the communal teasing that had been drawn by the other couples. Martha saw the eyes drop to her skirt, and looked down, and saw that the hem was dragging heavy with red mud.

Marnie came running forward, exclaiming, "But Matty, your lovely dress, you've spoilt it . . ." She clucked over Martha for a moment, then tugged her through the house on her hand, saying, "Come and wash it off, before it dries."

Martha went, without so much as a glance at the unfortunate Billy, grateful for Marnie, who thus took her back into the group.

"You'd better take that dress off," said Marnie. "You're staying the night, so it doesn't matter."

"I forgot my suitcase," said Martha awkwardly, leaving herself completely in Marnie's hands. For she had forgotten to pack her night things; her imagination had reached no further forward than the dancing and the exaltation.

"Doesn't matter, I'll lend my pyjamas."

Mrs. Van Rensberg came fussing in, pleasant and maternal, saying she would ring Mrs. Quest. It seemed that Martha ruining her dress while making love to her son was the most natural thing in the world. She kissed Martha, and said she hoped she would sleep well, and she mustn't worry, everything was all right. The warm and comfortable words made Martha want to cry, and she embraced Mrs. Van Rensberg like a child, and like a child allowed herself to be led to her room, and left alone.

It was a large room, built to the back of the house, lit by two tall candles, one on either side of a vast double bed spread with white. The windows were open on the veld, which was already greying to the dawn, and the moon had a pallid, exhausted look. A sheet of silver, inclining at the end of the room, took Martha's attention, and she looked again, and saw it was a mirror. She had never been alone in a room with a full-length mirror before, and she stripped off her clothes and went to stand before it. It was as if she saw a vision of someone not herself; or rather, herself transfigured to the measure of a burningly insistent future. The white naked girl with high small breasts that leaned forward out of the mirror was like a girl from a legend; she put forward her hands to touch, then as they encountered the cold glass, she saw the naked arms of the girl slowly rise to fold defensively across those breasts. She did not know herself. She left the mirror, and stood at the window for a moment, bitterly criticizing herself for allowing Billy, that impostor, to take possession of her at all, even for an evening, even under another's features.

Next day she took breakfast with the Van Rensbergs, a clan of fifteen, cousins and uncles and aunts, all cheerfully mingled.

She walked home through the bush, carrying the dress in a brown-paper bag, and, halfway, took off her shoes for the pleasure of feeling the mud squeeze and mould around her feet. She arrived untidy and flushed and healthy, and Mrs. Quest, in a flush of relief, kissed her and said she hoped she had enjoyed herself.

For a few days, Martha suffered a reaction like a dulling of all her nerves. She must be tired, murmured Mrs. Quest, over and over again, you must be tired, you must sleep, sleep, sleep. And Martha slept, hypnotized.

Then she came to herself and began to read, hungrily, for some kind of balance. And, more and more, what she read seemed remote; or rather, it seemed that through reading she created a self-contained world which had nothing to do with what lay around her; that what she believed was separated from her problems by an invisible wall; or that she was guided by a great marsh light—but no, *that* she could not afford, not for a moment, to accept. But not merely was she continuously being flooded in by emotions that came from outside, or so it seemed; continuously other people refused to recognize the roles they themselves had first suggested. When Joss, for instance, or Mr. Van Rensberg, posed their catechisms, and received answers qualifying her for their respective brotherhoods, surely at that moment some door should have opened, so that she might walk in, a welcomed daughter into that realm of generous and freely exchanged emotion for which she had been born—and not only herself, but every human being; for what she believed had been built for her by the books she read, and those books had been written by citizens of that other country; for how can one feel exiled from something that does not exist?

She felt as if a phase of her life had ended, and that now a new one should begin; and it was about a fortnight after the Van Rensbergs' dance that Joss wrote: "I heard there was a job going, at the firm of lawyers where my uncles are both partners. I spoke to them about you. Get a lift into town and interview Uncle Jasper. Do it quickly. You must get yourself out of this setup. Yours, Joss." This was hastily scribbled, as if in a hurry; and there followed a neat and sober postscript: "If I'm interfering, I'm sorry."

She wrote back that she would at once apply for the job, and gratefully thanked him. She sent this letter by the cook, so urgent did it seem that he should at once know her reaction.

With Joss's letter in her hand, she walked onto the verandah, and informed her parents, in a hasty, offhand way, that she was taking a job in town; and she hardly heard their startled queries. It all seemed so easy now. "But you can't expect me to stay here for the rest of my life!" she demanded incredulously, just as if she had not been "here" for two years, apparently as if she considered there could be no possible end to it.

"But why Joss—I mean, if you felt like this, we could ask our friends . . ." protested poor Mrs. Quest, helplessly.

She was thinking in terms of the future, something unpleasant to be faced, perhaps, next week; and when she heard that Martha intended to go into town, with Mr. McFarline, the very next morning, she said she forbade it. Martha made no reply, and she suddenly announced she was coming into town with her.

"Oh, no, you're not," said Martha, in the deadly tone of unmistakable hatred which always disarmed Mrs. Quest, who had never admitted that hatred inside a family was even possible.

Martha was not in the house that last afternoon, so Mrs. Quest went into her bedroom, and looked helplessly around it for some kind of clue to her daughter's state of mind. She found Joss's note, which struck her unpleasantly; she found the soiled white dress, still crushed into the paper bag and already going green with mildew; she looked at the books on the table by the bed, with a feeling that they must be responsible; but they were Shelley and Byron and Tennyson and William Morris; and though she had not read them herself since she was a girl, she thought of them as too respectable to be in any way dangerous.

Martha, in the meantime, was consciously bidding farewell to her childhood. She visited the ant heap where she had knelt in ecstatic prayer during her "religious phase"; she walked through the thick scrub to the quartz reef under which a spring came bubbling clear and cold, where she had lain thinking of the stream that must reach the sea hundreds of miles away; she walked through the compound, where she had secretly played with the native children against her mother's orders. She paid a last visit to the big tree. It was all useless; her childhood, it seemed, had already said goodbye to her, nothing had power to move her.

Next day she went to town with Mr. McFarline, who tried to impress her with the fact that he had just been elected member of Parliament for one of the city constituencies, but received only an abstracted politeness for his pains. She interviewed Mr. Cohen, the uncle, got the job, and found herself a room before nightfall. Her parents expected her home. She sent them a wire saying would they please send on her books and clothes. "Do not worry, everything fine."

And a door had closed, finally; and behind it was the farm, and the girl who had been created by it. It no longer concerned her. Finished. She could forget it.

She was a new person, and an extraordinary, magnificent, an altogether *new* life was beginning.

part two

The worst of a woman is that she expects you to
make love to her, or to pretend to make love to her.

BARON CORVO

1

The offices of Robinson, Daniel and Cohen were crushed into the top floor of a building on Founders' Street, a thoroughfare which marked the division between that part of the town built in the 1890s and the centre, which was modern. From the windows one looked away left over the low tin roofs and shantylike structures which were now kaffir stores, Indian stores, and the slum of the Coloured quarter. To the right rose gleaming white buildings fronted with glass, and at the end of the street was the rambling, pillared, balconied brown mansion known as McGrath's Hotel, whose erection was remembered by old inhabitants as a sign of the triumph of progress: the first modern hotel in the colony. Founders' Street was narrow and shabby; and though it was named to commemorate those adventurers who had come riding over the veld to plant the Union Jack, regardless of the consequences to themselves or to anybody else, it was now synonymous in the minds of the present citizens with dubious boardinghouses and third-rate shops. This building shared the doubtful quality. On the ground floor was a large whole-sale business, so that as one mounted the central iron staircase, which spiralled up like an outsized corkscrew, it was to look down on a warren of little offices, each inhabited by a man in shirtsleeves, half buried in papers, or by a girl with a typewriter; while at the back was a narrow strip of counter where the "samples" were stacked. With what relief did the romantic eye turn to that counter, past the hive of impersonal offices! For the half-dozen coloured blankets, the dozen rolls of material, which surely, from a practical point of view, were as good as useless, seemed to suggest that the owner, a brother of Mr. Cohen upstairs, a cousin of Mr. Cohen from the kaffir store, also felt a need to remind himself and others of the physical existence of machinery, textiles, and a thousand other fascinating things which were sold through this office by means of those little bits of paper. Perhaps Mr. Cohen, who had made his fortune in another small native store just down the street, regretted those days when he handled beads and bicycles and stuffs, and kept that counter embedded among the desks and filing cabinets as a nostalgic reminder of personal trading, trade as it should be. On that counter were big tinted pictures of shipping, locomotives, the ports of the world. No one seemed to penetrate to it save old Mr. Samuel Cohen himself, who might be observed (by someone climbing the iron staircase) handling the blankets and rearranging the pictures.

The first and second floors were let as rooms, and the less said about them the better. Clients ascending to the sober legal offices above might catch sight of a woman in a dressing gown hurrying (but aggressively, since she had paid her rent and had the right to it) to the bathroom. At night, working late, the partners had been known to telephone the police to quell a brawl or eject an improper person. In fact, this layer of the building was altogether undignified and unsuitable; but, as the partners were waiting to rebuild, everything was allowed to remain. Martha discovered a familiar atmosphere almost at once when she heard Mr. Cohen say to a client, "I must apologize for the surroundings, but we really aren't responsible." This although the building was owned and controlled by him; because he planned a change, he could not be considered as *really* being here.

On the other hand, the very age of the place gave it dignity. People from older countries might think it strange to describe a building dated 1900 as old; but it had been the first to raise its three stories above the bungalows and for this it was affectionately remembered, and one entered it with a comforting sense of antiquity —as in Spain one lifts one's eyes from the guidebook murmuring reverently, "This was first built three centuries before Christ, think of that!" and afterwards poverty and squalor seem merely picturesque.

This, the oldest legal firm in the city, was known as Robinson's on account of the first Mr. Robinson, now dead; for the young Mr. Robinson gave precedence to both Mr. Cohens, and to Mr. Daniel when he was there, which was seldom, for he was a member of Parliament, and therefore very busy. But all this became clear to Martha slowly; for she was too confused, to begin with, to understand more than her own position, and even that was not so simple.

The partners each had a small room, reached by squeezing through the main room, which was packed tight with typewriters and filing cabinets and telephones; but though this main room at first sight looked like chaos, holding as it did fifteen women of varying ages, certain divisions soon became apparent. The chief one was that the four senior secretaries sat at one end, with telephones on their desks; but Martha was so ignorant of office routine she did not at first notice this. She arrived on the first morning in a state of keyed desire to show impossible heights of efficiency: arrived half an hour before anyone else, and sat waiting for the demands on her to begin. But the other girls drifted in, talked a little; and then came the partners; and still no one asked her for anything. She was left sitting until a slight, sparrowlike woman, with bright fringed hair and round blue eyes, came past and remarked warningly that she should keep her eyes open and learn the ropes. From which Martha gathered that she had already failed in her first duty, and opened them again from a vision of herself receiving quantities of illegible scrawl and transforming it, as if by magic, into sober and dignified legal documents of the kind Mrs. Buss produced from her typewriter. She forced herself to watch what was going on around her.

At lunch hour she stayed at her desk, because she had ten shillings between herself and the end of the month, and told herself it would be good for her figure. She went from typewriter to typewriter to see what sort of work she would be asked to do, and felt dismayed in spite of her large intentions; for these legal documents—no, no, it was as if she, Martha, were being bound and straitened by the formal moribund language of legality.

Just before the others were due back, the door marked "Mr. Jasper Cohen" opened, and he came out, stopping in surprise when he saw her. He laid some documents on Mrs. Buss's desk and went back again. Almost at once a buzzer sounded, and then, while she confusedly looked for the right instrument, the door opened again and he said, "Never mind the telephone. You won't mind my asking—have you any money, Miss Quest?"

For some reason she protested, "Oh, yes, quite a lot," and then blushed because it sounded so childish.

He looked at her dubiously, and said, "Come into my office for a moment," and she followed him. It was very small; he had to squeeze past the corner of the big desk to the corner he sat in. He told her to sit down.

Mr. Jasper Cohen already owned her heart because of a quality one might imagine would make it impossible: he was hideously ugly. No, not hideously: he was fantastically ugly, so ugly the word hardly applied. He was short, he was squat, he was pale; but these were words one might as justly use for Joss, his nephew, or for his brother, Max. His body was broad beyond squareness; it had a swelling, humped look. His head was enormous; a vast, pale, domed forehead reached to a peak where the hair began, covering a white, damp scalp in faint oily streaks, and breaking above the ears into a black fuzz that seemed to Martha pathetic, like the tender, defenceless fuzz of a baby's head. His face was inordinately broad, a pale, lumpy expanse, with a flat, lumpy nose, wide, mauvish lips, and ears rioting out on either side like scrolls. His hands were equally extraordinary: broad, deep palms puffed themselves into rolls of thick white flesh, ending in short, spatulate fingers almost as broad as long. They were the hands of a grotesque; and as they moved clumsily in a drawer, looking for something, Martha watched them in suspense, wishing she might offer to help him. She longed to do something for him; for this ugly man had something so tender and sweet in his face, together with the stubborn dignity of an afflicted person who intends to make no apologies or claims for something he cannot help, that she was asking herself, What is ugliness? She was asking it indignantly, the protest directed against nature itself; and, perhaps for the first time in her life, she wondered with secret gratitude what it would be like to be born plain, born ugly, instead of into, if not the aristocracy, at least the middle classes of good looks.

He at last found what he wanted. It was a roll of notes, and he took five of them, sliding them free of each other with an awkward movement; and he said, "You are only getting a small salary, and so . . ." As Martha hesitated, he continued quickly, "It was my fault for not remembering you might be short of money, coming in from the farm like that. Besides, you are an old friend of my nephew." That clinched the thing for him; and Martha took the money, feeling guilty because she had not been a good friend to Joss. She thanked him with emotion, which seemed to upset him, and he said hurriedly, "In a day or two we'll give you something to do. Just pick up what you can, it must be strange to you if you've never been in an office before."

The interview was over. She went to the door and, as she opened it, heard him say, "I shall be pleased if you do not mention this to Mrs. Buss. There is no reason why she should know." She glanced incredulously at him, for he sounded apprehensive; she was even ready to laugh. But he was looking at some papers.

She went out, and met the other Mr. Cohen returning. She disliked him as much as she liked his brother. He was ordinary in appearance, smartly commonplace: a neat, pale, respectable Jewish-looking person, in a striped business suit, and his manner was snappy but formal, as if he tried to cover a natural ill-humour by the forms of good feeling. And where his brother swelled and protruded into large shapes, he seemed concerned to give the opposite impression. His hair lay in a smooth black cap; his hands were neatly moving, and weighted on either little finger with a heavy signet ring; his tie lay safely behind a narrow gold chain; a gold watch chain confined his neat little stomach.

Martha returned to her desk as the other girls came in, and spent the afternoon watching them. There was no need to be told (as Mrs. Buss made a point of telling her) that this was an easy office to work in. There was no feeling of haste; and if they paused in what they were doing for a chat, or a cigarette, they did not pretend otherwise if one of the partners came through. When Mr. Max Cohen entered with work for his secretary, he asked politely, "Would you mind doing this for me, when you've finished your tea?" And his secretary finished her tea before even looking to see what he had brought her to do. All this was strange to Martha, although she had not known what she must expect. Perhaps she was remembering what her father had said of his days in an office in England, for it was to escape from that office that he had come farming: "I simply couldn't stick it. Day in and day out, damned routine, and then, thank God, there was the war, and then, after *that*, going back to the office was nothing but purgatory, sitting at a desk like a mouse in a hole." So it may have been that Martha was unconsciously expecting a purgatory, and had now found this pleasant working place; but of course she had not yet so much as lifted her fingers to the typewriter.

Two incidents occurred that first afternoon. At a table near the door where the clients came in sat a young woman whose task it was to take money from debtors. They came in, one after another, white, black and coloured, to pay off small sums on what they owed. The young woman was strictly impersonal; and because of this, Martha's first impulse towards pity was dulled. But almost immediately after the midday break a shabby woman entered, with a small child on either hand, and began to cry, saying she could not pay what was due and perhaps her creditor would let her off that month? The im-

personal young woman argued with her in a warningly low voice, as
if to persuade the shabby one to lower hers. But all the typists were
watching, and Martha saw they glanced towards Mrs. Buss.

Sure enough, it was not long before the dues collector went to
Mrs. Buss and said, "Can you talk to Mr. Cohen? You know, she
really does have a hard time, and she's having another kid, too."

Mrs. Buss said flatly, "Well, whose fault is it she has a new kid
every year?"

"But—"

"I'm not going to ask Mr. Cohen, he'll give in to her again, and
anyway she's a fraud—she was drunk in McGrath's last night, I saw
her."

The shabby woman began to cry. "Let me explain to Mr. Cohen,
just let me explain," she pleaded.

Mrs. Buss kept her head stoically down over the typewriter and
her fingers drummed angrily, until the door behind her opened and
Mr. Jasper Cohen came out.

"What's all this?" he enquired mildly.

"Nothing," said Mrs. Buss indignantly, "nothing at all."

Mr. Cohen looked over the listening heads of his staff to the weeping woman.

"Mr. Cohen," she wept, "Mr. Cohen, you've got a good heart, you
know I try my best, you can put in a good word for me."

"You did promise, you know," said Mr. Cohen, and then hastily:
"Very well, don't cry, I'll write to our clients. Make a note of it, Mrs.
Buss." And he escaped quickly into his room.

The woman left the office, wiping her eyes, with a triumphant look
at Mrs. Buss; while Mrs. Buss let her hands fall dramatically from
her machine, like a pianist at the end of a piece, and exclaimed,
"There, what did I tell you?"

The dues collector looked positively guilty under that blue and
accusing stare, and murmured, "Well, he's got a right to decide."

"Yes," said Mrs. Buss tragically. "Yes, and that's what always happens. I do my best to protect him, but . . . Well, when we get into
the new offices this sort of thing won't happen, believe *me!*" And
she lifted her hands to the keys again.

The second incident was similar. Charlie, the office boy, came
round with a tray of tea, and then went to speak to Mrs. Buss, while
she let those dedicated hands rest on the keys like someone not prepared to be interrupted.

"No," she said loudly, "no, Charlie, it's no good." And she began
typing.

Charlie raised his voice over the noise; she typed faster; he cried, "Madam!"

She stopped suddenly, in a dramatic silence, glared at him, shouted "*No!*" and at once rattled on.

Charlie gave an immense, good-natured shrug, and went out. Immediately, Mrs. Buss rested her hands, looked around the office, and demanded breathlessly, "What do you think of that for cheek?" The girls laughed sympathetically and, it seemed, did not need to be told why it was cheek.

Martha, who was at sea, looked closely at Charlie when he came back to collect the empty cups. He was a tall and handsome young man, with a dark, bronze skin, a small toothbrush moustache, and careless eyes. He was whistling a dance tune under his breath.

Mrs. Buss watched him over her jigging hands, and then protested sharply, "Charlie!"

"Yes, madam?" he answered at once, turning to her.

"We know you're a dancing champion, you don't have to whistle like that," she said, without expecting an answer, for she tore a sheet of paper out of her machine and inserted another without looking at him.

Charlie stopped his muted whistle; and then, with his black and gallant eyes fixed on her, sidled past her towards Mr. Cohen's door.

"It's all right, I'll get his cup," she said firmly, flushed with anger. She glared at him; he looked back with, it seemed, appreciation of the duel, for his eyes were snapping with amusement.

"Charlie," she said furiously, "you're not to ask Mr. Cohen for that money!"

"No, madam," he agreed, and gave a large and fatalistic shrug. With a humorous look at her, he went out and began a shrill whistle just outside the door.

"Did you ever see anything like it?" asked Mrs. Buss, faint with indignation. "He'd go past *me*, into Mr. Cohen's office, and ask for an advance!"

Suddenly Martha asked, "What does he earn?" and knew at once she should not have asked, or at least not in that tone of voice.

Mrs. Buss said aggressively, "He earns five pounds a month. It's more than he's worth, by about four pounds. Have you ever heard of an office boy earning that much? Why, even the head cook at McGrath's earns only seven! Mr. Cohen's so softhearted . . ." She was overcome by inarticulate indignation, and continued to type like a demon.

Martha reflected uneasily that she herself was to earn twelve pounds ten shillings, and an altogether unreasonable protest was aroused in her; for if she supported the complete equality of all races, then she must applaud this small advance towards it. On the other hand, because of her upbringing, she was shocked. She asked the blond young woman next to her what Charlie did in the office, and was told that he delivered letters by hand, sent others to the post, made the tea and ran errands for the girls in the office.

"He's a real character, Charlie is," the girl added good-humouredly.

"Mr. Cohen makes a joke. He says, 'The two best-dressed men in the town are my brother'—that's Max, you know—'and my office boy.' " She looked at Martha to make sure she would laugh, and when Martha did she continued, "I like Charlie. He's much better than most of these niggers, and that's saying something, isn't it?"

Martha agreed absent-mindedly that it was, while she argued with the voices of her upbringing. She had never heard of a native being paid more than twenty shillings a month. Her father's boss-boy earned twenty, after ten years' service. With half her emotions she commended Mr. Cohen for his generosity, both to herself and to Charlie, and with the other she fought down an entirely new fear—new to her, that is: she could not help feeling afraid that the gap between her and Charlie was seven pounds ten shillings, in hard cash.

At half past four something happened which cannot be described as an incident, since she understood it occurred every day. The girls were covering their typewriters when the door swung open and in came a tall, fair woman, who simply nodded at Mrs. Buss and stood waiting. Mrs. Buss lifted her telephone receiver.

"Here's our beauty," muttered the blond girl to Martha. "I wouldn't mind her clothes, would you? These Jews always give their wives everything they want."

Well, of course; what could Mr. Cohen's wife be called, if not "beauty"? But Martha was troubled by something else—that she was not the only female creature prepared to overlook Mr. Cohen's appearance. It had never entered her head that there could be a Mrs. Cohen; but almost immediately the balance was redressed by a fresh conviction of injustice. Mrs. Cohen was not, Martha decided, in the least beautiful; whereas Mr. Cohen was—in any sense that mattered. Conventionally, she might be called tall, slim and elegant; Martha preferred to describe her as bony, brassy-haired and over-dressed. She wore a clinging white crepe afternoon suit, a white cap with dangling black plumes, and a great deal of jewellery. The jewellery was sound, but colourful. When Mr. Cohen came out, in answer to Mrs. Buss's call, Martha was still able to feel sorry for him; but she was at once forced to examine this emotion when she understood that all the women around her were feeling the same thing.

"Poor man," said Mrs. Buss calmly, as she came pushing her own narrow hips this way and that around the sharp desks, and pulling on black suede gloves. "Poor man. Oh, well, it's not my affair." And she went out, at a discreet distance from her employer and his wife, watching them jealously.

2

When Martha arrived in the room she was prepared to call home, her mother and father were there, and she was angry. She had not expected them for at least a week; it seemed to her monstrously unfair that she had been tormented for years by those terrible preparations for the excursions over a seventy-mile stretch of road, and now, it seemed, there was no more necessity for preparations. Mr. and Mrs. Quest, like anybody else, had "come in for the afternoon." Mr. Quest was talking about the Great War with Mrs. Gunn, the landlady, when Mrs. Quest gave him an opportunity, for she was concerned to get Mrs. Gunn to agree that girls were headstrong and unsatisfactory. Martha could hear this talk going on in the back verandah, through the fanlight of her room, which opened onto it. She sulkily refused to join them, but sat on her bed, waiting for what she expected would be a battle.

The room was large, and plainly furnished. The iron bed was low and spread with white, and reminded her of her own. There was simple brown coconut matting on the red cement floor, and a French door opened into a small garden filled with flowers. Beyond the garden lay a main road, and the noise was difficult for a country person who had learned *not* to hear only the din of thunder, the song of the frogs, the chirping crickets. As she sat waiting on her bed, Martha was conscious of strain. She understood that her ear-drums, like separate beings, were making difficult and painful movements to armour themselves against the sound of traffic. There was a quivering sensitiveness inside her ears. A big lorry roaring down the tarmac ripped across tender flesh, or so it felt; the *ching-ching* of a bicycle bell came sharply, almost as if it were in the room. She sat listening and painfully attentive, and at the same time marked the progress of the conversation next door. Her father was winning Mrs. Gunn's attention; it was becoming a monologue.

"Yes, that was two weeks before Passchendaele," she heard. "And

I had foreknowledge of it, believe it or not. I wrote to my people, saying I expected to be killed. I felt as if there was a black cloud pressing down on me, as if I was inside a kind of black velvet hood. I was out inspecting the wire—and then the next thing I knew, I was on the hospital ship."

That these words should be following her still made Martha feel not only resentful but afraid. In spite of herself, even as she isolated each traffic sound in a difficult attempt to assimilate it, even while she looked at the rough and hairy surface of the coconut matting, she was seeing, too, the landscape of devastation, shattered trees, churned and muddy earth, a tangle of barbed wire, with a piece of cloth fluttering from it that had once been part of a man's uniform. She understood that the roar of a starting car outside had become the sound of an approaching shell, and tried to shake herself free of the compulsion. She was weighted with a terrible, tired, dragging feeling, like a doom. It was all so familiar, so horribly familiar, even to the exact words her father would use next, the exact tone of his voice, which was querulous, but nevertheless held a frightening excitement.

When the door opened and her parents came in, Martha rose to meet them with the energy of one prepared to face the extremities of moral and physical persuasion; but all she heard was a grumbling note in Mrs. Quest's voice, as she said, "It wasn't polite of you not to come and have tea when you were asked." It was exactly as she might complain of Martha's rude behaviour to visitors on the farm; and Martha was surprised into silence. "Well, dear," continued Mrs. Quest, briskly, moving around the room as if it were her own, "I've unpacked your things and arranged them, I don't know whether you've noticed, and I moved the bed, it was in a draught, and you must be careful to sleep a lot." Noticing the look on Martha's face, she hurried on: "And now Daddy and I must go back to the farm, we really hadn't time to leave it, but you're such a helpless creature. you look tired, do go to bed early."

Martha, as usual, pushed away the invading feeling of tiredness and pointed out to herself that her sudden guilt was irrational, since she had not asked them to leave the farm and come in after her. She decided to leave this room at once for another which would be free of her mother's atmosphere and influence.

Mr. Quest was standing at the French door, his back to the women. "Mr. Gunn must have been an interesting chap," he said thoughtfully. "He was in the Somme country. Must have missed him by two weeks. Get Mrs. Gunn to tell you about him sometime, Matty, old chap. Died of gas from the war, she says. Pity those War

Office blokes never understood that people could be ill because of the war, and it only showed afterwards. He got no compensation, she says. Damned unfair." He turned himself around, and his face had put on its absorbed, devoted look. He reached for a bottle in the skirts of his bush shirt—he always refused to change from his farm clothes when he came into town—and stood holding it, helplessly looking around. "A glass?" he asked. Mrs. Quest took it from him, measured his dose at the washstand, and he drank it down. "Well?" he asked irritably, "it's quite a way back, you know, with our old car."

"Coming," said Mrs. Quest, guiltily, "coming." She moved Martha's things on the dressing table to her own liking, and changed the position of a chair. Then she went across to Martha, who stood stiffly in nervous hostility, and began patting her shoulders, her hair, her arms, in a series of fussy little pushes, as a bad sculptor might ineffectually push and pat a botched piece of work. "You look tired," she murmured, her voice sinking. "You look tired, you must sleep, you must go to bed early."

"*May!*" exclaimed Mr. Quest irritatedly, and Mrs. Quest flew to join him. Martha watched them drive away, the thatched, rattling, string-bound machine jogging through the modern traffic. People turned and smiled indulgently at this reminder that it was a farming country—even, still, a pioneer country. Martha could not manage a smile. She stood tensely in the middle of the room and decided to leave it at once.

Mrs. Gunn knocked. The knock, a courtesy to which she was not accustomed, soothed Martha, and she said politely, "Come in."

Mrs. Gunn was a tall, large-framed woman, with abundant loose flesh. She had faded reddish hair, pale, pretty blue eyes, and an air of tired good nature. "It was nice to speak to your mother," she said. "I couldn't help wondering, a young thing like you by yourself."

Martha was trying to frame words which would convey, politely, that she was leaving, and that it was no fault of Mrs. Gunn that she must. But Mrs. Gunn talked on, and she found herself without the courage to say it.

". . . your mother says you don't eat, and I must make you. I said you were providing for yourself, but I'd do what I could."

"There's no need, Mrs. Van Rens—" Martha stopped, confused. "I mean, Mrs. Gunn. I eat like a horse."

Mrs. Gunn nodded comfortably. "You look as if you had a head on your shoulders. I told her, girls have sense these days. My Rosie was out and about two years before she married, and I never had to raise my voice to her. The thing is, you must keep the men in their place, so they know from the start they're not getting something for nothing."

Martha was ready to be sarcastic at this remark; but Mrs. Gunn came over and kissed her, and she was warmed by gratitude into good humour.

"If you want anything, just come to me. I know young things don't want to be nagged at, but think of me like a mother."

"Thank you, Mrs. Van R—Mrs. Gunn," said Martha gratefully, and Mrs. Gunn went out.

Martha gazed around the room with as much dislike as if it had been contaminated. She looked into her drawers, and every crease and fold of her clothing spoke of her mother's will. But she had paid the rent till the end of the month, and she could not afford to move. She flung all the clothes out onto the floor, and then rearranged them to her own taste, though no outsider could have seen any difference; she pushed the bed back to what she imagined had been its old position, but she was unobservant and did not accurately know what that position had been. Having finished, she was very tired; and although it was early, she undressed, and stood by the door and watched the cars go racing past, while their lights spun over her in blotches and streaks of gold, and over the flowers in the garden, touching them into sudden colour. Beyond the garden and the street, there were black shapes of trees against a dim night sky. It was the park. And beyond, the city; but she imagined its delights in terms of what she had read of London or New York. She dreamed of the moment when she would be invited to join these pleasures, while her eyes remained on the trees and she unconsciously compared their shapes with those of the skyline on the farm; and soon it was as if the farm had stretched itself out, like a long and shadowy arm across the night, and at its end, as in the hollow of a large, enfolding palm, Martha stood like a pygmy and safely surveyed her new life. And when she woke in the morning, and saw the sunlight lying warm and yellow over the coconut matting, she wondered sleepily if the water-cart brakes had given, for it was making such a noise; and she sat up, while the new room rearranged itself about her; and now her ears had been informed by her brain that this was not the water cart but a delivery van, they began to ache in protest.

At the office that day, she was left to "keep her eyes open" until after the lunch hour. Then Mr. Max Cohen brought her a document to copy. She was so nervous, she had to start afresh three times; and when he came to fetch it, all that had been achieved were the words "Memorandum of an Agreement of Sale" typed raggedly across the top of the sheet. She shrank under his impatient assurance that it did not matter in the least, and she must take her time. Her fingers were heavy and trembling, and her head was thick. To type two pages of his small, neat writing into something clean and pleasant to look at seemed to her, just then, an impossibly difficult task. He went home without coming to her desk again; and she flung a dozen sheets of paper into the wastepaper basket, and decided she would come early next morning and do it before anyone else arrived.

Mrs. Buss, on her way out, asked, "Have you got any certificates?" Martha said no, she had learned to type at home. Mrs. Buss said nothing consoling, but merely nodded absent-mindedly, for her eyes were on the elegant Mrs. Jasper Cohen.

Martha left the office so humiliated she could hardly see where she was going. She was filled with a violent revulsion against the law and everything connected with it. What she said to herself was, I won't spend the rest of my life typing this stupid jargon.

She stood at a corner of the street, with Mr. Jasper Cohen's money —or rather, what was left of it—in her handbag, and watched a crowd of carefree young people going into McGrath's Hotel, and felt sick with envy. Then she crossed the street and went into the offices of the *Zambesia News*. She was going to see Mr. Spur, an old journalist, whom she had known "as a child"—that is to say, she had last spent a month's holiday with him and his wife about four years before. She was in the building about half an hour, and when she came out her face was hot with embarrassment. It had been so painful she could not bear to remember what had happened. What she must remember was that she had no qualifications whatsoever.

She understood, finally, the extent of the favour Mr. Cohen was doing her; and next morning she was at her desk in a very chastened frame of mind. Her eyes were certainly opened, but she had no time to use them, for long before that first document was finished several more arrived on her desk, and it was lunchtime before she knew it. She was very incompetent. She tried to persuade herself that the papers she sent in, neatly clipped and tied with green tape in the form of the exquisite, faultless documents Mrs. Buss turned out with such ease, were satisfactory. Mr. Max Cohen received them with a noncommittal glance and a nod; and later Martha saw Mrs. Buss doing them again. She was given no more. For a whole day she sat idle at her desk, feeling sick and useless, wishing she could run away, wondering what would happen.

The fair, plump girl, Miss Maisie Gale, who sat next to her said consolingly, "Don't lose any sleep over it. Just do what you can get away with, that's my motto."

Martha was offended, and replied with a stiff smile. Later, she was told to go to Mr. Jasper Cohen's office, and she went, while her heart beat painfully.

The ugly man was waiting quietly in his chair. It seemed to Martha that the pale face was paler than ever, and the flat, brownish-mauve lips moved several times before any sound came out. Then he pulled himself together. He settled the ungainly body firmly back in his chair, lifted a pencil with that fat, protuberant hand, and said gently, "Miss Quest, I think we were mistaken in putting you onto skilled work so soon. I thought you said you had learned to type."

"I thought I had," said Martha ruefully; and she was conscious that in using that tone she was again trading on the personal relation.

"Well, well, it doesn't matter; it couldn't have been easy, learning by yourself, and I propose to you the following course. Will you go down to the Polytechnic and take lessons in shorthand and typing for a few months, and in the meantime you can work with Miss Gale. You must learn to file too, and it won't be wasted, in the long run."

Martha eagerly assented, and at the same time registered the fact that working with Miss Gale was beneath her. She was surprised and flattered, for all the women in the office seemed so immeasurably above her, in their self-assurance and skill, that she saw them through a glowing illusion. She understood, too, that Mr. Cohen was now about to give her a lesson, very kindly and tactfully, and she must listen carefully.

"You see, Miss Quest, you are very young—you won't mind my saying that, I hope? It is obvious you are intelligent, and—well, if I may put it like this, you're not considering getting married next week, are you?" He was smiling, in the hopeful but uncertain way of a person who finds it hard to make amusing remarks; and Martha quickly laughed, and he gratefully joined in. "No. Of course not. At eighteen there's plenty of time. You shouldn't marry too quickly. In this country I think there's a tendency—however, that's not my affair. Well, most girls work in an office simply to pass the time until they get married—nothing wrong with that," he hastened to assure her. "But my policy—our policy—is, I think, rather unusual: that we do not believe married women make bad workers. Some firms dismiss women as soon as they marry, but you will have noticed that all our senior girls are married."

Martha saw, with fresh humiliation, that she had been expected to notice things of this sort, and she had not.

"My policy—our policy—is, that there is no reason why girls should not have a good time and work well too, but I would suggest to you that you don't get into the way of some girls we have—oh, they're very useful, and we couldn't do without them, but they seem to think that because they will get married one day, that is all that can reasonably be expected of them." Here Martha glanced quickly at him; there was a resentful note that could have nothing to do with herself. Again Mr. Cohen eased his great body in his chair, fingered the pencil, seemed to be on the point of speaking, and then said abruptly, "I think that's all. You will forgive me for making these remarks. I feel, we feel—in short, you have undoubted capacities, Miss Quest, and I hope you will use them, for efficient secretaries are rare. Which is remarkable, when you think of it, since most women these days seem to train to be secretaries?" On that query he paused and reflected, and then said, "I hope you don't feel that being a secretary is not a worth-while career?"

Martha assured him that she wanted to be an efficient secretary, even while she felt quite indignant; she felt herself capable of much more. She thanked him, went back to her desk, and once again sat idle. She was waiting for someone to direct her; then she understood she was now expected to direct herself, and went to Mrs. Buss, asking for information about the Polytechnic.

Mrs. Buss's face cleared into a gratified relief that seemed to Martha offensive; and she took a piece of paper from her desk, with clear directions as to classes and times. Then she delivered herself —with a pause between each, for assent—of the following remarks: "I'm glad you've got some sense. . . . You don't want to get like these girls here, sitting with their eyes on the clock, just waiting till their boy friends fetch them at half past four, and out all night and then so tired next day they just sit yawning. . . . There's plenty of work here, believe me, for those with the intention to do it." And finally, her china-blue eyes fixed on Martha's: "When you've got someone to work for as good as Mr. Cohen, then you work your best." Martha said yes; but it was not enough. "I've worked for my living since I was fifteen, and in England till two years ago, and in England girls are expected to be efficient, it's not like here, where they can get married for the asking, and I've never known anyone like Mr. Cohen." Martha said yes; and Mrs. Buss insisted challengingly, "He's got a heart as big as his whole body," and this time Martha said yes with real feeling, and she was released.

And now Martha was able to understand—but only since it had been pointed out to her—the real division in this closely packed mass of women. When Miss Gale leaned over and whispered, like a schoolgirl, "Get off easily?" she replied coldly, "I'm going to the

Polytechnic," and Miss Gale shrugged and looked indifferently away, like one who does not intend to show she feels her cause has been deserted. But Martha looked away from this group she had been put into with envy and admiration for the four secretaries and for the two accountants who sat side by side over their big ledgers. She intended, in fact, to emulate the skilled; and her eyes, when she regarded the complacent Miss Gale, were scornful. These women had in common not that they were younger, or even more attractive, than the others, but a certain air of tolerance; they were paying fee to something whose necessity they entirely deplored.

After work, Martha walked the hundred yards or so to the Polytechnic, which was further down Founders' Street. It was a low brown building, which looked as if it had once been a boarding-house, though now it swarmed with activity; and its front was barricaded by stacked bicycles. Martha, as usual doing nothing by halves, enrolled herself for classes which would take up every evening of her week, and walked home through the park, where the paths already glimmered pale among the darkening trees, her mind filled with visions of herself in Mrs. Buss's place, though they were certainly lit by the highly coloured experimental glow that had coloured earlier visions of herself as a painter, a ballet dancer or an opera singer, for like most people of her age and generation she had already tasted every profession, in mind at least.

When she reached her room, she imagined for a moment she had come to the wrong place, for through the light curtains across the French door she could see a shape she did not know. She hesitantly entered at last, and there stood a young man who asked, "Martha Quest? My mother had a letter from your mother and—" He stopped, and looked appreciatively at Martha; for until then he had been speaking with a politeness that said quite plainly, "I'm doing this because I've been told to."

He was a youth of about twenty. Martha, who had known only the physical, open-air men of the district, and the Cohen boys, who were all she had met of the student type, and her brother, who was a student because it was expected of him, found in Donovan Anderson something quite new. He was a rather tall, broad-framed, handsome young man, wearing a sharply cut light summer suit, and a heavy gold signet ring on one hand. She was not observant, but because of this impression of broad-shouldered masculinity she was instinctively looking for resemblances, and her eye lingered on the way his shirt front caved inwards under the flowing blue tie; for if Billy or her brother had been wearing that suit it would have bulged out, and the sleeves would have been filled with muscle. Looking upwards from the hollow chest, she received from that correctly arranged, healthily sunburned face—large nose, square jaw, open brow—an altogether incongruous impression of weakness.

He said gracefully, "We were expecting a nice girl from the wide-open spaces, we heard you were sporting and hunted big game."

At first Martha stared at the "we"; then she laughed, and averred that she loathed sport of any kind, as if this was a claim to grace in itself.

"That's a relief, because I'm ever such an indoor type, and I was expecting to have to take you to something energetic."

Martha said spitefully that she was surprised he did as he was ordered; to which he returned a politely appreciative laugh, and said, "Well, then, I'll take you to the pictures instead. You must come and meet my mamma. It is what both our mammas would expect."

Martha agreed that she would like to do this, and it was arranged that it would all take place the following evening—which, incidentally, meant that she must postpone her first lesson in shorthand. They informed each other that they insisted on being called respectively Don and Matty. His mamma, said Donovan, called him Donny, but one knew what mammas were. He most elegantly shook her hand, and told her that she must not be late tomorrow, for if there was one thing he could not endure it was being kept waiting by girls. He then took his leave.

Martha wandered around her room in a state of breathless exhilaration, already picturing Donovan as a lover, but in an extraordinarily romantic light, considering the nature of the books she read. The time between the present and tomorrow evening must be lived through; she felt she could not bear it, and just as she had decided she would go to sleep, in order to dispose of as much of it as possible in oblivion, Mrs. Gunn knocked and asked anxiously if she would like some supper. Martha refused, because of the anxious note, which automatically stiffened her resistance. Yet she had hardly eaten since she came to town; she had too little money to "waste on food"—in other words, she was by no means finished with that phase of her life when she was continuously thinking about food, not because she intended to eat any, but because she meant to refuse it. She would think of the next meal due to her according to convention, assess it in terms of flesh, and then nervously pass her hands downwards over her hips, as if stroking their outlines smaller.

Before she went to bed that night, she ironed the dress she intended to wear the following evening. An instinct she did not know

she possessed chose it from the point of view of a Donovan, and the
same instinct made the downward-stroking movement over hips and
thighs appreciative and satisfied. She had slimmed herself during
the past two years so that the bones of her pelvis were prominent,
and this gave her great pleasure; and she went to bed vowing she
must not put on weight.

At the office next day she helped Miss Gale with the filing, and
found that she liked her after all; for some reason, there was a flow
of sympathy between them, and more than once Mrs. Buss looked
sharply towards them and they lowered their voices guiltily.

Half past four soon came, and Martha flew home to dress, though
Donovan was not expected until six. She anointed and prepared herself with the aid of mirrors large and small, a bathroom next door,
and no Mrs. Quest likely to interrupt. She bathed, painted her fingernails and—for the first time, and with a delicious sense of sinfulness
—her toenails, powdered her body, plucked her eyebrows, which did
not need it, and arranged her hair; and all this under the power of
that compulsion that seemed to come from outside, as if Donovan's
dark and languid eyes were dictating what she must do, even to the
way her hair should lie on her shoulders. For the first time, she knew
the delight of dressing for a man: her father never noticed what she
wore, unless it was pointed out; her brother had not gone beyond
the stage of defensive derision, or at least not with her; and a Billy
Van Rensberg was likely to approve anything she wore.

But when Donovan arrived and she presented herself to him (still
in the power of that outside necessity), he behaved in a way she had
never imagined any man might behave. He looked at her, critically
narrowed his eyes, and even walked around her thoughtfully, his
head rather on one side. She could not resent it, for it was quite impersonal. "Yes," he murmured, "yes, but . . ." He lifted her hair back
from her face, studied her anew, then let it fall back, and nodded.
To Martha it was an extraordinary sensation, as if he were not only
receiving her appearance as an impact, but as if he were, for the
moment, herself, and her clothing covered him, and he felt the shape
and lines of her dress with the sympathy of his own flesh. It was like
being possessed by another personality; it was disturbing, and left
her with a faint but pronounced distaste.

Donovan emerged from this prolonged study, saying thoughtfully,
"You know what that dress needs, my dear? What you need is . . ."
He went to the wardrobe as if he had been using it himself for years,
flung it open, and searched for something that already existed in his
mind. "You must buy a black patent belt tomorrow," he announced

firmly. "About an inch and a half wide, with a small, flat buckle." And he was right, Martha saw that at once. "You must ask my mamma about clothes," he continued pleasantly. "She's very good at them. Now come on, she doesn't like being kept waiting." And he led the way to his car.

It was a small open car, dark green, shabby but highly polished; and when he climbed into the front seat and sat languidly waiting for her to join him, the man and the car instantly became a unit. "Like it?" he enquired indifferently. "Got it for twelve pounds ten last month. We junior civil servants must make do on other people's leavings." Yet he was indifferent because he knew he might be quite satisfied with both himself and the car.

They drove a short way out of town; that is to say, when they had left behind them the avenues of old houses that had been built between 1900 and 1920, there was about half a mile of tree-lined dust track to cover before they came to a signboard which said "The Wellington Housing Estate." Here they turned off onto another dust track which would one day be a street between houses, because the foundations of the houses were already lightly sketched, in cement, in the raw-surfaced earth; and piles of red brick lay everywhere.

"We got in early and bought the first lot while it was dirt cheap, but it's already expensive, this is going to be ever such a smart place to live," Donovan said; and she saw that he was politely pointing out what things she should admire, as he had done over the car. And so it was when they reached the house, the only completed house, which stood like a narrow brick box, spotted with round windows like portholes, and laced with a great deal of scrolled ironwork. "My mamma thought she would like a Spanish house," said Donovan, apparently meaning the iron; and again Martha knew she was being instructed.

Inside, while they waited for Mrs. Anderson, Martha was shown the ground-floor rooms, and found them smart and expensive, as Donovan said they were; and apparently he was satisfied with her response, for her politeness might easily be taken for the same thing as that negligence he was careful to maintain. Now, Martha was adapting herself to Donovan according to that outside pressure which said that she must; and yet this pliability was possible only because something was still informing her, in a small voice but a clear one, that this had nothing to do with her; in fact, it could be said she was so easy and comfortable with him just because of this fundamental indifference.

When they had finally settled in the big drawing room, an incident occurred which was final as far as Martha was concerned. She reached for a book from the big bookcase, to see what kind of people these were, as she always did in a new house, and heard Donovan say, "Oh, my dear, it's no use looking at the books. We have nothing new in the place."

Martha left her hand on the book, while she turned her stern, derisive eyes on Donovan as if she could not possibly have heard aright. "What do you mean, nothing new?" she enquired, in a voice he had not heard from her and was not likely to, or at any rate, not yet.

"My mamma forgot to send to England for the new books. All these are last year's best sellers."

Martha stared, then a movement of laughter disturbed her face, but at once vanished; she dropped her hand from the book, and in the same movement sank into a chair, in a pose that suggested a compliant willingness to be everything he might wish. And so Mrs. Anderson found them when she came sweeping into the room, her hands outstretched so that she might pull Martha to her feet and give her a quick, assessing glance that took in everything, before laying a perfumed cheek against hers, in lieu of the kiss which might disturb her make-up. Then she allowed Martha to fall back on the chair, and turned to her son so that he might kiss her.

She was a tall, large lady, firmly corseted, dressed in black-and-white silk, with waved fair hair and large, white, firm hands whose capability contradicted the rest of her appearance, which aimed at an impression of useless elegance. She placed herself on a low purple satin chair, and her son sat in another, immediately opposite, in a way which showed this was a habit with both of them. They proceeded to tease each other, good-humouredly affectionate, about his lateness that morning for breakfast, about her wasting the whole afternoon at the hairdresser's, about her dress, which, it seemed, was new and expensive. Martha listened, for she was excluded, though they did not mean to be impolite. She understood that this teasing was a way of finding out about each other's movements without direct questioning: for as soon as Mrs. Anderson had learned that Donny had not been late for the office, with which girl he had taken lunch, and what cinema he intended to visit with Martha, as soon as Donovan had told her she must go to bed early—"because old women need a good night's rest"—and had been scolded for his impertinence, she rose and kissed Martha again. Or rather, she made all the preparatory motions towards a kiss and concluded by faintly laying her cheek against Martha's; and asked to be forgiven, for she was going out to dinner, and the young people must amuse themselves.

She then asked Donovan to be sure a tray was sent up to his father, who did not feel like taking a proper dinner.

She was moving towards the door, with the voluminous lightness of a sailing ship, her skirts flowing, a scarlet chiffon handkerchief trailing from her hand, when Donovan asked, in a voice that held a grumbling, offended note that Martha had not yet heard, "Who are you going to dinner with?"

Mrs. Anderson paused, her back to them, a stiffened and wary back, and began touching some dark-yellow poppies that stood on a low table beside the door. "No one you know, dear," she replied cautiously, but with an unmistakably warning note. The scarf caught and dragged out a poppy, so that it lay in a pool of water on the polished table. Martha, who was watching, though Donovan could not since his face was sullenly averted, saw Mrs. Anderson's smooth and handsome face darken with anger. "Oh, damn," she muttered crossly, and glanced at her son; and then she hastily wiped away the spilt water with her handkerchief, and stood holding the crumpled ball of stuff delicately between finger and thumb, while a smile slowly spread over her face and she gave Martha a long, amused, but wickedly guilty look; and although Martha did not know what misdemeanour she was being invited to share, she could not help smiling back.

When Donovan saw Martha's smile, he turned to his mother, his eyes accusing. Mrs. Anderson came smoothly forward, holding the poppy. She bent over him, and inserted it in his lapel. "For my little boy," she murmured, and kissed the top of his head. Then she ruffled the carefully arranged hair with the tip of a long, firm finger, so that a lock of hair stood up, giving Donovan a ridiculous look. "He looks so beautiful," she said. Again, her tongue caught between her teeth, she smiled wickedly at Martha, allowed her eyes to return towards the accusing ones that were fixed on her, and suddenly flushed. "I'm late," she said firmly, and hurried out, her skirts disturbing the flowers for the second time as she passed them.

Donovan lay stiffly in his chair, frowning, smoothing back his hair with his manicured hand. Martha was astounded when he at last spoke, for this self-possessed young man sounded like a deserted little boy, his voice shrill and complaining. "She's out every night, and Father has to lump it. God knows what he does with himself all the time, reading in his room—" He stopped himself, leaped to his feet, and said, in a normal tone, "Well, let's go and see what my erring mamma has left us to eat."

They sat at opposite ends of a long dining table, served by a native in the conventional uniform: red fez, white starched tunic, an impassive face. This man brought in a tray for Donovan to examine. There was nothing on it but some bread, a boiled egg, and a lump of quivering green jelly.

"My father has ulcers," announced Donovan, as if this was a personal affront to himself. "Take it away," he said, waving his hand at the servant; then: "No, wait." The tray was returned for Donovan's inspection; and with a slow, wicked smile, very like his mother's, he took the yellow poppy from his lapel, tucked it into the napkin ring, and waved the tray away for a second time. "Well," he said with grumbling grace, "you have a glimpse of the home life of the Andersons."

But he looked at Martha challengingly, and Martha could not immediately meet the challenge. She was sorry for Donovan, but elderly ladies (she must be at least fifty) with the wayward charm of Mrs. Anderson had never come her way before. Also, the word "ulcers" had struck a deeper chord than she liked. At last she sighed and said, "Yes, it's all very difficult, isn't it?" But this was too strong a note, and he began to defend his mother and explain what a terrible life of it she led with Mr. Anderson.

When the meal was finished, he said, "And now we must hurry. I suppose I should take you to meet my papa? But no, you don't want to meet him, do you?"

Martha therefore followed him to the car; and during the weeks she was to visit this house, she saw the old gentleman no more than half a dozen times. He had been an important civil servant—something to do with finance, Donovan airily explained. If he came down to a meal, he sat silent, as Martha was accustomed to see a father behave, while Donovan and his mother kept up a lively conversation. In the drawing room he never appeared at all; there sat mother and son, on the low purple satin chairs, flirting, chattering, teasing, and always with a watchful look in their eyes. Martha was as relieved as they when he chose not to descend from his room, for a nerve in her, sensitized long before its proper time, predisposed her uncomfortably to watch Mr. Anderson, that morose, silent gentleman, rather like a dapper little monkey in his careful clothes—but an old and misanthropic monkey; she looked from him to the charming young man, his son, and wondered how soon the shrill and complaining strand in his character would strengthen until he too became like his father, a bad-tempered but erudite hermit among his books —but no, that transformation was impossible to imagine. And where did Martha gain the idea that Mr. Anderson was erudite? Simply from the fact that he spent his time reading. She had an altogether

romantic picture of him, and the background of that picture was
the wall of a library, sober with dark, leatherbound volumes.

One afternoon Martha came into the house to find it empty, and
climbed the stairs to Mr. Anderson's room, aided by the self-posses-
sion of an attractive girl accustomed to find herself welcomed, and
opened the door and went in—but she was not to be allowed into
this room under any such passport. Mr. Anderson was reading in a
big chair by a window which framed a view of veld crossed and
recrossed by telephone wires. When he demanded gruffly what she
wanted, she instinctively switched off the charming manner, sat
down, and asked him about his book, confident that *that* was the
key. But no, he thankfully laid the book aside. She saw it was called
Three Days to the Moon, and on the cover was a picture of something that looked like a bomb with a window in it, through which
peered a man and a girl, both half naked. Beside his chair were
stacked dozens of similar books. On the table, however, were blue-
books, reports and newspaper clippings; and she understood at last
where his heart was, when he began to talk of a recent Government
commission on population, and as abruptly stopped himself with the
bitter comment, "However, at sixty it seems I'm too old to take an
intelligent interest."

Rather nervously, she mentioned Donovan; and Mr. Anderson appeared to be dismissing both of them when he said gruffly, "Of
course, I suppose you find this sort of thing dull. But at his age . . .
However, nowadays it seems sex is enough." She was embarrassed,
but not for the reason he imagined.

There were voices and laughter downstairs, and she got up and
thanked him (automatically "charming" again, under the invisible
influence of mother and son, whom she was to join) for entertaining
her.

"Well, well," Mr. Anderson said forbearingly, and picked up his
science fiction again. She left him, with a pang for that window and
its view of the sun-soaked grasses; and another, much deeper one, of
fear that at sixty a window, some tedious reports and bad novels
were all that one could reasonably expect to enjoy.

But on that first evening, her idea of Mr. Anderson was crystallized by an invalid's tray, with a crumpled yellow poppy stuck into
a silver napkin ring.

When Martha asked what film they were going to see, Donovan
replied that he always went to the Regal, in his manner of pointing
out something she must copy. She was still silent, trying to approve
this way of choosing one's entertainment, when they arrived. The

Regal was a large, shabby building in the centre of town, decorated to surface splendour with coloured lights and posters of film stars. As they walked towards it, Donovan took Martha's arm, and she looked instinctively to see why, for this was not the sort of gesture one associated with him. She found they were progressing slowly through groups of people whom Donovan was greeting, and when she examined them she felt his obvious pleasure and excitement affect her: the pavement was a dull city pavement, the posters on the walls were garish, but the place was transformed into something very like one of her private dreams. Everyone was young, throngs of young men and girls were everywhere, and they all knew each other, or so it seemed; for as she and Donovan slowly pressed their way through, she found herself introduced to faces who smiled through a blur of excitement, she found herself shaking dozens of hands; and as they left the crowded foyer and climbed the staircase, she heard him say, "Well, you're a great success, Matty, they were all wanting to see the new girl come to town."

She was startled, and glanced back to see this crowd under the new light of a unifying "they," and saw that she was being watched by what seemed to be dozens of pairs of eyes. Straightening herself and tossing her hair back, she climbed onwards, still supported by Donovan's arm, which, however, withdrew itself the moment the crowd was left behind.

He said again, with his self-satisfied note, "There, now, you've made your debut."

Martha was resentful; or rather, a small critical nerve in Martha was struck unpleasantly. At the same time, excitement was flooding into her at the idea that she was being displayed; and this confusion of feeling persisted while they entered the cinema and once again Donovan began waving and calling to innumerable people. She was prepared to become absorbed by the film, for this was the first she had seen, apart from the few shown at school; but it soon became clear that seeing the film was the least of the reasons which brought Donovan to the cinema. While it was running, he talked to her and to the people behind him; in fact, there was a continuous murmur of talk, and when someone shouted "Hush!" it hushed only for a moment.

At the interval, Martha ate ice cream in the foyer with a group of young people to whom, it seemed, she had already been introduced; for they called her Matty, and knew not only where she worked but where she lived; and one youth asked if he might pick her up at Mrs. Gunn's the following evening, only to be informed curtly by Donovan that she was already engaged. Martha was annoyed. As they returned to their seats, he said, "You don't want to get mixed up in that Sports Club crowd, my dear, they're not in our line."

After the film was over, Martha found herself going into McGrath's together, it seemed, with everyone who had been at the cinema. McGrath's lounge was a vast brownish room, with a beige ceiling of heavy plaster divided into squares, like a mammoth slab of staling chocolate, which had been further moulded to form superimposed circles and scrolls and shells and flowers, and finally swabbed with pailfuls of gilt. The walls were also sculptured and panelled and made to glitter with gold. The room was divided down the centre with heavy fluted and gilded columns. But the floor of this old-fashioned room was crowded with slender black glass tables and chromium chairs, and these were crowded with young people. After some minutes, Martha realized that a band was playing, and on a platform decorated like an altar with flowers and statuary she saw half a dozen black-coated men making the movements of those who create music; and, straining her ears, she heard the ground rhythm of a waltz. The musicians were talking and laughing with each other as they played, and with the people at the tables under the platform; the waiters who hurried through the crowd carrying trays laden with glass mugs of beer smiled when they were hailed by their Christian names. It all had the atmosphere of a festival, and Martha found herself transported into delight, and forgot her resentment, and sat by Donovan drinking beer and eating peanuts and talking to the people around her so animatedly that she was not at first aware of Donovan's silence. When she looked around, he appeared sulky, and as soon as their beer was finished he refused to join in another round, and said, "Matty and I must be going." There were humorous groans from the young men; and Martha was astounded and infuriated to hear them calling out to the dignified Donovan, as he walked with her to the door, "Oy-oy! Spoilsport! Meany!"

On the pavement he said gruffly, "Don't take any notice." But he was certainly pleased; and that pleasure offended her; and she could not help glancing back to where the light spilled from the great columned door, with the music and the sound of laughter and young voices. They were singing now, inside; and unaccountably her eyes filled with tears. It seemed as if she were being snatched away from her birthright before she had even stretched out her hands to take it.

Donovan strolled beside her to the car, and said, "Well, it's quite early, what shall we do? Of course, we'll follow the custom. You haven't been up the kopje, have you? That's where all we boys and girls go, to look at the lights and hold hands." He was now light and careless again; and they found the shabby but correct little car and drove away downtown, through the slums and kaffir stores, until a low hill rose before them. They spiralled slowly up it; and near the top there was a flat space, filled with parked cars, lightless and apparently deserted. Donovan at once got out and led her to the edge of the flat space. For a moment Martha felt herself carried away, for it was with a violent mingling of fear and delight that she struggled with the sensation that she was back home, looking away over the darkened veld, under the stars. But now the great hollow before her was scattered with light—it seemed as if a large hand had flung down stars caught from the sweep of the Milky Way over her head, to mark the streets and houses of the little town. At her feet rustled the veld grass, and the scent of the violet tree swept across her face. But Donovan said, "And so here we are, we must admire the lights and feel romantic."

At once she sobered, and listened as he pointed out the compact blur of light which was McGrath's Hotel; an irregular dark space, surrounded by light, which was the park; and away over a blank darkness that seemed to suffuse with an internal blue glow, to the sparkle which was his own house, where the smart new suburb would soon rise from the veld grasses. What a small town it was, seen thus from above! and its smallness defined in Martha's mind what had till then mazed and confused in streets, parks, suburbs, without limit or direction. They were all here, her experiences of the last few days, shrunk to a neat pattern of light. They were dismayingly shrunk; and at once her mind tugged to soar away from Donovan and from the town itself; but he kept pulling her down, pointing out this building and that, once even gaining her willing attention by directing her gaze to a building that stood by itself, so brightly lit that even from here she could make out the tiny black strokes which were the pillars of the verandah.

"The Sports Club," he said, and she heard reluctance in his voice. "I'll take you there when there's a nice dance." She did not answer, but he continued, "And while we're about it, I'm booking the Christmas Dance, and the New Year's Dance, and the Show Ball." He added, grumbling humorously, "It's disgusting, booking a girl up months ahead, but what can one do, one must pay the penalty for living in the colonies, where there's a woman shortage."

She laughed and, examining her experiences of that evening, realized that in those crowds there had been far more men than girls; and immediately her heart lifted on a wave of reckless power. She laughed again, and there was an unscrupulous note.

"You'll get spoiled," said Donovan gloomily. "You all do. All the same, it does go against the grain to book one's girl up a year in advance."

It was in this manner that Martha learned she was Donovan's girl; and instinctively she turned towards him, in a moment of swelling gratitude and warmth; she was prepared to accept him, in short, as her man, since he had laid that claim on her; but Donovan was standing there, hands in his pockets, staring moodily down at the lights of the town. The moment passed, and she was left feeling blank, rather foolish, and unaccountably tired.

"Well," he remarked, "so now we've done the expected. Come on."

They stumbled back over the stony ground, past a big beacon, a great post stuck into a heap of whitewashed stones. She stopped to look at it, and he said, giggling, "Just imagine the pioneers climbing all this way to stick the flag on the top of a kopje!"

As they descended, a curve of the hill shifted slightly, and she saw below her another expanse of sparsely lit country, though this time there was no neat pattern of streets, only an apparently limitless darkness irregularly marked by small yellow lights. "The location," said Donovan indifferently. "Kaffirtown." Involuntarily, she stopped. "The cemetery's this side of it," he added. "Come on, do, Matty, it's getting late." She followed him obediently, with a glance down-wards at Kaffirtown. Her social conscience was troubling her, point-ing out that she should remonstrate with Donovan; it was also say-ing that Donovan was an unworthy successor to Joss—she had for-gotten Billy altogether by this time. However, follow him she did, for she was intoxicated.

They were now passing the silent and darkened cars, and, as if he was reminded by them of something he should do, he put his arm carelessly about her, and so they went to theirs. At the door of her room, he kissed her lightly on the cheek, which Martha accepted as the seal she was instinctively waiting for.

"And now," he said firmly, "let's fix up." He took a little book from his pocket and turned so that the light from the street lamp might fall on it. "Tomorrow evening?" he enquired.

"I'm going to take lessons at the Polytechnic," she replied uncer-tainly; and she would have thrown it all up at a word from him.

But no: he said approvingly, "That's a good girl, we must all get efficient and earn lots of money." He considered for a moment, and said, "You must arrange to be finished by seven every evening, other-wise it will be ever such a dull life for both of us. I'm supposed to be studying for some kind of an exam myself. We can fit it in." He put away his book, waved a cheerful goodbye, and went away to his car, leaving Martha to go to bed if she chose.

But she could not. She was walking, in that familiar dazed and delirious condition, for some hours around her room; it was not until the stars were dimming that she dragged herself unwillingly to bed; and she was late for the office next morning.

Maisie was a few minutes later; and, as always, she walked composedly through her already busy companions, pulling off her white beret and smiling in vague goodwill. She lazily settled herself, took off the cover of her typewriter, and lit a cigarette, which she smoked to the end before beginning work. The main filing cabinet was in front of Martha's desk, and as Maisie pulled out the drawers and began sorting files, she said pleasantly to Martha, "Well, did you have a good time last night?"

"Why—were you there?" asked Martha.

"You didn't see me," said Maisie, laughing suggestively. "And you looked through me at McGrath's, too."

"I'm sorry."

"It's O.K." She laughed again, and said, "So our Donny-boy's got hold of you, has he?"

This had more than a suggestion of contempt, and Martha replied quickly, "My mother knew his mother."

Maisie worked for a few moments in silence, humming under her breath. She wore a tight white linen dress, and as she lifted her arms to slide the drawers the soft bulges of flesh above her petticoat, and the lace of the petticoat itself, showed clear through the thin white. Also, there were large wet patches under her arms, and the tendrils of loose hair on her neck were damp. From time to time she paused, and gazed out of the window in gentle reflection towards the kopje that rose above the dingy, slumlike streets, while she rested her hand on the edge of a drawer. Those damp patches, and a dust mark on the white skirt, seemed inoffensive, even attractive, on this cheerful slattern whose whole appearance, way of talking and happy-go-lucky movements took their assurance from the life she led outside the office. And when Mrs. Buss asked, with indignant politeness, if the filing was finished, she replied, "It's going along fine," and gave a calm laugh. Before she sat down she enquired, "Good-looking young lad, our Donny?" and waited for an answer.

Martha assented, though oddly enough she had not thought of Donovan as good-looking; and now she was asking herself why she had not, since of course he was—now it had been pointed out, she could see it. Could it be that this had something to do with that notion (firmly inculcated in her by her mother, whether she liked it or not) that one loved a man not for his looks, but for what he *was*?

Mrs. Quest, who believed this, had married an extremely good-look-ing man—but this was an altogether unsettling line of thought, and Martha's mind refused to follow it; for it grew dim, and she shook her head to clear it.

Maisie said comfortably, "Well, we've only got one life, that's what I say, so let's enjoy it." She went back to her desk, where she lit an-other cigarette.

But Martha had resolved not to smoke in the office, and kept it up for half the morning; and she worked as well as she could for think-ing of the evening ahead of her. At half past four she went dutifully to the Polytechnic, and stayed there until Donovan fetched her at seven.

3

At the end of a month she found that she had passed one examina-tion, and moved to another room in the Polytechnic where she took shorthand from a Mr. Skye, a small, dark, restless man who encour-aged his pupils by taking it for granted that they would all, and very soon, be doing two hundred words a minute, as he could. This was friendly of him, but not the best method for someone like Martha, who already tended to think too much of an end before she had mastered a beginning. His restlessness fed itself by speeding up his girls; for after reading a long passage (which he must have read a thousand times before) he would say impatiently, "Now, that's fine. You did that in ten minutes. You did get it, didn't you? Now let's speed it up." There were good-natured groans, but everyone picked up her dulled pencil and flew after his reading. At the end he came round, glancing rapidly for form's sake over their shoulders, saying, "Fine, fine, you did get it." And by this means, when Mrs. Buss asked her how she was getting along, Martha was able to say that her speed was one hundred and twenty.

"You're a fast worker," said Mrs. Buss unbelievingly, and Martha laughed and said that she was. Mrs. Buss spoke to Mr. Cohen, and Mr. Cohen invited Martha into his office for dictation, which she managed better than he had expected but much worse than she had. So she was now promoted, not to the status of the skilled, but some-where in between: half her time she spent helping Maisie with the filing and copying, and for the rest did easy letters for Mr. Cohen, and even, when Mrs. Buss was pressed, some of the more simple documents. She felt an altogether unreasonable astonishment that the work she had put in at the Polytechnic had, in fact, lifted her one degree up the ladder towards efficiency; as if the process of painfully learning a thing could have nothing to do with her dreams for herself. But it was considered to be only a beginning; she felt it to be a beginning—and yet . . .

The truth was, she was slackening off. She was really tired; and she had every reason to be. Since she had come to town, she had been carried on the same impulse which had first made her take flight from the farm. She had never paused to think where she was going, she was too busy. She woke early for the delight of finding herself alone and no pressure on her but the necessity to be at the office more or less on time. She forced herself to give as much attention to the dry legal stuff as she could, pretending that it did not bore her intolerably. She ate sandwiches at lunchtime, and read alone in the office. After work in the afternoon she went, most days, to the Polytechnic, was picked up by Donovan and went on with him to a sundowner party, where they ate as many peanuts and snacks as they could, since, as Donovan pleasantly but frankly pointed out, they got them for nothing. She was seldom in bed before one or two in the morning. She even woke hungry.

This business of food: how little one should take it for granted! For it might be considered strange that until thirteen or fourteen Martha's appetite was so hearty it was positively embarrassing; and now that hungry and affectionate child had vanished so completely that she could not eat without feeling guilty and promising restitution to herself by giving up the next meal. On the other hand, she would suddenly turn aside into a shop, without even knowing she had intended to, and buy half a dozen slabs of chocolate, which she would eat, secretly, until she was sickened and very alarmed, saying she must be careful, for she would certainly lose her figure if she went on like this. And when her mother sent in parcels of butter, fresh farm cheese, eggs, exactly as she had when Martha was at school, Martha gave them to Mrs. Gunn, saying airily that it was a nuisance to have the smell of food in her room. But, for all this, she was putting on weight; for if she did not eat she drank, as everyone did. From the first sundowner, gulped down hastily to give her vitality after the hours of work, she drank steadily through the evening until she arrived back in her room in the small hours, slightly tipsy, if not drunk. She was only doing as everyone else did; and if someone had pointed out to her, "You are living on sandwiches, sundowner snacks and alcohol, you are sleeping three hours a night," he would probably have got for his pains a dark and uncomprehending stare; for that was not how her life felt to Martha: it was a rush of delicious activity, which, however, was just beginning to flag.

It was six weeks or so after she had come to town that Joss walked into the office, in the same dark businessman's suit he had worn in the red dust of the station and behind the counter of the kaffir store; and, as he passed through, asked her to come and have tea with him. He was leaving that night for Cape Town, where the university term was just starting. He dismissed Martha's rather embarrassed objections, saying that of course old Uncle Jasper wouldn't mind. He went into his uncle's office.

Maisie said, without envy, "You've got all sorts of irons in the fire, haven't you?" She was smiling at Martha, while she filed her nails.

But Martha said indignantly, "I've known Joss for years."

Maisie nodded. "I've known marriages come out of boy-and-girl romances before." She held up her white hand and looked at it critically, flicked a bit of cuticle dust from a shining red nail, and added, "Of course, romancing with a Jew-boy is one thing, and marrying's another, I can see that." She glanced up, and her frank blue eyes grew startled: what had she said to earn that deadly and contemptuous stare from Martha? "It's not my affair, of course," she said hastily, looking hurt.

Joss returned, saying, "It's O.K." Martha picked up her bag and followed him out. They went to McGrath's lounge, which in the morning was filled with shopping women. The band played, the palms quivered as the great doors unceasingly swung; and Martha ordered beer, from habit, when asked what she would have. Joss had been going to have tea, but ordered beer, and then looked straight at her and demanded, "What's the matter with you? Don't tell me my uncle is working you too hard? You look like something the cat's brought in."

She did not have to mind this, for he looked concerned and affectionate. She said, laughing, "Your uncle's an angel. He's the sweetest thing that ever lived."

He drank his beer and regarded her, half with admiration and half critically. Martha knew this criticism was of the new skilled vivacity which was part of her equipment as girl about town; she had not learned it, it had offered itself to her, together with a new vocabulary and the ability to drink all night without showing it unpleasantly.

"You look to me as if you could do with some sleep," he remarked.

"I could," she laughed. "I'm exhausted. You've no idea how exhausting life is."

She chattered on and he listened, nodding from time to time; and when she paused, thinking it was his turn to be self-revealing, he replied to the real sense of what she had said: "So now you've got all the boys queuing up, eh?"

She coloured, because now she could see she had been boasting, and he went on:

"It's all very well, Martha Quest, but—" He stopped, looking annoyed, and added, "It's nothing to do with me."

She wanted it to be his affair, and said, "Go on."

"Who's the boy friend?" he asked bluntly.

"I haven't got one," she said quickly; and it was true, for, sitting with Joss, the sober, the responsible, the intelligent and manly Joss, how could she own to Donovan?

"Good," he said simply, without impertinence or self-interest. "You'd better be careful, Martha. After all, if you wanted to get married, you could have stayed on the farm."

"But I'm not getting married," she laughed; and he said quietly, "That's the ticket," and looked at his watch. "I've got to pack. My mother's busy settling in the new house. They've bought a plot in a new suburb called Wellington or something like that, but in the meantime they've got something temporary. Our store has got 'Sock's Kaffir Emporium' written over it now," he ended, looking at her so that she might share his regret and amusement, which she did.

"I wish you weren't going away," she said impulsively, holding out her hand; and he took it and squeezed it before replacing it gently in her lap, as if rebuking her for being careless with it. "When are you coming back? Are you going to work with your uncles when you've finished university? Will you be away long?" she chattered, in an effort to keep him.

"My uncles want me, but I want to go overseas," he said.

"Ah, *yes*," she breathed out, and with such envy that he glanced quickly at her and said gently, "Never mind, your turn will come." She found her eyes swimming; it seemed to her, just then, that Joss was the only person she had ever known who knew exactly how she felt, with whom she might behave as she liked—*and get away with it*, a critical voice added inside her.

He came with her to the door of the office. "And how does my Uncle Jasper strike you?" he asked.

"He's very nice," she said, but he pointed out impatiently, "Surely you can see he's very ill?"

"I didn't know."

He gave her a rather irritated look. "My cousin's business isn't helping much—though of course Abe was right to go."

She looked at him helplessly.

"Surely you know about my cousin?"

"No one ever mentioned him," she excused herself.

"My Cousin Abraham went off to Spain last year, and no one's heard a word from him for months."

"The Spanish Civil War?" she asked doubtfully.

Again that look. "What's the matter with you? A bit out of touch, aren't you?" She nodded guiltily. "Well, my aunt treats my Uncle Jasper as if it was all his fault. And it is, too—*her* son would never have the guts or intelligence to know one side of the Spanish business from the other . . ." Here Martha looked down, blushing. "But Uncle Jasper may be a slow old man, but he's all right. And Abe's all right, too," he concluded, and sounded envious and sad. "I should have gone. If it wasn't for my parents, I'd have gone. I should have gone in any case." Here he stopped, looking guilty. "Even that romantic fool, my brother, had that much sense."

"You mean Solly's in Spain?" she asked incredulously.

"No, he got as far as England and then he got mixed up with some girl, and now he's on his way back. But at least he started in the right direction."

"Give Solly my—regards," she said reverently.

"I'll give him your love," he said promptly; and she was delighted to hear that he sounded grudging. "He always had a soft spot for you. God knows why," he added, smiling; and this shy smile completely transformed what was a rather solemn and stiff face. "Good luck," he said, and walked away from her. He called back, "I've given your name to some friends of mine." And he ran quickly down the iron staircase.

Back at her desk, she repeated to herself that Joss was going away, going away; to her, he was off overseas, Cape Town being merely a resting place in his voyaging; she thought of him as a citizen of Europe, with the freedom of the big cities, and melancholy and envy fused into a bitter, frustrated sadness. And yet, while she was seeing herself, attractive and intelligent Matty, caged behind the desk of a legal office, she heard Maisie ask, "Pleasant dreams?" and understood—even as she indignantly asked, "What do you mean?"—that she had been smiling. Maisie only gave her good-natured laugh, and yawned.

Under the spell of Joss, Martha completely repudiated Donovan; and this revulsion lasted through that day and the next, when there was the following letter for her:

Dear Martha,

I enclose a list of various people you should look up. There's a discussion group, Left Book Club, they only talk, but it's better than nothing. My Cousin Jasmine might be worth your while, she's in a receptive state due to being heartbroken over my Cousin Abraham. Who else? I'm afraid stony soil, but even in the provinces (!) there is work to do, and you might perhaps lead that ass Robinson to a meeting or two, he's going into Parliament, so it would be a good idea if he had at least one or two ideas in his head. As for my Uncle Max, he's a born fascist, so don't waste your time.

Sincerely,
Joss

Martha read this letter with difficulty—as an English person reads Scots dialect, for instance. There were a number of assumptions in it that it seemed Joss took for granted were hers as well; and this was flattering, but she felt ignorant. He made no secret of the fact that he considered her lazy, but at the same time it appeared she possessed a quality which would enable her to influence others. What quality, then, was it? It was as if he were handing on a torch. Reading the letter again, she was struck by a grudging and acrimonious undertone, and when she came to the word "fascist" it sounded exaggerated, so that she suddenly giggled, and Mrs. Buss looked enquiringly over the desks.

She glanced down the list of addresses, seven of them, and felt a curious disinclination, as mental images of seven (at least) new people to be approached and known rose in her mind. Martha Quest, who thought of herself as so adventurous, so free and unbounded—the fact was, even the idea of picking up a telephone and making herself known to a new person troubled her: she made excuses, she could not do it.

But the difficulty was solved when the telephone rang and a small, precise, slow voice introduced itself as Jasmine's, with the suggestion that Martha should go to such an address on the following afternoon. It was not a meeting, but Martha might find it interesting. There was a lazy, even slighting, tone to this voice, which struck Martha: Jasmine, like Joss, seemed more struck by what this new group of people lacked than by what they possessed; and this contempt extended itself, or so it seemed, to Joss himself, for when the name was introduced the voice poised on an upward note, as if it expected Martha to join in a good-natured laugh. Martha did not laugh, feeling indignant on Joss's behalf; but she said she would be there tomorrow.

She told Donovan, when he telephoned to book her for the usual sundowner party, that she was engaged; and even was irrational enough to feel hurt when he remarked huffily that in that case he would take someone else.

On the following afternoon she spent a long time getting dressed; and then, ten minutes before she was due to be fetched, flung off the clothes that had been suggested, even created, by Donovan—white linen slacks and a checked shirt—in favour of a simple dress. In her mind, the man who was coming to fetch her was identical with Joss; they stood for the same thing. What social current, flowing through such devious channels, reached this room, so that Martha felt that the casual, gaminlike appearance Donovan liked was wrong—even that the linen dress as arranged by Donovan was too sophisticated? She arranged a coloured scarf loosely around her neck, clasped an embroidered belt at her waist, and let her hair fall in untidy curls. There was a touch of the peasant in her now, and she went to meet Mr. Pyecroft with confidence. At once she was disappointed, for he struck her as elderly. As they drove uptown, she chattered in her "attractive" manner, although she felt obscurely, without being able to alter it, that there was a discrepancy between her appearance and the manner that had been brought into being by Donovan.

It was a beautiful afternoon: there had been a storm, and the sky was full and clear, with shining masses of washed clouds rolling lightly in bright sunlight. The trees in the park glistened a soft, clean green; the puddles on the pavements reflected foliage and sky; and as the car turned into the grounds of the school where Mr. Pyecroft was headmaster, these puddles became ruffled brown silk, and above them, all down the drive, grew massed shrubs, glistening with wet. On a deep-green lawn were several deck chairs. From them two men rose as Martha approached; and again she thought, disappointedly, But they are old.

They were, in fact, between thirty and forty; they wore flannels, open shirts, sandals; they were of the same type: all long, thin, bony men, with intellectual faces, spectacles, thinning hair. It would be untrue to say that Martha made any such observation, or even compared them with Joss. When she met people, she felt a dazzled and confused attraction of sympathy, or dislike. Now she was in sympathy; she responded to the half-grudging deference older men offer a young girl. She answered their questions brightly, and was conscious of her appearance, because they were.

Mr. Pyecroft said that his wife would not be long, she was giving the children their tea; the other two men also apologized for the absence of their wives, and Martha accepted these social remarks not at their social value, but with the statement which she imagined sounded light and flippant, but actually sounded hostile: "Children are a nuisance, aren't they?"

Soon three women came from a verandah of the big school building, shepherding half a dozen children and two native nannies to
another lawn, about a hundred yards away, which was sheltered by
a big glossy cedrelatoona tree. As soon as the women appeared, the
voices of the men acquired a touch of heartiness that had not been
there before, grew louder; and they turned their shoulders on these
domestic arrangements with an uneasy determination which at once
struck Martha, for she felt it herself. She was watching the scolding
and fussy women as if her eyes were glued to them in fierce horror;
she said to herself, Never, never, I'd rather die; and she reclined in
her deck chair with a deliberate coolness, a deliberately untroubled
look.

When Mrs. Pyecroft, Mrs. Perr, and Mrs. Forester came to join the
men, they apologized, laughing, together and separately, for being
a nuisance, and explained how the children had been troublesome,
and went into details (and in a way that made it seem as if it were
an accusation against the men themselves) of how Jane was off her
food, while Tommy was in a trying psychological phase. The men
listened, politely, from their chairs; but they were not allowed to
remain in them, for it appeared that the whole group must be rearranged, an operation which took a good deal of time. Martha was
more and more hostile and critical—the women seemed to her unpleasant and absurd, with their fuss and their demands; she was as
much on the defensive as if their mere presence were a menace to
herself.

She looked at their dresses, as Donovan had taught her to look,
but understood at once that here was a standard that refused to
acknowledge Donovan. Their appearance had something in common which was difficult to define; Martha made no attempt to define it, she merely felt derisive. They were not at all the unashamedly
housewifely women of "the district"; nor were they fashionable—
clearly, they disdained fashion. Their dresses tended to be discordantly colourful, and too long for the year; their hair was looped or
braided or fringed, in a consciously womanly way; they wore bright
beads and "touches" of embroidery—Martha found herself fiddling
with her embroidered belt and with her scarf, which was now uncomfortable. She was stifled by it.

A native servant rolled a waggon with tea things across the lawn,
and there began a business of pouring, handing cups and passing
cakes. Martha joked and lit a cigarette, and said she was slimming.
The women looked sharply at her, and said that at her age it was
ridiculous; they looked at the men for support, and did not find it.
If there was an edge on their voices when they spoke to her, they

could hardly be judged for it; for Martha's gaze was expressing the most frank criticism, even scorn; and she, in her turn, ranged herself with the men as if it were her due to have their support.

With the arrival of the ladies, the rights of the intellect were at once asserted; and Martha was informed of times of meetings, the origin of the Left Book Club, the courage and force and foresight of a Mr. Gollancz, and that "we" were trying to raise aid for Spain. But no sooner had this conversation begun than the children began to shriek, and all three women rushed off, as one, to the rescue, in spite of the two native nannies, who might have been considered sufficient to deal with them. And so it went on: the three women came back, hurriedly apologizing, firmly took up the threads of their respective remarks, a general conversation began to develop, and then either a child would come rushing across the lawn, shouting "Mummy, Mummy!" or one, or all, of the women found it necessary to go to the children.

And Martha heard that fierce and passionate voice repeating more and more loudly inside her, I will *not* be like this; for, comparing these intelligent ladies, who nevertheless expressed resentment against something (but what?) in every tone of their voices, every movement of their bodies, with the undemanding women of the district, who left their men to talk by themselves while they made a world of their own with cooking and domesticity—comparing them, there could be no doubt which were the more likeable. And if, like Martha, one had decided to be neither one nor the other, what could one be but fierce and unhappy and determined?

She did not know when she had spent a more uncomfortable afternoon. It was not until the women had gone off, saying brightly and irritably, "Well, I suppose now we've got to return to our chores," and Martha was left with the men, that she felt at all at ease, but by now the men had acquired, in her eyes, a pathetic and hangdog look, and she was impatient.

She rose, saying, "I'm afraid I must go, I've got a sundowner party."

There was a slight hesitation before Mr. Pyecroft enquired, in the humorous light tone which was the counter of conversation among the men (though certainly not the women), "And so I take it you agree with us?"

Martha replied, even rather offended that the question could be put at all, "But of course."

"And we can expect you at the meetings?"

"Oh, yes," said Martha lightly; but more was being asked of her than that light statement.

"What newspapers do you take?" asked Mr. Perr suddenly. She had gathered that he was the chairman of the Left Book Club, the leader of the group. His length of body and face, his bony look, his humorousness, were distinguished from the others' by an emphasis in everything. He must be well over six feet, the flesh of his face was hollowed over big bones as if by a bold sculptor, and everything he said had a cautious space around it, while he curled his large mouth in a deprecating smile. "Newspapers are everything," he remarked humorously. "One must be certain of the complete impartiality of one's sources." And he spoke as if he were amused at himself, and at the idea of any newspaper, or in fact anything at all, being taken seriously.

"I—I read the *Observer*," confessed Martha, understanding that he did not mean local newspapers.

They involuntarily exchanged glances. Mr. Pyecroft said reproachfully, "But, Miss Quest, surely . . ."

Martha flushed and said quickly, "But I've never been introduced to any other."

At the appeal, the men looked relieved, and were able to say protectively that this was easily remedied. Mr. Pyecroft picked up a journal that was lying on the grass by his side, apologized that it was damp, and offered it to her. "I think you will find you will never read another," he suggested.

Martha thanked him and said goodbye, and suggested she should walk home. Mr. Pyecroft would not hear of this, so she said goodbye again and they went to the car.

Inside, she looked at the paper and saw the name *New Statesman and Nation*. It was familiar, because the local newspaper used it whenever it wanted to frighten its readers with a suggestion of sinister lawlessness. They were bad words, like "Fabian" or "Communist." Martha felt that warmth of recognition with which one greets a person one has heard about from friends.

She was leafing curiously through it when Mr. Pyecroft said, "Here's our Jasmine," and drew the car in under a tree. Walking slowly towards them was a small, dark girl in orange slacks and a purple sweater. At first glance she might be taken for a child, she was such a miniature figure, her black hair curled all over her head and held with a ribbon. But the walk was composed and mature, even dignified; and Mr. Pyecroft said with a laugh, "Our Jasmine always takes her time." It was a critical laugh; and Martha, in her turn, was critical that every member of this group seemed to find the others absurd, or, at the most, tolerable.

Jasmine at last came to a stop beside the car door, and said, "Hya."

This bizarre greeting was made additionally extraordinary by the careful way she used it; it was as if she were saying, very formally, "Good afternoon." To Martha she said, with casual dignity, "Oh, hullo, so there you are at last," and added some information about the next meeting. It appeared she was secretary and intended to behave only in this capacity, for, having told Mr. Pyecroft that she was having some trouble with the press—information which he understood at once, for he nodded casually—and that these reactionaries were getting her down, she said, "Well, I'm in a terrible hurry," and nodded and walked on, with neat, slow, precise steps.

"Our Jasmine is an interesting figure at the moment, because her great love has gallivanted off to Spain," said Mr. Pyecroft, as he started the car; and he said it with what can only be described as a sneer.

Martha was altogether at sea. If Abraham was not to be approved, who was? "Don't you like Abraham?" she enquired, like a child.

Mr. Pyecroft glanced at her, and said immediately in a sentimental voice that Abe was a fine chap, an altogether unusually intelligent chap; he added at once, however, in his customary light, denigrating way, that all one had to do these days to be a hero was to go dashing off to Spain. He glanced again at Martha, inviting her to laugh with him, and saw her huddled away from him, inside her shawllike scarf, which she was holding close around her throat as if she were cold, her eyes bent down, her face puzzled and frowning.

He was silent, waiting for the self-possessed young woman to reappear, for this stubborn child was not at all to his taste.

As for Martha, she had discovered she disliked Mr. Pyecroft. She thought dimly, It's all very well for these old people . . . and sympathetically dreamed of Jasmine, who loved a modern hero.

When they reached her room she was opening the car door, prepared to thank him politely and get out, when he asked, "Perhaps you'd like to come and have supper with me one evening?"

She was struck by an eager but uneasy look on his face. At once she went scarlet, and said quickly, "I'll be seeing you at the meetings, I expect." She ran away from the car, repeating to herself, "Dirty old man"; and she did not look around until the car, after a long silence, began to grind its gears. "Disgusting, filthy, horrible," she muttered angrily to herself, inside her room; and poor Mr. Pyecroft had assumed, in her eyes, the very figure of an old lecher. But in her hand was his *New Statesman,* and she went to the telephone and left a message with Mrs. Anderson that she was ill and could not go to the sundowner party with Donovan.

Then she lay on her bed and read the journal; for she had already decided to cancel the *Observer* and order this instead. Perhaps it is not correct to say that she read it, for unfortunately the number of people who actually read magazines, papers or even books is very small indeed. As she turned the pages and the lines of print came gently up through her eyes to her brain, without assault, what she gained was a feeling of warmth, of security; for here were ideas which she had been defending guiltily for years, used as the merest commonplaces. She was at home, she was one of a brotherhood. Yet when she laid down the journal she could not have said in detail what she had read, what were the facts; but she gave, unconsciously, a great quivering sigh, and lay back on her bed, eating chocolate and dreaming of a large city (it did not matter which, for it shared features of London and New York and Paris, and even the Moscow of the great novelists) where people who were not at all false and cynical and disparaging, like the men she had met that afternoon, or fussy and aggressive, like the women—where people altogether generous and warm exchanged generous emotions.

And from this dream she passed to her older one, so much older than she knew, of that golden city whose locality was vague, but until now had been situated somewhere between the house on the kopje and the Dumfries Hills (which area was in fact inhabited by the Afrikaans community), the white-piled, broad-thoroughfared, tree-lined, four-gated, dignified city where white and black and brown lived as equals, and there was no hatred or violence.

Towards morning she awoke, rather cold and stiff, and went to the French door which stood open to the garden. She leaned her head against the doorframe, and shivered at the cold and starlit sky. There was no moon. Along the silent street came the clop-clopping of hooves. A small white donkey glimmered into sight, and behind it a milk cart, rattling its cans, and behind that ran a small and ragged piccanin, a child of perhaps seven years, whose teeth were rattling so loudly they sounded like falling pebbles even across the width of the garden. She felt sad and depressed; the ideas with which she had fallen asleep seemed ridiculous now; she thought dimly that if the world was going to be changed it would not be changed by the people she had met the previous afternoon, and at that decision she became even sadder. She shut the door and decided that, since it was already four o'clock and she must be at the office by eight, it would be a waste of time to sleep. She looked for a book among the piles on the dressing table, the table, even on the floor. She wanted something which would include that deprived black child, her own fierce unhappiness (which was likely at any moment, as she knew, to turn into as fierce a joy), even the unattractive and faithless group of people whom Joss very properly despised. She wanted it all explained. The titles of her books seemed faded, what the print said had nothing to do with her life; and as the sun rose, Martha was lying fully dressed on the floor, copying out titles of books advertised in the *New Statesman*, which had no better recommendation than that their names were included in the glow which surrounded that magic title.

She had decided she would go to the next meeting of the Left Book Club, but would treat Mr. Pyecroft coldly, as he deserved, for even the thought of him filled her with the most violent disgust.

She was just about to telephone Jasmine, when the phone rang for her; but not at all as simply as that statement sounds. First, the instrument on Mrs. Buss's desk gave a shrill and prolonged peal, so that Martha, who had been about to pick it up, jumped and went back to her desk, already jarred, even apprehensive. She saw Mrs. Buss give her an interested and then emotional look as she switched the instrument through to Mr. Jasper Cohen. Mrs. Buss continued to type, her vivid, but now professionally reticent, gaze hovering around Martha. Then the machine clicked, Mrs. Buss listened again, and switched it through to Mr. Max. Finally, Martha was called into Mr. Jasper Cohen's office, where she was told kindly that her father was ill and she must hurry back to her room, where her mother was waiting for her. Martha's irritation that her mother's sense of drama had succeeded in disturbing two busy men, and in fact the whole office, over something which should concern herself alone, was only just allayed by concern over her father. She left the office with all those interested eyes following her, while she instinctively modulated her walk to one of deprecating dignity. Mrs. Buss did not fail to point out that this was the second time within a week that Martha had allowed "personal matters" to call her out of the office, and Mr. Cohen was kindness itself.

Martha walked as fast as she could along the few streets which led to her room, and found her mother there alone, waiting at the door, restless with energetic excitement.

"So there you are," she exclaimed reproachfully, and, as she kissed her daughter's cheek, announced, "Your father's really ill, he really is very ill, Matty."

Martha felt guilty, as usual, and enquired, "What's the matter?"

She expected to hear of some crisis in the diabetes; but Mrs. Quest said, "Well, we're not quite sure, they're finding out at the hospital. I've left him there for the day." Mrs. Quest was drawing on her gloves, and was looking at a list of things she must do, which she had taken from her bag.

"Why did you call me out of office, then?" enquired Martha sullenly.

"I don't like driving in town, you can drive for me," said Mrs. Quest, and Martha said angrily, "I can't just leave the office to act as your chauffeur."

"But your father's ill," said Mrs. Quest antagonistically; and Martha exclaimed, *"Mother!"* Mrs. Quest, evading the accusing eyes, said briskly, "I must go and see Mrs. Anderson, she wrote to me, and I think it would be nice if you were there, too."

"Mother, what is the matter with Daddy?"

"I've told you, they're finding out. He's having a barium meal," announced Mrs. Quest, using the technical words with a satisfaction which reminded her daughter that she had been a nurse.

Hastily, in order to avoid the repulsive details which would certainly follow, described with the same cool satisfaction, Martha said, "I can't possibly spend all day having tea and gossiping. You didn't tell Mr. Cohen you wanted me as a chauffeur, did you?"

"He was very kind," said Mrs. Quest, smiling. "And now let's go quickly, Matty, because it will be too late for morning tea otherwise."

"I'm not taking you to tea with Mrs. Anderson, what do you want to see her for—" She stopped, on the verge of saying, "behind my back." As usual she was feeling the impotent resentment that as soon as she made a friend, created anything of her own, her mother followed her, assuming first place. She spoke as if she had been an intimate friend of Mrs. Anderson for years, whereas they had not seen each other since they met on the boat when the Quests first arrived in the colony.

"Don't be so unreasonable, Matty. It's only natural the two mothers should want to talk over their children." And she even looked suggestive and coy.

"What have you got into your head now?" asked Martha disgustedly; but Mrs. Quest, not at all upset, said impatiently, "Oh, come along, Matty, don't waste time."

"I'm not coming," said Martha, with calm fury.

Seeing her face, Mrs. Quest said hurriedly, "Well, you needn't stay, just run me out and leave me there. You can walk back, it isn't far." She looked into the mirror, composing her face and adjusting her hat, which was a severe navy-blue felt and suited her regular, dominant features. Her suit was of navy linen, squarely cut, and she looked altogether an efficient woman, a committee woman. Martha thought of the perfumed, billowing Mrs. Anderson, and wanted to laugh. On a wave of good spirits, inspired by the malicious thought of "the nice talk" the two ladies would have, she became suddenly amenable, even affectionate and she drove Mrs. Quest without protest to the Andersons' house, where she left her, and walked quietly back to the office.

And here she leaned her head on her hands, oblivious of the interested eyes of the other women, who were longing to be sympathetic if she would only give them the chance, and thought miserably of her own lack of feeling. She only felt resentful that her father was ill (only she did not believe he was as ill as her mother said); she felt resentful that at any moment it might be used as an emotional argument against her. She knew she should be thinking of Jasmine, and making arrangements to know her better, and yet all she could think of was her mother, at that moment discussing her with Mrs. Anderson. She knew that because of her mother's interference something unpleasant would happen, because it always did. Why had she not said that she had quarrelled with Donovan? It was as good as the truth. Why . . . But soon she ceased to think, she merely waited, in a condition of locked and irritable unhappiness.

Later that afternoon Jasmine telephoned her and asked her to come to tea. She heard Martha's remote, nervous voice saying yes, she would try, but it was difficult, and perhaps it would be better if . . .

Jasmine, who had telephoned the ladies Forester, Pyecroft and Perr for what she described half humorously as "a report" on Martha, had been told she was conceited, affected, and her level of political understanding was indicated by the fact that she read the *Observer*. The last was the contribution of Mrs. Pyecroft, who added that Joss must be influenced by Martha's looks: Martha would be quite attractive if she weren't so conscious of being attractive. Jasmine therefore gave Martha up as a waste of time, on hearing those ineffectual excuses.

By now Martha was nearly hysterical, for she had been sent a letter, by office boy, from Donovan, saying she must meet him at McGrath's immediately after office, because it was very urgent.

And when she threaded her way between the crowded tables, smiling automatically, like royalty, at the people who greeted her, shaking her head with playful regret when they asked her to join them, she could see Donovan energetically defending the empty seat beside him, and knew that he was very angry: he looked exactly like his father, morose and bad-tempered.

"Matty *dear*," he said shrilly, as she struggled to her seat, "what's all this about your mamma and my mamma? My mamma has telephoned me for the third time, and she is really furious."

"I'm not responsible for my mother," Martha said flatly, and added, "For God's sake get me a drink."

He ordered two enormous glass jugs of the strong local beer, and went on: "What are we to do, Matty? I told my mamma that I hadn't seen you for as good as a week, you've practically thrown me over, but she wouldn't listen."

This was an invitation to confess what she had been doing, but Martha said impatiently, "Yes, but what's happened?"

"Why haven't you been seeing me? A little bird told me that you were all mixed up with the local Reds, and that won't do you any good, Matty dear. Did you know the police go to their meetings? They'll be put in prison one of these days."

Martha laughed crossly, and said, "Oh, don't be such a baby."

The beer was slammed down in front of them by one of the hurrying waiters, and Martha seized hers and drank half of it.

"You're getting quite a little toper, Matty dear," said Donovan unpleasantly.

"Well, one must do something," said Martha defensively. She unconsciously glanced at her fingers: on both hands, they were stained to the middle joints with nicotine. As she decided she would cut down smoking, she reached for her bag and lit a new one from the stub of the last, and thought, I'll stop smoking when this business with my mother is settled.

"They're a bunch of Jews, too," said Donovan gracefully. "After knowing me for so long, you should have learned discrimination."

"But they aren't all Jews—" Martha began, and stopped, furious with herself. "I thought you had asked me here to discuss our respected parents?" she enquired at last, and with that rueful smile she knew put him at a disadvantage.

"You're a naughty girl," said Donovan, more gently. "My mamma says she wants to see us. It's a crisis, Matty, a crisis."

A group of lads in black-and-white-striped jerseys and white shorts, which exposed what seemed to be several yards of long, thick, red-brown thighs, entered the lounge and emitted a series of shrieks and yodels, began slapping the seated men nearest to them across the shoulders, and bending over the girls with yearning, sentimental faces.

"Now here are the Sports Club crowd," said Donovan sulkily. "If you let them sit here, it's the end, really it is."

Seeing Martha, the lads let out a yell expressing agonized frustration, and came pushing towards her. "Matty, Matty," they moaned inarticulately, "beautiful Matty." They were watching a passing waiter, and, even as they paid their fee to beauty, reached out for mugs of beer and turned their backs as the waiter protested, "Baas, baas, someone else paid for this beer."

"Beautiful," continued the ringleader, ignoring the waiter, "why are you so toffee-nosed, why—"

"This table is engaged," said Donovan, rising to the bait, as he had been intended to do.

"Keep your hair on," said the sportsman, and he lifted his glass mug and tilted his head back, exposing a long, lumpy throat, and began to drink.

"Down, down, down," chanted the people at the tables nearby. "Here's to Donny, drink it down . . ." The Adam's apple moved steadily up and down, the golden liquid sank in its foam, and everyone began to clap. The young man set down his mug, which had held nearly a quart of beer, and looked about proudly, so that the applause grew louder. Then he shook his hands together in self-congratulation over his head, and, his eyes happening to fall on Martha, turned up his eyes and staggered away, clutching his brow in a parody of despair. Everyone laughed, while Donovan sat moodily silent.

"If you can tear yourself away from these fascinating athletes, Matty darling, let's go and face my mamma."

"I still don't know what we have to face," said Martha, rising.

They went out, while Martha acknowledged the homage from various young men, who were putting on the despairing faces required of them by convention, with a careless smile.

"It must be so nice to be such a success," said Donovan spitefully, as the swing doors revolved behind them, for Martha had a self-satisfied look on her face, although she was reminding herself that it was a convention and meant nothing.

They drove in silence to the Andersons' house, where a message had been left by Mrs. Quest: "Sorry have no time to see you again, must go and get Daddy from hospital, such a pleasant morning with Mrs. Anderson, will let you know the result of the test."

With this piece of paper in her hand, Martha followed Donovan into the drawing room, and found Mrs. Anderson poised amid clouds of mulberry chiffon on her purple satin chair. She was smiling, but looked annoyed.

"Now, I want to speak to you young people frankly," she began, and Donovan muttered, "Oh, hell," and flung himself down on a settee and took up *Vogue*. "No, Donny, it's for you too, and you must listen. Now, both of you must realize that you are very young and . . ." Here she paused, gave them a doubtful glance, and took a cigarette from a tortoiseshell cigarette case. She lit it slowly, and it appeared that the impulse of anger that had carried her thus far was already failing her.

Martha sat on the end of the settee, at Donovan's feet, and tried to smile. "I don't know what my mother has been saying," she said, "but I think you are jumping to conclusions."

"Yes, yes," interrupted Mrs. Anderson impatiently, though she sounded relieved. "I expect you think I'm an interfering old lady—" here she laughed and looked flirtatiously at Donovan, who was looking at her coldly, "but I feel that your mother has perhaps—I mean—" She paused and sighed. "Oh, dear," she said, and she put her hands to her forehead in a helpless way, "I'm so tired and cross and . . ." Impulsively she rose, came to Martha and kissed her, but Martha accepted the embrace stiffly. "Well, I daresay I got the wrong idea," she murmured, and looked in appeal at both of them.

"I think you have, Mamma dear," said Donovan icily, throwing aside *Vogue* and sitting up. "Matty and I are ever so platonic, you've no idea, and it's very upsetting to have you two dirty-minded old girls behaving like this."

"*Donny!*" gasped Mrs. Anderson, and she began to cry, pressing a piece of ivory-coloured silk to her eyes in such a way that it would damage neither the silk nor her make-up. Donovan, with elaborate courtesy, handed her a handkerchief, and now she began to cry in earnest, in great shuddering sobs. "I'm so sorry, darling," she wept. "You must forgive me. I don't know why, but I was so upset, and Mrs. Quest was—I mean—"

"Well, don't cry, Mamma," said Donovan gracefully. "But I really do think you should tell us what this is all about. You can't summon Matty and me for an audience, and then get us all upset, and suddenly say that you're sorry and leave it like that."

He stood poised on one hip, a brown suede shoe extended easily in front of him, looking sternly down at his mother, who shook herself, laughed as she saw the black streaks on the handkerchief, dabbed her eyes again and said clumsily, "Mrs. Quest was talking as if you were getting married. I told her that you were both too young, and that we hadn't the money for Donny to marry—"

Here Martha flushed with annoyance, and exclaimed, "It really is the limit!"

"Yes, Matty, I'm sorry—but . . . Oh dear, it is so difficult. You see, we are really very poor and . . ."

Matty suddenly laughed, thinking of the oblique semipoverty of her home, and of this expensive house, and of the secret luxurious life of Mrs. Anderson: also, like a black screen against which this minor anomaly was exposed stood that knowledge she had brought with her from her earliest years: the fact that the poverty of the Quest family represented unimaginable and unreachable wealth to the black serfs who supported them.

"It's not a joke, Matty," said Mrs. Anderson, who was annoyed, although she smiled in the rueful, charming way that Martha herself used when pleading false claims. "After all, Mr. Anderson's retired, and we're not rich. I have some money, but not much, and living is so expensive these days, isn't it?" So too the millionaire, indicating his several houses, his cars, his yacht: "But it all costs a lot to keep up," he says indignantly.

"Well, Mamma," said Donovan, giving judgment, "I think you're a very naughty old girl, and I'm cross with you."

Mrs. Anderson brightened and reached up to kiss him. He generously extended his cheek. "I'm afraid I have a dinner engagement," she said in her normal gracious tone, standing up. "You two can look after yourselves. Don't forget Mr. Anderson's tray—tell the boy scrambled egg, he's sick of boiled eggs, he says." She smiled humorously. "Good night, dears, and forgive a silly old woman." And she swept out, touching her hair delicately with one hand and her smudged and blackened eyes with the other; she was frowning now, at the thought of the time it would take to do her face, for she was very late.

Martha and Donovan, left alone, did not immediately look at each other. They were both irritable. They understood that this scene had raised certain problems; and Martha, for her part, was waiting for him to put these problems into words—for a man should surely take the initiative?

And so he did, but not as she expected. "Well, Matty," he remarked at last, plucking at the beautiful rose and copper gladioli whose arrangement must have cost Mrs. Anderson so much trouble, "well, it seems that we're supposed to make love," and he looked at her gloomily, even resentfully.

She gave a snort of astonished and offended laughter. She stopped, then laughed again. She looked at Donovan, who was regarding her with puzzled annoyance, and went off into a peal of laughter that grew hysterical, and broke into a fit of coughing. And then silence. She sighed; she was very tired and depressed.

"It's all very well," said Donovan resentfully, "it's all very well." Again that critical, almost angry look; and now there was anger in the look she directed at him; for a few moments their eyes challenged each other, and then dropped away; and if Mrs. Quest or Mrs. Anderson had looked in then, she might have been surprised, and even disappointed, to find this couple separated by several feet of carpet and apparently on the verge of a bad quarrel.

"I suppose we had better eat," said Donovan at last.

With the relieved knowledge that the moment of crisis was postponed, they went to the dining room, where Donovan regained his good humour ordering his father's scrambled eggs. And after that they went as usual to the pictures; and, again as usual, on to McGrath's, where Donovan seemed to find no objection to sharing a large table with about a dozen others.

"Our Donny-boy's in good form tonight," said Maisie, who happened to be near Martha, under escort of one of the sportsmen.

And Donovan was—gay, malicious and amusing. He seemed determined to eclipse the sportsmen; he made fun of them, told spiteful stories at their expense, and then took the sting from it by telling stories against himself; and at midnight withdrew triumphantly with Martha, saying, "And now, Matty, you must get your beauty sleep, or you'll lose your looks, and then none of us will love you any more."

The sportsmen gallantly insisted that they would love Matty, and all their girls, forever; but without their usual assurance, and this was not only because of Donovan's triumph but because of the discordant note he always introduced.

On the pavement he said lightly, with the astonishing frankness which was possible only because he could not hear the discordancy, "You must admit, Matty, that I'm much more entertaining than these oafs who have all their brains in their thighs?" And when she assented he continued, "I really think you'd better stick to me, you know. The last girl I took out deserted me for them, and really you should have seen her, she was so bored I could have cried for her."

"And what happened to her?" asked Martha curiously.

"She got married—a businessman from Nairobi," he said, as if this served her right, a sentiment which Martha could not help sharing; though she began to dissent from it when he continued, "All you girls get married, you have no strength of mind at all. I really do feel that all this sex is overrated, don't you?"

"I don't know," said Martha humorously, "I haven't tried yet."

But he would not accept the humour. He pressed her arm urgently, and looked down into her face and insisted, "Well, don't you think so? All you girls want to be made love to, and really . . ." His face faded in disgust.

Although Martha had every intention of agreeing for the sake of good nature, she began to laugh; and he waited until this rather strained laughter was finished, and muttered bad-temperedly, "Women are oversexed, that's what I think."

She began to chatter, in her social manner, about a book on the sexual customs of the Bantu, which she had just read; and thought it ill-tempered of him not to accept what she imagined was a pleasant way out of personal comment: she was saying that among primitive races girls were judged to be sexually mature long before they were in civilized communities.

But he remained silent until he dropped her at her door, and slid his customary good-night kiss on her cheek, saying, "Well, Matty, I've decided to take you to a dance at the Sports Club next Saturday, and risk all; I can see you are tugging at the leash."

"Poor Donovan,' said Martha, and she laughed again, she could not help it. Suddenly what she at once described to herself as a mischievous impulse (since she was immediately overwhelmed by embarrassment at herself) made her say, "Kiss me properly, Don." She held her face invitingly under his, and half closed her eyes, thankful it was dark, for she could feel a hot flush creeping up her cheeks. She waited, watching his furious eyes through her lashes, until he clasped her and shook her hard.

"Now, stop it, Matty," he said firmly. "I will not be teased. You must behave yourself, or I won't take you to a dance."

On this note they parted. In her room, Martha first was angry, and then, since it was her instinct to adapt herself, saw herself through Donovan's eyes and became humiliated. Behind this confusion of feeling was another: she murmured to herself that one felt so safe with Donovan; she was relieved she was going to the Sports Club with him; and for a girl whose first article of faith was that one was entitled to lose one's virginity as romantically and as soon as possible, this was surely an odd thing to think? The fact was, the thought of making love with Donovan was rapidly becoming impossible, even indecent: she had several times called him Jonathan, and never noticed the slip of the tongue.

part three

*In the lives of most women everything, even the greatest sorrow,
resolves itself into a question of "trying on."*

PROUST

1

The Sports Club had come into existence about five years before,
and in a way characteristic of the country. For when it was first suggested, at a ladies' bridge party, Mrs. Maynard said, "What a pity
there isn't a sports club in this town," and the others assented, without feeling it necessary to point out that there were several; they belonged to the employees of the railways, the post office, various businesses. From half-past four until sundown, every open space in the
city was crowded with young people engaged in violent activity.

Mrs. Maynard was large, strong-minded, black-browed and energetic, the wife of a magistrate; and she was a lady. That is, in England, where she married Mr. Maynard, she had belonged to the gov-
erning class by birth. Mrs. Lowe-Island was a lady only because she
had married Mr. Lowe-Island, whose family had connections with
the English aristocracy. She was a vulgar, spiteful woman who did
not pride herself on saying just what she thought, because it had
never entered her head there were occasions when one should not.
She at once said, "I quite agree with you, dear. We need a place
with some class. There should be somewhere for civil servants and

people like us." Mrs. Maynard, who, because of her upbringing, understood first of all the arts of suggestion, was naturally pained at having her thought so crudely expressed; but she did not snub Mrs. Lowe-Island, because she was unsnubbable, and because in her secret heart she considered her hardly worth the effort. A third lady, Mrs. Talbot, was so dissimilar to the other two that her continued friendship with them was a tribute to their mutual passion for bridge. She was a charming, elegant lady, whose chief interest was her delicate and artistic daughter; and she now murmured, with a kind of laughing tolerance which was an appeal to her companions, that it would be nice for the children to have a place where they could play games; and it is a remarkable fact that until they were mentioned the claims of youth had not occurred to the other women. Mrs. Knowell, the fourth, at once exclaimed warmly and generously, "Oh, yes, we must do something for the young people, my Douggie loves rugger, though I keep telling him he'll break his neck."

There was a silence, for it was apparent that here was a conflict in intention. But Mrs. Knowell was aflame with excitement, and soon began talking again, and in a few minutes the Sports Club was built and furnished, and in the throes of an inaugural ball. They laughed at her, teased her; particularly Mrs. Maynard and Mrs. Lowe-Island, for they had imagined the Sports Club as a large shadowy verandah, with native servants standing like willing statues around the walls, plenty of sundowners, and that laughter which is the result of personal comment, while behind this imaginary verandah was a bridge room, filled with elderly ladies.

That evening Mrs. Maynard talked to her husband, who expressed agreement by saying it was a paying proposition; Mrs. Lowe-Island talked until Mr. Lowe-Island said he was no snob, but there were times when . . . Mrs. Talbot told her daughter tenderly that it was bad to spend so much time on her water colours, a game of tennis occasionally would help avert the migraine and fainting fits to which, like a Victorian maiden, she was addicted. And Mrs. Knowell telephoned her son at the office, which he had forbidden her to do, and irritated him until he said, "Yes, but for goodness' sake, Mater, tell me another time."

All these ladies were adept at raising money for good causes, and they found it even easier to raise a large sum for what would be a paying proposition; and very soon there was a large committee of about thirty people, not one of whom was under forty-five. They all had determined ideas about the number of bridge rooms, sundowner lounges and bars the place should possess; and they were on the verge of buying a site which would have room for a club building and perhaps one tennis court, when a new factor entered the situation—which is a mild phrase for what happened when Binkie Maynard picked up the architect's plans (marked "Sports Club") and went off into loud laughter.

"What's this, a home for retired civil servants?" he demanded.

His mother reproached him; his father regarded him with a certain practised apprehension; and Binkie looked at the plans with a growing interest, until at last he said, "What-ho, chaps, this has got something—got something, hey?" He flapped the plans in the air, let out a whoop, and flew out of the house in search of a fellow spirit.

Binkie had first given signs of what he was destined to become when, at the age of four, plated into tight sky-blue satin, he climbed onto the bride's table at his sister's wedding among the flowers and ribbons, and piped, "And now it is my turn to give you a toast . . ." He was lifted down, kicking and bawling. At school he was at the bottom of his class, and useless at games, but he organized clubs and societies of all kinds. When he left school, his father put him into the civil service, where at least he could come to no harm, and there he soon arranged clubs-for-having-sandwiches-at-lunchtime and associations-for-saving-money-for-buying-presents-on-retirement.   He was the thorn in his father's flesh, his mother's pride, the despair of his chief. He was a large, ungainly, red-faced, black-locked youth of twenty when those plans fell like manna from heaven into his hands and gave him the outlet he needed for his genius.

He said to his father next day, "I say, it isn't fair, you need the young element, I mean to say." His father could hardly disagree.

At the next committee meeting, Binkie, Douglas Knowell, and half a dozen other young men took the floor. Binkie was chairman, not because he had been elected, but by virtue of his deadly single-mindedness. At the second meeting, there were several girls in shorts and sweaters, who were polite to the elderly ladies and coy with the old men, but treated them as if they hardly had the right to be there at all.

Mrs. Lowe-Island got up (for she had not understood, as the rest had, their complete rout) and said that she was no snob, but the club must be restricted; and Binkie climbed to his feet before she had even finished, and with those large, black, indignant eyes fixed on her said he was upset, yes, really upset to hear that anyone, even Mrs. Lowe-Island, who deserved three hearty cheers for what she had done, could make remarks that really—he didn't think anyone would disagree with him—were not in the spirit of the country. This wasn't England, he meant to say, this was a new country; he wasn't used to making speeches, but really, he was going to suggest that the club should be free to anyone who could find twenty shillings a year, which was a lot of money to some people, though some people (he meant no offence) might not believe it, and that's all he wanted to say, and that was enough. Here there was a murmur of passionate agreement from all the golden girls and boys; and there was never another suggestion about snobs or restrictions.

From that time, and for several months, the Maynard house swarmed day and night with young men and women. Committee meetings were held, but as a matter of form, and to satisfy and support and confirm arrangements already made by Binkie.

There was one afternoon when Binkie caught sight of his mother playing bridge in a corner of the verandah with three other ladies, all huddled forward to escape the pressure from a throng of shouting and arguing youth; and a pang of contrition must have assailed him, for he said to his father afterwards, "I say, I hope you don't think we've been shoving our way in. I mean, it is a *sports* club, isn't it?"

Mr. Maynard, a suave and cultivated man, raised his eyebrows slightly and smiled; but, finding this gesture insufficient, he murmured, "My dear Binkie, I cannot tell you what a relief I find it that you are not, as I was beginning to suspect, without a natural bent. You have my blessing—if it turns out you cannot dispense with it, which I am afraid I find it hard to believe."

Binkie, after a pause, gave an uncertain smile, and said heartily, "Oh. Well, that's all right, then, isn't it?"

"So I gather you will have no objection if I resign from the committee and devote myself to reducing my handicap at golf—may I point out that you have made no provision for a golf course in your plans for the Sports Club?"

"That's not fair," said Binkie, in an aggrieved voice. "We've got first refusal on the land just behind the building site, and it'll fall vacant in six months, so I reckon there'll be a full-size golf course in a year's time."

"My apologies," said Mr. Maynard. "I withdraw completely. But, as to my first point, I suggest that I and your mother be allowed to resign. No ill feeling on either side, but now you've agreed that there may be a small side room where the ladies may play bridge, and I'm assured of my golf course, I feel our usefulness is at an end."

"I say!" said Binkie reproachfully. "That's not the spirit, Dad."

"But you've my blessing, as I've already said. After all, we're more of a hindrance than a help."

"But who's going to raise the money?" asked Binkie. "We need another ten thousand at least if we're going to have four squash courts and proper changing rooms, and the golf course won't get built for nothing."

"Let's get this clear," said Mr. Maynard. "You want myself and your mother to remain on the committee to raise money for you?"

"You can resign if you like," said Binkie kindly, "but we must have the finance committee, mother and Mrs. Lowe-Island and the rest, to fix the money."

Mr. Maynard's cheeks swelled, buttoned in by a tight and commenting mouth, while his eyebrows rose like black kites: it was an appearance he had evolved for use in the law courts, where he was magistrate, to oppress native offenders into an awe-ful frame of mind; but Binkie merely looked impatient. He allowed his brows to fall and his cheeks to deflate. "Well, well, well," he murmured. He nodded slowly again. "Tell me, what makes you think ten thousand'll be enough? Where did you get the figures?"

"Oh, I can show you the figures, if you want. It's ten thousand six hundred and fifty-four pounds ten shillings and fourpence."

"You worked that out? You worked it out yourself with estimates and a piece of paper and a pencil?"

"I've no head for figures," said Binkie good-naturedly. "I got Douggie to do it. He's the tops with figures."

"Well, well, well, the born organizer. Who'd have thought it? Well, it's worth it. I should have put you into industry," said Mr. Maynard.

"I say," said Binkie, annoyed, "you're not going to start changing jobs for me now? I haven't got time, I'm busy with the Club. Besides, they're going to put me up a grade at Christmas. After all, you've got to say that for the Service, they have to put you *up*, it's only fair."

In 1935 the Sports Club site marked the division between the old residential quarter of shady avenues and rambling verandahed houses and the naked veld. Its boundary fence ran along North Avenue; and for many years people had used the phrase "North Avenue" adjectivally. "She's ever so North Avenue," Donovan might say approvingly. Here lived senior civil servants, the Cabinet ministers, even the Prime Minister. But now they looked across the street, through the tall creamy trunks of a double line of gum trees, over the playing fields, to the club house. It was a noble building, in the Cape Colonial style, of smooth dark-red brick, with a green roof all curves and gables, and a deep verandah supported on stately white pillars. The playing fields, several acres of them, were smooth emerald in the rains, but a scurfy brown in the dry season, in spite of the perpetually working hoses, which were dragged all day like thick black coiling serpents into different positions by a team of half a dozen natives.

Inside there was a large, high-ceilinged room with a polished dark-wood floor, comfortable chairs, and a fireplace at each end; and this room was cleared two or three times a week for dances. Off this room, on one side, were a series of bars and sundowner lounges; and on the other, hidden among changing rooms, a small room which could be used for bridge—though any ladies reckless enough to settle themselves in it for a comfortable afternoon were likely to find Binkie's shock head poked through the door at them, with the firm injunction, "The squash rackets committee will be wanting this in ten minutes, I'm just giving you fair warning." For at about four in the afternoon, the Club, comparatively deserted until then, suddenly surged with young men in white flannels and striped jerseys, and girls in gym tunics, shorts, or coloured dungarees; and waiters ran to and fro, staggering under trays loaded with the ubiquitous glass mugs of golden beer. The verandah was crowded; dozens of bare, red-brown, hairy legs, male and female, dangled over the edge; all eyes, devoted, expert, and earnest, followed the hockey and rugger, and from time to time the sound of clapping fell thinly across the wide field, or the cry: "That's *it*, Jolly, old man," or a moan, "Betty, Betty, you'll *kill* me with that pass"; and an anxious youth might fall backwards, with an exaggerated loosening of his limbs, to lie on the verandah, murmuring, "That kid Betty'll kill me, she'll kill me, I say!" He lay waiting until someone took the cue and hastened to him with beer, when he slowly sat up, his eyes roving anxiously around his audience to test the effect of his performance, saying apologetically, "These kids, these girls! I can't stand it, no, they kill me." And he thoughtfully drank his beer, amid sympathetic laughter, perhaps even applause, with the modest air of a good actor who knows he has been on the top of his form.

And through these groups moved Binkie, the now kingly Binkie, a carelessly generous, untidy, beer-fat young man, his black eyes always on the watch for any sign of dissidence or discord. He would stop beside a young man, murmuring, "If you've a moment, there's that business of the shower . . ." And the youth would at once move away with him, and the two stood rather at a distance from the others, with a conscious though deprecatory importance, discussing the machinery of living. Or he would saunter down the length of the verandah, nodding here and there, the busy man for once at leisure, while the girls offered, tentatively, "Hullo, Binks!" "Hullo, kid," he returned, kindly, and at last might come to a standstill beside one, and put his arm about her, and his face would assume the agonized, frustrated look which was obligatory, while he said, "You're killing me, baby, you're killing me. Who's your boy friend, let me kill him for you." She remained passive, with the equally obligatory look of maternal indulgence, while the other girls laughed: they were flattered, for this was a mark of attention to them all; she was their representative. But even as Binkie moaned and offered homage, his eyes were roving in a sharp lookout for the next thing that must claim his attention; and suddenly he straightened, patting the girl lightly, as if to say, "Well, so much for you," and on he strolled to tell the next group that they must drink up, they'd had the same round for half an hour, and the Club'd go bankrupt if everyone didn't pull their weight. "You're not cooperating," he would say earnestly. And automatically the hands reached out for the mugs. "Waiter!" shouted Binkie, waving a lordly hand. "Waiter, fill up here!"

But the Club was flourishing. The subscription might be low, but there were few people under thirty in the city who were not members. For that matter, there were few under sixty, for, while a casual visitor might assume that this was devoted to youth, such was the prestige of the place that people felt impelled to join. "There's the New Year's Dance," they said. "It's worth it, just for that. It's such a nice atmosphere—not noisy, like McGrath's."

But it was nothing if not noisy; what they meant was that the section of the community which the bridge-playing ladies had at first hoped would exclusively use it did in fact come to the big dances, although in closed groups. The important civil servants, the big businessmen, with their wives and daughters, sat at large tables, smiled with a not too obvious benevolence, and tended to leave unobtrusively at midnight, before "things began to break up."

"Here, break it up there," Binkie yelled, or: "Come on, let's—tear—it—to—pieces!" And this meant that the groups, the couples, were expected to abandon any remnant of partiality and throw themselves into the dancing, yelling crowd, while Binkie stood, dripping with perspiration, his tie crooked, waving his beer mug and ordering the waiters to fetch free drinks for the band, who played and smiled, smiled and played, until their jaws and arms must have ached; and when, at two o'clock, they smiled and shook their heads and began to pack their instruments, they were at once surrounded by a crowd of remonstrating, reproachful young men, bribing them with drink for just one more, one more, always one more; while the girls stood smiling a little self-consciously, and, if the band were adamant, said soothingly, maternally, "Now, kids, it's late, you know, we've got to get to work tomorrow."

In 1935, "the gang" were certainly all kids, between sixteen and twenty-one or -two. And in 1938 they still called themselves kids, though in the daytime, between the hours of eight and four or four-thirty, these children were ambitious young businessmen, rising civil servants, and the girls were their secretaries; and if someone demanded, "Where's Bobby, why haven't we seen Bobby lately?" the girl who felt herself responsible for him would say with a faraway, devoted look in her eyes, "He's got an exam," and everyone nodded understandingly, with a sympathetic sigh.

The girls were, it was assumed, responsible for the men. Even the child of seventeen who had left school the week before, and was at her first dance, taking her first alcohol, would instinctively assume an air of madonnalike, all-experienced compassion; she did not giggle when this wolf or that moaned and rolled his eyes and said, "Beautiful, why haven't I seen you before, I can't take it, I'm dying," as he clutched his forehead and reeled back from the vision of her unbearable attractions. She smiled a small, wise smile, and might, even before her first visit into the grownup world was over, find herself exhorting him to "go on the tack," with a flushed, earnest look of sisterly regard. For they were always going on the tack; a dozen pairs of sympathetic eyes would follow the consciously heroic youth as he wandered down the verandah with a glass of orange juice in his hand; and they asked anxiously, "How goes it, Frankie?" "Keeping it up, Jolly?" And he would shake his head, and groan and suffer, with one experienced eye on his public—since he was bound to have done this at least a dozen times before.

The public: it was all so public, anything was permissible, the romances, the flirtations, the quarrels, provided they were shared. These terms, however, were never used, for words are dangerous, and there was a kind of instinctive shrinking, an embarrassment, against words of emotion, or rather, words belonging to that older culture, to which this was an attempt at providing a successor.

If two young men were seen in angry argument, Binkie or one of the older members would hastily go to them, saying sentimentally, "Break it up, old man, break it up, kids," and the contestants would be led back to the flock, smiling apologetically, smiling if it killed them. When a couple remained too long together, dated each other too often, half a dozen self-appointed guardians of public safety would watch them, and at last surround them, with "Hey, hey, what's this?" A young man would say, "You can't do this to me, Betty," and for the moment he represented all the young men; and a girl would say, in sour warning (and that sour personal note held a deeper note of danger), "And who were you with last night?," smiling at the culpable youth with the assurance of a representative, so that he accepted the rebuke as a public one, though with unacknowledged resentment because it was also personal.

This system of shared emotion might have been designed to prevent marriage; but if by chance a couple managed to evade Binkie's vigilance and the group jealousy, and presented themselves as engaged, they would be received with a groan of protest; it was felt, deeply, as a betrayal; and if they braved it out, shaking their heads smilingly at Binkie's private warnings that "Man, your work'll suffer," and "You don't want to tie yourself down to kids at your age, baby," then the group, like one of those jellylike spores which live by absorption, swelled out and surrounded the couple, swallowing the marriage whole. They might marry provided they married from the Sports Club, with Binkie or one of the senior wolves as best man, and rejoined the Club at once after the briefest possible honeymoon, prepared to share their joys and sorrows with the rest. But these marriages tended to dissolve rather quickly. There were more than one couple, now returned to the fold as units, who danced with their ex-husbands, ex-wives, in the usual sentimental good-fellowship, even made love to them afterwards, though within the prescribed limits, and in the prescribed place, a parked car; and if these limits proved irresistibly piquant, after the freedom of marriage, so that the couple seemed inclined to link up again, Binkie was likely to take both aside, but separately, saying, "Now, you've tried it once, it didn't work, now don't fall for it again." And then, as a desperate second best: "At any rate, have a bang with someone else. There's Tom" (or Mabel, as the case might be). "Now, Tom's a good sort, why don't you have a bang with him?"

There were already half a dozen children, club children, who slept in their prams through sundowners and dances, and grew up on the verandah among the hockey sticks, beer mugs and bare legs, like a doom made visible.

A newcomer, hearing the sentimental refrain, "Look, there's Betty, a nice kid, Betty," would turn to see a tall young woman in brief shorts and sandals, her face brown and dried by a thousand afternoons of hockey and tennis, her hair tied on the top with a pink or blue ribbon, and imagine that the "kid" was the small girl she led by the hand, who was likely to be wearing the same coloured shorts above fat and dimpled legs, and a hair ribbon tied in exactly the same way as her mother's.

And so it all went on, through '35, '36, '37, '38; during that Christmas season of 1938, it was as if the Club had existed forever, that it would exist forever; it was like a fairy story, drenched in nostalgic golden light, where everyone is young, nothing changes. The tranquil blue gums at the foot of the playing fields, the banked jacarandas at the back of the golf course, the hedges of hibiscus, splashed with vivid scarlet over the glossy thick green—these enclosed a magic circle, and inside it nothing could happen, nothing threatened, for some tacit law made it impossible to discuss politics here, and Europe was a long way off. In fact, it might be said that this club had come into existence simply as a protest against everything Europe stood for. There were no divisions here, no barriers, or at least none that could be put into words; the most junior clerk from the railways, the youngest typist, were on Christian-name terms with their bosses, and mingled easily with the sons of Cabinet ministers; the harshest adjective in use was "toffee-nosed," which meant snobbish, or exclusive; and even the black waiters who served them were likely to find themselves clapped across the shoulders by an intoxicated wolf at the end of the dance: "Good old Tickey," or "There's a good chap, Shilling," and perhaps even their impassive, sardonic faces might relax in an unwilling smile, under pressure from this irresistible flood of universal goodwill.

2

On that Saturday morning, Martha was embarrassed because she wanted to leave at twelve instead of at one, and did not like to ask the favour of Mr. Cohen. She was in an almost agonized condition, out of all proportion to the cause; partly due to the fact that she had hardly been near the Polytechnic for a week. With one part of her mind she was making resolutions to do nothing "for at least three months" but study shorthand and speed typing; while with the other she guiltily imagined herself walking into Mr. Cohen's office and telling him about the dress she wanted to buy: for she intended to use the charm, the almost stammering diffidence, which she knew she should banish from her personality here at work.

At twelve, when she at last rose to her feet, gripping the desk because her knees were shaking, Mr. Robinson's door opened, and he called through it, "Come here a moment, Miss Quest." He added impatiently, "If you don't mind," conforming to the etiquette imposed by Mr. Cohen.

Martha went to his office and found she was being given a long and complicated document; on a closer look, she found it was one she had already typed that morning.

"Miss Quest," said Mr. Robinson, with a rather strained smile and embarrassed look, "you must have been thinking about something else when you typed this."

Mr. Robinson was a young man about twenty-five, and he was serving his articles. There was nothing youthful about him. He was lean, of middle height, of the athletic build, though he tended to carry himself in an energetic curve, like a half-tensed bow. He was altogether grey and legal-looking; his light hair lay stiffly back, brushed with oil to a dun conformity; his mouth was thin, set, impatient; and his fine grey eyes, deep-set and intelligent, had not yet learned to soften into tolerance. He had a good knowledge of the law, but he was not yet a good lawyer, and would find it hard to become one. He tended to get impatient with difficult clients, and more than once he had emerged from his office looking prickly and bitter, after the women had listened for some minutes to his angry voice shouting against another, saying, "In university they don't tell you that the greater part of the law is learning to tolerate fools." With the women, he was curt, and then softened his orders and reprimands with a stiff smile. It was understood that when Martha was really efficient she would become Mr. Robinson's personal secretary; but neither of them looked forward to this arrangement. He liked Mrs. Buss, whom he overloaded with work, although she was supposed to work exclusively for Mr. Cohen.

Now he was trying his best to be pleasant, but failed; and Martha withdrew with the spoilt document, looking as irritable as he did.

She was relieved. Now she would not be in time to buy the dress before the shop closed. She was saved from spending twenty pounds on a model dress, which she would pay for at the rate of ten shillings a month. The decision had been made for her, her mind was set free, and she typed out the document almost as fast and neatly as Mrs. Buss, and returned to lay it on Mr. Robinson's desk well before one o'clock.

"Wait a minute," he snapped; then, hastily: "Please." He reached for the document, read it through, then looked up at her with his awkward smile. "If you can do it like this now, why couldn't you before?" he demanded.

Martha hesitated, then watched herself rushing gaily into a story about the dress; she wanted to stop, for she should never have started; the fatal nervous compulsion, similar to that which had made her tease Donovan to kiss her, had her in its grip, and she could neither stop nor speak naturally. He was uncomfortable, for he could never tolerate the personal, and by the time she had come stammering to an end they were both red and uneasy.

"If you'll take my advice, Miss Quest—though it's nothing to do with me, of course—you'll keep clear of these sharks who try and get you girls in their grip. I get them here as clients, crying their eyes out when it's too late. A dress for twenty pounds—it's ridiculous for a child your age," he finished, as if he were an old man himself. Then, with a glance at her sulky face: "Well, it's your affair. Please send Mrs. Buss in. If she's got time, of course."

Martha went out and found the big office half empty. She took her bag, and quickly left by herself, avoiding the others, and hurried along Main Street to the window where the dress was displayed.

Just before the war women were supposed to be tall, broad-shouldered, slim-hipped, long-legged. Martha's room may have been littered with books, but it was also plentifully supplied with magazines, where all the women conformed to that shape, and when she saw her reflection, when she imagined herself in this dress or that, she continually strained her mental image of herself upwards, thinning it, posing it; when she saw herself ideally, crossing a room, under fire from admiring eyes, it was in the guise of this other, imposed woman. As for Donovan, he saw her as so much raw material for his own needs. This dress, however, had the power to destroy these false images, and she examined it with love, almost with physical pain, for the shop was closed, and now she would never buy it. She knew that the moment this dress clothed her body she would be revealed to herself, and to others, as something quite new, but deeply herself. That dress was made to clothe the person she knew herself to be. It was of a brilliant dark blue, of fine, transparent silky stuff. Its bodice was close and moulded, lightly sewn with tiny brilliants, and the skirt had knots and ribbons of the same brilliants gleaming from the folds. It was a romantic dress, with its lightly draped shoulders and great flowing skirt; but as she tested the word "romantic" she could not help thinking of Donovan, and at once began to feel uncertain, for she knew it was not what he would have chosen for her.

And as she thought, dubiously, of Donovan, she heard a car hooting, and turned to see Donovan himself, trying to keep his place in the stream of Saturday lunchtime traffic. The street was a river of hot and shining metal, the cars were creeping, nose to tail, and she ran along the kerb until she was able to leap in beside him.

"What are you doing daydreaming beside our wicked Mr. Louise's window, Matty dear?" he enquired.

She explained, making herself sound flippant, and disguising all she really felt about that dress; and he said, "But, Matty, you know you must have my personal supervision. I saw that dress this morning, and really, Matty, you should have learned better by now. It's very pretty and womanly and all that, but it's not smart. Now, don't worry. I'll come home with you, and you'll see, I'll make you the belle of the ball."

She laughed, and after a moment submitted herself to him, and felt grateful; for a moment, however, she had felt the beginnings of something very different, a strong resisting dislike of his pressure on her.

In her bedroom, he took out the two evening dresses she owned, and laid them on the bed, and at once became serious and thoughtful. He sat beside them, fingering the material, and frowning; it was a physical communion between those dresses and himself, from which she was excluded.

There was a knock on the door, and Mrs. Gunn came in, and Martha knew it was because she had heard a man's voice.

"Oh, it's you, Mr. Anderson," she said, in doubtful relief.

Donovan, with hardly a glance at her, said that he was busy.

At a movement of Mrs. Gunn's head, Martha followed her on to the back verandah. "You won't take it amiss," said Mrs. Gunn, "but my daughter made it a rule never to have a man in her room. Not that I'd say a word against Mr. Anderson, but . . ."

Mrs. Gunn's pale and fleshy face was glistening with sweat, her dry reddish hair was dark in streaks, her dress was soaked from the armpits to the waist: hers was not a type to stand the heat. She went on complainingly, "I had a letter from your mother, she worries about you, I said I'd look after you, but . . ."

Martha said angrily that she could look after herself.

Mrs. Gunn was hurt, and said she didn't want to interfere. Martha replied that in that case she might refrain from doing so.

Their voices had risen, and they heard Donovan calling, "Matty, come here, I want you."

The two quarrelling women, who liked each other and knew it, exchanged an apologetic and humorous smile.

Mrs. Gunn said plaintively, "It's the heat, Matty. My temper's awful this weather."

Martha felt an impulse to kiss her, but it was impossible for her to kiss women; she said rather drily that she did not think there was any need to worry about Mr. Anderson.

Mrs. Gunn's pale and worried eyes lit with malicious speculation; they met Martha's, and suddenly both women began to laugh. "You're all right," said Mrs. Gunn, laughing hoarsely, with a helpless shaking movement of her big tormented body. She put her arms round Martha and kissed her, and Martha tried not to stiffen against this damp, strong-smelling embrace. "You're all right," said Mrs.

Gunn again, and Martha nodded and laughed, and with a guilty look rejoined Donovan.

"When you disgusting girls have finished," he said in a light but gruff voice. "You're as bad as my mother, she's always giggling with *women*. You have no discrimination, Matty. I've told you that before. You always get yourself mixed up with people."

Martha shrugged impatiently and went to the French window. The lunchtime traffic had thinned to an occasional car that raced past impatiently. The tarmac road glistened oilily, the sun poured down, there was a strong smell of warm tar. The sky was ominous, spaces of intense hot blue between heavy thunderheads. The trees in the park were motionless, the flowers in the garden hung stricken, with curling leaves. Martha was now both irritable and sad. She did not want to go to the dance, everything disgusted her. Worse, she did not understand these violent fluctuations of mood; it was as if half a dozen entirely different people inhabited her body, and they violently disliked each other, bound together by only one thing, a strong pulse of longing; anonymous, impersonal, formless, like water. She stood there, silent, at the open door, while gusts of hot, tar-smelling air came off the street. Slowly she settled into a mood of rich melancholy, where at least she felt at home, though she distrusted it so persistently: thus had she stood, as a child, watching the slow changes of the veld, where the cloud shadows dissolved like flocks of birds, watching the movements of rain along the hills: at *that* moment she saw herself as a lethargic person, doomed, without energy.

She wished Donovan would go away, for she knew that soon she must rouse herself to meet his wishes; for of course she would go dancing that night, and, long before then, would be vividly, electrically excited. The thought of this other person she would soon become exhausted her anew, and she said crossly to Donovan, "I do wish you wouldn't fuss so. What does it matter what I look like?"

He did not reply, and she looked over her shoulder to see an expression on his face which meant "These female vagaries"?—but no, it meant "Coquetry"! And he was impatient of it. "*Really*, Matty," was all he said; and then: "And now come here, I'm ready to start work."

She went listlessly to his side, but he said, "Now take off your dress, Matty—no, don't start these girlish giggles, I really do find them so tiresome."

She slowly removed her dress, pointing out to herself that this was the first time she had been seen undressed by a man, and wishing that it did not seem so unimportant. Standing in her petticoat, she saw Donovan scrutinizing her shoulders and arms, and he even put out his hand and slowly turned her round, to examine her back.

"That's a good girl," he said approvingly, screwing up his eyes with a professional look.

He led her to the mirror, lifted her arms, and gently pulled over her head the white cotton dress she had made for the Van Rensbergs' dance. "This has distinct possibilities, Matty, but you must leave yourself in my hands. It was quite pretty, but anyone can look pretty." He crouched at her feet and shook out the skirt, and Martha saw a pale, tired-looking girl with untidy hair looking back at her from the mirror. "Now just look at it," said Donovan. "You see?"

She saw that it was similar in shape to that dark-blue dress she coveted; it was, if one may use the term of something which has so many forms, the basic type of an evening dress: small fitting top, full skirt; but the blue dress took its beauty from the fine material, and the delicate tracery of glinting beads, and the suggestion of half-concealed shoulders. Obstinately, despite what he said, she yearned for it; and submitted to being shaped into something very far from the girl who could wear that soft, flowing gown.

Donovan kneeled below her and worked on the white dress. He was quite absorbed, and she turned passively between his hands like a dummy. She felt not a trace of self-consciousness when he reached up to pull the stuff across her breasts, even pushed them up with his hands, high into the stiff sharp folds with which he intended to emphasize them.

Mrs. Gunn knocked again, and entered with a big parcel. She was panting, her hair was falling damply across her face, and though she summoned energy enough to look drily at the absorbed young man on his knees in front of the girl, her remark, "My God, isn't it awful?" referred to the heat. "It's going to rain, shouldn't be surprised," she said, going out. Thunder was rolling gently among the banked clouds overhead.

Martha looked down at Donovan's dark head, usually so sleek and close. A strand of the rather coarse hair had fallen loose, and hung stiffly over his forehead, and for some reason Martha found that stiff lock repulsive; also the plane of forehead, which showed reddish, coarse-grained, and wet with sweat. There were flakes of sodden dandruff on the line of the parting, which showed dead white, like the belly of a fish. She began to move irritably under his working hands, and restrained herself with difficulty when he said, "Now, then, Matty, we must suffer in the cause of beauty, be a good girl."

She told herself that she was bored, looked away, and saw the parcel lying on her bed. Books. Cautiously, she leaned the top half of her body sideways, and extended an arm to pull the parcel closer, and Donovan said, "Matty, there's a time and a place for everything."

She remained exasperatedly patient.

"What books have you ordered?" he asked.

"I don't know what's come," she replied evasively, with the feeling that this, at least, should be her own.

"Why don't you arrange your books in a nice case so that people may see them when they come in? It's no good having books under the bed. And you're really a clever girl, Matty, but you talk just like everybody else. You'd impress people if you tried."

Martha put on a sarcastic expression for his benefit, but he was not looking at her.

"Now, take Ruth Manners. She went home to England with her mamma, and she's come back ever so intelligent, she went to the theatres and the galleries, and you've no idea, she's so North Avenue these days— Turn around a little, Matty, lift your hip—that's right. You do slouch, you know, but not in the right way, it's very sexy to slouch, if you know how. Well, it's done everything for Ruth. You haven't got a rich mamma to buy you clothes, but at least you've read everything; but you don't know how to make the best of yourself— Let your shoulders forward a little—you should learn to stand with your bottom tucked *in*, and your hips forward, and your shoulders slightly curved, but held so that your breasts stand out. Like *that*, Matty."

He rose to his feet in front of her, and with one hand pressed in her buttocks, and with the other pressed down her shoulders so that her breasts came forward, almost against his. His frowning eyes met her antagonistic ones, and he dropped his hands, and his handsome face, now showing coarse-featured, fleshy, shiny with heat and effort, slowly went a sullen red. "I know what you're thinking," he said, with an attempt at grace. "Well, I promise I'll make love to you, Matty, I will, really, but not now." He looked at his watch, and became himself. "Now you will lie down and sleep, because you really look awful, you know. I will come and dress you at six. You must have a bath at five, but don't touch your hair, I'll do it." Waving a cheerful good-bye, he hastened away, and Martha lay obediently, shuddering with dislike of him, and also with gusts of hysterical laughter.

She did not sleep. Soon she rose and filled the bath, and lay in it while the water cooled, listening to the iron roof creeping and tensing with the heat. Through the open fanlight she could hear Mrs. Gunn's sighs and complaints, where she sat on the verandah. The thunder muttered and growled like an animal. Soon she fell to inspecting her own body according to that other standard, "long, lean, narrow," but it was difficult to respect that standard when she saw herself naked, and soon, with frank adoration, she fell into a rite of self-love. Her limbs lay smooth and light in the water, her thighs seemed to her like two plump and gleaming fishes, she scattered water over her white belly, and watched the drops fall like rough jewels and slide to a perfect quivering silver globule in her navel. Meantime, her body lay unmoved and distant, congealing into perfection, under the eyes of this lover; while Martha thought of Mrs. Gunn's groaning sweating body, and was fiercely grateful for her own; she thought of the ugly scar across her mother's stomach, and swore protectively to her own that it would never, never be so marred; she thought of Mrs. Van Rensberg's legs, and with tender reassurance passed her hands over her own smooth brown legs, murmuring that it was all right, all right, nothing would harm them.

A few heavy drops fell like stones on the iron roof; there was a swish and a swirl of rain and wind and dust; the thunder cracked overhead and the rain plunged like a steel barrage. Her spirits rose like a kite, till she was singing inside the din at the top of her voice; and faintly, through the thunder, the crashing rain, the gurgling bath water Mrs. Gunn could be heard chanting relief like a prayer of thankfulness to the rain god. Martha left the bathroom, her depression flooded away with the bath water, and found that around the table on the back verandah Mrs. Gunn and her daughter were drinking tea, their faces bright and soft and smiling. Martha stood by the table in her red dressing gown and drank tea with them, and they talked and watched the rain drive in gleaming spears beyond the faded green mosquito gauze, and the irritable tension of the early afternoon was so far away there was no need to apologize for it. Mrs. Gunn put her arm around Martha's hips and said she was her girl, she was her daughter, now that her own had left her; and the young woman at the end of the table laughed, and they all laughed, and the rain fell, fell endlessly, everything rushed and gurgled and swam, and they laughed again when the thunder came crashing dangerously over the roof like armies, so loud that they could hear no sound of voices, though they were shrieking at each other like grinning maniacs. With a pantomime of laughing regret, Martha indicated she must go and dress; and was sorry to leave them. She could not understand how she had so disliked Mrs. Gunn earlier; and Mrs. Gunn's daughter, who had a new baby, and was therefore usually an object of repulsion to Martha, seemed delightfully simple and womanly as she sat there beside her mother, nursing the dribbling, mouthing infant.

She wanted to go to that dance more than she had ever wanted anything; her whole being was poised and dedicated; and when Donovan came in, shrieking with laughter over his damp evening clothes, he found Martha bright-eyed and chattering and amenable, ready to be sewn into her dress.

But it took such a long time. Donovan wiped off her make-up, and made her shut her eyes while he painted her face again. He arranged and rearranged her hair. She was compliant, but impatient. At the end, he led her triumphantly to the long mirror, and said, "Now, then, Matty . . ."

Martha looked, and, in spite of her pleasure, was uneasy. It was not herself, she felt. The simplicity of that white dress had been given a touch of the bizarre—no, *that* was not it; as she regarded herself, she was instinctively forming herself to match the young woman in the mirror, who was cold, unapproachable, and challenging. But from the cool, remote face peered a pair of troubled and uneasy eyes.

As she saw that glance—her own, it seemed—Donovan came forward quickly, and said, "Now, listen, Matty, you really must see that you should change yourself for a dress like this. Don't you see?" He bent towards her, his hand hovering, ready to seize on what was wrong. "Look," he said finally, "your eyes too. Lift your head." As she remained motionless, his palm raised her head. "With those cheek-bones," he said, "look, your eyes should be like this." With something like horror, Martha saw him slide his own eyes slantingly sideways, into a languid, distant gleam. "You *see?*" he demanded triumphantly. He did it again. For the flash of a second, he was terrifyingly herself; and she stared at him in fascinated disgust. This time her laugh was nervous, and he dropped his hand, and looked at her and flushed

"You really are—extraordinary," she said at last, slowly; and the dislike she felt was strong in her voice.

The silence was a long one; it was a moment of decision between them. Martha, looking helplessly at him, saw, but remotely, that if she was confused and unhappy, so was he; he had a sullen and little-boy look about him that should have claimed her pity, but merely irritated her; and across this barrier flowed a faint guilt that she could not, for the life of her, say something comforting; it was terrifying, in a different way, to see that assured young man so distressed and lost.

At last he sat himself down, flinging one leg moodily over the other, and he remarked, "I should have been a dress designer. I would have been a very good one, Matty dear." That light, "Matty dear," fed back his self-belief; he was already recovering. "But if one is raised in the colonies, then what can one do but go into statistics

and wait for one's chief to retire!" Here he laughed with genuine bitterness; and Martha understood that if anything bound them it was
their mutual conviction that *if* they had been born into other circumstances, *if only* . . .

"Well," she said awkwardly, "don't let's quarrel. You'd better give
me up as a bad job, you know. I don't think I'm cut out for a manne-
quin!" She was laughing at him, but she longed for—what? Some gesture that might express that thing they shared? She felt he should
put his arms around her in a light and brotherly way, and thus the
whole incident would have been put behind them.

Instead, he laughed again, angrily, and said, "Oh, well, to hell with
everything, Matty. Let's go to the party, and astonish them all."

At the door, she saw that the rain had stopped. A dusky sunset was
reflected in the lake which lay between them and the gate.

"I suppose you expect me to carry you, like a he-man on the films,"
he said. "But I shan't. Now, don't let the mud get your skirts."

He shrieked in gay alarm as she began balancing her way cautiously from the step to a rocking stone, and from there to a small
point of brick that stood blackly amid the rosy waters. And here she
stood, precariously, laughing at herself, and at him, for he was agitatedly dancing on the steps, saying, "Matty, Matty, do be careful."
There was something about that shrill and helpless exhortation
which turned her mood into defiance. She looked calmly about her:
there were six feet of muddy water between her and the gate. "To
hell with it," she remarked; and fell all at once in her element. She
lifted her crisp white skirts in a bunch around her waist, and composedly walked in her gold shoes, the water lapping cool around her
ankles, to the sidewalk, saying, "Oooh, it's lovely, it's lovely, Don,"
like a child paddling.

In a series of leaps, he came splashing across to join her. "Matty,"
he said, in distressed and incredulous astonishment, "Matty, you're
mad. I suppose you haven't even paid for those shoes yet."

"Of course not," she said recklessly, letting her skirts fall, and
laughing at him, despising him, most sincerely, from the bottom of
her heart.

"But your feet are wet," he complained.

"My feet are so wet," she mimicked him cruelly. "Oh, dear, I might
get a *cold*." She stopped, already feeling herself uncertain. After all,
the shoes were expensive; after all, it was rather childish. "Oh, don't
be such an old woman," she said crossly, and got into the car. "They
won't notice my feet," she said coaxingly at last. "They'll be looking
at your beautiful dress." She lifted her feet and examined them. The
gold leather had dulled, and was crinkling; there was a faint brown

tidemark around her ankles. She could not help looking at them with satisfaction; the elegant, cool white dress seemed quite remote from her, a mere surface to her body, which continued strongly upwards from those reckless, strong ankles.

She shook her head to loosen her hair, and laughed heartlessly when he said, "You look like a nice open-air girl, if that's what you want. But for heaven's sake, Matty, do move carefully, I've just tacked you into that dress so as not to spoil the line, and if you bounce about it'll fall off. I suppose you'd like that."

"Of course," she said lightly; but she imagined herself thus suddenly exposed, and laughed on a thrill of excitement. "Of course," she said again, and saw his face darken with irritated annoyance.

They arrived at the Club. The verandah was illuminated by strings of coloured lights, and a large electric sign said: "Three Weeks to Christmas—Let it Rip, Boys and Girls."

The large room was cleared for the dance, and was empty. On the main verandah young men and women were drinking, some in evening dress, some not yet changed from their sports clothes. Martha knew most of them by sight, and was greeted by intimate sisterly smiles from the girls, the usual howls and whistles from the men. Her resentment at this had been not so much dulled as pushed away into that part of herself she acknowledged to be the true one. As for Donovan, she saw he was being received with queries: "Well, stranger, you back?"—statements, in fact, which meant that in spite of what he said he was no stranger to the Club. She expected they would sit by themselves, if she expected anything at all—for this way of hers, submitting herself to a person or a place, with a demure, childish compliance, as if she were under a spell, meant that she did not consciously expect or demand; she might dream about things being different, but that, after all, commits one to nothing.

Far from leading Martha away from the others, Donovan held a court for a few minutes, while he debated aloud, gaily, with a frank rudeness, whether Binkie's table or another's would suit him best. At last he took Martha's hand and seated her at a table where Binkie and his lieutenants and their girls were drinking and eating peanuts, saying, "And now here you are, Matty, all among the huskies."

He then sat himself between two girls, and ignored Martha completely, which at first annoyed her, and then relieved her, for now she was free to behave as she pleased.

It was about seven in the evening. Beyond the dark spines of the blue gums, the sunset faded in a hushed and tender glow; the playing fields were shimmering green under water; the clubhouse itself was surrounded by a churned mass of red mud. It was the cloistral hour, the hour of silence, as if the very fact that in the trees, and in the veld that was no more than half a mile's walk distant, the little creatures and birds were sinking into sleep aroused in these people, though briefly, the memory of that other cycle submerged in their blood. The lights were not switched on; they sat in a flushed half-dark, and unconsciously their voices lowered, though they were teasing each other over the mud on their clothes and because some were reluctant to cross the mud to the cars so that they might go and dress. Martha showed her shoes and made a funny story out of wading through the water; halfway through it she became nervous, because she realized it put Donovan in a bad light, but continued, avoiding his eyes; and the young man next to her said that if he had been there he'd have carried Matty in his arms through the flood. He was a big, blond-fleshed youth, his fair hair crinkled tight over his head, with a reddish glint in it; and in a square, burnt, determined face were blue and direct eyes. Martha thought it remarkable that this young man, whom she knew to be manager of a big insurance company, should be content to appear like a buffooning schoolboy. She began talking to him, rather awkwardly, about a book she had just read. He answered reluctantly. When she persisted, he gave a public sigh, which drew all the expectant eyes towards him, and said mournfully, "Baby, baby, you'll be the death of me." Then he indicated Martha with an outstretched thumb, and said, "She's intelligent. This baby's got brains." And he laughed and rolled up his eyes, and shook his head with a kind of subsiding shudder into himself. Martha flushed, and, as soon as the conversation had got under way around them, began talking "amusingly," as she was expected to do. The uneasy blue eyes fixed on her in relief; his face cleared, and she understood that all was well. Soon he got up, saying that he must go and change; but Matty must remember he would die for her, she killed him, and he insisted on the first dance.

Soon the verandah was half empty, and there remained a few couples in evening dress. Martha was feeling a little sick, for she had hardly eaten all day; but Donovan was talking to the two girls, who were leaning towards him and laughing with a flattering attention; and so she gave up all idea of dinner, pulled a plate of potato chips towards her, and began eating them with the ruminant concentration which means a person is eating not for pleasure but for necessity.

She heard laughter, glanced up, and saw that the people around her were amused. "I'm starved," she said firmly, and went on eating.

Binkie got up from his chair, came to hers, and crouched beside her, his arm lightly about her waist. "Beautiful," he said, "we can't have this, we'll give you some dinner."

She looked hesitatingly towards Donovan. She had never said to herself that he was mean; and it was with another shock that she saw that here he was known to be, for the glances people directed towards him were spitefully amused. She was hurt for his sake, and said gaily that no, she didn't want dinner, Donovan was quite right, she was slimming and—

Donovan waved a careless hand towards her, and said, "Matty dear, do go, if you want to." Hurt again, this time on her own account, she got to her feet, and thanked Binkie, and said she would like to have dinner with him. And so it was that, at the very beginning of the evening, she was separated from Donovan; it was rather as if he had pushed her away, for she left, smiling an apologetic farewell, and he did not so much as look at her.

Martha walked beside Binkie with the same gentle, submissive gesture that had until five minutes before been Donovan's due; the mere fact that he had asked her to dine with him was as if her emotions had been gathered up, twisted together, by him. And he certainly put his arm around her as they went down the verandah, crooning, "My baby's having dinner with me"; but the circular look he directed around the verandah over her head was keen and critical, and he was summoning his subjects by a nod or a wave of his free hand; for having dinner with Binkie was a communal affair.

A dozen wolves, therefore, with their girls, crowded into cars, and drove down to McGrath's dining room, which they entered royally, welcomed by hosts of waiters. For Binkie's "gang" might go berserk, had been known to wreck the dining room, but they paid liberally, tipped fabulously. On the other hand, McGrath's was the senior hotel in the colony, and here came important visitors from England and the Continent; McGrath's must maintain its reputation, and therefore the waiters' welcome was apprehensive.

They were given a centre table in the big room, which was chocolate brown and gilt, like the lounge. It was already decorated for Christmas. The headwaiter and the wine waiter, both white men, greeted each wolf by name, were offered Christian names in return, and were slapped across the shoulders. They took orders in voices that were pointedly lowered; while the deferential eyes implored, Please, Mr. Maynard, do please behave yourself, and persuade your gang to do likewise! The headwaiter, Johnny Constuopolis, even pointed out to Binkie that Mr. Player, who was the head of the big company which in fact controlled the colony, was sitting with his wife in a corner under the palms by the band. But at this information Binkie leaped to his feet, and roared out a greeting to Mr. Player, so loudly that everyone in the room looked round.

Johnny was distressed, not merely because of the danger that other respectable clients might be annoyed, but because his feeling for the important Mr. Player was prayerful; the dark, suave, tired little Greek served the great man with the exquisite tact that had gained him this position; and from Mr. Player's table he crossed continually to Binkie's, whose father, he knew, was also an important man, an educated man; and in his heart he shuddered with amazement and awed fear, as at madness. These young people were all mad. They spent money like dirt; Binkie might throw away twenty pounds on one of these dinners; he owed money everywhere, even to Mr. Player himself; they all behaved like licensed lunatics, as if there was no future, as if they had no plans to become important men themselves, with wives and children. And their idea of themselves seemed to be accepted by everyone else. Johnny knew that if this was going to be one of the evenings when the wolves decided life owed them a holocaust, and began singing and tearing down the decorations, and dancing on the tables, then the other people, including Mr. Player, would regard them with the pained tolerance due to a pack of momentarily overexcited children. Strange and even terrible to the little Greek, who had left his beloved country with his family twenty years before, to rescue them all from a poverty so profound that it haunted him even now. Never would Johnny the Greek lose his fear of poverty; never would he lose the knowledge that from one minute to the next a man might lose his precarious foothold among the fed and honoured living, and slip down among the almost nameless ghosts. Johnny remembered hunger, that common denominator; his mother had died of tuberculosis; his sister had died of starvation in the Great War, a weightless bundle of rags. At Johnny's shoulder was always this shadow, this fear; and now he stood behind Binkie Maynard's chair, in McGrath's dining room, very slightly bowed forward, and took orders for the meal, while he kept his dark and sorrowful eyes carefully veiled, lest what he felt might show.

He knew that he must spend time taking orders, while the wolves yearned over the girls, insisting that their slightest wish should be fulfilled; but once this ritual was over, it did not matter what food was actually brought, for they would not notice. They did not care about food, or even about wine. If they ordered wine, they might spend five minutes debating about a title on the wine list, and forget what they had ordered when the bottle arrived. They did not understand, they understood nothing, they were barbarians; but they must be given reverence, for one day (though the gods alone knew how this metamorphosis was to be effected) they would be the grave and responsible fathers of the city, and these girls their wives.

Martha ate the hotel dinner with appetite, if not with enjoyment. The menu was long and in French, and this was the most expensive meal the colony could offer.

They ate a thick white soup, which tasted of flour and pepper; round cheese puffs, the size of cricket balls and tasting of nothing in particular; boiled fish with gluey white sauce; roast chicken, hard white shreds of meat, with boiled stringbeans and boiled potatoes; stewed plums and fresh cream; and sardines on toast. They were all drinking brandy mixed with ginger beer. Halfway through, Binkie began urging them all to "put some speed into it, kids"; for he was already anxious because the dance might begin without him.

At the end, he flung down silver, handfuls of it, while the waiters smiled and bowed towards him, though their intent eyes were already calculating how much silver, and how it would divide between them. The girls were protesting, as usual, with maternal pride, that Binkie was a crazy kid. They returned in a body to the Sports Club. Martha was thinking, with guilty affection, of Donovan, but could not immediately find him. She was already claimed by Perry, the large blond athlete.

The Club was now filled with people in evening dress, and the band was playing. She found Donovan sitting with a girl whom Martha knew to be Ruth Manners. He waved his hand towards her, like an acquaintance, while he cast a disparaging look at Perry. Martha looked for help to Binkie, who said with that disconcerting frankness, "Better off with us, baby, he doesn't even feed you properly." But her eyes were still appealing; and they groaned and sighed and shrugged, and fetched chairs and placed tables together, until Donovan was at the head of a large circle of people, and Martha was facing him.

Ruth Manners was a thin, delicate girl with a narrow white face, short dark springy hair, long nervous hands. Her features were irregular: the thin scarlet mouth twisted to one side when she smiled, her thin nose was a little crooked, her narrow eyebrows were like circumflex accents, sharp and black over pale and watchful eyes. She spoke carefully, with controlled vowels, she moved with care; at every moment, she was conscious of how she must appear. And this consciousness, together with the delicate look—her eyelids were slightly reddened and heavy, the white cheeks had an irregular fading flush—gave her an intellectual look. Yet she was very elegant, with an elegance that none of the other women present could approach. She wore a jade-green dress of a heavy thick crepe, which was pleated loosely from the waist, and held around the narrow figure with a flame-coloured sash. The top was cut low, front and back, the material lying lightly over small flat breasts that were like a child's. Her shoulders and neck were thin and bony, of a frail whiteness that looked as if it might so easily flush, like her cheeks, into unbecoming red. And yet, though she was not pretty, and her body—so Martha jealously said to herself—would be better covered up, she undeniably possessed that quality that Donovan admired so much. Her assurance seemed to say, One doesn't have to be attractive, one may have an undesirable body, but what of it? I have this other thing. And Martha, because of that assurance, lost hers. She felt herself to be dowdy and altogether lacking, in spite of the homage of the wolves.

Ruth and Donovan made a pair, and knew it. They talked easily to each other, where they sat side by side at the head of the table, in a light, flirtatious, bantering way that was so much *not* the way of the Club that the rest were a little subdued, listening with uncomfortable attention.

Seeing that he had an audience, Donovan leaned back in his graceful way, and took Ruth's hand and said, "Well, girls and boys, we should all go to England. You see what it does for us? Now, look at Ruth's dress, Matty dear—you see? It's got what we poor colonials can't achieve."

Ruth laughed and said, "Poor Don, but you were in England yourself last year."

Now, Martha had never been told that Donovan had been to England, and she found this extraordinary. She saw that he was annoyed; for he frowned, and hesitated, before making the best of it and saying, "Yes, Ruthie, but I had no opportunities to improve myself, for I went under escort with my mamma, and she was much too busy buying clothes in Harrods and Derry and Toms, and I had to go with her, because she can't buy anything without me, as you know."

These two shops, which had been presented to Martha all her childhood as synonyms for "niceness," now lost their dull sound, for they could also provide Mrs. Anderson's conventional smartness. But Ruth looked amused and tolerant at the names; and there was an allowance of spite in her careful drawl, which said plainly that she found Donovan a little ridiculous. "But surely you couldn't have spent three months doing nothing but buying clothes—even at Harrods?"

Donovan was annoyed, but he maintained the light note. "My dear

Ruthie, you have the advantage of a mamma who wants to do her best for you. You should have pity for us less fortunate breeds."

"Poor Donny-boy," said Ruth, with her short laugh.

"Yes," said Donovan, now launching himself on the effort to be amusing, even at his own cost. "Yes, it was a great disillusion to me, going to England. You know the way we all think of it—but after all, when one gets there, there are certain limitations one overlooks beforehand. I sat in the Cumberland—because we colonials always go to the Cumberland, and nothing will make my mamma see that there is no need to emphasize an already too obvious fact—and I ate ravishing cream cakes all day, with my father, who grumbled all the time because he said England was overcivilized, though I don't think for a moment he knew what he meant by that. We sat and waited for Mamma to return, laden with yet fresh parcels, from various little expeditions of her own—because my mamma can always be trusted to amuse herself, wherever she is. It was the only time I can ever remember that my papa and myself had anything in common. I said, "Pappa dear, you may like the wide-open spaces, and you're welcome to them, but as for me, I'm simply made for decadence. Why don't you give me some money, and I shall apprentice myself to some dress designer, and thus find my niche."

"Poor Donny-boy," said Ruth again, this time sincerely.

"So my papa said nothing would give him greater pleasure, he disliked anomalies like myself, but unfortunately, since Mamma had spent the money destined to last three months in the first three weeks, and he had had to cable for more, there was none left over for either of us." Donovan ended on a squeal of laughter, which sounded so resentful that only Ruth was able to join him. The others sat silently watching; and Martha heard Perry mutter, "For crying out loud, for crying out loud, come and dance, I can't take it." He roughly pulled Martha up, and they went inside to dance; and again he complained, "For crying out loud," with a reminiscent disgust, as they took the floor.

Perry, because of the character imposed on him, was obliged to stop every few moments, shoot up his arms, and yell like a tormented soul, while people turned to laugh; or he broke suddenly into writhing jive, his head crushed back on his neck, his eyes closed, while he crooned, in a thick, blind, whining voice, in imitation of a Negro singing. In between, he pushed Martha conventionally around the room, in a rectangular progress, and the straight blue eyes assessed her, while his face held its sentimental look.

Martha watched his eyes; she was becoming obsessed by the need to look at the eyes of these people, and not their bodies; for they were serious, anxious, even pleading; while all the time their bodies, their faces, contorted into the poses required of them. It was as if their surfaces, their limbs, their voices, were possessed, it was an exterior possession that did not touch them, left them free to judge and comment. Martha continually felt a shock; looking from Perry's eyes to his jerking, shuddering impersonations of Negro singing, she felt uneasy. In the meantime, she danced, smiling brightly, replying to him in the jargon. Towards the end of the dance, encouraged by the intelligent seriousness of the blue eyes, she rebelled, and talked in her normal voice, about Donovan, about Ruth, while she felt his arms tightening, his eyes clouding. But she went on; she was resentful because he would not accept her as *herself*—whatever that might mean; for was she not continually at sea, because of the different selves which insisted on claiming possession of her? She meant, she wanted to establish contact with him, simply and warmly; she wanted him to recognize her as a reasonable being. When he rolled up his eyes, and pretended to shudder, and said, "Oh, baby, but the way you talk," she kept a determined smile, and waited until he finished, and continued with what she was saying. And, slowly, she succeeded. He was beginning to talk normally, if in a gruff and unwilling voice, when the music stopped, and they had to return to the verandah. There Ruth and Donovan still sat by themselves; and now their voices were lowered, and they looked unwelcomingly around at the invasion of returning dancers. They went on talking. But if their earlier sophisticated talk had upset Binkie because it disturbed the atmosphere, this exclusiveness was much worse. When the music struck up again, Binkie went to dance with Ruth. He hated dancing, but it was his duty; he never danced unless there was a couple too much occupied with each other.

It was quite early; people were still arriving, and remained, as they settled themselves, in their parties or couples, though these couples might join others, or a girl from one group pass naturally to another. It was all so easy and friendly and informal. The waiters came with tray after tray of beer and brandy. Martha, drinking brandy and ginger beer as usual, was instinctively regulating the flame of her intoxication: the men might get staggeringly drunk, the girls should be softened by alcohol, not dissolved in it. Binkie, having returned Ruth to Donovan, switched the lights out in the big dance room, and swirled coloured lights steadily across it, in a slow persistent rhythm, which dulled the mind, and heightened the senses.

Martha danced in turn with Binkie, who seemed to think that more than one dance with Perry was dangerous, with Perry, with

Donovan. But it did not matter with whom one danced; it was all impersonal: one moved trancelike from one man to the next, one danced cheek to cheek, intimately, body to body, and then the music stopped, one drank again, chattered a little, and plunged back into the hot, coloured darkness of the dance room, while the music throbbed. Three times Martha found herself drawn onto the verandah by one or other of the wolves (afterwards she had to remind herself who they had been) and kissed; and always in the same way. Abruptly, without any sort of preface, she was held rigid against a hard body, whose lower half pushed against hers in an aggressive but at the same time humble way; and her head was bent back under a thrusting, teeth-bared kiss. Afterwards, he breathed heavily, like a runner, and sighed, and said, "I'm terrible, hey? Forgive me baby, you'll forgive me." And to this the spirit of the place made Martha reply graciously, "It's all right, Perry," or Douggie or Binkie; "it's all right, don't worry." She should have said, "Don't worry, kid"; but that word would not come off her tongue. She wanted to laugh; at the same time she found it revolting that they should become so humble and apologetic, while in those humble eyes was such an aggressive gleam. Each kiss was a small ceremony of hatred; and at the fourth occasion, when some anonymous youth began compulsively tugging her towards the verandah, she resisted, and saw his baleful glance.

"Toffee-nosed, hey?" he demanded. And afterwards, at the table, he indicated Martha to the others, and said, "This baby's toffee-nosed, she's . . ." And he made a show of shivering and holding a coat around him and chattering his teeth.

Donovan suddenly called, "Well, Matty dear, and how *are* you?" and it was only after she had seen a couple of the young men exchange grimaces in the direction of Donovan that she understood Donovan had been watching her all evening, that for some reason these young men's attentions to her were a challenge to Donovan. She saw, too, that he was pleased because she had been found lacking. She sat quietly at the end of the table, feeling hurt, and confused; her own idea of herself was destroyed. That other veiled personage that waits, imprisoned, in every woman, to be released by love, that person she feels to be (obstinately and against the evidence of all experience) what is real and enduring in her, was tremblingly insecure. She hated Donovan, with a pure, cool contempt; she looked at the young men, and despised them passionately.

When Perry, for the second time, danced her out of the big room, through the dancing couples on the verandah, and to the steps, she went with him easily. "But it's muddy," she said, laughing nervously, looking out at the playing fields, which were saturated with water and moonlight.

"Never mind," said Perry. "Never mind, baby." He tugged at her arm, and, when she did not follow him, picked her up, and lifted her down. She could hear his feet squelching through the heavy mud. He carried her around the corner of the building, and without putting her down kissed her.

This was something different, being suspended strongly, in space. Perry, the individual, was merging easily into that ideal figure, a young strong man, who wooed that other ideal person within her (veiled, but certainly lovely), when she suddenly cried out, "Perry, my *dress!*"

"What is the matter, kid?" asked Perry, annoyed but devoted. "What have I done?"

She felt a coldness strike down her thigh, and, peering with difficulty over the thick curve of his arm, said, "My dress is torn." And it was.

"Baby, I'm sorry, I'm a clumsy brute," said Perry sentimentally; and he carried her back to the verandah, squelch, squelch, through the moon-gilded puddles. There she stood, on the steps, examining the damage.

She understood there was a silence, people were watching. Her spirits rose in a defiant wave of elation, and she cried gaily, "Don, you were quite right, my dress is torn." She walked calmly to the table, holding the gaping cloth together over her naked thigh, and stood beside Donovan, while Perry followed, muttering, "Kid, I'm sorry. You kill me. You'll be the death of me."

Donovan was silent for a critical moment, then he shrieked with laughter. Everyone joined in. It was a relieved laughter, a little hysterical. Donovan said, "Well, I can't do anything without a needle and thread."

Binkie told a waiter to go and get these things. The waiter protested, sulkily, that he did not know where to find them, and was dismissed peremptorily with "Go on, Jim. Don't argue. If I say needle and thread, then get them." He waved his hand dismissingly, and the waiter went away; and returned after a few minutes with the things.

Donovan, again master of the situation, laughed, and stitched up Martha's dress, while Ruth blinked her shortsighted eyes and watched in her quiet interested way, and Donovan said that Martha was a disgusting girl, she had mud on her dress. For some reason, this incident had released them all into gay amity. Martha sat beside Donovan, who held her hand; Ruth held Donovan's, on the other side; Perry lounged beside Martha, watching her curiously. Outside, between the verandah pillars, the moon flooded wild and fitful light over the ruffling dark water. The gum trees moved their black hulking shapes over the stars. The music came pulsing steadily from inside. It was midnight. Some of the older people were going home, smiling in a way which suggested that while youth must have its due, it should not, nevertheless, demand too much. Binkie was muttering, like a storm warning, "Let's break it up, kids, come on, let's break it up."

Inside, during the next dance, they broke it up. Whooping and yelling, stamping and surging, they flung themselves indiscriminately around the room, while the band played and played and played, pulling rhythm from their instruments with steady fingers, smiling with conscious power, as if it were they, the human beings, who directed the movements of jerking, lolling marionettes below. Martha caught a glimpse, over Perry's arm, of Donovan, dancing loose-limbed, like a jointed doll, flinging out his arms and legs around him, his black hair falling in thick locks over his face, and smiling in a way which plainly said, "This is quite idiotic, I'm doing it because it's the thing." Ruth, now no longer cool and possessed, jerked unregarded in the pumping arms of Binkie, with a look of patient suffering on her face. And Martha realized that the ridiculous suffering look was the same as that on her own face; she did not like this, she could not let herself go into it. At the moment she became aware of that critical and untouched person within herself, she looked at Perry, and thought in a flash, Despite what he wants us to think, it's the same with him. Perry, apparently, was in a trance of violence. He was letting his shoulders rise and fall convulsively; his eyes rolled to the ceiling, darted sideways with a flash of white eyeball, and settled glazedly in a stare at the floor. His whole body shuddered and rocked and shook; and all the time, he was quite unaffected, for when, by chance, Martha encountered for a moment those blue eyes as they rolled past her, she saw them possessed only on the surface, for underneath they were cool and observant, absorbed in appreciative direction of his frenzy. "Look how madly we are behaving," that deep gleam seemed to say. At the same time, it disliked being noticed: during that second when Martha's eyes and Perry's met, it was exactly as if two people, supposed to be wholly absorbed in a religious ceremony, turn to spy on each other, and are annoyed and embarrassed to see the other's treachery. She wanted to giggle; she did laugh, nervously; and he pressed her close, as if to say, "Do be quiet," and said, "Baby, you're killing me." He let out an agonized groan, which made her laugh again.

No, like Ruth, she could not enjoy it. At the end of the first dance —that is, the first dance of abandon—she went back to the table on the verandah, leaving Perry to find someone else, and saw Donovan, already calm and composed, his black hair sleek as ever, sitting with Ruth.

"Really, Matty dear," said Donovan peevishly, "these orgies don't do anything for you. You'd better comb your hair—no, let me do it."

But she did it herself, rather perfunctorily, while the stampede continued inside, and she listened, half scornfully, half regretfully, because of this self-exclusion, which left her cool and mistress of herself, listening while Donovan talked to Ruth.

Soon she heard Donovan let out a graceful yell, and saw two people, thus arrested, pause, laugh, and come towards them. One was a small, striking-looking dark-eyed Jewish girl, dressed in tight striped satin, and the other, in striking contrast to her smooth, smart, woman-of-the-world look, a rather large and clumsy man, with a craggy-featured Scots face and blue shrewd Scots eyes.

This couple, it seemed, not merely "knew" Donovan, but were great friends of his; they sat down, ordering drinks while they protested they must go at once. Her name was Stella, his Andrew; they were married, and very pleased about it—these facts Martha gathered before the music stopped again and she found Perry beside her. He groaned perfunctorily that she had deserted him, she was killing him; but she could no longer keep it up. She laughed at him, and, keeping her eyes fixed on his, began talking naturally—about what? It did not matter, it was her tone that mattered; she could no longer maintain that maternal indulgence. She watched him grow uneasy, even half rise, with a trapped look, before he sank down again; she had won. She felt a reckless triumph that she had coaxed one of the wolves, Binkie's senior lieutenant, into treating her seriously! And it appeared that he was astonished himself; for when Donovan and Ruth, Stella and Andrew Mathews rose and announced they were going to the Mathews' flat, Perry followed Martha across the big dance room, contracting his face comically as he shouted out to the distressed Binkie, "This baby's got me, I'm lassoed, I'm done for!" And they drove off, Martha with Perry in the back of Donovan's car, while Ruth sat with him in front, thus acknowledging the change of partners.

Donovan and Ruth flirted pleasantly; as for Perry, he did not even attempt to hold Martha's hand. He allowed that great blond athletic body of his to shake gently with the car's movement, as if all the virtue had gone out of him; and while his head shook where it rested on the back of the seat, he looked at Martha, and said protestingly,

"Hey, baby, what are you doing to me?" while she laughed at him. And when they reached the big block of flats, whose fame was due to their being six stories high, higher than any other building in the town, he followed her meekly from the car, a tamed and uneasy wolf; and so they all went up, in their couples, to the Mathews' flat.

The flat was bright, modern, compact. The small living room had striped curtains, pale rugs, light modern furniture. Coming into it was a relief; one enters a strange place feeling, To what must I adapt myself? But there was nothing individual here to claim one's mood, there was no need to submit oneself. In this country, or in England, or in any other country, one enters this flat, is at home at once, with a feeling of peace. Thank God! There are enough claims on us as it is, tugging us this way and that, without considering fittings and furniture: who used them before? what kind of people were they? what do they demand of us? Ah, the blessed anonymity of the modern flat, that home for nomads who, with no idea of where they are travelling, must travel light, ready for anything.

The windows were open; the lights of the city spread glittering below; it seemed very high—like a platform lifted precariously in the great darkness, with nothing but a thin shell of concrete between the lit space and the black and sweeping winds. For the wind was strong again. The sky, cleaned by rain that same afternoon, was already tumultuous with moon-sculptured cloud. The clouds went rolling steadily but swiftly overhead, to bank themselves high under a slanting Southern Cross, in mountainous heaps of black. It was warm; although Martha was naked save for her slip of a dance dress, the tendrils of wind that clung to her shoulders were as soft as fingers. Thunder muttered softly, like something half asleep; a heavy cloud bucketed and rolled like a ship in the hands of a driving wind, its undersurface profound and dim, its upper reaches white and illuminated. The moon went out, and there was a smell of fresh rain pouring across the dark.

Martha turned from the windows, and found Andrew serving drinks. It seemed that, every place one entered, no sooner had one arrived than out came the alcohol. What would happen, she wondered, if for some terrible and unforeseen reason it did not? But the critical thought lasted just so long as the influence of the night outside; soon she was wholly confined to that small lit space, the Mathews' living room, and she reached out her hand for a brandy, and listened to what was going on.

Here it was not Donovan, or Ruth, or herself, who played lead. It was Stella. She sat on the arm of a chair, talking vivaciously, while her dark eyes glowed, resting on the faces of her audience, seeming to pull them into the circle of her magnetism. She was telling how Andrew's father had forbidden him to marry a Jewess, how they had married secretly, and thus seemed to be living together without grace of state or church, until the old man had come imploring them to marry, because this disgrace was more than his respectable Scotch soul could bear. Then they had told him they had been married all the time, given him a whisky, and asked him to stay to dinner. It wasn't the story itself that they listened to, laughed at; for Stella was displaying herself, as it were, with her husband for foil. She poised herself on the chair arm, in her tight bright satin, and her sleek, smooth, golden-fleshed body seemed to speak to every person there in a language of its own. She was alive from her naked silk-covered toes—she had flung off her shoes—to her smooth dark hair, which seemed so sophisticated, though it was arranged as her grand-mother's might have been, parted in the middle and coiled behind in a simple bun. Her face glistened with animation, her plump tawny arms flung out and gestured until at the end, where she described her father-in-law's collapse, she let them fall, and dropped her voice to a meek, womanly demureness. "And now everything's all right. The hell is over. It's not right for a son to quarrel with his father."

There was a short, astonished silence, while everyone looked at the smooth, down-drooping face in its madonna pose; and Andrew said crudely, "Fat lot you care," and gave a sardonic laugh.

But Stella was conscious that this apparent lack of sympathy was only on the surface a discord. She laughed, gave another conquering glance around, and then waited, as if to say, "Well, I've done my turn, the young married turn, and now are you ready to do your part?" She sat drinking, in silence, waiting for someone to take up the torch, of conversation. But no one did. So she continued: Now that she was openly married, she had had to give up her job—her firm did not employ married women; they were very, very poor. (She said this was an appropriate sigh.) Even the furniture would have been hire-purchase but for the grace of Andrew's father, who had come round with it as a belated wedding present. Really, things had been so bad (here she gave a long, dark, liquid look sideways at her craggy and forthright husband) that positively it had almost come to sleeping on the floor; she had been prepared to sleep on the floor, to be with her chosen. But here Andrew gave another sardonic snort, which checked her for a moment, and she smilingly took a sip of her drink, and looked with satisfaction down at her extended naked toes —she had beautiful, small feet. Then she complained gently that this was a terrible place to live in, because the neighbours kept protesting because of their parties—but really, one couldn't end a party before dawn, how could you? Everyone went to bed so early in this country, and—here she hesitated the briefest moment before smoothly switching the talk into a more reckless channel—really, what with one thing and another, she and Andy were reduced to making love only in the afternoons, and on Saturdays at that, because the neighbours . . .

And now everyone laughed, with relief, for this note united what she actually said with that other conversation her body held, on its own, with everybody, man or woman; and Andrew said gruffly that she was a disgusting wench, and a damned liar, because he couldn't imagine her starving on love once a week; and here she gave a high yell of laughter, and said he was a hypocrite.

Martha, even while she was slowly involved in this, the new atmosphere, with its taboos and licence, based on the young couple, understood (though with difficulty, since she had not encountered it before) that the grudging practical look of Andrew, his gruff, protesting voice, was only assumed; or if not, he was letting that part of himself out on leash; he was not only prepared to see his wife display herself thus to others, but he was an accomplice. Such a reversal was it to Martha's instinctively held ideas, that she was continually, surreptitiously looking to Stella for signs that she resented being shown off. For she was remembering her own continuous half-suppressed resentment of the way Donovan showed her off.

And in the meantime Donovan was curiously silent, for him; he lounged and watched, and laughed admiringly at Stella; Ruth smiled carefully, blinking her red-rimmed, watchful eyes; Perry sat stiffly in a shallow chair which looked as if it would splay out under the weight of his big body, and listened unsmilingly, while from time to time—at those moments when laughter was jerked out of him by Stella—he threw back his head with a sudden dismayed movement, and flung half a glass of liquor down his throat.

Soon, when the subject of love-making lost its piquancy, Stella put on a womanly, serious look, and began talking to Donovan. They were the greatest friends in the world, it seemed; they knew everything about each other, and yet they had not seen each other for six months, and that was at another party. Similarly, Martha found herself being treated with the same simple, affectionate intimacy by Andrew; she soon felt as close to him as to an old, old friend. And Perry too: when it was his turn to be charmed by Stella into the circle of amity, he turned his great body over sideways in the fragile little chair, and allowed himself to be coaxed by Stella's merry, warm glance into what was almost loquacity. He was uneasy, he did not like it, but he allowed Stella to hold his hand, and at the same time (as if her naked, gleaming shoulders, that small white hand, could have no connection at all with the words they were using) talked to her slowly, seriously, about the finances of the Sports Club, and listened solemnly to her tales of Hong Kong, where she had been brought up.

It was getting late, and cold too; for outside it was raining from the now slow-moving masses of ragged, fitfully moonlit cloud. But when Stella caught herself in a yawn, she cried out that it was impossible to go to bed and she was starving. They therefore descended through the bowels of the building again, in the big lift, and ran through the rain to the cars, and so off down to the hot-dog stands. The town was dead and asleep, under the slow cold rain; but the hot-dog stands were like a small gypsy camp that had sprung up in a side street. All along the pavement, night after night, until dawn, these small high rooms, lit with swinging hurricane lamps, perched on their wheels, and supplied food to the taste of all comers: big mixed grills, rolls filled with eggs, ham, sausages, cups of hot weak coffee or very strong tea, and there were shelves piled with tinned food, which would be opened to order. Martha had often come here to eat, with Donovan, after the pictures.

Stella did not want to leave the car to join the crowds at the stalls. She was in a sentimental mood. She leaned her graceful head against her husband's shoulder, and, it appeared, was no longer hungry, for she did not eat. No one was particularly hungry. But an inertia had settled on them, they could not bear to go to bed, and all around the stalls were ranks of cars filled with people similarly afflicted. It was four in the morning, neither day nor night; the lights of the stalls glimmered weakly; the black waiters stood yawning over their trays, or beside the stoves; and half the youth of the town ate and drank, watching the sky for that first spear of red light which would release them, so that they might go to bed, saying they had been up all night. But the sky was obscured. The moon appeared briefly, small and hard and bright in the welter of wet dark cloud, and vanished, this time finally. It rained steadily, making an illuminated yellow mist around the lamps. Martha yawned, and was chided for letting the side down; and they ordered more rolls, more coffee; and at last a grey damp light grew along the streets, the houses seemed to darken, harden into shape, and a weak pallid glow in the sky announced the dawn, which must be plunging in violent rose and gold above the clouds, but here was no more than a reflection of imagined splendour. And now they could go home.

Martha was dropped at the kerb from Donovan's car, but it was Perry who came to the door and kissed her; from which she understood she was now Perry's girl and not Donovan's. She was alone, it was five in the morning, and there was no point in going to bed if one must be up again in a couple of hours.

She opened her parcel of books and yawned till her jaws ached, and drank tea, sitting on the floor; and reflected that Stella and Andrew—an already sufficiently interesting combination—and Donovan and Ruth, and she and Perry, six people so ill-assorted it might seem they would have nothing to say to each other, not only had spent a pleasant evening together, but were planning to be together the following evening. For it had been taken for granted, under the spell of that intimacy, that of course they must be together; they could not bear to be separated. They would go dancing, having first taken sundowners in the Mathews' flat; they would then . . .

And here Martha, feeling chilled, moved from where she leaned against the bed, and sat in the elongated square of weak, wet sunlight that already lay across the matting, and slowly succumbed to disgust that deepened coldly within her as her flesh warmed to the warming sunlight. She was thinking that she had not been in town more than a few weeks and already she was bored and longing for something different; also, she was consumed by such a passion of restlessness that the conflict made her feel weak and sick. She was thinking that at any moment during the last evening, had she been asked, she would have replied that she was bored; yet, as she looked back on it, her nerves responded with a twinge of excitement. She knew that the coming evening would be as barren, and yet she could not think of it without pleasure.

Even more painful than this cold-minded analysis was the knowledge that it was all so banal; just as the stare from that dispassionate cool eye, which judged herself as adolescent, and therefore inevitably contradictory and dissatisfied, was harder to bear than the condition of adolescence itself. She was, in fact, suffering from the form of moral exhaustion which is caused by seeing a great many facts without knowing the cause for them, by seeing oneself as an isolated person, without origin or destination. But since the very condition of her revolt, her very existence, had been that driving individualism, what could she do now?

Slowly, and after a long interval, she began to think of Joss, who was never in any doubt about what was the right thing to do. Joss would say it all served her right, this was what she could expect; she should have telephoned Jasmine, and joined the Left Book Club —and at this point she began to laugh with the nervous helplessness that is the result of an anticlimax. For that was how she felt it: that all the terrific, restless force embodied in her was too powerful to be confined in the Left Book Club, and she began to feel critical and hurt at Joss, as if he had been unsympathetic, unfeeling, as if he had misunderstood her. She was mentally criticizing him, exactly as if he were responsible for her, and her failures and triumphs should belong to him. Since this criticism received no reply, her mental image of him remained stubbornly, sorrowfully silent; her mind slipped into a heightened mazy condition, and in a fevered daydream she imagined that some rich and unknown relation would come forward with a hundred pounds, and say, "Here, Martha Quest, you deserve this, this is to set you free."

For there was no doubt that the root of all this dissatisfaction was that she deserved something life had not offered her. The daydream locked not only her mind, but her limbs; soon she was cramped and stiff, and she had to get up and move about the room, till the blood flowed back, and she went to the door to receive the flood of now soft and hotly welcoming sunlight. It was as if the night had never been; for the light was heavy and rich and yellow, the sky was as thick with rain clouds as it had been yesterday, there was still the oppressive atmosphere of coming storm. There was the ringing of hard boots on tarmac, and the soft padding of bare feet. She stood quite still while past her moved a file of men. First, two policemen, in the boots, their crisp khaki tunics belted tight, their buttons shining, their little hats cocked at an angle. Then perhaps twenty black men and women, in various clothing, barefooted and shabby. Then, following these, two more policemen. The prisoners were handcuffed together, and it was these hands that caught Martha's attention: the working hands, clasped together by broad and gleaming steel, held carefully at waist level, steady against the natural movement of swinging arms—the tender dark flesh cautious against the bite of the metal. These people were being taken to the magistrate for being caught at night after curfew, or forgetting to carry one of the passes which were obligatory, or—but there were a dozen reasons, each as flimsy. Now, Martha had seen this sight so often that she was not dulled to it so much as patiently angry. She marched, in imagination, down the street, one of the file, feeling the oppression of a police state as if it were heavy on her; and at the same time was conscious of the same moral exhaustion which had settled on her earlier.

She was thinking, It's all so dreadful, not because it exists, merely, but because it exists *now*. She was thinking—for, since she had been formed by literature, she could think in no other way—that all this had been described in Dickens, Tolstoy, Hugo, Dostoevsky, and a dozen others. All that noble and terrible indignation had done nothing, achieved nothing, the shout of anger from the nineteenth century might as well have been silent—for here came the file of prisoners, handcuffed two by two, and on their faces was that same immemorial look of patient, sardonic understanding. The faces of the policemen, however, were the faces of those doing what they were paid to do.

And what now? demanded that sarcastic voice inside Martha; and it answered itself, Go out and join the Prisoners' Aid Society. Here she sank into self-derisory impotence, and, leaving the door, returned to her room. A clock was chiming hurriedly from the back verandah. Seven o'clock. She lifted the books from the floor, and looked through them as if she were looking for a kind of deliverance. An advertisement in the *New Statesman and Nation* had brought her certain poets; and she hastily opened some volumes and glanced through them.

Now the leaves are falling fast,
Nurse's flowers will not last,
Nurses to the graves are gone,
And the prams go rolling on . . .

She read it with deepening anger, for mentally she was still marching with that file of prisoners.

Did it once issue from the carver's hand healthy? demanded the black print silently; and Martha passionately averred that it had, it had—and turned the page quickly.

There is no consolation, no none
In the curving beauty of that line
Traced on our graphs through history where the oppressor
Starves and deprives the poor.

This poem she read through several times; and she watched herself sliding into that gulf of rich and pleasurable melancholy where she was so dangerously at home, while that sarcastic and self-destructive voice inside her remarked, Well, well, and did you see *that*?

The clock struck once, a clear dissolving note, and she thought, I must be quick, and snatched up another volume. Not the twilight of the gods, she read, but a precise dawn of sallow and grey brick, and the newsboys crying war . . .

The word "war" separated itself, and she thought of her father, and with irritation. He would like a war, too, she thought angrily; and she took her things and went to the bathroom. They say there's going to be a war because they want one, she thought confusedly; for since it was necessary to resist her parents, it was necessary to resist this voice too.

She lay yawning in the bath, and then heard herself thinking, What if there is a war? What would happen here? She was thinking that she would take lessons in nursing, and volunteer for service overseas—her blood quickened at the idea of it—and she was picturing herself a heroine in the trenches; she was leaning over a wounded man in the slime and debris of no man's land—the phrase gave her a pang of poetic delight; she would . . . But she suddenly leaped out of the bath in disgust at herself, saying, "I'm doing it, too." She was not only furious, she was puzzled. These highly coloured fantasies of heroism and fated death were so powerful she could only with a great effort close her mind to them. But shut them out she did; and came staggering out of the bathroom, telling herself she had a right to be tired, she had not slept that night.

She found Mrs. Gunn on the verandah wearing a faded pink nightgown that dragged over her huge sagging breasts. Her dull red hair was uncombed and her eyes bloodshot. "Well, dear," she asked, interest beginning to rouse her, "did you have a nice time?"

For a moment Martha wondered what she meant; then she said brightly, "Yes, lovely, thank you."

Mrs. Gunn nodded enviously. "That's right dear, you must enjoy yourself when you're young."

Martha laughed, at once animated in response to this demand that she should be. "I'm going out again tonight," she said, and spoke as if she could hardly bear to wait for that night to begin.

3

In this town, due honour was paid to holidays. Every year, from the beginning of December, work in the offices began perceptibly to slacken. Young Mr. Robinson, for instance, would return hurriedly at four in the afternoon, just to sign his letters, after an early festival lunch. Mr. Cohen announced that every girl might take three mornings off (in rotation, of course) to do Christmas shopping. Charlie was kept running to and from the post office, with sacks full of Christmas cards. And that Christmas of 1938 had a feverishness, almost a desperation, about it that seemed to involve the whole town. There were dances every night, often three or four of them, at McGrath's, in the Sports Club; while the Knave of Clubs, the city's only night club, was open every evening instead of twice a week.

There was a new, dangerous spirit in the Sports Club itself. An incident occurred that would have seemed incredible only a few weeks before. Two of the wolves were found fighting, publicly, over a new girl just arrived in town, Marnie Van Rensberg; a shocked and fearful Binkie appealed to them, exhorted—and, for once, failed. The young people of the Club saw something quite new: two wolves not merely not on speaking terms, but with packs of followers who tended to wrangle over the rights and wrongs of the case at the bar, even at meetings which were ostensibly about tennis courts or hockey fields. And they saw it passively—that was the extraordinary thing; this new wind blowing, this disruptive force, was so strong that it even seemed proper and normal that three couples should suddenly get married, that the young men should fight, and with real passion: Binkie had a bruise on his cheek, from trying to separate them.

Meantime, all over the Club were large notices: "Christmas 1938, Enjoy Yourselves" and "Give the New Year a Bang of a Start!" and "Let's Give it Stick!"

That dance Martha attended was the last at which Binkie was to give the signal to "break it up"; there was already too much of a breaking-up spirit. The Club was full of invisible tensions. That cold orgiastic spirit which he deliberately invoked of a Saturday evening, had been invoking for years, was a pale wraith beside the brooding excitement that was clear on every face. And although the unwritten law still held—though it would not for long—that there should be no politics in the sacred circle, there was one evening when a girl remarked aloud, in a silence, in a sudden dreamy voice, as if she had not known she was going to speak at all, "Well, this may be the last Christmas . . . I mean to say—" Then she blushed, and looked guiltily about her. Binkie exhorted her hastily to play the game, that wasn't the spirit; but no one else spoke, and eyes met thoughtfully, in swift glances, and turned away, frowning in deeper speculation. And these faces wore, though unconsciously, a new look: there were moments when they were stern and dedicated, as if they were listening to a distant bugle. It was a look which had the power to pierce like a warning. Binkie, seeing it, would yell to the band, who were perhaps already packing away their instruments, to give them a break, man, give them another tune. The band would most likely oblige. Although, once, two o'clock had been the limit, at two o'clock the musicians had firmly but gently shaken their heads and gone home, now they might play until half past two, even three, in the morning. Afterwards, everyone went down to the Knave of Clubs. No one slept, it seemed. Night after night they were up till the sun rose, they went to work as usual, and they met again by five in the evening. For into this timeless place, where everything continued dreamlike year after year, had come, like a frightening wind, a feeling of necessity, an outside pressure.

And during those heightened, tense days, Stella and Andrew, Donovan and Ruth, Martha and Perry went about together everywhere, for no better reason than that chance had brought them together, and a kind of inertia made it impossible for them to part. They were friends, they loved each other, a gentle, tender nostalgia made every meeting as vivid as a parting. They met in the Mathewses' flat immediately after work, and drank and danced or talked until morning, when exhaustion at last caught up with them, and they would fall like logs around the flat, and sleep on the floor, in chairs, or even tumbled across the big double bed, three or four of them together, in a sexless affection—or perhaps it would be more true to say that during that time the forces of sex hung balanced so precariously that no member of the group of six dared to make a movement one way or the other. During that three weeks, Martha might drive to a dance inside the circle of Donovan's arm, and return from it enclosed within the same gentle protective pressure—this time, from Perry. She might dance half the evening with Andrew, locked in that tender nostalgia, and watch Stella across the room, cheek to cheek with Donovan; she might fling herself down on the divan for an hour to catch some sleep, on coming to the flat straight from the office, and wake up to find beside her any one of the three men, who roused himself good-naturedly at her stirring, and then hastened to fetch her, and himself, a brandy. And so it went on. Such dreamlike, compelled amity, such good nature, such tender appreciation, had surely never existed? They felt as if something miraculous had descended upon them; and yet it all vanished, and from one moment to the next.

It was at the Christmas-night dance at the Sports Club. The band played until three; and at the moment the music finally stopped, Stella was with Donovan under the musicians' platform. The pair sang "God Save the King" hand in hand; and then, in terror lest the evening might end, Stella leaned over to one of the musicians and said, "Come and join us, Dolly—and bring your girl, if you've got one." He nodded with a grateful smile, and indicated that he would come when his violin was safely stowed away. Martha, who was with Andrew, linked arms with Stella, and, as Ruth and Perry came alongside Andrew, and the six of them, pressed side to side, danced slowly across the floor to the table, Martha heard Donovan say in a low grumbling voice he had not used for so long she was startled, "Why did you ask that damned—I mean, why did you make him come?"

And if Donovan's voice was bad-tempered, Stella's was tart. "You were going to say 'damned little Jew,' I think?"

"Jew or not, who cares," said Donovan, so unwillingly that Stella's eyes hardened, and she took her arm away from his. "He's loathsome. Adolph *King*—trying to pretend he's not a Jew."

"Here, you two," said Andrew pleasantly, but warningly. "What's going on?" He dropped Martha's arm, and went between his wife and Donovan, and began to laugh them out of their anger. And so they reached their table; and it was so long since this mood of tenderness had been disturbed by even a word or a jarring silence, that all six were troubled, and waited apprehensively for the arrival of Adolph King, who apparently had the power to stir up trouble.

Soon he came, a small, compact man, with a pale face that now glistened with the hours of music-making, smallish eyes of that red-brown, hot colour that goes with a smouldering temperament, and small, pale, rather beautiful hands; while his smile was eager and grateful, but indicated he was ready to take offence at a word.

He stood smiling uncertainly by an empty chair, which Stella pushed out towards him with a warning look at the others from her expressive eyes. Too expressive: he saw that look, and the smile was like the baring of a dog's teeth. But only for a moment; the gratitude settled back as he took his chair. Now, this gratitude had nothing to do with his position as music-maker; for all the members of the band also belonged to the Club, and, on evenings when they were not playing themselves, might stand with the crowd, urging their colleagues to play one more, just one more, exactly as if they too, and perhaps the next evening, would not be shaking their heads with that same smiling obduracy. So the uneasy gratitude was altogether troubling, and Martha felt it as she watched him talk with Stella. They were all watching, Donovan's face dark and hostile, Andrew quiet, supporting his wife by an occasional remark which caused Adolph to turn that quick smile in his direction, while Perry, lying back loosely in his chair, glanced alternately at Adolph and Donovan. He seemed to be remembering how much he disliked Donovan.

Donovan made a remark to Ruth in a low voice, and then let out that squeal of laughter; she answered shortly, seeming not to agree. Then Donovan turned to Martha and said, "Well, Matty, what do you think of Jew-boys who change their names?"

She replied coldly that she did not see why they should not; though in fact she was struggling with a feeling that it was cowardly—she was remembering what Solly had said about Jews who changed their names. She turned to Perry and asked him, "Do you know him? Is he nice?"

Perry remarked indifferently that Dolly was a nice kid, he was good-natured too, he often played on by himself when the rest of the band had packed up and gone home. "He's a good violinist," he added appreciatively, as if unaware of what all this feeling was about.

Donovan was furious. After a few moments' silence, he said loudly to Ruth, "Shall we go?" Ruth looked round slowly, blinking her tired, heavy-lidded eyes, and nodded. She and Donovan rose, and once again Stella's eyes sparkled indignation and reproach. But Donovan lounged over to her, kissed her cheek, and said, "We'll drop in tomorrow, Stella dear." He turned away, ignoring Adolph.

Ruth said goodbye to every person individually, smiling especially at Adolph, which caused him to flush and make an instinctive movement as if he were going to rise from his chair. Ruth ignored this movement, and, smiling her steady social smile, followed Donovan.

Martha and Perry, at the other end of the long table, were now by themselves.

"A precious plant, our Donny-boy," said Perry at last, giving considered judgment, and for himself, not out of that compelled group amity in which he had been stuck with the rest of them, like flies in treacle, for the three weeks which seemed like so many months.

Martha said hurriedly, "You should remember his—he has a bad time at home," though until she spoke she had not known she thought he had a bad time.

Perry's blue eyes rested on her thoughtfully, while he crooned, "You've a good heart, baby, you stick up for your friends."

Involuntarily, she frowned, and looked away; things hung on balance. For the first time in weeks she was thinking, What am I doing here?

Then Perry said in a low voice, "Come home with me now, baby?" She hesitated, looking up the table to where the group of three were now laughing together, a little too loudly. "Come on, they're all right," Perry said urgently, and hauled that long body of his to its feet; he always looked as if he were troubled by his own size, as if he must keep firmly in his head, which was such a long way from his feet, that those feet were too big and might get him into trouble.

Martha also stood up, saying, "I think I'll be getting home to bed."

Stella and Andrew at once exclaimed in dismay that it was too early, she must see Boxing Day in, they must all come and have breakfast at the flat. Martha shook her head, smiling, feeling her arm gripped tight by Perry's big paw.

"I'll drop in tomorrow," she said, as Donovan had done, and then, afraid that her going might be interpreted in the same way as his, walked up the length of the table to the man they called Dolly, held out her hand, shook his, and said that she hoped she would see him again. She saw Stella's approving nod, and Andrew smiling at her. As for Dolly himself, she was embarrassed by that effusively grateful smile.

She went out with Perry, feeling nervous and excited, for she felt the pressure of his eyes on her. She was wearing a dress of flowered crepe, which she had bought on an impulse, and which was neither what she liked nor what Donovan liked, for all he had said when he saw it was, "Well, Matty *dear!*" It was going to cost her ten shillings a month for the next year, and she regretted buying it. But the pressure of Perry's arm around her waist seemed to absolve her of bad taste.

They drove in silence back to her room, and he got out of the car without speaking and followed her to the door. She was looking for her key, hoping that no one they knew might choose that moment to drive down the street. A couple of cars from the Club swept by, hooting a greeting, and she muttered a bad-tempered "Damn!" as she fitted the key, and hastily went in. Again she hesitated, and found the problem solved by Perry, who simply lifted her up and carried her to the bed.

"Shhhh!" she could not help warning him; for Mrs. Gunn slept the other side of the thin wall.

"Never mind, kid," Perry crooned, and leaned over her admiringly. He looked for so long that she began to see herself through his eyes, approving the flushed face, heavy eyes, loosened hair. He bent to kiss her, and she let this image of herself dissolve, and shut her eyes, preparing to be lost. But the kiss persisted, and its hardness seemed to demand resistance, his mouth was boring down into hers so that it hurt, and as her mind remarked, He's calculating, he's testing me, she flashed awake and became conscious again of every part of herself as he might see it. She was locked in watchful resistance. He lay down beside her, and began pressing her to him. Her mind was schooled in poetic descriptions of the love act from literature, and in scientific descriptions from manuals on sex; it was not prepared for the self-absorbed rite which he was following. When he reached for her hand, and pulled it towards the front of his body, it stiffened; he pulled harder, and moaned, "Give me a break, kid, give me a break"; while at the same time he fumbled with her breasts.

She sat up, and demanded angrily, "What the hell is it you want me to do?" An entirely rhetorical remark, which he was taking seriously; for he was adjusting his face to that look of doglike and abashed devotion which exasperated her, and she hurried on, examining with hostility the hostile look in his eyes: "You're absolutely disgusting!" And then, realizing she was misunderstood, she stood up, shook back her hair, and said coldly, "It's quite all right to mess around, like kids, but to—to make love properly, I suppose you'd be shocked!" She was furious. She saw him slowly gather that great body of his to a sitting position, and thought, How silly he looks. He was so astonished that he had not yet time to be shocked, so she hurried on: "I wonder how many years you've been—messing with girls in cars. After dances there's nothing you don't do—but the thing itself." His inarticulateness, which was after all verbal, and nothing to do with the way he thought, was affecting her, for as each precise phrase came to her mind, licensed by her reading, she could not help discarding it, under compulsive pressure from a nervous prohibition; she was slowly growing furious with herself because of her clumsy, childish speech.

By now he had become shocked, and knew it. He was standing up, and his large, strongly featured face was hard, and his eyes had a look of lost illusions. He said warningly, still a little sentimental, "Kid, you'll get yourself into trouble."

She gave a snort of scornful but agitated laughter, and demanded, "What sort of trouble?"

He said, "I wouldn't have believed it of you, kid, I wouldn't have believed it." At the same time, the aggressive blue eyes were staring and uneasy. They were staring at her in the most perplexed way— here was a new phenomenon, it seemed; for he said slowly, "I like you, kid, I like you, let's get hitched."

And now she stared incredulously at him, and began to laugh. She shook with helpless laughter, while he slowly reddened, and his eyes narrowed, and onto his face came a most unpleasant anger. Then he muttered something, flung himself out of the room and slammed the door.

As soon as she heard that slam, she remembered Mrs. Gunn, lying on her respectable widowed bed next door, and hoped she had not woken. She heard the stealthy creak of springs, and thought, Oh, damn him! And then, shaken with anger, scorn, and discomfort, she reminded herself (for it seemed it was necessary to do this) that she was in the right, while he was revoltingly in the wrong; while she slowly and neatly undressed, folded her clothes across a chair, and got into bed. She said to herself that she would sleep the clock round, she would make up for weeks of sleeplessness.

But she could not sleep at once. She was hot and restless and writhing with shame. She thought of Joss, and was reassured, for she was convinced that her ideas were his also. She said to herself that Perry and all the rest of them were a bunch of kids, messing about for years with every girl in the Club, saying "Forgive me, kid," and "Please give me a break, kid"—and then he dared to look at her like that—and then asking her to marry him, as if—he was mad, he was crazy.

At last she sat up, to light what must have been the fiftieth cigarette since sundown the evening before. The door opened, and the pale, apprehensive face of Mrs. Gunn appeared, followed by her body.

"Come in," said Martha, in a hard voice.

"I thought I'd bring you in some tea," said Mrs. Gunn, advancing with a brimming cup. She was looking furtively around the room—for *evidence*, thought Martha with angry scorn. "I heard voices," said Mrs. Gunn delicately. "Did you have visitors?"

"A young man brought me home," said Martha, "and he's only just gone." Make what you like of that, she thought, staring at Mrs. Gunn, who sighed, evaded her eyes, and said it looked like rain again, look at that sky! She added that Martha hadn't been sleeping in her bed much lately, and . . . She glanced at Martha, who returned a calm look of defiance.

Martha finished the tea and handed back the cup, thanking her landlady, and, saying she intended to sleep until tomorrow morning, lay down and turned her back. Mrs. Gunn pulled the curtains across, shutting out the first gleams of sunlight, and murmured that she looked as if she could do with some sleep and that was a fact. She shuffled herself around the room in her loose slippers, stared at Martha's clothes lying neatly over the chair, and seemed to find comfort in them, for she said dubiously that she expected Martha could look after herself, and withdrew with the empty cup. Martha was already asleep.

She woke to find Stella shaking her, saying gaily that she was a lazy girl, it was six in the evening, time for a drink, and afterwards they were going to the pictures. Martha grumblingly got out of bed and dressed. She did not ask who "they" were; she was still thinking in terms of the group of six.

"What happened with you and Perry?" asked Stella jealously, with a gay laugh.

Martha laughed uncomfortably, and said they had quarrelled, to which Stella replied calmly that Perry was a great lump of a thing, anyway, and too dumb for Martha. Thus supported, Martha finally went out to the car, where Andrew and Donovan were silently waiting. Ruth, it seemed, was being kept in bed by her mamma. "One knows what these mammas are," Donovan said automatically, and gave his shrill laugh, but it was no good. They were flat and tired; it was all an anticlimax; even the vivacious Stella was daunted, and they separated early, after the pictures, irritable with each other and with themselves.

Martha was thinking that it appeared she had quarrelled finally with Donovan, for he was cold and sarcastic with her, and Perry of course would avoid her in future.

She went to bed determined to devote the first months of the new year to the Polytechnic; she reminded herself that in a month of really hard work she had accomplished more than many girls do in a year. Well, then, it needed only determination. Determination, therefore, was what she intended to keep; and she went to the office next morning flat but calm in mind, saying to herself that the New Year's festivities must be ignored. She would work on New Year's Eve, she told herself, and believed she meant it.

That same afternoon she was called to the telephone, to hear a voice she did not know. It was hesitant, and flattened, in the South African singsong manner, it was precise and formal, yet managed to leave the suggestion of something unpleasant, like a snigger. When Martha understood this was Adolph, her first impulse was to say no, she was engaged. Instead, she agreed to go out with him that evening. She put the telephone down thinking that her new regime would begin after the New Year.

When he called for her, he had no plans for their evening, so she suggested they might go to the Mathews' flat. He agreed, but in a way which made her ask doubtfully, "But you're a friend of theirs, aren't you?" He shrugged, in a large fatalistic manner, and its exaggeration made her stare at him.

"Why did you ring me up?" she asked in that direct way of hers, for he looked anything but pleased with the situation; his reddish-brown eyes flickered continually towards her, while he drove in a way which suggested he was surprised to see her here. She was half offended; perhaps she had become affected, after all, by the adulation of the Sports Club men.

"Why did you come and shake hands with me?" he countered, turning those eyes full strength, very aggressive, onto her.

"Shake hands—where?" she stammered; for she was unaccountably offended that he mentioned the incident at all.

"When I came to that table you were all thinking, Here comes that Jew," he said unpleasantly, but at the same time gave her a look which pleaded that she might deny it.

She denied it at once, even more hotly because it was half true.

He laughed disbelievingly, and said, "It was nice of you to shake hands with me like that."

"You exaggerate everything," she said uncomfortably. Then, when he laughed again, she said, "You talk as if—I mean, there are Jews at the Sports Club, aren't there?" For she had not noticed whether there were or not.

"Oh, they tolerate me, I play for them when the rest of the band has had enough," he said sarcastically.

"I think you're unfair," she said, really offended, remembering Perry's attitude.

They were at the block of flats, and Dolly brought the car to a rest, holding it on the brakes, with the engine still running. "Well, shall we go up?" he demanded.

Again she was puzzled, because he was making a challenge out of it, and asked, "But you are a friend of theirs, surely?"

He frowned, and then swiftly backed the car out again, saying, "I'll take you down to the Knave of Clubs, Mrs. Spore is a friend of mine."

"But it's only six," she protested.

"It's open for me," he said, and it was a boast. They drove in silence along the five miles of tree-lined tarmac to the night club, a barn of a place—which had in fact been a tobacco warehouse—built against a low kopje. A black sign, "The Knave of Clubs," was tied by fencing wire to the gate. The space in front of the building was filled with flowering cannas, red and yellow and orange—those fleshy, vulgar unambiguous plants whose masses of clear bright colour, showing against a building, or in a park, are as good as a sign, "For the Public." Jacarandas, now in heavy green leaf, surrounded the garden. Inside, the brick walls had been left bare. Fine sacking was slung across the ceiling and held in place by wire, between which it bulged downwards. There was a bare wooden floor, and in one corner a large radiogramophone.

Martha sat on a wooden chair by a bare wooden table, while Adolph went to a door at the back, where he knocked. An elderly female head came out, pale-grey flesh around which hung pale-grey locks; and a pair of large black eyes surveyed Martha. "We want to dance a little," he said; and the woman called out, "Excuse me, duckie, I didn't get the crowd out till six this morning, everyone's mad this year, and I'm sleeping it off." The head disappeared, and Adolph came back, with that uneasy set smile of his.

"Like dancing?" he asked.

Martha hesitated. She did not feel easy about dancing; all she knew was that there were people with whom she could dance, and those who froze her into clumsy stiffness, and this had nothing to do with whether or not they were good dancers. "I can't dance," she said hopefully at last; but he said, "I've watched you at the Club. You've got to learn to relax."

She laughed nervously, and fell back on the excuse that she'd never been taught.

"I'll teach you," he promised, smiling, while his eyes watched her closely in a way that made her uncomfortable. Never had a man looked at her in just that way, though she had not the experience to describe, even to herself, what "that" way was. She was, however, different from the young girl in earlier generations, in that she knew that everything was allowable. Now she was conscious of her body, and suppressed an impulse to close the opening of her dress, which was impossible in any case, since it was designed to stand open, showing her throat. She forced herself, then, to seem unconscious of his scrutinizing eyes, and felt the warmth of what she hoped was not a bright flush creep up over her face. He was smiling; he had noticed the blush, and was pleased; at once she made an angry movement—so angry she was surprised at herself, for what was there to be angry about? Almost at once, however, his face fell back into the uncertain smile; he unconsciously put out his hand, pleadingly, to check her movement away from him. They looked away from each other uncomfortably.

A waiter came from the back premises, bowed over them, and said that Missus Spore had told him to come and ask what they wanted. His manner said that he resented being sent out before the proper time—no one came here before ten in the evening. He did not wear the white uniform, only a white cotton singlet and rather soiled long white trousers. But Adolph spoke to him in a friendly, almost intimate way, and asked after his family, so that the man began to smile. He took the liberal tip Adolph slid over to him, and said he could sell them a bottle of brandy, if they wanted. Adolph said yes, but he wasn't going to pay more than in the shops, a joke which the waiter accepted as such, for he merely grinned, and soon the bottle of brandy arrived, with glasses and sandwiches.

Martha sipped her brandy, feeling that her escort would offer her no further entertainment until it had done its work; this, as usual, made her feel resentful, and as usual she suppressed it. Soon he put on a rumba and made her dance. She felt self-conscious, dancing alone in the big bare, ugly room, and with someone who was expert. For he said he had been a professional. She knew at once that this was a man with whom she could not dance; her limbs were awkward and heavy, and the more she tried to loosen, the more she became conscious of every joint and muscle of her body.

A tango was playing, and he was instructing her. "Look, your knees should be like this. Drop your shoulders like that."

It reminded her of Donovan, and suddenly she stopped, shook back her hair, laughed and said, "I'll never make a dancer, you'd better resign yourself to it." Feeling, for some reason, triumphant and self-confident, she walked away from him back to the table. She was thinking that she did not like this man, and she wanted to go home.

As this thought showed on her face, he said humbly, "I'm no company for you, am I?"

The way he said it, half pleading and half sullen, struck her again. She was feeling very sorry for him, in an impatient, contemptuous way.

"If the crowd at the Sports Club saw you with me, they'd be annoyed," he offered, hoping she would contradict him.

"What have the Sports Club crowd got to do with it?"

"And your friend Donovan Anderson?"

This seemed to her merely irrelevant; but she unconsciously rose to go, and he followed her, bringing the bottle of brandy.

Again they drove silently. It was dark, the stars flashed out, the hills over which the town sprawled were defined by a deeper, intense black, and over them rose the luminous velvet black of the sky. She was frowning ahead of her; he kept glancing at her furtively.

As he drove slowly past McGrath's, he said, "You wouldn't be seen dead with me in there, would you?"

She replied coldly that she did not understand him; and it was true that it would not have occurred to her to be ashamed of him unless he had pointed it out; though this attitude was at bottom a sort of *noblesse oblige*—he had abased himself so thoroughly that she was feeling like a princess being kind to a ploughboy. She was quite unconscious of it, however; she only knew she was very sorry for him.

"You seem to like being a pariah," she said, ironically; and now he laughed in appreciation of the irony, but at once slid back, and added aggressively that he was not ashamed of being a Jew. "No one suggested that you ought to be," she pointed out, again cold.

Altogether, she was getting more and more angry and uncomfortable; and she walked into McGrath's in a way which was, whether she knew it or not, defiantly calm. She waved to the people she knew, and when she saw Perry she smiled at him as if nothing had happened, receiving in return a curt nod. She found herself wondering whether if perhaps not only Perry but all the others were colder, less welcoming; she saw their eyes following not her but Adolph, who walked behind her; she dissolved in pity, and turned, protectively, so that they might walk through the room side by side, talking. But he did not hear what she said; on his face was that small, self-conscious smile; and she wanted to shake him into pride.

When they were seated, he said, "I've played in this band."

She was going to reply, as if accepting information, "Have you?" Then she understood, and said, with a dry smile that was already, after knowing him not more than three or four hours, like a tolerant, ironic comment, "Well, and why shouldn't you?"

Again his face was tormented by mingled sarcasm, gratitude and relief. Soon her impatience grew intolerable, and she suggested they should leave. The place was half empty, everyone was dancing up at the Club. Irrationally, she longed to be there.

He said quickly, "You'd like to be dancing with the others, wouldn't you?"

"I could have gone if I'd wanted," she said, and got up from her chair, adding that she was tired and wanted to go to bed.

She went home, and spent the evening reading. She hoped nervously that he had found her dull, and would not attempt to get in touch with her again. She even brought herself to believe this, so that she succeeded in feeling surprised when the telephone rang next day and he asked her to spend the evening with him. Because of this surprise she felt, she accepted, but in a hasty, confused way, which he complained about the moment he set eyes on her again.

"Why did you sound so cold on the telephone?"

"I didn't—I didn't mean to," she apologized.

Again they went to the night club when it was still empty; and afterwards to the pictures, reversing the usual procedure; and again she said she wanted to go to bed early. By now she was in a condition of bewildered apathy; her emotions were in a turmoil. By turns she pitied him, hated him, felt protective, despised him, while all the time her imagination was at work, making him into an interesting and persecuted figure. She told herself he was intelligent, meaning, simply that her image of him had this dubious, fantastic quality. She had discovered, through persistent questioning, that he was a Polish Jew, that his parents had emigrated to South Africa during the gold rush, that his father had been a jeweller in Johannesburg. All this had a romantic air, she was fascinated, and tried to make him talk of it, but he answered stiffly and reluctantly. Finally, he doused the fires of her imagination, by saying, like any conventional British colonial, that he had come to this country at the earliest opportunity because it was British. He was now naturalized. Martha was thinking of the Cohen boys, she was wondering at the difference between them and this man; but by now her feelings were so deeply involved that she could not afford to think very clearly. She pitied him too much to say he was unpleasant and cowardly; she was ready to fight the world on his behalf—or at least her world.

On the third evening of their acquaintance, she was sitting with him at McGrath's when she understood that someone must be staring at her, because of her strong desire to turn her head. She turned it, and saw Stella and Andrew and Donovan, sitting by themselves in a corner and smiling pointedly at her. She waved and smiled; but Stella made insistent signs that she wanted to speak to her. Martha thought this was an invitation to both of them, and looked at Adolph, who, however, was watching her with a fixed and deadly smile.

"Go on," he said. "She wants to speak to you."

Martha flushed at his tone, and promptly rose and went across to the other table, where she stood waiting by Stella's side.

"You're a naughty girl," began Donovan. "You just have to be different, don't you, Matty dear?"

"Different about what?" she said coldly, and turned pointedly away from him, looking at Stella. "What's the matter?"

"You shouldn't be here with Dolly," said Stella, in that discreet womanly voice of hers, which was several tones lower than her usual one.

Martha elaborately raised her eyebrows and glanced at Andrew. He, however, looked away; he was obviously embarrassed. "Why not?" she asked bluntly.

Stella's colour was higher than usual, and her eyes were evasive. At the same time she managed to look both sympathetic and self-righteous. It was this look that Martha could see embarrassed Andrew. "You should take our word for it," said Stella softly. "We're older than you."

This was a fatal argument to use to Martha; and she looked direct at Stella, meaning to convey by that look that she was shocked by what seemed to be disgraceful dishonesty. Stella maintained the responsible, womanly dignity, while her eyes shone with scandalized delight. Martha therefore said shortly that she was a big girl now and could look after herself. She said goodbye formally, and returned to Adolph, wishing that she did not so vividly feel the glances she received as disapproving. She told herself she was being influenced by Adolph's persecution complex.

She sat down beside him, smiling tenderly for the benefit of observers, but this smile fled as he said, "Well, they've warned you not to be seen in public with a disgusting Jew."

"You seem to forget Stella's Jewish herself."

"Yes, but she's from an old English family, she's not scum from Eastern Europe, like me."

Martha stared, coloured, then laughed scornfully. "Really, you are ridiculous," she said, not realizing that this cold scorn was possible only because she saw these distinctions from the heights of her British complacency. She laughed, but immediately checked herself, for there was a look of such hurt on his face that she could not bear it. "Don't take any notice," she said protectively. "Come on, let's get out of here."

He rose at once, in that obedient way, and they left the hotel; and this time she did not say she wanted to go to bed early. Instead, she assented when he suggested they might drive for a bit, and found herself pouring scorn on Stella and Donovan (she omitted Andrew, for some reason) for being Philistines, and on the whole Sports Club crowd for being . . . Here she hesitated, before she was off down that slippery slope of compelled confession that was like a moment of madness, but she did not know the words for what she felt; she was thinking of Perry. The men of the Sports Club were disgusting, they were like little boys, they just messed about and . . . Her voice lamely faltered into silence. She was blushing painfully, and hoped it was too dark to show. Adolph was watching her intently, and after a moment showed that he had understood her only too well, by saying that it was all very well, but she was rather young. This was unbearable; she protested that she wasn't young; then laughed, remembering that she was, after all, eighteen. But the word "youth" meant to her only something defiant, a reminder of her right to do as she pleased. Again his quickness took her off guard, for he nodded and said, "Well, if you know what you are doing." This checked her; and she did not reply.

He turned the car at a corner, and began driving back to town. She was wondering why she must always rush into these moments of urgent speech; she was feeling lost, self-abandoned; and she glanced at Adolph, half hoping that he was taking her back to her room, so that she might evade the choice. Then another emotion, a fearful, clutching need to grasp whatever came her way, made her hope that he was taking her to his; it never entered her head to ask him into her room, the idea would have seemed preposterous.

Soon, outside a big house gleaming with lights which fell across a wide shadowy garden, he stopped, with that characteristic gesture of holding the car on its brakes while he let the engine purr a little louder than usual, as if he would take an opposite course at the drop of her hat. "Coming in?" he suggested in a soft, suggestive voice.

This tone offended her, and she hesitated. At once he said, "Please come in," and she saw it as a challenge to her generosity.

"Of course," she said gaily. She was now on a wave of elation, and walked up the path between flowerbeds, talking rather too loudly, while he followed in silence. There was a side verandah, and he unlocked a door and they went into a large room that had curving windows all around the front, overlooking the garden. This gave a tweak at her memory; and she stood still, frowning, wondering why nostalgia was sickening her nerves, and looked at those curving windows— "like the prow of a ship," she thought vaguely. Then she knew he was watching her, and instinctively intensified the dreamy absorption of her face for his admiration.

He said, with that uncertain laugh, "Don't look so aloof," and, stung, she turned swiftly, smiling, to see that his smile had already gone from his face: he could never maintain any sort of criticism for longer than a moment, it vanished instantly, in fear of a snub; and at this thought she again dissolved in pity for him.

He was sitting on the extreme edge of his bed, that small dark man, with his watchful eyes and cautiously poised head, the suggestion of dammed power in the taut limbs. She became nervous; as usual, he was waiting to see what *she* would do. Since she did nothing, he said softly, forcing himself into direct speech, and letting the last words die away into a hesitating mumble, "I suppose you've changed your mind."

"About what?" she asked swiftly and quite sincerely, for it is true, though it might seem unlikely, that she had never directly admitted to herself why she was here.

He was now able to be sarcastic, and it was without any hesitation of manner that he said, "Of course, I knew you wouldn't."

Recklessly she walked across to him, feeling that again, as usual, she was being pulled down a current which she did not understand, and stood beside him, laughing. He half violently, half doubtfully pulled her to the bed, arranged her on it, looked at her, kissed her in an experimental way, looked at her again, hesitated, then muttered an excuse, and went to the dressing table, from which he returned loosening his tie with one hand while he held in the other a packet that he had taken from a drawer. He sat on the edge of the bed, pulled off his shoes, laying them neatly side by side, and began unbuttoning his clothes. Martha lay as if her limbs had been struck by a nervous paralysis, conquering the impulse to avert her eyes, which might have been interpreted by herself, if not by him, as prudishness. There was something dismaying about these methodical preparations. Like getting ready for an operation, she thought involuntarily.

Then, having made sure that everything was satisfactorily arranged, Adolph swung his legs up so that he lay parallel, and began to make love to her, using the forms of sensitive experience, so that she was partly reassured and partly chilled, while she arranged the facts of what was occurring to fit an imaginative demand already framed in her mind. Nor was she disappointed. For if the act fell short of her demand, that ideal, the-thing-in-itself, that mirage, remained untouched, quivering exquisitely in front of her. Martha, final heir to the long romantic tradition of love, demanded nothing less than that the quintessence of all experience, all love, all beauty, should explode suddenly in a drenching, saturating moment of illumination. And since this was what she demanded, the man himself seemed positively irrelevant—this was at the bottom of her attitude, though she did not know it. For this reason, then, it was easy for her to say she was not disappointed, that everything still awaited her; and afterwards she lay coiled meekly beside him like a woman in love, for her mind had swallowed the moment of disappointment whole, like a python, so that he, the man, and the mirage were able once again to fuse together, in the future.

Almost immediately he remarked that her friends at the Sports Club would be furious if they knew.

"I expect they would," said Martha indifferently. The Sports Club people, and Stella and Donovan and Andrew, seemed immeasurably distant. The act of love had claimed her from them, and she now belonged to this man. She remained silent, looked at his smooth, dark-skinned body; he was not fat or plump, but the flesh lay close and even over the small bones, like a warm and darkened wax, the dark tendrils of hair on his chest glistened, and she played with them, after an initial reluctance—the thought had flashed through her mind that this man's body was wrong for her, that she was having her first love affair with a man she was not the slightest in love with. She suppressed it at once, and when they rose and dressed she maintained that simple and demure manner, as if she were altogether at his disposal; and ignored a slow and persistent resentment that was beginning to flood out every other emotion.

They went down to the Knave of Clubs. Martha wondered why it was that before he had always hastily left when the crowd came in; now he remained, dancing every dance, smiling his uncertain smile, in which there was more than a hint of triumph. It annoyed Martha. Every time she lifted her face and saw that small gleaming smile, she had to smother anger. She was dancing badly; she simply could not dance with him; but she lay smoothly in his arms, her hand meekly lying on his shoulder, in the correct attitude for dancing as shown on the films or in magazines. But he seemed quite indifferent as to whether she danced well or not; when she stumbled over an attempt to follow his elaborate steps, he quickly righted them both, and his eyes were roaming over her head, around the faces of the other people.

At the end of perhaps the fifth or sixth dance, when it was still early, about midnight, she pulled away from him and said in a bad-tempered voice that she wanted to go home. He hastened to take her, without a word of protest. She went to bed persuading herself that she loved him, that he was intelligent (the two things were necessarily connected), and that he was in every way superior to the Sports Club men. She was annoyed because she wanted to cry; she indignantly swallowed down her tears.

Every evening, they went to the Knave of Clubs; for in this shabby place, into which one sank, in a haze of brandy and churning music, as if half stunned, Adolph seemed as much at ease as he could ever be. Mrs. Spore treated him with affectionate indulgence; the waiters, whom he tipped so heavily, hurried to greet him, to bring him what he wanted. For Adolph was very generous. Martha, who had grown used to Donovan's frank stinginess, felt herself royally treated, though it was not long before she began to demur, saying that he should not spend so much money on her. He was some kind of a senior clerk for the municipality, his salary could not be so large; and yet he surrounded her with boxes of chocolates and silk stockings, and grew annoyed when she was embarrassed.

New Year's Day they spent in his room, lying on the bed and eating chocolates. They were silent, for they had quarrelled the evening before. He had criticized her floral dance dress, but not in a way she would have been pleased for him to use. She knew it was dowdy; if he had laughed at her because of her mistake, she would have felt more easy about it. When he took her home he said that she should make it tighter, and showed what he meant by lifting handfuls of material away from her hips. "You want me to look like a tart," she said indignantly, to which he replied by calling her a prude. She asked how he would like her to look, and he suggested Stella Mathews. To this she said, "There you are, then." She had not known that she thought Stella in bad taste, but now it became a conviction strong enough to quarrel over. They had parted without sleeping together.

This morning the omission was almost at once made good, he being in a possessive, bullying mood, and she feeling dimly guilty, though she could not have said why. Afterwards, she tried again to make him talk about his childhood in the big city down south, but he answered shortly. There was a long silence.

Suddenly he asked her if she had slept with Donovan. She laughed, and said he had good reason to know she had not. And now he said spitefully that he had thought she was not a virgin. She replied, accusingly, that he had hurt her badly that first time. He said, again brutally, How was he to know? She was now so indignant that she remained silent, her face turned away, and he began to tease her, in his half-brutal, half-deferential way, into good humour. He interrupted himself to ask, as if the question had been wrung out of him, "Do tell me, I won't mind. *Did* you sleep with Donovan?" In spite of her annoyance, and the conviction of injustice, the idea of sleeping with Donovan seemed so absurd that she laughed wholeheartedly. He grew angry and said that Donovan was her type, while he, Adolph, was not. "If you say so," Martha said coldly, and refused to be coaxed out of her bad humour.

At five that evening, when he suggested they should go to dinner, she said she wanted to go home, she needed to sleep early, "for a change." Then she added hastily that in any case, now the New Year season was over, she would not be able to see so much of him, because she must study at the Polytechnic.

"That's right," he said, grinding his teeth slightly as he looked furiously at her, "I knew you wouldn't last long."

"It's only till seven at night, I'm free every evening at seven," she said, frightened into compliance by the spark of anger in his eyes.

Every evening at seven, then, he was waiting for her in his car. She came out gaily, grateful because of the man waiting patiently, only to find that gratitude vanishing in ill-humour as he began to question her about Mr. Skye: Was her instructor attractive, did he try to make love to her?

When she had turned sullen and uncommunicative, he asked her what she would like to do that evening. This always confused her; she looked back appreciatively at Donovan, who simply informed her what they were going to do. She would reply to Adolph that she did not mind; there was always a long moment of indecision, which was like a conflict between them, while they both assured the other they did not mind in the least what they did. At last she assented hurriedly to the first challenging proposal he made: Did she want to go to McGrath's and drink? Did she want to go to the night club? This manner of his, putting himself at her disposal, offended her, as if it were an insult. At the pictures, if she lost herself in the film, she would turn with an uneasy feeling that he was watching her; and yes, he would be leaning back sideways in his seat, his shoulder turned to the screen, while he smilingly watched her. "Why don't you look at the picture, don't you like it?" she asked brightly; and he replied, "I like looking at you"; which flattered her, but also made her feel lost and confused: she felt as if she were something that must be humoured, that he considered himself quite unimportant.

In fact, they were increasingly uncomfortable together, except during those moments immediately after love-making, when she lay quietly beside him, in a devoted, childlike way. She told him then that she loved him; she found herself saying all sorts of things that it embarrassed her afterwards to remember at all. For, lying close up against that warm, sleek body, which apparently had such a powerful claim on her, waves of emotion came over her which she longed might continue over those other uncomfortable times in between.

Once she murmured, not knowing she was going to say it, "I should like to have your children."

"You don't have to say that," he said sarcastically; and she was hurt, for she had been sincere for that moment.

He laughed unpleasantly, and said he would never have any children.

"Why not?" she asked, now deeply ashamed, because he had shattered the emotion which had made the words true.

He said shortly that the women he liked would never marry a man like him. Because of these pathetic words, she began to comfort him, reassure him; but next day he remarked, "I wonder what will happen to you. I wonder where we will both be in ten years' time." This filled her all at once with a terrible feeling of loss and impermanence; for once his tone was pleasant, and tender.

"Why shouldn't we get married?" she asked, her heart sinking at the thought of it.

He laughed at her, and smoothed her hair back, gently, in a paternal way, and said she was crazy. Then, a suggestion of cruelty returning, he held her hair close around her throat, so that it slightly choked her, and said that she would marry a good city father and become very respectable and have five nice, well-brought-up children.

She shook herself free, and said that she would rather die. The suggestion made her furious, he might have been insulting her. Afterwards, looking back on it, she marked that moment as the real end of their affair; at the time, she felt resentment, and under the resentment the old fear of loss, as if she were being cheated out of something.

This occurred about ten days after they first made love.

Two or three days later—it was a Saturday—when he asked her

what she would like to do, she said that she didn't always want to make the decisions, that she would like to do something he enjoyed, for a change.

"Very well," he said, and they spent the afternoon at the races; which revealed to Martha something quite new, a circle of people quite different from the regular Sports Club crowd.

The big oval of the racecourse, fringed and tasselled by rich green grass, banked by trees in full leaf, was a little way out of the town; and outside the clubhouse strolled a crowd of people dressed like those in the magazines from England. Adolph kept pointing out important personages, whose commonplace appearance naturally disappointed Martha, who until then had assumed that the famous must necessarily reflect all one's ideas about them, instead of insisting on mirroring forth their own. The man who caused Adolph the greatest excitement was a Mr. Player, whose name was used by the people of the colony in that spitefully humorous, grudgingly admiring way that is the tribute offered to real power. Mr. Player, said Adolph, knew more about horses than anyone else here.

Adolph hung about, waiting to catch the great man's eye, and when he did he offered an effusive smile, and received a careless nod in return. Mr. Player was fat and red-faced, and Martha thought him repulsive, but Adolph said admiringly that he had an eye for the women, he got all the really attractive women in the town sooner or later; which information caused Martha to look disbelieving, for while she knew, theoretically, that women slept with men for money, she could not imagine herself doing it, which is as good as saying she did not believe it. She therefore decided that Mr. Player must be kind and generous and perhaps intellectual, otherwise there was no explaining his reputation.

When Mr. Player had moved out of their neighbourhood, Adolph began wandering through the crowd, his eyes busily searching; and when he had found the right kind of face, he would appear to stiffen and wait, that almost servile smile steady on his lips, until he had got what he wanted—a hurried, sometimes annoyed acknowledgment of his presence, which he received gratefully. It annoyed Martha and made her feel uncomfortable. But when the first race began, she saw Adolph transformed. For the first time, she saw him shed his awful burden of self-consciousness. He stood by the rail, forgetting her, forgetting everything, absorbed in the horses that pranced and curvetted at the starting line, gleaming in the bright sunlight, and when they streamed into movement he leaned forward, his eyes following them, his hands gripping the rail; and when it was all over, he remained motionless for a few seconds, breathing heavily, before he turned to her, with a sigh, and said, "If I had the money . . ."

He took her to the stables, where he knew all the attendants and the jockeys, knew each horse by name. He stood by a big black powerful horse for nearly half an hour, his hand lying reassuringly on its neck, talking to it in a tone Martha had never heard. It touched her deeply, this passion was something she could respect, she felt a new tenderness for him, even while she wondered at his readiness to give up his regular attendance at the racecourse "simply to be with me," she said with genuine humility, instinctively seeing that whatever he might feel for her was nothing to this abiding emotion.

But when they returned to the crowd, and he resumed his game of stalking the great for recognition, her irritation came back. At the end of the afternoon, he told her sarcastically that she had been bored; she was insincere when she protested she had enjoyed it. And the racing itself did bore her, she was unable to care which horse came in first. The crowd interested her, the clothes of the women— but most of all, and for the wrong reasons, Adolph's behaviour. He knew this instinctively. She assured him again that she had loved every minute of it; he said roughly that she had no feeling for racing and she was a hypocrite.

When they left the racecourse, with the other cars, he drove past McGrath's. She waited, her nerves on edge, to hear him say that of course she wouldn't be seen dead with him in there, now it was filled with the smart crowd from the racecourse. He said it, and she found herself replying irritably that if he didn't behave like a dog who expected to be kicked, no one would treat him like one. It was the first time she had acknowledged that he was, in fact, disliked; and no sooner were the words out than guilt overwhelmed her.

"Look," she said gently, "think of Mr. Cohen, for instance. When he comes to the Sports Club, no one dreams of thinking, Look at that Jew!"

He laughed in a hurt, strained way, avoiding her eyes, and said, "Which Mr. Cohen? Those lawyers, maybe, but the Cohen who runs the wholesale business wouldn't dare show his nose in the place."

"Then it's nothing to do with being Jewish," she persisted, being reasonable at all costs; and he merely laughed again, and said she was a baby and knew nothing about life, which naturally touched her on her weakest spot, and made her cold and hostile.

She walked in front of him into McGrath's lounge, greeting the people she knew, as usual, but understood that their smiles, their waving, was no longer approving; there was no doubt of it: the

Sports Club crowd were watching her in a way which politely did *not* pass comment.

She chose a table, and waited for him to join her, which he did, smiling sheepishly. They were silent, and drank rather more quickly than usual, and when he suggested, as soon as their glasses were empty, that of course she wanted to leave now, she rose at once, and walked out.

He ran up behind her, saying, "Come home with me now?" It was more than his usual hesitating suggestion, and she replied quickly that she must go home, there were letters to write.

She had never seen him so black and stubborn as he insisted, between set teeth, "Now—I want you to come home with me now."

He had never insisted before; it had always been left to her to make the decision; and now she stiffened into resistance. "No," she said coldly, "I'm going home."

He grasped her wrist, and said, "You never come when I want you to, only when you feel like it."

Now, this struck her as unfair; she thought of herself as soft and compliant, because she saw the whole affair only in the light shed by those tender moments after love. She pulled away her wrist, moved away from the side of his car, where she had been standing, and said she would walk home. He came hurrying after her, already nervous and apologetic.

"You only want me to come now because—well, because you want to prove something to yourself!" she stated, and his face darkened, and all at once it became so urgently necessary for her to escape from the whole situation that she simply turned her back on him and said, "Leave me alone." As an afterthought, she flung back over her shoulder, "I'll see you tomorrow."

So she walked steadily down the main street, until she heard a car draw up behind her, and hastened her steps, thinking that he had followed her; but Donovan's gay, hard voice called out, "Matty, where are you off to?"

She stopped, adjusting herself to the idea of Donovan, and he said, "Yes, Matty dear, I've been looking for you. Come on, jump in."

She got into the car, asking, "What do you want me for?"

"*I* don't want you, *dear* Matty. Stella wants to speak to you about something. I said I'd never be able to tear you away from your fascinating new friend, but, as luck had it, we passed you engaged in your lovers' tiff, so I seized the opportunity."

"But *why* does she want to see me?" Martha sounded like a sulky child, and Donovan did not reply, but drove steadily along.

A car passed them, and she involuntarily glanced to see if it was

Adolph. Donovan said, "If you want to locate your admirer, surely you know where to find him?"

"What do you mean?" she enquired.

They were at an intersection; her room was perhaps two hundred yards down, one way, and the Mathewses' flat a couple of blocks further on. "Your fascinating admirer waits here for you," said Donovan, indicating a vacant and grass-grown lot at the corner. "Yes, Matty dear, when you've gone to your virgin bed, he sits here, in his car, watching your room to make sure of your exclusive interest in him—the whole town's laughing its head off about it," he added cruelly, and glanced swiftly sideways to see how she would take it.

She took it badly. She was stunned. Then she muttered, "I don't believe it."

He laughed. "Look over your shoulder."

She looked. A couple of blocks behind them crawled Adolph's car. The mere sight of it caused her annoyance, and she involuntarily gave an impatient movement as if shrugging off a burden. She said coldly, however, "That doesn't prove anything."

They had reached the flats. Donovan quickly stopped the car and jumped out. She saw he was waving to Adolph; the car wavered, appeared to be turning into a side street, and then adjusted itself and came straight on. Donovan, looking very manly and decided, strode a few paces to meet it, checked it with an imperiously raised hand, leaned inside the car, and spoke to Adolph; Martha caught a glimpse of Adolph's defenceless smile.

Donovan returned, and she said, "What's going on?"

"Never mind, Matty dear, you come and talk to Stella, you'll find out."

They avoided looking at each other as they went up in the lift. Martha hated Donovan, and was thinking of Adolph: she was saying to herself that it would be impossible for him to spy on her, while an inner voice was replying that it was only too likely—it seemed consistent with what she knew of him. Fighting against this new conviction, she entered the flat, and found Andrew, looking very embarrassed and concealing it with an assumption of responsibility, and Stella seated waiting on the divan as if the act of waiting was in itself a torment. She leaped up, and came to kiss Martha.

Martha allowed herself to be kissed, and asked, "What's the matter?"

Stella led her to the divan, her arm around her shoulders with a gentle pressure that said, Be patient; then she went to sit opposite, leaning forward. She was wearing a black cocktail dress with sequins on it, which Martha's eye noted and criticized as too bright even while she was waiting agitatedly for what Stella was going to say. Her hair was newly done, lying smooth and glossy on her small head; her oval face was tinted to an even apricot flush; her eyes glittered with excitement. At the same time, she was trying to subdue this excitement and appear deprecatingly womanly.

She said, in a low, dignified voice, which Martha at once resented as a dishonesty, "Matty dear, we really feel it our duty to tell you— no, don't speak for a moment." For Martha's eyebrows had involuntarily risen at the word "duty." "Let me finish, Matty."

Martha glanced at Donovan, who was watching avidly; at Andrew, whose face suggested that he was bound to agree with his wife, even if what she said continually came as a surprise to him. He refused to meet Martha's eyes, which were an appeal.

"Matty," continued Stella with that effusive gentleness which was like an irritant, "you're very young, and you've made a terrible, terrible mistake. You should have listened to us. That man has a bad reputation, he's immoral and—"

Here Martha laughed involuntarily, thinking of the atmosphere of sex that Stella exuded like a perfume.

Stella said hurriedly, "No, Martha, you mustn't laugh. He's not a nice man. He's been talking about you publicly, boasting everywhere."

This was another shock. Martha could not immediately speak. That inner voice was saying firmly, No, *that's* not true; but she was confused, thinking that if he could spy on her, which she believed, then he might also boast. She sat frowning, looking ,with dislike at Stella's triumphant face.

They were all gazing at her. In astounded horror of herself, she felt her lips beginning to tremble; the thing wavered this way and that, and then Stella expertly tightened the screw: "Talking about you all over the *town*, Matty." And Martha burst into tears. Her chief emotion was anger at herself for crying, for now she was lost. Through her tears, she saw the glint of cruelty in Stella's bright eyes; she saw Donovan smiling, though he at once adjusted his look to sternness. A glance at Andrew showed him to be extremely uncomfortable. He got up, came over to her, and pushed away Stella, putting his arms around Martha.

"Now, don't cry, it's all right," he said nicely, and looked angrily at his wife, who smiled and stood smoothing her hair reflectively, watching Martha's face.

Almost immediately, much too soon to please Stella, Martha pulled herself together, trying to laugh, and asked brightly for a handkerchief.

"You're not the sort of girl who should cry," said Donovan, handing her his. "Stella, now, looks divine when she cries. For goodness' sake powder your nose, Matty dear."

"That's enough," said Andrew, annoyed. "Let's call it a day now, shall we? Let's all have a drink." He went to pour them.

Stella took over again. "And now we want you to come with us while we go and talk to him."

"What for?" protested Martha sullenly. She had imagined it was all over.

"You don't want him ruining you, we must stop him talking, the whole town is gossiping," cried Stella indignantly.

"I don't see any necessity to go and see him," said Andrew stiffly.

But Stella and Donovan were already on their feet, waiting, and Andrew rose, too, in spite of himself.

"I don't think we should," said Martha faintly. "He won't be in, anyway," she added hopefully, and this rider was her undoing; for she understood suddenly that Donovan had arranged that he should be in, when he spoke to him in the car. The sense of elaborate preparations, discussions, intrigues which she had not begun to comprehend kept her silent while Stella impatiently pulled her up from the divan and said, "Oh, come on, Matty, he's expecting us."

As they drove the few blocks to Adolph's room, Martha, from her worried preoccupation, dimly heard Stella chattering animatedly about how easy it was for a young girl to go astray; it sounded like a magazine story. She looked incredulously at Stella, thinking surely this was an act, but Stella was carried away by the drama, and when Martha glanced towards Andrew, thinking that at least he must be amused, no, he was silent; his wife's self-righteousness seemed to have infected him, for he sentimentally pressed Martha's hand, and said, "You see, it's all disgusting, isn't it?" Stella promptly said, with a relieved look at him, that yes, it must have been a great shock to Martha. Martha understood that they meant sex; and an uncomfortable but derisive grin appeared on her face, and she turned her face away to hide it, for she felt guilty because she could smile at all; she was by now bitterly regretting being here, and hoped that Adolph would have the sense to avoid this ridiculous scene.

But of course he was waiting. As the four entered the big room with its curved windows—and for the first time it flashed into Martha's mind that the reason she had been so drawn to them was because they reminded her of home—Adolph was standing in the centre of the room, watching them, a small, ugly smile on his face. He looked caged; he stared helplessly at Stella, after a quick resentful glance at Martha, who even found herself signalling with her eyes, Don't take any notice of them.

But he could not take his eyes off Stella, and it was she who conducted the interview, while the two men remained standing in the background, waiting.

Stella began, in that womanly voice, "You know why we've come."

"I'm afraid not," said Adolph, with his scared smile.

Stella drew in her breath, outraged by the hypocrisy. "I've come to speak to you, because I feel it to be my duty. I'm a Jew myself and I feel—"

"*Stella!*" protested Andrew and Martha together.

Stella impatiently motioned them to be quiet, and went on, smoothing her black silk skirt with a hand that looked curiously agitated, in contrast with the bland smiling face. "You know quite well what people say, then why do you add ammunition to it, seducing an innocent English girl."

"Stella," said Martha again, but by now neither of them was interested in her.

Adolph moved his lips in his scared, guilty smile, and Martha thought, Why don't you stand up to her? Don't look so crestfallen. She was sick with anger at this scene, and with her part in it.

"You married a Scotsman," said Adolph at last, weakly.

Stella straightened herself, and said with dignity, "I married him. I didn't drag down my people to be gossiped about."

Adolph suddenly let out a nervous giggle; his face was dull purple, his eyes went from one to another of the group in front of him, in angry appeal. And since he said nothing, Stella lost poise; her body was tense with the desire for a good vulgar scene, but it seemed there would be no scene.

She dropped her voice and cooed reasonably, "You must see you've behaved shockingly."

There was a silence. Then Andrew said angrily, "Oh, come on, Stella, that's enough, this is all off the point."

And at last Adolph flashed into anger, and ground out, "And may I ask what this has got to do with you?"

"Because I'm a Jewess," said Stella, with dignity. "Because I've a right to say it."

It seemed Adolph had exhausted his anger; and after a pause, Stella rose calmly, remarking, "I'll leave it to your conscience, then."

She walked to the door, shepherding her flock before her. Donovan, looking moodily irritable, went out first. Andrew followed, saying uncomfortably to Adolph, "Goodbye." There was no reply. Martha looked swiftly over her shoulder at Adolph in guilty apology, and saw his eyes so filled with hatred that she averted hers, and hurried out.

No one spoke. In her mind, Martha was framing words to express what she felt: she wanted to say this was the most dishonest, disgraceful scene, she wanted to ask sarcastically why Stella had not said any of the things she had protested she intended to say. A glance at Stella's satisfied face silenced her, and a kind of tiredness came over her.

They went to the car and drove in silence uptown. At the intersection Martha said, "I should like to get out and go home."

"No, Matty dear," said Stella maternally. "Come home and have some nice supper with us."

"Let her go home," said Donovan unexpectedly. His voice was sulky, his heavy black brows were knitted together over his eyes; he was scowling.

Andrew stopped the car, and Martha got out. Stella leaned persuasively out of the car, and said, "Now, go to bed early, Matty, don't worry, you need some sleep, it's all over and no harm done."

Martha saw that Stella was waiting to be thanked; but the words stuck on her tongue. "Goodbye," was all that she could get out; and she sounded cold and reproachful. She was reproaching herself for being a coward.

Stella leaned further out, and said gaily that Martha must look on their flat as a home, she must come and see them next day.

Martha nodded, with a stiff smile, and went home.

And in her room she was so ashamed she could hardly bear her own company. She said to herself wildly that she must rush down to Adolph's room and say she was sorry, that it had had nothing to do with her, she had not known it was going to be like that. But at the back of her mind was a profound thankfulness that it was all over. There was no doubt that it was a relief that she need not see him again. And so, after a while, she soothed her conscience with the thought that she would write to him, she would apologize. Not now —tomorrow, later; she would write when a letter no longer had the power to bring him back.

part four

But far within him something cried
For the great tragedy to start,
The pang in lingering mercy fall
And sorrow break upon his heart.

EDWIN MUIR

1

Martha was alone in her room. She felt exposed, unable to bear other people. She wished she were ill, and so able to stay away from the office for two or three weeks. Soon she did feel a vague, listless aching, rather like an illness. Her mother had sent her a thermometer to "help her look after herself." She took her temperature. It was a little over normal. She assured herself that a temperature might be low in the morning and high in the afternoon, and got Mrs. Gunn to telephone the office, saying she was unwell.

In the afternoon, she was standing by the door, with the thermometer in her mouth, when she saw herself from outside, and at the same time remembered her father, medicine bottles stacked in hundreds by his bed—her father, whose image persistently composed itself in her mind as a worried, inward-looking man, standing moodily at a window but seeing nothing out of it, holding one wrist between the fingers of his other hand, to measure his pulse. The thought frightened her; she whipped out the thermometer, and stood hesitating, thinking, I'll throw the thing away. She glanced at the silver thread, for she might as well have a look at it first, and then it slipped from her hand and broke. Before it fell, she had seen that it stood at a hundred. Well, she had a temperature, she was justified. Soberly, she swept up the glass, and said consolingly that she would never buy another thermometer, she would not fuss over her health. But it was a relief, nevertheless, to be slightly ill, to be able to go to bed.

To bed she did not go. She put on a dressing gown, arranged books, and prepared for a few days' retreat from the world.

A few days: looking back on that period of her life afterwards, what she felt was wistful envy of the self she had been; she envied her lost capacity for making the most of time—that was how she put it, as if time were a kind of glass measure which one could fill or not.

She had left the farm a few weeks before; but put like that it was nonsense. Those few weeks seemed endless, one could not think of time—which is an affair of seconds, hours, days—in connection with it. It seemed she had been in town for years—no, that was another term for the divisions of the clock. What she had experienced since she got that momentous letter from Joss, which had released her from her imprisonment like the kiss of the prince in the fairy tales, was something quite different from the slow, measured years she had spent on the farm.

She thought of farm time, that strict measuring rod, where life was kept properly defined—for there could be no nonsense when the seasons were used as boundaries. On the farm, it was January, she told herself, it was in the middle of the rainy season. After the rainy season came the dry season; and after that, again, the rains. But when she came to think of it, it was not so simple. What of the season of veld fires, which had a climate of its own: lowering, smoky horizons, the yellow thickness of the middle air, the black wastes of veld? It was an extra season inserted into the natural year. What of October, that ambiguous month, the month of tension, the unendurable month? Again, it was neither dry season nor wet, for how can a month be called dry that is spent, minute by dragging minute, thinking of the approaching, inevitable rain, watching a sky banked with clouds which must break, must break soon? October was another season that was given, offered free, as it were, to vary a climate which is thought of as "dry season, wet season." And so the rains break at last, if not in October, then in November, or even, when it comes to the worst, in December; the word "October" does as well as any other to fix the terrible, beckoning period of tension which comes in every year, comes inevitably; one cannot have the breaking of the rains without the time of preparation and agonized waiting to which one gives the name "October." And the word "October" gave off to Martha (her birthday was in that month) a faint marshlight from

another world, that seemingly real but illusionary gleam from literature: overseas, October was the closing of the year, in a final blaze
of cold-scorched foliage followed by the ritual lighting of the fire on
the hearth. No, it was not easy, not easy at all, to moor oneself safely,
with words that meant one thing only, to use names like lighthouses;
these rocks shifted, as if they too floated treacherously on water.

But now it was January. Christmas was over. Martha stood at her
doorway behind a rather soiled lace curtain, and looked at the street.
It was hot and wet. The puddles in the garden never had time to
dry—to sink into the earth or lose themselves in the air. The sky
sweltered with water; several times a day the clouds drove incon-
tinently over the town, everything grew dark for a few minutes in a
sudden grey drench of rain, and then the sun was exposed again, and
the tarmac rocked off its waves of wet heat, the trees in the park
quivered through waves of rising moisture. January, January in the
town.

On the farm, everything was vivid, a violent green, while the
earth was a blaring red. The sky from Jacob's Burg to the Oxford
Range, from the Dumfries Hills away back, over the unbounded
north, was a deep, soft hall of blue; and the clouds wheeled and deployed and marched, day and night, flinging down hail, storming
down rain, rolling and rocking to an orchestra of thunder, while the
lightning danced about the thunderheads and quivered over the
mountains. On the farm, the bush on the hill where the house stood
was so soaked and lush that walking through it meant red mud to
the ankles, and saturated branches springing loads of sparkling water
at every step. On the farm, the cattle were grazing with nervous
haste on the short, thick grass, which they knew would be tough
and wiry in so short a time. For this was the season when it was impossible to remember the burning drought of the long dry season.
The veld was like those blackened brittle sticks one picks off a rock
on a kopje, apparently dead and ready to rot, which one places in
water, only to find, an hour later, that this lifeless twig has burst into
crisp, vivid little leaves. In January, the drought-ridden, fire-tortured
veld was as teeming and steamy and febrile as a jungle. In the rot-
ting trunks of trees the infant mosquitoes wriggled like miniature
dragons; one might find the energetic creatures in the hollow of a
big leaf, or in the imprint of a cow's foot or the tangled wetness of
a low-growing clump of grass.

Last January, Martha's eyes (fixed as usual on some image of herself in an urban setting—a college girl in Cape Town, perhaps?) were
caught by a slow squirm on a branch which she was just about to
allow to splash, like a sponge, across her already drenched head, and

she saw, as if the deep-green substance of the leafage had taken on another form, two enormous green caterpillars, about seven inches long, the thickness of a wrist; pale green they were, a sickly intense green, smooth as skin, and their silky-paper surfaces were stretched to bursting, as if the violence of this pulsating month was growing in them so fast (Martha could see the almost liquid substance swimming inside the frail tight skin) that they might burst asunder with the pressure of their growth before they could turn themselves, as was right and proper, into dry cases, like bits of stick, and so into butterflies or moths. They were loathsome, disgusting; Martha felt sick as she looked at these fat and seething creatures rolling clumsily on their light frond of leaves, blind, silent, their heads indicated only by two small horns, mere bumpish projections of the greenish skin, like pimples—they were repulsive, but she was exhilarated. She went home singing.

One might imagine I was homesick! she said to herself drily; for she could not return to the farm again, not if it were the last thing she did. And yet, for the moment, it seemed she could not face the town either, for here she was, shut into her room with a dubious illness that could be described by courtesy as malaria. Why not? She had had malaria as a child, and everyone knew that "once it was in your blood . . ." She had a "touch" of malaria, then—as one might speak of a "touch" of the sun—and she was not homesick. Everything was satisfactory, for she was telling herself that her experience with Adolph could be justified as such; one is not an honorary member of the youth of the 1920s without knowing that one is entitled to experience, if to nothing else. And it was true she was not ashamed of the affair with Adolph; she was ashamed—to that point where one bursts into inarticulate exclamations of disgust, alone in one's room, one's face burning—because of that scene with Stella. She told herself that never, not on any account, would she go near the Mathews' flat again.

On the third day of her retirement, she received a large and expensive bunch of flowers from Stella and Andrew, with a gay note saying that they had telephoned the office and heard she was ill. Martha was warmed by this kindness, but no sooner had she become conscious of the flush of gratitude through her veins than she remarked to herself irritably, in the old way, Nonsense, what is kindness then? She just does as comes easiest, and then . . .

She wrote a little note to Mr. Jasper Cohen, in the humorous vein she knew she should not use, because it pleaded special privilege; for she needed a doctor's certificate to stay at home any longer.

Then she returned to resume that other journey of discovery which alternated with the discoveries of a young woman loose in town: she returned to her books. She was reading her way slowly and vaguely from book to book, on no better system than that one author might mention another, or that a name appeared in a publisher's spring list. She was like a bird flitting from branch to darkening branch of an immense tree; but the tree rose as if it had no trunk, from a mist. She read as if this were a process discovered by herself; as if there had never been a guide to it. She read like a bird collecting twigs for a nest. She picked up each new book, using the author's name as a sanction, as if the book were something separate and self-contained, a world in itself. And as she read she asked herself, What has this got to do with me? Mostly, she rejected; what she accepted she took instinctively, for it rang true with some tuning fork or guide within her; and the measure was that experience (she thought of it as one, though it was the fusion of many, varying in intensity) which was the gift of her solitary childhood on the veld: that knowledge of something painful and ecstatic, something central and fixed, but flowing. It was a sense of movement, of separate things interacting and finally becoming one, but greater—it was this which was her lodestone, even her conscience; and so, when she put down this book, that author, it was with the simplicity of perfect certainty, like the certainties of ignorance: It isn't true. And so these authors, these philosophers who had fed and maintained (or so she understood) so many earlier generations, were discarded with the ease with which she had shed religion: they wouldn't do, or not for her.

In the meantime, she continued with the process of taking a fragment here and a sentence there, and built them into her mind, which was now the most extraordinary structure of disconnected bits of poetry, prose, fact and fancy; so that when she claimed casually that she had read Schopenhauer, or Nietzsche, what she meant was that she had deepened her conviction of creative fatality. She had in fact not read either of them, or any other author, if reading means to take from an author what he intends to convey.

Those "few days" were one of those periods which recurred in her life when she read like a famished person, cramming into the shortest possible time a truly remarkable quantity of vicarious experience. She emerged from it on the Sunday evening, restless with energy, knowing she must go back to work the following day. It was almost February; already a month had gone from the new year. She must go back and work at the Polytechnic, she must fulfil all her good resolutions, so that by the end of the year she would be embarked properly on a career and know where she was going.

The two authors she brought with her from that period of reading were Whitman and Thoreau—but then, she had been reading them for years, as some people read the Bible. She clung to these poets of sleep, and death and the heart—or so she saw them; and it did not occur to her to ask, not until long afterwards, how it was that she, not more than a few weeks in time from the farm, hardly separated from it in space (since this little town was so lightly scratched on the surface of the soil that one could see the veld by lifting one's eyes and looking down to the end of the street, while the veld grasses sprung vigorously along the pavements)—why it was that she read these poets as if they were a confirmation of some kind of exile?

When she returned to the office, she found that Mr. Jasper Cohen had gone abruptly on holiday. His son had been killed in Spain—he had been shot, near Madrid, rather more than a year before; a friend of his had written, on returning safe to England, to tell his father so.

The office was concerned not so much over the death of a hero as over the new regime; for Mr. Max Cohen, now in charge, had dismissed three girls, one of whom was Maisie. Mr. Max Cohen and young Mr. Robinson allowed it to be seen how much they did not approve of Mr. Jasper's methods. Martha was interviewed and asked perfunctorily after her health (she looked extremely well) and told that "we" were so pleased that she was persevering at the Polytechnic, because the office could no longer afford unqualified girls.

Maisie, placidly under sentence of dismissal, had already found herself another job, at an insurance office; she told Martha that she had taken four days off herself, for the Christmas season had nearly killed her—she had slept for three days without stopping. She manicured her nails, dreamily attended to the filing, and smiled with the pleasantest good nature at Mr. Robinson and Mr. Max, who were even more annoyed because she seemed not to regard being dismissed as a disgrace. The other two girls had left already, in a fit of outraged *amour propre*, and were employed elsewhere.

"Wait till *our* Mr. Cohen comes back," said Maisie calmly. "They'll catch it. Nothing but slave drivers." But it was unlikely that Mr. Jasper would be back for some months. It was not only the shock of his son's death; his wife—or so said rumour—was going to divorce him, for she felt that it was all her husband's fault that Abraham had been killed, and the office appeared to agree with her.

Mrs. Buss said with mournful satisfaction that if you were going to mix yourself up with the Reds, then you got what you asked for; she couldn't understand Mr. Cohen allowing Abraham to get mixed up with that bunch. Martha had her first political argument in the office; she pointed out hotly that it was not the republicans who were the rebels, but Franco. She was well armed with facts from the *New*

Statesman. She was even better armed by the conviction of being in the right, but what is the use of being right if one is faced by the blank, unaltered stare of satisfied ignorance? Martha was so new to the game that she was surprised by Mrs. Buss's calm remark, "Oh, well, everyone's entitled to their ideas." She said it was not a question of ideas, but one of fact. Mrs. Buss said tartly that in any case everyone knew what Communists were. Martha said the Government in Spain was not Communist, but liberal. Mrs. Buss looked blank for a moment, and then said that was what she had said all the time, the Government was liberal, so why did Abraham have to go and fight it? Martha was confused; then she understood, and said that Mrs. Buss was making a mistake, Franco had never been elected, but . . . Mrs. Buss listened, frowning doubtfully, while her hands rested on the keys, her bright little face looking stubborn. She repeated, with a toss of her head, that she was entitled to her opinions, and added that politics bored her, anyway, and at once rattled on with her work, to stop Martha arguing. Martha was furious, chiefly because Mrs. Buss not only was inconsistent but didn't mind being inconsistent.

After work, she walked down to the Polytechnic, still angry, and very grieved for Mr. Cohen, that kind gentleman whose only son was dead, and his wife on the point of leaving him. She decided that she would borrow some money from somewhere and go to Cape Town: if only she could speak to Joss, he would know at once what it was she ought to do! Finally she settled herself to take shorthand, and tried to concentrate while Mr. Skye dictated a long piece about the prices of cotton waste. She gave up the attempt rather early, and left the Polytechnic, to find Donovan waiting for her in his little car. He said graciously that he would take her to the Sports Club, where there was a dance. Martha said that she did not feel like dancing, half hoping that he would take this as a snub. But no, he seemed relieved, and said that in that case they would go and watch the others dancing, he much preferred watching, for dancing was an overrated amusement. Martha understood that she was provisionally forgiven. She was, however, in no mood to feel penitent.

On the way through the darkening streets, he asked in a falsely casual voice, "And so now you know all about the facts of life, you naughty girl, and I suppose you are pleased with yourself."

Martha felt that he wanted her to talk about the details of the affair; she felt repelled, and said sulkily that Stella had behaved disgracefully, and that he, Donovan, was a hypocrite. He was almost angry, but decided against it; after a quick look, he laughed, and said that she did not deserve a good friend like Stella. To this Martha maintained a strong dissenting silence, and looked out of the window.

She felt she should not have agreed to go to the Sports Club. On the other hand, there would have been something childish in refusing.

They reached the Club without having exchanged another word. The big room was cleared for the dance, but everyone was either down at McGrath's, having dinner, or in the bar. Donovan said they might as well fill themselves on sundowner snacks, there would be sandwiches later on, if they got hungry. Martha indifferently agreed. They sat in moody silence on the verandah, drinking brandy.

Soon a group of men came from the bar and joined them, greeting Martha with that stereotyped emotion. She realized that she had fallen from grace, but not disgraced, no, from this circle one could hardly be cast out; it depended on her to redeem herself, for her mere presence here was as good as a sign of penitence. She listened to their talk, and was astonished to find them discussing war. Not the Spanish war, nor the Chinese war, nor Mussolini's adventure in Abyssinia—these wars had had no existence, in this place. They were saying, devoutly, that things looked like trouble; they did not define this, for it meant what it would have meant to Mr. Quest—they would shortly be expected to defend the honour of Britain in some way or another. It would have been difficult for them to define it in any case; they never read anything but the newspapers, and the newspapers were still placating Hitler, while the word "Russia" was not so much the name of an enemy to be fought immediately (though of course it would be, one day) as it was a synonym for evil.

Soon, however, one of them said that if there was going to be a war, then there would be trouble with the niggers. His voice had that intense, obsessive note which means that the speaker desires a thing although he may be claiming the opposite. Martha found herself remarking belligerently that she did not see why there should be "trouble" with the natives; and the young men turned, rather startled, for they had forgotten there was a girl present. Their voices lowered to a sentimental level, and they assured her as one man that if there was, by God, the kaffirs would be taught a lesson, and there was nothing for *her* to worry about, and that was the truth.

Martha said coldly that there was certainly nothing for her to worry about, but there might be something for them to worry about unless—but at this point Donovan rose, looked at his watch, and said to Martha that if they wanted a nice table they'd better look for one now, before they were all filled.

She followed him, they settled themselves, and then he remarked, "You're in a most unpleasant mood, Matty dear."

She said that she was, and found herself telling him about the death of Abraham Cohen. Why? Did she expect him to sympathize?

Of course he replied grumpily that if people wanted to get mixed up with the Reds . . . Martha, who had apparently exhausted the possibilities of indignation with Mrs. Buss, shrugged and said sweetly that he was so well informed he left nothing to say.

Donovan did not react to this, because he did not notice sarcasm. He replied, "I told you before, Matty, that you can't possibly do better than me. Now, if you don't let yourself get carried away by another fascinating Jew-boy, then we might do quite well."

This astonished Martha into silence; she had not understood that he was proposing they should carry on as before; she was flattered, and at the same time she despised him. So she did not reply. They were in the half-dark of the verandah, where they could see into the dance room through the open door. She was being greeted by the people she knew, but in a muted, watchful way which reminded her again that she was on trial. Several wolves came up, yearned over her, and departed again; but it was not the same; this was the routine homage; she was no longer something special, she was being treated like the other girls, who had been currency in the Club for years. She realized this fully when Marnie Van Rensberg came onto the verandah wearing a bright floral evening dress, into which the projecting shelf of her breasts and her jutting hips were fitted like the slack bulging shapes of loosely filled grain sacks. Marnie smiled her good-natured, half-abashed smile, to a chorus of moans and whistles. She was the new girl, she was the fresh arrival, she had taken Martha's place, and this had nothing to do with her looks or her personality. Martha saw this, with a mixture of shame that she had ever been affected by the adulation, even slightly, and resentment that she could be deposed by a Marnie Van Rensberg.

This last feeling vanished in guilt as Marnie, giggling helplessly, which showed she was as little fitted to adjust herself to the atmosphere of the Club as Martha, came over to her, and said hurriedly, "Matty, man, so you're here, hey? They said you came here sometimes, and I didn't see you till just now."

Martha said she was glad Marnie was in town, and hoped she was enjoying herself. Mrs. Quest had said in a letter than the Van Rensbergs were furious with their daughter for taking a job suddenly in town, without consulting them, it was all a result of Martha's bad example. So Martha was prepared to join cause with her against the older generation.

But Marnie said indifferently she was having a fine time, and added, "Heard the news? I'm engaged!"

"Oh, that's nice," Martha said, and quickly added, "I'm very glad," when she saw Marnie disappointed at her lack of warmth. "Who to?"

She was unconsciously looking around the Club, trying to pick the man likely to be attracted to Marnie.

"No, Matty, I'm marrying a boy from home. I'm getting married in church next week."

Martha introduced her to Donovan, who was polite but cool. So she turned her back on Donovan, pressed Marnie down into a chair, and began talking about the district. The two girls said, "Do you remember . . . ?" for a few minutes, as if the district were years behind them, instead of weeks. But what they were really saying was a continuation of that childhood dialogue: Marnie was saying proudly that she had got herself a man, only to find this achievement losing glory under Martha's polite indifference. But they liked each other; while they made small talk, their eyes expressed regret—for what? That they could not be friends? Marnie said at last, with a giggle, that Billy sent his love, and then, hastily, that she must get back to her table. They clasped hands impulsively, then loosed them again as if there might be something wrong with this contact, and Marnie went back across the dance floor, blushing scarlet embarrassment in reply to the wolves' attentions.

"Did you hear, Matty dear? Andy and Patrick were rolling on the floor and biting each other, all for love of Marnie, only two weeks ago," said Donovan spitefully.

"What?" exclaimed Martha involuntarily, thinking of Marnie's graceless body.

"Yes, it's quite true. There was such a scandal! Just look at the sensation you girls make when you first come into town. And now you're a back number, Matty, and must make way for youth."

Martha could not help laughing, and for a little while they liked each other. But not for long.

At twelve o'clock the band stopped, for it was not a special dance; Adolph took up his violin, and played for about half an hour, his small gleaming smile fixed like hatred on his lips, while his eyes searched through the dancers: when they came in Martha's direction, she pretended not to see him. She felt guilty, and decided that she would write him that letter of apology next day. But when he had shaken his head for the last time, and climbed off the platform, there was no more music. Then Martha and Donovan, who had been thinking of going down to the Knave of Clubs with the crowd, saw groups forming themselves in a big circle around the dance floor. There was laughter.

"Come along, Matty," said Donovan hurriedly. "We're missing something."

They squeezed their way into the big circle. Everyone was laughing and watching Perry, who was doing his usual act—imitating an American Negro singing. He strummed an imaginary banjo, while he rolled up his eyes and jerked and splayed out his knees. It was funny, but he had done it often before, and it was not enough. So after a few minutes Perry let out a high quivering yell, which was immediately understood: he was no longer an American Negro, he was an African. But for this he could not be alone, he must be in a group, while the banjos and the melancholy sad wail from over the Atlantic were out of place. And soon a group of the wolves, headed by Perry, were stamping with bent knees, arms flexed and slightly held out, in a parody of a native war dance. "Hold him *down,* the Zulu warrior, Hold him *down,* the Zulu chief . . ." they grunted and sang, while the wide circle of people clapped accompaniment to the thudding feet.

Outside this circle of white-skinned people, the black waiters leaned at the doors or against the walls, looking on, and their faces were quite expressionless. And soon this new amusement worked itself out to boredom, and again the singing and stamping died away. Perry, the indefatigable, stood marking time, as it were, frowning thoughtfully, slightly jerking out his elbows, lifting his heels back alternately, humming under his breath, "Hold him *down* . . . boom-alaka, boomalaka . . ." He stopped and shouted to one of the waiters, "Hi, Shilling!"

The waiter thus indicated straightened a little, frowned, with a quick glance over his shoulder as if he wanted to escape, and then came towards Perry rather slowly.

"Come on, dance," said Perry. "Come on, man."

The man hesitated; he was smiling in an annoyed way; and then he shook his head and said good-naturedly, "No, baas, must work for the bar."

"Come on, come on," urged everyone, pressing around. It was all good-humoured and persuasive; they had narrowed to a small space, in which Perry and the black man stood. They were packed six deep, peering over each other's shoulders.

"War dance, war dance, come on," grunted Perry, hunching himself around on his heels, and levering out his elbows—all in an encouraging and paternal way. Then he stopped, took the waiter by one arm, urged him into the middle of the clear space, and stood back, clapping.

"No, baas," said the waiter again. Now he was annoyed, and intended to show it.

"Come on, man, I'm telling you," said Perry. "I'll lose my temper, I'm warning you."

So then the waiter, in a perfunctory and hurried way, began jerking his arms, and listlessly pounding his feet, while he let out a few grunts. And now Perry was annoyed. He shouted, "Come on, damn it, don't play the fool." He rolled his big body loosely into position, and demonstrated again, with his intense, emotional, self-absorbed parody of dancing, while the waiter remained silent, watching; and then, when Perry straightened himself out and waited, he made the same actions himself. It was not a parody of Perry, a mockery; he was simply trying to get the thing over as quickly as he could, and his eyes flickered worriedly over the heads of the white people to where his fellows stood, watching. Perry tried again; this time the waiter performed a mere sketch of the dance, hardly moving his feet. A girl laughed, on a high, foolish note.

"Come on, damn it," said Perry, frowning. He stood staring at the waiter as if he simply did not understand, while the man avoided his eyes. Then the blood rushed to Perry's face, and he muttered, "You damned black . . ." He had lost his temper completely.

The waiter shrugged, a controlled disdain, and walked towards the white wall of people, which divided instinctively to make way for him. He strolled through, and when he was near a door he suddenly broke into a run and vanished; he had been afraid.

"Gently, kid," said one of the girls maternally, clutching Perry's arm. "Don't lose your temper, it's not worth it, kid."

Perry stood breathing heavily, and even looked rather puzzled. "All I wanted was him to dance, that's all, for crying out loud," he said noisily, looking around him for appreciation and support. There were consoling murmurs from the girls. "That's all I asked, that's the bloody kaffirs all over, I ask him to dance and he gets cheeky." He looked towards the doors, but there was not a waiter in sight, they had all vanished.

And the white people were left unaccountably bad-tempered, and rather sorry for themselves. They drifted off in groups. Martha walked away with Donovan, who had not said a word. And it was not until they reached his car that he said coldly, in that well-bred, indifferent voice, "I suppose you're feeling sorry for the kaffir."

For a moment Martha was silent; what struck her was the deliberate way he said it, as if intending to provoke her. And the scene had made her very angry; also, which was worse, had made her afraid. What was terrible, she felt dimly, was the sentimental grievance of Perry and his friends: they really felt ill-used and misunderstood. It was like a madness.

"Not at all," she said, intending not to quarrel; but then she could not help adding, "I'm sorry for us, I think it's disgusting."

"I thought you would," said Donovan coldly.

They did not speak again for a few moments; they were both thinking of things to say.

"I suppose you thought it was a charming idea to ask him to sing 'Hold him *down,* the Zulu warrior,'" said Martha angrily, giving in to the silence; and she rather clumsily mimicked the pseudo-manly tone of the "hold him *down.*"

At once he said, "If you're not careful, Matty dear, you'll become a proper little nigger-lover."

At this she laughed in astonishment: it was his inevitable fatal false note. Now she had the advantage, and she went on: "Dear, dear *me,* how *awful,* isn't it, I should be such a naughty, *naughty* girl to have such wicked, unpopular opinions, and just *think* what people might *say!*"

And now he was furious, for she had minced out the sentence with a really unpleasant parody of his mannerisms. She had wounded him in his vanity, and so it was no longer a question of her opinion or his. They drove for a block or so in silence, while she waited for the thunderbolt to fall. She glanced at him nervously, wondering why he was so silent, but he frowned blackly, his face averted.

Then he said, "Well, Matty, we don't seem to do together at all, do we, I'm simply not broadminded enough for your Jews and your niggers."

And now she was very angry. She said, "You needn't flatter yourself you have a mind at all." It sounded so childish, she would have recalled it, if she could, in favour of something calm and dignified. But it was too late.

The moment the car stopped, she jumped out, and went to her room, without even looking at him. She was furious with herself; alas, with what self-command do we conduct these arguments in imagination!

"Well," she said finally, in a mood of wild elation, "that's over, I'm finished with *that.*"

And what she meant was, she was finished with the Sports Club, and everything it stood for.

2

Martha was again solitary, for a few days. She told herself it was only February, to still her extraordinary panic; she was so restless she could hardly bear to sleep; she would start awake after an hour's light doze, feeling that life was escaping her, that there was something urgent she should be doing. She flung herself into work at the office, which all at once seemed easy instead of tedious; she studied at the Polytechnic with all her concentration, and was commended by Mr. Skye. Afterwards, avoiding speaking to anyone, she walked home to her room through the park. There was a drought; the sun shone steadily all day, the sky was strong and blue, there was a smell of dust. (On the farm, the scents and wet heat of the jungle had vanished, and the grass was yellowing.) She tried to read, and could not. While the darkness settled over the town, she stood at her door, listening. For, night after night, music came from across the park, from down the street, from the hotel half a dozen blocks away: the whole town was dancing. The dance music flowed from all over the town, like water throbbing from dark sources, to mingle in a sound that was not music but could be felt along the nerves like the convulsive beating of a vast pulse. And there stood Martha at her doorway, carefully keeping out of sight behind the soiled lace curtain, watching the cars pass and hoping that none would stop, for she feared being dragged back to the compulsion of pleasure, saying that she should be studying—but what?—and feeling like a waif locked out of a party; she was missing something vitally sweet.

During those few days she made various inconclusive attempts to escape. At a sundowner party weeks before, she had met a young woman who dressed windows for one of the big stores. Martha, buoyed as usual by the conviction that there was nothing she could not do, given the opportunity, sought out this young woman, and went to interview a certain Mr. Baker, who owned the biggest store in town, offering herself as a potential window dresser. Mr. Baker, far from being discouraged, seemed to approve; and it was not until the unpleasant subject of money was approached that Martha realized she was being engaged for the sum of five pounds a month, which, Mr. Baker blandly assured her, was the salary all his girls were first employed at. Martha asked naïvely how it was possible to live on it. The gentleman replied that his work girls lived at home, or, if this were not possible, he arranged for them to live in a certain well-known hostel. Now, Martha knew this hostel was run on charity, and that Mr. Baker was a town councillor, a very influential person. She was young enough to be surprised and shocked that he should get his labour cheap by such methods. Mr. Baker, who had imagined that he was on the point of getting a young and attractive girl "of a good type" (this was his particular euphemism for the uncomfortable word "middle-class") for five pounds a month, was astounded to find this same apparently mild and amenable person suddenly half inarticulate with fury, informing him in short and angry jerks that

he ought to be ashamed of himself. Mr. Baker at once grasped the
situation, said to himself that this spirit could be useful if properly
handled, and, in the suave and reasonable voice of an experienced
handler of labour, began handling her. He said her views did her
credit, but that she was mistaken. His salesgirls were contented and
happy—why, they stayed with him for years! After all, if one was
training to become a servant of the public, one expected to pay for
that training: if Martha was going to be a doctor, for instance, she
would have to spend thousands on it, whereas he was offering to *pay*
her (though admittedly not enough to live on) to learn a skilled job.
Surely Miss Quest was reasonable enough to . . . Martha could not
stand up to this urbanity. She collapsed, not into agreement, but into
a stubborn silence, trying to find reasonable words to express her
anger. Why, it was only last week that Mr. Baker had made a compassionate speech appealing for public money to support the hostel
"for those unfortunate girls at the mercy of . . . ." She could not
speak, but she abruptly left, slamming the door, only to collapse immediately afterwards into a most familiar rage at herself for her in-
effectiveness.

She paid a second visit to the *Zambesia News*. Mr. Spur was delighted to see her. She was cool, like an acquaintance, though one
day she would remember with gratitude that it was in his library she
had first heard the words, "Yes, my child, you must read. You must
read everything that comes your way. It doesn't matter what you
read at first, later you'll learn discrimination. Schools are no good,
Matty, you learn nothing at school. If you want to be anything, you
must educate yourself." But that remark had been addressed to a
child, whose affectionate admiration she now entirely disowned. She
was, however, troubled by a vague feeling of indebtedness.

Mr. Spur said that since her shorthand was now passable, and her
typing fast, if inaccurate, she could certainly have a job with the
woman's page. But—how it happened she did not know—she found
herself arguing with half-inarticulate anger about the capitalist press.
The *Zambesia News* was a disgrace, she said; why didn't it print the
truth about what was happening in Europe? Mr. Spur said, half annoyed, that the truth was always a matter of opinion; and then, controlling himself, said with the humorous gentleness of old age that
on the woman's page she would be corrupting no one.

"The *woman's* page!" said Martha indignantly.

It was only afterwards that it occurred to her that he might perhaps have enquired, "Why do you come asking for a job when you
despise the paper so thoroughly?" But there was only one paper; if

she was going to be a journalist, then she would have to make use of it.

She went back home, and dreamed of herself as a journalist, as a window-dresser, applied for a job as chauffeur to a rich old lady, and was thankful when she was turned down, on the grounds of her youth. She decided she would become an inspired shorthand writer, like Mr. Skye; and answered an advertisement to help a mother across the sea to England with her three young children. This woman, a rather supercilious middle-class female whom Martha instinctively loathed, asked Martha if she liked children. Martha said frankly that no, she did not, but she wanted to go to England. The woman laughed, and there was a moment of indecision, which was ended when the lady noticed her husband's eyes resting on Martha with rather too much appreciation. Martha was naïve enough to think she had lost this opportunity because of her clumsy answer, and once again made resolutions, in privacy, to control her tongue, to behave sensibly.

But she was still working at Robinson's; she was, in fact, neither a journalist, a chauffeur, a shorthand writer, nor on her way to England.

For a few days then she dreamed of herself as a writer. She would be a free lance. She wrote poems, lying on the floor of her room; an article on the monopoly press; and a short story about a young girl who . . . This story was called "Revolt." She despatched these to the *Zambesia News*, to the *New Statesman* and to the *Observer*, convinced that all three would be accepted.

She remembered that as a child she had had a talent for drawing. She made a sketch there and then of the view of the park from her door; it really wasn't too bad at all. But the difficulty with being a painter is that one must have equipment. Ah, the many thousands of hopeful young writers there are, for no better reason than that a pencil and writing pad take up less room than an easel, paints, and drawing boards, besides being so much less expensive.

Martha, then, would be a writer: it came to her like a revelation. If others, then why not herself? And how was she to know that one may live in London, or New York, a village in Yorkshire, or a dorp in the backveld, one may imagine oneself as altogether unique and extraordinary (so powerfully does that pulse towards adventure beat), but one behaves inevitably, inexorably, exactly like everyone else. How was she to suspect that at least a hundred young people in the same small town stuck in the middle of Africa, kept desks full of poems, articles and stories, were convinced that *if only* . . . then they could be writers, they could escape into glorious freedom and untrammelled individuality—and for no better reason than that they could not face the prospect of a lifetime behind a desk in Robinson, Daniel and Cohen.

Almost immediately, the article on the monopoly press was returned from the *Zambesia News,* and the rejection slip dismayed Martha so much that she let the idea of being a free-lance writer slip away.

And all the time that she dreamed with a fierce hunger of escape, of doing something vital and important, the other secret pulse was beating. There she stood, behind the curtain listening to the slow throbbing of the dance music, and wanted only to dance, dance all night; not at the Sports Club, but with some group of young people who were faceless, almost bodiless, imagined as a delicate embodiment of the dance music itself.

About ten days after she had quarrelled with Donovan, she was telephoned at the office by Perry, to ask if she were free the following evening, for there was a visiting team of cricketers from England; would she like to be one of the girls?

Martha refused. She was now finally sickened by her own inconsistency—so she said, as she proudly put down the receiver, suppressing a surge of longing and regret that she was wilfully refusing an evening of delicious pleasure. Nonsense, she told herself, it would not be pleasure, she would be bored. The thought that remained in her mind was that she was now casually rung up to fill in—to be "one of the girls."

That evening, however, there was a letter from her mother. She picked it up gingerly. She was accustomed to reading the first paragraph of a letter from home and then flinging it, in a crumpled mess of paper, into the wastepaper basket.

My Darling Girl,

I sent Sixpence in to the post this afternoon, expecting a letter from you, and there wasn't. It really is unfair of you, I've not heard for a week, and you know how worried Daddy gets over you, he can't sleep at night worrying about you, and besides, we cannot afford to send boys in like this, and I've only got three now, I sacked Daniel for stealing, I missed my pearl brooch and I know he took it, but of course he denied it, though I sent for the police, and they gave him a good hiding, and they searched his hut, I expect he's hidden it in the thatch, so I have a lot of work to do, my new cook can't even boil an egg, they really are an ignorant lot, and so it's not fair of you to make me send in the boy for nothing.

I had a letter from Mrs. Anderson, she told me she hasn't seen you,

I wrote to her asking about you, since you never say anything, and if you've quarrelled with Donovan, I do think you might have told me, because it puts me in a false position with his mother. She seemed to think you might marry, she was pleased, though of course you are too young, but he's such a nice boy, one can see that, and of course there's money there too . . .

Martha threw away the letter; there were twelve pages of it, crossed and recrossed like the letters one reads of in Victorian novels —the letters of leisure. But as the crumpled ball flew across the room and landed rather short of the wastepaper basket, a postscript written in darker ink caught her eye, and in unwilling curiosity she went to pick it up.

I found my brooch this morning, it fell into a flour sack in the storeroom. But he's a thief in any case, I know he took my silver spoon, though of course he said he didn't. They're all thieves, every one, and the trouble with you Fabians is that you're all theory and no practice. One has to know how to handle kaffirs. The *Zambesia News* said last week the Fabians in England were complaining in Parliament again about how we treat *our* niggers! ! ! ! I'd like to get a few of them here, and then they'd see how filthy and dirty and disgusting they all are, and thieves and liars every one, and can't even cook, and then they'd change their tune! ! ! !

The effect of this letter on Martha was hardly reasonable. After half an hour of violent anger, a feeling of being caged and imprisoned, she went to the telephone, rang the Sports Club, asked for Perry, and told him she would be delighted to help entertain the visiting cricketers tomorrow.

3

In the event, the visiting sportsmen seemed disinclined to make much use of the girls provided for them.

The dance was held at McGrath's. The big dining room now showed its oblong of bare boards, for the tables were pushed back against the wall, their stained brown surfaces showing faded rings from wet glasses. The musicians were on the platform in their bower of ferns and potted shrubs. The tables in this room were mostly occupied by the young married crowd, while the cricketers, with the Sports Club men and the girls, were in the lounge, around a long improvised table that stretched almost from wall to wall of the enormous room. But the cricketers drifted off to the bar and remained there, and the girls, who were after all not forced by any pressure from statistics into being good-natured wallflowers, soon drifted off in the arms of the local men, who had come prepared to remain womanless for the evening. Martha danced when she was asked, and quite late in the evening returned to the table to find that half a dozen or so of the cricketers were now seated at the table, for the girls had become absorbed elsewhere. They did not seem to mind, they were drinking and talking and looking at their watches, though one of them rose and asked Martha to dance. She tried to talk, but found it difficult, and, being the prig that she was, was disgusted that people whose names were commonplaces in the news, idols of England, talked of by the Sports Club crowd with reverence, were like schoolboys in conversation. She was surprised, in short, that athletes were not intellectual, for somewhere within her was still a notion that famous people must necessarily be brilliant in every way. Besides, only that morning the *Zambesia News* had devoted three columns to the opinions of the captain of the team: the international situation, he said, was uncertain, but if sportsmen of all countries could play together regularly, unhindered by their governments, peace would be assured; all day businessmen, Rotary members, and civil servants had been quoting this judgment with approval and saying, Yes, he must be a fine chap.

Martha danced with this same man later, and was piqued that he was as bored as she—or rather, his attitude was so different from the Colonial men that she at first thought he was bored. She was accustomed to wait for attentive appreciation, while he, it seemed, wanted her to flatter him. When the dance was over, she sat down, shaking her head at an invitation to dance again, and reminded herself that "millions of women" would envy her, but was unable to find pleasure in the thought. For McGrath's was ugly, the band was bad, and though she was drinking steadily as usual, her brain was critically alert. She wished herself back in bed. At the same time, she observed herself chatting brightly, her face stretched in a smile, just like the few other girls who remained; and when a pert "amusing" remark ended unexpectedly in a yawn, she shook herself irritably into attention, and rearranged the smile.

Maisie, who happened to be there, remarked in that indolent voice, "Ohh, our Matty's been having too many late nights." This was offered to general entertainment, and received with laughter, while Maisie was teased about her own popularity. Through this she smiled sleepily, and then she said in a low voice to Martha, "For crying out loud, these English boys give me the pip, they're so stuck-up, you'd think they were doing us a favour." She then got up to dance with one of them, offering herself to him with a meekly submissive movement of her body as she slid into his arms, while her eyes drooped upwards in attentive silence. Over his shoulder she winked at Martha, which lit her face into spiteful but resigned mockery. She was danced away, the very image of a willing and admiring maiden.

It was at this point that Martha found herself addressed by the routine "Hullo, beautiful, why haven't we met before?" She got up to dance, the responsive smile already arranged in her eyes. She saw that this was a young man she had seen occasionally at the Club. His name was Douglas Knowell, which inevitably became Know-all. He was a cheerful, grinning young man, of middle height, rather round than lean, with a round fleshy face, light-blue eyes, a nose that would have been well shaped had it not been flattened by an accident of sport, and palish hair plastered with water into a dull sodden mat. He bounced rather than danced Martha around the room, and from time to time let out a yell of triumph, while Martha automatically soothed and admonished him into civilized behaviour.

"Who are you?" she asked at last flirtatiously, and he said, "Ah, that's asking, but I know who you are."

"Then you have the advantage," she said, wanting him to tell her his name, for she was perhaps a little piqued that he had not made any attempt to get to know her before.

"Adam," he said, twinkling his blue eyes at her in a consciously merry look; and Martha glanced at him, startled, for this was more literary than one might expect from a wolf, and she knew that he was one of the senior members of the pack: he had helped Binkie start the Club, so she had been told.

"What a pity I can't be Eve, since you know my name," she said, and instinctively dropped, without knowing it, the maternal note from her voice.

"Oh, but you can be Eve, you are," he shouted, drawing her closer, in his reckless bouncing dance around the room.

When the band stopped playing, Martha was startled that it was so late; she had enjoyed herself. Douglas told her it was a matter of luck he had come at all, he had not been going out much recently. "So I'm in luck, because you are rather-rather a fine," he said, with a beaming pressure from his eyes.

"I'm what?" she asked, startled.

"You're really a fine," he said again, using the adjective as a noun, which was a trick of his, as was his way of isolating each word as if considering it, so that his slangy speech had a curious effect of pedantry.

She asked him why he had not been going out, why he was so seldom at the Club, and he replied, quite in the code of the pack, that he was studying for an exam, and besides, he was on the tack.

Habit almost made Martha approve, "That's the ticket, kid, that's the style," but instead she asked bluntly, "Why, do you drink too much?"

He replied seriously that now he was too old for rugger, he was not as fit as he had been, he must keep his weight down, and besides, the doctor said he was getting an ulcer. Now, most of the men at the Club had stomach ulcers, and they all spoke of it in this same way, a protective way; they said, "No, that's not my line, I can't eat that," or "My ulcer won't allow me that," like a mother crooning over a baby. They addressed that part of themselves which was the ulcer as if promising to protect and look after it. They sounded proud of it.

She said flippantly, "Having ulcers is positively an occupational disease of a wolf."

"What's that?" he demanded quickly, ready to be offended; then he laughed and repeated, smiling with his eyes, "Yes, you-you are really-really rather a fine." And now Martha noted that stammer which was no stammer, not a nervous thing, but a trick of speech.

But she liked him, she was warmed by him; she went home looking forward to having tea with him next day. "Having tea," too, was exciting. One did not "have tea" with a wolf, it was a meal that had no social place in their lives. Douglas was already appearing to her as something new and rare, he was so different from the Sports Club men!

And so they ate strawberries and cream at McGrath's, and she insisted on paying for her own, for he had said casually he had sold his car, he could not afford it. If one could not afford a car, that was a confession of poverty indeed; for a reliable secondhand car could be bought at twenty-five pounds, and the most junior clerk owned one as a matter of course. Martha pitied him for this cheerful confession, and wondered at what must be a romantic reason for it, because he was fairly high in his department; at his level in the Service, one was not poor. But all this was confused in her mind, she was always vague about money; all she felt was a pitying admiration; and after tea, when he asked her to walk with him to the office, as he intended to work late, she went willingly.

When they reached the big block of Government offices, it was natural she should go in with him. His office was a large and airy room overlooking the tree-lined avenue. She wandered around it, trying to be interested in calculating machines and the other appurtenances of finance; for she always felt an instinctive revulsion when confronted with what she still referred to as arithmetic. In fact, it chilled her so much that she was wondering if she might politely take her leave, when she caught sight of a magazine lying on the desk, and darted forward to pick it up, exclaiming, "You didn't tell me you took the *New Statesman!*" She might have been saying, "Why, we are members of the same brotherhood!"

"Yes, I do take it, it's a fine-fine paper," he said.

She looked at him with wide and delighted eyes; she even unconsciously went across to him and took his hand. "Well," she said inarticulately, "how nice, well, then . . ." Suddenly she saw herself behaving thus, and flushed, and dropped his hand, moving away. "All the same," she said resentfully, "it's nice to meet someone who— In the Club, everyone is practically mentally deficient!"

He laughed with pleasure at this sincere flattery, and they began to talk, testing each other's opinions. Or rather, Martha flung down her opinions like gauges, and waited for him to pick them up; and when she said aggressively that she thought the natives were shockingly underpaid, and waited for him to say, "It's no good spoiling kaffirs, they don't understand kindness," and he said instead; "Oh, yes, it would be desirable if there were a change of policy," she gave a large, grateful sigh, and relapsed into the silence of one who has at last come home. But it was an expectant silence. It seemed to her that now their friendship was on an altogether new plane; and when he said, "I ought to be doing some work," she exclaimed, as if he were insulting their friendship, "Oh, no, you must come home with me to my room, I've just got a new parcel of books from England, I wired for them."

And so he went with her, not so much surprised as bewildered. For Martha had all at once turned into something quite different. She would have been indignant had anyone told her that weeks of the Sports Club atmosphere had altered her manner. Martha Quest, at McGrath's or at a dance at the Club, was either a bored, sullen, critical young woman with a forced smile or a chattering ninny with a high and affected laugh. Now her acquired manner dropped from her, and she could be natural. She was herself.

"Herself," in her room, making him tea, and then sitting on the floor with the new books spread out all around her, was completely childlike. Her hair fell out of the careful loose waves and was pushed hastily back, her eyes were bright and fixed on his with a delighted wonder; she talked quickly, as if the shock of finding a fellow spirit was so exquisite that she could not hurry fast enough to the next confirmation of it. She was altogether confiding and trustful. Not to tell him *everything* would have been a betrayal of their relationship; she

felt as if she had known him forever; the world was suddenly beautiful, and the future full of promise.

And it was the future they spoke of; for she found he was as dissatisfied as herself with the present. He wanted to go to England, he
said; he had plans, too, to live in the South of France and become a
wine farmer. That would be the life; one could live cheaply and be
free, and his father had been a farmer: he wanted to get back to the
soil.

She urged him to describe these plans in more detail, but since
they were still hazy, she made them for him. He must borrow a little
money, enough to get over there—fifty pounds would be enough,
living was so cheap in France, everyone said, all one had to do was
to get there, and then life would begin.

It was midnight when he said he must leave; which he did reluctantly. A serious, responsible young man, he seemed to Martha,
with his warm and approving blue eyes, and that touch of hesitation
in his speech, which made everything he said so deliberate, so considered.

Martha told herself fiercely that he was a man, at least, and not a
silly little boy. And so intelligent too! She slept that night deeply
and dreamlessly, for the first time in weeks; she did not start up, half
a dozen times, with the feeling that there was something she ought
to be doing, if she only knew what it was; she woke on a delicious
wave of anticipation, the day beckoning to her like a promise. But
she did not say she was in love. For of course, she was going to have
a career. Besides, when she said, "He's a man, at least," that "at
least" was by no means rhetorical. She was still capable of being
critical. For several days they were together all their leisure time,
and she looked surreptitiously at him, with a feeling of disloyalty,
and the round, rather low forehead struck her unpleasantly—there
was something mean about it, something commonplace; the shallow
dry lines across it affected her; as for his hands, they were large and
clumsy, rather red, heavily freckled, and covered with hair. Soon she
averted her eyes from his hands, she did not see them; she did not
see his forehead, with those unaccountably unpleasant lines, like the
lines of worry on an elderly face. She saw his eyes, the approving and
warm blue eyes. She had never known this easy warm friendliness
with anyone before; she could say what she liked; she felt altogether
approved, and she expanded in it delightedly, and her manner lost its
half-timid aggressiveness.

Also, he was so sensible! When she told him, making a funny story
of it, how she had nearly gone to England as a nursemaid, he listened
seriously, and said she should not go to England without being sure

of something to go to; and that it was "ill-advised" to become a chauffeur, because the job had no prospects; while at her remark that she thought of becoming a free-lance writer, he produced all kinds of practical objections, the least of which was the question of talent, for it seemed he had once had the same notion himself, had "gone into the question from every angle," in fact. He found a folder packed with sketches she had made of the wardrobe, the flowers in the garden, and evolved a most sensible plan. She should take a course in commercial art at the Polytechnic, and then she would be equipped to move from country to country as she liked. And Martha caught at this with enthusiasm, the idea gripped her completely for a couple of evenings. Then she began to condemn herself bitterly, as usual, for indecision; a creeping reluctance came over her at the mere idea of two or three years' serious study. But what she was thinking involuntarily was, What's the use of it?—meaning the war. "Two years?" she murmured, looking at him evasively. That knowledge of urgency was in her, stronger than ever. Unconsciously, the coming war was there, before her, like a dark chasm in her spirit. And when he said, "Well, two years isn't long," she laughed suddenly, and the maternal note was back in her voice, so that they both felt uncomfortable. It was a discord in their relationship. And they continued to talk, like two children at college, about growing grapes in France, or going to America, delightedly planning half a dozen different careers at once.

And this continued for what seemed to be a long time, though it was not much more than a week. And then one evening they had returned from the pictures, and were walking slowly towards his room under the long canopies of heavy leafage, and she was telling him, for some reason, about Perry, and how he had flung out of her room "in a rage," as she explained laughing. Douglas exclaimed, "You really are rather-rather a fine . . ." and kissed her. This was no romantic kiss, but more a friendly and companionable one; they clung together, and what she was most conscious of was the warmth of his arm against her back. And then she was flung into dismay because he broke away with a sigh, and muttered, frowning, "I shouldn't . . ." He walked on a few steps, and the boyish face was troubled, his eyes clouded.

"Why ever not?" she demanded, laughing, running up to overtake him, for now she felt that of course, since he had kissed her, he had in some way claimed her, and they would make love.

He looked embarrassed, so that she gave an uncomfortable laugh. She was offended.

"I—well—I . . ." He looked away, his face clenched in indecision;

then he again turned to her, and kissed her, muttering, "Oh, to hell with it, let them all go to hell." She hardly heard this; she was now possessed by a fierce determination not to be deprived of what was her right. He had kissed her, that was enough.

They reached his room locked together, their steps lagging, and he did not switch on the light. He took her to the bed, and they lay on it. He began to kiss her, caressing her arms and her breasts with a hard and trembling hand. She was ready to abandon herself, but he continued to kiss her, murmuring how beautiful she was. Then he smoothed her skirt up to her knee, and stroked her legs, saying over and over again, in a voice troubled by something that sounded like grief, that her legs were so lovely, she was so lovely. Her drowning brain steadied, for she was being forced back to consciousness. She saw herself lying there half exposed on the bed; and half resentfully, half wearily partook, as he was demanding of her, in the feast of her own beauty. Yes, her legs were beautiful; yes, she felt with delight (as if her own hands were moulding them), her arms were beautiful. Yes, but this is not what I want, she thought confusedly; she was resenting, most passionately, without knowing that she resented it, his self-absorbed adoration of her, and the way he insisted, Look at yourself, aren't you beautiful? Then he raised himself and pulled back the curtains. Immediately the trees in the street outside lifted themselves in moonlight, moonlight and yellow street light fell over the bed in an unreal flood of glamour, and in this weird light her bronze legs, her tumbled skirt, her loosely lying brown arms, lay like a statue's. He pulled aside her dress, and fell in an ecstasy of humble adoration on her breasts, cupping them in his hands and exclaiming how they were so sweet. During this rite, she remained passive, offering herself to his adoration; she was quite excluded; she was conscious of every line and curve of her own body, as if she were scrutinizing it with his eyes. And for hours, or so it seemed, he kissed and adored, pressing his body humbly against her and withdrawing it, and she waited for him to sate his visual passion and allow her to forget the weight of her limbs, her body, felt as something heavy and white and cold, separate from herself. At last, her spirit cold and hostile, she said she must go home, and sat up brusquely, jumping off the bed. He came to her and helped her button up her dress, still self-absorbed in his fervent rite of adoration.

"How sad-sad to shut them away," he said, closing the material over her breasts, and she felt as if they were burying a corpse. She thought angrily, *Them*—just as if they had nothing to do with me! Yet as she crossed in front of a mirror, she glanced in, from habit, and straightened herself, so that the lines of her body might approximate to those laid down by the idea of what is desirable. She settled her shoulders, so that her breasts, *they,* should stand out; and, with a rather impatient movement, she walked away from Douglas, who followed her meekly. But when they reached the gate and were ready to walk down the road, some kind of guilt, like a tenderness, made her slide obediently into the curve of his arm.

The moon stood high and cold, above a flood of stars, the trees glittered off a greenish light, the street shone like white sand. Suddenly she heard him say, in a different, half-sniggering voice, which struck her apprehensive with shock, "I-I can't-can't walk." He gave her a guilty, aggressive glance, and laughed. "Never-never mind," he said, still laughing suggestively. "But that-that was rather-rather a strain."

She did not understand him. She looked at him, bewildered. Also, she was disgusted and impatient. Her own body was aching, even her shoulders ached, and her breasts felt arrogant and chilled. But she was bound to love him, that claim had been laid on her. Yet she resented him so terribly, at that moment, she could not look at him. She was remembering Perry. She was wishing that men were not like this. She did not know, clearly, what she wished; all she knew was that she ached, body and spirit, and hated him. She walked silently down the moonlit street, looking ahead of her.

He said unexpectedly, without stammering, "I ought to tell you that I'm engaged to a girl in England."

Martha stared at him. She thought scornfully, How conventional. She despised him even more. She shrugged, as if to say, "What of it?" The girl in England seemed remote, quite irrelevant. At the same time, she felt all at once deprived and lost and unhappy, a flood of unhappiness came into her, so that, watching it from outside, as it were, she said irritably of herself, What's the sense of *that?*

To him she said sarcastically, "I suppose now you think everything's all right, you can say to her quite truthfully that you've been faithful."

He laughed uncomfortably, pressed her arm to his side with a quick, nervous squeeze, and said, "No—no, I didn't think, I was waiting all the time for you . . ."

"Waiting?" she asked, again at sea. Then she shrugged again. She said to herself, Oh, to hell with him. What she meant was, To hell with men.

When they reached her home, she nervously said good night, and turned to go in. But her coldness troubled him; he stopped her, holding her irresolutely for a moment. Then he said inarticulately again, "Oh, hell with it," and came in with her.

She thought, amazed, Surely he's not going to make love to me *now?* For it seemed quite outrageous, even insulting, that he should. The moment had passed. But he did. She acknowledged to herself that this was quite different, not at all the same thing as with Adolph. Then she suppressed the disloyal thought. Afterwards he remarked, with a proud, shy laugh, "You're the first girl I've made love to."

"*What!*" she exclaimed indignantly. She felt furious. She suppressed that too.

"Well, there was a prostitute in Cape Town, but I was drunk and . . ."

The prostitute seemed neither here nor there. "How old are you?" she asked bluntly.

"Thirty."

She digested this information silently. She was shocked. But it was not so easy to be shocked, for that claim on her was so strong. She stroked his head, acknowledging the claim, and thought uneasily that he had been messing about with the Sports Club girls for years. It was so unpleasant, she immediately forgot the fact. Then, like a ribald and mocking spirit housed somewhere disconcertingly within her, the thought arose: Gallantly preserving himself for the *right* girl! How touching. How disgusting! She tried to shut a lid on this disconcerting spirit, and succeeded, but not before it had said derisively, in a pious voice, Keeping himself clean for his wife. She turned towards him, and began caressing his head and hair in a passion of tenderness.

After a while she told him about Adolph. Now, this was no confession, but a statement of fact. And whatever Douglas might naturally have been inclined to do, such as forgive her, for instance, was put on one side, for if one has a relationship with a girl based on an assumption that one is in all things free and unprejudiced, and she remarks, taking it for granted that it has nothing to do with you, that she is not chaste, and it is to her a matter of no importance one way or the other, then a man can hardly do otherwise than conform. Douglas accepted the statement, in the spirit in which it was offered. Soon he was comforting her; Martha was sitting up in bed, her voice wrung with anguish, saying, "I can't understand how I behaved so terribly, I can't bear to think of it." He understood she did not mean sleeping with Adolph, she was ashamed because of something else. He comforted her, though it was not clear to him what it was all about. Finally he said, "Well, I know old Stella, she's a good sort, she's a good kid, she meant well." Martha did not reply, she withdrew from him into that glacial region where it seemed he was hardly worth criticizing. Soon he kissed her, and went home.

In the morning Mrs. Gunn was acidly correct, but Martha no longer cared about Mrs. Gunn. She was extremely depressed.

After work that day, Douglas waited for her, and took her to his room at once, saying that it was necessary for them to discuss a certain matter. She had not seen the room by daylight. It was quite large, an ordinary furnished room, with cretonne-covered chairs, a cretonne-covered daybed, coconut matting on the red cement floor. There was a writing table against one wall, however, and this was piled with ledgers and files from the office. She admired this, her respect for him was instantly restored. She was seeing him again as a sober, responsible man to whom she could defer.

He remarked nervously that he was in a hell of a fix. He moved around the room, stopping for a moment at the window, staring out of it, returning to the desk to finger a ledger or pick up a ruler. Martha watched him move, and what she felt was, This won't last long. She meant that her will was set hard on his saying he would give up the girl in England. It was remarkable that it had never entered her head to feel guilty about the girl in England; no, Martha was in the right, the other girl was the interloper. If someone had asked her, just then, if she wanted to marry Douglas, she would have exclaimed in horror that she would rather die. But she sat there quietly, her face troubled and her eyes thoughtful, and at the same time every line of her body expressed quiet, set determination.

As for Douglas, he looked altogether like a rather worried boy. He wore an old pair of flannel trousers, a white shirt rolled up at the sleeves and open at the neck. There was a fresh cleanliness about him. Martha was already feeling maternal. She sat and waited.

He began to talk, in an absorbed, troubled way. He was talking to himself, trying to present the problem to himself, as it were, with Martha as passive audience. He said he had met the girl in Cape Town. She had been on holiday there with her aunt. "Come out to get herself a husband in the colonies," Martha thought scornfully. He had taken her out several times. Then his leave was finished, and she returned to England, and he to his home town. Then, afterwards, he had written to England, asking her to marry him.

"You mean you *wrote*—you got engaged by *post?*" asked Martha in a scandalized voice.

"Yes. Yes. She was ever such a fine. She was such a sweet." He half stammered, looking as bewildered as she. "I told her," he added, suddenly quite firm, and speaking without a suggestion of hesitation, "that we could not marry yet, I can't afford it, we must wait two or three years."

She was silent. Again she was wondering why he was so poor. She asked hesitantly, not wanting to "interfere," "Why are you—I mean, why couldn't you marry?"

"Well, the Sports Club racket is a helluva expensive. You can't save money if you're in the Club much."

"Do you owe money?"

"No, I don't owe-owe money. But I thought, if I was going to marry, I ought to offer her a proper home." This last was said as if quoted.

She shrugged, dismissing the question of money. She felt there was some kind of discrepancy, but could not be bothered to think it over. What does money matter? she thought dimly.

He came to her helplessly, saying appealingly, "I don't-don't know, Matty."

She comforted him. Soon they made love. Physically it was a fiasco, which only made her more tender. By the end of the evening, it was decided they would marry. When she went home, she walked with calm angry contempt into the back verandah, informed a silent and critical Mrs. Gunn that she was going to get married, and turned on her heel and went out before there could be any reply. She then sat down and wrote to her parents that she was marrying "a man in the civil service," that they would be married in ten days, and she would bring him out to the farm "for inspection" the following weekend. "It went without saying" that they would marry at a registry office.

On the following morning she woke in a panic. She told herself she was mad, or rather, had been, for now she was quite sane. She did not want to marry Douglas, she did not want to marry at all. With a cold, disparaging eye, she looked at the image of Douglas and shuddered. She told herself that she would ring him from the office and tell him they had both made a terrible mistake. Calm descended on her, and she went to the office, spiritually free once again. In this mood she walked into the office, and was greeted by congratulations.

"But how do you know?" she asked, annoyed; although warmth was already rising in her, in answer to the spontaneous pleasure on every face.

It appeared Maisie had telephoned Mrs. Buss from the office where she now worked.

"But how did Maisie know?" enquired a completely bewildered Martha.

"She said your—your fiancé was up at the Club last night, he was giving it a real bang, he's off the tack again."

Martha nodded, and began taking the cover off her typewriter, to give herself time. Douglas had taken her home at midnight. He had then gone up to the Club? She could imagine the scene only too vividly; and disgust and anger, heightened by a sickly, unwelcome excitement, began plucking at her nerves.

The telephone rang for Martha. It was Maisie, being calmly, amusedly informative. Having congratulated Martha on "hooking Douggie—no one ever thought Douggie'd get hooked," she went on to say that the wolves had practically wrecked the town, they'd torn up the whole place. There was a chamberpot on the statue of Cecil Rhodes that morning, and all the lampposts were slashed with red paint. Perry, Binkie and Douglas had spent the hours between four and seven not in a prison cell, which was hardly fitting for people of their standing, but drinking brandy with the policeman on duty at the charge office. They had been fined ten shillings each, and presumably were now back administering the affairs of the nation.

"Douglas was *with* them?" said Martha, dumbfounded.

"You're telling me he was with them, you haven't seen our Douggie when he gets going."

Martha put down the telephone, and found Mr. Robinson waiting to congratulate her. There followed Mr. Max Cohen. Both shook her hand, smiling with an altogether new emphasis, like those welcoming a new member. (But of what?) She understood, however, that she had done well for herself. That was implicit in every smile, every gesture, every inflection of their voices. Mr. Robinson smiled continually, the same eager, interested, rather wistful smile that Martha was to see on every face for the next few weeks. He said, "Your young man has just telephoned me. Off with you and enjoy yourself. You only get married once—or so I hope," he added, with a glance at his girls, and they laughed dutifully.

Martha lingered in the cloakroom, powdering her face, while she tried to examine the idea that she was doing well for herself. It made no sense to her. And in any case, of course it didn't matter. So she went downstairs, and found Douglas on the pavement. He was transformed. Martha felt a disgust at the first glance, which she immediately banished. He was red-eyed, his plump cheeks were darkened with stubble, his clothes were crumpled.

"Come on," he cried, "we'll give it a bang." He gave a whoop, standing there on the pavement, so that people turned around and smiled: it appeared that everyone in the city knew. "I haven't been in bed yet," he said triumphantly; and she laughed, even while she felt a stab of irritation at the self-satisfied look on his face.

Martha found herself being led to the Mathews' flat. She hung back, protesting. But it appeared that Stella had known Douggie for years, they were the greatest of friends, Stella had rung Douggie at nine that morning to ask the happy couple to lunch.

In the flat, Stella took Martha into a warm embrace, her eyes shone with tender emotion, and even tears; she murmured, "I'm so glad, Matty dear. Now everything's all right, isn't it." The slightly sustained pressure of her embrace was the only reminder, for that moment, of the incident with Adolph, though at any point in the conversation where there might be an opportunity for remembrance Stella smiled in a secret, warm conspiracy over at Martha. Martha did not return these smiles; this was the only way in which she remained loyal to herself.

They drank all morning. Long before lunchtime, Martha was gone on the tide. She was wildly elated. They had a long and alcoholic lunch at McGrath's, where they were interrupted every moment by people coming with congratulations; and no sooner had lunch finished than they went to the Sports Club, where the crowd was arriving, for it was then four o'clock. At the Club, Martha and Douglas were kissed and clasped and slapped by dozens of people; they were half drowned in champagne, to the refrain, "I never thought anyone'd hook our Douggie."

Binkie danced with Martha several times, in a puzzled, angry sort of way, repeating that she was a nice kid; then he gave it up, with the remark that there was something in the air, everyone was getting married, he'd have to get hooked himself in self-defence soon, though of course now Matty was out of the question there was no point in it. And he heaved a large sigh, which was genuine; he had lost control of his Club, and he knew it.

The party went down to the Knave of Clubs at four in the morning, and at sunup returned to the flat, where Martha and Douglas collapsed on the divan and slept. They woke to find Stella, attractively sluttish in a rather soiled purple satin dressing gown, her ropes of dark glistening hair falling like a corrupted schoolgirl's over her shoulder, waiting with cups of tea, and suggestive jokes, because the loving couple had been sleeping back to back, with several inches between them.

Douglas told Stella that she was a dirty-minded girl, which was an echo of Donovan that made Martha cold and thoughtful. Douglas followed Stella to the kitchen, where the pair of them cooked breakfast and flirted until Andrew became annoyed. Miraculously, Stella transformed herself into the image of a quiet, devoted wife ministering to others. She served the breakfast, garbed in a white linen dress as simple as that of a nurse. Her hair was now coiled meekly around her exquisite head. She was so attractive that neither her husband nor Douglas could take his eyes off her. Martha did not notice this, for she was sunk in depression. But soon after that late breakfast they began to drink again, and again Martha was elated.

And so it went on for the whole of that week. In the office Martha was treated like a queen, she was allowed to come late, to stay away three hours for lunch, even not to come at all. The four of them spent their time together, while Stella's calm assumption that she was in some way fitted to lead the couple along the flowery road to matrimony was accepted by them quite naturally. And Martha was completely swept away by it all. There were occasional cold moments when she thought that she must somehow, even now, check herself on the fatal slope towards marriage; somewhere at the back of her mind was the belief that she would never get married, there would be time to change her mind later. And then the thought of what would happen if she did chilled her. It seemed that half the town was celebrating; she had not begun to realize how well known Douglas was; the Sports Club were magnificently marrying him off, with a goodwill in which there was more than a hint of malice. The wolves feted him and toasted him; several times in an evening he was rushed at by a group of them, and tossed protesting and laughing into the air, while Martha stood by smiling uneasily, feeling that she must be perverse to dislike what everyone else thought so amusing and natural. But she was uneasy about Douglas himself. The quiet, responsible, serious young man she had imagined she was marrying had vanished, for the time at any rate. He was jocular, he wore a steady smile of triumph that deepened self-consciously when he entered a room with Martha; and towards the end of an evening he was likely to vanish into a pack of stamping, yelling young men who moaned inarticulately in an ecstasy of frustrated energy, "We'll tear the place up, we'll give it a bang." Martha thought secretly that there was something very strange about it all, for if the point of this public orgy was sex—which surely it must be, judging from the meaning smiles, the jokes, and the way Douglas was continually taken aside by a young man, and teased until he began directing uneasy, proud, guilty looks at Martha which she tried hard not to hate him for—then sex, the-thing-in-itself, had mysteriously become mislaid in the publicity. For after a dance the couple found themselves back in the Mathews' flat, half drunk, completely exhausted, and Douglas in this mood of jocular triumph was so repulsive to her that she nervously protested she was tired, and he at once dropped off to sleep as if the thing were of no importance. She was, in fact, already feeling a creeping disgust of him. It would, however, all be all right when they were married. It was odd that Martha, who thought of the wedding ceremony as an unimportant formula that must be gone through for the sake of society, was also thinking of it as the door which would enclose Douglas and herself safely within romantic love; in fact, in a contradictory, twisted way, while she slept limb to limb with Douglas every night, she was thinking of that unimportant wedding ceremony rather as her mother might have done. Naturally this comparison wouldn't have dared to enter her head. She thought of the marriage as of a door closing firmly against her life in town, which she was already regarding with puzzled loathing. She was longing for the moment when it would no longer have anything to do with her.

By the Friday of that week, Martha was tired and irritable. She was also persistently depressed, which no one would have guessed from her smiling face. On that evening she was unresponsive when Douglas suggested they should go and see Stella, and said she would rather stay in her room.

"Come on, you only-only get married-married once," he said coaxingly; so they went to the flat and drank, but when Stella suggested they should go and dance, Martha said she was tired, and wanted to go to bed.

"Ooooh, naughty, naughty Matty," sang Stella, waving her tinted forefinger at the couple, her eyes bright with complicity and curiosity.

Douglas smiled and said proudly, "Give-give us a break, Stell."

They went home. There Douglas produced a book, and said, "We can't go wrong with this, can we?" It was Van der Velde's treatise on marriage. It may be said that few middle-class young couples dare marry without this admirable handbook; and as Douglas had seen it in his young married friends' bookcases, he had bought it.

Now, the sight of the scientific and modern book had a double effect on Martha. (She had of course read it.) It gave her assurance and made her feel a woman experienced in love, while at the same time she felt unaccountably irritable that Douglas should produce it now—Like a cooking book, she remarked to herself, before that persistently disagreeable voice was silenced by an effort of will. On the one hand, the gleam in Douglas's eyes excited her to try . . . , but here that irritating voice remarked, Position C, subsection (d); and once again it was squashed. She was adapting herself compliantly to Douglas's attitude (the book was lying open at the chosen recipe) when suddenly a wave of exasperation swept over, and she said angrily that she was tired, she was exhausted, she was fed up with the whole thing; she sat up with a jerk, and burst into tears.

Douglas was astounded. However, the thought that women are . . . came to his aid; he asked her nicely what was the matter, said

"Don't cry," and comforted her like a brother. Martha wept unrestrainedly, loved him for his kindness; and in due course they made love, and for the first time, and without the aid of the book, in a way that pleased them both.

He went home early, saying she needed sleep. He promised not to go to the Sports Club, which for some reason seemed important to her, though he could not imagine why. Martha woke with the feeling of a prisoner before execution, and said to herself that she would ring him up and say that she could not possibly marry him.

When she got up, there was a letter from her mother, ten pages of every sort of abuse, in which the phrases "you young people," "the younger generation," "freethinkers," "Fabian sentimentalists," and words like "immoral," were repeated in every sentence. Martha read the first page, flew to the telephone, and implored Douglas to come to her at once. He came, within fifteen minutes, to find Martha in a state of locked hysteria. She was dangerously calm, very sarcastic, shooting out epigrams about virtue and conventionality like bullets. She then burst into tears again, and said, half crying and half laughing, "How dare they? How dare she? It's not as if . . . If only they—well, it's not as if they cared a damn *really* one way or the other, and . . ."

Douglas calmed her, but did not make love to her, thinking this was hardly the moment, poor little thing. Martha was soon calm again, and Douglas was perturbed that now it seemed she was cold with him as well as with the rest of the world. However, he used the ancient formula, She'll be all right once we're married, and reminded her that today was the day they had arranged to go to the farm.

She seemed to feel annoyed that he thought it necessary to remind her. He went to fetch Binkie's car, which he was borrowing, and when they had packed their things they started, Martha rather subdued and silent, he transformed back into the serious and sensible young man whom it was so easy to love.

The road drove straight across country, twinkling off sunlight from the marbling lanes of asphalt, up the side of a vlei, down the next, between low walls of yellowing grass whose roots were still cluttered and bedded in the mess of last year's subsiding growth—that is, save where the veld fires had swept and left blackened soil (charred and cracked even after the drenching rains), so that new stems rose glistening, as clean as reeds from water. The sky was as deep and blue and fresh as a sweep of sea, and the white clouds rolled steadily in it. The veld, so thickly clothed with grass, broken with small tumbling kopjes which glittered with hot granite boulders, lifted itself unafraid to meet that sky. This naked embrace of earth and sky, the sun hard and strong overhead, pulling up the moisture from foliage, from soil, so that the swimming glisten of heat is like a caress made visible, this openness of air, everything visible for leagues, so that the circling hawk (the sun glancing off its wings) seems equipoised between sun and boulder—this frank embrace between the lifting breast of the land and the deep blue warmth of the sky is what exiles from Africa dream of; it is what they sicken for, no matter how hard they try to shut their minds against the memory of it. And what if one sickens for it when one still lives in Africa, one chooses to remain in town? Living in town, Martha had forgotten this infinite exchange of earth and sky. She met it again as if she had returned from the North, where veils of mist and vapour and pollution hang over the land, where a dim and muted sunset seems to be taking place in another universe, the sky is self-contained, it broods introspectively behind its veils, the sun shines, the rain falls, but absently, dreaming, and the people on the earth accept what comes, with hardly a glance at their cold partner. And Martha came out of the town into the veld like an astonished stranger; she had been shut from it by a matter of a few weeks among the shells and surfaces of brick and concrete. She might have been in another country.

She was hurtled along this straight road, and it seemed as if the framework of the car hardly existed; she was carried along on movement itself, the sun immediately above, naked and powerful, the loins and breast of light, while the earth's heat rose to meet it, in a rank and swelling smell of growth and wetness. The car flung her, so it seemed, through the air; and other cars, flying past, signalled the recognition of travellers in space with the flash of sunlight from hot metal. On and on; the town was a long way behind, the farm was not yet reached; and in between these two lodestones, this free and reckless passage through warmed blue air. How terrible that it must always be the town or the farm; how terrible this decision, always one thing or the other, and the exquisite flight between them so short, so fatally limited . . . Long before they had reached the station, the wings of exaltation had sunk and folded. Martha was bracing herself to meet her parents. She was going to fight and win. They tore through the station. She noted briefly that not only the Cohens' store had "Socrates" written over it; the Welshman had gone—it was Sock's Imperial Garage now. The puddle by the railway lines was brimming. The sky shimmered bluely in it, and through this illusory sea floated some fat white ducks, each leaving a ruffling wake of brown water.

The car turned, with a bounce, into the farm road. In the dry season, it was thick brown dust. In the wet, it was a lane of rich, treacly red mud. Now, in a short drought, the mud had hardened in deep fanged ruts where the waggons had passed. Binkie's town car began to groan and rattle.

"You can't go so fast over this road," said Martha, and it was the first remark she had made for half an hour. She added nervously, "You know, I think I ought to say . . ." She stopped, feeling disloyal to her parents. It flashed across her mind that Douglas might be shocked by their poverty; but since she was now allied to him, and she would have scorned to be shocked by anyone's poverty, this was a new and confusing sort of disloyalty. She left this problem to fend for itself, and finished what she had intended to say. "About my father. He wasn't actually wounded or anything, or at least not much, just a flesh wound, but—well, the war seems to have got hold of him. He doesn't think about anything but war and being ill," she concluded defiantly.

Douglas said pleasantly, being the decent young man he was, "Well, Matty, I'm marrying you and not your father."

She reached for his hand. Clinging to it, she allowed herself to be comforted into security. Suddenly they reached that spot where the road entered the big field. "I say, this is-is something like," approved Douglas, slowing the car. The maize was strong and green, a warm green sea glancing off golden light, while the dark-red earth showed momentarily along the dissolving lanes as the car crawled past. But Martha was looking apprehensively at the house. Now the trees had filled with leafage, the house was crouched low among them, nothing but a slope of dull thatch. She said to herself, Now, don't let yourself be bullied, don't give in. And with Martha in this defiant mood, they reached the homestead.

Mr. and Mrs. Quest were standing waiting outside the house. Mr. Quest was smiling vaguely. Mrs. Quest's smile was nervously welcoming; and at the sight of it, Martha began to feel uneasy. All through her childhood, at school or when she was away staying with friends, those letters had been flung after her, terrible letters, so that reading them Martha had cried, She's mad, she must be mad! She had returned determined to resist the maniac who had written those letters, only to see her mother smiling uncertainly, a tired-looking Englishwoman with unhappy blue eyes. And so it was now: before Martha had even got out of the car, she knew a most familiar feeling of helplessness. Douglas glanced at her, as if to say, You've been exaggerating, and Martha shrugged and looked away from him.

Douglas shook Mr. Quest by the hand and called him "sir"; when he reached for Mrs. Quest's hand, she bent forward and kissed his cheek. She was now smiling a timid welcome.

"Well," she said humorously, "and so you crazy youngsters have come, I'm so glad."

Martha, stunned as usual, was kissed by her mother, and received a pleasant "Well, old son?" from her father. Then he said, "If you don't mind, it's time for the news, I must just go inside for a minute."

"Good heavens," said Mrs. Quest, "so it is, we can't miss that."

They went inside to the front room, and turned on the wireless. Mr. and Mrs. Quest leaned forward in their chairs, listening intently, while an announcer repeated Hitler's assurances that he intended no further conquests in Europe. When the announcer began to talk about cricket, Mrs. Quest turned the wireless down, and said with satisfaction that it wouldn't be long now before war started. Mr. Quest said that if Chamberlain didn't listen to Churchill, England would be unprepared again, but it didn't matter, because England always won in the end.

Martha was opening her mouth to join in angry argument, when she noted that Douglas was politely agreeing with both her parents. She therefore deflated, sat back, and listened while Mr. Quest explained to Douglas that, according to prophecy, Armageddon was due almost immediately, there would be seven million dead lying around Jerusalem, the Mount of Olives would be split in twain (probably by a bomb) and God would appear, to separate the believers from the faithless. Here his voice changed, and he remarked, with an irritated eye fixed on Martha, that Douglas might not know it, but Martha was not only a socialist, which was not important, since it was only a disease natural to her age, but an atheist as well.

Martha was expecting Douglas to say that he was also an atheist, but he merely said that he thought what Mr. Quest said was so interesting, and perhaps he could borrow some pamphlets sometime.

Martha therefore sank into comforting dependence on Douglas, although somewhere within her was a protesting voice remarking that he needn't treat her father as if he were a child. Then she told herself that he *was* a child, and Douglas was quite right. At the thought, she felt sad, and looked unhappily at her father, for he seemed even more distracted than before. He seemed to be thinner, and his hair was greying fast. The handsome dark eyes peered with a remote and angry gleam from under shelves of bristling white hair. Surely, wondered Martha, he has not changed so much in a few weeks? Was it that she had not noticed, living so close to him, that he was becoming an old man? At the thought that her father was old, her heart contracted painfully; and she said to herself, Nonsense, most of his diseases are imaginary, and anyway, people can live for years and years with diabetes. In fact, because *she* could not endure the thought that her father might die, she assured herself he was hardly ill at all. All the same, she longed to comfort him, but this was impossible, for one half of her attention was still standing at the alert, waiting for the scene which surely was due to start at any moment. She was nervously watching her mother, but quite soon Mrs. Quest said she must go and give orders about lunch, the new boy was so stupid he couldn't even lay the table, and she had to do everything herself.

Mr. Quest, having finished a long explanation of how Russia was the Antichrist, and therefore the war could not start until the sides had become reshuffled in some way, remarked, "Well, there was something I wanted to say." He glanced apprehensively over his shoulder towards where his wife had gone, and said, "I didn't want to say anything in front of your mother, she's not—well, she doesn't understand this kind of thing." He paused, staring at the ground for a few moments, and then went on, as if there had been no interruption: "I suppose you two are not getting married because you've got to? Matty isn't in any sort of trouble?" He looked uncomfortably at the silent couple, the frail white skin of his face flushing. He does look old, thought Martha miserably, trying to look courageously at this new vision of him; for, in spite of everything, she had always thought of him as a young man.

Douglas said, "No, sir, there's nothing of the kind."

Mr. Quest stared disbelievingly at him. "Well, why get married in such a hurry, people will talk, you know."

"*People*," said Martha scornfully.

"I daresay," said her father angrily. "Well, I don't care, it's your affair, but what people say causes more trouble than you seem to think." He paused again, and said appealingly, "Matty, I wouldn't like to think of you getting married when you didn't really want to— of course, this has nothing personal in it, Douglas." Douglas nodded reassuringly. "Because if you are in the family way, then we'll do something about it, provided your mother doesn't know," he said aggressively, with another glance over his shoulder.

The words "family way" caused Martha acute resentment, and with a glance at her face, her father said, "Oh, very well, then, if it's all right, I'm glad to hear it." He then began telling Douglas about his war, while Martha waited, with her nerves on edge, for him to say, "But that was the Great Unmentionable, and of course you don't want to hear about that, you're all too busy enjoying yourselves."

Douglas said politely that he was very interested in everything Mr.

Quest said; and Mr. Quest's face brightened, and then he sighed, and said, "Yes, it's starting again, and I'm out of it, they wouldn't have me, I'm too old."

Martha could not endure this. She abruptly got up and went out.

Her mother was returning from the kitchen. Martha braced herself for the opposition that must come, but Mrs. Quest hurried past, saying, "I must get him his injection, and there's his new tonic, oh, dear, and where have I put it?" But she checked herself, and came back, saying quickly, with a downward look at Martha's stomach, "You're not—I mean, you haven't . . . ?" Her eyes were lit with furtive interest.

Martha snapped out coldly, with as much disgust as Mrs. Quest might have considered due to the cause of the possible event, "No, I'm not pregnant."

Mrs. Quest looked abashed and disappointed, and said, "Oh, well, then, if you are—well, I mean, but your father shouldn't know, it would kill him." She hurried away.

At lunchtime Mrs. Quest enquired whether they wanted to be married at the district church, and Martha said hotly that they were both atheists, and it would be nothing but hypocrisy to be married in church. She was expecting an argument, but Mrs. Quest glanced at Douglas, and sighed, and let her face droop, and finally muttered, "Oh, dear, it really isn't very nice, is it?"

That evening, when Martha went to her bedroom, she sat on the edge of her bed, and pointed out to herself that not only had her parents accepted the marriage, but she could expect her mother to take full control of the thing. In fact, she already felt as if it concerned her mother more than herself. The door opened, Mrs. Quest entered, and she said that she was going to come into town with Martha on Monday to buy her trousseau. Martha said firmly that she didn't want a trousseau. They wrangled for a few moments; then Mrs. Quest said, "Well, at least you should have a nightdress." She blushed furiously, while Martha demanded, "Whatever do I want a nightdress for?"

"My dear child," said her mother, "you must. Besides, you hardly know him." At this she blushed again, while Martha began to laugh. Suddenly good-natured, she kissed her mother and said she would be delighted to have a nightdress, and it was very nice of her to suggest it.

But Mrs. Quest hesitated, and then asked, "What kind of an engagement ring is he getting you?"

Now, neither Martha nor Douglas had thought of an engagement ring, and Martha said, "There isn't any need for an engagement ring. Anyway, he can't afford it."

Mrs. Quest took a diamond ring from her finger, and said nervously, sounding guilty, "Now, do be sensible, think what people will say, wear it for my sake, so people won't think . . . I mean, Marnie had such a lovely ring, and . . ."

The usual anger rose in Martha, succeeded by a kind of apathy. She took the ring, and slipped it on her engagement finger. It was a fine ring, a conventional five-stoned affair, but it had no beauty; it was a ring that said, Here are five expensive diamonds displayed in a row. Martha thought it unpleasant; besides, the cold metal sank into her flesh like a chain. She hastily took it off, and handed it back, laughing weakly and saying, "Oh, no, I don't want a ring."

"Now, please, Matty," said Mrs. Quest, almost in tears.

Martha looked at her mother in astonishment. She shrugged, and put the ring back, while Mrs. Quest embraced her, and again there was a guilty look on her face.

When her mother had gone, Martha removed the ring and laid it on the dressing table. She was now feeling lost and afraid. She was vividly conscious of the night outside, the vast teeming night, which was so strong, and seemed to be beating down into the room, through the low shelter of the thatch, through the frail mud walls. It was as if the house itself, formed of the stuff and substance of the veld, had turned enemy. Inside the thatch, she knew, were a myriad small creatures, spiders, working ants, beetles; once a snake had been killed—it was coiled between the thatch and the top of the wall. Under the thin and cracked linoleum that clothed the stamped mud floor, the shoots from trees cut two decades ago were struggling upwards, sickly white, to seek the light. Sometimes they pushed the linoleum aside, and had to be cut level. Martha, hating the room, went to the window. The light of the stars was strong and white, there was a sheet of white hazy light over the mealie fields. She was even more afraid. She looked at the door leading to her parents' room. It was open. It had stood open all night ever since she could remember. She thought now, with a half-derisive grin, how often her father had complained, "Can't we shut the door now, May? The kids are old enough, they won't choke in their sleep." But Mrs. Quest could never bring herself to treat that door as one that might be shut. The other door, which opened into the end room, had also stood open. In fact, it could not shut, because the lintel had swollen to a bulge. Now, however, this door was closed and fastened with a heavy padlock, of the kind that was used to secure the storeroom against the native servants. Martha went silently to examine this door, and found that the lintel had been planed flat, showing startlingly white, like new wood.

She slipped out of the door that led into the garden, receiving a drench of glittering starlight faintly perfumed with geranium. She looked over the landscape of her childhood, lying dark and mysterious, to the great bulk of Jacob's Burg, and tried to get some spark of recognition from it. It was shut off from her, she could feel nothing. There was a barrier, and that barrier (she felt) was Douglas. And as she thought of him, she turned sharply at a sound, and he came towards her, grinning, from the end bedroom.

He slipped his arm around her, and said, "You mustn't get so prickly with your parents. After all, we've rather sprung it on them, and they've been very decent."

She assented, and could not help feeling that even this mild protest was in some way a betrayal to their side.

"You'll see," said Douglas consolingly, "it'll be ever-ever such a fine wedding, and you'll like it."

Again she assented. It had been arranged that they would be married by Mr. Maynard, Binkie's father. He would marry them, as a favour, in their own flat—the flat which Douglas had already found for them "from a pal." Afterwards they were going off on a honeymoon with Stella and Andrew to the Falls. She had hardly listened to these arrangements, because all these formalities were so unimportant.

He remarked, "I must say, all this looks as wild as hell, gives me the creeps." She said yes, rather forlornly, for it did look wild and lonely; and she had never felt lonely in the veld before. The pressure of his arm on her shoulder suggested she should move beside him back to his room, and she went, gladly, with the warmth of his arm as guide.

She said passionately, "I wish it was all over." She repeated it desperately, as if she were talking about an unpleasant if not dangerous operation.

But inside the end room, which had been her brother's, she began to laugh at herself. One could almost think of this room as disconnected from the rest of the house. It was small and quiet, with whitewashed walls, and the glistening thatch slanting low over a small window. The low hissing of the oil lamp was soothing, and she sighed comfortably when she heard an owl hooting from the trees.

Douglas was a wall of strength; and from her clinging to him, and his calm reassurance, their love-making flowed out, and died into sleep. The "act of love"—that fatally revealing phrase—was no act at all tonight, if one gives to the words what is due to them of willed achievement. For both these people were heirs, whether they liked it or not, of the English puritan tradition, where sex is either something to be undergone (heard in the voices of innumerable chilled women, whispering their message of endurance to their daughters) or something to be shut out, or something to be faced and overcome. At least two generations of rebels have gone armed to the combat with books on sex to give them the assurance they did not feel; for both Martha and Douglas, making love when and how they pleased was positively a flag of independence in itself, a red and defiant flag, waving in the faces of the older generation.

In the morning Martha woke first, and found herself curled delightfully against Douglas's inert and heavy body. She was floating free and away from all the strained preoccupation of the day before. She thought with good humour of her mother's absorption in the wedding arrangements, and with amusement of her father, who would probably not notice the wedding ceremony at all if not reminded to do so. She lay gently, feeling the slow rise and fall of the warm flesh, and listened to the servant chopping wood outside, and watched the light from the window deepen on the white wall to a reflected yellow glow from the warming soil. Then the yellow patch began to shake and tremble—the sun had risen to the height of the tree outside; and slowly a pattern of leaves grew dark against a clear, luminous orange, and trembled as if a breeze were flowing through the room itself.

Douglas stirred and greeted her with an affectionate "Well, Matty." Then he turned over, and her body began to tense into waiting. "Let's try like this," he said with determination, and she caught a glimpse of his face, which was rigid with concentration, before she closed her eyes and lay alertly ready to follow what he intended to do. What she was thinking was, and with a really extraordinary resentment, Why does he have to spoil last night? Her attention was so strained to miss no new movement of his, for she was terrified he might find her lacking, that the end came unexpectedly for her, and left her reassuring him, as usual, that all was well. She was very tender and consoling, and lay stroking his hair, while she thought, Well, it was lovely last night, at any rate. Now, last night she had not been conscious of anything very much; she was in fact arranging the dark, underwater movements of last night into a pattern to measure against this morning's failure. She was also thinking worriedly about her mother. It no longer seemed unimportant or amusing that her parents were as they were. She was apprehensive. Back in her room, she looked at the open door into her parents' room, which had the force now of a deliberate reproach, and waited until Douglas was ready to go with her to the breakfast table, so that she need not face her parents unsupported.

That her mother had been in her room during the night Martha could see from her look of strained curiosity. And yet, this was surely more than could be expected from a conventional middle-class matron concerned that her daughter might go to the altar, or rather the table at the registry office, a virgin? That square, vigorous, set face, the small blue eyes, always clenched under a brow of worry, were now directed persistently towards Douglas. Mrs. Quest could not take her eyes off her daughter's young man. She talked to him like a reproachful but eager girl, there was an arch and rather charming smile on her face, even while the gaze was persistent, tinged with guilt. She looked as if she had been done out of something, Martha remarked unpleasantly to herself; and she knew that immediately after breakfast her mother would come to her, on some pretext or another, but really fulfilling a driving need to talk about what had happened. Martha felt exhausted, a dragging tiredness overcame her at the idea of it, and as soon as they all rose from the table she attached herself to her father; and at last Mrs. Quest went off with Douglas, since it seemed Martha was deaf to any suggestions that it would be nice to discuss the wedding.

Mr. Quest took his deck chair to the side of the house, and leaned back in it smoking, gazing over the slopes of veld to Jacob's Burg. The great heave of blue mountain was this morning towering up into a blue sky, and wisps and wraiths of cloud dissolved around it. Martha sank down beside him, with the comfortable feeling of repeating something she had done a thousand times. The sunlight slowly soaked into her flesh, she felt her hair grow warm around her face, she sighed with pleasure, and prepared to let the morning slide past, while her thoughts drifted away—not towards the wedding, that annoying incident which must somehow be accepted, but to the time afterwards. They would go to England, or to the South of France; Martha dreamed of the Mediterranean while her father thought of—but what was it likely to be this morning? After a while he began talking, after the preparatory "Well, old son!," and she listened with half her mind, checking it up, as it were, on the landmarks of his thought. He was thinking of her brother who (lucky devil) would be allowed to fight in this new war. From there he slid back into his tales of the trenches, of the weeks before Passchendaele, from which he had been rescued by that lucky flesh wound:

none of his company had come through it, all were killed. From there he passed to the international situation.

Martha lit another cigarette, lifted her skirt so that the sun might deepen the brown of her legs, and asked suddenly, "Do you like Douglas?" She might have been talking about an acquaintance. When she heard the tone of her voice, she felt guilty, because of this unwelcome, deep understanding with her father that lay beneath "all this nonsense about the British Israelites and the war"—the understanding that made Douglas seem like a stranger whom they might discuss without disloyalty.

"What?" he asked, annoyed at being interrupted. Then he collected himself, and said indifferently, "Oh, yes, he's quite all right, it seems." After a pause he said, "Well, as I was saying . . ."

Some minutes later Martha enquired, "Are you pleased I'm getting married?"

"What's that?" He frowned at her, then, seeing the sardonic lift of her brows, said guiltily, "Yes—no. Oh, well, you don't care what I think, anyway." This had the irritability due to the younger generation, and she giggled. Slowly he began to smile.

"I don't believe you've even understood that I'm getting married in five days," she said accusingly.

"Well, what am I expected to do about it? There was one thing I wanted to say. What was it, now? Oh, yes. You shouldn't have children—I mean, that's in my view, it's not my affair, but there's plenty of time."

"Of course not," said Martha vaguely. That went without saying.

"What do you mean, of course not?" he said crossly. "You may think you're better men than your parents, but we didn't mean to have you, the doctor said we were neither of us in a fit state, but you happened along nine months to the day. But then we didn't anticipate the wedding ceremony. We were both having severe nervous breakdowns, due to the Great Unmentionable"—he snarled this phrase over at her, but without any real emotion, so that she smiled patiently—"so we were taking all the necessary precautions, or rather your mother was, she's a nurse, so it's in her line, that sort of thing. So I thought I'd better point out, children have a habit of resulting from getting married."

Since her earliest years Martha had been offered the information that she was unwanted in the first place, and that she had a double nervous breakdown for godparents, and so the nerve it reached now was quite dulled; and she merely repeated casually that she had no intention of having children for years and years.

Mr. Quest remarked with relief that that was all right, then, and—his duty as father done—began talking about what they would do when they left the farm. If Martha had been listening, she might have noted that these plans were much more sensible and concrete than they ever had been; but she was not listening.

Soon the sun grew too warm, and they moved their chairs under the sheltering golden shower, and now faced outwards to the Dumfries Hills. They were low and clear today; the rocks and trees showed across the seven miles of distance as if the height of this hill and the height of that range shared a dimension where the ordinary rules of space did not apply. Martha felt she could lean forward over the lower slopes of ground between (where the Afrikaans community lived) and stroke the bluish contours of those brooding sunlit hills.

The servant brought morning tea, with the message that the Little Missus and the Big Baas must take it by themselves, for the Big Missus and the New Baas had gone off to the vegetable garden.

"He's being awfully tactful, isn't he?" remarked Mr. Quest half sarcastically, "He's being so well behaved. Well, I daresay that's the way to get on in this world." This was the nearest he had got to comment or criticism; and Martha invited him to continue with a glance and a receptive silence. He said: "Sex is important in marriage. I do hope that is all right. Your mother, of course . . . However . . ." He paused, with a guilty glance at her, and Martha was filled with triumph, though she could not have said why. "All your generation" (and the usual irritation was applied to the surface of his words) "take it in your stride, or so I understand." The look he gave her was an unwilling enquiry. How much she would have liked, then, to talk to him! She had even leaned forward, opened her mouth to begin, though she did not know what it was she was going to say, when he said hastily, "So that's all right, then, isn't it?" He handed her his cup for some more tea. There was a silence, but it lagged on unbroken. Martha was now restrained by that reiterated "young people," "your generation"; she owed it to her contemporaries to treat the whole subject with nonchalance. And soon he began talking about a girl he had been in love with before he met Mrs. Quest. "Lord, I was in love," he said longingly, trying to sound amused. "Lord, Lord, but I had a good time—but that was before I married, before the war, so it wouldn't interest you." He was silent, smiling thoughtfully over at the Dumfries Hills, his whitening eyebrows lifted in a perverse and delighted comment, while he occasionally glanced towards Martha, and then withdrew his eyes as if those glances were the results of thoughts he would rather not own.

As for Martha, she was now unhappy and restless, and wished that Douglas would return from the vegetable garden.

Immediately after lunch, it was time for them to go back to town. During the drive, Martha was telling herself that the last hurdle was past, she had "obtained her parents' permission." She used the phrase half humorously, half with spite, for she was feeling, contradictorily enough for a girl who refused formalities with such vehemence, that surely there had been something wrong with that weekend at home? Surely (or so she dimly felt) she should have had to fight, face real opposition, only to emerge a victor at the end, crowned by the tearful blessings of her father and mother? Surely there should have been some real moment of crisis, a point of choice? Alas for the romantic disposition, always waiting for these "moments," these exquisite turning points where everything is clear, the past lying finished, completed, in one's shadow, the future lying clear and sunlit before! For, looking back on the weekend, Martha felt nothing but that she had been cheated; her mother's attitude and her father's seemed equally wrong and perverse.

So, as usual, she gave an impatient shrug, and dismissed the whole thing; soon that door would be closing on her past; all the mistakes and miseries of her time in town would be forever behind her. She had merely to live through five days to the wedding. She asked Douglas what her mother had arranged with him, intending that the undertone of sarcasm should provoke him, but he did not hear it. He replied enthusiastically that everything would be fine, everything would be satisfactory. He continued to talk of various details, and Martha understood, and with amazement, that she would not be getting married under the ægis of the Club; she had had a vague idea that surely they would all be there, wolves and virgins. For Douglas was remarking casually, as if he were not a senior member himself, that they "must keep it dark, we don't want that crazy bunch spoiling it." He added with mixed pride and shame that if Binkie knew the exact time and place he'd turn it into a proper-proper scrum. Mr. Maynard, it seemed, had promised to keep it all secret, even from his son.

As they entered the town, rather late in the evening—for they had stopped to visit a tobacco-farmer friend of Douglas on the way—Martha happened to glance down towards the Club, and saw a crowd of people massed under the illuminated trees. "Let's drive past," she suggested, and they did so. "What on earth is going on?" There were three packing cases stood on end on the pavement, and on these stood three men. "An open-air meeting?" she suggested;

and Douglas said critically, "Gang of cranks." She asked coldly why one shouldn't have an open-air meeting, but he was frowning, and looked disturbed.

He stopped the car at a small distance, and they leaned out; the moon was pouring out light, and it was easy to see. The crowd was entirely white, save for half a dozen native stragglers who were on the outskirts of the crowd, ready to move off if challenged. Policemen stood waiting, white policemen, and their expression of scandalized interest was shared by most of the listening people. The speaker on the tub was a short, strongly built man with rough copper-coloured hair; fragments of Irish speech came floating over the heads of the crowd; "humanity," "drift to war," "fascism," Martha heard, and looked to Douglas to share her excitement. But his expression was that of an official faced with something new. It was not usual to have open-air meetings, there was something lawless about them, and therefore he disapproved. It was as simple as that. Martha felt her heart sink, looking at the frowning, rather pompous face. Then she turned to look again. It was rather beautiful. The trees were shining with an intense green, like trees seen through water, and they shook in a faint wind. Overhead, moon-illuminated clouds drifted quietly. The light shone on the rough copper hair of the speaker, and his eyes glittered steadily. Martha could hardly hear what he said. He was speaking about the necessity for making a pact with Russia to defeat Hitler; the faces of the audience had the passive, watchful look of public opinion faced with something it allows but does not approve. Then Martha, looking into the shadows behind the three men on the boxes, saw Joss, and Solly, and Jasmine Cohen; they were with the people Martha had met at that tea party at the school; there was also a rather slight, tall young woman with fair hair wound around her head in plaits, like a schoolteacher's; and Martha found herself vividly jealous of this girl. She longed to leave the car, to go over to the Cohens, and stay with them. The impulse to do so surged up in her, and died in a tired shrug at the thought of undoing all the arrangements that had been made. She turned away quickly, afraid that they might have seen her. She was afraid of how they might criticize Douglas; she could see him through their eyes only too clearly.

She saw Douglas was looking at her with a cold antagonism. "Finished?" he enquired, as if he had been listening only to please her. He started the car.

"How conventional you are," she remarked acidly, as they went down the street.

"Trying to draw attention to themselves," he said, for some reason red with anger, his eyes protruding. She had never seen him like this.

She said, with quiet dislike, that the essence of a public meeting was to draw attention to oneself.

He was feeding the petrol into the car so fast that it choked, spluttered, stopped. They rolled down the street in silence, while he tried to start the car. When it started, he turned to her, and demanded like a child in a temper, "If you've changed your mind, Matty, now's the time to say so," and she enquired, "About what?" though she knew quite well. His face grew more red, and seemed to puff out; his eyes were inflamed. She was now wondering sincerely why he was so extremely angry. She asked, reasonably, if he thought there was any necessity to lose his temper over a meeting he did not agree with. He was silent, breathing heavily; she was more and more astonished; at the same time, she was revolted; she thought he looked vulgar and ugly, puffed out and red with temper, his neck swelling over his collar. She said to herself that now she could free herself, she need not marry him; at the same time, she knew quite well she would marry him; she could not help it; she was being dragged towards it, whether she liked it or not. She also heard a voice remarking calmly within her that she would not stay married to him; but this voice had no time to make itself heard before he turned to her, and asked again, this time quietly and pleasantly, for his anger had subsided, whether she wanted to change her mind. She replied that she did not.

They went straight to the Mathews' flat, where they were welcomed with food and, above all, drink.

Next day Martha and Douglas moved into their new flat, so that Binkie and his lieutenants could not find them; and lived there like people under siege, while the Mathews brought them supplies. All four spent that time in a state of wild excitement, like a permanent picnic. Also, there were curtains to hang and furniture to arrange, which Stella took it for granted was her prerogative. Martha was rather surprised at the way Douglas recklessly bought whatever took his fancy or hers; the delivery vans were rolling up several times a day with carpets and cupboards and bales of stuff, and when she said nervously, "Look, darling, if you're broke, there's no need to have all this stuff, surely?" he exclaimed with a whoop that one only got married once. "But you did say you were short of money," she suggested, still nervous, for she could not rid herself of the feeling that to make detailed enquiries about his finances would be an unpardonable interference. Besides, he was paying the forty pounds she owed as a result of not being able to live on her salary, and she felt guilty about it. Douglas said that he had saved some money, he had about a hundred pounds, and he was heavily insured and could borrow on it. In fact, what he said now was in contradiction to what he had said before, but Martha as usual shrugged her shoulders. For the Quests' attitude towards money could hardly be described as practical.

This letter arrived from Mr. Quest on the day before the wedding:

Dear Douglas,

My wife tells me I should make enquiries as to your financial position, which I forgot to do; she, however, seems to have fairly accurate information, so I take it everything may be considered satisfactory [*At this point, that prickling irritability that always lay in Mr. Quest, like a poisoned well, made itself felt through the words of the letter.*] At any rate, under instructions, I am making a formal enquiry as to whether you are able to properly keep and maintain my daughter; which you are quite entitled to resent, since I have never been able to maintain her properly myself. I expect my wife will discuss the whole thing with you in due course. I am informed we are providing the linen and blankets, but since my debt to the Land Bank is due for repayment, I trust you will discourage my wife in any unnecessary generosity.

Yours sincerely,

Alfred Quest

P.S.—I do hope everything goes well with the arrangements. I am persuading my wife not to come in to town until the day itself. I take it this will meet with your approval.

This letter was read by Douglas with an amused grin; while Martha hoped nervously that her father's persuasions might in fact keep her mother out of town, though she doubted it. Then he let out a whoop, and did a war dance around the room among the bottles and ham rolls and eggs, and said, "*We're* all right, aren't we?"

For he was very pleased with everything. The wedding was working out well, for the arrangements were by no means as casual as might appear.

The people who were to be invited were all "old friends" of his whom she had not been told of until that moment. Mr. Maynard, for instance, that respected magistrate; Douglas's voice had a ring of satisfaction when he mentioned him. There was a Mrs. Talbot too; Martha knew of her as a very rich and respected lady, who, it seemed, had known Douglas since he was a child. She was giving them a generous cheque. There was to be present, too, a certain member of Parliament, a Colonel Brodeshaw, who had been a friend of Douglas's father. The head of the department and his wife were to drop in for a glass of champagne afterwards; for there was to be a garden party at Government House that same afternoon, which it was hardly reasonable to expect them to miss, even for a wedding.

It was being impressed on Martha that the wolves, though it seemed Douglas did not consider himself to be one, were also the rising young men of the town, with futures to consider. It made her uneasy, until she comforted herself with the thought, Well, we're leaving the town, anyway, we're going to Europe.

When Douglas asked her whom she wanted to invite, she looked at him in amazement, and replied that she didn't mind. For she persisted in feeling that all this was quite unimportant, her only part in it was to get through with the distasteful business as quickly as possible. And since this feeling remained with her to the end, there is very little to say about the wedding itself. Mrs. Quest, certainly, was too upset to describe her emotions when she arrived at ten in the morning in order to "dress the bride," and found that most of the wedding guests were already seated around the bedroom—where Martha was trying to pack—perched on the bed, on top of the dressing table, even on the floor.

Martha was "quite wild with happiness." This is what Stella and Mrs. Quest told each other, as they fought, with deadly politeness, over who was to arrange the buffet. The two women loathed each other at first sight, and, in consequence of this passion, were inseparable all day. Martha and Douglas were laughing and making jokes against themselves and this unorthodox wedding, trying to finish packing amid clouds of confetti, and drinking champagne in tumblers. At lunchtime about twenty people, already slightly tipsy, were seething about the tiny flat, eating sandwiches and drinking, while Mr. Quest, looking resigned but slightly irritated, sat in a corner, flirting with Stella when she came near him, which was not often, since she had to keep an eye on Mrs. Quest.

It could be said, then, that the wedding began at about ten in the morning; there was no *moment* at which poor Mrs. Quest might emotionally take leave of Martha. Shortly after lunch, Mr. Maynard arrived, looking urbane. He shook Douglas by the hand and called him "my boy," was pleasant to Martha, and then suggested that as he had to marry four other hopeful couples that afternoon he would be obliged if they might get it over, otherwise he'd never get finished with the business. Mrs. Quest hurried her husband into a position where he could give Martha away, for she had not understood that it was unnecessary in this kind of ceremony.

There was a long pause of unwillingly suspended emotion while

Martha signed about nine different documents—"In triplicate, too!" she exclaimed aloud, exasperatedly, while her mother said, "Hush, dear," and Douglas said soothingly, "It's all right, Matty, I thought we might as well get it all done with." What the documents were she had no idea.

Mr. Quest, seeing that his presence was not needed, retired to stand by Stella, who could now give her attention to fascinating him, and succeeded completely. This afternoon she was brilliantly attractive. She wore sleek black, and a hat streaming with bright-green feathers, and supplied a cosmopolitan smartness to the dowdy colonial gathering. Martha was atrociously dressed, and knew it, but had decided it was of no importance.

Mrs. Quest waited anxiously immediately behind Martha's left shoulder, and at the crucial moment when the ring must be put on she grasped Martha's elbow and pushed forward her arm, so that everyone was able to see how Martha turned around and said in a loud, angry whisper, "Who's getting married, me or you?"

The group then dissolved in tears, kisses, congratulations, and alcohol. In this manner, therefore, was Martha Quest married, on a warm Thursday afternoon in the month of March, 1939, in the capital city of a British colony in the centre of the great African continent. Afterwards she could remember very little of the occasion. She remembered a wild elation, under which dragged, like a chain, a persistent misery. She remembered (when time had sorted out what was important from what was not) that someone had been saying that Hitler had seized Bohemia and Moravia, while everyone exclaimed it was impossible. She had heard the information with the feeling she must hurry, there was a terrible urgency, there was no time to waste.

She remembered, too, that as she and Douglas, Stella and Andrew were about to leave on their joint honeymoon (for, as Stella was explaining to everyone, she had never had a proper honeymoon before) Mrs. Quest stood shaking Mr. Maynard by the hand, her face lit by the timid charming smile which was so strange a contrast with the formidable masculine face, while Mr. Maynard smiled his usual tolerant comment on life and people.

"Mr. Maynard, you must agree with me, it's *such* a relief when you get your daughter properly married!"

And Mr. Maynard replied, "Unfortunately I have no daughter, but if I had, it would be my first concern." He involuntarily frowned as he glanced at his watch, and added, "I must ask you to excuse me, I'm late for my next, I cannot understand what is coming over our gilded youth, I've never known such a year for weddings." He hastily flung a handful of confetti in the direction of the departing car, and hurried off on foot to the Magistrate's Court, which was just down the road.

Halfway there, he saw the wedding car trying to turn down a side street, away from half a dozen pursuing cars. "The pack are on the scent," he murmured, as he caught sight of Binkie leaning out of the front car, his mouth open in a yell, his eyes staring excitement. The car recklessly shot across the corner of a pavement. It skidded. The following car collided with it. There was a general screeching of brakes, a smashing of glass, and yells and shrieks of all kinds. The Mathews' car, hooting derision, sped rocking down the main road south.

Mr. Maynard scrupulously averted his eyes from the accident, for he was likely to have to judge it in court—if it came to court, which he hoped they would have the sense to avoid. Really, he thought, it would be the limit if he had Binkie up in front of him on a charge of—what? He glanced over his shoulder. The cars, locked together, were surrounded by a mass of humanity, girls and boys; but they were not arguing with each other, but standing over a black man, who had apparently been knocked down. "Damn the boy," said Maynard furiously, meaning his son. From behind a building, he peered out cautiously. No, the native was getting to his feet and shaking himself. And now it looked as if silver rain were falling from heaven around the man, for the wolves were flinging handfuls of money at him, slapping him on the shoulder, and assuring him he was all right, no bones broken. They were already climbing back into the undamaged cars, to resume the chase after the Mathews' car.

Mr. Maynard walked on, very shaken, very unhappy. No sense of responsibility, completely callous, thought they could do anything if they could buy themselves out of it afterwards . . . His thoughts turned to what was happening in Europe. His views were liberal, in the old, decent sense; he hoped there would not be war, he knew there would be. Suddenly he found himself thinking, Poor kids, let them enjoy themselves while they can— He shook himself furiously; this was a first infection from that brutal sentimentality which poisons us all in time of war. He recognized it, and dismissed it, and walked on, more slowly. Four more weddings to get through. Well, he thought cynically, that would be four divorces for him to deal with, in due time. Five, counting the one he had just finished. Marry in haste, repent in leisure: he believed this firmly, though he had been engaged to his own wife for over a year and knew that he had disliked her for the past fifteen.

He thought, Well, Douggie's got married, that's a step in the right direction; more than I can hope for Binkie. He began thinking, with the wistfulness of a lonely and ageing man, of possible grandchildren; for to a man like Mr. Maynard a son like Binkie is as good as having no son at all.

TWO

A PROPER
MARRIAGE

part one

"You shouldn't make jokes," Alice said, *"if it makes you so unhappy."*

LEWIS CARROLL

1

It was half past four in the afternoon.

Two young women were loitering down the pavement in the shade of the sunblinds that screened the shopwindows. The grey canvas of the blinds was thick, yet the sun, apparently checked, filled the long arcade with a yellow glare. It was impossible to look outwards towards the sun-filled street, and unpleasant to look in towards the mingling reflections in the window glass. They walked, therefore, with lowered gaze, as if concerned about their feet. Their faces were strained and tired. One was talking indefatigably, the other unresponsive, and—it was clear—not so much from listlessness as from a stubborn opposition. There was something about the couple which suggested guardian and ward.

At last one exclaimed, with irritated cheerfulness, "Matty, if you don't get a move on, we'll be late for the doctor."

"But, Stella, you've just said we had half an hour to fill in," said Martha, as promptly as if she had been waiting for just this point of fact to arise, so that she might argue it out to its conclusions. Stella glanced sharply at her, but before she could speak Martha continued, deepening the humorous protest, because the resentment was so strong, "It was you who seemed to think I couldn't get through another day of married life without seeing the doctor, not me. Why you had to fix an appointment for this afternoon I can't think." She laughed, to soften the complaint.

"It's not so easy to get an appointment right away with Dr. Stern. You're lucky I could arrange it for you."

But Martha refused to be grateful. She raised her eyebrows, appeared about to argue—and shrugged irritably.

Stella gave Martha another sharp look, tightened her lips with calculated forbearance, then exclaimed, "That's a pretty dress there. We might as well window-shop, to fill in the time." She went to the window; Martha lagged behind.

Stella tried to arrange herself in a position where she might see through the glass surface of reflections: a stretch of yellow-grained canvas, a grey pillar, swimming patches of breaking colour that followed each other across the window after the passers-by. The dresses displayed inside, however, remained invisible, and Stella fell to enjoying her own reflection. At once her look of shrewd good nature vanished. Her image confronted her as a dark beauty, slenderly round, immobilized by a voluptuous hauteur. Complete. Or, at least, complete until the arrival of the sexual partner her attitude implied; when she would turn on him slow, waking eyes, appear indignant, and walk away—not without throwing him a long, ambiguous look over her shoulder. From Stella one expected these pure, unmixed responses. But from her own image she had glanced towards Martha's; at once she became animated by a reformer's zeal.

From the glass Martha was looking back anxiously, as if she did not like what she saw but was determined to face it honestly. Planted on sturdy brown legs was a plump schoolgirl's body. Heavy masses of lightish hair surrounded a broad pale face. The dark eyes were stubbornly worried, the mouth set.

"What I can't understand," said Martha, with that defensive humour which meant she was prepared to criticize herself, even accept criticism from others, provided it was not followed by advice—"what I can't understand is why I'm thin as a bone one month and as fat as a pig the next. You say you've got dresses you wore when you were sixteen. Well, this is the last of mine I can get on." She laughed unhappily, trying to smooth down crumpled blue linen over her hips.

"The trouble with you is you're tired," announced Stella. "After all, we've none of us slept for weeks." This sophisticated achievement put new vigour into her. She turned on Martha with determination. "You should take yourself in hand, that's all it is. That hair style doesn't suit you—if you can call it a hair style. If you had it cut properly, it might curl. Have you ever had it properly cut—"

"But Stella," Martha broke in, with a wail of laughter, "it needs washing, it's untidy, it's . . ."

She clutched her hair with both hands and moved back a step as Stella moved forward to lay her hands on it in order to show how it should be arranged. So violent and desperate was her defence that Stella stopped, and exclaimed with an exasperated laugh, "Well, if you don't want me to show you!"

In Martha's mind was the picture of how she had indubitably been, not more than three months ago, that picture which had been described, not only by herself but by others, as a slim blonde. Looking incredulously towards her reflection, she saw the fat schoolgirl, and shut her eyes in despair. She opened them at once as she felt Stella's hand on her arm. She shook it off.

"You must take yourself in hand. I'll take you to have your hair cut now."

"No," said Martha vigorously.

Checked, Stella turned back towards her own reflection, And again it arranged itself obediently. Between the languidly enticing beauty who was Stella before her glass and the energetic housewife who longed to take Martha in hand there was no connection; they were not even sisters.

Martha, sardonically watching Stella in her frozen pose, thought that she would not recognize herself if she caught a glimpse of herself walking down a street, or—a phrase which she saw no reason not to use, and even to his face—managing her husband.

Stella saw her look, turning abruptly, and said with annoyance that they would go that moment to the hairdresser.

"There isn't time," appealed Martha desperately.

"Nonsense," said Stella. She took Martha's hand in her own, and began tugging her along the pavement: an attractive matron whose sensuality of face and body had vanished entirely against the greater pressures and pleasures of good management.

Martha pulled herself free again, and said, "I don't want to have my hair cut." Then, as a final appeal: "I'll miss my appointment with Dr. Stern."

"You can have an appointment with Dr. Stern any time. I can always fix it." Stella, preoccupied, frowned at Martha, and commanded, "Just wait for me here, I'll go and tell Mrs. Kent you're a friend of mine, she'll do it as a favour." With this she hastened over the street and vanished into a door under the sign "Chez Paris. Coiffeuse."

Martha remained on the street's edge, telling herself she should hurry after Stella and put her foot down. A familiar lassitude overcame her, and she remained where she was, wishing that Stella would leave her alone and return to her own life—if she had one at all. But this spiteful final jab was rather as if she were sticking a pin into her own image; for whose fault was it, if not her own, that she had spent most of the last month with Stella, that the four of them had even gone off together on what was virtually a honeymoon for four? "After all, I don't even like her," muttered Martha obstinately, thus committing herself to the acknowledgment, always imminent the moment she was left alone, that she didn't like any of the things she had become obliged to like by the fact of marrying. The communal exaltation, like a sort of drunkenness, vanished the moment she was alone, leaving her limp with exhaustion. But she had not been alone for five minutes since her marriage.

Feeling her back stung by the sun, she moved into the shade of a pillar to wait. She was looking along a pavement backed by low buildings. Half a mile away, at the end of the street, a glint of waving burnished grass showed the vlei. The urban scene, solid and compact in the main streets, tended to dissolve the moment one moved into the side streets. The small colonial town was at a crossroads in its growth: half a modern city, half a pioneers' achievement; a large block of flats might stand next to a shanty of wood and corrugated iron, and most streets petered out suddenly in a waste of scrub and grass.

Outside a sprawling shed that was a showroom for agricultural implements lounged a group of farmers in their khaki; past them came a city man in smooth grey flannel. Martha's eyes followed this man, the only moving object in the heat-stilled street. She was deep in worried introspection. Into this grey lake plopped the thought, I know that man, don't I? It was enough to restore a little sight to her eyes, and she watched him coming towards her, while with another part of her mind she was thinking, When Stella comes out I shall tell her I won't have my hair cut—as if this act of defiance would in itself be a protest against her whole situation.

The man was tall, rather heavy; the grey flannel which encased him was like a firm outer skin to his assurance. His large elderly face had the authority of a commanding nose, jowled cheeks, strong hazel eyes deep under thick black brows. It was that English face which, with various small deviations, has been looking down so long from the walls of countless picture galleries and country houses. Handsome it was, but more—every feature, every curve, had an impressive finality, an absolute rightness, as if the atoms which composed it had never had a moment's hesitation in falling where they did.

Martha thought: here is another person who is *complete*—finished in his way as Stella is in hers. Whereas she herself was formless, graceless, and unpredictable, a mere lump of clay. She rejected even the sight of him, and returned to her own preoccupations.

Mr. Maynard was also preoccupied, whether pleasantly or not could be deduced only by a certain sarcastic twist of the lips. He noticed a girl standing listlessly by a pillar, and was about to walk past her, when he slowed his pace: he ought to know her. Then he remembered that less than a week before he had married her to her husband. She was looking through him; and at once he was annoyed that she should not remember such an important figure at what was surely an important occasion. This annoyance was succeeded by a more sincere pressure: she, if anyone could, would be able to tell him where his son Binkie was.

He stood firmly before her, blocking her preoccupied stare, and said, "Good afternoon, Mrs. Knowell."

Martha glanced hastily sideways to see whom he was addressing, then blushed. She looked closely at him, and then exclaimed, "Oh— Mr. Maynard!"

"And how," enquired Mr. Maynard, cutting short this mutual embarrassment, "do you find the married state?"

She considered this seriously, then said, "Well, I've only been married five days."

"A very sensible attitude."

She looked at him and waited. He was struck by her tiredness, and the unhappy set of her mouth. That critical look, however, checked in him the instinct to instruct. He was not a magistrate and the descendant of magistrates and landowners for nothing. He found himself searching for the right tone.

She saved him the trouble by asking, "Has Binkie come home yet?"

"I thought you would be able to tell me."

"The last we saw of him was when we left the Falls at two last night. He said he was going to swim across the Falls if it was the last thing he did. It probably would be, too," she added dispassionately.

Mr. Maynard winced. "He was drunk, I suppose?"

"Not *drunk*." This, it seemed, she found crude. But she added, "No more than usual."

Mr. Maynard looked sharply at her, saw this was not criticism but information willingly given, and said, "I suppose the fact that the river is full of crocodiles wouldn't deter him?"

"Oh, I'm sure he wouldn't really do it," she said quickly, on a maternal note. "They rushed off in a horde saying they would. Three years ago they say one of them tried to jump across to that little island—you know the one, when the river is low—and he went over the edge. We reminded them about it just as they left. Besides, Binkie's far too sensible."

"Binkie's *sensible?*" exclaimed Mr. Maynard, very bitter.

Martha, feeling that she was included in the bitterness, moved slightly away with "Well, I'm not responsible for Binkie."

He hesitated, then again moved in front of her. "Young woman, it would interest me very much to know why you think Binkie is sensible. He drinks like a fish. He never does any work if he can help it. He is continually either giving it a bang or tearing the place to pieces." He heavily isolated these last phrases, and handed them to her, as it were, like a challenge.

After a pause for reflection Martha observed, "He always knows what he's doing." This comment, it appeared, was enough.

"You amaze me. You really do amaze me, you know." He waited for more.

Martha offered him a sudden friendly smile, and said, "I shouldn't worry. In twenty years' time he'll be a magistrate, too, I shouldn't wonder." She laughed, as if this in itself was funny.

"My youth was not misspent. We neither gave it a bang nor tore the place to pieces."

Martha's eyebrows at once went up. "Really? I understood that you did—judging from novels, at least. Though of course in England you'd call it something else probably, you people."

"Who is 'you people'?" he asked, annoyed.

Martha looked at him as if suspecting a deliberate dishonesty, and then remarked, blushing because she had to put it into words, "Why, the upper classes, of course, who else?"

Ironically stiff, he remarked, "My son Binkie also uses the phrase 'you people'—and in the same way."

"For all that, he'll end up by being a magistrate." And Martha laughed with real enjoyment and looked straight at him, expecting him to share it.

He did not laugh. He was hurt. "You are exempt from this law?"

The shaft went home at once. She lost her shell of confidence, her face contracted, she looked at him from a haze of anxiety before turning away from him. He had no idea why this should be so.

He was contrite. Then he said apologetically, "Well, thank you.

I daresay Binkie will turn up at midnight again. I don't know why he imagines he can miss three days at the office without even ringing up to apologize—his chief rang me this morning." He heard his own voice coming so bitter that he hastened to restore his balance by sarcasm. "Don't imagine I am enquiring on my own account. As far as I am concerned, I decided long ago it would be no loss to society if Binkie did fall prey to the crocodiles. But my wife will have a sick headache until he returns."

Under the impression that he had ended the interview on a note which must leave him whole in her eyes, he was about to turn away with a "Good afternoon," when he saw her offering him a look of such ironic pity that he stopped.

She smiled and he found himself returning her smile. "Well, Mr. Maynard," she remarked in precisely his own tone of cool self-punishing sarcasm. "If Binkie has learned to ignore sick headaches, then it must be because he knows he'd be doing someone out of a pleasure if he did not." But this logical sentence crumbled, and she added awkwardly, "I mean, everyone knows about sick headaches . . . Besides—they're so old-fashioned," she went on angrily. And then: "Not that everything doesn't just go on, even when one might think they had no right to exist any longer."

Ignoring the last part of this, he seized upon the first with an ironical "Well, well!" His relations with his wife had been conducted on this principle, but he would have considered it unchivalrous to do more than talk blandly about "the female element" when with his male friends. Yet here was a representative of this same element who seemed to feel no disloyalty in putting what he had imagined to be a male viewpoint. It occurred to him, first, that he was out of touch with the young; secondly, a note had been struck which he instinctively responded to with gallantry.

Instilling gallantry into his voice, and a gleam of ironic complicity into his eyes, he moved nearer and said, "You interest me enormously."

At once she frowned, and even moved away. He dropped the tone; but held it in reserve for a later occasion.

Then he lowered his voice like a conspirator and enquired, expanding his eyes with a look of vast enquiry, "Tell me, Mrs. Knowell, is it the fashion now for young people to take their honeymoons in crowds? In my young days a honeymoon was an opportunity to be alone."

"You know quite well we did our best to get away without Binkie and the gang," said Martha resentfully.

"I was referring to the other couple, the Mathews."

For a moment it was touch and go whether she would repudiate them; but another loyalty was touched, for she laughed and asserted that they had all had a marvellous time and it was absolutely gorgeous.

Mr. Maynard watched her, then raised his heavy brows and said drily, "So it would appear."

He had expected her to succumb in confusion to this pressure; instead she suddenly chuckled, and met his eyes appreciatively. He said quickly, "Our generation has not made such a success of things that we can expect you to follow our example." This seemed to him the extreme of magnanimity, but she smiled sceptically and said, "Thanks."

There was another pause. Martha was thinking that his eighteenth-century flavour had, after all, its own piquancy—not fifty yards away the farmers still lounged and argued prices and the weather and the labour question, while almost at their elbow arched the great marble doors of the cinema.

But surely Stella should be returning by now? And all this talk of generations had a stale, dead ring. Martha reacted violently against Mr. Maynard, particularly because of that moment when he had invited her to flirt a little. She thought confusedly that there was always a point when men seemed to press a button, as it were, and one was expected to turn into something else for their amusement. This "turning into something else" had landed her where she was now: married, signed and sealed away from what she was convinced she was. Besides—and here her emotions reached conviction—he was so old! She wished now, belatedly, that she had snubbed him for daring to think that she might have even exchanged a glance with him.

He was enquiring, in a voice which engaged her attention, "I wonder if I might take this opportunity to enquire whether 'the kids'—or, if you prefer it, 'the gang'—behaved so badly that I may expect a bill for damages."

This was, underneath the severity, an appeal. Martha at once replied with compassion, "Oh, don't worry. I'm sure it will be all right."

He retreated from the pity into gruffness, remarking, "I live in terror that one day Binkie'll behave in such a way that I'll have no alternative but to resign—not that you would see any misfortune in that," he added.

Martha conceded that she was sure he was a marvellous magistrate; she sounded irritable. Then, as he did not move, she began to speak, giving him the information he was obviously waiting for, in the manner of one who was prepared to turn the knife in the wound if he absolutely insisted. "Binkie and the gang caught up with us that night about twelve. We shook up one of the hotels and made them open the bar . . ."

"Illegal," he commented.

"Well, of course. We—I mean the four of us—sneaked out while the gang were 'giving it stick' "—here she offered him an ironic smile, which he unwillingly returned—"and we drove all night till we reached the hotel. The gang came after us about eight in the morning. Luckily the hotel wasn't full and there was room for everyone. The gang didn't behave so badly, considering everything. The manager got very angry on the last day because Binkie—you remember those baboons that come up to the hotel for food? Well, Binkie and the gang caught one of the baboons and made it drunk and brought it onto the verandah. Well, it got out of control and started rampaging. But they caught it in the end, so that was all right. The baboon was sick," she added flatly, her mouth twisting. "Binkie and the baboon were dancing on the lawn. It was rather funny."

"Very funny."

"It was—very. However," she pointed out coldly, "since the gang have been tearing the place to pieces for years, and no one has got hurt, they can't be so crazy as they make out."

"Except for young Mandolis, who went over the edge of the Falls three years ago."

She shrugged. An allowable percentage of casualties, apparently. Then she added, in a different voice, hard and impatient, "There's going to be a war, anyway."

"Since this will be my second world war, I have the advantage of knowing that those follies we commit under the excuse of wartime are not cancelled out when it's over. On the contrary."

Again he had made a remark at random which went home. Mr. Maynard, whose relations with his fellow human beings were based on the need that they should in some way defer to him, found that this young woman, who until now had clearly recognized no such obligation, was all at once transformed into a mendicant. She had come close to him, and was clutching at his sleeve. Her eyes were full of tears. "Mr. Maynard," she said desperately, "Mr. Maynard . . ." But he was never to know what help she was asking of him. Afterwards he reflected that she was probably about to ask him if he could divorce her as rapidly and informally as he had married her, and was irrationally wounded because it was in his capacity as a magistrate that she was demanding help.

A loud and cheerful voice sounded beside them. "Why, Mr. Maynard," exclaimed Stella, grasping his hands and thus taking Martha's place in front of him. "Why, Mr. Maynard, how lovely to see you."

"How do you do?" enquired Mr. Maynard formally; in his manner was that irritation šhown by a man who finds a woman attractive when he does not like her. He moved away, smiling urbanely at Martha. "I shall leave you in the hands of your—matron of honour?" With this he nodded and left them. He was thinking irritably, Wanting it both ways . . . And then: Am I supposed to supply the part of priest and confessor as well? She should have got married in church. Nevertheless, he was left with the feeling of a debt undischarged, and he glanced back to see the two young women crossing the street, and apparently engaged in violent argument.

"But I've just made the appointment," said Stella angrily. "And she's had to cancel someone else. You can't change your mind now."

"I'm not going to have my hair cut," said Martha calmly. "I never said I would. *You* said so." It was perfectly easy to resist now; it had been impossible ten minutes ago. She gave a glance over her shoulder at the firm and stable back of Mr. Maynard, who was just turning the corner.

"She's a very good hairdresser, Matty—just out from England. Besides," added Stella virtuously, "you look awful, Matty, and it's your duty to your husband to look nice."

But at this Martha laughed wholeheartedly.

"What's funny?" asked Stella suspiciously. But she knew that this amusement, which she never understood, was Martha's immunity to her, and she said crossly, "Oh, very well, I'll cancel it again."

She went into Chez Paris; and in half a minute they were continuing on their way.

"We'll be late for the doctor," said Stella reproachfully, but Martha said, "We are ten minutes early."

The doctor's rooms were in a low white building across the street. Looking upwards, they saw a series of windows shuttered against the sun, green against a glare of white.

"Dr. Stern's got the nicest waiting room in town, it's all modern," said Stella devotedly.

"Oh, come on," Martha said, and went indoors without looking back.

On the first floor was a passage full of doors, all marked "Private." Stella knocked on one of these. It opened almost at once to show a woman in a white dress, who held its edge firmly, as if against possible assault. She looked annoyed; then, seeing Stella, she said with nervous amiability, "It's lovely to see you, dear, but really I'm busy."

"This is Matty," said Stella. "You know, the naughty girl who married Douggie behind everyone's back."

The young woman smiled at Martha in a friendly but harassed way, and came out into the passage, shutting the door behind her. She pulled a half-smoked cigarette from her deep white pocket, lit it, and puffed as if she were starved for smoke. "I really shouldn't, but the doctor'll manage," she said, drawing deep breaths of smoke. She was a thin girl, with lank wisps of thin black hair, and pale worried blue eyes. Her body was flat and bony in the white glazed dress, which was a uniform, but no more than a distant cousin of the stiff garments designed by elderly women to disguise the charms of young ones. "My Willie knows your Douggie—they've been boys together for years," she said with tired indulgence.

Martha was by now not to be surprised at either the information or the tone, although she had never heard of Willie.

"My God, but I'm dead," went on Alice. "Dr. Stern is my pet lamb, but he works himself to death, and he never notices when anyone else does. I was supposed to leave an hour ago."

"Listen," said Stella quickly, "that's easy, then. Just slip Matty quickly in for her appointment, then we'll all go and have a drink."

"Oh, but I can't, dear," said Alice feebly; but Stella gave her a firm little push towards the door; so that she nodded and said, "All right, then, there's lots waiting from before you, but I'll manage it." She slipped the crushed end of cigarette back into her pocket, and went into the room marked "Private."

Martha followed Stella into the waiting room. It was full. About fifteen or twenty women, with a sprinkling of children, were jealously eyeing the door into the consulting room. Martha edged herself into a seat, feeling guilty because she was about to take priority. Stella, however, stood openly waiting, with the look of one for whom the ordinary rules did not apply.

Almost at once the consulting-room door opened, and a bland voice bade a lady goodbye; she came out blushing with pleasure and giving challenging looks to those who still waited.

"Come on," said Stella loudly, "now it's us."

She pushed Martha forward, as Alice looked around into the waiting-room and said in the kindly nervous voice which was her characteristic, "Yes, dear—it's you, Mrs. Knowell."

Stella went beside Martha to the door; but there Alice held out one barring hand, with a professional look, and pulled Martha forward with the other. The door shut behind Martha, excluding Stella.

This was a large, quiet room, with a white screen in one corner which was bathed in greenish light from the shutters over the window. An enormous desk filled half the outer wall, and behind it sat Dr. Stern, his back to the light. Over an efficient white coat a smooth pale heavy-lidded face lifted for a moment, the pale cool eyes flicked assessingly over Martha, and dropped again as he said, "Please sit down."

Martha sat, and wondered how she should start: she did not really want any advice. She looked at the top of Dr. Stern's head, which was bent towards her as he flicked quickly through some papers. He had a mat of thick black crinkling hair; his neck was white, thin —very young. She saw him suddenly as a young man, and was upset. Then he said, "If you'll excuse me for one moment . . ." and glanced up again, before continuing to leaf through the papers. The upwards look was so impersonal that her anxiety vanished. She yawned. A weight of tiredness settled on her, with the cool silence of the room. A patch of yellow sunlight slanted through the slats of the blind onto the desk. Her eye was caught by it, held. She yawned again. She heard his voice: "Allow me to congratulate you on carrying off young Knowell—I've known him quite a time." He sounded quietly paternal; and she was reminded again that he was probably no older than Douglas, who had agreed enthusiastically to Stella's insistence that Martha should see the doctor at once: "Yes, Dr. Stern's just the ticket—yes, you go along, Matty, and get to know him, he'll show you the ropes."

Yet, since Martha knew the ropes, there was nothing to say. Her eyes still fixed by the yellow patch of light, she let herself slide deeper into the comfortable chair, and Dr. Stern enquired, "Sleepy?"

"Haven't had much sleep," she agreed, without moving.

Dr. Stern looked at her again and noticed that she, in her turn, was unhappily regarding Alice, who was folding something white behind the white screen.

"It's all right, Mrs. Burrell, just go next door for a moment. I'll call you." Alice went out, with a kind, reassuring smile at Martha. "And leave the door open," said Dr. Stern, for Martha's benefit, which she did not appreciate: she would have preferred it shut.

And now Dr. Stern, whose handling of the situation had been by no means as casual as it appeared, gave a swift downwards glance at his watch. Martha noticed it, and sat herself up.

"Well, Mrs. Knowell," he began smoothly, and, after a short silence, went on to deliver a lecture designed for the instruction of brides. He spoke slowly, as if afraid of forgetting some of it from sheer familiarity. When he had finished, Martha said obstinately that according to authority so and so another method was preferable. He gave her a quick look, which meant that this was a greater degree of sophistication than he was used to; almost he switched to the tone he used with married women of longer standing. But he hesitated. Martha's words might be matter-of-fact, but her face was anxious, and she was gripping her hands together in her lap.

He went off at a tangent to describe a conference on birth control he had attended in London, and concluded with a slight risky joke. Martha laughed. He added two or three more jokes, until she was laughing naturally, and returned to the subject by a side road of "A patient of mine who . . ." Now he proceeded to recommend the method she had herself suggested, and with as much warmth as if he had never recommended another. His calm, rather tired, remote voice was extremely soothing; Martha was no longer anxious; but for good measure he concluded with a little speech which, if analyzed, meant nothing but that everything was all right, one should not worry, one should take things easy. These phrases having repeated themselves often enough, he went on to remark gently that some women seemed to imagine birth control was a sort of magic; if they bought what was necessary and left it lying in a corner of a drawer, nothing more was needed. To this attitude of mind, he said, was due a number of births every year which would astound the public. He laughed so that she might, and looked enquiringly at her. She did laugh, but a shadow of worry crossed her face. He saw it, and made a mental note. There was a silence. This time his glance at his watch was involuntary: the waiting room was full of women all of whom must be assured, for various reasons, that everything was all right, there was nothing to worry about, of course one did not sleep when one was worried, of course everyone was worried at times—of course, of course, of course.

Again Martha saw the glance and rose. He rose with her and took her to the door.

"And how's your husband keeping?" he asked.

"Fine, thanks," said Martha automatically; then it struck her as more than politeness and she looked enquiring.

"His stomach behaving itself?"

"Oh, we've both got digestions like an ostrich," she said with a laugh, thinking of the amount they had drunk and eaten in the last few weeks. Then she said quickly, "There's surely nothing wrong with his stomach?" Her voice was full of the arrogance of perfect health. She heard it herself. "What's the matter with him?" she repeated. The solicitude in her voice rang false.

"I believe I've been indiscreet," said Dr. Stern. "But he is silly not to tell you. Ask him." And now he smiled, and held out his hand, saying that if she wanted help, if she just wanted to drop in for a chat, she must give him a ring. Martha wrung the hand, and left his room with the same look of soft, grateful pleasure that the previous patient had worn.

The other women watched her critically; they found that confused, self-confessing smile ridiculous. Then, as Stella rose to join her, they lost interest and turned their eyes back to the closed door.

"Well, was he nice, did you like him?" asked Stella urgently; and Martha said reticently that he was very nice.

Nothing more, it seemed, was forthcoming; and Stella urged, laughing, "Did you learn anything new?" And it occurred to Martha for the first time that she had not. Her sense of being supported, being understood, was so strong that she stopped in the passage, motionless, with the shock of the discovery that in fact Dr. Stern had said nothing at all, and in due course Douglas would be sent a bill for half a guinea—for what?

Stella tugged at her arm, so that she was set in motion again; and Martha remarked irritably that Dr. Stern was something of an old woman, "sitting all wrapped up behind his desk like a parcel in white tissue paper, being tactful to a blushing bride."

At once Stella laughed and said that she never took the slightest notice of what he said, either; as for herself and her husband, they had used such and such a method for three years, and she distinctly remembered Dr. Stern telling them it was useless.

"Well," asked Martha ungratefully, "what did you send me for, then?"

"Oh!" Stella was shocked and aggrieved. "But he's so nice, and so up to date with everything, you know."

"He can't be much older than you are," remarked Martha, in that same rather resentful voice. She was astounded that Stella was deeply shocked—at least, there could be no other explanation for her withdrawal into offended dignity: "If you don't want a really scientific doctor, then . . ." Belatedly, Martha thanked her for the service; but they had reached the door marked "Private," where they must wait for Alice; and Stella forgot her annoyance in the business of wriggling the door handle silently to show Alice they were there.

On the other side of the door, Alice was holding the handle so that it should not rattle, and watching Dr. Stern to catch the right moment for announcing the next patient. Usually, having accompanied a patient to the door, he went straight back to his desk. This time, having shed his calm paternal manner over Martha's farewells, he went to the window and looked down at the streets through the slats in the shutter. He looked tired, even exasperated. Alice expected him to complain again about being a woman's doctor. "I can't understand why I get this reputation," he would grumble. "Nine tenths of my practice are women. And women with nothing wrong with them."

But he did not say it. Alice smiled as she saw him adjust the shutter so that the patch of sun, which was now on the extreme edge of the desk, should return to the empty space of polished wood nearer the middle. He turned and caught the smile, but preferred not to notice it. He frowned slightly and remarked that in three months' time Mrs. Knowell would be back in this room crying her eyes out and asking him to do an abortion—he knew the type.

Alice did not smile; she disliked him in this mood. Her eyes were cold. She noted that his tired body had straightened, his face was alert and purposeful.

He seated himself and said, "Make a card out for Mrs. Knowell tomorrow." He almost added, laughing, "And book her a room in the nursing home." But he remembered in time that one did not make this sort of joke with Mrs. Burrell, who was sentimental; his previous nurse had been better company. All the same, he automatically made certain calculations. January or February, he thought. He even made a note on his pad; there was a complacent look on his face.

"That will do, Mrs. Burrell. Thank you for staying over your time— you mustn't let me overwork you." He smiled at her; the smile had a weary charm.

Alice did not respond. Her criticism of him formed itself in the thought, He has to have his own way over everything. And then the final blow: Heaven preserve me from being married to *him,* I wouldn't have him as a gift.

"Who's next?" he asked briskly.

"Mrs. Black," said Alice, going to the other door to call her in.

"She ought to be starting her next baby soon," he remarked.

"Have a heart," she said indignantly. "The other's only six months old."

"Get them over young," he said. "That's the best way." He added, "You ought to be starting a family yourself."

Alice paused with her hand on the knob of the door, and said irritably, "The way you go on! If I catch you with less than five when *you* get married . . ."

He looked sharply at her; he had only just understood she was really annoyed; he wished again that he might have a nurse with whom he did not have to choose his words. But she was speaking:

"You Jews have got such a strong feeling for family, it makes me sick!"

He seemed to stiffen and retreat a little; then he laughed and said, "There's surely every reason why we should?"

She looked at him vaguely, then dismissed history with "I don't see why everybody shouldn't leave everybody else alone."

"Neither do I, Mrs. Burrell, neither do I." This was savage.

"You're the sort of man who'd choose a wife because she had a good pelvis," she said.

"There are worse ways of choosing one," he teased her.

"Oh, Lord!"

"Let's have Mrs. Black. O.K.—shoot."

Alice opened the door and called, "Mrs. Black, please." She shut the door after the smiling Mrs. Black, who was already seating herself; and, as she crossed the room on her way out, heard his voice, calmly professional: "Well, Mrs. Black, and what can I do for you?"

She joined Martha and Stella, saying, "Wait, I must tell the other nurse . . ."

She came back almost at once, pulling out the frayed cigarette stub from her pocket and lighting it. Then she began tugging and pushing at the wisps of black hair that were supposed to make a jaunty frame for her face, but were falling in lank witch locks. "Oh, damn everything," she muttered crossly, pulling a comb through her hair with both hands, while the cigarette hung on her lip. Finally she gave a series of ineffective little pats at her dress, and said again, in a violent querulous voice, "Oh, damn *everything*. I'm going to give up this job. I'm sick to death of Dr. Stern. I'm just fed up."

Martha and Stella, momentarily united in understanding, exchanged a small humorous smile, and kept up a running flow of vaguely practical remarks until they had reached the hot pavement. They glanced cautiously towards Alice: she had apparently recovered.

Stella immediately dropped the female chivalry with which women protect each other in such moments, and said jealously, "I wouldn't have thought Dr. Stern would be so hard to work for."

"Oh, no, he's not," agreed Alice at once, and without the proprietary air that Stella would have resented. "Anyway, I'm really going to give it up. I didn't train as a nurse to do this sort of thing. I might as well be a hotel receptionist."

"You're mad to work when you're married," said Stella. "I've given notice to my boss. Of course, we're quite broke, but it's too much, looking after a husband and then slaving oneself to death in an office."

Alice and Martha in their turn exchanged an amused smile, while Stella touched it up a little: "Men have no idea, they think housework and cooking get done by miracles."

"Why, haven't you got a boy, dear?" enquired Alice vaguely, and then broke into Stella's reply with "Do you like Dr. Stern, Matty? If not, I shan't bother to make out a card for you."

"One doctor's as good as another," said Martha ungraciously. "Anyway, I'm never ill."

"Oh, but he's very good," exclaimed Alice, at once on the defensive. "He's really wonderful with babies."

"But I'm not going to have a baby, not for years."

"Oh, I don't blame you," agreed Alice at once. "I always tell Willie that life's too much one damned thing after another to have babies as well."

"What do you do?" enquired Martha direct.

Alice laughed, on the comfortable note which Martha found so reassuring. "Oh, we don't bother much, really. Luckily, all I have to do is to jump off the edge of a table."

They were at a turning. "I think I'll just go home, dear, if you don't mind," said Alice. "Willie might come home early, and I won't bother about a drink."

"Oh, no," protested Stella at once. "We'll all run along to Matty's place. You can ring Willie and tell him to come along."

And now Martha once again found herself protesting that of course they must all come to her flat; an extraordinary desperation seized her at the idea of being alone; although even as she protested another anxious voice was demanding urgently that she should pull herself free from this compulsion.

"Oh, well," agreed Alice good-naturedly, "I'll come and drink to your getting married."

Martha was silent. Now she had gained her point she had to brace herself to face another period of time with both Stella and Alice. She thought, Let's get it over quickly, and then . . . And then would come a reckoning with herself; she had the feeling of someone caught in a whirlpool.

The three women drifted inertly down the hot street, shading their eyes with their hands. Alice yawned and remarked in her preoccupied voice, "But I get so tired, perhaps I'm pregnant? Surely I'm not? Oh, Lord, maybe that's it!"

"Well, jump off a table, then!" said Stella with her jolly crude laugh.

"It's all very well, dear, but this worrying all the time just gets me down. Sometimes I think I'll have a baby and be done with it. That'd be nine months' peace and quiet at least."

"What's the good of working for a doctor if he can't do something?" suggested Stella, with a look at Martha which said she should be collecting information that might turn out to be useful.

Alice looked annoyed; but Stella prodded, "I've heard he helps people sometimes."

Alice drew professional discretion over her face and remarked, "They say that about all the doctors."

"Oh, come off it," said Stella, annoyed.

"If Dr. Stern did all the abortions he was asked to do, he'd never have time for anything else. There's never a day passes without at least one or two crying their eyes out and asking him."

"What do they do?" asked Martha, unwillingly fascinated.

"Oh, if they're strong-minded, they just go off to Beira or Johannesburg. But most of us just get used to it," said Alice, laughing nervously, and unconsciously pressing her hands around her pelvis.

Stella, with her high yell of laughter, began to tell a story about the last time she got pregnant. "There I was, after my second glass of neat gin, rolling on the sofa and groaning, everything just started nicely, and in came the woman from next door. She was simply furious. She said she'd report me to the police. Silly old cow. She can't have kids herself, so she wants everyone else to have them for her. I told her to go and boil her head, and of course she didn't do anything. She just wanted to upset me and make me unhappy." At the last words Stella allowed her face and voice to go limp with self-pity.

"The police?" enquired Martha blankly.

"It's illegal," explained Alice tolerantly. "If you start a baby, then it's illegal not to have it. Didn't you know?"

"Do you mean to say that a woman's not entitled to decide whether she's going to have a baby or not?" demanded Martha, flaring at once into animated indignation.

This violence amused both Stella and Alice, who now, in their turn, exchanged that small tolerant smile.

"Oh, well," said Alice indulgently. "Don't waste any breath on that. Everyone knows that more kids get frustrated than ever get born, and half the women who have them didn't want to have them, but if the Government wants to make silly laws, let them get on with it, that's what I say, I suppose they've got nothing better to do. Don't worry, dear. If you get yourself into a fix just give me a ring and I'll help you out, you don't want to lose sleep over the Government, there are better things to think about."

Stella said with quick jealousy, "I've already told Matty, I'm just around the corner, and God knows I've got enough experience, even though I'm not a nurse."

Surprised, Alice relinquished the struggle for the soul of Martha— she had not understood there was one.

"Well, that's all right, then, isn't it?" she agreed easily.

They had now reached the flats. They were a large block, starkly white in the sunlight. The pavement was so heated that its substance gave stickily under their feet; and its bright grey shone up a myriad tiny oily rainbows. A single tree stood at the entrance; and on this soft green patch their eyes rested, in relief from the staring white, the glistening grey, the hard, brilliant blue of the sky. Under the tree stood a native woman. She held a small child by one hand and a slightly larger one by the other, and there was a new baby folded in a loop of cloth on her back. The older children held the stuff of her skirt from behind. Martha stopped and looked at her. This woman summed up her uncomfortable thoughts and presented the problem in its crudest form. This easy, comfortable black woman seemed extraordinarily attractive, compared with the hard gay anxiety of Stella and Alice. Martha felt her as something simple, accepting—whole. Then she understood she was in the process of romanticizing poverty; and repeated firmly to herself that the child mortality for the colony was one of the highest in the world. All the same . . .

Alice and Stella, finding themselves alone in the hall, came back and saw Martha staring at the tree. There was nothing else to look at.

"It's all very well for us," remarked Martha with a half-defiant laugh, seeing that she was being observed. "We're all right, but how about her?"

Alice looked blank; but Stella, after a spasm of annoyance had contracted her face, broke into a loud laugh. To Alice she said boisterously, "Matty is a proper little Bolshie, did you know? Why, we had to drag her away from the Reds before she was married, she gets all hot and bothered about our black brothers."

She laughed again, insistently, but Alice apparently found no need to do the same.

"Come along, dear," she said kindly to Martha. "Let's have a drink and get it over with, if you don't mind."

Martha obediently joined them. But Stella could not leave it. She said brightly, "It's different for them. They're not civilized, having babies is easy for them, everyone knows that."

They were climbing the wide staircase. Alice remarked indifferently, "Dr. Stern has a clinic for native women. Every Sunday morning. I tell him he's so keen on everybody having babies that he can't even give Sunday a rest."

Stella involuntarily stopped. "Dr. Stern treats kaffirs?" she asked, horrified. It appeared that he was in imminent danger of losing a patient.

"He's very goodhearted," said Alice vaguely. The words restored her own approval of Dr. Stern. "He only charges them sixpence, or something like that." She continued to drag herself up the staircase, ahead of the others.

Stella was silent. Her face expressed a variety of emotions, doubt being the strongest. Then Dr. Stern effected in her that small revolution in thinking which crosses a gulf to philanthropy. She remarked, still dubiously, "Well, of course, we should be kind to them."

Martha, three steps below her, laughed outright. Alice looked at her in surprise, Stella with anger.

"Well, if everyone was like you, they'd get out of hand," Stella said sourly. "It's all very well, but everyone knows they are nothing but animals, and it doesn't hurt them to have babies, and . . ." She added doubtfully, "Dr. Stern is always modern."

"He's making a study about it," said Alice. She was waiting for them on the landing. "It's not true they are different from us. They're just the same, Dr. Stern says."

Stella was deeply shocked and disturbed; she burst into her loud vulgar laugh. "Don't make me laugh."

"But it's scientific," said Alice vaguely.

"Oh, doctors!" suggested Stella, in precisely the same indulgent tone Alice had previously used for "the Government."

Martha, arriving beside them on the landing, said bitterly, "It seems even Dr. Stern is only interested in writing papers about them."

Alice was offended. "Well, so long as they get help, I don't suppose they mind, do you? And he's very kind. How many doctors can you think of would work as hard as he does all the week and every night and then spend all Sunday morning helping kaffir women with their babies? And for as good as nothing, too."

"Well, sixpence is the same for them as ten shillings would be for us," protested Martha.

Alice was really angry now. "It's not the same for Dr. Stern."

"Whose fault is that?" demanded Martha hotly.

Stella cut the knot by opening the door. "Oh, let's have a drink," she said impatiently, "Don't take any notice of Matty. Douggie'll put some sense into her head. You can't be a Red if you're married to a civil servant."

They went inside. Martha was acutely depressed at the finality of what Stella had said. She began to take out glasses and syphons, until Stella took them impatiently out of her hands. She sat down, and let Stella arrange things as she wished; with the feeling she had done this many times before.

Alice was unobservant and relaxed in a deep chair, puffing out clouds of smoke until she was surrounded by blue haze. "For crying out loud, but I'm tired," she murmured; and, without moving the rest of her body, she held out her hand to take the glass Stella put into it.

The room was rather small, but neat; it was dressed with striped modern curtains, light rugs, cheerful strident cushions. Stella's taste, as Martha observed to herself bitterly, although telling herself again it was her own fault. Well, she'd be gone soon, and then . . .

She took the glass Stella handed her, and let herself go loose, as Alice was doing.

Stella, accompanied apparently by two corpses, remained upright and energetic in her chair, and proceeded to entertain Alice with an amusing account of "their" honeymoon.

". . . And you should have seen Matty, coping with the lads as if she were an old hand at the game. No wedding night for poor Matty, we were driving all night, and we had two breakdowns at that—the funniest thing you ever saw. We got to the hotel at two in the morning, and then all the boys arrived, and it wasn't until that night we all decided it was really time that Matty had a wedding night, so we escorted them to their room, playing the Wedding March on the mouth organs, and the last we saw of Matty was her taking off Douggie's shoes and putting him to bed." She laughed, and Martha joined her. But Alice, who had not opened her eyes, remarked soothingly that Douggie was a hell of a lad, but Matty needn't worry, these wild lads made wonderful husbands, look at Willie, he'd been one of the worst, and now butter wouldn't melt in his mouth.

The thought of her husband made her sit up, and say in a determined voice that she really must go; Willie was a pet lamb, he never worried about anything—but all the same, she wasn't going to start setting a bad example. She struggled out of her chair, drained her glass, and nervously pressed Martha's hand. "Sorry, dear, but I really must—I'll see you soon, I expect, my Willie and your Douglas being such friends. And now I really . . ." She smiled hastily at Stella, waved vaguely, and hurried out. They could hear her running down the stairs on her high heels.

"Alice is just an old fusser," said Stella, settling herself comfortably. "If Willie isn't tied to her apron strings she can't sit still." Martha said nothing. "That's no way to keep a man. They don't like it. You should manage them without them knowing it."

Martha observed irritably that Stella and Alice talked about husbands as if they were a sort of wild animal to be tamed.

Stella looked at her, and then remarked in an admonishing way that Martha was very young, but she'd soon learn that the way to keep a lad like Douggie was to give him plenty of rope to hang himself with.

Irritation was thick in the air, like the tobacco smoke that now made a heavy bluish film between them. Martha was praying, I wish she'd go.

Stella made a few more remarks, which were received in silence. Then she looked angrily across and said that if she were Matty she'd have a good sleep and then take life easy.

She rose, and stood for a moment looking at the mirror inside the flap of her handbag. Everything in order. She shut the handbag, and gazed around the little room; she adjusted a cushion, then turned her gaze towards Martha, who was sprawling gracelessly in her chair.

Martha looked back, acknowledging the discouragement that filled her at the sight of this woman. Stella must have gained this perfect assurance with her maturity at the age of—what? There were photographs of her at fifteen, showing her no less complete than she was now.

It appeared that the moment for parting had at last arrived. Martha struggled up. And now Martha was filled with guilt. For Stella's face showed a genuine concern for her; and Martha reminded herself that Stella was nothing if not kind and obliging—for what was kindness, if not this willingness to devote oneself utterly to another person's life? Martha was too tired even to instil irony into it. She kissed Stella clumsily on one of her smooth tinted cheeks, and thanked her. Stella brightened, blushed a little, and said that any time Matty wanted anything she had only to . . . At last she left, smiling, blowing a kiss from the door, in precisely that pose of competent grace which most depressed Martha.

The moment she was alone, Martha rummaged for a pair of scissors and went with determination to the bathroom. There she knelt on the edge of the gleaming and slippery bath, and in an acutely precarious position leaned up to look into the shaving mirror. It was too high for her. There was a large mirror at a suitable height next door, but for some reason this was the one she must use. Nothing in her reflection pleased her. She was entirely clumsy, clodhopping, graceless. Worse than this, she was filled with uncomfortable memories of how she had looked at various stages of her nineteen years —for she might be determined to forget how she had *felt* in her previous incarnations, but she could not forget how she had looked. Her present image had more in common with her reflection at fifteen, a broad and sturdy schoolgirlishness, than it had with herself of only six months ago.

Her dissatisfaction culminated as she put the scissors to the heavy masses of light dryish hair that lay on her shoulders. She remembered briefly that Stella had laid stress on her hair being *properly* cut; but the mere idea of submitting herself to the intentions of anybody else must be repulsed. Steadily, her teeth set to contain a prickling feverish haste, she cut around her hair in a straight line. Then she fingered the heavy unresponsive mass, and began snipping at the ends. Finally she lifted individual pieces and cut off slabs of hair from underneath, so that it might not be so thick. From the way the ends curved up, she could see that Stella might be right—her hair would curl. At last she plunged her head into water and soaped it hard, rubbing it roughly dry afterwards, in the prayerful hope that these attentions might produce yet another transformation into a different person. Then she swept up the cushions of hair from the floor and went into the bedroom. It was after six, and night had fallen. She switched on the light, to illuminate a cheerful room whose commonplace efficiency depressed her; and stood in front of the other mirror, trying to shape the sodden mass of hair into waves. She thought her appearance worse than before. Giving it up in despair, she switched off the light again and went to the window. She was thinking with rueful humour that now she was undeniably longing for Douglas to come so that he might reassure her; whereas for most of the last week she had been struggling with waves of powerful dislike of him that she was too well educated in matters psychological not to know were natural to a newly married woman. Or, to put this more precisely, she had gone through all the handbooks with which she was now plentifully equipped, seized on phrases and sentences which seemed to fit her case, and promptly extended them to cover the whole of womankind. There was nothing more paradoxical about her situation than that, while she insisted on being unique, individual, and altogether apart from any other person, she could be comforted in such matters only by remarks like "Everybody feels this" or "It is natural to feel that."

She leaned against the sill, and tried to feel that she was alone and able to think clearly, a condition she had been longing for, it seemed, for weeks. But her limbs were seething with irritation; she could not stand still. She fetched a chair and sat down, trying to relax. Behind her, the two small and shallow rooms were dark, holding their scraps of furniture in a thinned shadow, which was crossed continually by shifting beams of light from the street. Under her, the thin floor crept and reverberated to footsteps behind the walls. Above her, feet tapped beyond the ceiling. She found herself listening intently to these sounds, trying to isolate them, to make them harmless. She shut her mind to them, and looked outwards.

The small, ramshackle colonial town had become absorbed in a luminous dark. A looming pile of flats was like a cliff rising from the sea, and the turn of a roof like a large elbow half-blocking the stars. Below this aerial scene of moon, sky, roofs and the tops of trees, the streets ran low and indistinct, with lights of cars nosing slow along them among the isolated yellow spaces which were street lamps. Whiffs of petrol-laden dust and staled scent from flowers in the park a hundred yards away drifted down past her towards the back of the building, where it would mingle with a heavier, composted smell: that smell which comes rich and heavy out of the undertown, the life of African servants, cramped, teeming, noisy with laughter and music. Singing came now from the native quarters at the back; and this small lively music flowed across the dark to join the more concentrated bustle of noise that came from a waste lot opposite. The fun fair had come to town; and over the straggling dusty grass, showing yellow in the harsh composite glare from a hundred beating lights, rose swings and roundabouts and the great glittering wheel. Once a year this fair visited the city on its round of the little towns of southern Africa, and spilled its lights and churning music for a few hours nightly into the dark.

The great wheel was revolving slowly, a chain of lights that mingled with the lamps of Orion and the Cross. Martha laid her wet and uncomfortable head against the wall, and looked at the wheel steadily, finding in its turning the beginnings of peace. Slowly she quietened, and it seemed possible that she might recover a sense of herself as a person she might, if only potentially, respect. It was really all quite simple, she assured herself. That this marriage was a foolish mistake must certainly be obvious to Douglas himself; for if humility can be used to describe such an emotion, Martha was genuinely humble in thinking of him and herself as involved in an isolated act of insanity which a simple decision would reverse. His personality and hers had nothing to do with it. The whole graceless affair had nothing to do with what she really felt or—surely?—what he felt, either.

The dragging compulsion which had begun to operate when they met, which had made it impossible for her to say no at any stage of the process, seemed broken. It would be easy, she thought, to tell Douglas when he entered the room that they must part at once; he must agree. For since he shared her view that the actual ceremony was no more than a necessary bit of ritual to placate society, it followed he would view a divorce in the same light.

Thus Martha—while her eyes hypnotically followed the circling of the great wheel. But at the back of her mind was an uncomfortable memory. It was of Stella roaring with laughter as she told the story, while her husband laughed with her, of how she had, a day after their wedding, run back to her mother, because she had decided she didn't want to be married at all, and most particularly not to Andrew; after some months of marriage, it seemed that Stella found this mood nothing but a joke. The fact that what she was feeling now might be nothing but what everybody felt filled Martha with exhaustion. She remained clinging to the sill, while tiredness flowed into her, an extreme of fatigue, like the long high note on the violin that holds a tension while the ground swell of melody gathers strength beneath it. Her limbs were so heavy she could hardly prevent herself from sliding off the chair; while her mind, like a bright space above a dark building, was snapping with activity. The small, clear picture of Stella laughing at her own story was succeeded by another: she saw Binkie, large, fat, heavy, grotesquely dancing with the baboon on the lawn outside the hotel; she saw herself laughing at the scene, arm in arm with Douglas. Finally, she saw a small yellow flower on the very edge of the Falls, drenched with spray and tugging at its roots like a flag in a gale, but returning to its own perfect starred shape whenever the wind veered. She could not remember having actually seen this flower. It was frightening that she could not—yet there was something consoling about it, too. She tried again and again to place the moment she had seen it; her mind went dark with the effort, as if a switch had been turned down. Then she heard, with a movement of slow, swelling sadness, the music from the amusement park. And now she understood that she was looking back at the hectic elation of those four days with regret—nostalgia was invading her together with the rhythm of the false cheap music. Yet the truth was she had disliked every moment of the time. She jerked herself fully awake; *that* lie she had no intention of tolerating. She stood up, and told herself with a bleak and jaunty common sense that she needed a good night's sleep.

The outer door crashed open; the lights crashed on. A cheerful young man came towards her, whirled her up in his arms, and began squeezing her, saying, "Well, Matty, here we are in our own place at last, and about time, too!" With this he gave her a large affectionate kiss on the cheek, and set her down, and stood rubbing his hands with satisfaction. Then it seemed that something struck him; doubt displaced the large grin, and he said, "But, Matty, what've you done to yourself?"

Turning quickly away, Martha said, "I've cut off my hair. Don't look at it now, it'll be all right in the morning."

Taking her at her word, he said, "Oh, all right, changed your hairstyle, eh?" And he rubbed his hands again, with pleasure: she could see he took it as a compliment to himself that she should. "Sorry I was late, but I ran into some of the boys and I couldn't get away. Had to celebrate." His proprietary look half annoyed her; but she could feel the beginnings of fatal pleasure. From the way he looked at her and rubbed his hands, she knew that he had again been congratulated on his acquisition; and while she puzzled over the knowledge that this could have nothing to do with *herself*, she could not help feeling less heavy and unattractive.

"They think I'm a helluva lucky . . ." he announced; and at the thought of the scenes in the bar with the boys, a reflection of his proud and embarrassed grin appeared on his face. He swooped over at her, ground her tightly to him, and announced, "And so-so I am."

Then, still holding her, but loosening his grip because his mind was on them and not on her, he began telling her some of the things they had said, in a comradely way, sharing the pleasure with her. At first she said, half anxiously, half pleased, "And what else?" "And what did they say then?" Until suddenly she jerked away from him, angry and red, and said, "I don't think that's funny, that's disgusting."

The very image of an offended prude, she turned her back on him; while, half shamefaced, half sniggering, he looked at her and said at last, "Oh, come off it, Matty, don't put on an act."

Martha undressed in silence, flinging crumpled blue dress, knickers, petticoat, in all directions. She stood naked. In the mood she was in, it had nothing to do with coquetry.

To Douglas, however, this was not apparent. He found the naked and angry girl an argument for forgiveness. Flinging off his own clothes, he bounced onto the bed, and moved over to give her room. Still frowning, she moved chastely in beside him; for the fact that they were annoyed with each other made the act of getting naked into bed on a level with sitting beside him at breakfast. She was irritated to discover that he did not understand this. She was on the point of turning over away from him, when the instinct to please turned her towards him. Love had brought her here, to lie beside this young man; love was the key to every good; love lay like a mirage through the golden gates of sex. If this was not true, then nothing was true, and the beliefs of a whole generation were illusory. They made love. She was too tired to persuade herself that she felt anything at all. Her head was by now swimming with exhaustion.

"God, but I'm tired, Matty," he announced, rolling off her. He yawned and said with satisfaction, "How many hours have we slept during the last fortnight?"

She did not reply. Loyalty towards love was forcing her to pretend that she was not disappointed, and that she did not—at that moment she was sick with repulsion—find him repulsive. But already that image of a lover that a woman is offered by society, and carries with her so long, had divorced itself from Douglas, like the painted picture of a stencil floating off paper in water. Because that image remained intact and unhurt, it was possible to be good-natured. It is that image which keeps so many marriages peaceable and friendly.

She listened, smiling maternally, while he calculated aloud how many hours they had slept. It took him several minutes: he was nothing if not efficient.

"Do you realize we couldn't have slept more than about three hours a night during the last six weeks?" he enquired proudly.

"Awful, isn't it?" she agreed, in the same tone.

After a pause: "It's been lovely, hasn't it, Matty?"

She agreed with enthusiasm that it had. At the same time she glanced incredulously at him to assure herself that he must be joking. But he was grinning in the half-dark. She simply could not comprehend that his satisfaction, his pleasure, was fed less by her than by what other people found in their marriage.

Her silence dismayed him. He gripped her arm, pressed it, and urged, "Really, everyone's been awfully good to us, haven't they, Matty? Haven't they? They've given us a hell of a start?"

Again she enthusiastically agreed. He lay alert now, feeling her worry and preoccupation. Then he suddenly enquired, "Did you see the doctor? What did he say?"

"Oh, nothing much," she said, sleepy and bad-tempered. "He doesn't seem to know more than we do, only he does the big medicine-man act awfully well."

But Douglas could not agree with this. "He's very good, Matty—very good indeed."

Her motherliness was warned by his anxiety, and she at once assured him that he had been very kind and she liked him enormously.

"That's all right, then. You'll be all right with him." A pause. "Well, what did he recommend? Those effells are a pain in the neck, only for bachelors." He laughed proudly.

"He made a joke about them."

"What did he say?" She told him. "He's a helluva lad, Dr. Stern, isn't he, Matty? Isn't he?"

She hesitated. Besides, she did not want to think now about the machinery of birth control, which suddenly appeared to her distasteful. But since from the beginning it had been a matter of pride to be efficient, gay and matter-of-fact, she could not say that she detested the jellies and bits of rubber which from now on would accompany what Dr. Stern had referred to as her love life (as if it were some-thing separate from life itself); she could not now say what for the moment was true: that she wished she were like that native woman, who was expected to have a baby every year. She wished at the very least that it should not all be made into a joke. She wanted to cry her eyes out; nothing could be more unreasonable.

Suddenly Douglas observed, "We've just done it without anything. I suppose that's a bit silly, eh, Matty?"

"Oh, it'll be all right," she said hastily, unwilling to move. She felt it would be "all right" because since the "act of love" had been what Dr. Stern described as unsatisfactory, she felt it had not occurred at all. She was unaffected, and therefore it would be unfair, if not un-natural, that a child might result from it.

"Because you'd better get out of bed and go to the bathroom," he suggested uneasily.

"Judging from the book of words," she said, with a dry anger that astounded even herself, "those little dragons of yours go wriggling along at such a rate it would be too late by now."

"Well, maybe it would be better than nothing," he urged.

"Oh, I'm too tired to move," she said irritably. "Besides," she added firmly, "I'm not going to have a baby for years. It would be idiotic, with a war coming."

"Well, Matty . . ." But he was at a loss for words in the face of this irrationality. "At any rate," he announced firmly, "we mustn't take any more chances at all. Actually we're being helluva fools. It's not the first time."

"Oh, it'll be all right," she agreed amenably, quite comfortable in the conviction, luckily shared by so many women who have not been pregnant, that conception, like death, was something remarkable which could occur to other people, but not to her.

"Did you tell Dr. Stern about your periods?" he persisted.

"What about them?" she asked irritably, disengaging herself from his arm and lying parallel to him, not touching him.

"Well, you did say they were a bit irregular."

"Oh, do stop fussing," she cried, tormented. "According to the book of words thousands of women have irregular periods before they have a baby and it doesn't mean a thing."

"But, Matty, do be reasonable," he implored.

She was silent. Even more did she want to weep. But this would have meant abandoning herself to him, and to explanations of what she could not explain herself—a feeling of being caged and trapped. Until two weeks ago, her body had been free and her own, some-thing to be taken for granted. She would have scorned to fuss about, or even to notice, a period that was heavy or one that chose not to come at all. And now this precious privacy, this independence, so lately won from her mother's furtive questioning, was being threatened by an impertinent stranger.

"Matty," he said again, "don't you think you're being unreasonable?"

"I'm so tired I could scream," she muttered defiantly.

Silence. Music from the waste lot came throbbing into the room. The big wheel, glittering with white lights, revolved steadily. Like a damned wedding ring, she thought crossly, abandoning herself to anger, since she was not free to cry.

"I do hope you'll be in a better humour in the morning," said Douglas coldly, after a pause.

Her mind began producing wounding remarks with the efficiency of a slot machine. She was quite dismayed at the virulence of some of the things that came to her tongue. She cautiously turned her head and saw his face showing thoughtful in the steady flicker of lights. He looked young—a boy, merely; with a boy's sternness. She asked, in a different tone, "Dr. Stern said something about your stomach."

His head turned quickly. Guardedly he said, "What did he tell you?"

"Nothing—only mentioned it. Why didn't you tell me?"

"Oh—I don't know."

The pride that concealed a weakness appealed to her. She reached out her hand and laid it on his arm above the elbow. It stiffened, then responded.

"I've an ulcer—nothing much. I just go on the tack when I feel it."

She could not help a pang of repulsion for the idea of an ulcer; then another of pity. "I thought you had to have special diet for ulcers?"

"Oh—don't fuss." He added, contrite, "I lay off fats when it starts up."

"You're very young to have an ulcer," she remarked at last. Then, thinking this sounded like a criticism, she tightened her fingers about the thick warm flesh. It was slack. He was asleep, and breathing deeply.

2

When Martha woke, she knew she had slept badly. Several times she had half roused, with the urgent knowledge that she ought to be attending to something; and this anxiety seemed to be of the same quality as that suggested by the great dragging circle of lights, which continued to flicker through her sleep like a warning. The ceiling of the small bedroom spun with light until after midnight, when the wheel was stilled; then bars of yellow light lay deep over the ceiling, over the bed, across Douglas's face, from a room opposite, where a man must be lying awake reading, or a woman keeping vigil with a sick child.

At six she was fully awake. The sky outside was a chilly white-gold haze; winter was coming. She leaned on her elbow to look out at the wheel; in this small colourless light it rested motionless, insignificant, and the machinery of the fun fair beneath it seemed tawdry and even pathetic. It no longer had the power to move her; and the fact that it had so disturbed her sleeping was absurd. But Martha had been born—or so it seemed—with the knowledge that the hours of sleep were long, busy, and of the same texture as the hours of waking. She entered sleep cautiously, like an enemy country. She knew, too, however, that for most it was a sudden dropping of a dark curtain, and regarded this other family of mankind with a simple envy, the result of her upbringing so far away from the centres of sophistication, where she would have learned to use the word "neurotic" as a label that would make any further thought on the subject unnecessary, or as a kind of badge guaranteeing a superior sensibility. She was in that primitive condition where she was able to pay healthy respect to—Douglas, for instance.

She looked at him now with a rather wistful curiosity. He lay on his back, easily outstretched among the sheets and blankets. He was handsome when he slept. His face was open and rather flushed. An outflung arm, as if it had just fallen loose from the act of throwing something, lay in a calm, beautiful line from waist to shoulder. The upper part of his body, emerging from the clothes, was solid, compact, the flesh clear and healthy; a light sprinkling of freckles over a white, bright skin. He looked stern and dignified, sealed away from her in sleep, and restored to the authority of good sense. Martha's respect for him was now deep and genuine. She thought, with a simplicity which was authorized and confirmed by the dignity of his face, I shall say we must stop being married; he won't mind.

When he woke, everything would be explained and settled.

Waiting for him to wake, she sat up and looked out. The town, no less than the fun fair, looked small and mean after the hazy splendours of the night. The two big blocks of flats opposite rose white and solid, but rain had streaked their sides into dinginess. Their windows were dead and asleep. Beyond them, half a dozen business houses, their surfaces clean with paint, glossy with money; and beyond these again,

the tin-roofed shanties of the Coloured town, which marked the con-
fines of order; for on two sides of this organized centre stretched the
locations, or straggling slums where the Africans were. From a single
small window she could overlook at least three worlds of life, quite
separate, apparently self-contained, apparently linked by nothing
but hate. . . . But these familiar ideas, sprung in her mind by the
simple act of looking through a window, were too much of a burden
this morning. First Douglas should wake, and then it would be time
to look out of the window. She might suggest to him, for instance,
that he should at once throw up his job, and they should go and "live
among the people."

She sprang out of bed, but noiselessly, and went next door to the
living room. There, as she expected, lay a small heap of letters
where Douglas had flung them down the night before. She carried
them back to bed with her. Most were of that sort which people
write to those getting married, in order that they may say with
pride, "We have had so and so many letters of congratulation." At
least, Martha could not yet see letters of politeness in any other way.
She therefore tossed them aside, and took up one from her brother,
now at the University of Cape Town. It was a good-humoured letter,
full of a determinedly humorous tolerance; their relations were always harmonious; in order that two people may quarrel they must
have something in common to quarrel over.

The next, also from the university, was from Joss Cohen. She
opened it with the most vivid delight; she even held it unopened for
a moment, to delay the pleasure of reading it. What she expected
from it was—but what did she *not* expect from Joss Cohen! At last
she opened it. Four lines:

Dear Matty,
    Your brother mentioned that you got married last week. I must admit
this was something of a surprise. However, please accept my congratulations. I hope your marriage will be happy and prosperous.
                                                        Yours,
                                                        Joss

She put it down slowly, flushing with hurt anger. It was that word
"prosperous" which stung her. Then she reread it, trying to revive
him as he really was, since these colourless lines could have no power
to evoke him. She admitted at last that she felt abandoned because
he had not thought her worth even the trouble of a sarcastic phrase.
Very well, then: she dropped the letter into the pile of purely formal
ones.

The third was from Marnie Van Rensberg, on blue paper with a pink rose in one corner.

Dear Matty,
  Mom told me your news this morning. She heard it from your Mom at the station when she went in to get the mail. I am so happy Matty now we are both married. I hope you will be very happy. I am going to have a baby in October. The doctor says November, they think they know everything. I hope it will be a boy because Dirk wants a boy. I don't mind what it is, but for my sake I hope it's a girl really, but who would be a woman in this world. Ha. Ha.
                              Affectionately, your old pal,
                                        Marnie

The fourth was from Solly Cohen, and from the moment Martha opened it she knew she would find in it everything Joss had refused.

  Well, well, Martha Quest, I'm not surprised, you are a born marrier, and I always told Joss so when he insisted something might be done with you. I hear high civil service, prospects, pension, and no doubt a big house in the suburbs. If not yet, it will come, it will come. Well, well. You'll have to be a good girl now, no naughty ideas about the colour bar—no ideas of any kind, for that matter. If there is one thing you can't afford, dear Matty, in the station of life into which you've chosen to marry, god help you, it is ideas.
  Well, as you will see from the address, I'm not in Cape Town any more. The higher education, being nothing but sh—, is not for me, though Joss is apparently prepared to go through with it. I'm making an effort towards communal life in the Coloured quarters of our great metropolis, a small light in a naughty world. All the boorjoys are very shocked, of course. I shall naturally not be allowed to have visitors of your sort, but if at any time you feel like dropping a line from your exalted world of tea parties, sundowners and sound incomes, I shall be pleased to read it.
                                        Yours,
                                        Solly

  (I am not supposed to have letters unless the whole group approves, but I shall explain that a certain amount is due to you as a victim of the system.)

At first Martha allowed herself to feel angry and hurt, but almost at once she laughed, with the insight of fellow-feeling. She read it again, isolated the word "god," with a small g, and then the word "boorjoys." That's what you are doing it for, she thought maliciously. At once Joss seemed infinitely better than his brother; Solly was

nothing but a child beside him. But at the same time she was thinking of this communal household as a refuge for herself. She had decided she would go there at once, that very morning, and ask if she
might join them. She yearned towards it—a life of simplicity, conversation and ideals. And in the Coloured quarter, too . . . she was
about to leap out of bed to pack the suitcase which would be the
most final of arguments against being married, when she saw there
was another letter lying among the folds of the bedclothes. It was
from her mother.

My dear Girl,
   I do hope you enjoyed your honeymoon, and are not too tired after
it. I am just writing to say that we have finally decided to sell the farm,
we have had a good offer and shall settle in town. Somewhere near you,
so that I can help you now that you are married and . . . [Here a line
was carefully scratched out, but Martha made out the word "baby,"
and went cold with anger.] At any rate, perhaps I can be of use.
   No more now, affectionately,
                                        Mother

This letter affected Martha like a strong drug. She threw herself
on Douglas.
   "What's the matter?" he jerked out, as he woke. He looked at her
closely, and at once sat up. He yawned a little, warm and easy with
sleep, then he smiled and put his arm around her.
   "Douglas," she announced furiously, "do you know, I've had a
letter from my mother, and do you know, they're moving into town
after me, just in order to run my life for me, that's all it is, and—"
   "Hold your horses," he demanded. He absorbed this information,
and said at last, "Well, Matty, they were bound to move in sometime,
what of it?"
   She froze inwardly; and after a pause, moved away again. He
moved after her, and began patting her shoulders rhythmically: he
was calm, matter-of-fact, sensible.
   "Now, look here," he went on. "I know you have a thing about
this, but you seem to think fate's got it in for you specially or something of the sort. All girls quarrel with their mothers, and mothers
interfere—you should have seen my sister and my mother before
Anne went to England. They were like a couple of cats. Of course
your mother's a bit of a Tartar. Just don't take any notice. And in any
case"—here he laughed good-temperedly—"you'll be just as bad at
her age," he teased her.
   These sensible remarks struck her as the extreme of brutality; but
no sooner had she felt a rush of emotional indignation than a sin-

cerer emotion took hold of her. What Douglas had said, phrase after phrase, struck straight at her deepest and most private terrors. For if she had remained in the colony when she had wanted to leave it, got married when she wanted to be free and adventurous, always did the contrary to what she wanted most, it followed that there was no reason why at fifty she should not be just such another woman as Mrs. Quest, narrow, conventional, intolerant, insensitive. She was cold and trembling with fear. She had no words to express this sense of appalling fatality which menaced everyone, her mother as well as herself. She wriggled off the bed, away from his warm and consoling hand, and went to the window. Outside, the sunlight was now warm and yellow, everything was activity.

"Look," she said flatly, "it's like this. Ever since I can remember, they've been on that farm, stuck in poverty like flies on flypaper. All the time, daydreams about all kinds of romantic escapes—for years I believed it all. And now suddenly everything becomes perfectly simple, and don't you see, it was all for nothing. That's the point—it was all for nothing."

She heard her voice rising dramatically, and stopped, irritated with herself.

Douglas was watching her. There was a look in his eyes which struck her. She looked down at herself. She was wearing a thin nightgown. She saw that he was finding her attractive in this mood. She was completely furious. With a gesture of contempt she picked up a dressing gown and covered herself. Then she said flatly, "I can see I am being ridiculous." Then, since he looked hurt and shamefaced, she began hurriedly, in an impulse to share it with him, "The whole point is this: if it wasn't sweepstakes, it was a gold mine or a legacy. In the meantime, nothing but the most senseless poverty—"

But again she heard that dramatic note in her voice, and stopped short. *That* was not what she felt! She was unable to say what she meant in a way that sounded true. Silence—and she was filling with helpless exhaustion. Suddenly she thought, It's all so boring. She felt obscurely that the whole thing was old-fashioned. The time for dramatic revolts against parents was past; it all had a stale air. How ridiculous Solly was, with his communal settlements, and throwing up university—for what? *It had all been done and said already.* She had no idea what was the origin of this appalling feeling of flatness, staleness and futility.

"Oh, well," she began at last, in a cheerful, hard voice, "it all doesn't matter. Nothing one does makes any difference, and by the time we're middle-aged we'll be as stupid and reactionary as our parents—and so it all goes on, and one might as well get used to it!"

"Now Matty!" protested Douglas, helplessly, "what on earth do you expect me to do about it? I'll stand by you, of course, if that's what you want." He saw her face, which wore an unconscious look of pure hopeless fear, and decided it was enough. He got out of bed, and came to her. "Now, don't worry, I shall look after you, everything's all right."

At this Martha clung to him. "I'm sorry," she said brightly and falsely. "I'm an awful fool."

He kissed her, patted her here and there in an affectionate and brotherly way, and then said, "For God's sake, I shall be late for office. You should have woken me before." He went whistling into the bathroom, and began shaving.

She went back to bed, propped a hand mirror on a ridge of blanket, and tried to brush her hair into shape. She did not want to be noticed, and each time Douglas came in to fetch something she hastily turned away. But when he at last came in, fully dressed, he remarked, "Your hair doesn't do too badly like that." He was now in very good spirits. He announced, rubbing his hands, that he must not be late. There would be some sort of show at the office for him— this was the first day he would be at work since his marriage. As he picked up some papers, and gave his usual efficient glance around to see what he might have forgotten, he remarked, "And don't forget the sundowner party tonight at the Brodeshaws'."

Martha said quickly, "Douglas . . ."

He stopped on his way out. "I'm awfully late."

"Douglas, why can't we go to England—or somewhere?" she enquired resentfully. "After all, you said . . ."

But he cut in quickly. "There's going to be a war, and we can't take chances now."

The newspaper was lying over the bedclothes—one glance at the headlines was enough. But she persisted. "But it would be much better there than here if the war comes—at least we would be really in it."

"Now look, Matty, I really am late." He went out, hastily.

For some time she remained where she was, surrounded by the lanky sheets of newsprint, by scraps of letter, by the hand mirror, the brush, a tangle of the new white wedding linen. The headlines on the newspaper filled her with nothing but the profoundest cynicism. Then she saw a small book lying open on the bed, and pulled it towards her. She saw it was Douglas's engagement book, and left it; for it was certainly her strongest principle that a wife who looked at her husband's letters or pockets was the blackest sort of traitor to decency. But the little book still lay open, at arm's length. It was, after all, only an engagement book; and these engagements would concern herself. Compromising with her principles by not actually touching it, she moved closer and read the entries for the next two weeks. There was not a day free of sundowner parties, dances, lunches. Most of the names she did not know. The little book, lying beside the crumpled newspaper with its frightening black headlines, provided the strongest comment on her situation. She saw Solly's letter, with its emphatic scrawl of an address, foundering among billows of sheet. Her anxiety focused itself sharply with: I've got to get out of it all. She got up, and dressed rapidly. Her clothes were all crushed from packing; there was nothing to wear but the blue linen from yesterday. But what she looked like, she assured herself, would be quite irrelevant to Solly, who was now monastic and high-minded in his communal settlement. In a few minutes she had left the untidy flat behind, and was in the street.

And no sooner had she turned the corner which shut out the flats, than it seemed as if not only they but her marriage did not exist—so strong was her feeling of being free. She was regarding her marriage, the life she was committed to, with a final, horrified dislike. Everything about it seemed false and ridiculous, and that Matty who apparently was making such a success of it had nothing to do with herself, Martha, now walking at leisure down this street on a cool fine morning. It was only a short walk to the Coloured quarters, and she went slowly, loitering along the pavements under the trees, picking off leaves from the hedges, pulling at the long grass which forced itself up wherever there was a gap in the pavement.

What puzzled her most was that she *was* a success. The last few weeks, confused, hectic, hilarious, had one thread running through it: the delight of other people in this marriage. How many had not embraced her, and with the warmest emotion! Everyone was happy about it—and why? For—and this was surely the core of the matter? —how could they be so happy, so welcoming, when they didn't know her? She, Martha, was not involved in it at all; and so in her heart she was convicting them of insincerity. They could not possibly mean it, she concluded at last, dismissing all these friends and acquaintances, the circle into which she was marrying. The whole thing was a gigantic social deception. From the moment she had said she would marry Douglas, a matter which concerned—and on this point she was determined—no one but their own two selves, some sort of machinery had been set in motion which was bound to involve more and more people. Martha could feel nothing but amazed despair at the thought of the number of people who were so happy on their account.

And now she began walking as quickly as she could, as if running away from something tangible. She was already, in mind, with Solly, who would most certainly help her, rescue her; she did not quite know what he would do, but the truth of her relations with the Cohen boys, difficult sometimes, but at least based on what they really thought and felt, could not possibly betray her now.

The street he had chosen to live in was in the most squalid part of town. She could not help smiling sourly as the poverty deepened around her: nothing less than the worst would do for Solly! Once these houses had been built for the new settlers. They were small and unpretentious, simple shells of brick covered with corrugated iron. Now each house held half a dozen families. Each was like a little town, miserable ragged children everywhere, washing hanging across doorways, gutters running filthy water. Between two such concentrated slums was a small house high on its foundations, in the centre of a fenced patch of garden. There were no other gardens in the street, only untidy earth, littered with tins, bits of cloth, trodden grass. Here, inside the new fence, was rich dark earth, with neat rows of bright-green vegetables. The gate was new, painted white, and on it was a large board which said "Utopia." Martha laughed again: that touch of self-derision was certainly Solly's, she thought.

She was opening the gate when she heard a voice. A youth with a watering can emerged from a small shed and demanded what she wanted.

"I've come to see Solly Cohen," she said, with a touch of defiance, for she had not, until now, remembered those other members of the community who might forbid her.

He was very young, Jewish, and every inch of him an intellectual, though it appeared he wanted to look like a peasant. After a pause, he nodded reluctantly, and turned away.

Martha went on up the path. There was a smell of hot sun on hot earth, the smell of evaporating water. Small bunches of brilliant-green lettuce studded the dark earth, drops of water hung glistening in their leaves. They had just been watered: she could hear the deep soft drinking sound of water being sucked into dry soil. She walked slowly, for the pleasure of hearing it. She remembered how on the farm, after a storm, the tiny mealie plants held in their centres a single round, perfect drop of glittering water . . . But she was being observed, and by someone who resented her being there. She hurriedly climbed the steps. Whatever squalor had been here was cleaned away. The verandah, a small patch of dark-red cement between low grey walls, was polished and gleaming. The front door was newly painted a bright, strong blue. New paint, and cleanliness, and the windows were sparkling! She opened the blue door and found herself in the living room. It was empty. It was not a large room, but looked so because it had so little in it. The red cement floor had a piece of striped purple-and-yellow matting on it. There were half a dozen low wooden chairs, painted yellow. The walls had books all round them. That was all. To find this room in this street . . . But at this moment, a door was pushed open and Solly entered. His face showed blank surprise; then he hastily adjusted his expression.

"What are you doing here?" he asked unwillingly.

Martha sat down without being asked. "Do you mind my coming to see you?" she asked. It sounded rather aggressive.

He could only reply that he did not. He sat down himself, with the air of one being polite against his will. Martha looked to see how he might have changed. Since she had seen him last, he had been to the university, quarrelled with his family, made a trip to England, *almost* got to Spain, had a love affair, returned, thrown up university for good. None of this showed on his face. He was exactly as he had been, tall, very thin, with a loose knobby look about his movements. His face was as sharp-featured and bony, with the look of the young intellectual Jew: lively and critical, but with an additional sarcastic hostility about him. His clothes were different, however. He wore very short dark-blue shorts and a rusty-brown shirt, falling loose. He was tanned a dark brown.

"I like the name you've chosen for your communal settlement," said Martha, ready to laugh with him.

"We didn't choose it. It was the name before."

"Oh!" Then: "Do you mean the Coloured people called it Utopia?" she asked, dismayed and touched.

"That's right. Stoo-pid, isn't it?"

She saw he was jeering at her, and came back with "I thought you had the grace to laugh at yourselves, at least."

But he was not prepared to be provoked. In any case Martha blurted out, "Can I come and live here, too?"

He looked at her, first grinning, then grave. "Well, well," he commented at last. Then, cautiously: "I thought you'd just got married?"

"I have. But I want . . ."

But it was impossible to make explanations. "I shouldn't have got married, anyway. I would like to come and live here. Why shouldn't I?" she demanded like a child.

Here Solly, who had been preparing some gestures of amazement or amusement, simply shrugged.

"But you can't do that," he said reproachfully at last.

Martha was indignant. "Why did you write me that letter, then?" she asked naïvely.

"But, Matty . . ." Here he relapsed into his old manner. He was going to be simple and natural. "But, Matty, you can't go getting married one week and throwing it up the next." He was looking at her enquiringly; his face showed an intelligent comprehension—but not kindness.

Martha's spirits were sinking lower and lower. She saw she had been extremely foolish. However, she continued lamely, "You mean, *everyone* feels like this, it's like measles, one just has to go through with it?"

"Having never been married myself . . ." he began portentously, but dropped the manner at once. "What did you get married for?"

"I have no idea," said Martha ruefully.

"Anyway, you can't live here," he announced at last. "For one thing, there aren't any women."

Martha felt herself blushing, and was furious. For the first time it occurred to her that Solly might be taking this as a personal interest in himself. It was intolerable! She exclaimed belligerently, "You keep out women?"

At once Solly recovered his jaunty manner. "We did ask some girls. Unfortunately none of you can be torn away from your bright lights and your clothes. I suppose you understand that here everything is in common—books, money, everything. And we don't smoke and we don't drink."

"And you are all celibate?" she enquired sarcastically.

"Naturally." Then he added, "But marriage is allowed."

But now she laughed scornfully. "Anyone'd see that married couples would wreck it."

"Luckily we are none of us intending to get married, so that's all right." She was sitting upright in her chair, eyes bright with anger, face flushed—he deliberately lounging in his, with an appearance of conscious ease. "And you're not Jewish either," he said. He sounded embarrassed.

This was something she had not thought of; and she saw at once it was unpardonable of her. She flushed deeper; her face was burning steadily, so that she would have liked to hide it. She wanted to say something like "So now *you're* being exclusive," but an awkward guilt stopped her. "Well, that's certainly final," she said, trying to sound light and casual. And then, seeing that he was still a little embarrassed, she went on: "How many of you?"

"Four, at the moment. We are modelling ourselves on the settlements in Israel."

"Israel?"

"Palestine to you," and he could not help a sudden savage grin.

"But what will you do when the war starts?" she asked awkwardly.

"When the old men have finished their diplomatic fiddling and we can see what they're up to, we'll decide. I shall be a conscientious objector if they turn the war against the Soviet Union, and I shall fight if it's against Hitler."

She felt very small beside this enviable clarity of mind. "How nice to have everything so tidily planned, how nice to be so sure about everything." She tried to jeer at him, but it sounded thin.

"There's nothing to stop you," he said.

She got up, and with a familiar gesture turned to look at the bookshelves. She had only the time to see the names of books she had not heard of, authors that were new, when he said, trying to make a joke of it, "No, Matty, you can't borrow books here. It's a joint library."

"I wasn't going to." She moved towards the door. "Well, I'll go back home, then."

But now he was obviously contrite. "You don't have to run away. We won't eat you."

After hesitation, she returned to her chair. They were now warm with friendship for each other. They were both remembering how often they had sat thus, in a small room filled with books, at the station; outside, the ox waggons rolled heavily through clouds of red dust, and the farmers in their loose working khaki hurried from store to garage, from garage to post office, with their letters and groceries; outside, the black people swarmed around the door of the store, fingering their bits of money and talking excitedly about the bargains they would make. Martha looked out of the window: a mass of dirty little houses, swarms of brown-skinned, poverty-ridden children; but under the window a Jewish youth was hoeing a patch of potatoes.

"You have no servants?"

"Of course not."

"Well, I don't see what you're going to achieve by it," she said doubtfully. "Except, of course, you'll have a lovely time yourselves." Her tone suggested that this was an aim she was prepared to approve of; but his black eyes watched her sarcastically as from an inner truth she could not be expected to see.

Silence, and the hoe rose and fell in the soft earth outside, with a thud, thud, thud. Someone turned a tap on somewhere close inside the house; the water rushed loudly, then it was cut off—silence again.

"You study all day, you discipline yourselves, you work hard?" Martha attempted again.

"That's right."

"You might just as well be—up in the white town. Why do you have to come and live here?"

"We have contacts with the local people," he said defensively; it seemed this was a weak point.

"You could have classes for them," she said excitedly.

But at this he laughed heavily. "That's right, so we could. As for you, you'll be dishing out charity to the poor from your lofty position in the civil service, inside five years."

She shrugged this off impatiently, untouched by the gibe.

"What sort of—contacts?" She used the stiff, impersonal word with difficulty, trying to make it into a picture: Solly and his friends, talking, in this room, with some of the poor Coloured people she could see out of the window.

"Actually," he announced briskly, "the Coloured community are a waste of time. In their position halfway between the blacks and the white Herrenvolk, they are bound to be unstable, they are petty bourgeois to the core, all of them."

He was jettisoning them all! Martha, very shocked, said feebly, "They are human beings, after all."

"So they are," he said with his brisk jeer, his black eyes snapping scorn. "So they are. We are all human beings, and everyone is as good as everyone else, all born equal in the sight of God."

"Well, you brought in God, I didn't. What's God got to do with it?"

They were now as awkward with hostility as they had been a few moments before with friendship.

"Anyway, there are a few hundred Coloureds, and several million Africans—what's the point of it?"

"We'd have lived in the location, but it's against the law. So we chose the next best thing."

"Rubbish, you only came to live here because people'd be shocked, that's all."

He tapped the long bony fingers on the arm of his chair and yawned. It was not for some seconds that she realized the yawn was deliberate. At once she got up and said, "I'll go. I've got things to do."

"Your housewifely duties?" he asked sarcastically.

She stood behind her chair, looking regretfully at this pleasant room, the books, feeling the atmosphere of dedicated freedom, feeling herself an exile. But she felt something else too: a deep pity for him. He seemed all at once very young and absurd.

"Well," she said flatly, "when the war comes, that'll be the end of it. But it'll be nice while it lasts."

He regarded her in silence, apparently considering whether she was worth the trouble he might decide to take. Then he said, "Now, listen, Matty, I shall now give you a short lecture on the international situation." He grinned savagely, and she smiled back gratefully. She noted at the same time, half consciously, that he, unlike his brother, could take nothing seriously. That was hòw she felt it: the jaunty self-consciousness, the invisible quotation marks around his phrases, the drawled "situ-a-tion," gave her a strong feeling of disbelief.

She stood, however, behind her chair and listened. He spoke for some ten minutes, as if he were delivering a lecture, but in the harsh, flat language of controlled cynicism, which chimed in very well with what she felt herself. And although the picture he presented of what was happening in Europe was cold, simple, and logical, that harshness and cynicism could only feed her own. So that when he had finished she said drily, "Well, whichever way it goes, there'll be a war, won't there?"

"Well?"

She shrugged, avoiding the hard aggressiveness of that black stare.

He began to jeer again. "Yes, poor Matty, life is hard, life isn't easy. People get killed, the cows get into the rose garden, violence keeps popping up its ugly head."

She remarked irrelevantly, "My father was in the last war. He talks about it."

He stared. "Well?" Then, in a flat, angry voice, quite different from any she had heard from him—for the first time carrying the conviction of deep personal feeling: "And the Jews are in the concentration camps. Who cares? Do you? If the British Government wanted, they could stop it all in a month—if they wanted. As for you," and here he mimicked her doubting, hesitant voice, "all you say is, Don't let's have any nastiness, please let everything be comfortable."

She was now so confused by all this hostility—for it was clear that she had become for him the enemy he hated most—that she could only say, "Well, Solly . . ." and tailed off into silence.

He was now waiting for her to go. She asked, "What do you hear from Joss?"

"We don't write."

She went towards the door.

"He's joined the Communist Party," she heard.

"Well, I thought he was a Communist anyway."

"He's joined it, that's quite different from talking."

There was such spite in his voice that she turned and enquired, "Why, do you mind him joining?" Then she saw it was directed against herself. He picked up a newspaper from beside him and handed it to her. It was a thin, limp paper. She looked at it dubiously. It was called *The Watchdog*. The headlines, large and strident, assaulted her mind. She heard him laugh, and saw that she was holding the thing as if it might explode in her face. She smiled ruefully.

"Nasty crude paper," he said. "You don't want to be seen with it. What would your new friends say? Let alone your nice husband."

Since she did not feel at all identified with her husband or his circle, she let this pass. She looked down again at the paper. The exclamatory style, the hectoring language, affected her uncomfortably, as if her whole system had been injected by some powerful irritating substance that it must throw off. But she looked at it steadily and saw that what it was saying was no more than Solly's just-concluded lecture on the international situation.

He summed up her thought by saying, "It's all right if you hear it all said in nice intellectual language in a nice comfortable room, but it's quite different like that, isn't it?"

She laid it down on a chair and looked at him. She needed to wound him as he was wounding her. She asked, "Why don't you join the Communist Party, then?" He simply maintained his steady grin; she realized that he must have joined it, otherwise he would not look so satirical. After a moment, she tried another tack: "Who's paying for this house and this quiet intellectual existence?" He reddened; and she persisted. "Your four fathers, no doubt. So your share of it comes from the profits made out of the kaffir store in the district. I don't see that you are any better than I am, if it comes to that." He was waiting for a chance to get in at her, but she went on hastily, delighted with her advantage: "So I'll leave you to your *independence,* until the bull gets into this rose garden."

She quickly shut the door behind her, and walked rapidly down the garden. All vegetables, of course, she thought, trying to be spiteful, but on the verge of tears. No flowers for the high-minded, naturally! While she had been inside, the earth around the little green clumps of lettuce had dried. Small granules of grey earth lay evenly over the base of wet dark richness. The youth was steadily hoeing potatoes at the far end of the garden. He did not lift his head as she came past. Then she heard her name called: Solly stood on the verandah.

"Matty—would you like to come to a meeting here tonight?"

She hesitated, then called back sardonically, "Unfortunately I have a sundowner party—" But she was unable to finish. Solly was doubled up in a pantomime of laughter.

She turned her back on him and walked away under the trees that shaded the pavement. It was some minutes before she was able to smile at herself and at him, her regret at having to leave was so

strong. She felt forsaken; and nothing but the memory of Solly's savage farewell laughter prevented her from hurrying back and saying
that of course she would come to the meeting. When she reached the
flat, she occupied herself with altering a dress to fit her for the sundowner party that night, and with an ironical consciousness of how
Solly would see this proceeding. But there was something much
stronger, a feeling of Well, then, I'll show him! The showing him consisted in making the dress and herself as attractive as she knew how.
It was not until she realized this that she remembered the moment
when she had felt he might be thinking that she had come to him as
a man, and not as a person in that romantic thing, a communal settlement. She burned with embarrassment; she could not forgive him.
Now, looking back at the meeting, she could see the thing in no
other way; everything they had said was permeated with this other
emotion; to it she attributed his aggressiveness and that sarcastic
stare. She was hating him quite vividly. In a short while, the memory
of that interview had become quite unbearable; and she was putting
stitches into the fabric of her dress with strong stabs of the needle,
while she muttered incoherently, Idiot! Conceited idiot! And even:
Can't they ever see us differently?

When Douglas returned that afternoon, he was welcomed by an
extremely cheerful young woman, who proceeded to amuse him with
a satirical account of how she had rushed down to see Solly—all intelligent in blue trousers and sunburn—and how she had wanted to
join the settlement. Because, as everyone knows, we girls go through
these moments of not wanting to be married.

"And me too," confessed Douglas, apologetically, kissing her with
a rueful laugh. This mutual confession delighted them. They were
back together in the warmest affection, which almost at once led to
the bed—there was half an hour to fill in, as he pointed out. The
half hour was hilarious. In a mood of tearing gaiety, they experi-
mented with a couple of new positions sanctioned by the book, and
were freshly delighted with their efficiency. Then, seeing the time,
six o'clock, that hour sacred to sundowner parties, they hastened off
the bed and got dressed. They drove off to the party with the look of
competent unconcern that they had both already learned to wear in
public.

Colonel Brodeshaw's house was in the part of the town which had
been the most fashionable before the new suburbs began to spread.
There were several avenues of big sprawling shady houses in big
gardens—these were the nearest approach to an individual architec-
ture the colony had achieved. They had been built for comfort, for
the climate, by people with money and enough self-confidence not

to need the extra boost of that kind of smart house which was now being built. They were the natural expression, in fact, of the type of English person whose families have been in the habit of administering this part or that of the British Empire, accustomed to making themselves comfortable in a difficult climate. Comfort was their keynote. The servants' quarters, built in a row along the end of the back garden, and reminiscent of stables, were vast—not because these people intended to make their servants comfortable, but because they meant to have plenty of servants. The rooms were large and cool, the verandahs enormous; whatever these houses might look like from outside, sprawling, shapeless, often shabby, they were a delight to live in.

The young Knowells drove through several avenues filled with such houses, and were able to feel a pleasant regret for the past. They murmured that it was a pity people did not build like that these days. They parked the car with a dozen others in the ditch outside a flaring hibiscus hedge, and walked up a narrow drive that was like a green tunnel. Through gaps in the foliage, hoses could be seen playing on a smooth green lawn, and beyond that the garden was bounded by a warm red-brick wall draped with morning glory, a vivid sky blue which was beginning—the sun was setting—to show edges of white. Soon it would be as if scraps of limp dirty-white linen hung among the green. A few steps further, and the front verandah was in sight, a garden inside a garden, for it was filled with painted tubs of flowering plants, and festooned with golden shower. People too, of course; but the verandah was as big as a large room, and able to absorb large numbers of people among the columns of brick and tubs of flowers.

From outside, Martha caught a glimpse of faces she knew, and felt a stab of disappointment: she could not rid herself of the belief that being married would introduce her to something new and exciting. She could see Donovan, and Ruth Manners; and was looking for others, when Douglas remarked, "Mr. Player is going to be here, I believe." He tried to sound casual, but could not prevent a note of pleased deference.

Martha was looking for Mr. Player when they arrived at the top of the steps and were met by Colonel Brodeshaw and Mrs. Brodeshaw. The Colonel was a tall, thin, bent man, with a small dark moustache and mahogany skin, so much the colonel in manner and appearance that it must save Martha the effort of looking for further individuality. His wife was competently dispensing hospitality in a black-and-white flowered dress, a colonel's lady, clipped, brisk and smiling.

Martha had not taken two steps before she was absorbed into the warm embrace of Mrs. Talbot, and welcomed with a warm but timid smile by Mrs. Talbot's daughter. Martha knew that of all the people who were being made happy by this marriage, Mrs. Talbot was perhaps the happiest. She had received no less than three charming notes from her in the last week, welcoming her into—what? And now she was putting her arm around Martha's shoulders, turning her away from other groups on the verandah, and leading her to a chair beside her own. Over her shoulder she smiled and murmured to Douglas, "You really must allow me to deprive you of Matty for just a few minutes." And Douglas, smiling and touched, seemed prepared to wait.

Mrs. Talbot was, above all, a lady of charm. In each movement, each tone of her voice, was this suggestion of deferential murmuring grace; and as she seated herself beside Martha she did so with a hurried, almost apologetic movement of her hindquarters, as if even this personal necessity was something deplorable because it detracted from the wholehearted attention she was determined to bestow upon Martha. Both she and her daughter then leaned towards her, smiling with warm friendship, and proceeded to tell her how happy they were that Douggie was married at last, how wonderful, how suitable, how . . . As one woman arrived at the end of a breathless phrase, searching for the superlatives that could not express what she felt, the other took it up; it was a duet of self-immolation towards Martha.

Martha, seated, smiling a little awkwardly, looked from one to the other, trying to *see* them, for she felt herself in danger of being smothered by this perfumed attack. She was able at last to see Mrs. Talbot as a tall, fair-haired woman, slight, pliant, with a smooth oval face tinted uniformly pink, like a fine breathing enamel. Everything, hair, face, dress, was so smoothly perfect, so exquisitely created, that one felt impelled to look at the daughter to find the raw materials from which this work of art had been begun. Elaine was like her mother, a slight, graceful creature, but the oval face, the large grey eyes, showed signs of strain and ill-health. The skin was pale, flawed; there were faint blue shadows under the eyes. Martha looked from one to the other, noting the looks of affectionate reassurance that continually passed between them, and thought only that for a girl of eighteen to be so close to her mother must in itself be perverse. She felt herself menaced by it. But since there was no need for her to say anything but "Thank you" and "How very kind of you," she allowed her attention to pass to that other problem which was so much her preoccupation. For the spiritual hangers-on which every marriage attracts must certainly expect to suggest the question, What is it they themselves have found, or lack, in marriage? Since Mrs. Talbot and her daughter could not be delighted that it was *Martha* who had married Douglas—they did not know her, as Martha reminded herself—it must be the idea of marriage that fed this delight? Martha tried to form some sort of image of Mr. Talbot, and it was only then that she realized that she did not even know whether there was one. She had heard a great deal about Mrs. Talbot during the past weeks, but it was always "Mrs. Talbot and Elaine," "Elaine and Mrs. Talbot" —that was how the world spoke of the Talbot family. Together they enveloped Martha in caressing affection, and together they rose, after a long, smiling, intimate look at her which—even in this small matter of agreeing that it was time to release Martha—overflowed into a glance of understanding between them. The young Knowells were invited to spend the evening very soon with Mrs. Talbot and Elaine, and (for of course he was so happy about the marriage, too) Mr. Talbot—if he wasn't out ("He always has so much to do"); and the two women withdrew into chairs further away, where they proceeded to allow their reservoirs of charm to overflow onto Douglas.

Martha was therefore left alone for a moment, looking down the great verandah, which was like a room with three walls of green leaves. The last rays of sunlight fell through the leaves, patterning the faces of the guests. Perhaps forty people were sitting, with glasses in their hands, in this green-dappled glow. Martha could see Donovan poised on the edge of his chair, addressing Ruth Manners. "But, my dear, it was the funniest thing you ever saw," she heard his light voice say, before he let it drop and leaned forward to continue the sentence in a lower key; it was a bit of gossip: the discreetly malicious smile on Ruth's face showed it. Beside Ruth sat a young man whom Martha had not seen before. She immediately recognized him as being fresh from England, because of his pink-faced, cautious look of one on trial. From the way he and Ruth smiled at each other, it was clear they were a couple.

Far down the verandah, in a well of green shadow, Mr. Maynard was surveying the guests with his look of sardonic but controlled comment. Beside him was that formidable lady his wife, who in a high, firm, commanding voice was saying the last word about something she felt strongly: "And so I said to her, 'It is quite out of the question!'" She turned to look at her husband, commanding agreement; but Mr. Maynard continued to gaze in front of him, lightly flipping his fingers against the glass he held. The clink, clink, clink, came travelling softly down among the voices and laughter, like irritation made audible; and Martha looked at this black-browed energetic woman, and remembered, with a strong feeling of incongruity, that sick headaches were her weapon of choice. She was convicting Mrs. Maynard of having no sense of period, when she saw Mr. Anderson, sitting not far from his son, a small dapper man radiating bad temper because it was necessary to be here at all and to make conversation. He was making it, Martha saw with surprise, to Mrs. Anderson, who sat near him. The fact that Mr. Anderson could be persuaded to leave his solitude reminded Martha that this was an important sundowner party, and she searched for Mr. Player. Remembering a brief glimpse of a large, redfaced man, she searched in vain—he could not have arrived.

The chair beside her was still empty. Donovan rose from his place and joined her, remarking gaily, "Well, Matty, so here you are nicely settled at last." This reference to her marriage she let pass; she was looking to see if there was anything in his face which might suggest that he remembered the ugliness of their last meeting. But it seemed not. He proceeded to entertain her with a scandalous story about their hostess. To which Martha replied that the moment he left her he would undoubtedly make a spitefully funny story about her marriage. He giggled gracefully and said that he had been dining out on stories about her for the last week. "Really, Matty, why do you waste such an occasion for being on show? Now, look at Ruth, she's got herself engaged, and she's having a nice engagement party, and we'll all give her expensive presents, and everything so satisfactory for her and her friends."

"On the other hand, there won't be any funny stories about her wedding," she pointed out. "You can't have it both ways."

"True," he conceded, "true."

He was looking among the guests to see if there might be someone to inspire an anecdote, when Martha enquired, "What's Ruth's young man like?"

"On the way up. Secretary to the secretary of Mr. Player. Money, family, everything." Then, with his usual gay spite: "One could hardly expect less of Ruth, after all, considering what's been done for her."

"Yes, but what's he like?" enquired Martha naïvely, looking at the neat little English face, all the features correctly in place, the small fair moustache, the sober clothes that succeeded in suggesting only what the limbs and body must be like underneath—correct, controlled, adequate.

Donovan grinned pleasantly; then he said in a soft lowered voice which for the first time allowed that they did, after all, know each other quite well, "Really, Matty, you'll never learn! Surely that's enough!"

Here she laughed with him, in genuine appreciation of that wit which, however, he was determined should never be more than socially agreeable. But he went on, with the astounding frankness with which he said what he really felt: "Anyway, Matty, if a girl marries a man with money and so on, what more can she want?" He sounded really aggrieved. She let out a snort of laughter; saw him flush, and then he rose gracefully. "Well, Matty, I shall now leave you." His smile was cold; their eyes met unpleasantly; then he sailed, in a way which was reminiscent of his mother, across the verandah to another empty chair.

Martha's glass was refilled for her. She was becoming depressed as the alcohol took effect. She was disappointed that there was anyone here that she knew; and looked back to her first weeks in town, when the people she met seemed like glorious and disconnected phenomena, meteors and rockets that went shooting across her vision, only to disappear. But certainly not tamely connected in social circles. That Donovan, Ruth, even Mr. Maynard, should be brought to this verandah on this evening by a mysterious connection gave her a feeling of oppression. She could feel the nets tightening around her. She thought that she might spend the rest of her life on this verandah, or others like it, populated by faces she knew only too well. It was at this point, and for the first time, that she found herself thinking, The war will break it up, it won't survive the war. Then she was sincerely dismayed and ashamed. She said it must be her own fault that she could see no face, hear no voice, which could make her happy at the idea of being here.

Half a dozen chairs away, Mrs. Talbot and Elaine were discussing with a third lady a new method of cutting sandwiches, and, Martha noted, with precisely the same allowance of deferential charm that they had given her marriage. Opposite them, two ladies were arguing—what else? the iniquities of their servants. Mrs. Maynard, at the other end of the verandah, and at the top of her confident voice, was discussing hers. Mr. Maynard, from the depths of his resigned boredom, took up the theme with a slow, deliberate account of a case he had judged that morning. A native youth had stolen some clothes from his employer; the question before him, the magistrate, had been: Should the sentence be prison or an official beating? He told his story with a calm objectivity that sounded brutal. But Martha, as she watched that heavy and handsome face, saw the full, authoritative eyes move slightly from one face to another, saw suddenly that he was using this audience, which, after all, was not so arbitrarily associated, as a sort of sounding board.

Everyone was listening now, waiting to jump into the discussion with their own opinions; for certainly this was a subject, *the* subject, on which they were all equipped to speak. But Mr. Maynard was not yet ready to throw the ball out for play. Having concluded with the bare facts of the case, he turned to a similarly large and authoritative gentleman in a neighbouring chair, and remarked, "It is a question, of course, of whether a sentence should be regarded as a punishment or a deterrent. Until that is decided—and they certainly haven't decided it even in England—I can hardly be expected to have any opinions."

The half-dozen people who had been leaning forward, mouths half open, ready to say what they thought, were taken aback by the depths of intellectuality into which they were expected to plunge. They waited. One lady muttered, "Nonsense, they should all be whipped!" But she turned her eyes, with the rest, towards the gentleman appealed to.

He appeared to be thinking it over. He sat easily in his chair, an impressive figure, his body and face presenting a series of wide smooth surfaces. His corpulence was smoothly controlled by marvelous suiting, the fat areas of cheek and chin from a distance seemed scarcely interrupted by the thin pink mouth, the small eyes. When he lifted his eyes, however, in a preliminary circling glance before speaking, it was as if the bulk of ordinary flesh, commonplace cheeks, took an unimportant position behind the cold and deliberate stare. Those eyes were not to be forgotten. It was as if the whole personality of this man struggled to disguise itself behind the appearance of a man of business who was devoted to good, but good-natured, living—struggled and failed, for the calculating, clever eyes betrayed him. He said in a casual voice that in his opinion the whole legal system as affecting the Africans was ridiculously out of date and should be radically overhauled.

One could hear the small suppressed gasp of dismay from his listeners. But Mr. Maynard kept his full prompting eyes fixed on the cold grey ones, and merely nodded; whether in agreement or not, he intended to convey, was quite unimportant, for it was his task to administer the law and not to change it. Martha was expecting an outburst from these people; she had not spent the greater part of her nineteen years listening to talk about the native problem for nothing. She was astounded that they remained silent.

It was Mrs. Maynard who spoke for them; it was the politeness of her disagreement that told Martha that this fat pig of a man must be Mr. Player. She could not easily believe it; a man cannot become a legend without certain penalties, and it seemed to her altogether too simple that people so inevitably become like the caricatures that their worst enemies make of them; besides, it was hard to connect the groomed pink face with that large hot red one she had once caught a glimpse of on a racecourse. Mrs. Maynard was announcing firmly that it was obvious the natives were better served by being whipped than being sent to prison, for they didn't mind prison, it was no disgrace to them. They were nothing but children, after all. At this, a dozen ladies angrily flung out their agreement. Martha listened with tired familiarity—this was something one could always be sure of. One after another, it was stated in varying ways that the natives should be kept in their place—and then Martha lost a few remarks, because she was considering something she had just realized. Two familiar words had not been used: *nigger* and *kaffir*; either this was an evolution in opinion or this circle of people were different and less brutal than those she had been used to.

There was a silence in progress when Martha became attentive again. Then the second camp made itself heard. It was Mrs. Talbot who said, with a breathless air of defiance, that the poor things shouldn't be whipped, everyone should be kind to everyone else. Her daughter murmured agreement, and was rewarded by a glance of grateful affection from her mother, who was flushed by her own daring. For while "poor things" was certainly not a new note, the suggestion that poor things and children should not be whipped for their own good was.

At this point, the young man from England, the secretary of the secretary, gave it as his opinion, with a quick and rather nervous glance towards Mr. Player, that public opinion in the colony was behind the times. The silence that followed was a delicate snub to the newcomer because of the burden of problems that they all carried. Ruth remarked in a detached voice that progressive people thought that whipping only made people worse. The word "progressive" was allowed to pass; she was very young, and had been educated largely in England. Then Douglas stoutly averred, with the slight stammer which Martha was only just beginning to see could be a delicate compliment to superiors, that what was needed in the colony was good housing and good feeding, and the colony could never move forward while the bulk of the population was so backward. A silence again, during which Martha looked with grateful affection towards him; and everyone looked towards Mr. Player.

The great man nodded affably towards Douglas, and said, "I quite agree." Again he allowed a pause for considered thought, for that slow, circled grey stare. Then he began to speak; and Martha heard with amazement the liberal point of view expressed by this pillar of reaction, this man who was a symbol of "the Company." It was a shock to everything she had believed possible. And now many people who had been silent came in. Martha looked from face to face and tried to see what connected the champions of progress. At first she failed. Then she saw that mostly they were "business" as opposed to "civil service." The talk went on, and it was not until she had heard the phrases "greater efficiency," "waste of labour," etc., etc., often enough, that she understood.

What she had understood was finally crystallized by Mr. Player's summing up. He said that the whites were ruining their own interests; if the blacks (Martha noted that his use of the emotional word was calculated) were not to revolt, they must be fed and housed; and he, Mr. Player, blamed above all the editor of the *Zambesia News*, for persistently feeding the public with nonsense. For the last ten years, said Mr. Player, ignorance had been pandered to by a policy that could only be described as monstrously stupid; any expression of a desire for improvement on the part of the natives was immediately described as impertinence, or sedition, or even worse. We were, after all, living in the twentieth century, concluded Mr. Player, while he directed his grey stare towards a man halfway down the verandah.

Following the searchlight of that stare, Martha saw at the end of it an uncomfortable, flushed gentleman angrily clutching at a glass of whisky. Since it was obvious that Mr. Player did nothing casually, it followed that this gentleman must be connected with the press. As soon as Mr. Player had finished, he remarked aggressively that the press was not concerned with fostering the interests of any particular section of the population. His look at Mr. Player was pure defiance.

Mr. Player stared back. Then he said that it was in no one's interest that the blacks (this time the word was a small concession to the press) should be ill-fed and ill-housed into a condition where they weren't fit for work. He paused and, having narrowed his eyes for a final stab, said, "For instance, I hear that on the Canteloupe Mine a policy of proper feeding and housing is gaining quite remarkable results." He elaborated this policy for some time. It occurred to Martha belatedly that this same mine was almost certain to be connected with the Company, and that Mr. Player himself had originated this enlightened policy. The gentleman of the press listened, frowning, looking at his glass. Mr. Player redirected his stare towards him, and remarked, "Some people might wonder why something that is after all an experiment is not considered newsworthy by a paper which claims to represent everybody."

The victim grew redder, resisted for a moment, then said clumsily, "Well, of course, we are always ready to print genuine news."

At once Mr. Player removed his gaze and elaborated his theme in a different key for a while, then passed to another. He did not look towards the *News* again. They all listened in silence—the Service, business, two members of Parliament, the press—while Mr. Player continued to express views which ninety per cent of the white population would consider dangerous and advanced. Obstinate, even ironical faces seemed to suggest that it was all very well for Mr. Player, who did not have to answer to this same ninety per cent, but only to investors overseas. One felt that no slighter provocation than this could have provoked them even to think of these investors, particularly as such thoughts were likely to be followed by others—such as, that the Company indirectly owned a large part of the *News* and most of the businesses who used its advertising space.

A telephone rang inside the long room which could be glimpsed through the open French windows. A native servant emerged, anonymous in his white ducks and red fez, to say Mr. Player was wanted on the telephone. The secretary of the secretary made a movement towards rising; and subsided as Mr. Player rose with a sharp look at him. He sat stiffly beside Ruth, discomforted. There was a long silence, while they listened to the voice inside. Then Mrs. Brodeshaw remarked with a smile that Mr. Player had a horse running in a race in England. There was a burst of relieved, admiring laughter.

Martha was looking at Mr. Maynard, who did not laugh, but appeared bored and indulgent. Her persistent, speculative stare had its effect, for he got heavily to his feet and came down towards her. He sat down, saying, "If you young women will change your hair styles every day, what can you expect?"

"I cut it," said Martha awkwardly—everyone had watched him coming to join her. Then Mrs. Brodeshaw mentioned her roses, and conversation began again.

"Did Binkie come back?"

"He returned last night," said Mr. Maynard. A glance at him showed his face momentarily clenched; a second, blandly indifferent. "His mother is a different woman as a result," he remarked; but at this point Mr. Player returned. Everyone looked expectantly prepared to triumph or commiserate over the horse in England, but Mr. Player sat down, and leaned over to murmur something to the young secretary. He was pink with importance.

Mr. Maynard watched the scene, holding his glass between two loosely cupped hands, and said, "That is a very pretty young man."

"Oh, very!" she agreed scornfully.

"Have you noticed that the type of immigrant is changing? The era of the younger sons is passing. A pity—I am a firm believer in younger sons. Now we have what the younger sons, such as myself, for instance, left England to escape from." The idea of Mr. Maynard as a younger son made Martha laugh; and he gave her a quizzical look. "Now, in the old days—but you wouldn't remember that." He glanced at her and sighed. Martha felt she was being dismissed. He did not continue. Instead he asked, in a casual but intimate voice that referred to yesterday's encounter, "Well, what do you make of it all?" He glanced around the long verandah and then at her.

Martha blurted out at once, "Awful. It's all awful!"

He gave her another glance and remarked, "So I thought. I have been looking at you and thinking that if you must feel so strongly you'd better learn to hide it. If I may give you advice from the height of my—what? fifty-six years."

"Why should I hide it?" she demanded.

"Well, well," he commented. "But it won't do, you know!"

"You didn't even know it was me, you didn't recognize me," she accused him.

"I have noticed," he swerved off again, "that at your age women are really most extraordinarily unstable in looks. It's not till you're thirty or so that you stay the same six months together. I remember my wife . . ." He stopped, frowning.

There was a conversation developing at the bottom of the verandah. Martha heard the words "the war," and sat up.

"Mr. Player must naturally be concerned with the international situation," remarked Mr. Maynard. "A man who controls half the minerals in the central plateau can hardly be expected to remain unmoved at the prospect of peace being maintained."

Martha digested this; what he was saying had, to her, the power to blast everyone in this house off into a limbo of contempt. It was more difficult for her to understand that for him it was enough to say it. She could find nothing polite enough to express what she felt. He looked at her again, and it disconcerted her because he saw so clearly what she would have liked to say.

"My dear Mrs. Knowell, if I may advise you—" But again he

checked himself, and said, "Why should I? You'll do as you like, anyway."

"What advice?" she asked, genuinely.

But now he fidgeted his large and powerful dark-clad limbs in his chair, and said with the gruffness which was his retreat, "Let's leave it at this: that I'm profoundly grateful I'm nearly sixty." He paused and added scathingly, "I can leave it all safely in the hands of Binkie."

"There are other people," she remarked awkwardly; she was thinking of Joss and Solly. Suddenly it occurred to her that there was an extraordinary resemblance between this dignified man and the rebel in the settlement in the Coloured quarters. Of course! It was their savage and destructive way of speaking.

But now he remarked, "I daresay one attaches too much importance to one's own children." He sounded tired and grim. She was immediately sorry for him. She was trying to find words to express it, when he nodded down towards the end of the verandah to direct her attention there.

Colonel Brodeshaw was speaking. ". . . a difficult problem," she heard. "If we conscript the blacks, the question of arming them arises. It'll come up before the House in due course . . ." Once again, this gathering was being used as a sounding board. This time there was no doubt, no cleavage of opinion, no need even for discussion. From one end of the verandah to the other, there was a murmur of "Obviously not. Out of the question." It was so quickly disposed of that Colonel Brodeshaw had the look of an orator on a platform who has been shouted at to sit down in the middle of a speech. He murmured, "Well, it'll not be settled as easily as all that." People looked towards Mr. Player; it appeared he had no views on the matter. Mrs. Maynard announced finally, "If they learn to use arms, they can use them on us. In any case, this business of sending black troops overseas is extremely shortsighted. They are treated as equals in Britain, even by the women." There was no need to say more.

Mr. Maynard remarked, "One of the advantages of living in a society like this, though I don't expect you'll appreciate it yet, is that things can be said. Now, in Britain it would take a very stupid person to talk in such a tone. In the colonies there is an admirable frankness which makes politics child's play in comparison."

"It's revolting," she said angrily.

"Well," he said, flipping his forefinger against his glass again, "well, when this colony has reached the stage where a gathering like this talks about uplifting the masses of the people, you'll find that politics will be much more complicated than they are now."

"Mr. Player has just been talking about it."

"But with what engaging truth, with what disarming frankness. Enlightened self-interest—it has taken us long enough to reach it. Why, only a year ago, I remember, the suggestion by dieticians that Africans were not conveniently equipped by nature to subsist healthily on mealie meal and nothing else was treated as the voice of revolution itself. We advance, we advance! Now, in my youth, my 'class' —as you so refreshingly have no inhibitions in putting it—were for the most part outspokenly engaged in putting the working classes in their place. But when I paid a visit to England last year, how different things were! The working classes were undoubtedly just where they used to be, but everyone of my 'class' seemed concerned only to prove not only that they were entitled to a good life, but that they had already achieved it. Further, it was almost impossible to hold a conversation with my friends and relations, because their speech was full of gaps, pauses, and circumlocutions where words used to be. With what relief did I return to this country, where a spade is still called a spade and I can use the vocabulary that I was taught to use during my admirable education. I can no longer say, 'The kaffirs are getting out of hand,' that is true. But I can say, 'The blacks need firm treatment.' That's something. I am grateful for it."

Martha did not know what to say. She could not make out from this succession of smooth and savage sentences which side he was on. As she put it, with a straightforwardness which she imagined he would commend, "If you think it's terrible, then why do you . . .?"

"But I didn't say I thought it was terrible. On the contrary, if there's one thing my generation has learned it is that the more things change, the more they remain the same."

Martha reached out her hand to take his glass. "You're going to break it," she warned. He had in fact broken it—there was a mess of wet glass in his hand. He glanced at it, with raised brows, then reached for a handkerchief. Martha was looking around to see if the incident had been noticed. But everyone was listening to Mrs. Brodeshaw, who was explaining how she was forming a woman's organization in preparation for the war.

A servant came forward to remove the bits of glass.

"We old men," Mr. Maynard said apologetically, "are full of unaccountable emotions."

"I know," said Martha at once. "You're like my father—what upset you was the 1914 war, wasn't it?"

He looked exceedingly uncomfortable, but assented.

"You really seemed to think it was going to change things, didn't you?"

"We did attach a certain importance to it at the time."

She heard her name called. Donovan was grinning at her with a gay spite which warned her. "You don't agree, Matty dear, do you?" he was calling down the verandah.

"I wasn't listening."

Mrs. Talbot called out with apologetic charm, "Donovan was telling us that you were a pacifist. I don't blame you, dear, war is so utterly dreadful." She broke off with a confused look around her.

"But I'm not a pacifist," said Martha stubbornly.

Mr. Maynard broke in quickly with "All my generation were pacifists—until 1914."

There was a burst of relieved laughter. Donovan looked at Martha; she looked back angrily. He turned back to Ruth with a gay shrug.

Martha saw that Mr. Maynard had been protecting her. She said in a low voice, "I don't see why one shouldn't say what one thinks."

"Don't you? Oh, well, I'm sorry."

This depth of irony succeeded in making her feel very young and inadequate. It was a snub to those *real* feelings she was convinced she must share with everybody, nothing less would do! After a moment she said, "All the same, everyone here is planning for the war, and we don't know yet who the war is going to be fought against."

She had spoken rather more loudly than she had meant; the gentleman from the press had heard her. He said irritably, "You'd agree, I hope, that one must be prepared for a war?" This was the substance of the leader in that morning's *News*.

Mr. Maynard answered for her, in a smooth voice, "I daresay the younger generation, who will have the privilege of being killed, are entitled to know what for?" He had acquired another glass, and was engaged in flipping this one too with his fingernail. The journalist's look was caught by the gesture; he watched it for a moment; then some women sitting near asked him deferentially for his opinion on the international situation. He proceeded to give it. Martha listened to his string of platitudes for a few moments, then heard Mr. Maynard again: "Another of life's little disillusionments: you'll find that the newspapermen are as stupid as they sound. One reads what they say, when young, with admiration for the accomplished cynicism they display; when one gets older one discovers they really mean what they write. A terrible blow it was to me, I remember. I had been thinking of becoming one myself. But I was prepared to be a knave, not a fool."

He had meant her to laugh, but she was unable to. She wanted to protest. Fear of his contempt for her clumsiness kept her silent. She was prepared to be thought wrong-headed, but not naïve. He was using much more powerful weapons than she was to understand for a very long time.

"Come," he said, "let me fill up your glass." It was her third, and she was beginning to be lifted away from herself.

"Tell me," he enquired, having refilled his own, "if it is not too indiscreet, that is: What decided you to get married at the age of— what is it? Seventeen?"

"Nineteen," said Martha indignantly.

"I do apologize."

She laughed. She hesitated a moment. She was feeling the last three months as a bewildering chaos of emotion, through which she had been pulled, will-less, like a fish at the end of a string, with a sense of being used by something impersonal and irresistible. She hesitated on the verge of an appeal and a confession; an attempt, at the very least, to explain what it had been like. She glanced at him, and saw him lounging there beside her, very large, composed, armed by his heavy, sarcastic good looks.

"If I may say so," he remarked with a pleasantly pointed smile which was like a nudge to proceed, "ninety-nine people out of a hundred haven't the remotest idea why they got married—in case you are under the illusion that you are a special case."

With this encouragement, she took a sip from her brandy and ginger beer and began. She was pleasantly surprised that her voice was no less cool, amused and destructive than his own. She noted, also, that words, phrases, were isolated in deprecating amusement— as Solly had used the language that morning. It was as if she was afraid of the power of language used nakedly. "Well," she began, "not to get married when it is so clearly expected of us was rather more of an act of defiance than I was prepared to commit. Besides, you must know yourself, since you spend most of your time marrying us, that getting married is our first preoccupation—the international situation positively demands it of us. Who one marries is obviously of no importance at all. After all, if I'd married Binkie, for instance, I'm sure that everyone—with the exception of your wife, of course— would have been just as delighted . . ."

He laughed: "Go on."

"Though it would have been no less potentially disastrous than the marriage I'm committed to. Love," she noted how she isolated the word, throwing it away, as it were, "as you would be the first to admit, is merely a question of . . ." "In short," she concluded, after some minutes of light-hearted description of the more painful experiences of the last few weeks, "I got married because there's going to be a war. Surely that's a good enough reason." There was not even an undertone of dismay to be heard in her voice.

"Admirable," he commented. Then: "Entirely admirable. If I may give you some advice."

"Oh, I do assure you that I've taken the point."

He looked at her straight. "And I assure *you* that you will find it much more tolerable this way."

"I don't doubt it," she said angrily.

He was on the point of making some further attempt, when she felt a hand on her arm. It was Douglas. He looked rather nervous, first because he was disturbing her conversation with Mr. Maynard, secondly because she was looking so guilty. She felt very guilty. She jumped up quickly as he said, "Matty, we should be going."

Mr. Maynard released her courteously, and returned to his chair beside his wife. They stood at the door shaking hands with Colonel Brodeshaw and his wife. Mrs. Brodeshaw took the opportunity to ask, "My dear, I wonder if you would like to help on the committee for organizing the ladies . . ." It took Martha by surprise, and Mrs. Brodeshaw swiftly went on: "Though of course, my dear, you don't want to be worried by all this sort of thing yet, do you? It's not fair, when you're just married. We'll leave you in peace for the time being," she promised, smiling. Then she added, "There's a suggestion of starting a committee to investigate the conditions of the Coloureds—"

"I was down there this morning," remarked Martha.

Mrs. Brodeshaw looked startled, then said, "Oh, yes, we know you are interested."

Douglas came quickly in with "Perhaps we can fix it later, when we're more settled."

Again Mrs. Brodeshaw retreated gracefully. They said goodbye. Douglas and Martha went to the car in silence. She saw he looked annoyed, and wondered why.

"You know, Matty, I think you might have been a bit more pleasant about it."

"Charity?" said Martha angrily.

"It's not such a bad idea, you know." He was referring to her being "in" with the Brodeshaws.

"Charity," she said finally. It dismayed her that he might even consider it possible. Then she felt sorry for him—he looked utterly taken aback.

"But, Matty . . ."

She took his arm. She was now lifted on waves of alcohol: she was recklessly happy.

"Mr. Maynard was having a long talk with you?" he enquired.

"Yes. Let's go and dance, Douglas."

"The Club? What? With the gang?"

"The gang," she mocked. "We've put up with them for long enough, haven't we?"

"Let's have a night by ourselves."

But by now she could not bear to go tamely back to the flat. There was something in the talk with Mr. Maynard which had unsettled her, made her restless—she needed to dance. Besides, she was instinctively reluctant to go now, in this mood of disliking him, which she did unaccountably, to spend an evening with Douglas.

"Come on—come on," she urged, tugging at him.

"All right, then, we'll go and beat up Stella and Andy—and let's get Willie and Alice. We'd better buy some brandy . . ."

But she was hardly listening. She was wildly elated, she could feel that she was very attractive to him in this mood; it intoxicated her and deeply disturbed her that he should find her desirable when she was engaged in despising him. "Come on, come on," she called impatiently, and ran off down the path through the bushes to the car. He followed, running heavily behind her. It was dark now. The gateposts reflected a white gleam back to a large low white moon. The town had lost its ramshackle shallowness. A mile of roofs shone hard and white like plates of white salt, amid acres of softly glinting leaves. The road lay low and grey, with a yellow glimmer of light from the street lamps.

3

"Well, Matty, and now you'll be free to get on with your own work."

It was with these words that Douglas dropped his parting kiss on her cheek when he left for the office each morning, and with a look of pure satisfaction. The kindly, confident young man crossed the untidy bedroom towards the door, bouncing a little from the balls of his feet, smiling backwards at Martha, who was sitting in a tangle of crumpled and stained silk in a mess of bedclothes, and vanished whistling down the corridor. The gleam of proprietary satisfaction never failed to arouse in Martha a flush of strong resentment, which was as unfailingly quenched by a succeeding guilt. To account for the resentment, for above all it was essential to account for every contradictory emotion that assailed one, she had already formed a theory.

After Douglas had left, she kicked off the bedclothes, and allowed herself to fall backwards on the cooling sheets and pillows. She lay quiet. Opposite her, two neat squares of bright-blue sky, in one of which was suspended the stilled black wheel of the fair; reflected sunlight quivered hot on the wall. From all around, from above, from below, the sounds of voices, a broom swishing, a child crying. But here, in the heart of the building, two rooms, white, silent, empty. And, on the bed, Martha, uncomfortably fingering the silk of her nightdress, trying most conscientiously to relax into the knowledge of space and silence. At the same time she was thinking of Douglas, now already at his office; she could see the self-conscious look with which he allowed himself to be teased; every night he came back to share with her his pleasure in how the office had said this or that. And how she hated him for it! And it was her husband about whom she was feeling this resentment, this violent dislike.

Martha, ignoring the last few months in town before her marriage, because she could not bear to think about them, went back to that period when she was a girl on the farm. From this, several incidents had been selected by her need for a theory. There had been that young man who . . . and the other one . . . and that occasion when . . . After hours of determined concentration she would emerge with the phrase, "Women hate men who take them for granted." It would have done for a story in a magazine. But that impersonal "women" was a comfort—briefly, for no sooner had she reached it than she saw the image that the words conjured up: something sought, wooed, capricious, bestowing favours. No, there was something extremely distasteful about that capricious female; no sooner had Martha caught a glimpse of her than she must repudiate her entirely; she was certainly from the past! The suggestion of coyness was unbearable. Yet she and Douglas had achieved a brotherly friendliness almost immediately; and when he bounced cheerfully into bed, clutching her in a cheerful and companionable act of love that ignored the female which must be wooed, she undoubtedly loathed him from the bottom of her heart—an emotion which was as inevitably followed by a guilty affection. The situation was, as she jauntily and bleakly put it, unsatisfactory.

She therefore got out of bed and went into the living room, and knelt in front of the bookcase. Books. Words. There must surely be some pattern of words which would neatly and safely cage what she felt—isolate her emotions so that she could look at them from outside. For she was of that generation who, having found nothing in religion, had formed themselves by literature. And the books which spoke most directly were those which had come out of Western Europe during the past hundred years, and of those, the personal and self-confessing. And so she knelt in front of a bookcase, in driving need of the right arrangement of words; for it is a remarkable fact that she was left unmoved by criticisms of the sort of person she was by parents, relations, preachers, teachers, politicians and the people who write for the newspapers; whereas an unsympathetic description of a character similar to her own in a novel would send her into a condition of anxious soul-searching for days. Which suggests that it is of no use for artists to insist, with such nervous disinclination for responsibility, that their productions are only "a divine play" or "a reflection from the creative fires of irony," etc., etc., while the Marthas of this world read and search with the craving thought, What does this say about my life? It will not do at all—but it must be admitted that there always came a point where Martha turned from the novelists and tale tellers to that section of the bookcase which was full of books called *The Psychology of . . ., The Behaviour of . . ., A Guide to . . .,* with the half-formulated thought that the novelists had not caught up with life; for there was no doubt that the sort of things she or Stella or Alice talked about found no reflection in literature—or rather, it was the attitudes of mind they took for granted that did not appear there, from which she deduced that women in literature were still what men, or the men-women, wished they were. In this other part of the bookcase, however, were no such omissions; she found what she was thinking and feeling described with an admirable lack of ambiguity. And yet, after hours of search among the complexities and subtleties of character, she was likely to return to her bedroom profoundly comforted, with some such resounding and original remark as "The young husband, therefore, must be careful to be especially understanding during the difficult weeks after marriage." For, since Douglas, the young husband in question, so logically insisted on relying upon the common sense *she* insisted on, she must with some part of herself take his place by being understanding, compassionate, etc. Martha was able to preserve an equilibrium because of an observing and satirical eye focused upon her own behaviour from a superior vantage point that was of course in no way influenced by that behaviour. She achieved quite extraordinary degrees of self-forbearance by this device.

In the bedroom the bedclothes were still lying dragged back, clothes lay everywhere; the morning was slipping past and she was not dressed. And now this question of work fronted her. She had understood she was not alone in her position of a woman who disdained both housework and a "job," but was vaguely expected by her husband—but only because of her own insistence on it—to be engaged in work of her own. Both Stella and Alice had claimed the state. Martha had heard their respective husbands speak to them in precisely the same tone of pride and satisfaction that Douglas used to her. Their wives were not as those of other men.

Feeling the distant pressure of this "work," Martha dutifully went to the bathroom to equip herself to face it.

The bathroom was modern. A high window showed yet another angle of clear blue sky, together with the tops of the trees in the park. A large white bath filled with heavy greenish water where spangles of light quivered, white cabinets, white shelves—it was all a gleam of white enamel. Martha took off her nightdress, and was alone with her body. But it was not that calm and obedient body which had been so pleasant a companion. White it was, and solid and unmarked—but heavy, unresponsive; her flesh was uncomfortable on her bones. It burned and unaccountably swelled; it seemed to be pursuing ideas of its own. Inside the firm thick flesh, a branch of bones which presumably remained unchanged: the thought was comforting. Martha looked down at her shape of flesh with the anxious thought that it was upon this that the marriage depended; for this, in fact, they—she and Douglas—had been allowed by society to shut themselves away in two high rooms with a bathroom attached. It was almost with the feeling of a rider who was wondering whether his horse would make the course that she regarded this body of hers, which was not only divided from her brain by the necessity of keeping open that cool and dispassionate eye, but separated into compartments of its own. Martha had after all been provided with a map of her flesh by "the book," in which each area was marked by the name of a different physical sensation, so that her mind was anxiously aware, not only of a disconnected partner, a body, but of every part of it, which might or might not come up to scratch at any given occasion. There were moments when she felt she was strenuously held together by nothing more than an act of will. She was beginning to feel that this view of herself was an offence against what was deepest and most real in her. And again she thought of the simple women of the country, who might be women in peace, according to their instincts, without being made to think and disintegrate themselves into fragments. During those first few weeks of her marriage Martha was always accompanied by that other, black woman, like an invisible sister simpler and wiser than herself; for no matter how much she reminded herself of statistics and progress, she envied her from the bottom of her heart. Without, of course, having any intention of emulating her: loyalty to progress forbade it.

At that hour of the morning the sun fell in bright lances through the high window. Martha stood where they might fall on her flesh; her skin shone with a soft iridescence, the warmth kneaded together her unhappily disconnected selves, she began to dissolve into well-being. But first there was another ritual to be gone through. From the high cupboard she took down the cans and rubber tubes pre-scribed by Dr. Stern, and washed away the sweats of love in the rocking green water. Then she refilled the bath for what she thought of as her own bath. In this she wallowed, while the sunlight moved up over the sides of the bath and into the water, and she was whole and at peace again, floating in sunlight and water like a fish. She might have stayed there all morning, if there wasn't this question of work; so she got out too soon, and thought with vague anxiety that those areas of tenderness on breasts and belly were no more than what was to be expected after such an intensive love life. The thought of pregnancy crossed her mind; and was instantly dismissed. She felt that it was hard enough to keep Martha Quest, now Kno-well, afloat on a sea of chaos and sensation without being pregnant as well—no, it was all too difficult. But her dress was tight; she must eat less, she told herself. Then she made tea and ate bread and but-ter with satisfaction at the thought that she was depriving herself of a meal.

And now it was ten in the morning, and her day was her own. Her work was free to start when it would. Martha went to the other room, and arranged herself comfortably on the divan. Or rather, it was with the intention of comfort, for the divan was a high, hard mattress on a native-made bed covered with a loosely woven brown linen. Comfortable it was not; but it suitably supported the rest of the room, and Martha chose it because one might sit there without surrendering to the boundaries of a chair.

Into this little box of a room had flowed so many different items of furniture—and then out again. Now two small jolly chairs were set at neat angles on a clean green rug. A new table of light wood, surrounded by four chairs of the same, filled the opposite corner. The curtains, of that material known as folk-weave, whose rough grain held pockets of yellow light, were of the same brown she sat on. It was safe to say that the furniture that had flowed in and out of this room with the restless owners of it was indistinguishable from what filled it now. This thought gave Martha an undefined and crav-ing hollowness, a sort of hunger. Yet everything was so practical and satisfactory! She looked at this room, from chair to window, from

table to cupboard, and her eyes rested on nothing, but moved onwards hastily to the next article, as if *this* might provide that quality
she was searching for.

It was not her flat; it belonged to that group of people who had
seen her married. Almost at once her thoughts floated away from
this place she sat in, these white boxes in the heart of the building,
and slowly she tested various other shells for living in, offered to her
in books. There were, after all, not so many of them; and each went
with a kind of life she must dismiss instantly and instinctively. For instance, there was her father's childhood in the English country cot-
tage, honest simplicity with the bones of the house showing through
lath and plaster. Outside, a green and lush country—but tame, tamed;
it would not do at all. Or—and this was a dip into the other stream
that fed her blood—a tall narrow Victorian house, crammed with
heavy dark furniture, buttoned and puffed and stuffed and padded,
an atmosphere of things unsaid. If that country cottage could be
acknowledged with a self-conscious smile, like a charmingly naïve
relation, this narrow dark house could not be admitted—too close it
was, too dangerous. And that house which was being built now
everywhere, in every country of the world, the modern house, cosmopolitan, capable of being lifted up from one continent and
dumped down in any other without exciting remark—no, certainly
not, it was not to be thought of. So there remained the flat in which
she was in fact now sitting? But she was not here at all; she did not
live in it; she was waiting to be moved on somewhere. . . .

At about eleven in the morning she roused herself. For she knew
that since both Stella and Alice were as free for their own work as
she was, either or both were likely to drop in. She therefore put the
kettle on and made sandwiches, prepared to spend the rest of the
morning gossiping, or—as pleasantly—alone.

By now the stores would have delivered by native messenger the
groceries, meat, and vegetables she had ordered by telephone; putting away these things interrupted work for a few minutes. Preparing a light lunch for Douglas could not take longer than half an
hour. In the long interval before lunch, Martha drifted once more in
front of her mirror, with her air of one prepared to be surprised by
what she saw there. And from this, as a natural consequence of a
long and dissatisfied examination of herself, she collected scissors
and needles and material, and in a few moments was at the table
with the sewing machine. And now her look of vagueness had vanished; for the first time since she had risen that morning, she was
centred behind what her hands did. She had the gift of running up
sundowner frocks, dance dresses, out of a remnant from the sales,

even discarded curtains or old-fashioned clothes that her mother had kept. She could transform them without effort—apart from the long, dreamy meditations which might fill half a week; for when a woman claims with disarming modesty that she has run up this dress for ten shillings, the long process of manipulating the material around her image of herself, those hours of creation, are not taken into account. Very few women's time is money, even now. But while the clothes she made for after dark were always a success, it seemed her sureness of touch must desert her for the daytime. Her friends might exclaim loyally that her morning dress was absolutely wonderful, but it was only over the evening clothes that their voices held the authentic seal of envy. From which it follows?

The fact is that as soon as Douglas returned from the office for lunch, the day was already nearly at evening. For he returned finally at four; and after that, it was only a question of time before their eyes met on a query: at the Sports Club, everyone they knew would be delighted to see them, and afterwards there would be dancing there or at the hotels. It seemed as if the day was only a drab preliminary to the night, as if the pageant of sunset was meant only as a curtain-raiser to that moment when the lights sprung up along the streets, and with them a feeling of vitality and excitement. For in the hotels, the clubs and the halls, the orchestras struck up at eight, and from every point in the town dance music was flowing like water from a concealed reservoir of nostalgia hidden below it. These were the nights of African winter, sharp, clear, cold, a high and luminous starlit dark lifting away from the low, warm glitter of city lights. In the white courts of the hotels, braziers offered a little futile heat to the cold dry air, and groups of young people formed and dissolved around them: there was no room for everyone inside, there was no room for all the people who needed, suddenly, to dance.

Night after night, they moved from the Club to the Plaza and on to McGrath's; and the self-contained parties that began the evening expected to dissolve into a great whole as midnight approached. By midnight they were dancing as if they formed one soul; they danced and sang, mindless, in a half-light, they were swallowed up in the sharp, exquisite knowledge of loss and impending change that came over the seas and continents from Europe; and underneath it all, a rising tide of excitement that was like a poison. Uniforms were appearing here and there, and the wearers carried themselves with self-effacing modesty, as if on a secret mission, but conscious that all eyes in the room were fixed on them. The rumours were beginning. This regiment was going to be called up, they were going to conscript the whole population; but the question of conscription was surely an irrelevance when every young man in the town was thinking only of the moment when he could put on a uniform—and that before it was decided what the war was to be fought about. They were all longing to be swallowed up in something bigger than themselves; they were, in fact, already swallowed up. And since each war, before it starts, has the look of the last one, it did not matter how often stern and important young men assured hushed audiences that the world could not survive a month of modern warfare, they would all be bombed to pieces by new and secret weapons; it was necessary only for the orchestra to play "Tipperary" or "Keep the Home Fires Burning"—which they did on every conceivable occasion—for the entire gathering to become transformed into a congregation of self-dedicated worshippers of what their parents chose to remember .of 1914.

In between dances, groups formed to discuss what was happening in Europe—or rather, to exchange the phrases they had read that morning in the *Zambesia News*. The fact that this newspaper was contradicting itself with the calmest of assurance from day to day did not matter in the least; there was going to be a war, and night after night youth danced and sang itself into a condition of preparation for it. Their days and work, their loves and love-making, were nothing but a preparation for that moment when hundreds of them stamped and shouted in great circles to the thudding drums, felt less as sound than as their own pulses; this was the culmination of the day, the real meaning of it, the moment of surrender.

Then the music stopped suddenly and disastrously, the managers came forward bowing with strained politeness, ignoring the pleas and imprecations about their hardheartedness—and the masses of young people streamed out into the still, frostbound air, under the glitter of the Cross. It was at this point that Martha and Douglas were reminded that they were married; for "the gang"—those of them that remained unbound to the girls whose one preoccupation it was to get married to the doomed as quickly as possible—went off shouting and stamping to the fun fair, which they kept going until early morning. The young married couples departed to one of the flats; and it was then that it became apparent there was a certain difference of viewpoint between husbands and wives. Stella, Alice, Martha, might have been part of that single yearning heart only half an hour before, but now they tended to fall silent, and even exchanged tolerant glances as their respective young men held forth on their plans for joining up. For it is a strain on any marriage, which after all is likely to begin with the belief that it must provide satisfaction and happiness for at least a few years, when one of the

partners shows signs of such restlessness to "rush off to the wars"—
as the girls acidly put it—the moment a war, any war, offers itself.

By the time Martha and Douglas reached home, reached the small,
brightly lit, untidy bedroom, still littered with their day clothes and
filled with the loud, sad, bitter music from the fun fair—for the wheel
was still dragging its glittering load of cars in its circle—by this time,
their elation was flagging, and there was a feeling of anticlimax.
Now, drenched and submerged by the music, which it was impossible to keep out even with shut windows, Martha crept closer to
Douglas and demanded the assurance that he did not really want to
leave her; just as Stella and Alice were doing in their bedrooms.
Douglas, manfully clasping Martha to him, murmured reassurances
and looked over her head at the glitter of the wheel. He had not
known how intolerably boring and empty his life was until there
was a chance of escaping from it; and the more fiercely he determined not to be left out of things, the more tightly he held Martha and
consoled her. He was holding a warm, confiding bundle of female
flesh, he wished only to love her and be proud of her—for, above all,
his pride was fed by her anxious demands for his love; but it was
all no use. For, just as he was playing a role which was surely inconsistent with what he thought—the young hero off to the wars for adventure—so she began to speak in the ancient female voice which he
found utterly irritating. After a long silence, during which he hoped
she might have gone to sleep so that he might dream of adventure
without guilt, a small, obstinate, ugly voice remarked that there
would be wars so long as men were such babies. At this point he
would loosen his grip and lie stiff beside her, and begin to explain
in an official tone that surely, Matty, she must see they must be prepared . . . But it was no use; that official tone carries no conviction
any longer, not even to the people who use it. She sniggered derisively; and he felt foolish.

They rolled apart and lay without touching; even apologizing in
an offhand, hasty way if they happened to touch by accident. Douglas soon fell asleep. Martha could not sleep while the wheel turned
and churned out music. She was in a mood of angry self-contempt for
being infected by that dangerous undertow of excitement. For she
had caught herself daydreaming of being a nurse, and no less than
a ministering angel. But, alas, alas, we know all about that ministering angel; we know what she comes to in the end; and Martha could
only return to thoughts of her father. She considered the undoubted
fact that while Mr. Quest might expatiate about the inefficiency and
corruption of the leaders of his war, about the waste of life, the use-
lessness of the thing, while he might push into Martha's hands books

like *All Quiet on the Western Front* with an irascible command that she should read it and understand that *that* was war, while he might talk of that war with the bitter, savage consciousness of betrayal, yet there was always an undercurrent of burning regret. Then he had been alive. "The comradeship," he would exclaim, "the comradeship! I've never experienced that since!" And then the terrible *"It was the only time in my life I was really happy."*

When the wheel stilled at last, Martha was able to sleep; and in the morning she was a different creature, easily able to withstand the insinuations of the ministering angel in the white coif, and prepared to look soberly at the alternatives—or rather, at a single alternative, for the possibility of in fact settling down to a life of tea parties, sundowners, and in due course children, was out of the question. She was trying to form the confusion of feelings that afflicted her to fit the sharp, clear view of life held by Solly and Joss—that was how she saw it. What she actually wanted, of course, was for some man to arrive in her life, simply take her by the hand, and lead her off into this new world. But it seemed he did not exist. And so she read the newspapers, and enjoyed the cynicism they produced in her. There was the *Zambesia News*, for instance, at that period in a state of such uneasy uncertainty. On the one hand it was reminding its readers about the atrocious nature of Hitler's Germany; on the other it seemed to be suffering from a certain reluctance to do so. Hard to forget that these same atrocities, concentration camps and so on, had been ignored by the *Zambesia News*, as by its betters, until it was impossible to ignore them; while even now, like those great exemplars overseas, it showed real indignation only over Hitler's capacity for absorbing other countries. Nor was she able to feel any less derisive when she read the great exemplars themselves, the newspapers from Home. As for that other, deeper knowledge, the pulse that really moved her, gained from her almost religious feeling for literature, a knowledge that amounted to a vision of mankind as nobility bound and betrayed—this was vanishing entirely beneath the pressure of enjoyable cynicism which was being fed by everything about her, and particularly by her own behaviour. For despite all her worried introspection, her determination to act rationally if only it was possible to find out what rational behaviour should be, the fact was that her sluggish days were nothing but a preparation for the first drink at sundown, which led to that grand emotional culmination at midnight, when she joined the swinging circle of intoxicated dancers controlled by the thudding of the drums.

It was about six weeks after her marriage that all this confusion was shaken into a single current by the fact that she was violently sick one morning. Lethargy caused her to murmur consolingly that it must be the result of not sleeping enough—probably nothing but a hangover. But she succeeded in forgetting it.

Two days later, in Stella's flat, after a dance, it happened that Maisie was there. She was wearing a dress of white tulle, frilled and flounced like a baby's bassinette, and from it her plump shoulders, her lazy pretty face, emerged with a placid enjoyment of life which apparently had not been disturbed by the fact that she had become engaged to one of the young men who was training to be a pilot. She came to sit by Martha, murmuring vaguely, "Well, Matty . . .," as if they saw each other every day. In fact they did, at dances, but from across the room. She bent down to rip off a strip of dirty white from the bottom of her dress where it had been trodden on, rolled it up, and tossed it into the corner of the room; and sat looking speculatively at Martha, her fair face flushed and beaded with the heat. "You look fine, you don't show yet," she remarked good-naturedly, looking frankly at Martha's stomach.

"What do you mean?" asked Martha.

Maisie was startled. "I'm sorry," she apologized hastily. "I thought . . ." Someone spoke to her, and she took the opportunity to get up and si† somewhere else. From time to time during the rest of the evening, she glanced towards Martha, but with the determination not to catch her eye. She left before Martha did, arm in arm with her pilot, including Martha with the rest of the room in a large, vague smile of farewell.

Afterwards Martha said indignantly to Douglas that it was the limit, people were saying she was pregnant. To which he replied a little awkwardly that some of the lads from the Club had suggested this was the case.

"Do you mean to say they think we got married because we *had* to?" she exclaimed, furious; for she felt this as an insult towards them as free beings able to do as they wished.

But he misunderstood her indignation, and said, laughing, "After all, Matty, since most of the people who get married get married because they have to . . ."

She laughed, but she was very uneasy.

Again she forgot about it, until there was a letter from her mother, which immediately caught her attention because of its casual tone. At the end of it was an enquiry as to how she felt. Again she burned with indignation—there was a conspiracy against her!

For some days, there was no reason to think of it; then she got a charming letter from Mrs. Talbot, which had the same hurried apologetic manner as her speech. She asked why dear Matty did not drop into see her one morning, she would so like to have a proper talk.

The letters were always on thick white paper, in a fine-pointed black hand; they gave an impression of casual elegance which made Martha curious, for never had she known anyone whose letters were not utilitarian. The letters, like Mrs. Talbot herself, spoke of an existence altogether remote from this colonial town. But what was this life which Mrs. Talbot seemed so anxious Martha should share? And what was this proper talk?

"We have supper or spend the evening with them at least two or three times a week," Martha pointed out to Douglas, quite bewildered.

"Oh, go and see her, Matty, she'll be pleased."

Martha had discovered that Mrs. Talbot was not, as one might infer from her appearance, about thirty-five, but over sixty; she was very rich, but in a way that seemed to apologize for the unpleasant fact that there was such a thing as money in the world at all. During those evenings, she would take Douglas—apologizing first—into an inner room, and they would discuss investments and properties. "There are no flies on Mrs. Talbot," he said appreciatively. And then, always: "She's an absolute marvel, a wonder! Why, Matty, would you think she was a day over thirty? Isn't she terrific?"

"But Elaine . . ." pointed out Martha jealously.

"Oh, Elaine's all right, she's a nice kid," said Douglas, dismissing her.

That Elaine should be thought a nice kid made Martha laugh—it was easier to tolerate the amazing Mrs. Talbot. For at the bottom of an uneasy disapproval of that lady was Martha's physical arrogance—the pride of the very young. *She* was young and whole and comely; secretly she felt a fierce, shuddering repulsion for the old and unsightly. For a brief ten years—she was convinced that thirty was the end of youth and good looks—she was allowed by nature to be young and attractive. For Mrs. Talbot to be beautiful at sixty was not fair.

"She *can't* be sixty," she had protested hopefully. But she was.

Martha told Douglas that she didn't want to have a proper talk with Mrs. Talbot; but on the morning after getting the letter she found herself disinclined for that "work," and set off on an impulse for Mrs. Talbot's house. It was half past nine; the morning was well advanced for a society which began work at eight. Martha walked through the park and along the avenues: the house was one of the delightful houses of the older town. It was almost hidden from the street by trees and flowering bushes. The door opened immediately from the garden path, and not off a wide verandah. The house had an introspective, inward-turning look because of this discreet black door with its shining door knocker. Mrs. Talbot's house, like herself, could not help suggesting the England one knew from novels. That door might be flanked on either side by poinsettias, ragged pointed scraps of scarlet silk fluttering on naked shining silken stems, but one felt they were there only to suggest an ironical contrast.

Martha rang, and was admitted by a native servant, and shown into a small side room kept for just this purpose. She summoned her memories of what she had read, and then saw, as she had expected, a tray on a stand, littered with visiting cards. At this it occurred to her that the phrase "dropping in" might have a different meaning to Mrs. Talbot than it had for herself and her friends. Before she could recover herself, Mr. Talbot came in. She had seen very little of him; he went to the Club in the evenings when his wife entertained. He was wearing a dark silk dressing gown, was tall and heavily built, with a dark, heavy face, and he came stooping forward with his hand outstretched, apologizing for his dressing gown. She was embarrassed because of her thoughts about him. She did not like him. She did not like the way he would come into his wife's drawing room, on his way out, a man paying forced tribute to women's amusements; besides, he suggested a spy—his look at Mrs. Talbot always made her uncomfortable. Finally, he was an old man, and distasteful because he had a sardonic, intimate manner with her that made it impossible to dismiss him so easily. He was forcing her now to think of him as a man, and she stammered a little as she said she had come to see Mrs. Talbot. He said very politely that he didn't think his wife was up yet, but that Martha might care to wait?

She said at once, no—of course not; she was only on a walk, and she would come up another time.

He held her eyes with his while he enquired if she would like to see Elaine.

Martha said yes, she would like to very much.

Mr. Talbot stood aside for her to precede him out of the door, and she felt uncomfortable as she passed him, as if he might suddenly put out his hands and grasp her. In the passage, he indicated the drawing-room door, and apologized again for his dressing gown. Then he opened another door; Martha caught a glimpse of a large brown leather chair, a pipe smoking on a small table, a litter of newspapers; he went inside, having held her eyes again in another direct glance.

She went into the drawing room, feeling its contrast with the brown masculine study he had gone into. It was large, low-ceilinged, rather dim. It was carpeted from wall to wall with a deep rosy, flow-

ering softness that gave under her feet. It was full of furniture that
Martha instinctively described as antiques. It was a charming room,
it was like an Edwardian novel; and one could not be in it without
thinking of the savage country outside. Martha kept looking out of
the windows, which were veiled in thin pale stuffs, as if to assure
herself this was in fact Africa. It might have vanished, she felt, so
strong was the power of this room to destroy other realities.

Elaine came forward, from a small sunny verandah enclosed by
glass and filled by plants in such a way that it suggested a conserva-
tory. Elaine was wearing a loose linen smock, and she was doing the
flowers.

She asked Martha, with charming formality, if she would like to
come to the sun porch, and Martha followed her. There was a small
grass chair, and Martha sat on it and watched Elaine fitting pink and
mauve sweet peas into narrow silver vases like small fluted trumpets.

Elaine said that her mother was never up before eleven, and accompanied this remark by a small smile which did not invite shared
amusement, but rather expressed an anxious desire that no one
should find it remarkable. Elaine, standing by her trestle, with her
copper jugs for water, her shears, her rows of sweet peas and roses,
her heavy gauntlets, had the air of a fragile but devoted handmaid
to her mother's way of life. Martha watched her and found herself
feeling protective. This girl should be spared any unpleasantness
which might occur outside the shining glass walls of the sun porch.
Her fragility, her air of fatigue, the blue shadows under her eyes,
removed her completely from any possibility of being treated by
Martha as an equal. Martha found herself censoring her speech; in a
few minutes they were making conversation about gardening. Then
a bell shrilled from close by, and Elaine hastily excused herself, laid
down her flowers, and went to a door which led to Mrs. Talbot's
bedroom.

In a few minutes she came back to say that her mother was awake
and was delighted to hear that Martha had come to see her. If dear
Matty did not mind being treated so informally—and here Elaine
again offered a small anxious smile, as if acknowledging at least the
possibility of amusement—would she like to come into the bedroom?
Martha went to the door, expecting Elaine to come with her; but
Elaine remained with her flowers, a pale effaced figure in her yellow
smock, drenched in the sunlight that was concentrated through the
blazing glass of the sun porch.

Martha's eyes were full of sunlight, and in this room it was nearly
dark. She stood blinded just inside the door, and heard Mrs. Talbot
murmuring affectionate greetings from the shadows. She stumbled

forward, sat on a chair that was pushed under her, and then saw that
Mrs. Talbot was up and in a dressing gown, a dim figure agitated by
the delight this visit gave her, but even more agitated by apologies
because she was not dressed.

"If I'd known you were coming, Matty darling . . . But I'm so
terribly lazy, I simply can't get out of bed before twelve. It was so
sweet of you to come so soon when I asked you—but we old women
must be allowed our weaknesses. . . ."

Martha was astounded by that "old women"; but there was no
suggestion of coyness in it. She tried to peer through the dark, for
she was longing to see how Mrs. Talbot must look before she had
created herself for her public. All she could see was a slender figure
in an insinuating rustle of silks, perched on the bed. Mrs. Talbot lit
a cigarette; almost at once the red spark was crushed out again;
Martha saw that this flutter was due simply to a routine being upset.

"I rang up my hairdresser when I heard your voice, I told him not
to come this morning. I'm sure it won't hurt me to show an inch or
so of grey just for once. When you reach the age of going grey,
Matty darling, don't be silly and dye your hair. It's an absolute mar-
tyrdom. If I had only known. . . ."

Martha was now able to see better. Mrs. Talbot's face came out of
the shadow in a splash of white. It was some kind of a face mask.
"Shall I go out till you are dressed?" she suggested awkwardly.

But Mrs. Talbot rose with a swirl of silk and said, "If you don't
mind it all, Matty, I'd adore you to stay." There was a nervous gasp
of laughter; she was peering forward to see Martha, to find out her
reaction. It occurred to Martha that the apology, the deference, was
quite sincere and not a pose, as she had assumed. Mrs. Talbot's nerv-
ousness was that of a duchess who had survived the French Revolution and timidly continued to wear powdered curls in the privacy of
her bedroom because she did not feel herself in the new fashions.

Martha saw the slight figure rise, go to the window, and tug at a
cord. At once the room was shot with hazy yellow light. Mrs. Talbot
was wearing a shimmering grey garment with full flounced sleeves;
she was covered in stark-white paste from collarbones to hairline,
and from this mask her small eyes glimmered out through black
holes. Her pale smooth hair was looped loosely on her neck; there
was no sign of grey. She sat before a large dressing table and dabbed
carefully at her face with tufts of cotton wool. The room was long,
low, subdued, with shell-coloured curtains, dove-grey carpet, and
furniture of light, gleaming wood which looked as if it had been
embroidered; it had a look of chaste withdrawal from the world; and
Mrs. Talbot was a light, cool, uncommitted figure, even when she

was poised thus on her stool, leaning forward into her mirror, her submissive charm momentarily lost in a focus of keen concentration. Her skin was emerging patchily from under the white paste, and she muttered, "In a minute, Matty."

Soon she rose and went to an old-fashioned washstand, where a graceful ewer stood in a shining rose-patterned basin. It was clear that taps running hot and cold would be too much of a modern note in this altar to the past. Mrs. Talbot splashed water vigorously over her face, while the air was pervaded by the odour of violets. In the meantime Martha, still examining every detail of the room, had noticed the bed. It was very big—too big, she thought involuntarily, for Mrs. Talbot. Then she saw it was a double bed, with two sets of pillows. She must re-admit Mr. Talbot, whom she had again forgotten. This bed, untidy and sprawling, gave Martha the most uncomfortable feeling of something unseemly: it was, she saw, because a man's pyjamas lay where they had been flung off, on the pillow. They were of maroon-striped silk, and strongly suggested the person of Mr. Talbot, as did a jar of pipes on the bed table. So uncomfortable did this make Martha that she turned away from the bed, feeling her face hot. Mrs. Talbot, however, returning from her ablutions, could not be aware of how Martha was feeling, for she carelessly rolled these pyjamas together and tucked them under the pillow, observing, "Men are always so untidy." Then she sat herself on the edge of the bed, with the air of one prepared to devote any amount of time to friendship.

And now they must talk. There would follow the proper talk. Martha saw the gleam of affection in Mrs. Talbot's eyes and was asking herself, Does she really like me? If so, why? But Mrs. Talbot was talking about Douglas: how he was such a dear boy, how he was always so clever and helpful, and with such a sense for these horrid, horrid financial things; and then—impulsively—how lovely it was that he had married such a sweet girl. At this Martha involuntarily laughed; and was sorry when she saw the look of surprise on this delightful lady's face. She rose from her chair and began walking about the room, touching the curtains, which slipped like thick silken skin through her fingers, laying a curious finger on the wood of the dressing table, which had such a gleaming softness that it was strange it should oppose her flesh with the hardness of real wood. Mrs. Talbot watched her without moving. There was a small, shrewd smile on her lips.

"Are you shocked, Matty, at all this fuss?" she asked a little plaintively; and when Martha turned quickly to see what she could mean, she continued quickly, "I know it all looks so awful until it's tidied up; Elaine is so sweet, she comes in and tidies everything for me, and then this is a lovely room, but I know it must look horrid now, with face creams and cotton wool everywhere. The trouble is . . ." Here she tailed off, with a helpless shrug which suggested that there was nothing she would like better than to relapse into the comfortable condition of being an old woman, if only she knew how. Martha involuntarily glanced at Mr. Talbot's side of the bed and then blushed as she guiltily caught Mrs. Talbot's eye. But it was clear that this was one thing she could not understand in Martha; she looked puzzled.

After a short pause she said, "I hope you'll be friends with Elaine, Matty. She's such a sweet thing, so sensitive, and she doesn't make friends easily. Sometimes I feel it is my fault—but we've always been so much together, and I don't know why it is, but . . ."

Now Martha's look was far more hostile than she had intended; and Mrs. Talbot's thick white skin coloured evenly. She looked like an embarrassed young girl, in spite of the faint look of wear under her eyes. Martha could not imagine herself being friends with that gentle, flower-gathering maiden; she could not prevent a rather helpless but ironical smile, and she looked direct at Mrs. Talbot as if accusing her of being wilfully obtuse.

Mrs. Talbot cried out, "But you're so artistic, Matty, and you would have so much in common."

Martha saw tears in her eyes. "But I'm not at all artistic," she observed obstinately—though of course with a hidden feeling that she might prove to be yet, if given the chance!

"But all those books you read, and then anyone can see. . . ." Mrs. Talbot was positively crying out against the fate that persisted in making Martha refuse to be artistic. "And Elaine is so sweet, no one knows as well as I do how sweet she is and—but sometimes I wonder if she's strong enough to *manage* things the way all you clever young things do. You are all so sure of yourselves!"

Here Martha could not help another rueful smile, which checked Mrs. Talbot. She was regarding Martha with extraordinary shrewdness. Martha, for her part, was waiting for the proper talk to begin; what was it that Mrs. Talbot wanted to say to her?

Mrs. Talbot sighed, gave the shadow of a shrug, and went back to her dressing table. Here she applied one cream after another, with steady method, and continued to talk, in between pauses for screwing up her mouth or stretching her eyelids smooth. "I would so much like Elaine to get married. If she could only get properly married, and I needn't worry any more . . . There is no greater happiness, Matty, none! She meets so few people, always my friends, and she is so shy. And you meet so many people, Matty, all you young people are so brave and enterprising."

For the life of her Martha could not see Elaine with the wolves of the Club, with the boys, the kids and the fellows. "I don't think Elaine would like the sort of men we meet," observed Martha; and she caught another shrewd glance. She felt there were things she ought to be understanding, but she was quite lost.

"There's your Douglas," said Mrs. Talbot, a trifle reproachfully. "He's such a nice boy."

Surely, wondered Martha, Mrs. Talbot could not have wanted Douglas for Elaine? The idea was preposterous—even brutal.

"So kind," murmured Mrs. Talbot, "so helpful, so clever with everything."

And now Martha was returned, simply by the incongruity of Douglas and Elaine, into her private nightmare. She could not meet a young man or woman without looking around anxiously for the father and mother: that was how they would end, there was no escape for them. She could not meet an elderly person without wondering what the unalterable influences had been that had created them just so. She could take no step, perform no action, no matter how apparently new and unforeseen, without the secret fear that in fact this new and arbitrary thing would turn out to be part of the inevitable process she was doomed to. She was, in short, in the grip of the great bourgeois monster, the nightmare *repetition*. It was like the obsession of the neurotic who must continuously be touching a certain object or muttering a certain formula of figures in order to be safe from the malevolent powers, like the person who cannot go to bed at night without returning a dozen times to see if the door is locked and the fire out. She was thinking now, But Mrs. Talbot married Mr. Talbot, then Elaine is bound to marry someone like Mr. Talbot, there is no escaping it; then what connection is there between Douglas and Mr. Talbot that I don't see?

But Mrs. Talbot was talking. "I'll show you something, Matty— I would like to show you, I don't everyone."

Mrs. Talbot was searching hurriedly through her drawers. She pulled out a large, leather-framed photograph. Martha came forward and took it, with a feeling that the nightmare was being confirmed. It was of a young man in uniform, a young man smiling direct out of the frame, with a young sensitive, rueful look. "Hardly anybody knows," Mrs. Talbot cried agitatedly, "but we were engaged, he was killed in the war—the other war, you know—he was so sweet, you don't know. He was so nice." Her lips quivered. She turned away her face and held out her hand for the photograph.

Martha handed it back and returned to her chair. She was thinking, Well, then, so Elaine must get engaged to *that* young man; is it conceivable that Mrs. Talbot sees Douglas like that?

But more: her mother, Mrs. Quest, had been engaged to such another charming young man. This boy, weak-faced and engaging, smiled up still from a small framed photograph on her mother's dressing table, a persistent reminder of that love which Mr. Quest could scarcely resent, since the photograph was half submerged, in fact practically invisible, among a litter of things which referred to her life with him. Martha had even gone so far as to feel perturbed because this boy had not appeared in her own life; she had looked speculatively at Douglas with this thought—but no, weak and charming he was not, he could not take that role.

She sat silent in her chair, frowning; when Mrs. Talbot looked at her, it was to see an apparently angry young woman, and one very remote from her. She hesitated, came forward, and kissed Martha warmly on her cheek. "You must forgive me," she said. "We are a selfish lot, we old women—and you probably have troubles of your own. We forget . . ." Here she hesitated. Martha was looking through her, frowning. She continued guiltily: "And to have children—that's the best of all. I wish I had a dozen, instead of just one. But Mr. Talbot . . ." She glanced hastily at Martha and fell silent.

There was a very long silence. Martha was following the nightmare to its conclusion: Well then, so Elaine will find just such a charming young man, and there's a war conveniently at hand so that he can get killed, and then Elaine will marry another Mr. Talbot, and for the rest of her life, just like all these old women, she'll keep a photograph of her real and great love in a drawer with her handkerchiefs.

"There's nothing nicer than children, and you look very well, Matty," said Mrs. Talbot suddenly.

Martha emerged from her dream remarking absently, "I'm always well." Then she heard what Mrs. Talbot had said; it seemed to hang on the air waiting for her to hear it. She thought tolerantly, She's heard a rumour that I'm pregnant. She smiled at Mrs. Talbot and remarked, "I shan't have children for years yet—damn it, I'm only nineteen myself."

Mrs. Talbot suppressed an exclamation. She surveyed Martha up and down, a rapid, skilled glance, and then, colouring, said, "But, my dear, it's so nice to have your children when you're young. I wish I had. I was *old* when she was born. Of course, people say we are like sisters, but it makes a difference. Have them young, Matty—you won't regret it." She leaned forward with an urgent affectionate smile and continued, after the slightest hesitation, "You know, we old women get a sixth sense about these things. We know when a woman is pregnant, there's a look in the eyes." She put a cool hand to Martha's cheek and turned her face to the light. Narrowing her eyes so that for a moment her lids showed creases of tired flesh, she looked at Martha with a deep impersonal glance and nodded involuntarily, dropping her hand.

Martha was angry and uncomfortable; Mrs. Talbot at this moment seemed to her like an old woman: the utterly impersonal triumphant gleam of the aged female, the old witch, was coming from the ageless jewelled face.

"I can't be pregnant," she announced. "I don't want to have a baby yet."

Mrs. Talbot let out a small resigned sigh. She rose and said in a different voice, "I think I shall have my bath, dear."

"I'll go," said Martha quickly.

"You and Douggie'll be coming to dinner tomorrow?"

"We're looking forward to it very much."

Mrs. Talbot was again the easy hostess; she came forward in a wave of grey silk and kissed Martha. "You'll be so happy," she murmured gently. "So happy, I feel it."

Martha emitted a short ungracious laugh. "But, Mrs. Talbot!" she protested—then stopped. She wanted to put right what she felt to be an impossibly false position; honesty demanded it of her. She was not what Mrs. Talbot thought her; she had no intention of conforming to this perfumed, silken bullying, as she most deeply felt it to be. But she could not go on. The appeal in the beautiful grey eyes silenced her. She was almost ready to aver that she wanted nothing more than to be happy with the dear boy Douglas, for Mrs. Talbot; to have a dozen children, for Mrs. Talbot; to take morning tea with Elaine every day, and see her married to just such another as Douglas.

Mrs. Talbot, arm lightly placed about her waist, gently pressed her to the door. She opened it with one hand, then gave Martha a small squeeze, and smiled straight into her eyes, with such knowledge, such ironical comprehension, that Martha could not bear it. She stiffened; and Mrs. Talbot dropped her arm at once.

"Elaine, dear," said Mrs. Talbot apologetically past Martha to the sun porch, "if you'd like to run my bath for me."

Elaine was now painting the row of pink and mauve sweet peas in the fluted silver vases. "Ah!" exclaimed Mrs. Talbot delightedly, moving forward quickly to look at the water colour. She leaned over, kissing Elaine's hair. The girl moved slightly, then remained still under her mother's restraining arm. "Isn't this lovely, Matty, isn't she gifted?"

Martha looked at the pretty water colour and said it was beautiful. Elaine's glance at her now held a real embarrassment; but she remained silent until her mother had gained her meed of admiration.

Then Mrs. Talbot waved goodbye and returned to her bedroom; and Elaine rose, and said, "Excuse me, Matty, I'll just do Mummy's bath—she likes me to do it, rather than the boy, you know." Martha looked to see if there was any consciousness here of being exploited, but no: there was nothing but charming deference.

They said goodbye, and Martha, as she turned away, saw Elaine knocking at the door that led into Mrs. Talbot's bedroom. "Can I come in, Mummy?"

Martha walked away down the street, thinking of that last deep glance into her eyes. Nonsense, she thought; it's nothing but old women's nonsense, old wives' superstition. There seemed nothing anomalous in referring to the youthful Mrs. Talbot thus at this moment. "How can there be a look in my eyes?"

When she reached home, it was nearly lunchtime. The butcher's boy had left a parcel of meat. For some reason she was unable to touch it. The soggy, bloody mass turned her stomach—she was very sick. But this was nonsense, she told herself sternly. She forced herself to untie the wet parcel, take out the meat, and cook it. She watched Douglas eating it, while she made a great joke of her weakness. Douglas remarked with jocularity that she must be pregnant. She flew into a temper.

"All the same, Matty, it wouldn't do any harm just to drop along to old Stern, would it? We don't want kids just when the war's starting, do we?"

That afternoon, since Stella was not there to gain priority for her, she sat out her time of waiting with the other women; and in due course found herself with Dr. Stern. He gave her instructions to undress. She undressed and waited. Dr. Stern, whose exquisite tact had earned him the right to have his waiting room perpetually filled with women who depended on him, explored the more intimate parts of Martha's body with rubber-clothed fingers, and at the same time made conversation about the international situation. Finally he informed Martha that he did not think she was pregnant; she might set her mind at rest.

He then made the mistake of complimenting her on her build, which was of the best kind for easy child-bearing. Martha was stiff-lipped and resentful and did not respond. He quickly changed his tone, saying that she needn't think about such things yet; and suggested that there was no reason why she should be pregnant if she had been carrying out his instructions? The query dismayed Martha; but she had decided to remember that he had been definite about it.

When she had left, he remarked to his new nurse that it was just as well for the medical profession that laymen had such touching faith in them. The nurse laughed dutifully and summoned the next patient.

Martha walked home very quickly; she could not wait to tell Douglas that everything was all right.

4

Officially pronounced not pregnant, Martha determined to use her freedom sensibly. But if there was a weight off her mind, her flesh remained uncomfortable. She might say that she would settle her future "once and for all"; but it was not so easy: she was feeling— but how did she feel? For no matter how many charts of her emotions and flesh she may be armed with, it is not so easy for a very young woman, newly married, to discriminate between this sensation and that. Her body, newly licensed for use by society, stimulated—as Dr. Stern had so humorously and succinctly put it—three times a day after meals, was in any case a web of sensations. Buzzings, burnings, swarmings: she was like a hive. And as for her tendency to feel dizzy or queazy in the mornings—what could one expect if one slept so little, ate so erratically, and, it must be confessed, drank such a lot? That is, regarded statistically, she drank a lot. But not more than everybody else. Still, from six in the evening until four the next morning she was unlikely to be without a glass in her hand, or at least, without a glass standing somewhere near. Drunk, no; one did not get drunk. A person who drinks too much is he who drinks more than the people around him. Besides, she was persistently tipsy as much from excitement as from alcohol; for the wave of elation which rose as the sun went down was as much the expectation of another brilliant, festive dancing night where the braziers burned steadily into the dawn. So Martha shifted the load of worry about how uneasy and unpredictable she felt onto how she was behaving, which she would have been the first to describe as idiotic. But then, it would not last long: the very essence of those exciting weeks was nostalgia for something doomed.

The town was restless with rumour. The voice of authority, the *Zambesia News,* faithfully reflecting the doubts and confusions of the unfortunate British Government, left ordinary people with no resource but to besiege the men in the know with questions. Every-one had some such person to whom they repaired for information. The young Knowells, for instance, had Colonel Brodeshaw; every-one knew a minor member of Parliament or a big businessman. Whenever Douglas returned from the world of offices, bars and clubs, it was with some final and authoritative statement, such as that conscription was imminent, or that people wouldn't stand for it; or that the British Government was about to declare war on Hitler the next weekend, or that—and this was very persistent during those weeks of June and July—Hitler and the British Government would together attack Stalin, thus ridding the world of what was clearly its main enemy.

But alas for the glamour and glory of great public events, their first results, regardless of how one may see them afterwards, "in perspective," as the phrase is, tend to show themselves in the most tawdry and insignificant ways. In this case, the business of collecting the latest news proved so fascinating that young husbands preferred the bars and the clubs of the city to returning home for lunch with their wives.

These three young wives reacted to this state of affairs according to their respective temperaments. Alice, after three or four days of nervous speculation over her apologetic Willie, arranged that she would meet him every day at one o'clock, and go with him on his rounds; which meant, of course, that the specifically male establish-ments were now out of bounds. But it was not her fault, she re-marked, with her vague good-natured giggle, if men were so silly as to exclude women. As for Stella, it was all at once made evident to everyone that she had a mother. A rich widow, she was living in the suburbs. Stella, like all these young women, had fought the good fight for independence, had routed her mother from her affairs as a question of principle, no less; but now, like the heroine of a music-hall joke, she rushed back to her. At five in the evening, when An-drew went home to find his wife so that they might start on the eve-ning round of dancing and drinking, she was not there; he had to drive out to the suburbs, where he found these two antagonists drinking tea and treating him with a calculated coolness, a weapon taken from Stella's mother's armoury of weapons against men. But this time it did not work. After some days, Andrew remarked with calm Scotch common sense: "Well, Stella, it's not a bad idea, your having lunch with your mother. It means you're not alone all day." Stella was doomed to a life always much less dramatic than she felt it was entitled to be.

As for Martha, whose first fierce tenet in life was hatred for the tyranny of the family, naturally she was barred from these contemptible female ruses. It was she who, after Douglas had rung up twice at lunchtime to say that he was just running off with the boys for a drink, and did she mind if he was a little late, suggested that it would be more interesting for him if he did not come home at all. He was surprised and grateful that his wife set no bounds to his freedom. It was an additional reason to be proud of his acquisition. But later in the evening, when he came home, there was perhaps a slightly resentful look on his face, as Martha enquired where he had gone and whom he had met—of course with the friendliest interest and without any suspicion of jealousy. She would then listen intently, making him retrace his conversations and arguments by the sheer force of her interest in them. It was almost as if she had been there in his place; almost as if *she* were putting the words into his mouth for future conversations. Tyranny, it seems, is not so easily legislated against.

Besides, Douglas, like all these other young men with wives, wore during these weeks a steady, if faint, look of guilt. It had become known that a dozen of the richer young men of the city had flown Home to England to offer their services to the Air Force. Douglas, Willie and Andrew, late at night, made reckless with alcohol, discussed hopelessly how they might do the same. But if it turned out there would be no war after all? They would be without jobs, without money; *they* were not the sons of rich fathers. But of course, if they had been free—if they had no responsibilities . . . Even alcohol, even the relaxed and intimate hour of four in the morning by the coffee stalls, could not release that thought into words. But the wives, listening with consciously sardonic patience, heard the sigh after lost freedom in every gap in the conversation.

"Men," remarked Stella to Martha, with charged womanly scorn, "are nothing but babies."

Martha disliked her own most intimate voice in Stella's mouth. But she was wrestling with a degree of contempt for Douglas that dismayed her. She could not afford it. She pushed it away. These young men, so eagerly discussing the prospects of being in at the kill, seemed to her like lumpish schoolboys. She despised them quite passionately: the nightly-recurring sight of Douglas, Willie and Andrew behaving like small boys wistful after adventure made her seethe with impatient contempt.

To Stella she said angrily, "If they knew they were going to fight for something, if they cared at all . . ."

To which Stella replied indignantly, after the briefest possible pause, switching course completely in a way which could hardly strike her as odd, since it was no more than the authorities did from day to day, "But it's our duty to squash Communism."

The Mathews' man in the know was an upper secretary in the establishment of Mr. Player; fed from this source, Stella was a well of good reasons why Communism should be instantly suppressed. It had flickered into Martha's mind that Andrew had talked of getting a job in the Player offices. She instantly dismissed the suspicion. It was one of her more pleasant but less efficient characteristics that she was unable to believe in that degree of cynicism from anyone. For naturally she persisted in believing that people should be conscious of their motives. Someone has remarked that there is no such thing as a hypocrite. In order to believe that, one must have reached the age to understand how persistently one has not been a hypocrite oneself.

Martha devoted herself to explaining to Stella how intolerable it was that she as a Jewess should have a good word to say for Hitler; while Stella, torn between persistent suspicions that there might be something in the rumours that Hitler ill-treated Jews and her terror that Andrew might not conform to Mr. Player's qualifications for a minor administrator, defended the Third Reich as an ally for Britain. That is, she continued to do so more or less consistently, interspersed with short periods when someone else's man in the know had supplied other authoritative information sufficiently persuasive.

It had reached the end of July. A second batch of young men left for England. It caused an extraordinary resentment. That there were no class distinctions of any sort in this society was an axiom; one was not envious of people who sent their children to university, or even—in extreme cases—to finishing schools in Europe; it was all a question of luck. But for some days now the young men who could not afford air fares, or to gamble with their jobs, spoke with a rancour which was quite new. Opinion seethed, and brought forth a scheme by which a sufficient number of young men should besiege their heads of department and employers to give them time off, so that they should be ready and trained for instant service when war started. This admirable scheme came to nothing, because the authorities in Britain had not yet made up their minds how the colonies were to be used. There was only one principle yet decided, and this was that the men from the colonies were clearly all officer material, because of lives spent in ordering the black population about. The phrase used was, "They are accustomed to positions of authority." It would be a waste for Douglas, Willie and Andrew to take the field as mere cannon fodder. But although the wave of determination disintegrated against various rocks of this nature, for at least a week the young men in question thought and spoke of little else. As a result, the women turned over various ideas of their own.

They were all sitting late one night in the Burrells' flat, which it is unnecessary to describe, since it was identical with the Knowells' and the Mathews' flats, when Alice remarked, with a nervous laugh, that it was no good Willie's thinking of dashing off to the wars, because she thought she was pregnant.

Willie was sitting next to her as usual; he squeezed his large sunburnt hand on her shoulder, and laughed, giving her his affectionate protective look. "It's all very well," persisted Alice. "Oh, well, to hell with everything." And she reached for a cigarette.

No one took it seriously. But a week later, when the Burrells were rung up to join a party for dancing, Alice remarked in a calm way that she had no time for dancing for a couple of days, because she had to do something about this damned baby. Douglas, returning from the office, reported to Martha that he had met Willie in the bar and Willie said it was very serious, no laughing matter at all. Stella, all delighted animation, rang up to offer her services. But Alice, the trained nurse, was vaguely reassuring. She was quite all right, she said.

Stella was offended, and showed it by saying that it was stupid to get pregnant when— But this sentence flowed into "And, in any case, she's only doing it to keep Willie from being called up." Martha said indignantly that anyone would think Alice was doing it on purpose. To which Stella replied with her rich, shrewd laugh. Martha was annoyed because she was associated with a sex which chose such dishonest methods for getting its own way.

"I bet she's not really doing anything about getting rid of it," said Stella virtuously. But one felt her energies were not really behind this indignation.

She and Martha were secure in a plan of their own. Martha had suggested they might go and take a course in Red Cross. It was on a day when the newspaper had warned them that an enemy (left undefined, like a blank in an official form to be filled in later as events decided) might sweep across Africa in a swastikaed or—the case might be—hammer-and-sickled horde. In this case, the black population, always ungrateful to the British colonists, would naturally side with the unscrupulous invaders, undermined as they were by sedition-mongers, agitators and Fabian influences from England. The prospect brightened the eyes of innumerable women; one should be prepared; and in due time Red Cross courses were announced.

"Matty and I are thinking of joining an ambulance unit," said Stella demurely. "After all, we won't have any responsibilities here if you go on active service, will we?"

Martha had dropped this suggestion in passing, just as she had tentatively suggested the Red Cross course, only to find it taken up and moulded by Stella. And the uneasy silence of their husbands contributed to their perseverance. At ten o'clock one morning, Martha and Stella were in their seats for the first of these lectures.

It was a large room filled with rows of school desks. They were crowded with about sixty women, who must be housewives or leisured daughters at this hour of the day. The lecturer was an elderly woman, fat, red-faced, with jolly little black eyes. Under the edges of her flowing coif showed flat scooplike curls of iron-grey hair, gummed against her cheeks; for, unlike the nuns whose garb this so much resembled, this woman was a female still—those curls proclaimed it. The masses of her flesh were tightly confined in glazed white, and supported on the large splayed feet which were the reward of her work.

This, then, was Sister Dorothy Dalraye, known for the last thirty years to her friends and colleagues, now numbering several thousands, as Doll. She introduced herself with the cheerful cry of "Well, girls, since we're all going to be together for six weeks, you must call me Sister Doll!" And proceeded to a series of bright remarks, infusing into her animated black eyes a look of insinuating suggestiveness, so that her audience instinctively listened as if some doubtful joke was imminent. But no: it appeared her innuendoes referred to the coming war—or rather, the enemy who was yet unnamed. Martha unravelled her ambiguities to mean that she, unlike Stella, hoped to fight Hitler and not Stalin; at last she made some references to "the Hun" which settled the matter. That this was a memory from the last war was made clear when she called it, just as Mr. Quest might do, "the Great Unmentionable," but without his bitter note of betrayal. Sister Doll had fought alongside the boys during the Great Unmentionable, and on various fronts. She named them. She produced anecdote after anecdote, apparently at random. But Martha slowly realized that this was not at all as casual as it looked. This gathering of some sixty women had ceased to be individuals. They were being slowly welded together. They were listening in silence, and every face showed anticipation, as if they were being led, by the cheerful tallyhoing of Sister Doll, to view entrancing vistas of country. Sister Doll was adroitly, and with the confidence of one who had done it many times before, building up a picture of herself, and so of them, as a cheerfully modest, indefatigably devoted minister of mercy who took physical bravery for granted. But behind this picture, absolutely genuine, was another; and it was this that beckoned the audience: adventure. Sister Doll was promising them adventure. Once again Martha heard the mud, the squalor, the slaughter, of the trenches re-created in the memory of someone who had been a victim of them —Sister Doll remarked in passing that she had "lost" her boy at Passchendaele—as cleanly gallant and exciting.

She spoke for some twenty minutes, this jolly old campaigner; then, judging it was enough, she proceeded to talk about discipline. It was clear that this was by no means as popular as those inspiring reminiscences—perhaps because these women, being mostly married women with servants, had reached the position where they believed their task was to discipline others and not themselves. In this they resembled Sister Doll. At any rate, judging from the critical and sceptical look on their faces, they were reflecting that the discipline of the nursing profession, like its uniform, was more hierarchic than practical. They were minutely observing Sister Doll's uniform, with its white glaze, its ritual buckles and badges, and its romantic flowing white veil, with the common sense of disparaging housewives. They began to cough and shuffle like a theatre audience. Not a moment too soon Sister Doll prevented them from separating again into a collection of individuals, by turning to her main topic for that day, which was how to make a bed properly. Not, however, without remarking with a sort of regretful severity, looking at the wall in case she might be accused of singling anyone out, that some people said, though of course she wouldn't know if it was true or not, that the young people of today hadn't the sense of vocation of her generation.

Martha had decided that she had no intention of devoting six weeks, although only a few hours a week were demanded of her, to the company of this elderly war horse who nevertheless continually suggested a happy hockey-playing schoolgirl. She therefore occupied her time in trying to decide what was the common denominator of this mass of women; for certainly there must be a special kind of woman who rushes, at the first sound of the bugle, to learn how to nurse "the boys." There was no doubt that this was how they were picturing themselves, and how Sister Doll was encouraging them to think; a white-garbed angel among wounded men was the image that filled their minds, despite this talk of a threatened civilian population. But she could only conclude that the difference between them and herself was that they were all taking down minute notes about the correct way to fold bedclothes.

She looked towards Stella, who was coiled seductively on the hard bench, head propped on slender hands, eyes fixed on Sister Doll. It was clear that she was not listening to a word. It looked as if she was deliberately trying to present the picture of a detached observer. She happened to be wearing a white linen dress, whose severity was designed to emphasize her slim curves; or perhaps it was that she had felt white to be more "suitable" for a nursing course than any other colour. But her small, apricot-tinted face with its enormous lazy dark eyes, the soft slender body in its white, were the cruellest comment on the only other white figure in the room, fat and perspiring Sister Doll, half a dozen paces away. It appeared that Sister Doll felt it, or at least her inattention; for during those pauses while she was waiting for her class to take down sentences such as "The greatest care must be taken to keep the patient's bed neat and tidy," she turned hot little eyes, full of rather flustered reproach, on Stella, who was regarding her with indolent enquiry. Catching Martha's eye, Stella made a small movement of her own eyes towards the door. Martha frowned back. Stella gave a petulant shrug.

The moment Sister Doll dismissed her class, Stella took Martha's arm and hurried her out. Her first words were, "Let's go and see Alice."

"Really," exclaimed Martha, her boredom and dissatisfaction exploding obliquely, "what a waste of time—all this nonsense about making beds."

"It's only just up the road." Stella tugged at her arm.

"And we've paid all that money for the course."

"Oh, well . . . Anyway, I expect there won't be a war anyway."

"Why not?" Martha stopped and looked at Stella, really wanting to know.

"Andrew says they won't start training them. Well, then, if there was going to be a war, they would train people like Douglas and Andrew, wouldn't they? He said so this morning. I thought they'd start playing soldiers any minute now." Stella dismissed the thing, and said, "Oh, come on, Matty, it's only just up the road."

"But she doesn't know we're coming. She doesn't want to see us."

"Nonsense," said Stella with energy.

The matter thus settled, they walked towards Alice's flat.

Stella knocked at the door in a manner that suggested discreet determination. Her eyes were alive with interest. There was a long silence.

"She's out," said Martha hopefully. She knew that Alice, like herself, preferred to take the more intimate crises of life in private.

"Nonsense," Stella said, and knocked again. A long silence. Stella changed the tempo of her knocking to a peremptory summons. "She's only trying to get rid of us," she remarked with her jolly laugh.

Alice opened the door sharply on that laugh. She was annoyed.

"It's us," Stella said, and walked blandly inside.

Alice was in a pale-pink taffeta dressing gown which had been bought for the fresh young woman she had been as a bride; now she was rather yellow and very thin, and her freckles seemed to have sprung up everywhere over the pale sallow skin. Her black hair hung dispiritedly on her shoulders.

"Well?" demanded Stella at once.

Alice regarded her from a distance, and remarked that she wasn't feeling at all well.

Stella, a little figure bristling with frustrated purpose, said, "Oh, stop it, Alice." Then she frowned, decided to change tactics, and said diplomatically, "Shall I make you a nice cup of tea?"

"Oh, do make it, dear. I'm really exhausted." And Alice subsided backwards into a chair, and lay there extinguished.

The moment Stella had gone to the kitchen, Alice opened her eyes and looked at Martha as if to ask, "Am I safe from you?"

Martha was equally limp in another chair. She enquired childishly, "Is it true you only have to jump off a table?" She meant to sound competent, but in fact her face expressed nothing but distaste. "Did you know I went to Dr. Stern and he said I wasn't?" she went on.

"Did you, dear?" This was discretion itself; it was the trained nurse remembering her loyalties.

But it was not what Martha wanted. "He said I was quite all right."

A short silence. Then Alice remarked vaguely, "You know, they don't know everything."

Alarm flooded Martha; she shook it off. "But he's supposed to be very good at—this sort of thing."

To this Alice could only reply that he was, very. Then Stella came in with a tray. She set it down, and proceeded to cross-examine Alice while she poured the tea. Alice replied vaguely with that good humour which is rooted in utter indifference. Vague as a cloud, lazy as water, she lay with half-shut eyes and let fall stray remarks which had the effect of stinging Stella into a frenzy of exasperation. At the end of ten minutes' hard work Stella had succeeded in eliciting the positive information that Alice believed herself to be three months gone.

"Well, really!" Horror at this incompetence shook Stella. "But three months!"

Clinical details followed, which Alice confirmed as if they could not possibly have any reference to herself. "Well, dear, I really don't know," she kept saying helplessly.

"But you *must* know," exclaimed the exasperated Stella. "One either has a period or one has not."

"Oh, well—I never take any notice of mine, anyway."

This caused Martha to remark with pride that she never did, either. For she and Alice belonged to the other family of women from Stella, who proceeded to detail, with gloomy satisfaction how much she suffered during these times. Alice and Martha listened with tolerant disapproval.

Checked on this front, Stella brooded for a while on how to approach a more intimate one. Martha had more than once remarked with distaste to Douglas that if Stella were given a chance she would positively wallow in the details of the marriage bed. This chance was not given her. Women of the tradition to which Alice and Martha belonged are prepared to discuss menstruation or pregnancy in the frankest of detail, but it is taboo to discuss sex, notwithstanding the show of frankness the subject is surrounded with. It follows that they get their information about how other women react sexually from their men, a system which has its disadvantages. More than once had Stella been annoyed by reticences on the part of Martha and Alice which seemed to her the most appalling prudery; an insult, in fact, to their friendship. But she did not persist now; she returned to ask direct what steps Alice proposed to take. Alice said with a lazy laugh that she had done everything. Cross-examination produced the information that she had drunk gin and taken a hot bath. Even more shocked, Stella delivered a short and efficient lecture, which interested Martha extremely, but to which Alice listened indifferently, occasionally suppressing a genuine yawn. Stella then supplied the names of three wise women, two Coloured and one white, who would do the job for a moderate fee. To which Alice replied, with her first real emotion that day, that she had seen enough of girls ruined for life by these women ever to go near them herself.

"Well, then, how about Dr. Stern?"

Alice said angrily, with the curtness of a schoolmistress, that if Stella wasn't careful she'd find herself in trouble, saying such things about honest doctors! Stella rose, red and angry, her tongue quivering with expert retaliations. Alice gave her a weary and apologetic smile, and said, "Oh, sit down, Stella, I haven't the energy for a row."

Stella sat. After a while she asked, in a deceptively sweet voice, on a note of modest interest, if perhaps Alice intended to have this baby after all?

Alice said good-naturedly, "We all have to have them sometime, dear, don't we?" Here she laughed again, and it was with reckless pleasure; at the same time her look at Stella was challenging, triumphant, very amused.

Stella, after a shocked and accusing stare, turned away, with an effect of indifference, and elaborately changed the subject.

Leaving the flat, Stella remarked coldly that it was utterly irresponsible of Alice to have a baby when they were so hard up; then that it was criminal to have a baby when war was starting; finally, after a long pause, that as for herself she was too delicate to have a baby, she would probably die in childbirth. There was a speculative look on her face as she said this, which caused Martha to remark, amused, that it would be awfully inconsistent of Stella to have a baby herself, after what she had said. Stella reacted with an affronted "It would be quite unfair to Andrew; I'd never do a thing like that."

The two young women parted almost at once, without regret.

Martha walked slowly home, thinking about Alice. Her emotions were violent and mixed. She felt towards the pregnant woman, the abstraction, a strong repulsion which caused various images, all unpleasant, to rise into her mind one after another. From her childhood came a memory of lowered voices, distasteful intimacies, hidden sicknesses. It was above all frightening that all this furtive secrecy, which she and all her friends so firmly repudiated, was waiting there, strong as ever, all around her, as she knew: Alice, because she was pregnant, was delivered back into the hands of the old people—so Martha felt it. She felt caged, for Alice. She could feel the bonds around herself. She consciously shook them off and exulted in the thought that she was free. Free! And the half-shaded flat she had left, with the pale, sallow, sick-looking woman in pink taffeta, seemed like a suffocating prison. But at the same time a deeper emotion was turning towards Alice, with an unconscious curiosity, warm, tender, protective. It was an emotion not far from envy. In six months, Alice would have a baby. Why, it is no time at all, she thought. But no sooner had she put it into words than she reacted back again with a shuddering impulse towards escape. She could see the scene: Alice, loose and misshapen, with an ugly wet-mouthed infant, feeding-bottles, napkins, smells.

Martha reached her flat, removed her clothes, and anxiously examined every inch of her body. Unmarked, whole, perfect—smooth solid flesh; there was not a stain on it. Here Martha gave an uncomfortable look at her breasts, and acknowledged they were heavier than they had been. There was a bruised, reddish look about them— here came a flood of panic, and then she subsided into perfect trust in Dr. Stern. She felt particularly supported by the knowledge that ever since her second visit she and Douglas had followed the prescribed rituals with determined precision. She was free. She continued to revel in her freedom all that afternoon, while underneath she thought persistently of Alice, and wondered why she was now so contented to have a baby, when, as short a time ago as a month, she had spoken of having one with vigorous rejection.

When Douglas returned from the office, she described the day's doings, passing over the nursing lecture as an utter waste of time, and laughing at Stella's frustrated homilies and Alice's vague determination. But Douglas, who had moments, which were becoming increasingly frequent, of remembering that he was a Government official, remarked rather officiously that Stella would get herself into trouble one of these days. It was illegal to procure abortions: that was the cold phrase he used. But at this Martha flew into an angry tirade against governments who presumed to tell women what they should do with their own bodies; it was the final insult to personal liberty. Douglas listened, frowning, and said unanswerably that the law was the law. Martha therefore retreated into herself, which meant that she became very gay, hard, and indifferent. She listened to his rather heavy insistence about what she intended to do in place of the nursing course, and understood that he was above all concerned that she should not be in the war—should not go in pursuit of the adventure he himself was quivering to find; he was even more reluctant because of his own daydreams as to certain aspects of that adventure.

He went so far, carried away by the official in him, as to make various sound remarks about the unsuitability of danger for women. She thought he must be joking; nothing is more astonishing to young women than the ease with which men, even intelligent and liberal-minded men, lapse back into that anonymous voice of authority whenever their own personal authority is threatened, saying things of a banality and a pomposity infinitely removed from their own level of thinking.

Martha was first incredulous, then frightened, then she began to despise him. She became even more gay and brilliant; he became fascinated; she despised him the more for being fascinated; he began to resent the offhandedness of her manner and retreated again into the official. She mocked at him recklessly, they quarrelled. As a result of this hatred, they spent a hectic evening, ending up at four in the morning at the fair, where Martha, sick and giddy, revolved on the great wheel as if her whole future depended on her power to stick it out. High over the darkened town—where a few widely scattered windows showed the points where revellers were at last going to bed —plunging sickeningly to earth and up again, Martha clung on, until the wheel was stopped, the music stopped churning, and there was literally nowhere to go but bed. From the bedroom window they could see the lights greying along the street. The native servants were coming in from the location in time to be at work.

She woke with a start; the bed next to her was empty. There were noises next door. Then she saw it was nearly eleven. While she still stood in her nightdress, fumbling at her dressing gown, the door began very gently to open inwards. Its cautious movement was arrested; then the person the other side dropped something; the door crashed back against the wall, and Mrs. Quest stumbled into the room, reaching out for parcels which scattered everywhere.

"Oh, so you're up," Mrs. Quest said sharply. "I didn't mean to wake you, I was coming in quietly." Then, retrieving a last package to make a neat pile on the bed, she added archly, "What a dashing life you lead, lying in bed till eleven."

This roguishness aroused the usual strong distaste in Martha; she had covered herself entirely with her dressing gown, buttoning it up tight from throat to hem.

"I thought you must be ill, I peeped in and saw you. Shall I go for the doctor, don't get up, stay in bed and I'll nurse you—for today, at least."

"I'm perfectly well," said Martha ungraciously. "Let's go and have some tea." Firmly, she led the way from the bedroom, but Mrs. Quest did not at once follow her.

Martha sat on the divan listening. Her mother was following the ritual that she had already gone through here, in this room. The flowers had been removed from their vases and rearranged, the chairs set differently, books put into place. Mrs. Quest had reassured herself by touching and arranging everything in the living room, and was now doing the same in the bedroom. Martha had time to make the tea and bring in the tray before her mother reappeared.

"I've just made your bed, your nightdress is torn, did you know? I've brought it to mend while I'm here, your bathroom isn't done, it's wet," Mrs. Quest remarked flurriedly. She had Martha's nightdress clutched in one hand. She glanced at it, blushed, and remarked coquettishly, "How you can wear these transparent bits of fluff I don't know."

Martha poured the tea in silence. She was exaggeratedly irritated. The violence of this emotion was what kept her silent; for she was quite able to assure herself that nothing could be more natural, and even harmless and pathetic, than this unfortunate woman's need to lead every other life but her own. This is what her intelligence told her; her conscience remarked that she was making a fuss about nothing; but in fact she seethed with irritation. The face she presented to her mother was one of numbed hostility. This, as usual, affected Mrs. Quest like an accusation.

The next phase of this sad cycle followed: Mrs. Quest said that it was unfair to Douglas not to sleep enough: she would get ill and then he would have to pay the bills. Martha's face remaining implacable, she went on, in tones of hurried disapproval: "If you'll give me a needle and thread, I'll mend your nightdress."

Martha got up, found needle and thread, and handed them to Mrs. Quest without a word. The sight of that nightdress, still warm from her own body, clutched with nervous possession in her mother's hands was quite unendurable. She was determined to endure it. After all, she thought, if it gives her pleasure . . . And then: It's not her fault she was brought up in *that* society. This thought gave her comparative detachment. She sat down and looked at the worn, gnarled hands at work on her nightdress. They filled her with pity for her mother. Besides, she could remember how she had loved her mother's hands as a child; she could see the white and beautiful hands of a woman who no longer existed.

Mrs. Quest was talking of matters on the farm, about the house in town they were shortly to buy, about her husband's health.

Martha scarcely listened. She was engaged in examining and repairing those intellectual's bastions of defence behind which she sheltered, that building whose shape had first been sketched so far back in her childhood she could no longer remember how it then looked. With every year it had become more complicated, more ramified; it was as if she, Martha, were a variety of soft, shell-less creature whose survival lay in the strength of those walls. Reaching out in all directions from behind it, she clutched at the bricks of arguments, the stones of words, discarding any that might not fit into the building.

She was looking at Mrs. Quest in a deep abstract speculation, as if neither she nor her mother had any validity as persons, but were mere pawns in the hands of an old fatality. She could see a sequence of events, unalterable, behind her, and stretching unalterably into the future. She saw her mother, a prim-faced Edwardian schoolgirl, confronting, in this case, the Victorian father, the patriarchal father, with rebellion. She saw herself sitting where her mother now sat, a woman horribly metamorphosed, entirely dependent on her children for any interest in life, resented by them, and resenting them; opposite her, a young woman of whom she could distinguish nothing clearly but a set, obstinate face; and beside these women, a series of shadowy dependent men, broken-willed and sick with compelled diseases. This the nightmare, this the nightmare of a class and generation: repetition. And although Martha had read nothing of the great interpreters of the nightmare, she had been soaked in the minor literature of the last thirty years, which had dealt with very little else: a series of doomed individuals, carrying their doom *inside* them, like the seeds of fatal disease. Nothing could alter the pattern.

But inside the stern web of fatality did flicker small hopeful flames. One thought was that after all it had not always been that these great life-and-death struggles were fought out inside the family; presumably things might change again. Another was that she had decided not to have a baby; and it was in her power to cut the cycle.

Which brought her back into the conversation with a question on her tongue.

Mrs. Quest was talking about the coming war. She had no doubt at all as to the shape it would assume. It was Britain's task to fight Hitler and Stalin combined. Martha suggested this might be rather a heavy task. Mrs. Quest said sharply that Martha had no patriotism, and never had had. Even without those lazy and useless Americans who never came into a war until they could make good pickings out of it, Britain would ultimately muddle through to victory, as she always did.

Martha was able to refrain from being *logical* only by her more personal preoccupations. She plunged straight in with an enquiry as to whether her mother had ever had an abortion. She hastened to add that she wanted to know because of a friend of hers.

Mrs. Quest, checked, took some moments to adjust to this level. She said vaguely, "It's illegal . . ." Having made this offering to the law, she considered the question on its merits and said, in a lowered voice, a look of distaste on her face, "Why—are you like that?"

Martha suppressed the hostility she felt at the evasion, and said, "No."

"Well, you look like it," said Mrs. Quest bluntly, with triumph.

"Well, I'm not." Martha added the appeal, "I do wish you'd tell me . . ." She had no idea what she really wanted to know!

Mrs. Quest looked at her, her vigorous face wearing the dubious, rather puzzled expression which meant she was trying to remember her own past.

Martha was telling herself that this appeal was doomed to produce all kinds of misunderstanding and discomfort. They always did. And what *did* she want her mother to say? She looked at her in silence, and wished that some miracle would occur and her mother would produce a few simple, straightforward remarks, a few *words*—not emotional, nothing deviating from the cool humorous understatement that would save them both from embarrassment. Martha needed the right words.

She reflected that Mrs. Quest had not wanted her. How, then, had she come to accept her? Was that what she wanted to know? But looking at her now, she could only think that Mrs. Quest had spent a free, energetic youth, had "lived her own life"—she had used the phrase herself long before it was proper for middle-class daughters to do so—and had, accordingly, quarrelled with her father. She had not married until very late.

For many years now, she had been this immensely efficient down-to-earth matron; but somewhere concealed in her was the mother who had borne Martha. From her white and feminine body she, Martha, had emerged—that was certainly a fact! She could remember seeing her mother naked; beautiful she had been, a beautiful, strong white body, with full hips, small high breasts—the Greek idea of beauty. And to that tender white body had belonged the strong soft white hands Martha remembered. Those hands had tended her, the baby. Well, then, why could her mother not resurrect that woman in her and speak the few simple, appropriate words?

But now she was turning Martha's flimsy nightgown between her thickened, clumsy hands, as if determined not to say she disapproved of it; and frowned. She looked uncomfortable. Martha quite desperately held on to that other image to set against this one. She could see that earlier woman distinctly. More, she could feel wafts of tenderness coming from her.

Then, suddenly, into this pure and simple emotion came something new: she felt pity like a clutching hand. She was remembering something else. She was lying in the dark in that house on the farm, listening to a piano being played several rooms away. She got up, and crept through the dark rooms to a doorway. She saw Mrs. Quest seated at the keyboard, a heavy knot of hair weighting her head and glistening gold where the light touched it from two candle flames which floated steadily above the long white transparent candles. Tears were running down her face while she set her lips and smiled. The romantic phrases of a Chopin nocturne rippled out into the African night, steadily accompanied by the crickets and the blood-thudding of the tomtoms from the compound. Martha smiled wryly: she could remember the gulfs of pity that sight had thrown her into.

Mrs. Quest looked up over the nightdress and enquired jealously, "What are you laughing at."

"Mother," she said desperately, "you didn't want to have me. Well, then . . ."

Mrs. Quest laughed, and said Martha had come as a surprise to her.

Martha waited, then prodded. "What did you *feel?*"

A slight look of caution came onto her mother's honest square face. "Oh, well . . ." But almost at once she launched into the gay and humorous account, which Martha had so often heard, of the difficulties of getting the proper clothes and so on; which almost at once merged with the difficulties of the birth itself—a painful business, this, as she had so often been told.

"But what did you *feel* about it all? I mean, it couldn't have been as easy as all that," said Martha.

"Oh, it wasn't easy—I was just telling you." Mrs. Quest began to repeat how awkward a baby Martha had been. "But it wasn't really your fault. First I didn't have enough milk, though I didn't know it; and then I gave you a mixture, and didn't know until the doctor told me that it was only half the right strength. So in one way and another I half starved you for the first nine months of your life." Mrs. Quest laughed ruefully, and said, "No wonder you never stopped crying day or night."

A familiar resentment filled Martha, and she at once pressed on. "But, Mother, when you first knew you were going to have a baby—"

Mrs. Quest interrupted. "And then I had your brother, he was such a good baby, not like you."

And now Martha abdicated, as she had so often done before; for it had always, for some reason, seemed right and inevitable that Mrs. Quest should prefer the delicate boy child to herself. Martha listened to the familiar story to the end, while she suppressed a violent and exasperated desire to take her mother by her shoulders and shake her until she produced, in a few sensible and consoling sentences, that truth which it was so essential Martha should have. But Mrs. Quest had forgotten how she had felt. She was no longer interested. And why should she be, this elderly woman with all the business of being a woman behind her?

In a short while she returned to the war, dismissed Chamberlain with a few just sentences, and recommended Mr. Churchill for his job. The Quests belonged to that section of the middle class who would be happy and contented to be conservatives if only the conservatives could be more efficient. As it was, they never ceased complaining about the inefficiency and corruption of the party they would unfailingly vote for if they lived in England.

Towards lunchtime she left, with the advice that Martha should go and see the doctor and get a good tonic. She looked dreadful—it wasn't fair to Douglas.

The result of that visit from her mother was that Martha decided again she must not sink into being a mere housewife. She should at once learn a profession, or at least take some kind of job. But this decision was not as firm as it might seem from the energy she used in speaking about it to Douglas.

She was gripped by a lethargy so profound that in fact she spent most of her time limp on that divan, thinking about nothing. She felt heavy and uncomfortable and sick. And she was clinging to Douglas with the dependence of a child. She was miserable when he left in the morning; she was waiting anxiously for his return hours before he might be expected. Pride, however, forbade her to show it, or to ask him to come home for lunch. At night, the loud sad music from the fair was becoming an obsession. She found herself waking from sleep and crying, but what she was weeping for she had no idea at all. She drew the curtains so that she might not see the great wheel; and then lay watching the circling of light through their thin stuff. She accused herself of every kind of weak-mindedness and stupidity; nevertheless, the persistent monotony of that flickering cycle seemed a revelation of an appalling and intimate truth; it was like being hypnotized.

During the daytime she sat with a book, trying to read, and realized that she was not seeing one word of it. It was, she realized, as if she were listening for something; some kind of anxiety rang through every limb.

One morning she was very sick, and all at once the suspicion she had been ignoring for so long became a certainty—and from one moment to the next. When Douglas came home that night she said sullenly, as if it was his fault, that she must be pregnant; and insisted when he said that Dr. Stern could not be wrong. At last he suggested she should go and talk to Stella, whose virtuosity in these matters was obvious. She said she would; but when it came to the point, she shrank from the idea and instead went to Alice.

It was a hot, dusty morning. A warm wind swept flocks of yellowing leaves along the streets. The jacarandas were holding up jaded yellow arms. This drying, yellowing, fading month, this time when the year tensed and tightened towards the coming rains, always gave her a feeling of perverted autumn, and now filled her with an exquisite cold apprehension. The sky, above the haze of dust, was a glitter of hot blue light.

Alice was in her pink taffeta dressing gown in her large chair. She greeted Martha with cheerful indifference, and bade her sit down. On the table beside her was a pile of books, called variously *Mothercraft, Baby Handling*, and *Your Months of Preparation.*

Martha glanced towards them, and Alice said, "The nonsense they talk, dear, you wouldn't believe." She pushed them gently away. Then she got up, and stood before Martha, with her two hands held tenderly over her stomach. "I'm as flat as a board still," she remarked with pride. She looked downwards with a preoccupied blue stare; she seemed to be listening. "According to the books, it doesn't quicken until—but now I've worked out my dates, and actually it quickens much earlier. At first I thought it must be wind," remarked Alice, faintly screwing up her face with the effort of listening.

"I think I'm pregnant, too," remarked Martha nervously.

"Are you, dear?" Alice sat down, keeping her hands in a protective curve, and said, "Oh, well, when you get used to it, it's quite interesting, really."

"Oh, I'm not going to *have* it," said Martha with energy.

Alice did not reply. Martha saw that she had gone completely into her private world of sensation, and that anything which happened outside was quite irrelevant. She recognized the feeling: what else had she been fighting against during the last few weeks?

After a pause Alice continued the conversation she was having with herself by remarking, "Oh, well, to hell with everything. Who cares, anyway?" She gave her dry, nervous laugh and reached for a cigarette.

"Well, you look very pleased with yourself," said Martha, half laughing.

Alice frowned as these words reached her, and said, "Help yourself to cigarettes, dear."

The morning drifted past. Alice, dim and safe in her private world, smoked constantly, stubbing out the cigarettes as she lit them, and from time to time dropped remarks such as "It ought to be November, I think." When Martha roused herself to go, Alice appeared to be reminding herself that she had not been as sympathetic as she could have been. She held the door half open, Martha already being outside it, and proceeded to offer various bits of advice in an apologetic voice, the most insistent being that she should at once go and see Stella.

Martha went home, reached for the telephone, but was unable to dial Stella's number. She shrank away from Stella with the most extraordinary dislike of her. She was thinking of Alice; and in spite of her own deep persistent misery, her knowledge that the web was tight around her, she knew, too, that she was most irrationally elated.

Anyone would think that you were pleased, she said angrily to herself. With an efficiency which Stella must have applauded, she put on her dressing gown, locked the door, and took the telephone off the hook. She then drank, with calm determination, glass after glass of neat gin, until a full bottle was gone. Then she lay down and slept. When she woke it was four in the afternoon, and she felt nothing but a weakness in her knees. She filled the bath with water so hot that she could not put her hand into it, and, setting her teeth, got in. The pain was so intense that she nearly fainted. She was going through with this, however; and she sat in the bath until the water was tepid. When she reeled out, she was boiled scarlet, and could not touch her skin. Having rubbed cream all over herself, she lay on her bed, shrinking from the touch of the sheet, and cried a little from sheer pain. She slept again. Douglas was rattling at the locked door when she woke, and she staggered to let him in.

Faced with a touzled, bedraggled, red-faced female, reeking of gin, Douglas was naturally upset; but he was informed in a cold and efficient voice that this was necessary. He sat wincing while Martha climbed repeatedly onto the table and jumped off, crashing down on her heels with the full force of her weight. At the end of half an hour he could no longer stand it, and forcibly put her to bed. In a small triumphant voice Martha informed him that if *that* didn't shift it nothing would.

In the morning she woke, feeling as if her limbs had been pulverized from within and as if her skin were a separate, agonized coating to her body, but otherwise whole. Douglas was astounded to hear her say, in a voice of unmistakable satisfaction, that she must be as strong and as healthy as a horse. He was unable to bear it: this female with set will, tight mouth, and cold and rejecting eyes was entirely horrifying to him.

"Well," demanded Martha practically, "do we or do we not want to have this baby?"

Douglas evaded this by saying that she should go forthwith to see Dr. Stern, and escaped to the office, trying to ignore the inescapable fact that Martha was contemptuous of him because of his male weakness.

Late that afternoon Martha entered Dr. Stern's consulting room, in a mood of such desperate panic that he recognized it at once and promptly offered her a drink, which he took from a cupboard. Martha watched him anxiously, and saw him look her up and down with that minute, expert inspection which she had seen before. On whose face? Mrs. Talbot's, of course!

Dr. Stern, kindness itself, then examined Martha. She told him, laughing, of the measures she had taken, to which he replied gravely, looking at her scarlet skin, that she shouldn't overdo these things. But never, not for one second, did he make the mistake of speaking in the anonymous voice of male authority, which she would have so passionately resented.

Finally he informed her that she was over four months pregnant; which shocked her into silence. Such was his bland assurance, such was the power of this man, the doctor in the white coat behind the big desk, that the words stammering on her tongue could not get themselves said. But he saw her reproachful look and said that doctors were not infallible; he added almost at once that a fine, healthy girl like herself should be delighted to have a baby. Martha was silent with misery. She said feebly after a pause that there was no point in having a baby when the war was coming. At which he smiled slightly and said that the birth rate, for reasons best known to itself, always rose in wartime. She felt caught up in an immense impersonal tide which paid no attention to her, Martha. She looked at this young man who was after all not so much older than herself; she looked at the grave responsible face, and hated him bitterly from the bottom of her heart.

She asked him bluntly if he would do an abortion.

He replied immediately that he could not.

There was a long and difficult silence. Dr. Stern regarded her steadily from expert eyes, and reached out for a small statuette which stood on his desk. It was in bronze, of a mermaidlike figure diving off a rock. He fingered it lightly and said, "Do you realize that your baby is as big as this already?" It was about five inches high.

The shock numbed her tongue. She had imagined this creature as "it," perhaps as a formless blob of jellylike substance, or, alternatively, as already born, a boneless infant in a shawl, but certainly not as a living being five inches long coiled in her flesh.

"Eyes, ears, arms, legs—all there." He fingered the statuette a little longer; then he dropped his hand and was silent.

Martha was so bitter that she could not yet move or speak a word. All she was for him, and probably for Douglas too, she thought, was a "healthy young woman."

Then he said with a tired humorous smile that if she knew the proportion of his women patients who came, as she did, when they found they were pregnant, not wanting a baby, only to be delighted when they had got used to it, she would be surprised.

Martha did not reply. She rose to leave. He got up, too, and said, with a real human kindness that she was able to appreciate only later, that she should think twice before rushing off to see one of the wise women: her baby was too big to play tricks with now. If she absolutely insisted on an abortion, she should go to Johannesburg, where, as everyone knew, there was a hospital which was a positive factory for this sort of thing. The word "factory" made her wince; and she saw at once, with a satirical appreciation of his skill in handling her, that it was deliberately chosen.

He shook hands with her, invited her to drop in and talk it all over if she felt like it at any time, and went back to his desk.

Martha returned to her flat in a trance of despair. Not the least of her bitterness was due to her knowledge that in some part of herself she was already weakening towards this baby. She could not forget that diving creature, bent in moulded bronze, about five inches long. In her bedroom, she found herself standing as she had seen Alice stand, hands curiously touching her stomach. It occurred to her that this child had quickened already; she understood that this long process had been one of determined self-deception—almost as if she had wanted this damned baby all the time, she thought quickly, and immediately pushing the idea from her mind. But how could she have mistaken those irregular but definite movements for anything else?

When Douglas came home she informed him that nothing would induce her to have this child, with which he at once agreed. She found herself slightly annoyed by this. It was agreed that she should go at once to Johannesburg. Douglas knew of an astounding number of women who had made the trip and returned none the worse for it.

Martha, left alone next day to make preparations for the trip, did nothing at all. Then her mother flew in. Against all her intentions, Martha blurted out that she was going to have a baby; and was immediately folded in Mrs. Quest's arms. Mrs. Quest was delighted; her face beamed pleasure; she said it was lovely, it was the best thing that could possibly happen, it would settle Martha down and give her no time for all her funny ideas. (Here she gave a small defiant, triumphant laugh.) Unfortunately, as she had to get back to the farm, she could not stay with her daughter, much as she wanted to. She embraced Martha again, and said in a warm, thrilled voice that it was the greatest experience in a woman's life. With this she left, wet-eyed and with a tremulous smile.

Martha was confounded; she sat thinking that her mother must be out of her mind; above all she was thinking angrily of the triumph she had shown. She roused herself again to pack and make telephone calls; but they again faded out in indecision. The child, five inches long, with eyes, nose, mouth, hands and feet, seemed very active. Martha sat feeling the imprisoned thing moving in her flesh, and was made more miserable by the knowledge that it had been moving for at least a week without her noticing it than by anything else. For what was the use of thinking, of planning, if emotions one did not recognize at all worked their own way against you? She was filled with a strong and seething rage against her mother, her husband, Dr. Stern, who had all joined the conspiracy against her. She addressed angry speeches of protest to them, fiery and eloquent speeches; but alas, there was no one there but herself.

Sometime later Stella came in, stepping blithely around the door, hips swaying lightly, eyes bright with interest. She had heard the news; the boys were already drinking Douglas's health in the clubs.

"Everyone's quite convinced that you *had* to get married," said Stella with a delighted chuckle.

An astonishing thought occurred to Martha for the first time. "Do you know," she cried out, half laughing, "if I'm as pregnant as Dr. Stern says I am, then I must have been when I got married!" At this she flung back and roared with laughter. Stella joined her briefly; then she regarded Martha impatiently, waiting for the rather helpless wail of laughter to end.

"Well," demanded Stella, "and what are we going to do about it?"

It was at this point that Martha, in the stubborn, calm voice of complete conviction, found herself explaining to Stella how foolish an abortion would be at this stage. Stella grew increasingly persuasive, and Martha obstinate. The arguments she now found for having this baby were as strong and unanswerable as those she had been using, only ten minutes ago, against it. She found herself intensely excited at the idea of having a baby.

"Well, I don't know," remarked Stella disgustedly at last. "You and Alice are mad. Both quite, quite mad."

She rose, and stood poised before Martha to deliver the final blow; but Martha intercepted it by suggesting teasingly that Stella herself ought to start a baby, as otherwise she'd be left out of it.

At this Stella allowed a brief gleam of a smile; but at once she substituted a disapproving frown. "I'm not going to have kids now, it wouldn't be fair to Andrew. But if *you* want to shut yourself into a nursery at your age, then it's your own affair." She gave the triumphant and amused Martha a long, withering look, dropped a goodbye, pulled on her gloves gracefully, and went out.

She sustained the sweep of her exit until she reached the street. She had meant to go shopping, but instead she went to Douglas's office. She told the typist to announce her, but was unable to wait, and followed the girl in, saying urgently, "Douggie—I must see you."

"Come in, Stell." He nodded to the typist, who went out again.

Stella sat down. "I've just seen Matty."

"Yes, it's a bit of a mess," he said at once. But he looked self-conscious, even proud.

Seeing it, Stella said impatiently, "She's much too young. She doesn't realize."

"Oh, I don't know—she's been putting the fear of God into me. She'll be ill. I wish you'd speak to her, Stell."

"But I have been speaking to her. She won't listen."

"After all, there's no danger in a proper operation in Johannesburg, but messing about with gin and all that nonsense . . ."

Stella shrugged this away, and said, "She's as stubborn as a mule. She's just a baby herself. She's pleased now, of course, but that's natural."

Douglas looked up sharply, and went red. His lips trembled. He stood up, then sat down again. Now he was white.

"What's the matter with you?" she asked, smiling but irritated.

"I'll talk to her again," he muttered. He understood. Now all he wanted was for her to go. For the first time he had imagined the baby being born. He was imagining himself a father. Pride was invading him. It had already swallowed up his small pang of hurt that Martha had made up her mind without him, his aggrieved annoyance at her inconsistency. He felt nothing but swelling exaltation.

Stella had risen. "You're both crazy," she said.

"There, Stella . . ." he said, hesitated, then kissed her.

"Well!" she exclaimed, laughing.

"Look, Stell, I'm awfully busy."

She nodded, and said, "Come and have a drink, both of you, this evening. We'll celebrate. Though I think you're both mad." With another unconsciously envious look at his flushed, proud face, she went out.

The moment she had gone he rang Martha. Her voice came gay over the air as she announced her conviction that having a baby was the most sensible thing they could both do.

"Why, Matty!" he shouted. Then he let out a yell of pure elation. He heard her laugh.

"Come home to lunch?" she asked. Then she added scrupulously, "Not if you're busy."

"Well, actually, I've got an awful lot of work."

"Oh, very well, we'll celebrate this evening."

"Actually, Stella asked us over."

"Oh, but Stella . . ." She stopped.

"We can decide that later." They each held the receiver for a while, waiting for the other to say something. Then he said, very stern and efficient, "Matty, you're quite sure?"

She giggled at his tone, and said derisively, "I've been perfectly sure for a whole hour."

"See you later, then." He put down the receiver—and nearly lifted it to ring her again. Something more, surely, must be said or done. He was seething with the need to release his elation, his pride. It was impossible to sit quietly working in the office. He walked across to the door of his chief's office, and stood outside it. No—he would tell him later. He left a message that he would be back in half an hour, and went into the street. He was walking towards the flat, he realized. His steps slowed, then he stopped. On a street corner he stood staring at nothing, breathing heavily, smiling. There was a florist's shop opposite. He was drawn to the window. He was looking at some deep-red carnations. He would send Matty some flowers— yes, that was it. But as he was about to go into the shop, he saw again her face as he had last seen it that morning—set, angry, stiff-lipped. He did not enter the shop. A big clock at the end of the street said it was after twelve. He hesitated, turned, and set off towards the flat after all. He would surprise her for lunch. Then again he stopped, standing irresolute on the pavement. Nearly, he went back to the office. Almost, he directed himself to Martha. He gave another long look at the mass of deep-crimson carnations behind the glass. Then he thought, I could do with a drink. He walked off to the Club, where he usually had a drink before lunch.

The first person he saw was Perry at the bar, eating potato chips with a glass of beer. They nodded, and Perry pushed the plate of chips towards him.

Douglas shook his head. "My ulcer's been playing me up again."

"The more I ill-treat mine, the more it likes it." Perry directed very bright hard blue eyes at him, and asked, "What are you looking so pleased about?"

"We're having a kid," said Douglas proudly. He knew tears stood in his eyes: it was the climax of his exultation.

"You're joking," said Perry, polite but satiric.

Douglas laughed, then whooped, so that people turned around to stare and smile sympathetically. "It's a fact." He called to the barman, "Drinks on me. Drinks all round." In a moment the two were surrounded and Douglas was being thumped over the shoulders and back. "Stop it, silly sods," he said, grinning, "stop it."

Then Perry, with a wooden face, deliberately reached into his pocket and fetched out papers. "You'll want to fix this up right away," he said, pushing the papers towards Douglas.

"Don't work so damned hard," said Douglas, laughing, pushing the papers back. Insurance policies—Perry worked as manager of a big insurance company.

"The finest policy south of the Sahara," said Perry. He pulled out a fountain pen and handed it to Douglas. "Sign on the dotted line."

Douglas pushed them back at him again.

But as they drank and talked, Douglas glanced over the papers, and as the two men left the bar he said, "I wouldn't mind having another look at that policy sometime."

"I'll send it over to you," said Perry.

"You think it's the ticket, hey?"

"It's the one I'd have if I was starting a kid."

Perry nodded and was walking away. Douglas thought, It'll be a surprise for Matty. He wanted to take something back to her. He called after Perry, and the two went together to the insurance offices. Douglas signed the documents then and there. He rang up his office to say that he would not be back this afternoon, and went home to Martha. He ran the last few yards of the way, and pounded up the stairs holding the packet of papers in his hand, grinning like a boy with pleasure at the thought of her face when she saw the policy.

part two

You must remember that having a baby is a perfectly natural process.
FROM A HANDBOOK ON HOW TO HAVE A BABY

1

Mrs. Quest joyfully ran into the house and announced they were to have a grandchild.

Mr. Quest lowered his newspaper and exclaimed, "What! Oh Lord!"

"Oh, my dear," she said impatiently, "it's the best thing that could happen, it's so nice for her. It'll settle her down, I'm so happy."

He listened for some time to his wife's cheerful planning of the child's future; it was not until the young man was due for university that he remarked uncomfortably, "It's all very well . . ."

But she swept on, illuminated by decision. The boy—he was to be named Jeffrey, after Mrs. Quest's father—was to be saved by a proper education from Martha's unconformities; he would be, in fact, the child Mrs. Quest had always longed for, the person her own two children had obstinately refused to become. Her eyes were wistful, her face soft. Mr. Quest regarded it with increasing discomfort, for it could not but bear witness to what he hadn't been able to do for her.

"I think on the whole Sandhurst would be better," she concluded at last. "We'll see that his name is put down in good time. I'll write tomorrow. My father always wanted to go to Sandhurst, instead of Uncle Tony—it was the great disappointment of his life."

Mr. Quest removed his gaze from the Dumfries Hills, whose blue coils were wreathed in smoke—a veld fire had been raging there unchecked for some weeks—and turned his eyes incredulously on his wife. Then he flung down his newspaper, and let out a short laugh. "Damn it all!" he protested.

Mrs. Quest was gazing at the great blue buttresses of the mountain range. She heard his voice; her smile became a little tremulous. She swiftly glanced at him, and dropped her eyes.

"One may presume the child's parents will have something to say in the matter?" he enquired. Then, dismayed by the pitiful incomprehension on her face, he suddenly put back his head and let out a roar of angry laughter.

"But I mean to say," she protested, "you know quite well what she *is*, she's bound to have all sorts of ideas . . ."

"Oh, well," he commented at last, "you fight it out between you." He lifted his paper. "It will be time for my medicine in five minutes," he added abstractedly.

Mrs. Quest continued to dream her dreams, while she watched the light change over the mountains. It was an hour of pure happiness for her. But her husband's withdrawal began to affect her. Soon the wings of her joy had folded. She sat in silence through supper; she looked like a little girl checked in what she most wanted. After the meal, she went to old chests and cupboards, and took out baby clothes she had kept all these years, and unfolded them, stroking them with remembering hands. Tears filled her eyes. Life is unfair, unfair! she was crying out in her heart, that lonely unassuaged heart that was aching now with its emptiness. For what her husband had said meant that, once again, she was to be cheated. She felt it. After a long time she carefully folded the clothes again, and put them away in their lavender and mothballs. It was time for bed. She went out in search of her husband to tell him so. He was not in the house. She looked out of the windows. Light streamed from them down the dark paths of the garden. The moon was rising over the Dumfries Hills. Mr. Quest stood, a dark, still shape beyond the reach of the streaming yellow house lights, watching the moon. She left the house and walked through the rockeries, where geraniums were a low scent of dryness rising from around her feet. She put her arm in his; and they looked out together towards the Dumfries Hills, which were now lifted towards the pale transparent disc of the moon by chains of red fire, and swirling in masses of red-tinted vapour.

"Beautiful," said Mr. Quest, with satisfaction. Then, after a pause: "I'm going to miss this." It was a half-appeal. Mr. Quest, who for years had been playing his part in framing the family's daydreams for escape to England or to the city, was longing for some reprieve now that the move to the city was certain.

Mrs. Quest said quickly, "Yes, but things will be much better in town."

Their thoughts moved together for a few minutes; and then he remarked unwillingly, "You know, old girl—well, she is awfully young, damn it."

Mrs. Quest was silent. Now, instead of the charming young man Jeffrey, she could see nothing but the implacable face of Martha.

The drums were beating in the compound. A hundred grass huts, subdued among the trees, were illuminated by a high flaring bonfire. The drums came strongly across the valley on the wind. The taste of wood smoke was bitter on their tongues.

"I'm going to miss it, aren't you?" he demanded savagely.

The sad knowledge of unfairness filled Mrs. Quest again, and she cried out, "But we can't die on this place, we can't die here."

Against this cry the drums thudded and the crickets chirped.

"It's time to go to bed," said Mrs. Quest restlessly.

"In a minute."

They remained, arm in arm, looking out.

"My eyes aren't so bad, even now," he said. "I can see all the Seven Sisters."

"Well, you can still see them in town, can't you?" She added, "It's getting cold," as the night wind came sharp to their faces from a rustling glade of drying grass.

"Oh, very *well*." They turned their backs to the moon and the blazing mountain, and went indoors. At the door he remarked, "All the same, I wouldn't be surprised if it wasn't more sensible for her not to have this baby."

"Oh, nonsense," she cried gaily. But she lay a long time in the dark, and now it was Martha's face she saw, set stubborn and satirical against her own outpourings of joy.

In the morning she rang up the neighbours to see if it was possible to get a lift into town. Nothing was said between husband and wife as she left but "Do what you can, old girl, won't you?" And she: "Oh, very well, I suppose you're right."

Two days after Mrs. Quest had heard the news from the bitter Martha, she marched into the flat to see her kneeling on the floor, surrounded by yards of white satin which she was fitting to a cradle. Martha swept away her mother's protests that it was absurd and impracticable to surround a baby with white satin, and in any case, why so soon? Martha had already bought flannel and patterns and had cut out nightdresses for the baby.

Mrs. Quest ignored the small protesting image of her husband, and disapproved strongly of the pattern for the nightdresses. She finished by enquiring, "Why not *blue* for the cradle?"

"Oh, so it's going to be a boy?" enquired Martha.

Mrs. Quest blushed. After a few minutes she conceded, "Why, are you going to have a girl, then?"

Martha said nothing, and Mrs. Quest understood that she had again confirmed her daughter's worst ideas of her. She said with an aggressive laugh, "Anyway, it's no good making up your mind you want a girl. I was sure you were a boy. I'd even chosen the name— and then look what I got!"

"I know, you mentioned it," said Martha coldly. She swiftly put satin, flannel, scissors and pins into a drawer, as if concealing them, and faced her mother like—the image came pat to Mrs. Quest—an animal defending her cubs.

The older woman said, laughing, "Well, there's no need to look like *that*. After all, I have had experience, and you have had none."

Again the vision of Mr. Quest hovered between them. Mrs. Quest, doing her duty, said like a lesson, "Your father says he thinks you are too young to have a baby, and you should consider what you're doing."

At this Martha flung herself into a chair, and laughed helplessly; and after a moment Mrs. Quest joined her in an enquiring peal.

"I'll make tea," said Martha, springing up.

They drank it while Mrs. Quest explained exactly how this child should be brought up. Martha said nothing. At the end of an hour she exclaimed abruptly, her voice seething with anger, "You know, this is *my* baby." At once Mrs. Quest's eyes filled with tears; she was the small girl who has been slapped for something she has not done. Martha felt guilty, and told herself that her mother could not help it. She said quickly, "You must stay and have lunch."

Mrs. Quest had planned to stay the day. But she rose and said unhappily that she had shopping to do. She left, filled again with the conviction of bitter injustice, her heart aching with love refused.

She went back to the farm and told Mr. Quest that as usual he had got hold of the wrong end of the stick, that Martha was quite wild with happiness. Then she went off into a long complaint of how Martha's ideas about children were absurd and she was bound to ruin them.

After listening in silence for some time, Mr. Quest rose and took out his writing things. "God knows why you two have to go on like this," he said bitterly. "Why? why? why?" His words drifted out of the window and died among the noises of owl and cricket. He sat stiffly holding the pen between his fingers, staring out of the window to where the Seven Sisters burned low over the glare from the fire-swept mountains, a pale smudge against that nearer conflagration which still sent wings of flame up into the great black starry vault of the sky. "One would think," he observed to this scene of splendour where his mind dwelt at ease, "that people would have some sense of proportion, considering the state the world's in."

A pause. He turned his pen angrily between his fingers. Mrs. Quest knitted behind him in silence; she had that evening begun on a jacket for the baby Jeffrey.

"But I suppose it makes no difference one way or the other," he went on. Mrs. Quest clicked her tongue protestingly.

Mr. Quest, with a final, confirming glance at the stars, the fiery mountain, the empty veld, murmured, "After all—those stars are millions of years away, so they say . . ."

"My *dear*," said Mrs. Quest again, uneasily.

Mr. Quest's pen was motionless in mid-air. His eyes were wide at the sky. "So if one damned foolish girl wants to make a mess of her life . . ." He lowered his pen carefully to the paper and began to write.

When her mother had left, Martha cupped her hands protectingly over her stomach, and murmured to the creature within that nothing would be allowed to harm it, no pressure would deform it, freedom would be its gift. She, Martha, the free spirit, would protect the creature from her, Martha, the maternal force; the maternal Martha, that enemy, would not be allowed to enter the picture. It was as one independent being to another that Martha spoke; and her hands on her flesh were light, as if even this pressure might be an unforgivable imposition.

To Douglas she forcibly outlined the things they must avoid in this child's future. First, even to suggest that the child might be one sex rather than another might have deplorable results—to be born as it chose was its first inalienable right. Secondly they, the parents, must never try to form its mind in any way whatsoever. Thirdly, it must be sent to a progressive school, where it might survive the processes of education unmutilated—for Martha felt, like so many others, that progressive schools were in some way outside society, vacuums of progress, as it were. If this last necessity involved their sending the child at an early age to a country where there *was* a progressive school, then so much the better; for a child without any parents at all clearly had a greater chance of survival as a whole personality.

To all this Douglas easily agreed. The ease with which he did agree disconcerted Martha slightly; for her convictions had after all come from the bitterest schooling, which he had escaped. He did remark at one point that the war might make it difficult to do as they liked about schools, but she waved this aside.

Douglas was very satisfied with Martha. There had been moments in the last few weeks when she had seemed unreasonable, but that had all vanished. She was now gay and amenable, and the whole business of having a baby was being made to appear as a minor incident, to be dealt with as practically as possible. Practicality was the essence of the business, they both agreed; and the completed cradle, a mass of icy white satin and lace, was a frivolous note of contrast to the sternness of their approach. For Martha, who was prepared to spend infinite emotional energy on protecting the child from her emotions, it was a matter of principle that the physical requirements should be as simple as possible. She took one look at the lists of things supposed to be needed for a small baby, and dismissed them with derision, as Alice had already done. By the end of a fortnight after she knew she was pregnant, she already had everything necessary to sustain that child for the first six months of its life. They filled a small basket. The child might be born now, if it chose. Martha even had the feeling that the business was nearly over. For she was once more in the grip of a passionate need to hurry. Impatience to be beyond this milestone was a fever in her. The five months between now and the birth of the child were nothing—five months of ordinary living flashed by so fast they were unnoticeable, therefore it was possible to look forward to the birth as if it were nearly here. Almost, it seemed to Martha that strength of mind alone would be enough to rush her through those months; even her stomach might remain flat, if she were determined enough.

In the meantime, she continued to live exactly as she had done before. She would have scorned to abdicate in any way, and in this Alice agreed with her: the two women, meeting at some dance or drinking party in the evening, congratulated each other on not showing anything; retiring into comfortable distortion would have seemed a complete surrender to weakness.

Almost at once, however, and it seemed from one day to the next, the wall of Martha's stomach pushed out in a hard curve, behind which moved the anonymous but powerful child, and Martha's fingers, tentatively exploring the lump, received messages that strength of mind alone was not enough. Besides, while Alice and she, the centre of a group of approving and envious people, insisted gaily that no fuss whatsoever was to be made about these children, that they were not to be allowed to change their parents' lives—and in their own interests, at that—it was obvious that both were very jealous of their privacy. Husbands and friends found these women admirably unchanged; during the daytime, they retired, and were irritable at being disturbed.

The moment Douglas had gone to the office, Martha drifted to the divan, where she sat, with listening hands, so extraordinarily compelling was the presence of the stranger in her flesh. Excitement raced through her; urgency to hurry was on her. Yet, after a few minutes, these emotions sank. She had understood that time, once again, was going to play tricks with her. At the end of the day, when Douglas returned from the office, she roused herself with difficulty, dazed. To her it was as if vast stretches of time had passed. Inside her stomach the human race had fought and raised its way through another million years of its history; that other time was claiming her; she understood the increasing vagueness of Alice's eyes; it was becoming an effort to recognize the existence of anything outside this great central drama.

Into it, like noises off, came messages from the ordinary world.

For instance, from her father. A few lines in his careful hand, dated three weeks back—clearly he had forgotten to post it.

My dear Matty,
   I understand you are going to have a baby. I suppose this is a good thing? Naturally, it is for you to say. Your mother is very pleased. What I wanted to say was, if there is anything I can do, I shall be glad. Children have a tendency not to be what you expect. But why should they be? Some damned kaffir has let a fire start on the Dumfries Hills. Extraordinarily pretty it is. We have been watching it at nights.

And then the careful close, the basic forms of the letters shaped and formal, with the capital letters all flourishes: "Your affectionate Father." After this, hasty and expostulating, one rapid sentence which said all that he had failed to get into his letter: "Damn it all, Matty, it's so damned inconsistent!"

Martha felt helpless with tenderness for him. She could see him writing it: the pen hovering before each word and dipped so reluctantly into the wells of feeling because duty demanded it of him; his mouth set in duty; and all the time his eyes straying towards the landscape outside. She wrote him a flippant letter saying she was apparently doomed to be inconsistent; she was terribly happy to be having a baby; she couldn't imagine why she had not wanted one!

And there was politics, in the shape of a twenty-page letter from Solly. Solly had been betrayed. The communal settlement, only three months old, had been blown into fragments by the Stalin-Hitler pact. Having read it twice, Martha pushed it aside, with every intention of writing to assuage the unhappiness it revealed. But after a day or so she was left not with the impression of unhappiness: she saw, rather, a dramatic figure on a stage. She did not understand it. If, however, she had remembered that with no personal memory of the Twenties she had succeeded in imaginatively experiencing the atmosphere of the decade from people who had, she might have looked forward to the time when the Thirties would be similarly reconstructed for her. As it was, she could only shrug. Solly—vociferous, exclamatory, bitter, had gone into the Cohen store as "the lowest-paid clerk," which, he seemed to feel, served history right. Also, he had taken a packing case to the market square where the Africans bought their vegetables, stood on it and harangued them for an hour on how they had been betrayed, they now stood alone, on their own efforts would their future depend. Apparently this throng of illiterate servants and casual labourers had listened with respect for his efforts, but without understanding, as they should instantly have done, the nature of the revelations being made to them. Solly had been taken off in a police van and—final insult—fined ten shillings for being drunk and disorderly. "As you know, I consider alcohol degrading." It all went to show the incredible stupidity of the authorities in not understanding their real enemies, personified by Solly.

Solly stood before the magistrate—as it happened, Mr. Maynard—and delivered a fine speech on the historical development of liberty. Mr. Maynard, interested but at sea, had suggested practically that it was a pity he didn't finish at the university; such talents should not be wasted. This was the final blow to Solly's pride.

Martha got a letter from Mr. Maynard, giving his version of the affair.

. . . A friend of yours, apparently? I took him out to lunch after the case, because of my insatiable interest in the vagaries of the young. His vagaries, however, do seem to me to be out of "historical context"—a phrase I learned from him. Surely behaviour more appropriate for England or Europe? One feels it is wasted on us. It would appear that he feels there is no hope for the world at all; I find it enviable that people should still care that this should be so. At my age, I take it for granted. He says he is now a Trotskyist. I said that I was sure this would be a great blow to Stalin, but that I would infinitely prefer my own son to be a Trotskyist rather than the town buffoon, it at least shows an interest in public affairs. This annoyed your friend exceedingly. He feels I should have sent him to prison for six months. If I had only known, I would have obliged him. Why not? But, as I pointed out to him, since the sons of our Chief Citizens think nothing of spending their nights in the custody of the police—Binkie was given a "shakedown," as he calls it, the other night in the company of some of the "lads"—the hands of the police are hardly the place for conscientious intellectuals. They wouldn't appreciate him, either.

Making feeble elderly jokes of this kind had the opposite effect to that I intended. He remarked darkly that the Revolution (which?) took too little heed of the differences in the degree of consciousness of the ruling classes. He said there was nothing he despised more than a reactionary who imagined himself a liberal. Could this mean me? He went on to say I was making a mistake to underrate him. I took *this* to mean that there must be a vast conspiracy under our noses among the blacks. My information, however, is that this is not the case. An interesting similarity, this: between the good ladies of the city, who are moaning with horror over their bridge tables about your friend Solomon's exploit, and your friend Solomon himself, whose imagination is no less romantic. However. I was writing to say that I am delighted you are having a baby. Since you are probably still bathed in the sweats of the honeymoon, you will not agree with me when I say that children are the only justification of marriage. I should like to be godfather to your (I hope) daughter. Naturally, I hasten to say, without the benefit of religion. If I'm not mistaken, this would be against your principles? I should like, however, to be "in" on it. I wanted a daughter more than anything.

This last sentence touched Martha deeply, coming as it did after the painful self-punishments of the rest of the letter. It was to the writer of that sentence she sent an affectionate reply, ignoring the rest.

Almost at once various other letters arrived, and, her nose being as acute as it was to sense any form of spiritual invasion, she was becoming aware that the people who are sucked irresistibly into the orbit of a marriage are by no means the same as those who respond to the birth of a child. Mr. Maynard, for instance, could be witty about marriages, but not about daughters. Mrs. Talbot was never anything but tender about daughters, sighed continually over the children she had not had, sent a charming note of congratulation to Martha, but for some weeks saw very little of the young couple, for she had become absorbed in the wedding of a friend of Elaine's, who needed all her attention. Various elderly ladies, scarcely known to Martha, rushed into her flat, folded her in their arms, offered her their friendship, and lingered, talking about their own children with the wistful, discouraged look which always made Martha feel so lacking.

Above all, the elder Mrs. Knowell, who had done no more than send sprightly telegrams of congratulation from the other end of the colony about the wedding, suddenly arrived in person. That creature in Martha which was the animal alert for danger against her cub waited tensely for the arrival of a possible enemy; and the other raw nerve was sounding a warning: this woman was likely to be a fore-cast of her own fate. For—she had worked it out with mathematical precision—since men were bound to marry their mothers, then *she,* in the end, would become Douglas's mother. But she was committed to be like her own mother. And if the two women were not in the least alike? That did not matter; in its own malevolent way, fate would adjust this incompatibility too, and naturally to Martha's dis-advantage.

As Mrs. Knowell entered the room, Martha's defences went down. They had been erected in the wrong quarter. She had been expect-ing something gay, jolly, with the self-conscious eccentricity of the letters and telegrams. Mrs. Knowell stood hesitating, kissed Martha carefully, and took her seat like a visitor. At once she took out a ciga-rette. Martha unconsciously curled out of sight her own stained fingers, and looked at the big, rather nervous hands, soaked in nico-tine. This was something altogether different from what she had been waiting for! Mrs. Knowell was a tall woman, big in the bone, yet with thick flesh loose about her. She had heavy brown eyes, the whites stained yellow; she wore a mass of faded yellow hair in a big untidy bun. Her skin was sallow, and a concession to what was ex-pected of her had put a hasty rub of yellowish lipstick across a full sad mouth. She wore a yellowish-brown dress. Nervous exhaustion came from her like a breath of stale air. She watched Martha as she made the tea, and made conversation, in a way which said clearly that she had come prepared not to interfere or infringe. It positively made Martha nervous. Her talk quite contradicted the heavy watch-ful eyes: it was gay and amusing; this was the personality which en-abled her friends from what she herself referred to as her "palmy" days to entertain her with a warm amused affection as a persistent *enfant terrible.* That gay old child, flitting erratically from one house to another, dropping in on a bridge game from a town seventy miles away, or suddenly taking flight in the middle of a two-week visit on an irresistible impulse to see a friend at the other end of the colony, was a creation of such tact that Martha found herself undermined by pity and admiration.

Mrs. Knowell was not of the first generation of pioneering women. She had ridden in covered waggons in the months-long journey from the south, but without need to take cover against hostile tribes. She had lived in the remote parts of the country, but the rifle which leaned ready against the wall was against wild animals and not a native rising. Her husband had been farmer, miner, policeman, businessman, as opportunity offered; he had made several fortunes and lost them in the casual way which was then customary. She had borne eight children, and kept two alive. The daughter in England was married to a small-town solicitor; they kept up a bright and entertaining correspondence.

Mrs. Knowell had succeeded in imposing on everyone who knew her this gallant and independent old lady, the jolly old girl; yet, if that heavy yellow stare, that tight defensive set of her limbs, that tired dry undercurrent to her voice meant anything, it was that her battles had been fought not against lions and flooded rivers or the accidents of a failing gold reef. She was in every way of the second generation; and Martha, impulsively ignoring the "amusing" remarks, as if she were insulted that such a fraud should be offered to her, spoke direct to what she felt was the real woman, out of her deepest conviction that anything less than the truth was the worst of betrayals, and more—that this truth should be an acknowledgement of some kind of persistent dry cruelty feeding the roots of life. Nothing else would do.

Mrs. Knowell responded slowly, with a nervous gratitude. She tentatively mentioned the baby; Martha talked of it without defences. Mrs. Knowell, released by this new baby into her memories of her own, spoke of them as she had obviously intended not to do. She began talking of the way they had died—blackwater, malaria, a neglected appendix. She began telling a long story, in a heavy, slow, tired voice, of an occasion when she had found herself alone on a farm, fifty miles from anywhere, her husband having gone to buy some cattle. She had been pregnant with her second child, her first having died. She had slept each night with locked and barricaded doors, a revolver under her pillow. In the day she had been frightened to move away from the house. Martha could imagine it, the lonely farmhouse, blistering in the heat, the empty veld stretching for miles all around. "Of course," said Mrs. Knowell, smiling drily, "I never told Philip I was lonely." Into this loneliness had come riding a young policeman on his rounds. "He was so kind to me, Matty—he was so kind." Martha, who had been expecting the story to continue, found it had reached its conclusion. Mrs. Knowell stirred herself, and remarked, "I don't know why I'm telling you this, I never talk about it." Martha, who was triumphant at that admission, which it was her need, for some reason, to gain, replayed, as it were, in her head, like a recording, that story of the weeks of loneliness, in the light of that final "He was so kind to me"—and found it enough.

She was being very kind to Mrs. Knowell. She liked her enormously, and knew Mrs. Knowell liked her. It was understood that Mrs. Knowell would stay to lunch, would spend the afternoon with Martha, and in the evening the three of them would go out somewhere. Into this scene burst Douglas, cheerfully rubbing his hands, and embraced his mother with the words, "Well, Mater, what have you been up to?"

There was a short pause, while the currents changed, and Mrs. Knowell visibly rallied the bright old lady. She offered some hilarious stories about the people she had just been staying with. Her weeks in that house had been one long picnic of jam-making, bottling, pickling. She had cut her finger—she wagged it before them, laughing. Now she was departing south, and had taken the opportunity to drop in and see the dear children.

Douglas invited his mother to admire Martha's health and attractiveness. She did so. Both Douglas and Martha became offhandedly practical about the whole affair; Douglas began to tease his mother about her preoccupation with such old-lady-like things as embroidered pillowcases and lace-edged dresses. Mrs. Knowell preserved her amused sprightliness for a while, but became noticeably silent, while Martha chattered brightly, in a hard voice, about unhygienic sentimentality—this was not at all as she had been alone with her.

After a while Mrs. Knowell suggested wistfully that it was such fun to make things for a new baby; and saw them exchanging glances in tolerant silence.

"But it is!" she cried out. "I'd love to have the chance of making little things again."

"Now come off it, Mater," said Douglas cheerfully. "We're not going to have any of *that*."

After a while she got up and remarked that as she was going to play bridge with Mrs. Talbot that afternoon she must hurry away.

Douglas, relieved, teased her about being a frivolous old woman. She bravely announced that she had taken one shilling and sixpence off Mrs. Talbot the last time she had played with her.

In a flurry of jokes, kisses, promises to meet soon, she departed. Martha was left with the memory of those yellowing tired eyes resting on her in hurt disappointment. She felt a traitor. And yet, by themselves, they had understood each other so well!

Douglas was speaking with grateful enthusiasm about his mother's capacity for enjoying herself so much at her age—Martha reminded herself that, after all, Mrs. Knowell was only fifty. Douglas went on to remark practically that at least they needn't expect any interference from her, she always had far too much on her own plate to bother about other people. Martha was on the point of repudiating this comfortable evasion of the truth, but let the moment go.

Mrs. Knowell departed from the city that evening, after sending a small parcel by Mrs. Talbot's houseboy, containing a dozen long muslin dresses, exquisitely embroidered and tucked, with a note saying: "These were Douglas's when he was a baby. I offered them to my daughter, but she said they were not practicable. But if you can't use them, then they'll do as dusters. I really haven't time to see you dear children again, I must get off to the Valley, they're having a picnic on Sunday, and I wouldn't miss that for worlds."

Later, Mrs. Talbot remarked that Mrs. Knowell had been as erratic as ever: she had promised to stay a week, and left after half a day. She was really so wonderful for her age.

Martha was sitting down the next morning to write a nice letter to the old lady, to make some amends for the unpleasant way she knew she had behaved, when a native messenger arrived from Douglas's office. There was a note saying: "Well, we're off! War's just been declared." After the signature, the words, "Matters appear extremely serious."

Martha tried to *feel* that matters were extremely serious. Outside, however, a serene sunlight, and the pleasant bustle of an ordinary morning. She switched the wireless on—silence. Then the telephone rang. Alice, in tears, repeating angrily, "And now Willie's bound to go and I'll be alone." Then Stella, who also wept: the situation demanded no less.

But, having put the receiver down, she stood listening to the silence as if there was something more, some other *word* that needed to be said; she heard now that same dissatisfaction in the voices of the two women who had ceased speaking, and were doubtless engaged in busily telephoning others to find whatever it was they all needed. "They say that war has been declared, Matty?" It was this incredulous query which floated in her inner ear. She was extremely restless. She looked at the blue squares of park and sky which opened the walls of the flat, and it seemed menacing that nothing had changed. She went out into the streets. There, surely, the war would be visible? But everything was the same. A knot of people in sober argument stood on the pavement's edge. She approached them and found them talking about the prices of farm implements. She walked through the streets, listening for a voice, any voice, speaking of the war, so that it might seem real. After a while she found herself outside the offices of the newspaper. There clustered a small crowd, faces lifted towards windows where could be seen the large indistinct shapes of machinery. They were hushed and apprehensive; here danger could be felt. But Martha saw after a minute that they were all older people; she did not belong with them.

She went home to the wireless set, which was playing dance music. It was now lunchtime, and she wished Douglas might come home. At the end of half an hour she was disgusted to find herself making angry speeches of reproach to him in her mind—a conventional jailer wife might do no less! Nothing, she told herself, was more natural than that he should find the bars and meeting places of the city more exciting than coming to her. She would do the same in his place. And so she waited until afternoon in a mood of impatient expectancy; and when the door at last opened, and he came in, she flew at him and demanded, "What's the news? What's happened?" For surely something must have!

But it appeared that nothing had happened. In both their minds was a picture of London laid in ruins, smoking and littered with corpses. But it seemed that while they thought of London, of England, the imaginations of most were moving far nearer home. Douglas announced ruefully that women were already sitting shuddering in their homes, convinced that Hitler's armies might sweep down over Africa in "a couple of days," and more—the natives were on the point of rising. In any colony, a world crisis is always seen first in terms of a native rising. In fact it seemed that the dark-skinned people had only the vaguest idea that the war had started, and the authorities' first concern was to explain to them through wireless and loudspeaker why it was their patriotic task to join their white masters in taking up arms against the monster across the seas in a Europe they could scarcely form a picture of, whose crimes consisted of invading other people's countries and forming a society based on the conception of a master race.

Douglas was stern, subdued, authoritative. Martha was only too ready to find this impressive. Almost, she found her dissatisfactions fed. But it was soon clear that Douglas too was waiting for that *word,* that final clinching of emotion. He moved about the flat as if it was confining him, and suggested they should drop across to the Burrells. They met the Burrells and the Mathews coming in. They went in a body up to the Sports Club, where several hundred young people were waiting for the wireless to shape what they felt into something noble and dramatic.

By evening, the hotels were full. To dance would be heartless and unpatriotic; but to stay at home was out of the question. The bands were playing "Tipperary" and "Keep the Home Fires Burning" to packed, silent masses of people who seemed to find it not enough. They stood waiting. They were waiting for the King's speech, and with a nervous hunger that began to infect Martha. The pillars of the long, low white dance room were wreathed in flags; when the band struck up "God Save the King" the wind of the music seemed to stir the Union Jacks hanging bunched over their heads. When the slow, diffident voice floated out over the crowd, it was noticeable that a stern, self-dedicated look was deepening on all the faces around her. Douglas, she saw, was standing to attention, his face set and proud. So were Willie and Andrew. Alice, however, appeared miserable; and Stella, whose facial muscles were set into a mould of devoted service, was steadily tapping her small gold-covered foot, not impatiently, but as if preserving some rhythm of her own. As for Martha, she found these three young men, stiff as ramrods, with their fists clenched down by their sides, rather ridiculous. After all, she was pointing out to herself, even while her throat muscles tightened irritably against an unaccountable desire to weep—she resented very much that her emotions were being roused by flags, music and solemnity against her will—after all, if any of these young men were to be asked what they thought about the monarchy, their attitude would rather be one of indulgent allowance towards other people's weaknesses. She glanced sideways towards Alice, and Stella: involuntarily they glanced back, and, not for the first or last time, acknowledged what they felt by a small, humorous tightening of the lips.

The speech was over. The enormous crowd breathed out a sigh. But they remained there, standing, in silence. The courtyards were packed, the bars crammed, the big room itself jammed tight. For some people it was clear that the word had been said—they were released. A few groups disengaged themselves from the edges of the crowd and went home: mostly elderly people. Everyone else was waiting. The band again struck up "Tipperary." Then it slid into a dance tune. No one moved. Stern glances assailed the manager, who stood in acute indecision by the pillar. He made a gesture to the band. Silence. But they could not stand there indefinitely; nor could they go home. Soon people were standing everywhere, glasses in their hands, in the dance room itself, the verandahs, the bars, the courts. The band remained on its platform, benevolently regarding the crowd, their instruments at rest. At last they began playing music which was neutral and inoffensive: selections from *The Merry Widow* and *The Pirates of Penzance*. And still no one went home. The manager stood watching his patrons with puzzled despair.

Clearly he should be giving them something else. At last he approached a certain visiting general from England, who was standing at the bar. This gentleman climbed up beside the band, and began to speak. He spoke of 1914. That date, and the words Verdun, Passchendaele, the Somme, were like a bell tolling, and led to the conclusion of the speech, which was: ". . . this day, September the third, 1939." Heightened and solemn it was; and the hours they had been living through, so formless and unsatisfactory, achieved their proper shape, and became a day they would remember always; it could be allowed to slide back into the past, and become another note of the solemn bell pealing the black dates of history.

There was nothing more to be said. The general, with a long, half-appealing look at his audience, as if to say "I've done my best," climbed from the platform, hastily adjusting his tunic. The band rose and gathered their instruments. Now they could all go home.

As the Knowells, the Burrells, and the Mathews reached the pavement, Stella remarked in a humorous, apologetic voice that she thought she was going to have a baby. It fell flat.

Alice said pleasantly, "That's nice, dear." She clutched her husband's arm, and said, "Do let's go home." Her voice had risen in a wail of tears.

The days went by slowly, as slowly as if people had been wrenched out of habit; as if to live in exactly the same way as before was in itself something unexpected and impossible. A ship was sunk thousands of miles away. An army crossed to France, arousing in the older people memories that apparently fed them with certainty about what was going to happen next. In Britain, the Government bickered, and the newspapers put it into the language of dignified disagreement. Anticlimax deepened. It was as if the date for the beginning of a tragic winter had been announced, and a late summer persisted in shedding a tentative sunlight.

Martha went back to her divan. Where the bright pinnacles of the trees in the park, persistent green against the persistent blue, showed in the open squares in the white wall, Martha sat watching patterns of sunlight shift and lengthen across the floor, watching the blue convolutions of smoke from her cigarette dissolve into a yellowish haze. Sometimes she stretched out her arm and received the warmth of the sun direct through her skin on behalf of the new creature within; it seemed to her that the sudden glow was answered by an increased vigour of its movements. Or, smoothing down the cotton stuff of her tunic over the swelling mound, she watched the wall of flesh pulse, or how the weight of flesh distributed differently—as if a sleeper turned in his sleep. It was as if on the floor of a dark sea a half-recognized being crouched, moving sometimes against the change of the tides. Or she looked at the blue vein on her wrist and thought it swollen, and was glad because its larger weight of impurities guaranteed the fresh strength of the new red current that fed the infant. She had succumbed entirely to that other time. She even tried to remember the flood of excitement that had swept through her, and so short a time ago, at the words: Only five months, four and a half months, four months . . . For now these seemed immensely long epochs; she could hardly see the end of a day from its beginning.

She was alone from early in the morning till dark. Douglas was spending all his time with the boys, rocking delightedly on every fresh current of rumour. It was understood that he would be going on active service very soon. He felt guilty at his own delight in it. He even felt uneasy because Martha concurred so easily. For he did not understand that five months, in this new scale of time, seemed so immensely long. It was as if he were planning to leave her in a distant future. Naturally he would go! To put any pressure on him not to would be unpardonable—she would always refuse to play any such role. But the fact was, the outside noises of war seemed like increasingly distant thunder.

One morning there came a little note from Mrs. Talbot saying it would give her great pleasure if dear Douglas and Matty would come with her to the station to see a friend off to England. Douglas reported that Elaine had become engaged to a young man from the Cape.

The long grey station was hot with evening sunlight. The train, that perfect symbol of the country, stood waiting. Behind the engine stretched the coaches; one or two white faces showed from the windows of each. At the extreme end, there was a long truck, like a truck for cattle, confining as many black people as there were whites in the rest of the train. In between, a couple of ambiguous coaches held Indians and Coloured people, who were allowed to remain provided no white person demanded their seats.

Halfway down the train was a concentration of white faces. These were young men, the sons of fathers who had been able to afford their learning to fly, but not to risk their jobs before the war actually started. Outside the windows stood groups of well-dressed elderly people. At a window away from the others leaned a youth of perhaps twenty, not more. He was slight and pale, with a shock of light straw-coloured hair. His face was sensitive and intelligent, his eyes direct and blue, very serious. Elaine stood beneath, looking up at him. So isolated were they, so still, that when Mrs. Talbot appeared at the station entrance, in an impulsive movement of love which would carry her across to join her daughter, she was checked. Her eyes overflowed. She turned to Douglas and held out her arms, in a helpless gesture of emptiness, before slowly letting them fall.

Douglas at once went to her, laid a hand on her shoulder, and said stoutly, "Bear up, Mrs. Talbot."

Her whole body shook; she let her head droop beside his for a moment; then she raised a sad set face. "It's awful—they've only been together a few days."

She looked across to where Elaine and her lover still gazed at each other. She took a step forward, and stopped as if afraid to disturb them. Douglas supported her and led her towards the window. Mr. Talbot emerged from the entrance. He nodded at Martha formally; again she felt herself instinctively shrink away from him. He was now looking at his wife. Douglas, with a small bow, released Mrs. Talbot to her husband's protection; but as Mr. Talbot showed no signs of supporting her as she needed to be, Douglas replaced his comforting arm. Martha watched Mr. Talbot's hard close look at his wife. Again she felt shrinking discomfort, which was almost fear. Experience gave her no clue to that jailer's look; but she could not remove her puzzled gaze from that saturnine pillar of a man who stood erect, dark, concentrated with watchfulness, just behind his wife. She felt protective towards Mrs. Talbot. He remained perfectly still, watching, while his wife allowed her head to fall in a momentary gesture of despair on Douglas's shoulder, and while Douglas squeezed and patted her shoulders consolingly and exchanged with her a smile of intimate sympathy. Finally Mrs. Talbot took two helpless steps forward by herself, and was within the orbit of the lovers. Elaine smiled quietly out from that charmed circle at her mother; but immediately turned her eyes back towards the young man.

A few paces away a score of youths were saying goodbye to their families, who were preserving a brave cheerfulness which was becoming increasingly unbearable.

The engine suddenly let out a long shriek. Elaine gathered herself up in a movement as if she would fling herself after her lover, but she let herself sink back. Mrs. Talbot was now clinging to the girl. The train moved; the sunlight flashed along its windows. A chorus of goodbyes broke out. They all watched the boyish, grave, charming face; then he lifted his hand in salute, and withdrew: the window was empty. Elaine remained standing on the extreme edge of the platform, stiff in the arms of her mother, gazing after the train, while the groups of people dissolved about them. Mrs. Talbot was weeping openly. Elaine seemed to awaken, she turned, smiled at her mother, put her arm about her, and walked beside her to the arched entrance: they went out of sight. Mr. Talbot, whose gaze had never left his wife, nodded formally to Martha, gave a stiff bow to Douglas, and strode after the two women.

Douglas remained gazing after the train, whose smoke was settled in sunlit clouds over the platform. Martha, who knew he was feeling nothing but envy of the young men who soon would be in the Air Force in England, looked away from him. Close by, she saw Maisie, shaking the hands of an elderly couple who were urging her to come home with them. Their smiles were stiff and determined: Maisie had married their son that morning. They had been prevented by the taboos from saying she was of the wrong class; now it was appropriate that their son's wife should come home "at least for the evening," as they repeated disapprovingly. "He would have wanted it," the lady had murmured, sighing, to her husband.

Maisie was standing lazily before them, her weight slumped onto one plump hip, her loose fair curls shining in a haze of sunlight. There was an ink mark on her yellow skirt. She was repeating with a forbearance as marked as theirs, "Thank you, thank you so much, but I have an appointment this evening." Her face continued polite; theirs were increasingly resentful. At last, putting an end to it, she said directly, "I am sure you mean it kindly." And turned away.

Her face changed into a strained blank gaze. Through it came a glimmer of recognition. She came walking towards Martha, the good-natured blue eyes heavy with shock. Martha instinctively put out a hand to steady her as she came to rest, still looking after the train.

"So they've gone, eh?" Maisie said. She was incredulous.

Douglas said kindly, "Bad luck, I'm sorry."

She looked through him, turned the round blue eyes on Martha, and said, "We got married this morning. I said to Dickie, 'What's the point? It makes no difference to us, and it only gets *them* down.'" She jerked her shoulder towards her parents-in-law, who were standing hypnotized, listening, a few paces off. "I said to him, 'After all, with their ideas from England, they can't help it, so why get them all upset for nothing?' But he'd got a bee in his bonnet, so I married him. Men are romantic, aren't they?" she ended on an enquiry, wanting confirmation from Martha. The parents-in-law were exchanging looks in which, as Martha could see, their intention to show a democratic forbearance was rapidly vanishing under fury that this young woman should have no idea of her good fortune. Maisie, who had forgotten them, went on: "As long as it made him happy, I don't mind. I wouldn't mind having a baby, really," she added, frankly inspecting Martha. "You don't show much, either, considering."

Her eyes moved past Martha to where the railway lines curved gleaming out of sight. Her mouth fell open, like a child's. "They've gone," she muttered again.

The parents-in-law exchanged another look, and moved away heavily with a look of patient endurance.

Martha and Douglas took an arm on either side of Maisie and moved her towards the entrance. She was heavy and inert.

Outside the station she seemed to recover. She shook herself free calmly, and remarked, "I've got a date tonight with Binkie. I don't really feel like it, but Dickie wouldn't like me to sit at home and mope." She nodded and smiled. The blue eyes were solemn and puzzled. "I suppose everyone else knows what the war's for," she remarked resentfully, as she turned away with a final wondering stare at the station, "but it's more than I do."

With this she walked off past the car where her new parents-in-law were sitting. She offered them a polite unhappy smile, and slightly increased her lazy amble along the street which led to Mc-Grath's. She was late for her date with Binkie.

2

Stella was now explaining to both Alice and Martha that it was the duty of young married couples to have children while they were young: their duty to the children, who would naturally prefer to have parents who were brothers and sisters to them. No one contradicted her. She went on to insist that to have a baby now, while the men were on active service, was the essence of good planning: the nursery stage would be over by the time they got back. To which Alice replied irritably, "They haven't gone yet, for crying out aloud!" And Martha, "But, Stella, that isn't what you *said.*"

Stella drew herself up; indignation flashed from every line of her charming body. She retreated to her own flat, sulking. As usual, neither Alice nor Martha seemed to understand the gesture. She emerged, at the end of a week, in full dresses, with a look of warm loosening fulfilment. After many hours before the mirror she had decided to pile her hair loosely on top of her head, like a busy mother too occupied to bother with personal attractions. Presenting herself thus, she earned from Alice the good-natured remark, "You look lovely, Stell." And from Martha, "But, Stella, why do you rush into smocks when you aren't even showing yet?"

Stella wept. Martha and Alice looked at each other in complete amazement. They offered handkerchiefs and the advice to take things easy.

Martha was feeling that of the three of them it was Stella who was really enjoying herself; for zest, always Stella's quality, was the one which neither she nor Alice possessed.

She was essentially divided. One part of herself was sunk in the development of the creature, appallingly slow, frighteningly inevitable, a process which she could not alter or hasten, and which dragged her back into the impersonal blind urges of creation; with the other part she watched it; her mind was like a lighthouse, anxious and watchful that she, the free spirit, should not be implicated; and engaged in daydreams of the exciting activities that could begin when she was liberated.

Into this precarious balance burst Mrs. Quest again and again, bright-eyed, insistent, stating continually that the deepest satisfaction in life was maternity and that Martha must sacrifice herself to her children as she had done, concluding always with the triumphant remark, "You won't have time for all your ideas when the baby is born, believe *me!*"

To which Martha reacted with a cold, loathing determination that she must keep brightly burning that lamp above the dark blind sea which was motherhood. She would *not* allow herself to be submerged.

To Douglas she cried continually, "Why can't she leave me alone?"

But one day he entered on a scene where Mrs. Quest, irritable, impatient, and insistent, was demanding that Martha should order a certain pattern of jacket rather than the one she preferred, while Martha was logically arguing that in Iceland, or perhaps it was Chile, babies wore no jackets at all, and therefore— He collapsed into a chair and laughed until his face was wet. Mrs. Quest regarded him with smiling forbearance. Martha, however, felt she had been betrayed. She looked forward to when her father would come into town; he, she was convinced, would support her against the forces of tyranny.

It was not long before the household had been moved, and she received the message she expected. Mrs. Quest said that her father had something important to say to her; she must come over at once.

Martha therefore walked across the park, and found Mr. Quest seated under a folded mass of purple bougainvillea, which in its turn was shaded by branches of jacaranda in full bloom. The masses of light-mauve blossom swayed over him; occasionally a flower detached itself and floated down. Mr. Quest, from a distance, looked as if he were seated in a clear blue lake.

"I wanted to say something to you, what was it?" he demanded, conscientiously turning his eyes on his daughter. He examined his future grandchild with the frank appraisal of a countryman, and remarked, "You're shaping nicely, all things considered. I can't remember what your mother said I should say, but you wouldn't take any notice anyway, so it doesn't matter, does it?"

Martha sat down. The house was of red brick, with verandahs flung out all around. A golden shower climbed the pillars in front, and laid heavy green arms over the corrugated-iron roof. Through the windows could be seen the furniture from the farm. Martha felt a sadness which she understood was shared by her father when he said, "It's all very well, we had a bad time on the farm, but I feel so damned *shut* in, with all these streets." The park opened its acres of green and flowers immediately across the street, the garden was shadowed by shrubs and trees from the bisecting street, but Martha felt an exile, as he did. She did not know how much it had meant that her parents, at least, had been on the land. Some balance had been upset in her. That fatal dichotomy, soil, city, had been at least held even by thinking of her father working his land. Now she felt altogether cut off from her roots, even more so because she disliked the idea of actually living on a farm so much.

"It's not that I enjoy all the inconvenience," went on Mr. Quest, looking over at her for confirmation. "It's not that at all. I don't see any point in lamps instead of electric light, or being miles from doctors, or no shops nearby. Some people seem to enjoy that sort of thing. But, damn it all, I liked knowing what was going on—you can't even see how the rain comes and goes here. I liked watching the rain coming across the hills."

Martha assented. What she was feeling was something like disloyalty: she could not share with her father her love for that particular patch of soil the farm, which in fact he was now aching after. She probed, "But it wasn't the same for you as England, was it? You know, when you used to go rabbiting in the fields, and then the horses . . ."

She waited. It worked, as it always did. Mr. Quest, eyes narrowed at the hard blue area of sky overhead, sighed. Then it was as if he expanded in water. He let himself fall back in the chair, and stretched his legs in front of him luxuriously. "Ah, well, now, that was a different thing altogether!" He looked at her suspiciously, and asked, "But I told you, didn't I?"

"I don't think so," said Martha quickly.

"I thought I had." He removed his eyes from her face, suppressed any thought that she might be tolerating an old man, and remarked,

"The rain is different there—things smell after rain. There's nothing like the smell of the earth after rain in England." To Martha, for whom the smell of this African earth after the first rains of the season was the keenest pleasure of the year, it was as if a door had been shut: she had invited it. "And then those long evenings, not like this damned country, where the night shuts down on you like—like—I can't bear being shut *in*," he said.

He continued to talk about England. He did not once mention the African farm on which he had lived for all those years. Martha listened, circling her stomach with her forearms, while with one half of her mind she saw a boy running wild across an English farm, fifty years before, and ran with him, tasting faint and exquisite dews, feeling long lush English grass around her ankles. With the other, she was indulging in the forbidden pleasure of nostalgia. The pang of lost happiness was so acute it shortened her breath. Then she asked herself if there was any moment of her childhood she would choose to live again, and she could only reply that no, there was not. If she burrowed back under the mist of illusion, she had felt a determination to continue, a curiosity perhaps, an intention to endure, but no delight. Yet that uncomfortably antagonistic childhood had over it a shimmering haze of beauty, it tugged at her to return.

She broke across her father's rambling monologue to enquire, "Were you happy as a child?"

He was checked. The bright vague eyes clouded over—irritation at being brought back to this garden, this sky. "What I liked best," he remarked, "were the horses. They don't have horses here, not like *those* horses!" He looked at her again. "Oh, yes," he said practically, "I've remembered what I wanted to say. Your mother thinks that you ought to come and have your baby here. Then she can look after you both."

He looked steadily at her. She looked at him.

"You must do as you think best," he said hastily. Then, after a long reflective pause, he enquired, "Did I ever tell you about the time I went to Doncaster with Bert's black mare?"

Soon after this, a letter, rather wistful, arrived from Mrs. Knowell, saying that if she wouldn't be in the way, she would like nothing better than to come and nurse mother and baby.

Martha immediately booked a room in the nursing home which she had sworn never to enter because it was almost inevitable that she must.

As for Alice, after discarding Dr. Stern as a possible assistant in the process of birth, which she felt she understood well enough to dispense with one, she gloomily accepted him with the remark that she supposed one doctor was as bad as another. She too hastily booked a room, after representations from her grandmother that she should instantly move to the city where that old lady was living, several hundreds of miles away.

"Really," she remarked with her familiar good-humoured giggle, "you'd think that they'd be pleased to be finished with the awful business, instead of rushing to start all over again with us."

The mere act of booking a room seemed to bring the day of birth nearer; Martha felt it was positively unnatural that the actual number of days on the calendar remained the same.

The rainy season began. The child would be born towards its end. Again she felt the discrepancy between the shortness of the rainy season, a handful of brief months in any ordinary scale of time, and the crawling days which she had to live through. She was consumed, several times a day, by a violent upsurge of restlessness. She could not keep still. She could not read. Above all, she felt there must be something wrong with her, to feel like this. For at the back of her mind was the vision of a woman calm, rich, maternal, radiant; that was how she should be.

She was very much alone.

Douglas, together with Willie and Andrew, was going through a crisis of his own. For authority had spoken, and as a result several hundreds of young men had achieved uniform. But not their age group. And it was the first time they had understood they were not the boys of the town, the golden youth. That was over. It had been a shock to find themselves thrust aside by these younger men. They were wearing the humorous, resigned look of middle-aged men called "sir" for the first time by their juniors. They would, however, be called up very soon, they already felt themselves to be cut off, in spirit, from the civilian population, and they filled the bars and clubs every moment they were free of work.

To Martha, Douglas suggested she should spend her time with Alice. To Alice, Willie said that Martha was a nice kid, and just the ticket as a companion. But for a long time the two women did not meet in the daytime. They liked each other, they understood each other very well; but something prevented them from mingling their daytime lives. It was that both felt they must be in some way unnatural; they did not want to expose what they felt to the other.

Then, one very hot morning, when Martha was seated under that square of blue sky, such a passion of rebellious restlessness took hold of her that she leaped up, ran downstairs, and got into the car. She was going to do something she had often been tempted to do before. She was going to look at the nursing home. It was five miles. She

parked the car on a small ridge half a mile from it, and looked longingly across the valley to where the building stood, neat in its white
paint and green shutters, on the opposite ridge. She felt that looking
at it thus might bring the day nearer. She felt that looking at it made
her one with the mysteries it sheltered.

Nevertheless, the sight of it awoke some unwelcome and far too
familiar thoughts. Scrupulously visualizing first a male child and
then a female one, she shaped that unborn being, now heaving and
bubbling continuously in its cage of ribs, into—Binkie Maynard, perhaps? Or one of the hockey-playing maternal amazons of the Sports
Club? That was even more intolerable. Yet even as she shuddered
away these possibilities, she was reminding herself that never, at any
time, had she had the intention of becoming what Solly so easily dismissed as a petty-bourgeois colonial, yet here she was; so it followed
that the child was doomed, also.

It was very hot. The whitish dust of the road glittered. Heat
poured down from masses of black cloud. In a haze of glare, a yellow
dazzle focused into her eyes. It was a car, gathering shape in seething clouds of white dust. She knew the car—Alice, now slowing to a
standstill. The two women looked at each other. Both blushed; then
they smiled confessingly. Alice awkwardly jumped out of the car, a
tall, lean creature from whose light frame of bones protruded grotesquely her child. Martha joined her. They examined each other
frankly, and exchanged heavy sighs which said that while they knew
they were committed to this absurd process, they at least intended to
remain ironical spectators of it.

"I thought I'd come and have a look at the place," Alice said, and
giggled suddenly.

Martha joined in with a laugh. "I can't bear the way time crawls,"
she complained, with a watchful eye on Alice's reaction. "I can't bear
any of it! I could scream!"

But Alice looked understanding and relieved. "Neither can I. I
wish I'd never started. If I'd known it was going to take so long . . ."

They looked across the intervening wastes of yellow grass to the
grove of blue gums, the white shining building where lay fortunate
women, already delivered of their burdens. They stood there a long
time, gazing at the promised land, until Alice said irritably, "Oh well,
I suppose this is just stupid."

Martha assented, and they returned in their separate cars to Martha's flat. The barriers had gone down.

Now they spent their days together. They did not talk much. They
smoked, sewed a little, or amused themselves by balancing some object on their stomachs, such as a box of matches, until a thrusting

limb or a butting head knocked it off onto the floor. Long periods of inactivity caused Alice to remark helplessly, "I suppose the little so-and-so's asleep. Well, good luck to it, it doesn't know when it's lucky." This was a reference to her misery because Willie, like Douglas, was so seldom at home.

Some person high in the Government, exasperated beyond endurance by the importunities of the young men, had cried out, "For God's sake, find something for them to do. Keep them quiet until we know what to do with them." As a result, the men of Willie's and Douglas's generation spent every afternoon after work deploying on a red dust square with various obsolete weapons, under an old sergeant from the last war who resented this occupation bitterly: he wanted only to be sent to the front somewhere. After an hour or so's drill the men went to drink. They were soldiers. They returned to their women late in the evening, cheerful strangers. Or at least that was how Martha felt it.

Alice greeted Willie with sardonic hostility; later she might weep and cling to him.

Martha was scrupulously undemanding, but enquired who had said what and when, until Douglas said impatiently, "Oh, it was all just as usual."

It was a heavy rainy season that year. Many afternoons the square was a squelching mass of water and red mud. Once Martha and Alice drove up to watch, which they did in derisive silence. The drill was impossible, so the soldiers were scrambling and fighting across the mud, throwing great handfuls of it into each other's faces, yelling and whooping, knocking each other over.

It was painful to the women, seeing their men turned into willing savages. They never told their husbands they had been up to watch. They never mentioned it again to each other; they did not even like to think of it. There was some sort of disloyalty to their husbands, and to their marriages, in remembering how the men had fought among the mud puddles with each other, their eyes gleaming with savage joy out of mud-streaked faces, because they were not allowed to go off and fight some enemy.

The women were very close together. It rained endlessly. They felt enclosed behind a high misty grey curtain which shut out everything.

Martha had no satisfaction from this rain, which drenched down and was stopped by surfaces of concrete, surfaces of brick. Half an hour after a storm, the town was clean but dry; the water had been repelled and was flooding off into swollen gutters away from the streets. In the park opposite, the soil received it, small acres of greenness in a waste of impervious streets. She leaned at a window, looking out into the swirling mists that rose faintly about the hard glittering rods which caught a gleam of light from a window, or a car nosing far below. She was helpless with melancholy, inert with waiting; for on such afternoons both women stiffened and listened at every sound outside—the men might perhaps be coming home, since it was surely impossible to drill. But the hours went by, it was dark before they came.

One afternoon Douglas rang to ask if the girls would stretch a point: he and Willie wanted to go on to some celebration. He was speaking in the overcontrite, almost mockingly pleading way men use when they band together against the impositions of their women. He had never spoken so before; Martha had always winced with angry distaste at hearing Willie speak so to Alice, or Andrew to Stella. Now, because Douglas was with Willie, in that atmosphere of men escaping their wives, he put on the tone with her. She was furious that he could do it. She assured him, gaily, that of course he must go with the boys, of course she didn't mind—as she always spoke on these occasions. But when she put the telephone down she was angry. It was all intolerable. She was shut in here, in this flimsy little flat, by the rain, because of the baby in her stomach, forced to accept that falsely humble voice from a young man who by himself would never think of using it: she was the wife of one of the lads. That was all.

Alice had sunk back into a chair, her face bleak and discouraged. "Oh, well," she said after a moment, with a bright unhappy laugh, "I suppose I don't blame the buggers. I suppose if I were a man I'd find us dull, too." The two women looked at each other, acknowledging frankly in this moment that they wished they had never married, wished they were not pregnant, even hated their husbands. They looked out again into the grey thick rain.

"Let's go out in it," said Martha on an impulse. Alice's face lit; she waited, though, for Martha to encourage her. "We'll go and drive in it," Martha said again excitedly.

Alice sprang up. They were now restored to their own self-respect. For to go out in the rain would be a gesture of defiance to their husbands, who were now so full of prohibitions and firm masculine attitudes about getting cold or tired: they had adopted this attitude because they were so little with their wives. The women had accepted the counterfeit, which was better than nothing.

They ran downstairs, hesitated a moment in the doorway, which glittered with stalactites of rain; then ran straight out into it, leaped across the gutter, and dived into Alice's car. The cars stood side by side in the gutter, water to the wheelhubs. Alice swore, because the size of her stomach made it hard to fit comfortably behind the driving wheel; then she stiffened her body and jammed it back repeatedly against the seat until it slid back. Her face was set, her eyes hard and lost-looking. She was putting far more force into the action than it needed. Martha saw that Alice, like herself, was thinking wildly that perhaps even now she might have a miscarriage, might be released from a position they found all at once humiliating and intolerable. Alice swung the car around and began driving recklessly through the downpour. The streets were a drumming haze of water; the headlights drowned in a wet yellowness half a dozen yards ahead. The water sliced up from the wheels in a beautiful solid, gleaming curve fringed with scattering white.

Alice took the road to the nursing home. On the small rise opposite it, they parked the car. They were shut into a small dry space inside the swirl and squelch of the storm. Through the greyness came a movement. It took shape, and they watched a single African workman come past, the water splashing up from his bare feet. His khaki pants clung to him. The water poured over his chest. He held his arms clenched across in front, for a little warmth, and walked head bent, his body tensed in a shiver. His eyes moved sideways towards the car, then returned to the road ahead. He was concerned with nothing but getting to shelter.

When the darker blot of his shape had been sponged into the downpour, Alice looked at Martha and said, "Well?"

She began taking off her clothes, with rapid clumsy movements. Martha did the same. They held the door half open, for a last look for any possible invaders, and then plunged across the road into the long grass on the other side. Immediately they were to their knees in water held by the rough wells of saturated grass. Martha saw Alice, a long, distorted female shape, pallid in the grey rain, before she vanished. She heard a shout of exultation. Then she too ran straight onwards, stumbling through the wet, dragging waist-high grass that cut and stung, through the deep drench of the rain which came hard on her shoulders and breasts in a myriad hard, stinging needles. She heard that same shout of triumph come from her own lips, and she ran on blindly, her hair a sodden mat over her eyes, her arms held out in front to keep the whipping grass off her face. She almost ran into a gulf that opened under her feet. It was a pothole, gaping like a mouth, its red crumbling sides swimming with red water. Above it the long heavy grass almost met. Martha hesitated, then jumped straight in. A moment of repugnance, then she loosened deliciously in the warm rocking of the water. She stood to her knees in heavy mud, the red thick water closed below her shoulders. She looked up through the loose fronds of grass at the grey pit of the sky and heard a mutter of thunder. She was quite alone. A long swathe of grass had been beaten across the surface of the water, and around its stems trailed a jelly of frog spawn. A bright-green frog sat six inches from her face, watching her with direct round eyes and a palpitating throat. The rain drummed on the surface of the water in a fury of white prancing drops. Martha put out her hand towards the frog. It took a clumsy leap into the froth of water, and came up to cling with its small human hands to the ends of the grass, watching her anxiously. Martha allowed herself to be held upright by the mud, and lowered her hands through the resisting water to the hard dome of her stomach. There she felt the crouching infant, still moving tentatively around its prison, protected from the warm red water by half an inch of flesh. Her stomach stretched and contracted; and the frog swam slowly across the water, with slow, strong spasms of its legs, still watching Martha from one bright eye. In the jelly spawn were tiny dark dots of life. She could see a large snail tilting through the grass stems, its pale-brownish shell glistening and beautiful, the horned stalk of its head lifted high. Then, across the white-frothed surface of the pool, she saw an uncoiling in the wet mat of grass, and a lithe green snake moved its head this way and that, its small tongue flickering. It slid down over the red pulpy mud, and, clinging with its tail to a clutch of grass, it allowed itself to lie on the surface, swaying its vivid head just above the water.

Thunder shook the clouds again; and Martha looked up and felt a lightening of the dark enclosing grey. She could hear nothing but the drumming of the rain, see nothing but rods of shining rain; but certainly it was clearing. All of a sudden she was panic-stricken. She must get back to the car before the rain stopped and she was exposed and visible. She struggled out of the pool, while the snake pulled back on its spring of a tail away from the rocking water and flickered its tongue a little. The frog hopped into the middle of the pool with a splash. She was red to her armpits; and she stood still, while the rain came down and drove the red off her into the grass and she was clean and shining. Carrying her belly proudly, she walked blindly back to where she thought the car might be. At last she came onto the road, and saw with a fresh panic that there the rain was sending down its last big drops. The car was a hundred yards away. Suddenly she felt that there might be hidden eyes anywhere in the trees or the grass. She ducked low into the stinging grass, and ran crouching along its verges until the car was opposite. She dived across the road and into the front seat.

Almost at once Alice appeared, looking apprehensively up and down the road. She too flung herself over the exposed road and into the car. They looked at each other, holding their mats of sodden hair away from their faces. They went off into fits of laughter at the sight of their large, aggressive swollen stomachs, streaked purple and red, resting with such self-satisfaction on their slender white legs. But they were covered all over with minute red scratches from the grass, and fragments of wet grass clung to them. Outside the car the rain had stopped, and a wash of strong orange sunlight was coming fast over the low, beaten grass, which was already slowly lifting itself, frond by frond, as the heavy sparkling drops sprang off. The women took their petticoats and scrubbed themselves. In a moment they were dry enough to put on their clothes—in the nick of time—for a crowd of labourers came along the road, gave a curious glance to the two bedraggled young women, and then averted their eyes.

They drove back through heavy sultry sunlight which dragged shining clouds of steam from the earth. Everything was saturated; everything shook off water; the road was still running a foot of water.

"Those potholes are probably filthy," said Alice all at once, with a nervous laugh.

Martha was thinking the same. Back in the neat enclosed car, with her clean clothes about her, that plunge into the wet soiled veld seemed to her exaggerated and unpleasant. But there was no doubt they were both free and comfortable in their minds, their bodies felt relaxed and tired: they did not care now that their men preferred other company to theirs.

As soon as Martha was home she rushed to wash off the experience in a deep clean bath. She now hated to think of the mud of the vlei in her pores. "Not," she remarked to the crouching baby, half visible through a bright cloud of fresh steam, "that it makes any difference to you whether it's clean or dirty water outside, does it?" The child lurched, and the whole balance of Martha's stomach changed as it went into a new position. The skin on the lower slopes was breaking into purple weals; on the upper part of the thighs were red straining patches. Her breasts were heavy, bruised-looking. But the woman who only a few months before had enjoyed such ecstasies of self-worship had apparently died. She felt no more than a pang for the lost perfection. She traced the purple stretch marks with one finger, and felt something like satisfaction mingled with half-humorous appreciation of the ironies of her position. She reminded herself that she would never be perfect again. She told herself that never again would she look herself over, finding not one mark or faulty line on her body. It was gone, that brief flowering. It crossed her mind that perhaps, when it came to being old—at thirty or even sooner, for she was still proudly revolting away from the thought of being old—when it came to that moment of renunciation, perhaps she would feel no more than this amused ironical appreciation? But it was an intolerable thought, to be pushed indignantly away.

Later, Willie and Douglas came in. It was nearly midnight, and they were rather drunk. They played the role of humble apologetic husbands for a little; then Willie went off to Alice, and Douglas reverted at once to his usual self. "Sorry, Matty," he said nicely, "but I didn't want to miss it—I knew you wouldn't mind."

By now she did not; the fact that she didn't was making him uneasy, she saw. An old instinct came up, and she found herself grumbling humorously: who would be a woman, stuck at home, while the boys go off and have fun. He brightened as he listened. Then he came over to her and put his arms about her.

3

Weeks before the babies were born, the two women sat waiting, while each twinge, each shift of pressure, a pang down the thigh, caused them to alert: was that the beginning of the pains? For both women had scorned Dr. Stern's calculations, and had arrived at dates a week earlier than his.

"It might as well be born now," said Alice. "I've only got to give the finishing touches, so to speak." From which Martha understood that her feeling was shared, an incredulous relief that she had so far successfully sheltered the creature and it was now a human being. The fact that it might be born safely now was merely a step to believing that it would be.

But every morning they awoke to deserts of time. Both would turn over, to sleep away another hour or so. At least when they were unconscious time resumed its proper shape.

Then Martha's self-allotted period was up. A day passed, then another. She rushed in a frenzy of disappointment to the other extreme, and exclaimed that there was no reason at all why she should not have to wait another month. Alice reached her day and passed it. Both women slumped into an irritated depression which made them snap at each other; they found each other repulsive to look at, exasperatingly self-absorbed. After spending every day together for months, they withdrew into solitude, alone with their swollen discomfort like animals in a cave.

One morning Willie rang to say that Alice had started pains at twelve the night before, and now had a son. At this announcement, making the extraordinary adventure so banal, Martha fell into a state of sullen resignation. She drove out to see Alice, entering the nursing home with the feeling of a rightful inmate unjustly treated as a visitor, and found her seated bolt upright in bed, looking flushed, bright-eyed and very pretty, her black hair curled for the first time in months. She greeted Martha with casual triumph, and announced that nothing would ever induce her to have another baby, and if women knew what they were in for, they'd think twice. Martha heard this as if it were meant for someone else. If she had ever thought of childbirth as an ordeal, it was—she was convinced—because people were weak-minded enough to allow it to be one. She watched the gay and elated Alice with a hurt conviction that she was betraying her, Martha, by so completely repudiating the condition she had been in only yesterday. She might never have been clumsy, heavy, waddling, misshapen.

Martha went home in despair. She informed Douglas that she was convinced the child would not be born for at least another month. Douglas pointed out that Dr. Stern had predicted tomorrow. But Martha scorned Dr. Stern. The contrast between Alice, now two beings, and herself, still one, was too great. Having finally given up, or so it seemed, the intention ever to have a baby at all, she spent the evening sorting books that would provide the basis for a study course on economics. She was sitting on the floor surrounded by them, when there was a small stabbing pain in her vitals. She frowned with alert concentration; then told herself that she was sick of imagining that every twinge was the herald of the end. She was about to get undressed when she felt another. There was no doubt it was of a completely different quality from all the other stabs and twinges. She prowled cautiously about the room, admonishing the child to keep still, so that she might listen better to the activities of her muscles. The child was seething and striving like a wrestler. It was stilled momentarily on a third stab of pain. Martha was lifted on a wave of excitement; she cried out, "Hurray, this is it!" and, like some sort of savage creature, proceeded to dance in heavy lopsided triumph around the room. Never had she felt such a soaring elation as this.

Douglas, who was on the point of sleeping, awoke at once, enquired practically if she was sure, and began to dress. He was delighted. It was a moment of pure delight for both of them, being alone thus, the lights of the city dimming all around them, while they were setting off on such an adventure. Martha announced her intention of walking to the nursing home. Douglas's satisfaction in a wife who had such a carefree attiude was submerged in concern. She was put into the car, together with the case which had been packed for the last two months, and driven rapidly to the home. She had established, by the time she had reached there, that the pains were coming every five minutes; it troubled her that this was not what the book said was correct.

The nursing home was flooded with light. From some room down the corridor came a subdued chorus: several scores of babies were yelling there. A door opened; the orchestra swelled up into a cacophony of protest. It shut; the sound subsided again. A very young nurse came hurrying past. She saw Martha, exclaimed, "Oh, damn, here's another!" then suggested impatiently that Martha should sit down and wait. Martha sat obediently, while the distant orchestra swelled up and down as the door opened and shut; and nurses in uniform went hurrying past, carrying half a dozen bundled babies each, with the satisfied proficiency of waiters balancing several piles of plates at once. Finally a large, fat nurse went briskly past, wheeling a tea trolley with six bundles of baby on the top layer and six on the bottom. Martha saw a dozen twisted searching heads, a dozen open mouths nuzzling for absent breasts. Doors opened and shut. The sound of hungry crying diminished. All at once there was silence over the building; the unshaded lights glared down into an intensity of stillness, long white corridors gleaming emptily away in all directions.

At last there emerged an immensely tall, thin, springlike woman, a long white glazed pillar of efficiency, from which peered two calm, brisk dark eyes. She laid her hand on Martha's shoulder consideringly, rocked her slightly back and forth a little, then said, "Let me see, what's next? Oh, yes, of course, the forms." Martha and Douglas were invited into an office, and found themselves engaged in that indispensable preliminary to every vital activity—filling in forms in triplicate. Douglas complied efficiently; Martha felt disappointed that this adventure should be interrupted by such banalities. When it was over, Miss Galbind told Douglas that he must go away and ring up in the morning. "Be a good boy, don't ring up every five minutes— we're coping with the Easter rush." While Martha subdued her indignation that she was included in anything so ordinary as an Easter rush, Miss Galbind received Douglas's conscious grin with a relieved and even coquettish smile. Encouraged, she proceeded, "Why you young people restrict your fun and games to certain times of the year I can't think."

Douglas laughed. The two stood together, laughing; while Martha waited on one side. She had decided that she wanted Douglas to go;

she noted that while Miss Galbind was made ageless by the uniform
—she could not be more than thirty-five—it also enabled her to call
Douglas a good boy and to flirt with him.

Douglas squeezed her shoulder encouragingly, and said he would
go off and find Willie so that they might give it a bang. With this he
departed, rubbing his hands. A nurse came rushing down the long
brightly lit corridor, calling out for Miss Galbind, who again invited
Martha to sit down and wait awhile—"Unless there is any hurry,
dear?" She went off on her soundless springlike feet. Martha was
again left alone in the entrance hall. She walked up and down for
some half an hour, from the big door that stood open, like the door
of a sanctuary, showing the star-crowded sky and the distant glow
of the city across the ridge, to another door—large, white, closed, on
which was painted "No Admittance." She was listening to the rhythm
of her muscles. Five minutes to the second. She was extraordinarily
impatient; it seemed to her intolerable that nature should be thus
bound by the clock; all the needs of her being demanded that this
baby should be born forthwith, without any further nonsense. In her
mind, it was already born. A nurse who came past, holding her face
down tenderly to a white silent bundle, aroused in Martha a flood
of impatient tenderness. It was reassuring to see that busy young
woman in a moment of love snatched from the white-glaring, painfully shining, bare, heartless efficiency. Martha wondered if Alice
was asleep. She wished she might go and talk to her. She looked
longingly towards the door of her room, but did not dare go towards it.

At last another nurse came hurrying along, and said in a harassed
way that she was terribly sorry to leave Martha so long, but there
were five babies being born, there wasn't a bed to put Martha in just
now—would she mind filling in time by having a bath?

Martha was shown into a bathroom, and told to ring the bell if she
needed anything. She was undressing when a second nurse put her
head around the door and said hopefully that she could see from Martha's face that she was the sensible sort, not like some, who carried
on in a way you wouldn't believe. As she spoke, a door opened somewhere near, and Martha heard a woman screaming on a high note,
"Mother . . . Mother . . . Mother. . . ."

"Listen to that!" said the nurse, a girl of perhaps twenty, with a
round, pink, disapproving face surrounded by light wisps of shining
fair hair. "And she's only just started."

Martha understood, from the fresh face, and the voice, that the
girl was newly from England; she at once felt the appropriate reaction: What right has *she* to criticize *us!* Besides, she was such a baby,

thought Martha, from the immense superiority of her proud belly, her primed breasts.

The girl gave Martha another encouraging smile, and said that if everybody was as sensible as Martha, life would be much easier. With this she left her alone.

Martha flung her cotton smock off, with the triumphant thought that she would never have to wear it again. She heaved herself into the deep hot water and looked at her stomach. It was now almost square, mottled and streaked purple, glistening with strain. The baby was as tense as a knot; and Martha's every muscle was braced with the intention of hurrying the process. She lay stiff in the water, her eyes on the watch. Five minutes. Five minutes. Five minutes. The pains came steadily, like the strokes of a bell, and, each time, Martha's whole body tensed against them.

She lay there for nearly an hour; the water was getting cold. The woman across the corridor was moaning steadily. The noise was beginning to get on Martha's nerves; or rather, her intention that it should not succeeded in fermenting in her an angry irritation. Five minutes—Martha found herself exhausted, and lapsed into tired indifference. It was into this lull of absence that there shot a new intense pain, strong enough to make her catch her breath. She got quickly out of the bath, and put on the ugly calico garment provided for her. She caught a glimpse in the steam-dewed mirror of a fat, bedraggled shining-faced slut with a look of frowning concentration. She combed her hair, and made up her face. Thus armed, she walked out into a deserted corridor, still gleaming timelessly with regular white lights. Lines of shut doors stretched to either side. She walked to the right, and was met with a door marked "Labour Ward." She stood there, listening to the woman moaning inside. It opened abruptly, and a nurse came out, who, seeing Martha, pushed her gently to one side, and then ran fast down the corridor and out of sight. Martha walked back in the other direction and found herself in front of an open door. Inside were half a hundred white cradles, silent under a low shaded light, and at a long central table sat the fat nurse whom Martha had seen wheeling the loaded trolley. She exclaimed, "What are you doing here?" then glanced keenly at Martha's face, and said in a different voice, regulated to kindness, "You fed up with waiting?" She regarded Martha cautiously over a poised needle. Then she inched the needle into the white stuff she held, and pushed it away over the shining table. Everything in that room shone, even in the subdued light. The walls were very white, the floor black, with pools of shining light moving over it. The cradles were white, the nurse's glazed uniform was white. Piles of white napkins, white baby clothes, were stacked everywhere. Martha suddenly found herself gripping the table's edge.

The fat nurse walked unhurriedly towards her, laid a hand on her shoulder, and waited till she straightened up. "That's right," she approved.

Again there was a keen, impersonal glance. Martha felt there was something in her face which should not be there, for the nurse said, "Cheer up, you'll have got it out by this time tomorrow. Nearly over!"

Martha felt her lips tremble. She would have liked to fling herself on that fat shining bosom. The impulse annoyed her.

"Can I see Mrs. Burrell's baby?" she asked timidly.

The nurse hesitated, then stepped along the lines of cradles. At the foot of each was a name on a card. She nodded to Martha, who followed her, and bent over a tightly stretched white blanket, where showed the top of a small red head that was crinkled and covered with loose dark fuzz. A powerful stirring of tenderness came into Martha; she resisted it; she felt it to be dangerous to her intention of concentrating on getting her own baby born.

The fat nurse sat down again, pulled the white stuff towards her, and said, "You'd better get back to your room, you know."

"I haven't got one yet," said Martha forlornly.

"Dear me," said the nurse. "Well, we're so full—it's the war. There's a crop of babies suddenly that took us all by surprise." She was sewing steadily, her needle going with flashes of light through the white stuff.

Martha drifted out again, and was standing in the corridor when the pink English girl came hurrying along. "Oh, there you are, you shouldn't have got out of that bath without me, you know," she reproved. "The doctor wants to see you."

Martha followed the pink nurse, who led her into another room marked "Labour Ward," and said, "You'll just have to make the best of this. There's nowhere else to put you till morning."

It was another gleaming white room, this time with the lights bulging down from the ceiling like eyeballs. There was nothing in it but trolleys full of sharp instruments, and two very high, very narrow white beds.

"Lie down," said the nurse, sharp with impatience.

Martha climbed with difficulty onto one of the high narrow beds, and almost at once Dr. Stern came in.

"Well, Mrs. Knowell? You girls all insist on having your babies in the small hours." She knew him well enough by now to understand that he had said this many times before. Once again she submitted to those skilled impersonal hands, while he remarked that it was a good time of the year for having babies, she had done well to arrange things thus. He then removed his hands, said "Fine, fine," and turned to depart. Martha, who had half believed that this was nearly over, demanded how long it would be; at which he remarked absorbedly, on his way out, that she must be a good girl, and be patient. The door swung silently shut behind him, and she was alone.

For some time she lay stiff on the very narrow slope of the bed, and waited. In this position, it seemed that the pains were worse. Or rather, that she could not command herself as well. She climbed down, and walked up and down the deserted room. Now it was every four minutes, and she was doubled up with them, shutting her teeth against the desire to groan, cautiously unfolding herself again. She noticed she was wet with sweat. It was very hot in the room. She went to the window and looked out. Across the faintly moonlit veld, the glow from the city burned steadily, swallowing a glitter of stars. The stars vanished in another hot wave of pain. This time she found herself crouching on the floor, astonished and indignant at the violence of it. The pain had swallowed *her* up; and dismay at having lost guard caused her to return to the bed, where she might keep her attention on the process, keep that sentinel alert against the dark engulfing sea. Tight, stiff, cautious, she felt the baby knot and propel itself down; it recoiled and slackened, and she with it. The pain had changed. She could mark the point at which, just as it had abruptly changed its quality a couple of hours before in the bath, so now it ground into a new gear, as it were. It gripped first her back, then her stomach, then it was as if she and the baby were being wrung out together by a pair of enormous steel hands. But still she kept that small place in her brain alive and watchful. She would *not* give in. She lay like a tight spring, with half her attention given to not rolling off the bed, or table—which was so narrow she could not have turned on it —and concentrated.

The baby-faced nurse hurried in, and enquired, "How are you doing?" And hurried out again. Martha, engulfed in a pain, most passionately resented that uncommitted virgin with her determination not to be disturbed by suffering. But it was to the practical cool little voice that she was submitted; and when, at some indeterminate time later, the nurse came back, to say that Martha was being a good girl, and in the morning she would have a comfortable bed, she was able to achieve a humorous gasp that she wouldn't mind a comfortable bed now.

"Well, what can we do?" demanded the pink girl. "We can't help it if all the babies decide to get born at once, can we?" She vanished again, remarking, "We've got three of them out, that's something. Let's pray no more of you come in tonight."

Martha no longer had the energy to achieve a mild amusement. The small lit place in her brain was dimming most alarmingly with the pains. Every time, the light nearly went out; always, it flickered precariously and shone up again. Martha noted that something new was happening to time. The watch that lay six inches from her nose on her crooked arm said the pains were punctual at two minutes. But from the moment that the warning hot wave of pain swept up her back, she entered a place where there was no time at all. An agony so unbelievable gripped her that her astounded and protesting mind cried out it was impossible such pain should be. It was a pain so violent that it was no longer pain, but a condition of being. Every particle of flesh shrieked out, while the wave spurted like an electric current from somewhere in her backbone and went through her in shock after shock. The wave receded, however, just as she had decided she would disintegrate under it; and then she felt the fist that gripped her slowly loosen. Through the sweat in her eyes she saw that ten seconds had passed; she went limp, into a state of perfect painlessness, an exquisite exhaustion in which the mere idea of pain seemed impossible—it was impossible that it could recur again. And as soon as the slow flush of sensation began, the condition of painlessness seemed as impossible as the pain had seemed only a few moments before. They were two states of being, utterly disconnected, without a bridge, and Martha found herself in a condition of anxious but exasperated anger that she could *not* remember the agony fifteen seconds after it had ended. She was lying now almost naked, her great tight knotted belly sticking up in a purple lump, watching with fascination how it contracted and strained, while she kept alert the determination not to lose control of the process; while she was lit with curiosity as to the strange vagaries of time and, above all, and increasingly, almost to the point of weeping fury, that all her concentration, all her self-consciousness, could not succeed in creating the state of either pain or painlessness while its opposite was in her. It was a complete failure of her, the free spirit: how was it possible not to remember something that had passed ten seconds before, and would recur so soon? The anger at her failure was strong enough nearly, but not quite, to quench that part of her mind which must stay alert. She sobered herself. When the wave of pain had receded, and she lay spent, she was grimly flogging her mind to *imagine* the quality of the pain that had just gone. Impossible. And when she was writhing in the grip of the giant fist, she was gasping with determination to *imagine* no pain. She could not. With all her determination, she could not. There were two Marthas, and there was nothing to bridge them. Failure. Complete failure. She was helpless with rage. She heard the pain-gripped Martha cry out, "Oh, God, oh, God!" and she was curious at the ancient being in her that cried out to God. Damned liar, coward, idiot! said Martha to herself from across the gulf. It only needs that you should call out "Mother!" And behold, Martha, that free spirit, understood from the exquisite shore of complete, empty non-sensation that she had been groaning out "Mother, Mother, Mother!" Without a flicker of feeling in any part of her body, she felt the tears of failure roll down her face; and looked up through them to see the pink nurse looking down at her with unmistakable disappointment.

"Well, dear," said the girl disapprovingly, "it's no good carrying on like that *yet*." Her plump little hands, tightly sealed in pink rubber, went plunging into Martha's body. "Not nearly yet, you know," she remarked, regarding Martha while she grunted and rolled in another pain. "And anyway," heard Martha, the young bright voice coming distorted through hot agony, "we've got to get this other baby born before we can attend to you. Do you think you could hold it a bit?"

Martha saw the door open, and a stretcher wheeled in. Suddenly the room was filled with people. She saw a woman, similarly grotesque, inhuman, grunting, being rolled over onto the other narrow high table, while Dr. Stern and a couple of nurses stood about with a look of intent concentration. Then the white screens went up and hid them. Martha looked away, and submitted to another trial. The woman on the other table seemed to be having pains about every half minute; what Martha's determination could not achieve, her nerves could: she suffered in her flesh that other woman's pains, like a counterpoint, a faint but faithful echo of her own, in jarring opposite to her own rhythm. Suddenly the sounds of striving flesh ceased, a faint smell of chloroform was in the air; Martha found herself avidly breathing it in. Instruments clinked; she heard Dr. Stern's voice giving orders; she heard the stiff rustle of starch. There was a gasp, and a baby started crying.

"For God's sake," nagged Martha to her child, "get yourself out of there quickly." The child, however, was crouched waiting for the next spring forward; and Martha watched the flesh shrink and harden in the new contraction. This time she heard herself give a shriek. She no longer cared at all. All she fought for was to drag herself as soon as possible out of each gulf, not to give in more than she had to. A long time passed; she rolled her eyes to the window and saw that it showed grey light; a single white star hung quivering; it faded; a pink flush crept up the sky. She heard the sound of a wet brush on a floor. It was a native woman, on her knees with a scrubbing brush. The screens had gone from the other white bed. Martha tensed and groaned, and the native woman raised her head, looked over, and smiled encouragement. There was no one else in the room. Martha could hear the cacophony of screaming babies from the other end of the building.

The native woman gave a quick look into the passage, and then came over to Martha. She was young, her dark face polished and smiling. She wore a neat white cloth on her head. She laid her wet dirty hand on Martha's striving stomach. "Bad," she said, in her rich voice. "Bad. Bad." As a fresh pain came, she said, "Let the baby come, let the baby come, let the baby come." It was a croon, an old nurse's song. Martha trembled with exhaustion, and tensed herself, but the woman smiled down and sang, "Yes, missus, yes, let it come, let it come."

Martha let the cold knot of determination loosen, she let herself go, she let her mind go dark into the pain.

"That's right, missus, that's right, that's right."

Suddenly the hand was withdrawn, leaving a cold wetness on her stomach. Martha looked, and saw that the native woman was on her knees with the scrubbing brush, and the young pink nurse stood beside her, looking suspiciously at the scrubbing woman. The brush was going slosh, slosh, wetly and regularly over the floor. Martha listened to the sound as if it were the pulse of her own nature, and did not listen as the pink nurse lifted her legs, levered them energetically up and down, and said, "That's the stuff, push!" Later, Martha heard the bright voice calling from the door, "Yes, doctor, she's ripe!" The room was full of people again. She was sucking in chloroform like an addict, and no longer even remembered that she had been determined to see the child born.

When her eyes cleared, she caught a glimpse of Dr. Stern holding up a naked pallid infant, its dark hair plastered wet in streaks to its head, mouthing frustratedly at the air. Martha momentarily lost consciousness again, and emerged, feeling it must be years later, to see Dr. Stern, in the same position, still holding the white baby, which looked rather like a forked parsnip and was making strangled, grumbling gasps. Two nurses were watching him. They looked triumphant and pleased. This humanity comforted Martha. She heard one say, "A lovely little girl, isn't she?" Then the pink nurse bent over her and began lifting handfuls of Martha's now slack stomach, and squeezing it like oranges. Martha shrieked, with the intention of being heard.

"Oh, drat it," said the nurse; and the dome of white chloroform came down again over Martha's face.

This time her eyes opened on a scene of white beds, and faces leaning against white pillows. After a time, she realized that she was pillowed at last in comfort. Five other women were in the beds. Excitement flooded her, and she attempted to sit up. The lower part of her body announced that it was bruised and sore, and did not want to move. Martha raised herself on her hands and the woman next to her asked how she felt. Martha was struck by the lazy self-absorption of that voice. She said she felt fine, and the woman nodded. But her eyes were on the door. It opened, and the pink nurse entered with five babies balanced all over her arms. They were yelling, with hungry open mouths. The babies were plopped neatly one after another onto the beds, and gathered in by the waiting mothers. The pink nurse, empty-armed, arrived at Martha's bed, and enquired, "Well, how are you?"

"Where's my baby?" asked Martha anxiously.

"She's having a nice rest," said the nurse, already on her way out.

"But I haven't seen her yet," said Martha, weak tears behind her lids.

"You don't want to disturb her, do you?" said the nurse disapprovingly.

The door shut. The woman, whose long full breast sloped already into the baby's mouth, looked up and said, "You'd better do as they want, dear. It saves trouble. They've got their own ideas."

Martha, cheated and empty, lay and watched the other women suckle their babies. It was intolerable that after nine months of close companionship with the creature, now announced as a girl, she might not even make its acquaintance. There was something impossible in the idea that yesterday the child had been folded in her flesh and it now lay rooms away, washed and clothed, in a cradle with its name on it. It made her uneasy; she wanted to see it—she even felt irrationally that the child might have died at birth and they were lying to her.

Then she remembered the moment when she had seen it lifted, mouthing and struggling for air, and winced suddenly with remembered pain. She had entered on a new state. The shadow of the pain she had felt, though not the terrible intensity of it, threatened her. She must not think of it, as otherwise the bruised flesh of her stomach began to contract in remembered waves of pain. Also, the absolute peace of those moments between the pains had gone. She was sore and aching, and her body was gripped tight in a stiff roll of stuff, under which she could feel the slack flesh folded together.

The babies lapsed into content all round her, and she watched them being taken away. The elation she felt, the achievement, slackened into disappointment.

When Douglas came in that afternoon, beaming, rubbing his hands with pride, smelling strongly of beer, her intention to appeal to him vanished in dislike. He announced with pride that he and Willie had been giving it a bang with the boys all night, he had not been to bed, he had rung up the home at half-hour intervals until Miss Galbind had told him he was a nuisance. He said, too, that the baby was fine.

"I haven't seen her," said Martha faintly.

"Oh, well, they know best," he said.

At this moment Mrs. Quest entered, tremulous with emotion, and said that the baby was beautiful, but that she was quite sure the nurses had no idea how to treat a new baby; she had a good idea to go to the matron. At this Martha reacted with the announcement that the nursing-home people certainly knew what they were doing.

When Douglas and Mrs. Quest left, Martha lay and quivered with anger and frustration. It was late afternoon. For the third time she saw the white bundles brought in and handed to the mothers, while she lay watching.

Late that evening, after the babies had been fed for the last time, Miss Galbind briskly entered and asked if everyone was happy, and Martha enquired when she could see her baby.

"You want to see her, do you?" enquired Miss Galbind reasonably. "Oh, well, I suppose you may as well." She departed, having shed friendly good nights around the room; and Martha raised herself, waiting for the moment.

But it seemed Miss Galbind was in no hurry; half an hour crawled by, while Martha watched the door. At last the pink nurse entered, with a tight white bundle, and deposited it carelessly on the bed. "There's your daughter," she announced. "Five minutes, now."

Under the jealous inspection of the pink nurse, Martha turned back the flap of blanket, and saw a tiny flushed sleeping face. Again curiosity flooded over into a passionate protective tenderness, and she held the baby close; but the nurse, restlessly hovering at the side of the bed, decided it was enough.

"Now, then," she announced, "you'll have enough of her in the next few months, I bet!" And with this she deftly removed the bundle, and went out with it, switching off the lights.

The other five women had already laid themselves down for the night. Martha, who to her fury once again discovered that she wanted only to cry, looked around for support. She caught the eye of the woman in the next bed, who said kindly, "It's no good getting upset. They'll let you have her in the morning, I expect." She turned herself carefully onto her side, and shut her eyes, in an obvious determination to submit to the routine and get it over. She remarked, with closed eyes, "This is my third. I always say I'll never come here again, but it's easier on the whole. You can do what you like when you get home, that's a comfort." She began breathing deeply.

Martha lay tensely awake. She heard a car drive up: another baby was due to be born; but already the condition of waiting for a baby to be born seemed far behind. She felt a calm superiority over the women who still had to go through with it. But when, later, doors opened and shut, feet hurried, and a woman began moaning down the passage, she had to bury her head in the pillow, because each moan seemed to drag a wave of pain out of her own stomach. She could not sleep. Excitement was beating through her. She was longing for the morning—perhaps then she might be allowed to feed the baby. The women slept heavily all around her, reminding her, with their heavy breathing, of cows on a dark hillside. But her mind was at the other end of the building, in the room full of babies. She watched the stars move across the windows, and wished they might hurry, hurry, hurry to the dawn. Then a baby began crying, a faint persistent wail, and soon they were all crying. The women began stirring and listening in their beds.

The woman in the next bed said in a resigned voice, "Well, they're as tough as anything, that's a comfort." She was lying tense; Martha saw she was crying. This upset her—the mother of three, calmly resigned, had given her strength to bear her own childish impatiences.

"What's the matter?" asked Martha anxiously. Then: "Are the babies hungry?"

The woman gave a weak laugh through her tears, and said, "They can't be hungry till six. It's against the rules." Then she turned herself over with another cautious heave, and remarked, "I always cry like a leaking tap for weeks after I have a baby. Don't take any notice."

For a while Martha saw how the women turned and tossed, listening; then the chorus of crying dimmed and they slept again. Martha heard the cocks crow, and then again. She could see the Seven Sisters, a faint clustering glow over a spiring black gum tree. The babies began to scream again. It was nearly dawn. The sky was lightening. The women sat up, blinking, as the lights came on and a bright gay voice shouted, "Get ready, girls." It was morning, though the stars were shining outside. It was half past four.

"What's funny is this," said the woman next to Martha, with tolerant good nature, "it's supposed to be six, but even the nurses can't stick it out, so they stretch it a bit."

Half an hour passed. "My breasts are dripping," said one woman. "Every morning my bed's flooded," said another. Martha was helpless with envy. Her breasts were still limp.

This time six small yelling bundles came in on a trolley. Martha received her daughter with trembling eagerness. The baby was crying; it looked, to Martha, distressed, hot and miserable. She took the little thing, and held the yelling round mouth to her nipple. It moved in sudden desperate silence this way and that, eyes showing anxious gleams of blue, and then—miracle!—the lips fastened and began to suck. Strong waves of suction passed through Martha and into her womb with contractions of pain. She did not expect this, and moved uncomfortably, gripping herself against it. The baby sucked steadily, small slits of hazy blue showing in the tiny red face. Martha daringly undid the tight roll, and the infant fell loosely into the shape of a baby, so that Martha was able to hold it to herself comfortably, instead of in the shape of a papoose. She moved it over to the other breast, admonishing both to be quick and supply milk.

Miss Galbind came springing silently in, and stood watchfully over Martha. "All right," she announced, after a minute, "she's a good sucker." With this she removed the child, rolled it again into the papoose of white blanket, and said, "That's enough for a start." She went out, the baby tucked under her arm like a long parcel sticking out behind.

"Don't worry," said the woman in the next bed, giving Martha an amused look. "You can do anything to a baby, even bounce it." Martha therefore lay back and refused to worry. She had accepted this woman as a guide; she was able to because she disliked the discipline as Martha did, and yet could dismiss it all as another of those unaccountable bureaucratic stupidities thought up to plague honest females—that was her attitude. Martha found the tolerant matron—she was perhaps thirty—frightening because she had three children and was so satisfied to be a maternal housewife, but at the same time inexpressibly comforting. Through her, Martha was accepted into this community of women, all so much older than herself, all absorbed into the rhythm of eating, sleeping and nursing.

When Mrs. Quest and Douglas entered that afternoon, it was as if foreigners had come from a strange country. A gay message from Alice in the next room meant more than Douglas's talk of parties at the Club; and Mrs. Quest's announcement that it was absurd to feed babies to the clock found Martha calmly determined that everything was as it should be.

Next morning, when she woke, her breasts were heavy, and she received the baby with pride that she had milk for her. She was now in a state of settled calm elation, she could not conceive that she had ever imagined anything but a girl child, or a child in the slightest way different from this one. A faint warning voice from the well of fatality did remark that a girl child was in the direct line of matriarchy she so feared, but it left her indifferent. This tiny, delightful creature, with its exquisite hands, its small round red face, cuddled with such perfect trust to Martha that she could not believe she could be anything but good for it, and to it.

She was now very uncomfortable with the pressure of the milk. Her breasts were swollen like two full skins attached to her body. Her determination, fed by the book, that it was her duty to femininity to preserve the shape of them fell before the surging plenty nature offered. In the night she woke, hearing the yelling roomful of babies down the corridor, and her breasts swelled and stung in answer; and she found her sides wet with useless milk. In the morning, the women would sit up in bed, helplessly laughing, as they supported their enormous breasts with their hands and let the milk spurt away in streams into the cloth that had bound them. And the babies, who had been restless and hungry for several hours, would come fighting to the engorged breasts and choke there. The faint sweet smell of milk filled the women's nostrils all day.

Soon Martha found herself light and easy in bed; slipping her hands down under the tight hard cloth over her stomach, she pulled in the muscles and felt them respond, a hard wall under the rolls of fat. Then the woman in the next bed announced to her doctor that five days in this factory was enough. She climbed unsteadily to her feet, and went. Martha noticed with a pang of apprehension that this woman, who in her bed had seemed so light and easy, on her feet was heavy and shapeless—a veritable wet nurse of a female. She missed her when she had gone. They put into her bed a girl having her first baby with precisely Martha's look of determined cheerfulness, under which showed anxiety. It upset Martha, that hard gaiety. Then Alice came to see her from the next room; and she saw her as not at all radiant and pretty, as she had been on the first morning after the birth, but pale, tired, bedraggled, with a loose stomach and full clumsy hips; Alice was unhappy. Her helpless giggle rang out repeatedly as she complained that she couldn't stick these damned women in uniform—the Lord help her, she said with a shocked smile; if she thought she had been as inhumanly efficient as that when she was a nurse, she'd hang herself. It was clear that she felt she had.

She complained they were never left in peace for half an hour together. If it wasn't cups of tea or bedpans, it was visitors, babies, or having to wash, she said; she couldn't sleep at night for listening for the babies crying. She burst into tears herself, and Miss Galbind, entering hastily, said, "Now, really, Mrs. Burrell! Surely you should know better than that!" Alice was led away, sobbing.

Martha was quite shocked at this collapse. The next day, however, she found herself heavy, languid, tired; the wings of elation had folded under her. She thought that when she got home she would be ugly and shapeless; she would be bound for months and months of servitude, without any escape from it; she found herself regarding the infant Caroline with a detached scrutiny that resulted in the faint, bored thought that this was a baby like any other, of no interest to anybody, not even herself. She would certainly grow up to be like these women about her, a dull housewife with no purpose in life but to continue the cycle of procreation. Martha found herself disliking the child, hating her swollen breasts, and filled with disgust at the way milk flowed over her a dozen times a day like a tide. She found herself no longer seated up in bed, bright and animated, chatting to Douglas about the parties, questioning him about what So-and-so had said, but lying flat on her back with no desire ever to sit up again.

Miss Galbind came in to ask how she did, and she was astounded to find herself in tears. But it seemed Miss Galbind found nothing surprising in this.

"It's the reaction, dear," she explained; and Martha, who could never feel anything but resentment at the idea that her emotions might be the result of predictable chemical processes in her body, said, "I don't care a damn what it is, but I wish I'd never had a baby at all."

Miss Galbind listened and clicked her tongue, clearly because she felt it might do Martha good to be disapproved of. Martha found that her things were being collected together, and she was invited to get out of bed and walk next door. Miss Galbind said it would be nice for Martha and her friend Mrs. Burrell to be together and cheer each other up.

Martha found that she and Alice had been put in a kind of enclosed verandah with glass around three sides. The sun came streaming into the white shining place. Alice lay in bed on her back, looking up at the ceiling. She rolled her eyes towards Martha, and remarked indifferently, "Oh, so it's you."

"It looks like it," said Martha, grimly.

Miss Galbind looked from one to the other, and remarked, "You'll both feel better in a couple of days."

Martha got into the new bed and lay flat. From depths of utter indifference to life, the two women lay and looked at a ceiling whose flat emptiness seemed to mirror their condition.

After some time Alice remarked, with a shocked giggle, "I hate that damned brat, and that's the truth."

"So do I," said Martha at once.

A pause. Then Alice let out a small resigned, chuckle, as a suggestion that she might, at some future time, be prepared to find her present mood ridiculous.

Martha said, "We might just as well be a couple of cows."

Into this shared misery suddenly entered Stella, with a cheerful matronly smile, bearing flowers, her plump body graceful even now in its folds of dark silk. Martha looked at her, and noticed that her reaction to the sight of Stella's protuberant stomach was one of repugnance; Stella was as distasteful to her as poor Caroline now was.

Stella looked at the two women and stopped abruptly. "What on earth is wrong with you? It's the first day they'd let me in, I've been every day to ask."

"It's no good coming to see us," remarked Alice flatly. "We both wish we were dead."

Stella gave them a shocked look, then sat midway between them, as if she were distributing her friendship equally.

"What's the matter? The boys said you were doing fine, and I've seen your babies. They're lovely. I do wish I'd started when you did, I'd have got it over by now." She was looking anxiously from one to the other; and recognition of duty to a fellow woman stirred in Alice and Martha simultaneously: they aroused themselves and thanked her for the beautiful flowers she had brought.

"Did you have an awful time in labour?" she asked, with bright eyes.

Alice said indifferently, "Oh—mine just fell out."

Martha said honestly, for now, at this wide distance of five days, she could barely remember the experience, "There's nothing to it."

After a pause Stella said jealously that Dr. Stern said she had narrow hips. Since there was only the disapproving silence that she was used to from these two unaccountable women, and which confused her, she went on to demand practically, "If it's easy as all that, why are you going on like this? And look at your hair!" she added disapprovingly. "You look awful, both of you."

Almost, Martha and Alice were stirred into their duty to be attractive at all costs. But they subsided again into lethargy. Quite soon, Stella, flushed with shocked disappointment, got up and said that if *she* had got it over and done with, they wouldn't find her behaving like this! "It's not nice for your husbands," she concluded on the familiar note, which succeeded only in eliciting a faint giggle from Alice and an exasperated sigh from Martha.

She was on the point of leaving, when both women felt guilty, and Alice spoke for them both when she raised herself in bed and said appealingly, "Now, look here, Stella, don't take any notice. We're in a bad mood."

Stella brightened, glanced gratefully towards them both, and left radiant with happy maternity.

They slumped back into the comfort of their beds.

"Poor Stella," remarked Alice. "Little does she know." Then she giggled, and suddenly burst into tears. She cried out that she wished she had never got married, she knew now that she had never loved Willie at all; she couldn't understand how she had been so crazy as to tie herself down to being nothing but a piece of livestock to be stuffed three times a week, and then swollen like dropsy, and then a cow streaming with milk, and her breasts were so sore she couldn't bear it. "Look at these silly bitches," she said, meaning the nurses, "all they have to think about is boy friends, and going out, and earning money and having nice clothes—they've got some sense, at least." Half crying, half laughing, she continued until the babies were brought in. Then she stopped herself, and fed her child with an air of tired endurance.

But later that afternoon Martha saw that she was being bad-tempered with Willie, and felt envious, because this was evidence of more emotional energy than she could command. Next morning, when the stars were extinguished as the electric light came plunging on, she noted that Alice immediately shot up in bed, then sat regarding her chest, which was padded tight in wads of wool, with a grim smile. She stripped off the wool, exposed the two knotted swollen breasts, and then remarked cheerfully, "Oh, well, who cares?" She combed her black hair, applied lipstick, and announced to Martha as she lit a cigarette that life wasn't as bad as she had thought.

From which Martha deduced that by the next day she, too, might be over "the reaction." And so it proved.

But in her gay competence of the next morning, she knew that she was left with a certain uneasiness. Nature, that great mother, might have done better, she felt. To remove the veil of illusion, to allow the sustaining conviction of necessity to fail, even for a moment, must leave her female children always helpless against a fear that it might happen again, and with as little warning.

4

On the same afternoon, Alice and Martha stood on the steps of the nursing home, expelled from the community of women back into ordinary life, each carrying a white bundle of baby, each clinging tightly to her husband's arm.

Willie remarked that there were dozens of aunts and so on waiting to welcome Alice home. She murmured, "Oh, God!" and emitted her high helpless giggle, looking enquiringly towards Martha for support; for Douglas had just told Martha that she must expect a similar ordeal. That it would be an ordeal was an axiom with them all.

Martha was just about to get into the car, when another drew up. She saw an immensely large young woman, surrounded by older women, go towards the building. She recognized Marnie Van Rensberg. She ran after her, and stopped her. At first Marnie did not seem to recognize Martha. Then she and her mother exclaimed and kissed her. Mrs. Van Rensberg was in black—black lace hat, black crepe, an enormous black bag stuffed with knitting. Marnie was as broad as a bed, and smocked in pink roses. Her honest, happy face beamed under crimped fair hair.

"You've got a lovely baby, Matty," she said enthusiastically; and for a moment Caroline passed from one to another of the attendant sisters and aunts. Then Marnie seemed to stiffen; she clutched her mother's arm for a few seconds, then she cried out, "Oh, Mom!"

"Quick," said Mrs. Van Rensberg. She hurried Marnie into the home, both women sending warm smiles back towards Martha as they went, Marnie's, however, rather strained. The flock of women entered the building; and were received by Miss Galbind. A young man, stiff in his Sunday suit, stood on the steps. Presumably the husband. He passed his hand nervously over his plastered-down hair, and went in. The steps were empty.

Martha went back to the car. Douglas said that they had all agreed it would do the girls good to drop in for a drink at the Club before going home. The Burrells' car was already departing down the avenue of frangipanis. Alice was turning to wave and smile back at Martha. Thus had they so often set off on one of those long nights of dancing. But it was not the same.

"Perhaps we could go to the Club after Caroline's asleep?" suggested Martha.

But Douglas said, "No, the boys want to give the kids the once-over. Just for a minute—it'll do you good after being cooped up for so long."

They arrived therefore on the verandah of the Club among the bare brown legs and the beer glasses, and were vociferously welcomed. Both babies had been celebrated continuously for some days now; their actual appearance was felt, at least by the mothers, to be an anticlimax. After a few minutes Martha's look at Alice received support for she rose, slightly unsteady, and said that it was time the little so-and-so was fed. Martha made a similarly cheerful remark; for a few minutes the two women stood clutching their babies amid a knot of admiring girls, and then the young couples separated to go home.

Next morning both were visited by the nurse appointed by the authorities for this purpose, Sister Doll, armed with pamphlets, charts, scales and an insistence that to "pick up" a crying child, or to feed it five minutes before the clock said it should be fed, would be —her tone, shocked and grave, conveyed it—no less than a crime against nature. Alice and Martha exchanged ribald scorn at Sister Doll over the telephone, but the fact was that their lives were now regulated by her weekly visits, periods which were broken not into days and nights, but into shorter intervals bound by the clock striking six, ten, two, six, ten.

They would sit, both tense in every nerve, in their separate flats, with their eyes on the clock, their breasts tingling with milk, while the infants screamed in their cradles for an hour, two hours, three hours—until the second hand touched the hour, and they might spring up and lift the child to be fed. The strain of it was something to be acknowledged only in half-humorous grumbling remarks over the telephone.

Alice, much weaker clay than Martha, broke first. She rang up one morning to announce, in the hushed shocked tones of one who is prepared to take the burden of a sin on herself, that she had fed the child in the night. Martha was silent and censorious.

Martha would lie awake for hours, listening to Caroline crying, smoking cigarette after cigarette, and responding gaily to Douglas's admonitions that she should bear up—for he sometimes woke. The most she would do was to feed the child a few spoonfuls of water, as the nursing home and Sister Doll recommended, in the hopes that it might be deceived into thinking itself fed. Those nights were a torture. She could not understand why the crying should so work on her nerves. Caroline had only to stir and let out a single cry, for Martha to spring tinglingly awake. She tried to pretend it was a child belonging to some other woman; after all, the baby through the wall in the next flat cried often, and Martha did not hear it. But it was good for Caroline to cry, Sister Doll said so; and her character would be ruined for life if Martha was to give in.

After a few days Alice—now almost hostile in her determination to break the taboos—rang up to say briefly to hell with everyone, she was putting her son on the bottle, she couldn't stand it any longer. Martha received this too with polite disapproval.

But now she began to worry that her own milk was getting less. She worried all through the day, listening, as it were, to the activities of her breasts as she had listened to the movements of Caroline in her body. By four every afternoon, with Caroline already screaming for food, she would anxiously hold her breasts, still limp and half empty; she would even, desperate with worry, lift the baby from her crib half an hour before the clock allowed, with an instinctive feeling that the warmth of the little thing against her might encourage the flow of milk.

Then Sister Doll weighed the child and found that she had achieved half an ounce of flesh less than was proper. Martha was quite frantic, and began drinking milk herself, pints of it, and horrid preparations of baked flour which were supposed to assist the process. And still Caroline cried, and Martha's nerves vibrated in extraordinary response, as if the child were connected to her flesh by innumerable invisible fibres. That energetic, angry wail seemed to scrape direct on her backbone like a sharp fiddle on a bone. She would hang over the crib, hands locked behind her back to prevent them from reaching out to the child, watching the scarlet little face moving openmouthed from side to side to find the breast, while her heart beat with anxious pity.

She would not, however, weaken like that traitor Alice, who had routed Sister Doll, and fed her child not only from the bottle, but regularly in the middle of the night, a practice which was bound to ruin its stomach. "Oh, well, dear," said Alice forbearingly, to Martha's disapproval, "I suppose you are right, but I just couldn't stick it, that's all."

And Martha looked secretly at the small Richard, and agreed that he seemed to be surviving under the treatment remarkably well.

From one day to the next, Martha changed front. Caroline let the breasts go without protest. She was taking the bottle inside twenty-four hours, and Martha had tied up her suffering breasts with linen—their work was over.

Peace at last.

Mrs. Quest looked at Caroline with an odd little smile, and then remarked with the bright guilty laugh in which was the note of triumph that always stung Martha, "I suppose you've been starving her as I starved you."

And now Martha was free again, she proceeded to starve herself. By dint of literally not eating anything, she had lost twenty pounds at the end of six weeks. Better, she had regained that slimness which had been hers before she had married. Looking incredulously into the mirror—for she never looked into one without preparing to be surprised at what she might see there—she confronted a slight, firm young woman with high breasts, a determined mouth, and tawny-coloured hair in rough curls all over her head.

She was herself, though a new self; and Caroline, as the rules said she ought to be, was content to take milk from bottles at stated hours. The nights were calm. Martha was lifting her head to look about her, with the burden of maternity properly regulated and herself free to see what life might have to offer, when authority spoke again: all of Douglas's generation were whisked into uniform and into a camp just outside the city. It was said they might train there for some months; that was the rumour. Martha was adjusting herself to a life which would receive a husband released for afternoons or an occasional weekend, when a fresh surge of rumours settled into a decision.

All the men were to be sent at once up north. At one stroke, two evenings from now, several hundred of them, the junior civil servants, administrators and executives, the clerks and the businessmen and the lawyers—that firm masculine cement that held the community safe and steady—would be sent away. After the long months of waiting for precisely this moment, of eagerness held in check but fed steadily by the phrases, the ritual dancing and drinking, it was as if a bell had struck, but on the wrong note. For, while it was understood that the boys would be given a bang of a send-off, and the clubs and the dance halls dedicated themselves for the occasion, it was observable that there was a curious look of uncertainty, even anticlimax, on faces hitherto lit by wild excitement.

Late that last evening, in the crowded gilded halls of McGrath's Hotel, while the band played from its bower of ferns, Binkie Maynard, his fat body encased in tight khaki, sat at the head of a long packed table, fingering a glass, his heavy reddened face solemn with thought.

"I don't get it," he observed, frowning. "*They* must know something we don't." Heads nodded around the table; to relinquish authority to *them* would come easily to none of these men. "I mean to say, what's the good of just getting us together and sending us off? Where are we going to be trained? It's not good enough, they don't tell us anything."

"It's wartime, kid," observed Maisie, who sat, plump and fair, beside him, smiling maternally.

"Well, but all the same. They're pushing us around. I'm not going to fight a parcel of . . ." But complete lack of information made it impossible to finish. "I mean to say, I'm all for fighting the Huns—" He paused; the words had given off the wrong echo. "The Jerries, I mean," he amended carefully. "They've got to be put in their place. They want to take our colonies away, that's all they're after. But there's the Wops—they're not even worth fighing, as far as I can see."

There was a pause. The fifty people listening waited hopefully for that one word from the pastor of their days of youth which would allow them with good grace to board that train the next day. The violins, which had been sobbing through the changes of "Black Eyes," stopped, were joined by a drum, and swung into "Run, Rabbit, Run." That song, whose impertinent, cocky mood expressed a Britain whose vigour was still in mortgage, sounded an alien note here. Half the table took it up; it petered out weakly.

"It's all very well," concluded Binkie indignantly, his black locks untidy over flushed civilian brows, his buttons undone, his shoulder tab crooked—Maisie reached over to straighten it—"it's all very well, but somebody's messed something up, that's what I think." Instantaneous agreement. It was the anguished wail of the administrator who must become a pawn, the administrator who has no reason to have much faith in the processes of government.

"What I mean to say," pursued Binkie with difficulty, "it's not fair!"

The band had exhausted "Run, Rabbit, Run," and offered "The Siegfried Line." It was no good—the mood was wrong. The violins retired a little, the drums and saxophones came forward and stood looking at Binkie.

Binkie tipped back his head, drained his beer, and produced automatically, "Well, to hell with everything!" Then, in a chant: "*I'm* all right, are *you* all right?"

The crowd chanted back, "We're all right, we're all right!"

Binkie, having abandoned the difficulties of politics to his betters for the duration, climbed on a chair. He raised his arms; his tunic strained; a button flew off and Maisie stooped to pick it up.

"Isn't he a crazy kid?" she crooned admiringly.

The room stilled, grinning at the familiar sight, waiting for the moment when those commanding arms would descend.

" 'Roll out the Barrel'!" shouted Binkie; and the obedient orchestra crashed into the familiar tune, as Binkie's arms descended, releasing the din of thumping feet and yelling voices.

Nobody went to bed that night. All over the city next day wives and mothers waited for the hour of sunset in the condition of hypnotized calm that the hilarious mood of the men made necessary.

The train was to leave at six. By five-thirty the long grey platform was packed. The train was waiting, its empty windows like so many frames waiting to be filled, and the sky over it tumultuous with a gold-and-crimson sunset. A band was playing, hardly audible in the din of talk and singing. A warm breeze smelling of sun and petrol stirred a hundred yellow streamers that idled above the heads of the crowd, which parted, shouting greetings, as the men in uniform came roaring through. They were all drunk and singing. With them came the girls, running alongside, singing and flushed with the same intoxication.

Someone had blundered again, for there were only five minutes before the train was supposed to leave. A wave of khaki washed up over the train; the frames were filled with grinning soldiers. The relatives and friends shook themselves out into groups below the windows. The band was playing "Tipperary."

There was a sardonic cheer. Binkie and Perry appeared on the roof of one of the carriages, and stood swaying there, grinning, arms outstretched.

"Go it, Binkie!" shouted a shrill voice. "Give the Jerries stick!" roared the female chorus. Meanwhile the sober families smiled steadily.

Binkie and Perry were doing a war dance, and singing "Hold Him Down, the Zulu Warrior"; while the band joined in half a bar behind. A group of officers, smiling but cautionary, appeared at the edge of the crowd; Binkie and Perry clung to each other in a parody of fright, and staggered up and down like clowns on a tight rope. The officers were shouting some orders; Binkie craned forward, blinking foolishly, one hand behind his ear. His foot slipped, someone shrieked; he rolled down over the roof into the crowd. Perry staggered back and forth like a man trying to get his balance, his great handsome blond face wooden with deliberate stupidity; then he took a neat nose dive off into a group, which caught him. For a moment Perry and Binkie were tossed up and down, yelling and laughing, while the officers gesticulated futilely on the edge of the crowd.

The train shrieked. Douglas, who was holding Martha's hand out of the window, was laughing appreciatively at Perry and Binkie. She held up her face, he bent to kiss it; but the train jerked forwards a foot, and they both laughed, while their eyes met in regret that it was impossible to be serious at this last moment. Two paces away, Binkie and Perry were locked in embrace, singing in thick wobbling voices, "Kiss me goodbye . . ." But the crowd took it up seriously for a few bars; then someone shouted, "Get onto the train, you silly buggers, it's going." Mr. Maynard stood forward and held out his hand to his son. Binkie dropped his fooling, and came to meet him, looking responsible. Mrs. Maynard, blinking away tears, impulsively flung her arms around him in a convulsive embrace. Binkie remained still, then made a joke in her ear, so that she stepped back, grimacing with laughter as the tears fell.

Binkie and Perry began running down the creeping train in slow motion, with exaggeratedly lifted legs and pumping arms. The train stopped again. A sardonic cheer from the soldiers in it, who were leaning out waving beer bottles. Perry and Binkie swung themselves onto the back bumpers. The train jerked, nearly flinging them off, then let out another shriek, and began to move in earnest. It rumbled along the platform with its burden of soldiers, who were hanging from their waists in every window or clustered on the foot plates. As the train gathered speed, Binkie and Perry appeared on the roof of the last carriage, through a cloud of filthy grey smoke. They were dancing and waving beer bottles. An epoch was going out to the strains of "Roll Out the Barrel"; and the crowd on the platform left facing the empty rails were silent.

The band stopped, then played "Show Me the Way to Go Home." The crowd eddied and thinned. In a few moments there remained a group of young wives with babies, looking with determined stoicism after their husbands. A group of girls who had run some way along the train now returned, wild-eyed, untidy, tipsy. Maisie was among them, and she greeted Martha cheerfully as she passed, with "So now we're all girls without men. What a life, hey?"

Stella, Martha, and Alice looked at each other, and smiled; smiled steadily. The train, a black snake blotched with khaki, was now far away over the veld. A wave of blue gritty smoke came drifting back. The sun, a heavy orange ball, dropped behind the mountain, and the white station lights came on. Yellow flags still idled under the roof; the band had gone.

Alice's face was white; but all she said was, "So that's that."

Stella suddenly collapsed into tears, and was led away by her mother. Martha and Alice left the station. Mr. Maynard stood on the pavement, beside a car where his iron-browed wife was weeping over the driving wheel.

"There, there!" he was saying. "There, there!" As Martha went past, he looked at her, suddenly produced a heavy sarcastic smile which was like a grimace of pain, and observed, "So much for the happy warriors!"

"Oh, the foolish, foolish boys," Mrs. Maynard cried out. "They'll all kill themselves before they even get to the fighting."

"I think not," said Mr. Maynard patiently. He had turned back to her, and Martha went on with Alice. The two women lifted their infants into their respective cars, and drove away home.

part three

When a person dies for his country, then you can say he loves it.

TURGENEV, *On the Eve*

1

The skies of Africa being for the most part blue and clear, and eminently suitable for aeroplanes, there were few cities in the subcontinent that did not hastily throw up on their outskirts camps of Nissen huts, hangars, runways and temporary houses, surrounded by fences and barbed wire and as self-contained and isolated as those other towns outside the city, the native locations.

For weeks before anything changed, the local inhabitants would drive out of a Sunday afternoon to watch the building; for weeks nothing was spoken of but that the Air Force was coming. That phrase, together with those others now constantly used by the newspapers, like "Knights of the Air" and "our boys," evoked in the minds of the population, which was now after all mostly female, an image of a tall graceful youth fitted neatly into sky-blue cloth. Certain poets were partly responsible for this charming figure—the newspapers are not to blame for everything. Besides, this was the period of the Battle of Britain; a need for heroism, starved so long, was being fed at last; it was as if the gallant youth from 1914 had donned a uniform the colour of the sky and taken wing. Their own young men who had left the colony in search of adventure were mostly dead, and killed in the air. The air was their medium, they felt. Useless to ask a country separated from the sea by hundreds of miles to think of itself as a breeder of sailors; and of that mass of young men who had departed north for land fighting, few had as yet actually fought. When they did, when those deaths and wounds were announced, the shock of it would breed a new image; in the meantime, it was an air war, and it was fitting that this colony should be asked to train airmen.

More than this lay behind their impatience for the moment when "the boys" should actually arrive. Few of them had not been brought up with the words "Home" and "England" continually in their mouths, even if they had not been born there; it was their own people they were expecting—and more: themselves, at one remove, and dignified by responsibility and danger. They knew what to expect: the colony was being fed month by month in peacetime by immigrants who were certainly of the stock which produced rather graceful young men, even if they changed in so few weeks into people like themselves—not charming, not—but the word "effeminate" was one the Battle of Britain made obsolete; it was conceded that the war and the number of deaths in the skies over London made those more sheltered cousins the equals of any veld adventurer or horizon conqueror.

But before an aeroplane can be sent into the air with its proper complement of highly trained young men, there must be so many others on the ground to provide for the welfare of both. It was this that the local people had not taken into account.

Suddenly, overnight, the streets changed. They were filled with a race of beings in thick, clumsy greyish uniforms; and from these ill-fitting cases of cloth emerged pallid faces and hands which had—to people who above all always had enough to eat and plenty of sunshine—a look of incompleteness. It was as if nature had sketched an ideal—that tall, well-fed charming youth, so easily transformed into a tough hero—and, being starved of material to complete it with, had struggled into what perfection it could. That, obscurely, was how they felt; they could not own these ancestors; their cousins from Home were a race of dwarfs, several inches shorter than themselves. They were not burnt and brown, but unhealthily pale. They were not glorious and rebellious individuals—for, above all, emigrants to the colonies have been that—but they had the look, as they strayed cautiously and curiously about the shallow little colonial streets, of a community whose oneness was only emphasized by the uniform.

In short, they were different.

It never entered their heads to apologize for being different.

They made no effort to become like their hosts.

Worse than anything, the faces of these new guests—a colonial people instinctively feel themselves as hosts—expressed nothing but a patient and sardonic criticism. They were unwilling guests.

These groundlings, dumped arbitrarily into the middle of Africa, strayed about the town, noted the two cinemas, half a dozen hotels, a score of bars; noted that the amenities usual for ten thousand white inhabitants were to be stretched to provide for them in their hundreds of thousands; noted that women would be in short supply for the duration; and, with that calm common sense which distinguishes the British workingman, decided to make themselves as comfortable as possible in circumstances fully as bad as they had expected. For a time the grey tide ebbed back from the city into the camps that were surrounded by the high, forbidding fences.

Not before a number of disturbing incidents had occurred. For instance, several innocent men had brought Coloured women into the bars of an evening, and had violently resented being asked to leave. Others were observed offering black men cigarettes on street corners, while talking to them, or even walking with them. It was rumoured that quite a number had actually gone into the homes of the servants of the city, in the native location. But this was not the worst; it was felt that such behaviour was merely the result of ignorance; a short acquaintance with local custom would put things right. No, it was something more indefinable, something inarticulate, an atmosphere like an ironic stare, which, since it was not put into words, could not be answered.

A group of airmen might be walking down the street, hoping that some diversion might offer itself, when their attention was drawn by the sound of a wild and urgent motor horn. An expensive car stood by them, in which a couple, smiling with fervent goodwill, urged they should enter. They climbed, therefore, into the car, and were whisked off to McGrath's Hotel, where drinks were called for all round. The orchestra still played, war or no war, from its bower of ferns. The native waiters came round with trays of beer. All was gilt and imitation marble. And this couple, so eager to be kind, were kindness itself. But why this positively effusive hospitality. Why? They might almost have been guilty about something. They talked about England: Do you remember, do you know, have you ever been to . . . But, but! the colonial's England is not the England that these men longed for, not the pubs and streets they were exiled from. They were kind enough not to point this out.

That *but* was felt like a piece of grit in the mouthful of honey which was this chance to be welcoming hosts. How seldom do colonials, starved in their deepest need to be hosts, get the chance to take to their bosoms not one or two but twenty thousand grateful guests at once? All over the city, in bars and hotel lounges and even in private drawing rooms, could be seen—in that first week or so—a couple, man and wife, entertaining anything up to twenty polite but determinedly inarticulate groundlings, who drank and ate all they could, since the pushed-around are entitled to take what crumbs fate offers them, but certainly did not return that loving approval which is what hosts most essentially ask in return. Yes, this was a fine country; yes, it was a grand town; yes, it was a wonderful achievement for half a century. But. But. But.

The tide receded. It would return. Thousands upon thousands more men were arriving every week from Home. From those first tentative contacts it was clear that there was a situation which should be faced by those whose task it was to administer and guide.

In every city there is a group of middle-aged and elderly women who in fact run it. The extent to which they are formally organized is no gauge of their real power. The way in which they respond to danger is that gauge; and from the frankness with which they express their intentions can be measured the extent of the danger. To students of "local politics" let there be recommended the activities of the mothers of the city:

About a week after the first grey tide, there occurred a conversation between Mr. Maynard and his wife, not on the pillow—they had not shared one for many years—but at the breakfast table.

Mrs. Maynard was the leader of the council of matriarchs. She was fitted for it not merely by character. The wives of prime ministers, Cabinet ministers, governors, mayors, because of the necessity that they should be above struggle and party strife, are precluded from certain positions. Far from envying such women, Mrs. Maynard rather pitied them. She could have been one had she chosen. As it was, she was the daughter of an English family who for centuries had occupied itself with "public work"; she was a cousin to the existing Governor, her husband was a third cousin to the Prime Minister of Britain; but he was only a magistrate; she was, so it was hoped it would be considered, not only reliable, but above all independent. Nothing she said would be taken as from the Government or a political party.

She remarked over the sheets of the *Zambesia News*, "It is quite disgraceful that the authorities are not doing anything about it."

Mr. Maynard laid down his paper and asked, "About what?"

"Millions of poor boys brought into the country and nothing whatsoever done for them."

"You exaggerate slightly, I think?"

"Well—fifty thousand, a hundred thousand. One thousand would be bad enough."

"There are cinemas and canteens in the camps, I believe."

"You know quite well what I mean."

Mr. Maynard stirred his coffee, and remarked, "Even in peacetime men outnumber women." He added, "I assume you are not suggesting a brothel—the churches wouldn't stand for it."

She coloured and tightened her lips; this mask of annoyed rectitude vanished as she smiled with dry appreciation. "Personally I'd rather brothels than—but that isn't what I meant." She frowned and said, "We should provide entertainment—something to keep them occupied."

"My dear Myra, save your trouble. Every woman in the town is already lost. Wait until the pilots arrive."

"I am thinking of the blacks," she said, irritated. A short pause. Then, as it were thinking aloud, "I heard from Edgar that they have no idea at all how to treat natives. Not their fault, of course, poor things. I suggested to him a course of lectures on native policy, that sort of thing, *before* they arrive in the country."

"So you are not concerned with the morals of our wives and mothers?" He smiled at her, the heavy urbane eyebrows raised.

She returned an equally bland smile. "I am concerned with both. The first thing should be a dance hall, with canteens, ping-pong—something like that."

"I have just understood that you intend me to sponsor it—is that it?"

"You would do very well," she suggested, for the first time with a touch of appeal.

"No," he said decidedly.

"You've got to do something. Everybody's doing something."

He continued to stir his coffee, and to look at her. It was a challenge.

It was met. "We are at war, you know!" she cried out at last, from her real emotions. She was now flushed, indignant, and with a hint of quivering softness about brows and mouth—a reminiscence of a certain striking dark beauty.

He smiled unpleasantly; apparently he felt this to be a victory.

But she did not attempt to quell her emotion. "Your attitude is extraordinary, extraordinary!" she said, lips quivering. "Don't you care that we are at war?"

"I care very much. But not enough to run a refined club for the boys," he added. Then: "I shall confine myself to keeping the native population in its place. Nothing could be more useful than that, surely?"

They exchanged a long married look, which held dislike, and re-spect. The two faces, both heavy, black-browed, commanding, con-fronted each other from opposite ends of the long table. It was, as always, a deadlock.

"Then I shall ask that old stick Anderson to run it."

"An admirable choice."

She rose, and went towards the door. His raised voice followed her: "As regards the problem of the dear boys and the native women, it is my personal view that—regarded from a long-term point of view, of course—a few thousand more half-caste children would be a good thing. It might force the authorities to provide better amenities for them. As things are, the Coloured community provides more petty criminals than any other section of the population."

This was designed to annoy. But one of the minor pleasures of power is to exchange in private views which would ruin you if your followers ever had a suspicion you held them. Mrs. Maynard let out a short dry chuckle and said, "There are surely simpler ways of get-ting better housing for the Coloureds than infecting all our boys with V.D."

Two days later a paragraph in the paper announced that three en-tertainment centres for the Air Force personnel were to be opened shortly under the experienced patronage of Mr. Anderson, late of the Department of Statistics, a well-known public figure.

A second grey tide flowed abruptly over the town. Not quite so grey: the idea of the blue air fed a tinge of blue into those stiff uni-forms, and now the hungry expectations of the people were assuaged, for these were the cousins, the welcomed relatives from Home—these, the aviators in person, recognizably the same species as themselves. They were perfectly at ease in drawing rooms, clubs, bars and dance rooms, where they at once appeared in their hundreds; and the city, long accustomed to indulging its young men in whatever follies they might choose to use, found nothing remarkable in their behaviour. They brought with them an atmosphere of dedication to danger, of reckless exuberance which—as every young woman in the city soon had reason to know—was covered by a most charming modesty; and this in its turn was a mask for a cynical nihilism which was more dan-gerously attractive than even recklessness. If the note of the First World War was idealistic dedication, succeeded by its mirror image, sarcastic anger, then the symbol for this period of the Second War was a cynical young airman sprouting aggressive but flippant mous-taches, capable of the most appalling heroism, but prone to surpris-ing lapses into self-pitying but stoic despair, during which moments he would say he hoped he would be killed, because there was no point in living, anyway. The truth of the morale of any army is most likely to be discovered between the sheets.

The danger of this mood, felt like a heightened pulse in the town, was expressed to Mr. Maynard at the breakfast table thus:

"It's all very well, but we have to think of our boys up north."

"I expect they are taking care of themselves in their own way."

"Have you heard about . . ." Here followed the names of about a dozen young women. "They are all losing their heads."

"Provided they don't lose them too far, I daresay all will be well at the armistice."

Mrs. Maynard looked sharply at him, tightened her lips, held his eyes steadily with her own. When this couple had come together in 1919 after years of separation, there had been incidents to overlook on both sides. Not forgiven—no. Mrs. Maynard could not forgive him that he had overlooked so easily. Yet what had happened? Nothing— she had never been unfaithful to him. There was simply a photograph of an officer, a cousin, among a bundle of old letters. As for him, he could not forgive that there was nothing to forgive. She had always fulfilled the letter of every agreement. But there burned in this handsome matron's heart a steady flame of romance; he knew it. She had given her heart to the dead and was thus free to deal with life as she felt was right. She had never done anything to be ashamed of.

After a few moments, he smiled and enquired, "What do you propose to do about it, my dear?"

Mrs. Maynard paid a number of visits, received others, was a good deal on the telephone. As a result, many young women got letters from various organizations suggesting that they might spend their time on such and such a form of war work. Strings invisibly tightened. Mrs. Talbot, wan and beautiful with her daughter's grief (the fiancé had been killed in the air over London during the Battle of Britain), dropped in to see Martha and suggested she should join the organization of women connected with the civil service.

Martha hardly listened. Such was her naïveté that she thought it odd, even interfering, of Mrs. Talbot, who had nothing to do with the Service. She gave Mrs. Talbot tea, told her what news there was of Douglas—very little, save that he had just finished leave with the boys in some town in Abyssinia. And that meant—Martha calmly stated it, apparently not noticing Mrs. Talbot's indrawn breath—that he was probably having dozens of love affairs. Happening to glance at Mrs. Talbot, she frowned slightly, and added that he was perfectly entitled to do so; they did not believe in jealousy. Mrs. Talbot was searching for the right words to express her disturbance of mind, when Martha, unaware that any were needed, began talking of something else. Martha's advantage in any such encounter was always her assumption that Mrs. Talbot (for instance) was bound to agree with her; any suggestion that her view might not be the right one was met with a critical, almost incredulous stare.

Some days later, Mr. Maynard himself came to see Martha. Mrs. Maynard had said that she intended to visit personally a number of girls who were not pulling their weight. Mr. Maynard had said hastily that he would see to young Matty Knowell himself. It was an instinct of protectiveness which he did not analyze.

As he climbed the stairs to the flat, he heard a child screaming; he had to knock several times before he was heard. Martha admitted him and asked him to sit down, announcing brightly that they would have to shout through the noise, if he didn't mind.

Mr. Maynard did mind. He said he was prepared to wait. He disposed his large body on one of the small chairs, and watched. He was adjusting his ideas to the fact that Martha was no longer a girl with a baby, that his godchild-without-the-benefit-of-religion was now a personality. He saw a small lively girl striving energetically against the straps that bound her to a high chair, her cheeks scarlet and tear-stained, her black eyes rebellious. Caroline was small-limbed, dainty, with a fine pointed face—a delightful creature. On the platform before her was a heavy china plate, and on that a squelch of greyish pulp. Martha, planted on her two sturdy legs, faced the child like an antagonist, her own lips set as firmly as Caroline's, who was refusing the food she was trying to push in between them. As the spoon came near, Caroline set up an angry yell, and bright sparks of tears gleamed through squeezed lashes; then the small white teeth closed tight on the metal. Martha was pale with anger, trembling with the contest. She even caught the child's nose until the mouth opened, and thrust in the spoon, leaving a mass of that unpleasant-looking pulp. Caroline choked, then began to cry differently—a miserable, helpless wail. Martha winced, then fumblingly loosened the straps, and caught Caroline up. "Oh, Lord," she cried helplessly, "I don't know what to do!" Caroline was twisting in the embrace; Martha set her on the floor, where she stood holding a chair and yelled defiance at her mother. Martha lifted her, with an impatient movement, and took her out to the verandah, came back and shut the door. Silence. She passed her hand across her eyes, reached for a cigarette, lit it, and sat down. She was now pale, tense and exhausted.

"Is all this really necessary?" enquired Mr. Maynard.

Martha laughed unhappily, and said that the book ordered that if a child would not eat it should not be forced, but Caroline had not eaten a mouthful for days.

She took great gulps of smoke, but seemed to be sitting on edge, as if waiting for the slightest sound from Caroline.

"She looks very well on being starved," observed Mr. Maynard.

Martha frowned, and was silent. He was reminding himself of that time—so long ago—when Mrs. Maynard was engaged in rearing Binkie. He could recall only his violent distaste at what had seemed an indefinite period of smells and mess; he remembered his puzzled respect for that tidy and fastidious lady his wife, who had apparently found nothing distasteful in soiled napkins and dribbling mouths. Now he looked at the high chair planted in the middle of the room, bathed in sunlight from the window. Scraps of brownish vegetable mush clung to it. There were bits of the stuff on the floor around it. Flies were settling over the plate. "Can't you remove that unpleasant object?"

Martha looked at him enquiringly, and then at the chair. She shrugged at male queasiness, and remarked, "If I take the chair out and Caroline sees it, she'll start screaming again." But she lifted it outside, without incurring any protest, hastily wiped the bits of mess off the floor, and sat down again, still smoking. Mr. Maynard observed that she was looking very attractive. She wore a slip of a yellow dress showing brown bare legs, brown well-shaped arms. Her fingernails and toenails were painted. She was scarcely recognizable as the pale plump schoolgirl he had married to her husband. She looked very young, self-contained, hard, unhappy. The dark speculative eyes watched him as if he might turn out to be an enemy.

The shell of bright confidence dissolved as she remarked humorously, "I believe firmly that children should be removed from their parents at birth in their own interests."

Mr. Maynard's thoughts, which had left the infant Caroline, were thus returned to her. He said that children survived anything, in his experience. And returned to considering the fact which appeared to him to be confirmed by Martha's careful attractiveness, that rumour must be right.

"What are you doing with yourself?"

"Nothing much."

"Having a good time?" he probed.

She said humorously, in a way which grated out resentment, that since children had to be fed three times a day and put to bed at half past six, there was scarcely much time left to enjoy oneself.

Mr. Maynard could not remember being discommoded by Binkie's infancy, so he again dismissed Caroline. "Do you go out much?"

"No," she said, biting it off. And then: "I am reading a lot."

But he did not take it up. He lay propped on the angles of the slight chair, like a broad solid grey plank, and observed her from his heavily accented eyes. He was convinced that no young woman living alone with a small child would go to the trouble of curling her hair and painting her twenty nails, unless it was for the purpose of attracting a man. He dismissed the reading as he dismissed Caroline, and came direct to his point. "It is being said that you are having an affair with an officer in the Air Force."

"I have no doubt of it." She was flushed with anger. "If I were, I think I should be perfectly entitled to."

"I am not arguing the matter from its principles," he began, regarding this as an admission. "I am merely suggesting that there are ways of doing things."

"Hypocrite!" Martha snapped out; then stiffly smiled. Her eyebrows were knitting and reknitting as if, above her gulfs of anger, tendrils of thought attempted to engage.

Mr. Maynard coloured slowly; such was the power of Martha on him: she paid no tribute at all to the authority he felt he enshrined. "My dear young woman, what is the point of infuriating people if an ounce of tact would save you from it?"

It appeared a fresh outburst was imminent; then she laughed and said, "As a matter of fact, I haven't had any love affairs with anybody."

"Having acknowledged your rights in the matter—" he began, with humorous conciliation, but was interrupted.

"Do you know what happened?" enquired Martha, poised on the verge of what she meant him to think an amusing story.

"I can't wait to hear."

"Well, I don't go out at nights much, because of Caroline."

"Why don't you ask your mother to take her?"

"No," said Martha quickly. "Well, I asked the woman across the corridor to watch her. She never wakes at night. There was a dance at McGrath's—an officers' dance, of course," she added disgustedly.

"Well, why not?"

She hurried past this point. "So they laid on the girls, as usual. You know how they ring you up and ask you if you'll be one of the girls."

"I don't see why not. As long as the boys are content to be boys, why shouldn't the girls oblige?"

She giggled. Then: "Well, you know how they go on—but I suppose if there is one thing we've all had plenty of experience in it is coping with the boys on the tear."

Mr. Maynard coloured again, and shifted his limbs uncomfortably. "Quite."

"There were half a dozen at my table—you know, all very *English*." She paused for words, while Mr. Maynard wondered what the word "English" meant to a girl, certainly English by parentage, who had never been in England.

"I am at a loss."

"Soft," said Martha, dismissing it. "You know, those deprecating types with moustaches."

"I hardly think it is the right word to use *now*," he observed.

She looked confused and guilty, but persisted. "Well then, heroes one and all, I know. But what is heroism, then?"

"Can't we leave that fascinating social question aside for the moment?"

"It's easy enough to let yourself be killed."

"There are hundreds of thousands of men who are doing everything to see they will *not* be killed—I do hope you don't admire them more."

"I didn't say so," she said sullenly.

Mr. Maynard waited.

"About twelve o'clock I was landed with one of them and he was terribly drunk. I mean, really drunk. He was swaying all over the table. I got a waiter to hold him upright. But all his brothers in arms were dancing or in the bar. I couldn't think of anything to do. So I pushed him into my car and brought him here. Well, I could hardly take him into the men's washrooms, could I?"

"I suppose not."

"So I brought him here and he was duly sick. Then I put him to bed on that divan there, and went to bed myself. About three in the morning, a vast horde of them burst in to claim him. Very solicitous they were about his condition. It appeared he was due to fly at five. He nearly pranged the morning before, he told me . . ." She tailed off. A note of defiant pity that had appeared in her voice must be disowned, apparently, for she continued, "They all thought it a hell of a joke."

This was the end of the story. Martha was scarlet with remembered humiliation. After a pause, Mr. Maynard said, "I don't see what you expect—you want to have it both ways."

"Why?" she enquired reasonably. She lit a cigarette. "If you want to construct a story that I am having an affair with the Air Force out of that interesting little incident, then you're welcome."

"I don't see why I should apologize when you think you're entitled to an affair any time you like."

"But I didn't!"

"When your practice catches up with your theory, all I want to suggest is a little more discretion."

"Did you come here to tell me that?" she asked, amazed.

He moved his limbs again, and said, "Well, no."

First she appeared angry; then, unexpectedly, moved. She leaned towards him and asked, stammering slightly, "Why—why do you care what I do?"

And again Mr. Maynard, having got through the defences of this armoured young woman, could not face the emotion he had found. He took a quick glance at her direct, enquiring eyes, averted his own, and remarked, "My dear girl, you can all go to the devil for all I care."

He was surprised and contrite that her eyes filled with tears. She got up abruptly, went outside, and returned in a few moments with the sleeping child. She sat, holding her in her arms, smoking over the soft nestling head. Mr. Maynard saw that ancient symbol, mother and child, through a pale blue fog shot with sunlight. He was extraordinarily moved. Martha seemed to him altogether more amenable, conciliating—safe, in fact—thus disposed.

He remarked, "A charming picture."

Martha was first puzzled, then embarrassed. She at once sprang up, and deposited the baby in a receptacle outside the door.

"Why did you do that?" enquired the elderly gentleman. "I meant it."

She looked at him sardonically. "I am so glad you find it so satisfactory." Then: "It's against the rules to cuddle a baby out of hours—the book says so."

At this point the door opened, and Mrs. Quest came in. "Matty, why don't you put your name on the door, I keep telling you—" She saw the magistrate, and greeted him warmly.

"I'm just going," said Mr. Maynard, "having spent a delightful half hour with your daughter."

"She's an awful scatterbrain," said Mrs. Quest instinctively, avoiding compliments to her own like a peasant afraid of the evil eye. "Have you ever seen such a mess as this place is in?" She began to set it to rights forthwith. Martha sat on the arm of a chair, puffing out smoke and looking stubbornly ironical.

"Would you like to come with me to a meeting of that Left group tomorrow night?" enquired Mr. Maynard.

Martha brightened. Mrs. Quest's face glazed—the pillars were rocking. She looked timidly at Mr. Maynard and said, "You don't mean that batch of Communists—someone said yesterday they have the

C.I.D. at all their meetings." She gave a short scandalized laugh.

"Oh, I don't think it's as bad as that," Mr. Maynard soothed. He looked enquiringly at Martha.

Mrs. Quest said, "I'll take Caroline, and you can go with Mr. Maynard, it's very kind of him."

Martha said nothing; she was looking angrily at her mother.

Mr. Maynard recognized the existence of one of the female situations which it was his principle to avoid, and said to Martha, "I'll pick you up tomorrow about eight—see you then, goodbye, ladies." And departed.

"I really don't see why you don't get a boy," said Mrs. Quest irritably.

"Why should I have a servant when I've nothing else to do?"

"Everyone has one."

"That's apparently final."

"Besides, you don't do the housework—I've never seen such a mess."

"Well, I live in it." But now appeared that old enemy to decision of character, who pointed out to Martha that this argument was ridiculous, not because she was not entirely in the right, but because it sounded so *banal*. She retreated to the divan which not so long ago had supported the inebriated limbs of the Air Force officer, and watched her mother sweep and tidy the flat.

Mrs. Quest, relieved by "doing something," began to chat good-humouredly about Mr. Quest—who was much better these days, he had dropped one of his medicines yesterday—and went on from there to Mr. Maynard, who must be misinformed about that Left crowd, because a man in his position couldn't afford to get mixed up with such people.

"Oh, Mother!"

"But everybody knows . . ." This was lost as she bent under a corner table to retrieve fallen papers. Martha sprang forward to take them from her. Mrs. Quest gave them up suspiciously. Martha put them into a drawer in such a way that she might have been accusing her mother of looking at them. Mrs. Quest, hurt, said she had no intention of prying into Martha's private concerns. This reminding her of nearer preoccupations, she enquired offhand, "And what's all this I hear of your going out gallivanting in the evenings?"

"I can only imagine."

"I thought you said you weren't going out—what did you do with Caroline?"

"She was not neglected, if that's what you mean."

"It's all very well," cried out Mrs. Quest, from the depths of her heart, "but when I dropped in yesterday, she was quite alone and crying. As I told Mrs. Talbot at bridge yesterday, you are really quite irresponsible."

Martha was now alert with anger. "I was only out for twenty minutes buying vegetables. And what's it to do with Mrs. Talbot?"

"You should get a boy, and then you wouldn't have to go out shopping. It's ridiculous, they'll deliver, anyway."

"I thought you said it was dangerous to have a boy in a place where there was a small girl, because he was bound to rape her?"

They were now on the verge of a real battle, when Caroline let out the sudden, startled wail of an infant woken too soon. Martha got up, but, seeing that her mother was there before her, sat down, telling herself it was all unimportant and she should learn not to mind.

Mrs. Quest brought in the small girl, and sat crooning over her, with an access of tenderness that touched and disarmed Martha; but Caroline was striving like an unwilling captive in the arms that held her. Mrs. Quest laughed ruefully and set her down, and she unsteadily staggered back to the verandah, while the two women watched her with the same small, proud smile, in which was a touch of regret.

"She's very small for her age," said Mrs. Quest dubiously. "I hope you are giving her enough to eat."

Martha jumped up as if stung. Mrs. Quest rose hurriedly, and said she might just as well take Caroline now for a few days, it would give Martha a rest. Martha nearly protested, then allowed herself to slide into apathy—for why not? Then Mrs. Quest added that Caroline needed to be fed up a little, and Martha turned away helplessly, silenced by the knowledge that she was certainly a failure, she could no more manage Caroline than Mrs. Quest had managed *her*. Grandmothers, she reflected, falling back with relief on the abstraction, are better with their grandchildren than with their own children. And she even dwelt wistfully on a charming picture, Mrs. Quest tenderly relaxed with Caroline, a picture that had the same soothing, ideal quality as what Mr. Manyard saw when he looked at *her* with the child.

In a few minutes Mrs. Quest had left with Caroline, and the flat was empty. Martha was, as always, uncomfortably surprised that as soon as Caroline was away from her it was as if she had never had a child at all; whereas as long as they were together that invisible navel string twanged like a harshly plucked string at every movement or sound the child made. She sat down and consciously tried to pull herself together; she felt herself to be a hopeless failure; she was good for nothing, not even the simple natural function that every female should achieve like breathing: being a mother. As she sat there, her eye came to rest on a half-closed drawer from which papers protruded. She jumped up, and, without reading what she had written, tore them up. It was a letter to Douglas. She had fallen into the habit of writing him long letters about—as she put it—what she really felt. The letters that reached him, however, were amusing accounts of Caroline's development, Alice's struggles with her son, Stella's enjoyable sufferings in childbirth. Pride forbade her to post her "real" letters, which were in effect passionate complaints that he had ever married her if he intended to leave her at the first opportunity; despairing admissions of incompetence with Caroline; and her hatred of the life she led.

The letters she got from him filled her with dismay she would not acknowledge. The incidents of his army life he found as humorous as she did hers. Besides, he continually urged her broad-mindedly, as was the spirit of their compact, to get out and have a good time; which she interpreted, from a deeper instinct than she would admit to possessing, as the voice of guilt itself.

She was about to sit down and describe the visit of Mr. Maynard in terms which would make him sound like an avuncular priest, when the telephone rang.

She approached it with caution. Since that moment three nights before when six or seven young men had burst in to claim their comrade, it had been ringing with suggestions that she might go to this dance or that. She had reacted with stiff coldness. She was hurt that the victim himself had made no sign. She had not told the whole truth to Mr. Maynard. Thomas Bryant had collapsed onto the divan in more than alcoholic breakdown. He had wept on her breast like a child—he had lost his nerve, he would never be able to go up again, he wished he had been killed when the aircraft had tipped over on its wing that morning. Martha had cradled him, and felt such a depth of emotion that afterwards she could not bear to think of it. It was terrible to her that weakness should have so strong an appeal. And yet it had been a perfect intimacy—for the few minutes before he went limp into sleep. That he should *not* have rung up seemed to her like a slap in the face. Now she took down the receiver, and a hearty embarrassed voice thanked her for holding his head; it was a jolly good show, he said. Then, after a short pause, he said it was a lovely day; Martha laughed in amazement; encouraged by this sound, he invited her for dinner that night. Martha agreed at once.

She ran off to prepare her dress and herself for the occasion: it was shortly after midday. While she bathed and curled her hair and anointed her body, her whole being was dedicating itself anew. She might have never been the wife of Douglas and the mother of Caroline. Her fantasies of the night ahead centred on the intimate talk, a continuation of that existing intimacy, a complete truthfulness which would sanctify what would follow. This, however, never approached even the threshold of consciousness. At the most she imagined a kiss. But until the kiss, fantasy must sleep. She was crying out for a romantic love affair; she had been waiting for months for just this moment; not for one second had the idea entered her head. There is no such thing as a female hypocrite.

When Thomas Bryant entered the flat at eight that night, she had been dressed and ready for over an hour. This was one of the evenings, she knew, when she was beautiful—though why the spirit of attraction should visit her as it did, she did not know; no man had ever explained it to her.

She welcomed him casually, like an old friend; she saw at once he did not recognize her. He looked uncertainly about the flat, and then at the divan on which he had slept.

"Mrs. Knowell?" he enquired formally.

Martha laughed involuntarily; saw his startled shamed look; then hastily covered for him: he remembered nothing of what had happened, and she must not tell him. "It was a terrible evening, wasn't it—we were all drunk as owls," she remarked flippantly, and saw the relief on his face.

"I'm very sorry," he said. "You must let me make amends."

She offered him a drink, and he arranged his length carefully on the divan, as if he distrusted it. He was very tall and rather slight, though broad-shouldered. He was fair, with a clear, ruddy English skin, and blue eyes inflamed by flying and late nights. They observed Martha with approval. The boys had told him she was a nice little piece; it was an understatement. He could not remember ever having seen her before; he remembered a crowd of vaguely amiable girls. He had decided to take her out to dinner somewhere where he would not meet his friends, behave pleasantly, take her home early, and take care not to see her again. Something like that was owed to a woman whom he remembered dimly as a maternal and practical presence. Now he changed his plans instantly: he would take his prize among his brother officers.

Martha, examining him, saw that he wore his uniform carelessly; that his whole person expressed a sort of humorous resignation to the absurdity of uniforms and war—a studied, self-conscious repudiation of anything serious, particularly his own death, which, since his training would be complete in a couple of weeks, was not likely to be delayed longer than a few months at most. She felt a pity for him which was betrayed even in the way she handed him a glass of whisky; he might already be a figure on a war memorial.

He tossed it down, and said, "Let's go." He stood up. "Shall we dance instead?"

She said immediately she would love to. Somewhere in her was spreading a shadow of desolation. She felt insulted. She became very gay.

All the way to the camp he asked her minute questions about the make of the car, its performance, how much it cost to run. She thought of cars as objects invented to take one efficiently from one place to another; she had never really believed anyone could be seriously interested in such matters. He was offering her the merest small change of conversation; and she answered politely.

At the gates in the great black fence, the sentry stood aside as the young officer held out a piece of paper. There was a newly built hall, surrounded by ranks of parked cars. They entered the hall. It was already full. A band of uniformed men played from a platform.

Martha looked around and knew all the women present. A year ago, they had been dancing in the arms of the local men; now they were moving with equal compliance in the arms of the Air Force, and using with perfect ease the new language. She saw Alice dancing past. She waved. Alice waved back, then stopped, spoke to her partner, and came over.

The young officer stood aside politely while Alice took Martha's elbow and said, "Hey, Matty, so we're back in circulation—it's awful, isn't it?" She let out her high giggle, and added, "I'm browned off with everything. I don't see why we shouldn't—God knows what Willie's up to up north."

Martha, who had felt a stab of jealous shock on behalf of the absent Willie, now agreed instantly that Douglas always said she must go and enjoy herself. At this Alice suddenly smiled, the women smiled ironically, exchanged a look, and separated.

Thomas Bryant returned to Martha, and edged with her around in the space between the dancers and the tables. She suddenly stopped. She had thought of this as going out with Thomas Bryant; she had imagined being with *him.* She saw a long table, around which sat a dozen young officers, half of whom had rung her during the last week. She looked at Thomas, unconsciously reproachful. He glanced curiously at her face: she was scarlet. He avoided looking at his friends, who had already made a space for them, and led Martha to another small table. They sat. Her back was now to the other table. Glancing at him, she saw him looking over her shoulder at his friends; she turned swiftly, and saw them grinning at him; his face expressed a half-sheepish triumph. She hated him. When he summoned the black waiter and suggested champagne, she said she would drink lemonade. They got up to dance, like two wooden things. He was drinking heavily again. After a few dances, he had sunk into the collective wash of emotion; the whole roomful of people was dancing in the anonymous throb of music. That was what he most wanted, she could see: not to have to think, to let himself go into it, to let his mind flow out and away from the terrible necessity of his days. And he wanted her to be a girl whose face he would not have to remember next day. Well, then, she would. She loosened and danced in the beat of the drums.

Quite soon, a grinning young man tapped Thomas on the shoulder. "Why don't you come and join us?"

He looked awkwardly at Martha; she said at once, "Why, we'd love to."

At the end of that dance she went easily with him to the other table. She disliked him now so much it did not matter what she did. She was now that woman who says, "So that's what you want me to be—very well, then, I'll show you how well I can do it." She danced cheerfully with the young men to whom she had been so cold on the telephone. Choosing a moment when Thomas was at the bar, she asked one of his friends to tell him she had a headache—she chose the most casually insulting formula she knew—and left, quickly, to find her car. She was now trembling—with cold, she told herself. It was a cold night, the great stars glittering in their patterns as they had on so many dancing nights.

As she got into the car, she saw two people sitting in the back seat. A young woman, lazily disposed in one corner, supported the head and shoulders of a young officer who lay stretched along the seat. Martha peered through the half-dark and saw that the girl was Maisie. Both were asleep.

She sat for a while, watching the bright soft dresses of the women flowing against the neat close shapes of the men as couples passed up and down the steps in the yellow light that fell from the apertures of the hall. Then she grew impatient, and leaned over and shook Maisie's bare white shoulder.

Maisie woke at once, opening her eyes straight into Martha's, and smiling in her easy friendly way. "Hey, Martha, have we been asleep?" She looked down at the man, whose face was half buried in her bosom, and yawned. "I picked your car because I knew you wouldn't mind. Lord, this boy's heavy."

"Who is he?"

"He's the Air Force."

"Well, of course."

"You know, Matty, I like those English boys, don't you? It'll be awfully hard to go back to our own after knowing them. They treat us quite differently, don't they?" A pause, and another yawn. "I never get any sleep. They read more books. They talk about things. They've got culture, that's what it is."

Maisie's husband had been killed flying in Persia. That was six months before.

"He's very nice, this one," she went on reflectively. "He wants to marry me. Men are funny, aren't they, Matty? I mean, the way they are always wanting to get married. I suppose it's because they are going to get killed."

"Are you going to marry him?"

"Well, I suppose so, if it's going to make him happy. I don't see the sense in it, myself. I look at it this way: Supposing he doesn't get killed after all—a lot don't, they just finish their turn, and then go to the ground. Well, then, he'll be English, and he'll want to live in England. But I like it here and then we'll be married and have to get divorced." She shifted herself, with infinite gentleness, into a different position, carefully catching her lower lip between white teeth as his head rolled into the crook of her arm. He opened his eyes, stirred, sat up.

"This is Matty. I told you—she's all right."

"How do you do?" enquired an educated English voice.

"How do you do?" said Martha.

"Do you mind giving us a lift back to town, Matty? That's why we came into your car. Don hasn't got to fly tomorrow. He's got a week-end pass."

Martha backed out, and drove through the big gates past the sentry. "When are you getting married?" she asked.

"Tomorrow," said the young man promptly, in a tender proprietory tone, to which Maisie responded good-humouredly, "Oh, you're a crazy kid."

Martha observed in the mirror that they were once more embraced, and was careful not to speak again. She was feeling cold and lonely and left out. Now she regretted behaving so stiffly with Thomas.

She was able to drive to Maisie's room without having to ask for instructions. She stopped outside another white gate, banked with shrubs whose glossy leaves glinted in the starlight. She waited for them to realize that the car was no longer in motion.

Maisie came unhurriedly out of the embrace, saying, "Thanks a lot,

Matty, do the same for you sometime." As she got out, linked to her young man, she enquired politely, "And how's our Douggie?"

"He's doing fine."

"Did you hear that a crowd of our boys tore Mogadishu to pieces a while back? You know how they are when they get into one of their moods."

Don politely thanked Martha. "It's very kind of you."

"Not at all."

He bent his head over Maisie's fair gleaming curls as they walked into the house where she had her room. Martha watched them going inside, cheeks laid together, dancing a half-mocking, half-dreamy sliding step. She wished that her principles would allow her to cry. But this would not do; she efficiently let out the clutch, and drove herself back to the flat, feeling herself to be the only cold, sober, isolated person in a moon-drugged city given over to dancing, love and death. She felt as if she had shut the door against her own release. Then she remembered that tomorrow night she would be taken to a meeting packed full—she hoped against hope—of dangerous revolutionaries. She was enabled to retire to bed alone with philosophy.

At half past seven the following evening Mr. Maynard folded his napkin and rose from the dinner table, although the meal had reached only the roast-beef stage and there were guests.

"Spending an evening with your chums?" enquired his wife briskly. The word "chums" was the one she used to deprecate that group of elderly gentlemen who were Mr. Maynard's favourite company, and whom she felt as an irritating but not dangerous comment on her own activities.

"No, I'm dropping down to the Left people."

The ladies let out arch little cries of dismay. They were Mrs. Talbot, pale in clouds of grey chiffon and pearls; Mrs. Lowe-Island, her stubby, sunburnt sixty-year-old body upright in pink taffeta; and Mrs. Maynard herself—sage-green lace and an amber necklace that fell to her waist.

Mr. Maynard was prepared to forgo his pudding, but not his brandy; he sipped it standing. Mrs. Lowe-Island, born to be that indispensable lieutenant who must say and do what her superiors find beneath them, cried, "Now that everything is so serious, and the Huns are attacking us in North Africa, I can't see how anyone can waste time with a bunch of agitators—it's encouraging them."

Mr. Maynard smiled, and set down his brandy glass. Mrs. Maynard was absorbed in her pudding, but it was to her that he remarked, "Even with the Huns at our gate, I feel we might keep a sense of proportion."

Mrs. Maynard took another spoonful, but Mrs. Lowe-Island said indignantly, "They might sweep down over the whole continent in a couple of weeks."

"I'm sorry you have so little confidence in our armies."

"Oh—but we know Hitler is quite unscrupulous."

Mr. Maynard laughed. He was on his way to the door.

His wife enquired, "You are taking that Quest girl?"

"You don't mean that young Mrs. Knowell?" exclaimed Mrs. Lowe-Island.

"She's a sweet girl," said Mrs. Talbot reproachfully. "She's a darling thing—and so artistic!"

Mrs. Lowe-Island quivered. Mrs. Maynard spooned in the last of her pudding in a way which said that the cook would be spoken to about it in the morning, and firmly rang the bell.

From the door, Mr. Maynard saw that in the centre of the living room stood a card table, with fresh packs of cards laid out; while on subsidiary tables here and there were piled dockets of papers, files, lists, pencils: his wife intended to indulge both her passions that evening.

"Who's your fourth?" he asked.

"Mrs. Anderson." The name was merely dropped.

"Ah," Mr. Maynard said, and looked curiously at his wife.

"Mrs. Anderson is such a sweet, dear woman," said Mrs. Talbot, fingering her thick pearls. "Now that her son is in uniform, she's taking such an interest in things. And when she's always so busy, too."

"Busy," cackled Mrs. Lowe-Island, flushing angrily. "We could all be busy if we took as much interest in men as she does."

"Oh!" breathed Mrs. Talbot.

Mrs. Maynard turned her head slightly, and surveyed the areas of wrinkled burnt skin above the ruched pink taffeta. "I should say that men took an interest in her," she observed suddenly, her lips compressed over a laugh. Mrs. Talbot and she exchanged a rapid malicious glance.

A short pause, while Mrs. Lowe-Island looked from one to the other, smiling sourly. She blundered on: "I hate to think what she spends on clothes."

Mrs. Maynard now surveyed the small puffed pink sleeves on Mrs. Lowe-Island's upper arms, and remarked, "It is so pleasant to sit through a dull committee with a woman like Mrs. Anderson, who is always a thing of beauty. It's a rare talent to dress suitably for one's age—it seems."

Again Mrs. Lowe-Island appeared puzzled. Mr. Maynard enquired, "So she's already on committees, is she?"

"She is coming to talk things over tonight," said his wife discouragingly.

"What! In the inner councils already?"

"Her husband is being so efficient with the recreation centres," said Mrs. Talbot.

"I can imagine. And what's she providing—the entertainment?"

Mrs. Maynard frowned. "Mrs. Anderson is really very efficient."

"I was always convinced of it. There's nothing I admire more than that kind of efficiency. The art of living in a small town is one of the most difficult to acquire. Or perhaps it is inborn?" Here he looked full at Mrs. Talbot; her eyes veiled themselves, she faintly coloured.

Alert to danger, Mrs. Maynard glanced from one to the other, and said energetically, "Perhaps you and Mrs. Talbot might discuss it later—privately. As you usually do," she added, with a pleasant smile. "Because you are going to be late for your meeting."

She saw Mrs. Lowe-Island's small black eyes fastened eagerly on Mrs. Talbot. Mrs. Maynard rose, and laid her hand lightly on Mrs. Talbot's shoulder. "Bless you, dear," she said. Mrs. Talbot's face did not change at all; her shoulder shrank away slightly, then stood firm under the slight pressure.

Mr. Maynard was looking warningly at his wife. She met his eyes, and raised her heavy black brows mockingly. Then she allowed her hand to slide away from the grey chiffon shoulder, and went towards the living room. They all followed her.

It was a long, low-ceilinged room, painted white, with pale rose-and-green hangings. It was a room appropriate for tea, cards and gossip; and in the middle of it stood Mrs. Maynard, upright, hands on her hips, looking at her card indexes and files.

"Mrs. Brodeshaw is probably dropping in later," she informed Mr. Maynard.

"So the Players are extending their scope?"

"Not Mrs. Player, Mrs. Brodeshaw," Mrs. Lowe-Island said, and stopped. Her stiff bulky little body quivered under the pink taffeta; the tolerant silence was another affront. She looked from one to another discreet face, and dropped into an ingratiating smile.

"I wish success to your councils," Mr. Maynard said, and strode off across the verandah.

"I do think it's odd that Mr. Maynard should go to the meetings of those people."

"So boring, I should have thought," said Mrs. Maynard casually. She seated herself at the card table, split the seal off a pack, and remarked, "It wouldn't be a bad thing if we could get a representative of the Left League, Book Council, whatever it is."

"Oh, yes, they are such terribly sweet people, really," urged Mrs. Talbot.

"You keep in touch so cleverly with everything."

Mrs. Lowe-Island flushed again and insisted, "They tell me they have niggers at their meetings."

Mrs. Maynard half closed her eyes, and remarked, "Aggie, dear, there are parts of Africa where *Africans* sit in Parliament."

"But we don't want that to happen *here*."

"It surely depends *how* it happens?" Her smile at Mrs. Lowe-Island was an invitation to allow the mills of thought to begin to turn; but Mrs. Lowe-Island snapped, "I wouldn't sit down in the same room with a kaffir."

"No one has asked you to yet."

Mrs. Lowe-Island swelled; then the round reddened little face twisted itself into a smile; the small black eyes wavered, uncertain.

"Will you cut?" enquired Mrs. Maynard.

"What I think is," breathed Mrs. Talbot, "everybody should get together and learn to like each other. I mean, when you meet anybody, you like them *really*—I don't see why people should dislike each other, and all this bickering . . ."

"Bless you, dear. Would you like a higher chair? Your pearls are getting mixed up with the cards."

Mr. Maynard, having looked at his watch and discovered he was late, amended his pace very slightly, and made his way under the moon-filled branches of the trees which lined the avenues that led towards young Mrs. Knowell.

His mind was working comfortably along two different channels. He was thinking that in the "Left Club" or "Socialist League"—his contempt for the organization was demonstrated by the fact that he could never remember, or rather, refused to use, its proper name—were some very able men, who, if the Government had any sense, would be made use of in this national emergency. For the purposes of his dissatisfaction he chose to think of the Government as some clearly defined machinery with which he had nothing to do. Besides, he was an amateur, a looker-on, a dropper-in; he was not implicated. Therefore he turned over in his mind the names of the men in question like a woman fingering silks she had no intention of buying. But there rose the vague thought, One might have a word with old Thompson-Jones.

At the same time, he was conscious of a steady chagrin which he defined as due to Martha. He was a handsome man; many women had found him so; Martha was an attractive young woman; there was nothing in the laws of nature to prevent her from thinking of him as a man: it was clear that never, not for a moment, had she done so. To that woman who makes a man feel for the first time that he is getting old is due a regard which is not so easily defined. He remembered the moment yesterday when she had leaned forward and asked emotionally why he cared about her; and thought of it as an opportunity lost. He knocked on the door of the flat, and waited, suitable remarks preparing themselves on his tongue.

Martha appeared at once, so that he was reminded he was late; and he apologized. He thought she looked very young, and rather appealing. He turned out the light for her, shut the door behind her, and, as they descended the broad stone stairs, tucked her arm under his. She suffered it to remain there a moment, then it dropped out from its own weight.

"You'll be cold," he remarked. She wore one of her slips of coloured linen, arms and legs bare.

"But it's so hot," she said.

He conceded to himself that for him a coat was something one put on when one went out in the evening. For Martha there was a different approach, apparently. He reflected that his wife had sets of clothes suitable for occasions; he could deduce from what she wore what she intended to do. That sage-green lace, for instance, was essentially for bridge with ulterior purposes; whereas, had she worn bunchy silver brocade, he would have diagnosed a late intimate call from the wife of the Prime Minister, or even the Governor's wife.

Whereas Martha might have been going shopping, for a picnic, or to the pictures.

She continued to walk beside him in silence. The moon was large, clear silver, directly above them. The little town was glaring white, black-shadowed, everything sharp and defined. The road glittered saltily. The street lamps were round bright-yellow globes.

"Do you often go to these meetings?" enquired Martha.

"Occasionally."

"What are they talking about tonight?"

Mr. Maynard considered. "I don't know." Then, seeing her surprise: "The deficiencies of education, I believe."

"Well, that should keep them busy."

"Surely education's better than it used to be?"

She was puzzled. "Oh, you mean in *England*."

"You consider they should discuss education here?"

"We live here."

Mr. Maynard considered this in silence.

Aggressively she said, "They just talk and talk."

"I apologize," he began, bringing unnecessary batteries of sarcasm to bear, "for taking you to a function of which you disapprove so strongly."

And now she slipped her arm into his. "It's very sweet of you. It really is."

At once he tightened the grip of his elbow intimately. She impatiently pulled hers away, then shot him an apologetic and embarrassed look. "It's so hot," she said again.

As they turned the corner of a street into that small area of the town which was the business area, she stopped and looked down a few hundred yards of shop fronts and office blocks. "It's growing with the war, isn't it?"

He had never really considered it as a town at all; he tried to see it through Martha's eyes, and failed. "You've never been out of the colony?" His voice was compassionate.

She burst out, "I hate it. I loathe it. I wish I could take the first train out of it. It's like a—Victorian novel. They talk about their servants at tea parties, and say the lower orders are ungrateful. They even go so far as to pay them twelve pounds a year, like our grandmothers, and say they are spoilt. It's all so boring, things happen the same way over and over again. And in fifty years' time, people will be saying about now, "How backward they were then!" But in the meantime, they fight and make speeches and write articles over every sixpence, and all the time with moral language, religion, and all the rest of it. What's it all about, that's what I want to know? It's all so stupid and unnecessary."

"We'll be late," he said, walking forward hastily—not away from the idea, which seemed to him sensible, but from the emotion she put into it. "For a girl of your age, I can think of better things to care about." There was no reaction to this. After a while he conceded, "I admit that this place is only to be borne by those, like myself, who have had their fill of big cities and know that there is really very little difference— We turn in here, I believe."

They were now in the street which lower down became very disreputable and petered out in the slums where the Coloured people lived. They entered a large old, ugly building, and began to mount a spiral iron staircase that was lit by one dull-yellow electric bulb.

"I worked here once," said Martha.

"When?"

"Oh, about two years ago." Clearly, it might have been a decade.

"You know what's so awful about you?" she enquired angrily.

"I shall be pleased to be told."

"You don't really care about anything." She was sullen and aggressive. Then, looking at him, she was overcome with discomfort, and let out a short embarrassed laugh which was half flirtatious. "Well, you don't, do you?"

They stood now on the second landing, which was in the darkness. Above them, over several twists of the iron stairway, came a glimmer of yellow. Doors stood shut and discreet all around them. There was a faint stale smell of urine.

Mr. Maynard suddenly put his arms about Martha, kissed her, and said, "So, I don't?"

She gave him a cold shocked look, pulled away, and went up the stairs in front of him. He followed resignedly.

On this third landing, the doors which studded the dim and dirty corridors stretching away all around them showed brown and peeling under that dingy yellow light. One door stood open, light spilled out, there were people inside. On the door was "Contemporary Politics Discussion Circle" in small white letters on the cracked brown paint. They entered. The meeting had already begun. They slipped into empty spaces separated from each other. Martha looked around, and saw faces she had seen before.

It was a large room, with discoloured whitewashed walls, a bare board floor, yellow electric-light bulbs hanging from loosely knotted flex. There were rough wooden benches all around the walls. A plain wooden table stood at one end, and from behind it spoke a long, bony, bespectacled figure—Mr. Pyecroft himself. He was speaking with great deliberation, mouthing over the long, many-syllabled words. There were about twenty people present, among them three young men in the grey-blue uniform.

On the walls hung two portraits, one of Mr. Nehru and one of Lenin. She had never seen a picture of Lenin before, and the name had had a flavour of something unpleasant, furtive, shady. She saw a strong man, gazing calmly into the future over his little pointed beard. The contrast between the two images confused her. She began to listen to what was being said. Mr. Pyecroft was talking about the provisions for education for village children in Wales in 1910; and although occasionally a match scraped or feet shifted, everyone was listening absorbedly. Martha thought that in 1910 Lenin was alive; she saw him against the background of Tolstoy and Chekhov; in 1910 children in Wales were suffering conditions not much better than Russian children—why, then, had there been no Lenin in Wales? And the way African children lived now . . . She looked around the room. If there existed a Lenin here, presumably he would be in this room? She looked from face to face, and her spirits sank; and she had again ceased to listen.

Opposite her she saw a small dark girl smiling, and recognized Jasmine. She smiled back. Jasmine's eyes turned with a look of enquiry towards Mr. Maynard, and Martha felt herself grow hot. She saw Mr. Maynard through Jasmine's eyes. She was embarrassed. He was seated on his part of the wooden bench stiffly, taking more room than anyone else, arms folded, legs stretched out in front, eyes lowered to the floor. The dark decided face showed no sign of emotion of any kind. Yet from time to time he lifted the bold hazel eyes and looked with a peculiar intentness at various people: Mr. Pyecroft himself, Mr. Perr, Mr. Forester. This intent gaze made Martha uncomfortable, as if she were responsible for it; then, seeing a derisive, critical smile on Jasmine's face, and one that was meant to be noticed, she reacted in the other direction: in comparison with these careless, nondescript people, Mr. Maynard was impressively dignified and sure of himself. If *he* were cut across, he would show solid clean grain right through; he was all of a piece.

But Mr. Pyecroft was still talking. He was now in Scotland and quoting a passage from Scott. People stirred and livened and laughed as Mr. Pyecroft read; a fresh current of life ran through them, and they shifted themselves more comfortably for another effort at listening.

Then Martha saw everybody's eyes turn towards the door. A tall, stooping man stood there smiling; he was an African, dressed carefully in shabby clothes that had been darned and patched everywhere. He carried a briefcase under his arm. Mr. Pyecroft stopped for him; he had continued talking as Mr. Maynard and Martha came in.

Everyone nodded and smiled, made way for him beside them. Half a dozen packets of cigarettes were at once stretched out towards him. He seated himself between Jasmine, who smiled at him like an old friend, and a small fair woman whom Martha remembered seeing before somewhere. He accepted a cigarette, and looked towards the speaker; at once everyone, reminded of their obligations, did the same. But Martha continued to look at him. This was the first time in her whole life, and she was now twenty-one—the first time in a life spent in a colony where nine tenths of the population were dark-skinned—that she had sat in a room with a dark-skinned person as an equal. Again her spirits lifted, and she felt these were people to live and die for. She looked with envy at Jasmine, and at the fair woman on the other side, who had been whispering something to him. She was a tiny, thin creature, with fair braids wound around her head. She had a small, round, bright-coloured face, small brown quick eyes, a big generous nose, a wide emotional mouth. On her other side sat a large, fattish young man, pale, with black-rimmed spectacles: Jewish obviously, and very much an intellectual. From her whispering to the African, she turned to him, the young man, and they exchanged a warm, intimate, deep smile. Martha saw they were in love; passion shone out all at once from the dingy room, and even from the measured sentences of Mr. Pyecroft. Martha warmed to them, warmed to them all. Then, directed by another cautious sardonic look, this time from the tiny fair girl's young man, she looked towards Mr. Maynard, who was steadily regarding the African under his heavy brows.

Martha caught a whisper from near her: some women were talking. One said, in a low humorous voice, "That's Magistrate Maynard —he fined Mr. Matushi two pounds or twenty days last week." "Dirty bastard," came the reply. A great many eyes turned towards Mr. Maynard, who was impervious to such atmospheres, obviously, for he remained calm and absent in his space of bench, a monument of detachment.

Mr. Pyecroft had raised his voice. "And now for my conclusions," he said. He took off his spectacles, paused, laid down his papers. Eyes which had been directed at Mr. Maynard, at Mr. Matushi, centred on him again. Martha found herself gripped by what he was saying. The dead statistics, cautious assessments, hedged facts, were flowing together outwards on words that had the nobility that emanated from the picture of Lenin, from the couple in love, from Mr. Matushi. She listened as if to her own deepest voice speaking. People, said Mr. Pyecroft, were warped and twisted by the system; vast capacities for good lay in everyone; only the tiniest proportion of humankind had ever been given what was needed to raise them from brutes; he painted a picture of the world crowded with miserable, stunted, light-starved creatures, like animalculae writhing under a stone which needed only to be removed. But by Mr. Pyecroft? If one shut one's eyes and listened to the words, then anything was possible, any belief, any vision of good; if one looked at him, that cautious lean gentleman, with his humorous, almost jaunty self-deprecation, the vision collapsed. He was finishing an extraordinarily moving description of new and ennobled humanity with the dry phrases, "And so much for the set piece of the evening; now I'll leave the subject open for discussion."

People stirred, and moved their limbs about: those benches were very hard. No one was eager to begin. After a long minute's silence, Mr. Pyecroft remarked humorously that it appeared he had exhausted the subject. At once Mr. Perr, in considered words, presented what he described as "a small contribution." It appeared that Mr. Pyecroft had misquoted some figures from Scotland. Then the young pale Jew next to the fair girl began to speak. His English was slow, correct, and he would pause without embarrassment for as long as he needed to find the exact word. He asked them to consider the following proposition: In countries where there had been education for the working classes for any length of time, no revolution had been achieved. Revolutions occurred in countries where the masses had "never been made—" he hesitated over the word—"moulded—*formed*," he brought out triumphantly, "by the ruling classes." Could there, then, be a case, he asked them to consider, for progressives such as themselves to fight against popular education instead of for it?

There was a small laugh around the room: it was an embarrassed one. Mr. Pyecroft smiled indulgently, and asked their good friend Boris from Poland to remember that this was a general discussion on education; it was not in their province to discuss the techniques of revolution.

The young man Boris said sarcastically that he should have thought it was a key question. A short silence ensued; Martha saw that the fair girl looked with passionate support into his eyes, and even touched his hand with her own. He remained passive but bitter for a few moments, until he flashed out a warm, grateful smile at her. Various people looked at them tolerantly, but with a touch of malice, as Martha noted angrily.

Since there seemed to be no further contributions, Mr. Pyecroft asked their good friends and visitors from the Air Force to contribute. Two looked at the floor to avoid the invitation. One, a bulky shockheaded mechanic, got up and said that he would like to take up Boris's argument, with which he disagreed, but he was forbidden while in uniform to discuss politics. Here he gave a rather sarcastic laugh, which provoked sarcastic laughter from everybody. He proceeded to describe his own education, which had finished at the age of fourteen, in London. When he modestly sat down, he was regarded with interest and compassion by them all: here was the subject of their discussion in person, the workingman from England.

All this time Mr. Matushi had been listening intently. Now he stood up and asked leave to speak. They all leaned forward to listen. He began by saying that he had heard with gratitude the address given by Mr. Pyecroft, he was sure everyone would be grateful to him for the trouble he had taken. But what had interested him very much was what the last speaker had said. Because it was always surprising and interesting to hear that white men were not always well educated and doing only nice work. (Here people looked at each other self-consciously, but with a certain satisfaction.) A great many of his people would not believe that in England white men lived in bad houses, and with not enough to eat, and had to dig coal and make roads. He wished very much that a great many of his people could hear what the last speaker had said. Then perhaps—he said this with a gentle humour—they might not be so hurt by the newspapers when they said all black men were centuries in evolution behind the white men. But what he really wanted to say was this: There was a problem that interested him even more than the wonderful and intelligent lecture of Mr. Pyecroft. It was the question of the education that African children were given—if you could call it an education, he added apologetically. It would give him great pleasure, he would be very grateful, if that problem could be discussed.

He sat down and looked at them in his characteristic way: patient, dignified, but stubborn.

Mr. Pyecroft at once rose, thanked Mr. Matushi for his contribution, and said they would certainly have a discussion on African education very soon. Here he looked at Jasmine. "In a month's time, Miss Cohen?"

Jasmine said it must be two months' time, since there was another meeting already arranged.

Mr. Pyecroft looked around, his hand resting on the table before him. "If no one wants to say anything?" he began; but Mr. Maynard remarked, "I should rather like to say something."

Close attention was focused on him. "I will be brief. The assumption behind the speaker's very interesting address was this and I want to challenge it: that education is a good thing. There is no evidence at all that sow's ears can be made into silk purses. Popular education in Britain has existed, such as it is, for some decades; are the people better or happier as a result? I doubt it."

There was a chorus of "Oh! Oh! Oh!"

Mr. Maynard waited until it had subsided, and said, "Is there any evidence whatsoever that a person educated in one way rather than another will have different qualities, different abilities? And is there any evidence that the mass of human beings are better than brutes!"

He paused. Everyone exchanged ironical glances. There was also a feeling of discomfort, due to his repeated use of the word "evidence": there was that gap between him and them that is always filled by silence; it was as if a peasant had asked them to prove that the world was round.

"I would be the first to admit that I am an avowed reactionary," said Mr. Maynard urbanely. There was a relieved laugh.

Mr. Perr the statistician rose eagerly. "This is my province," he said, and they laughed again. He was a thin, dark man, with close gleaming black hair and pale gleaming cheeks with a ruddy patch on each. He held himself in such a way that he looked as if he might suddenly fold up like a hinged ruler. He quoted statistics plentifully from various countries, which—if it were necessary—proved to everyone that Mr. Maynard was talking nonsense; Mr. Maynard was obviously unimpressed, however. He smiled ironically until people began chanting all around him in lugubrious tones, "The more things change the more they remain the same," and "Everything is the same under the sun."

"That is my contention," remarked Mr. Maynard.

The deadlock might have been prolonged indefinitely, to peter out, as they do, in frustrated anger and hostility. But Mr. Matushi, who had been regarding Mr. Maynard with a sorrowful face, stood up and began passionately, in marked contrast with his controlled speech of a few minutes before, "Our friend Mr. Maynard says that people don't need to be educated. Well, I know that our people suffer from not being educated. Perhaps Mr. Maynard has had too much education—then he doesn't want other people to be educated. All I know is that our children want to go to school, they want to learn, and they cannot because there are schools for a tiny number of them only."

"You misunderstand me," interrupted Mr. Maynard.

"Oh, no, no, no, I don't misunderstand you, I understand you very well," cried Mr. Matushi.

"Mr. Matushi . . ." said Mr. Pyecroft urgently, half rising from his seat.

Mr. Matushi hesitated, looking around him at faces which for the most part regarded him with interested compassion. He slowly seated himself. "If I am out of order, I am sorry."

"I think we should close the meeting," said Mr. Pyecroft. "Are there any announcements?"

Jasmine rose, in her demure, self-contained way, and laid a slip of paper before him, and returned to her seat.

Mr. Pyecroft read the slip, and then smiled in a way which prepared them all for a joke. "The next meeting, which will take place here four weeks from tonight, will be addressed by Mr. Dunhill." There was a titter. "Mr. Dunhill, who, as we all know, is from the C.I.D., has asked to address us on the comparative incidence of crime in industrial and agricultural areas in Britain."

They all laughed loudly, and looked at a smooth clerkly man who sat, self-conscious, in a corner. "It's a hobby of mine," he muttered.

Could this be all that was meant by the gossip that the C.I.D. attended all their meetings? Martha felt indignant and let down.

"It is now ten o'clock," said Mr. Pyecroft. "Before I close the meeting, there is the little matter of funds."

Discreet tolerant smiles were held while Jasmine, who had apparently been secreting it about her person, produced a cocoa tin with a jagged rent in its lid. It went from hand to hand about the room, to the accompaniment of the small tinkling of falling coins. This incident, like every other, seemed to provide everyone here with the comforting sense of repetition, the safe, the familiar. These people, who all knew each other so well, who exchanged understanding glances at a word, who knew at once at which points to laugh in discussion—these people had been meeting once a month for years, to reassure themselves that their ideas were shared by enough others to make them valid; for years they had discussed education in Chile, or medicine in India; and for years respectable tea tables had been humming with talk of their dangerous activities. Martha found herself succumbing to something rather like fear: the old fear as if nets were closing around her, that particular terror of the very young. This was such a small town—the size of a small market town in England, so they said; and yet it was possible for so many different groups to form themselves, to lead their own self-contained lives, without affecting, or so it seemed, the existence of any other. She was instinctively shaking herself free of this mesh of bonds before she had entered them; she thought that at the end of ten years these people would still be here, self-satisfied in their unconformity, talking, talking endlessly.

All about her she heard small jokes, half-finished phrases that needed only an understanding laugh to complete them. People were rising, going to find particular friends, making plans to meet for sundowners, tea, or children's tea parties.

Jasmine had crossed the room and stood before her, smiling in her quiet friendly fashion. "It's nice to see you here," she began, and involuntarily shot a questioning look towards Mr. Maynard, who was talking to Mr. Perr the statistician. Mr. Perr laughed; it had a note of flattered eagerness which Martha found unpleasant. She saw that Jasmine was observing the couple satirically.

"Did you enjoy it?" she enquired, turning her critical but patient attention back to Martha.

"Why England, why not Africa?" burst out Martha hotly.

Jasmine smiled her agreement, saying, "Well, there are some of us who feel the same way . . ." She glanced round, looking at Boris. "This crowd are a waste of time," she added. Someone grasped her arm. She smiled hastily at Martha, saying, "I'll get into touch with you," and turned away, having thus dismissed the organization for which she had been acting as secretary for some years.

Her place was taken by the fair girl, Betty, who eagerly clasped Martha's arm, searching her face with warm brown eyes; behind her stood Boris, smiling.

"Well?" demanded Betty urgently. "Jasmine's told us about you— we're pleased to see you here. How about coming to tea with us, and—"

"You are overwhelming the poor woman," said Boris humorously, in his clear, correct voice. Betty fell back, laughing, looking at him with eyes full of love. For a moment they smiled at each other, in a way which isolated them from everyone else in the room. A pang of pure envy shot through Martha: she immediately saw their relationship as something lofty, beautiful, on a plane infinitely higher than anything she herself had ever known.

Boris withdrew his eyes from Betty with difficulty, and said with the slow humour which made him sound pompous, "If you would care to come to tea with us and discuss certain matters? There might be a place, for instance, for a discussion group which is not quite so— cautious?"

"They're really too scared to live," flamed Betty. "They're so scared of the word 'Left' that they won't even use it in their name, and—"

They both fell back as Mrs. Perr came forward, shouldering them aside absently. Martha saw them exchange humorous glances.

Mrs. Perr, a tall, thin dark woman, with hair cut straight around her face like a Dutch doll, loose straight discordantly coloured clothes, and a large dry orange mouth, looked closely at Martha and said, "Oh—we've met before."

"Yes, about two years—"

"Well, we're pleased to see you again. I'll ask Jasmine to send you notices of the meetings."

"Thank you very much."

Mrs. Perr narrowed her eyes at her for a moment, in a way which suggested that she was mentally ticking off items on a list and said, "And, of course, there's the Book Club, if you want to join that." She glanced over her shoulder, frowned, then smiled with pleasurable malice. Betty and Boris were leaning against the wall on the other side of the room, talking in low voices, face to face. It was not only

Mrs. Perr who smiled in that discreet, faintly malicious way. "Betty does the books, but since she's been in love they're neglected. Betty!" she called.

Betty slowly turned and blinked across at them, her small, warm, delicately pink face illuminated.

Martha saw that Mr. Maynard was looking at her impatiently across the room, and said, "I'll have to go, anyway." She smiled apologetically at Mrs. Perr, whom she disliked quite finally for being malicious about love, and joined Mr. Maynard.

They went out into the long, dim, dusty corridor. The laughter and talk from the room they had left became a unit of cheerful sound, and Martha stopped, afflicted by the desire to return and belong to the warm community.

"And how did that strike you?" enquired Mr. Maynard affably.

Martha was not going to confess to the criticism that was at the root of her confused disappointment: while they were a community, each of them seemed anxious to repudiate the others to an outsider at the first opportunity.

"That man Perr has real ability," observed Mr. Maynard. "And so has Forester."

"And not Mr. Pyecroft?" Martha could see no difference between Forester, Perr and Pyecroft, all of them as far as she was concerned equally verbose, self-satisfied and elderly.

"Pyecroft has a head on his shoulders, but he's got bogged down in this talking shop. It's all very well as an amusement, but not as a lifework, after all." He added, "There is a certain type of man who leaves the common rooms and lecture halls of Britain simply because he will strike enlightened communities like this one as the last word in education and intellectual daring."

Martha was digesting this when he said, "I've never been able to understand why left-wing women choose to be so unattractive, A remarkable phenomenon."

"They might have better things to do."

"Conceivably."

Martha was thinking of the imposing Mrs. Maynard, who clearly regarded clothes as so many badges of office. She was wondering how Mr. Maynard saw his wife, when feet hesitated behind them. It was Mr. Matushi.

"Ah, Matushi," exclaimed Mr. Maynard, "I'm glad of the opportunity to talk to you."

They were on the dark platform of iron which was the landing on the second floor. This was where he had tried to kiss her. She would have liked to go quickly past it. But he waited calmly while Mr.

Matushi descended. She noted that Mr. Maynard did not use the "Mister," which the others had been so careful to do; she most bitterly resented, on Mr. Matushi's behalf, the casual, authoritative manner of Mr. Maynard.

Mr. Matushi was now standing quietly on the landing, drooping his length from his shoulders: he was a head taller than even Mr. Maynard.

"I understand you regard yourself as a kind of leader of your—compatriots?" Mr. Maynard enquired.

"Yes, I think that is so." The voice was soft, firm, a little hesitant.

"Well, then—there's this question of the war. Would you like to represent your—followers, on a committee for raising funds, eh?"

Mr. Matushi appeared to reflect. Then he said, "Our people all support the war against fascism."

Mr. Maynard let out a surprised grunt. "Eh?" It was the word "fascism"; as far as he was concerned, England was fighting Germany again. "So, you do, do you?"

"Our people are well aware of the danger Hitler represents to the civilized world."

"I don't suppose that more than half of one per cent know who Hitler is."

"In that case, it is not . . . democratic"—Mr. Matushi hesitated delicately over the word—"to make them soldiers in this war, is that not so, Mr. Maynard?" He stooped before Mr. Maynard, stubborn, gentle, expressing with every line of his body an infinite willingness to wait.

Mr. Maynard looked at him heavily, and said, "Be that as it may, it would be appreciated if a well-known and acknowledged leader—a man like yourself—would represent your people on the committee."

Mr. Matushi smiled gently. "Perhaps there might be a better man for the position? A person like myself, fined in the courts, might not be—acceptable?"

Mr. Maynard's black eyebrows shot up, and he said severely, "Matushi, if you don't keep the law, it's my job to fine you. That's all there is to it."

Mr. Matushi was smiling, biting his lips, smiling again; he shook gently with laughter. "But, Mr. Maynard, you are a very good magistrate, we all know that; we all know you as a very just man." There was no resentment in his manner, not even the impertinence which Mr. Maynard was certainly looking for—nothing, apparently, but that genuine bubbling amusement. Suddenly he stopped his long body from the slight pervasive shaking, and said, "Mr. Maynard, our people will do everything they can in this terrible war. They will fight well. It is only fifty years since we were honourably defeated by your soldiers. Our soldiers have already gone to fight with your soldiers against fascism for democracy." He waited, stooping and smiling.

"Good night, Matushi," said Mr. Maynard.

"Good night, sir." He stood to one side while Mr. Maynard and Martha went down the stairs before him, and then followed at a polite distance. They reached the street.

"What did you fine him for?"

"For not having a pass after nine o'clock."

Martha was silent with hostility.

"I don't make the laws, I am their servant."

Martha laughed angrily.

He looked at her in surprise. "Personally I should be in favour of issuing educated men—comparatively educated, that is—with a special pass to exempt them from carrying other passes. I believe it is under consideration now."

"Why not abolish passes altogether?"

"Why not? I suggest you put pressure on your Parliamentary representative to that effect."

Martha laughed again.

"I am firmly of the opinion that the sooner a middle class with privileges is created among the Africans, the better it will be for everyone. Unfortunately, the majority of the whites are so bogged down in intelligent considerations such as that they wouldn't have their sisters marrying black men, that they are too stupefied to see the advantages of such a course."

Martha was several years from understanding this remark, and felt herself to be as stupid as that majority he had dismissed so contemptuously.

They proceeded in silence down the empty moonlit street, Mr. Maynard strolling along, putting one firm leg before the other under a heavy, massive body, hands behind his back, narrowed thoughtful eyes directed ahead. "They are all the same, these African agitators. You can buy any one of them for ten shillings."

"Has Mr. Matushi been bought?"

"They all overreach themselves, if you give them time."

"One of these days they'll fight you with their bare hands."

"I don't doubt it. In the meantime I shall continue to do my duty in that station of life into which it has pleased God to call me."

Martha considered this for a time; and then enquired, really wanting to know: "I don't see why you go to these meetings?"

For the first time, Mr. Maynard showed signs of discomfort. He said hastily, heavily humorous, "I'm an interested observer of life."

"You behave as if you were God," said Martha at last.

They had reached the pavement outside the block of flats.

"If you are genuinely interested in uplifting humanity, which is right and proper at your age, then there are many things you could do."

"Oh no you don't," said Martha abruptly. Mr. Maynard raised his brows. Martha was embarrassed because of the hostility that had sounded in her voice; she did not really understand what she had said. "It was very sweet of you to take me out," she said like a schoolgirl.

"So you have already said. Are you going to ask me up for a drink?" he enquired, facing her massively, so that she had to look up into his face. She felt him to be powerful and dangerous; she remembered him on the second landing. She said, "Caroline wakes so early in the mornings."

Up went those brows. "But I thought Caroline was with your mother?" Then he said, "Well, I won't obtrude myself. Good night." He turned and went striding off along the street.

Martha went indoors in a ferment of embarrassment. He had made her feel gauche and unaccomplished. Yet there had been nothing of the ironical gentleman about him on the second landing among closed doors and the unpleasant, disreputable smell. She felt that that incident had been an insult to both of them. If she chose to remember it, she would never be able to feel liking for him again. She proceeded to forget it, with the vague thought, I suppose it's because he's so old; that generation—kissing hastily on staircases is the sort of thing they did.

She proceeded to think of Mr. Matushi; she could not understand his extraordinarily gentle amusement. If I were Mr. Matushi, she thought angrily, I would . . . But she could think of nothing but that she would have slapped Mr. Maynard's face. Which would have earned him a sentence for assaulting a white man.

She went to bed in a mood of severe self-criticism.

As for Mr. Maynard, he strolled through the moonlight, hands behind his back, and the memory of Martha's nervous hostility rankled. He felt he had been encouraged and then rebuffed. He proceeded to comfort himself by thinking of various romantic episodes. At the same time, he reflected on the meeting; he dwelt particularly on that moment when Mr. Perr had laughed when he remarked that he could not understand why left-wing intellectuals always insisted on being so uncomfortable when they met. The grateful, almost obsequious note in that laugh caused another, but quite disconnected, image to

float into his mind: the face of old Thompson-Jones, Minister for
Finance, with whom he would be playing golf tomorrow.

2

The two rooms at the top of the block of flats were filled with light
from the sky as soon as the sun, splendid, enlarged and red, swelled
up over the horizon of suburb-clotted hills, pulling behind it fila-
ments of rose-and-gold cloud. By half past five, fingers of warm
yellow were reaching over the big bed, over Caroline's crib. Martha
lay warm in the blankets, listening to Caroline wake. She always
woke the moment the child first stirred, as if an alarm had gone off;
she woke instantly if Caroline murmured in her sleep at night. Caroline gurgled, and strove with her limbs until the covers were off. She
sat up. Martha, through eyes kept half closed, saw the tiny energetic
creature in its white gown rolling over and stretching, two small
rosy feet playing in the air, while the voice tried itself: a soft
chuckle, then a deep, self-absorbed murmur; silence, and a sudden
shriek of triumphant vitality as the cradle shook and rattled with her
movements. The low meditative murmur began again; Caroline,
crouching on all fours, looked steadily at the white blanket while
she listened to her own voice; there was a look of thoughtful surprise
on the small face. She dropped sideways, rolled to her back, her
legs stuck straight up, she grunted and puffed while her face reddened. She lay there, rocking her legs from side to side, silent for the
moment, apparently waiting with docile patience to hear what new
sound her throat would bring forth. A high single note, like a bird's;
another, a fifth lower; a long silence, and again a high triumphant
yell. Caroline clambered resolutely to her feet, clutched the edge of
the cradle, put her chin on it, and looked out of the window at the
sun. The big yellow ball swam now in a clear sky. Caroline blinked
at it; beads of sweat clung under her short black curls. She squeezed
her eyes shut, and rocked, humming, from one foot to another, the
sun sharply etching her rosy face with shadow and warm light. She
opened her eyes cautiously; the sun still filled her eyes with its
dazzle. She turned her head slightly, and, frowning with determination, put up a clenched fist over one eye, and opened the other at
the sun: it was still there, hanging in the blue square of the window.
She stretched out one fist and spread it into a shaft of yellow light
that swam with golden dust; the small fingers moved wildly, then
clutch! they shut on nothing. Caroline looked down, puzzled, at her
empty palm. She tried again; her hand went clutch! clutch! at the

mote-filled sunlight. Then she stretched out both hands to the sun, a look of desperate desire on her face. She let out a high angry, baffled yell and shook the bars of her crib furiously. She lost her footing, rolled over, and lay on her back, legs waving comfortably in the warm sunlight, contentedly trying out her voice.

Martha shut her eyes and tried to sleep again. She could not. There was this band of tension, felt deeply as a web of tight anxiety, between her and the child. Every movement, every sound Caroline made reverberated through Martha. Relax! said Martha to herself, but she felt tension in every limb. She was waiting for that moment when Caroline's high shriek peremptorily sounded the summons for the day to begin.

And yet, during those three days while Caroline had been with her grandmother, Martha had slept, waked, gone about living as if Caroline did not exist, had never existed. Not for a moment had Martha felt anxiety; she had scarcely thought of the child. She came home; and again Martha was caught up into the rhythm of this other small life. Her long day was regulated by the clock to Caroline's needs; and she went to bed at night exhausted by Caroline's experience.

She lay now, eyes closed to a narrow slit, the sun making rainbows on her eyelashes, so that she might see it as Caroline had just seen it, and knew that her reluctance to get out of bed was simply boredom at the thought of the day ahead. She wished it were already the end of the day, and Caroline safely in bed and asleep. Then her, Martha's, life might begin. And yet the hours of evening were as restless and dissatisfied; she always went to bed early to put an end to them. Her whole life was a hurrying onwards, to get it past; she was back in the tension of hurry, hurry, hurry; and yet there was nothing at the end of it to hurry towards, not even the end of the war, which would change nothing for her.

At this point in her reflections, she again told herself to relax: her inability to enjoy Caroline simply filled her with guilt. Yet she could not relax into Caroline; that would be a disloyalty and even a danger to herself. Cycles of guilt and defiance ruled her living, and she knew it; she had not the beginnings of an understanding what it all meant.

Caroline was now chanting steadily, with a note of urgency in her voice that Martha knew. Her limbs involuntarily stiffened; she made them lie loose.

Caroline bundled herself over, dragged herself hand over hand up the bars of the crib, rested her chin on the rail and looked at her mother. Martha saw the small, white-gowned girl, her alert bright black eyes shrewdly watching her. Caroline let out a shriek of warning, and waited. Martha suddenly laughed, won over into tender amusement. Caroline surveyed her mother for a moment, and shook the bars like a monkey. In an instant, Martha had swung her legs over, lifted Caroline out and set her on the big bed.

The book prescribed rusk and orange juice. Martha fetched them. Caroline staggered around the room on her unsteady little legs, sucking the rusk into a sticky fawn-coloured paste.

The small white-painted room was filled with sunlight, like a glass bowl full of quivering bright water. Martha took a bath: the bathroom was shot with needles of sunlight; the water rocked in the white bath in spangles and opals of light. Then she dressed swiftly in one of the brief coloured dresses that gave her so much pleasure to wear. How lovely to wear so little, to feel her brown smooth limbs coming out of the slip of coloured linen; she was all free and her own again; she was light and supple, and the stains and distortions of pregnancy belonged to another epoch. How lovely then to wash the little girl, and see her in her fresh pretty cotton dress, the delicate pink feet balancing so surely and strongly over the floor.

By seven every morning Martha and her daughter were dressed and ready for the day, and they ate breakfast together; or rather, Martha drank tea and painfully did not care that Caroline would not eat.

Ever since the day Mr. Maynard had entered on the unpleasant scene of Caroline being fed, when Martha had seen it sharply through his eyes, she had forced herself, and with an effort that exhausted her, *not* to care about Caroline's eating. She must break this bond! That was how she felt it: as something compulsive and deadly that would most certainly affect the child's whole future. So Martha no longer cared, on principle. But at the beginning it had not been so easy. She prepared the messes suitable for Caroline's age, set them on the wooden platform before the child, put a piece of linoleum under the high chair, and retired with a cup of tea and a book, forcing herself not to look at her.

And now what contests of will followed! Caroline had been used to a forceful pillar of a mother standing over her with a glinting hard spoon full of stuff that she *must* eat, no matter how she tightened her lips and turned away her face; now she saw this same woman—and from one day to the next—sitting away from her on the other side of the room, not listening to her cries of rage and shrieks of defiance. Caroline picked up the bowl of porridge and flung it on the floor so that the greyish mess splashed everywhere; Martha turned a page and did not look. Caroline sparked her black eyes at Martha, let out short sharp cries of anger to *make* her look; then she picked up a mug of milk and poured it all over herself. Martha remained indifferent in her chair; but there was a tight-lipped tension about her that Caroline knew. She paddled her hands in a lake of soiled milk and rubbed them in her hair, singing out her defiance. And suddenly Martha became a whirlwind of exasperation. She jumped up and said despairingly, "Oh, Caroline! You are a naughty, naughty girl!"

The little girl, with blobs of porridge on her face, her hair plastered and dripping with milk, gurgled out triumphant defiance. Then she found herself lifted roughly from the chair; she yelled angrily while Martha held her kicking under her arm, and bent to fill the bath. She was dropped into the water, soaped hastily; she felt herself whirled into new clean clothes, and then she was dropped into her wooden pen, where she soon forgot all about it, and began playing with her toys.

In the meantime Martha was scrubbing porridge and milk off the floor, the furniture, herself. She was sick with disgust at the mess. She was asking herself why she had endured months of that other mess with only occasional lapses into distaste; a period when napkins and then clothes and blankets had been wet and dirty, without difficulty: the book had said so. The book and she had been admirably justified: Caroline was now, as the phrase went, perfectly clean. But that had been no problem; the battle centred on food. What is it all about? asked Martha in despair. She was furious with herself for losing her temper. She could have wept with annoyance. She was saying to herself, as she wiped off milk and grey pulp, Oh, Lord, how I do hate this business, I do loathe it so. She was saying she hated her daughter; and she knew it. Soon, the hot anger died; guilt unfailingly succeeded. Outside, on the little verandah which was like a wired cage projecting out into the sunlight—the sun was now pouring down from over the trees in the park—Caroline was cheerfully gurgling and singing to herself. Inside the room, Martha was seated, tired and miserable. Her heart was now a hot enlarged area of tenderness for the child whom she was so lamentably mishandling.

She went out into the verandah. Caroline, in her short bright dress, looked up with her quick black eyes, and made an enquiring noise. She was snatched up and held against Martha's bosom. At once she began striving free; Martha laughed ruefully and put her down; she staggered around the room, singing to herself.

But she had eaten absolutely nothing. Martha produced rusks, and left them surreptitiously about the room. Caroline seized on them and began chewing vigorously.

"Oh, Caroline," sighed Martha, "what am I going to do with you?"

She was forming the habit of talking to the child as if to herself. The small brain was receiving the sound of a half-humorous, resentful, grumbling, helpless voice rumbling away over her head.

"My poor unfortunate brat, what had you done to deserve a mother like me? Well, there's no help for it, you'll just have to put up with it. You bore me to extinction, and that's the truth of it, and no doubt I bore you. But as far as I can make out, one of the most important functions of parents is that they should be suitable objects of hate: if psychology doesn't mean that, it means nothing. Well, then, so it's right and proper you should hate my guts off and on, you and I are just victims, my poor child, you can't help it, I can't help it, my mother couldn't help it, and her mother . . ."

After a silence the voice went on, rather like Caroline's own meditative experimental rumblings and chirpings: "So there we are, and we'd better make the best of it. As soon as possible I'll send you to a nursery school where you are well out of my poisonous influence, I'll do that for you at least."

By nine in the morning, it seemed always as if long stretches of the day had been lived through. And yet it was three hours till lunchtime. Martha sewed—she and Caroline had dozens of cheap pretty dresses. She watched the clock. She cooked little messes for Caroline. She leafed hopefully through the book—or rather, whichever one of them seemed most likely to provide what she wanted—to see if she had overlooked some pattern of words that might help her to feel better. And at the least she felt she was being honest, that virtue which she was still convinced was the supreme one. Somewhere at the bottom of her heart was a pleasant self-righteousness that while she was as little fitted for maternity as her mother had been, she at least had the honesty to admit it.

She would watch lunchtime approaching with helpless despair. But she was determined to break this cycle of determination, which always ended in her own violent anger and Caroline's rebellious screams.

She learned to put Caroline's food in front of her and then go out of the room altogether. When she came back, she forbade herself to notice the unpleasant fly-covered mess on the high chair. She quickly lifted the child out, and washed her, and set her back in her pen without saying a word. Day after day, Martha lay face down on the bed at every mealtime, her fingers stuck in her ears, reading, while Caroline yelled for attention next door. Slowly the yells lessened. There came a point where the child received her food and ate it. Martha returned from her exile in the bedroom, the victory won. She had succeeded in defeating the demon of antagonism.

And now she was able to cook the food and serve Caroline with it and not care if she ate it or not. And, of course, now it was eaten. And Martha existed on hastily cut slabs of bread and butter and tea. She could not be interested in food unless she was cooking it for someone with whom she would share it afterwards. Women living by themselves can starve themselves into a sickness without knowing what is wrong with them.

Then she became perversely sad because she had won the victory. It seemed that something must have snapped between her and her daughter. It increased her persistent uneasiness, which expressed itself in those interminable puzzled humorous monologues: "It's all very well, Caroline, but there must be something wrong when you have to learn *not* to care. Because the trouble with me is not that I care too much, but that I care too little. You'd be relieved, my poor brat, if you knew that when you were with my mother I never thought of you at all—that's a guarantee of your future emotional safety, isn't it?" Silence, while Caroline pursued her own interests about the room; if the silence persisted, however, she cocked a bright enquiring eye towards her mother. "But what I can't understand is this: Two years ago, I was as free as air. I could have done anything, been anything. Because the essence of the daydreams of every girl who isn't married is just that: it's the only time they are more free than men. Men *have* to be something, but you'll find when you grow up, my poor child, that you'll see yourself as a ballet dancer, or a business executive, or the wife of a Prime Minister, or the mistress of somebody important, or even in extreme moments a nun or a missionary. You'll imagine yourself doing all sorts of things in all sorts of countries; the point is, your will will be your limit. Anything'll be possible. But you will not see yourself sitting in a small room bound for twenty-four hours of the day—with years of it in front of you—to a small child. For God's sake, Caroline, don't marry young, I'll stop you marrying young if I have to lock you up. But I can't do that," concluded Martha humorously, "because that would be putting pressure on you, and that's the unforgivable sin. All I can promise is that I won't put any pressure on you of any kind. I simply *won't care.* . . . But supposing that not caring is only the most subtle and deadly way of putting pressure on people—what then? . . . But what is most difficult is this: If you read novels and diaries, women didn't seem to have these problems. Is it really conceivable that we should have turned into something quite different in the space of about fifty years? Or do you suppose they didn't tell the truth, the novelists? In the books, the young and idealistic girl gets married, has a baby—she at once turns into something quite different; and she is perfectly happy to spend her whole life bringing up children with a tedious husband. Natasha, for instance: she was content to be an old hen, fussing and dull; but supposing all the time she saw a picture of herself as she had been, and saw herself as what she had become and was miserable—what then? Because either that's the truth or there is a completely new kind of woman in the world, and surely that isn't possible, what do you think, Caroline?"

All the morning, sunlight moved and deployed around the flat. After lunch the sun had moved away; the rooms were warm, airless, stagnant. And then Martha put Caroline into her push-chair, and filled in the time by wheeling her around the streets for an hour, two hours, three hours. Or she sat in the park under a tree with dozens of other young mothers and nannies, watching the children play. This period of the day seemed to concentrate into it the essence of boredom. It was boredom like an illness. But at six in the evening, Caroline was washed, fed, and put into her crib. Silence descended. Martha was free. She could go out, see people, go to the pictures. But she did not. She sat alone, reading and thinking interminably, turning over and over in her mind this guilty weight of thoughts, which were always the same. Those people who have been brought up in the nonconformist pattern may shed God, turn upside down the principles they were brought up to; but they may always be relied upon to torment themselves satisfactorily with problems of right behaviour. From these dreary self-searchings there emerged a definite idea: that there must be, if not in literature, which evaded these problems, then in life, that woman who combined a warm accepting femininity and motherhood with being what Martha described vaguely but to her own satisfaction as "a person." She must look for her.

Then one day she saw Stella in the street. They exchanged the gay guilty promises to come and see each other which people do who are dropping out of each other's lives. Afterwards Martha thought that Stella looked very contented. She had changed. Two years ago she had been a lithe, alive, beautiful young woman. Having a baby had turned her into a stout and handsome matron, very smart, competent and—this was the point—happy. Or so it seemed in retrospect. Thinking wistfully for several days about Stella's unfailing self-assurance, in whatever role life asked her to play, turned her, for Martha, into a symbol of satisfactory womanhood. On an impulse then she dropped Caroline in the house across the park with her mother, and drove out to the house in the suburbs where Stella now lived with her mother.

It was a very bright sparkling day, with a tang of chill in the air. The sky was glacially blue. The white houses in their masses of heavy green foliage shone in a thin clear light, with a remote, indrawn look, as if prepared to be abandoned by warmth for a short season. The wave of painful emotion that is a clearer sign of changing seasons than the loosening of a leaf or a clap of thunder after seven months' silence entered Martha suddenly with familiar and pleasurable melancholy—winter was coming. In such a mood, to enquire from Stella how one should live appeared absurd; nostalgia imposed different values—nothing mattered very much. Suppressing it, she drove on through the avenues, turned outwards over a narrow road through a shallow grass-filled vlei, and entered a new suburb; the town was spreading fast under the pressures of war. This suburb was a mile of new bungalows scattered hastily over a rock-strewn rise. Stella's mother's new house was at its limit; beyond stretched the unscarred veld; and the garden was bounded by heaps of granite boulders tangled over by purple bougainvillea. The bungalow was small, but no longer a Colonial bungalow. The verandah was a small porch, and there were green shutters to the windows, and there was a look of glossy smartness about it. Martha parked the car, went up prim steps, and rang the bell, feeling like someone paying a visit.

Stella appeared and cried out a gay welcome. She was wearing a handsome scarlet housecoat, and her dark braids fell down her back. In the living room her mother was playing with the baby. The room looked like an illustration from a magazine; it was all cream leather and red carpet. Through the cream-shaded windows a stretch of sere drying veld looked in and disowned the alien. Martha felt a sharp dislocation in her sense of what was fitting, as she always did with Mrs. Barbazon, who, with her careful dark eyes, seemed a stray from the capitals of Europe.

Stella flung back her dark braids carelessly, and, with her new look of matronly contentment, sat down, watching her child—a little girl, dark-eyed, slender, pale. Both women were competing for Esther's attention. Mrs. Barbazon was holding up her crystal beads and swinging them before the infant's moving eyes. Stella leaned forward and offered the end of one of her long thick plaits. Esther reached out for it, and with a satisfied smile Stella lifted her onto her own lap.

"How's Andrew?" asked Martha.

Without lifting her eyes from Esther's face, Stella said, "Oh—I haven't had a letter recently. I don't know." This was hard and careless.

"I heard from my brother that he'd met him somewhere up north."

Stella looked up quickly, searched Martha's face, asked, "What did he say he was doing?"

"Oh, nothing much, just that they'd met. My brother's with the South Africans."

"This terrible, terrible war," said Mrs. Barbazon.

"Oh, they seem to be having a good enough time," said Stella, with a careless laugh. Her face looked set for a moment; then she smiled at Esther, and began tickling her cheeks with the soft brush at the end of the braid.

"And how's Esther?"

Mrs. Barbazon, smiling reminiscently, opened her mouth to give information. Stella cut in first with a story of how the child had crawled this morning across her bed. Mrs. Barbazon said, "You should let her sleep with me—you'd get some rest."

"Oh, I've nothing else to do, and you're a good girl, aren't you, Esther?"

There was a silence. Martha felt the room oppressive. She could see that both women were devoting their lives to Esther; it was a close, jealous, watchful household.

"And are you having a good time?" asked Mrs. Barbazon, in a way which told Martha they had been discussing her unfavourably.

"I've got my hands full with Caroline."

"Oh, there's no time for anything else with a baby in the house."

"I had a letter from Andrew last month," said Stella casually. "He says the boys up north are all demoralized because their wives and girl friends are unfaithful to them with the Air Force."

"It's a terrible thing," said Mrs. Barbazon, "when our men are sacrificing everything to fight, and the women have no loyalty."

Here there was an inexplicable long look between Mrs. Barbazon and Stella; the older woman rose, and said, "I'll make some tea, the servants are out." She left the room with a small wistful smile in the direction of Esther.

As soon as her mother had left the room, Stella set the child on the floor and gave her attention to Martha. She asked if Caroline was walking yet; when Martha said yes, she said quickly that a year was early to be walking, from which Martha deduced that Esther had fallen behind schedule in her achievements.

Martha looked at Esther with detached criticism, in which was concealed the distaste that women feel for other women's babies while they are still closely physically linked with their own. Esther, she decided, was listless and heavy compared to the ceaselessly mobile Caroline.

Stella began talking of how she had had to wean the child after three months; her health had not permitted her to stand the strain of breast feeding; as she spoke, she unconsciously felt her now plump breasts with both hands. "Having babies ruins the figure, ruins it." She looked over at Martha and said, "You've lost the weight you put on."

"I didn't lose it," said Martha grimly, "I starved it off."

"Oh, I could never diet, I'm not strong enough. Anyway, Andrew always said he wished I was fatter." Stella sighed, and her face fell into dissatisfied lines. The beautiful dark eyes looked strained and shadowed. The remote exotic gleam had gone; the seductive quality that Martha had so envied, that had showed itself in her every glance and movement, had completely vanished; she was a good-looking housewife, no more.

The doorbell rang. Stella's eyes gathered life; she half rose, then said, "But I'm not dressed!"

"Leave it—I'll go," said Mrs. Barbazon from the kitchen.

Stella stood with her hands to her hair.

"You'd better get yourself dressed," said Mrs. Barbazon, as she came through to go to the door. There was a disapproving note in her voice which caused Martha to glance curiously at Stella.

A look of anger crossed Stella's face, then went. "Oh, yes, I can't be seen like this," she said, and went out quickly just before Mrs. Barbazon came back with a young officer.

He was a big, bulky, fairheaded man, blue-eyed, Northern-looking. He sat down, while Mrs. Barbazon moved and fussed about him. She sat down and began questioning him with the touching, self-immolating devotion which was what she offered to her daughter, about how the flying had gone yesterday, had he been sleeping better?

"Stella's just getting dressed. You know what things are with a baby in the house."

The newcomer, reminded of the household's obligations clucked at the baby. Mrs. Barbazon, seeing him occupied, went out and quickly returned with a tea-waggon. She began pouring.

A gay voice was heard outside. "Mother, where's my hairbrush?"

"I don't know." Mrs. Barbazon spoke sharply. She stood looking at the doorway, with the teapot held suspended in her hand. Stella, in a dress of apple-green linen which showed her apricot-coloured arms, was standing in the doorway, her loosened masses of hair about her face, apparently oblivious of the officer.

"Ah, there it is. Naughty Esther, you had it." Stella reached for the hairbrush, holding back her heavy hair with one hand. "Why, Rupert, is that you?"

Mrs. Barbazon steadily poured tea, her lips compressed.

"You know how things get all over the place, with babies in the house," said Stella with her jolly laugh. She stood in front of the big man, who had risen and was awkwardly facing her, and began brushing back the loads of glistening hair that slipped with a hiss over her shoulders. He could not keep his eyes off it. Her small smooth face emerged from the frame of falling hair, and Martha saw that the spirit of attraction had lit it again; Stella looked as she had done before the baby. She smiled and asked how he did, while he said, "Fine, fine, thank you," and his eyes followed the movement of the hair. She held the scene for a few moments longer; then, with a final swift toss of her head backwards, which flung the hair into an oiled, irridescent, dead-black curve, she said, "Excuse me, I'll just finish dressing."

The three sat and made conversation while the officer's eyes rested on the door through which Stella had gone. She returned in a few moments, the black hair done up demurely in its heavy knot, and sat down near him. Little Esther began tugging at the green linen. Stella put her hands down once or twice, and then said hastily, "Let's call the nurse—she can go out for a bit."

Mrs. Barbazon rose, picked up Esther, and went out. She did not return.

Martha soon got up and said she must go and feed Caroline.

At once Stella said, "Do come and see us again, Matty. You're a naughty girl, forgetting your friends like this." But she was looking at the officer even as she spoke; Martha felt something like pity for the big likeable man with the candid blue eyes.

Stella came with her to the door. "He's a nice boy," she remarked. "We try and make him feel at home. It must be hard for them, so far from their families."

Martha laughed. Stella looked at her, puzzled.

"He's a really nice boy, Mother says she feels towards him like a son," she went on, smiling a small, dreamy and quite unconscious smile.

Martha urged Stella with false animation to visit her soon. Stella again berated Martha for being so unsociable. They exchanged urgent invitations for a few moments, and parted, disliking each other.

Martha was feeling extraordinarily foolish as she drove home. The reaction against Stella sent her back to Alice. The two women had in common a basic self-absorption that made it possible to forget each other for weeks and meet again easily without any embarrassment. They understood each other very well. They would seek each other out for the sole reason that they needed a safety valve; they would discuss in humorous, helpless voices, for an hour or so, their boredom, the tediums of living alone, the unsatisfactory nature of marriage, the burden of bringing up children, and part in the best of humours with the unscrupulous and buccaneering chuckle that came of being so ruthlessly disloyal to everything they were.

Then each retired again into isolation. Alice was half crazy with being alone. She was very thin, her hair hung limp about her face, she neglected her clothes. From time to time she exclaimed defiantly, "Oh, to hell with everything," and rang up Martha to say she was going out with the Air Force. Martha always assured her that this was the least of her rights. Alice pulled out an old dance dress, combed her hair back, scrawled some lipstick across her face. She then set herself to be the life and soul of whichever party she happened to be at. Returned to her flat by some ardent young man, she allowed herself to be kissed and caressed for a while, as if she owed this to her self-respect, and then said, "Oh, well, that's that—thanks for a lovely time." With which she departed indoors, with a hasty apologetic wave. She never saw any young man for a second time. On these occasions Martha was likely to be rung up at three in the morning by Alice, who concluded her desperate, gay, rambling comments on the party by "The point is, once you've been married there's no point in it, I don't enjoy anything any more." And then, firmly: "But if Willie thinks I'm going to sit at home weeping for him, he'd better think again, after what I heard he was up to!" With this, she let out her high fatalistic giggle, and wished Martha a good night.

3

The airstrip was an irregular stretch of glistening white sand in the dull-green bush. As the aircraft turned in to land, the shadow of its wings dipped over an acre or so of tin-and-brick bungalows. The soldiers in the aircraft peered down past the tilting wings and suggested Lower Egypt, Abyssinia, Kenya, Uganda. It seemed that they had all seen this shantytown in the bush many times before.

The aircraft bounced a little as it landed, then slewed to a stop. A thick cloud of white dust drifted up. The door was kept shut till it cleared. Then they descended—half a dozen men on their feet. An ambulance was already motoring across the half mile between here and the red-brick shack that was an office, to pick up the stretcher cases. The half dozen stood on one side hopefully while the stretchers were slid inside the white car, but it drove off immediately. They walked across the white glisten of the strip, sand giving with a silken crunch beneath their boots, then through low dun-coloured bushes towards the office. Small paper-white butterflies hovered over the bushes, or clung with fanning wings. There was a hot, spicy smell of leaves. Over the squashed remains of a chameleon, spreadeagled on the sand like a small dragon's skin pegged out, was a thick black clot of ants. A stray kaffir dog, his skeleton showing clear through tight skin, lay in the pit of blue shade outside the verandah. They stepped over the dog and went in.

It was a single room. A South African sergeant sat behind a small deal table. A black man in a sort of orderly's uniform stood at ease beside him. The sergeant was pouring a glass of water from a bedroom decanter. He tipped back his head, poured the water into his mouth, wiped his hand across his mouth, looked at them and said, "So there you are."

Douglas said half facetiously, "Where are we, we'd like to know."

The sergeant thought, concluded that the information could not subvert the course of the war, and offered cautiously, "Nyasaland."

The men exchanged startled, bitter glances. "Pretty far from the front," said Douglas, his face hard.

A quick glance from the sergeant. He said officially, "Are you O.K. till you get into town? There's a car coming for you."

He nodded at a bench set against the wall. They did not immediately sit down. They stood tense, looking at each other, at the sergeant.

"Sit down," said the sergeant again, authoritative but uneasy.

They slowly walked over, dropped their packs by the wall, sat. Six men, all tough soldiers, very burnt, apparently fit for anything. Yet here they sat. They sat and waited with the patience which a year in the Army had taught them. Indeed, for that year they had done little else but wait. They had marched, drilled—and waited; slept under canvas or in the open—and waited; they had been told nothing, knew nothing. For the first time in their lives they had been *pushed around;* they were expected to wait. And now things were really happening up north, and they were back only a few hundred miles from home. They waited. The small brick room, unceilinged, was roofed with corrugated iron; the heat poured down. The brick at their backs burned through the thick khaki; they sat away and forward from the wall, looking out of the doorway into the sunlight. The aircraft looked like a small silver insect glittering off sunlight. It was apparently abandoned. A pair of hawks circled above on steady wings.

Douglas, at the end of the bench, blinked regularly out into the dazzle. Beside him sat Perry, legs sprawling in front of him, the big blond sun-reddened body tense. Douglas heard the breath coming fast and irregular, and glanced swiftly sideways; Perry was staring angrily at a map of Africa nailed to the brick wall opposite. Arrows of black ink showed the offensives and counteroffensives in North Africa. Their unit was—so they believed—combining with the Australians against Rommel at that moment. Perry's mouth, when closed, was a hard, lipless line; when slightly open, as now, it had a spoilt and peevish droop.

Douglas muttered with warning cheerfulness, "Hey, take it easy, man."

Perry moved his legs, showing mats of wet hair on reddened skin where they had adhered together. Sweat was dripping steadily off all of them. "There's been a balls-up, a mucking balls-up." The tone was one they all knew; legs shifted, bodies eased, all along the bench. The sergeant, seated behind his table, was writing a letter home, and did not look up.

Douglas got up, went to the table, reached out his hand, laid it on the decanter, and looked at the sergeant, who nodded briefly. Douglas took glass and decanter, and went along the line of men with it. Before he reached the end, the water was finished. He handed the decanter to the black orderly, who submerged it in a petrol tin covered with a wet sack that stood in a corner, and handed it back, dripping. The water hissed into the brick floor. Douglas returned the things to the table, and sat down again.

Perry's mouth and chin were wet with water. He raised his fist and rubbed it over the lower part of his face, then let it drop. The fist hung clenched. He banged it several times against the edge of the bench, and left it hanging. He looked at the map and said, "They told us we'd be examined. They've balled us up. What are we doing in this God-damned dump?"

Douglas hastily agreed, "Bloody mess," and looked at him with entreaty.

Perry writhed his big body frustratedly and jumped up. He went rapidly to the table, snatched at the decanter as the sergeant instinctively jerked up his head, dived at the petrol tin, filled the decanter, and poured it all over his head and shoulders. The sergeant turned his head to watch, then went on writing. Perry dumped the decanter down under the man's nose.

"Oh, sit down, damn it," the sergeant muttered uneasily.

Perry grinned slightly, and sat. They waited. The bricks hissed as the water sank in. Water dripped off Perry's neck and hair.

A lorry came bumping across the airstrip. But it swerved over to the aircraft. A couple of Africans got out, uncoiled a black hose, and began feeding petrol into it. The two hawks were now black specks high in the grey-blue air. The air between here and the aircraft swam in lazy hot waves. Then the aircraft began to shake. It turned, and trundled away up the strip for the take-off. They watched it turn and come roaring down the strip past them, and up. In a moment it was away over the trees, and its silver glitter was absorbed in the vast glitter of the sky. The two hawks continued to wheel on level wings.

"Mucking bastards, leaving us behind," said Perry suddenly, and his voice cracked.

The sergeant's cheek muscles showed tense, but he went on writing fast.

Perry got to his feet with slow deliberation, and slouched over to the table. "Sarge?"

The sergeant laid down his pen and looked at him. "Steady on, man," he said warningly, "I'm not responsible for it."

Perry, his face scarlet, his tunic soaked, drops of sweat and water scattering, leaned forward, suspending a big red hairy fist over the table. "I'm not going to be messed up," he said, in a quiet voice.

"I'm not messing you up," said the sergeant steadily. He looked past Perry to the bench, where the men sat watching. There were half-grins on their faces. The man at the far end, nearest the door, a lanky youth with a bony freckled face, was smiling hilariously. He looked as if he were about to cheer.

Douglas remained seated for a moment, but then got up and came forward, laying his hand on Perry's shoulder. "Now, come on, man, don't take it out on him." He sounded embarrassed.

Perry kept his shoulder still, then flung off the hand with a sudden heave. Douglas stood back a pace. Perry leaned both his fists on the table, and stared straight into the sergeant's face. "I'm going to break everything up if I don't get some sense out of you."

The table leaned over, the sergeant put his hands down to steady it, it slid roughly over the lump brick tight against the sergeant's stomach. He was now pinned back against the wall. The orderly stood, arms folded, watching with interest.

Perry deliberately pressed the table forward against the sergeant, who was pale and gasping, and trying to push it back again. "You mucking pen-pushing bastard . . ." Using all his strength, he forced the edge of the table into the sergeant. Ink, pens, paper, glass, decanter, went rolling and crashing.

Douglas made a movement of his head towards the others. After a hesitation, three of them rose, leaving the cheerful boy alone, and came over. "Now stop it, damn it, man," said Douglas.

Perry gritted his teeth, and heaved. The sergeant had lost his foot-ing, and was pinned in mid-air against the wall, straining for breath. His boots scraped wildly at the floor. Douglas nodded at the three; all four gripped Perry by the shoulders, with a sort of weary good humour, and pulled him back. A moment's scrape, struggle, heave— then Perry came staggering back, the sergeant found his feet, the table shot away. The sergeant stood blinking, trying to get back his breath without showing he had lost it. He smoothed down his tunic, pulled up the fallen chair, and sat down. He nodded at the African, who began picking up things off the floor.

"Look at him," gasped out Perry, "sitting there on his fat arse, pushing a pen." He shook off his captors, who had their hands laid warningly on various parts of his upper body. He looked at them, grinning. They grinned sheepishly back. Then they all turned sud-denly at the sound of a wild cry of laughter from the youth who had remained sitting. His face was flushed and incoherent, his eyes lit with a blue glare. He stamped his boots a few times on the floor, let out a "Hurray!" and all at once sat looking at them doubtfully, as if he did not know them.

"For God's sake," said Douglas in a rapid warning undertone, "he'll be off again." Immediately all five returned to their places on the bench, leaving a small space between the youth and the man next to him. Perry leaned back against the burning wall, and began a low hissing whistle between his teeth, to the tune of "Begin the Beguine." From time to time he banged his big fists on his knees, in a consider-ing way. His mouth drooped slightly open; but he looked cautiously over the youth, who was now staring straight in front of him, his clear blue eyes clouded with wonder, at the map on the wall. The African was sweeping the mess of glass, ink, and water from the brick with a fibre broom. The sergeant sat moodily, arms folded on the table.

"I could have you court-martialled," he observed bitterly at last.

No one said anything. Perry continued to hiss out "Begin the Be-guine."

"I'd be within my rights to have you court-martialled," insisted the sergeant.

"Discipline," said Perry. "Discipline is what this war needs." He turned his big head slowly towards the sergeant. He surveyed him steadily.

"Oh, for God's sake," said Douglas impatiently. "Don't start again."

The sergeant glanced involuntarily through the square in the wall that called itself a window, and exclaimed, "Your car's coming." His voice was eager with relief.

Perry lapsed back against the wall, his lips stretched in a small ugly grin.

A large army lorry stopped outside. The soldiers stood up, stretching themselves. When the distracted youth did not move, the man nearest to him unceremoniously heaved him up: he stood for a while, vaguely looking, then began with hasty officious movements to straighten his clothes and arrange his pack.

A young woman leaped down from the driver's seat, landing with a skid in the white sand, and came forward. She was clumsy in khaki, her cap on the back of her head, wisps of pale damp hair hanging beside her face.

At once Douglas let out a whoop, and began thumping her on her shoulders, while she stiffened herself, laughing, saying, "Hey, hey, steady now, boys." They crowded around her; she was one of the girls from the Sports Club. They had played hockey with her, danced with her, made love to her all through their glorious youth. "It's fine to see you here, Bobby," said Douglas. She received their kisses on her offered cheek.

She was a rather tall, lumpish girl, with pale fatty cheeks which were stained wild pink in patches from the heat. Her grey eyes were slightly protuberant. She had acquired a mannish stride and a new hearty voice. "Well, pile in, boys." She made a half-serious salute to the sergeant—who returned a grin and a nod—and turned towards the lorry. "Here, aren't you coming?" she shouted cheerfully at the youth, who had sat himself down again on the bench, and was watching the proceedings from a distance. Douglas significantly tapped his head, and she gave a stare of startled distaste at the youth. One of them went back, helped him to his feet, and came with him to the back of the lorry. He was heaved in. Bobby, Perry and Douglas stood beside the front seat.

"What the hell are you doing in this dump?" asked Douglas. "We heard you'd got up north."

"Join the Army and see the world. If I'd known I'd land in this mucking hole . . . But they're sending me up north next month, this bleeding place is being closed down." This slightly hoarse, good-fellow's voice, the way she carefully seasoned in her obscenities, caused Douglas and Perry to involuntarily exchange a look.

Perry suddenly remarked, "For Christsake, we haven't seen a woman in months." He sounded injured.

Bobby's pale cheeks crimsoned irregularly. She looked at them in appeal. Douglas, embarrassed for her, said quickly, "It's pretty good to see an old pal here, Bobby." She looked now in gratitude, then turned away, and climbed up into the cab. Douglas was about to climb up beside her, when Perry laid his arm across, like a barrier, and grinned at him fiercely. For a moment Douglas glared. Then he smiled, let out a short laugh, and said, "Go ahead."

Perry hoisted himself up beside the girl, shouting down, "You'll be seeing your wife tomorrow."

Douglas looked annoyed. He said through his teeth, "You'd better let up, Perry, I've just about had enough of you."

Ever since Perry had been officially informed that he had an ulcer, he had been breaking out. Douglas had been watching over him like a father. It was his turn to feel injured. He walked moodily back to the end of the lorry, and jumped in. There was no window between the back of the lorry and the driver's seat. But they could all hear Bobby's loud boisterous laugh, increasingly uneasy, as the lorry turned, bumped across the bush-covered sand, found the strip, raced along it at sixty and, with a swerve that sent them sprawling, turned onto a rough track that wound through the bush. They were silent, crouching with their backs against the sides of the lorry, holding tight as it bounced and rocked. The youth with the wild eyes had stiffened himself and was glaring at them all in turn. They were all afraid of him and ashamed to be afraid. The trees were growing thinner, and shacks of brick and tin flashed past. Then it was a proper street, tarmac, where the heat oiled and quivered, and stretches of whitish sand on either side; then Indian stores and native eating houses. Now they were in a broad empty space of dust, whose surface eddied and stirred. There was a biggish new white building, with a couple of jacaranda trees shading it. The lorry stopped with a jolt. They swore angrily under their breaths as they banged themselves on the sides. Bobby's loud and boisterous voice invited them to descend. They did so in silence.

Under one of the trees a native woman sat in the dust, draped in red cloth. She was suckling her baby. She looked at them indifferently. Some dogs lay stretched under the other tree, looking as if they were dead. The men stood in a group around Bobby; she seemed hot and flustered, and would not look at Perry, who was grinning savagely.

"Now, who's got what wrong with them?" she enquired. "We've got stomach and respiratory separate."

They all laughed disgustedly.

"For crying out loud," said Perry. "What, two beds each?"

"Well, Perry," said Douglas, "we're together." They stood off to one side.

Bobby looked at the other four. "What's wrong with you?" Their faces tightened. "Oh, very well," she said hastily. "I'll show you where to go. Perry and Douglas—over there, that house there. The doctor'll come over." She quickly turned her back on Perry, and went off with her four into the big building, the youth lagging behind and looking around him suspiciously.

Perry and Douglas crossed the dust towards a small wire-enclosed house. "Bloody skirts," said Perry.

"Oh, go on," said Douglas awkwardly. "She's a nice kid."

Perry spat and began whistling between his teeth.

The shack had a verandah closed in by greenish gauze. It was raised; three red cement steps led to the gauze door. On the steps sat a native orderly. He sprang up and stood to one side, quivering at attention. Perry heaved his shoulder dispassionately into the man's chest without looking at him, swung open the door and went in. The man saved himself from falling by clutching at the doorframe, nimbly straightened himself, and sat down on the steps, brushing whitish patches of dust from his khaki. He reached out for his hand piano where it had fallen beside the steps, and began playing it.

Inside on the verandah were four iron beds covered with neatly folded red blankets. There was no one in sight. Behind the verandah was a single room with a table and a chair in it. On the table stood a glass jar with some thermometers slanting up.

Douglas slung his pack onto one of the beds, took off his boots, and lay down on another, closing his eyes.

Perry heaved his pack beside the other, and let himself down flat on his back, his dusty boots side by side on the blanket. He waited, hands behind his head, a dangerous immobility about him.

It was about two in the afternoon. They had landed four hours ago. No one came. The expanse of dust outside the green gauze remained empty. Half a dozen native women came past with their children, chattering in their shrill voices. From a big msasa tree that shaded the verandah a pigeon was cooing regularly. The iron roof cracked in the heat. The hand piano tinkled.

"For crying out loud," began Perry suddenly.

Douglas hastily opened his eyes, swung his legs down, said, "I'll see if they can get us a bite." He called the native orderly. "Hey, Jim, where's the doctor?"

The orderly pointed at the other building cheerfully.

"Can you get us something to eat?"

"Yes, baas. Right away, baas."

He went through into the inner room, through that into the back. Silence again. The pigeon cooed on and on.

He came back with a tin tray. Fried eggs, bacon, fried bread. Perry raised himself, looked at it, looked at him.

"We have ulcers," he said. "Ulcers—diet—no fat." He flipped his hand up against the tray. It jerked, the plates slid, the orderly caught at it, steadied the plates into their pattern. Perry turned his back and was staring out through the green gauze at the sky.

"Can you boil us some eggs?" asked Douglas quickly.

"Boiled eggs? Yes, baas, right away, baas." The orderly went out with the tray at a half-run.

Perry did not move. He was looking at an officer walking across the dust towards them, who came up the steps, pushed the door open impatiently, then carefully closed it behind him. Perry turned himself over in one movement, and lay looking at him. Douglas, who had been going to salute, stood up, then sat down again.

"You're the ulcers, are you?"

"That's me," said Perry. "Just one big ulcer."

"Sorry I didn't get over before—was fixing those other chaps." He sat down on the edge of Douglas's bed, and looked at them. He was rather slight, with rough fair hair, grey straight eyes. He was reddened and sweating.

"You're English," remarked Perry.

"Yes, I am actually."

Perry turned on his back and lay looking at the iron roof.

The doctor smiled rather tiredly and said, "Well, how are things where you've come from?"

"Read the newspapers?" asked Perry.

"Pretty bad," said Douglas.

The doctor glanced at Perry quickly, then more slowly at Douglas.

"When am I going to be examined?" asked Perry dangerously.

"There's been a bit of a balls-up," said Douglas apologetically. "We shouldn't be here."

"What happened?"

"Well, it's like this—"

But Perry swung over again, and poked his head forward at the doctor: "He got it in for me. I'll get him when the war's over, I'm warning you. Officer—well, he won't be an officer when the war's over, he'll be my junior clerk." He dropped his head back again, and let his two fists dangle on each side of the narrow bed. They swayed back and forth over the floor.

"How about sleeping for a bit?" said the doctor. "Then we'll talk about it."

"I'm not going to sleep. I'm going to be examined—now."

Douglas again smiled his small apology. Perry's sideways flickering eyes caught the smile. "And I'll get you too, Douggie old pal. Arse-licker, that's all you are. Always were."

Douglas yellowed, but kept his steady, rather nervous smile.

The doctor sat in thought. He sighed unconsciously. Of the four men in the other building, three had threatened him and the commanding officers, then broken down and wept. Secret cabals of influence worked against them; life itself had it in for them. But he, Doc, was a good type who understood them. He had given them sedatives, and tomorrow they would go home with battle fatigue. The crazy youth had been quite amenable, then suddenly had begun climbing out of the window, shouting that he would kill himself. He was now under guard. He was all in line with what the doctor knew and could handle. But he could not understand these colonials, so tough, masculine, violent—and then the sudden collapse into self-pity. It seemed a well of self-pity lay in all of them, ready to overflow at any moment. Caught by accident in South Africa at the beginning of the war, he had been with South Africans all the time. They every one of them got drunk or broke down at some stage or another and confessed to a vast grievance against life. Extraordinary, he thought, remarkable. He looked at Douglas, and considered. Douglas filled him with confidence. He looked a round, humorous, cheerful soldier of a man; the round good-natured face was frankly boyish. The doctor felt he could rely on him. He turned to him and asked, "Tell me what happened?"

Perry stiffened, rolled his eyes sideways, but did not move.

"Well, I've had trouble with my stomach off and on for years," said Douglas, with a wary look at the braced Perry. "It flares up from time to time. I had a sudden bad go last week. Usually I just shut up about it and diet myself as well as you can on army food. But it was a really bad go—they got me into hospital. I'd only been there half an hour when orders came to evacuate. I was never examined. They flew a bunch of us down to the next town. We were evacuated from there again almost at once. The next thing was, we were all shoved onto a plane, and here we are. I'm sure I could carry on in the Army. I'm quite fit apart from the ulcer, and it's not bad." He ended on a frank appeal.

"You can't feed an ulcer in the Army," said the doctor pleasantly. "And you're better out."

Douglas's mouth was bitter. "No one examined me, I was just pushed off." Suddenly the lips quivered. He turned away, blinking. God help us! thought the doctor, astounded—here it is again.

Perry had slowly risen, was sitting on the edge of his bed. "Hey, what about me? What about me, Doc?" He rose, fists clenched.

Deliberately ignoring him, the doctor said to Douglas, "Get inside a minute, I'll call you." He was embarrassed at what he was going to do.

Douglas hesitated, then rose, then stood still. He was staring like a child at the doctor. At last he turned and stumbled indoors.

Perry, crouching low, was on the point of springing at the doctor. "Damn it," said the doctor easily, "take it easy, now." His voice was deliberately kind, paternal.

Perry quivered all over, then sat. His lower lip, thrust out aggressively, worked. Tears sprang from his eyes. The doctor moved over and put a hand on his shoulder. Perry seemed to swell, then subsided. The doctor sat beside him, arm lightly across his shoulder, and began to talk, in a low, persuasive voice.

Douglas, standing behind the gauze door, looking suspiciously out, was amazed and upset at the scene. Then he turned away, and sat on the table inside. He could still hear the doctor's almost maudlin voice soothing Perry like a child. He could hear Perry heaving up great sobs and complaining that the officer had it in for him, the sergeant had it in for him, he'd never had a chance.

The back door cautiously opened; the orderly's head came around it. He came in with a tray of boiled eggs, and laid it before Douglas. Seeing a dangerous gleam in Douglas's fixed blue stare, he hastily slipped out again.

The sentimental murmuring had ceased. Douglas looked out. Perry was lying face down on the red blankets. His fists, hanging down each side of the bed, were being banged slowly and with method on the floor—there was a streak of blood on the knuckles. The doctor was standing upright, filling a syringe against the light. Then he swiftly bent, jabbed the needle into Perry's forearm, and moved quickly back: clearly, he expected Perry to attack him. But Perry was whimpering, face down, "You're a good chap, Doc, thank you, Doc."

Douglas saw the doctor shut his eyes, sigh, and open them again, as he stood motionless, syringe in hand. If he sticks that thing into me I'll kill him, thought Douglas. But the doctor dismantled the syringe and put it away. Then he stood up and braced himself: there was still Douglas. He came into the inner room. Douglas stood waiting for him belligerently.

"He'll sleep for a couple of hours and then he'll be all right," said the doctor cheerfully.

"You're sending us home?" began Douglas, standing square in front of him.

The doctor suddenly snapped, "Yes, I am. I'm sick to death of the lot of you. You've no right to be in the Army in the first place. How did you get in? Told a lot of lies, I suppose. Bloody clever." He paused, and added, "Hundreds of pounds spent on you, you crack at the first strain, and you have to be sent back home. What do you think this is, a picnic?"

Douglas looked at him incredulously. Seeing the familiar swelling and reddening, the working lower lip, the doctor snapped, "Oh, shut up, shut up, shut up—go to hell and shut up."

"Who's in charge here?" asked Douglas after a pause, the official in him coming to the rescue.

The doctor stared, laughed angrily, and said, "You can go and see Major Banks if you like—he's over there." He pointed at the building opposite, picked up his case, and went out past Perry without looking at him. He strode across the dust and vanished into the building. Douglas looked at the eggs; he was unconsciously grinding his teeth. Then he followed the doctor out.

A deep shady verandah surrounded the main building; off it rooms opened. Inside one of them sat Major Banks under a spinning electric fan, dealing with piles of papers. He looked up, irritated, as Douglas strode in, slamming the door. His eyes narrowed. Douglas stopped in the middle of the room, saluted hastily, came forward.

"Well, Doug, how are you?" said the Major, rising and holding his hand out over the table. Douglas shook it. They had known each other for years. "Sit down." Douglas sat. He was looking at the papers, the files, the ink banks, the paper clips: the fetters from which he had escaped.

"The doctor's been talking to me about you," said Major Banks.

Douglas allowed himself a bitter smile. But he accepted a cigarette with a "Thank you, sir."

Major Banks was a lean, fibrous, olive-skinned man, with very keen, bright light-blue eyes: they looked odd in that burnt face. "Active service's out, Doug," he said finally. "But if you want me to fix you up on the administrative side, I'll do it."

"Thanks," said Douglas with hostility.

"You're wise. I'll be spending the rest of the war in happy spots like this one—nice prospect."

"If I've got to sit behind a desk I'd rather do it at home."

"They should never have let you go, anyway. I know your chief was sick when you left."

"They didn't let me go. I worked a point," said Douglas, grinning proudly.

"So I gathered," said the Major drily. He added, "How's your wife—she'll be glad to see you."

"Oh, she's fine, fine," said Douglas proudly. "We've a kid, did you know?"

"Lucky chap. Well—perhaps you'll join me for a drink later."

"Alcohol's out—I've got an ulcer."

"Bad luck." The Major picked up some papers.

Douglas rose. He saluted; the Major casually, half jocular, returned it. As Douglas reached the swing doors, someone started shouting from a room nearby. He stopped. The sound was disturbing for a reason he could not define.

"That's your pal Simmons," said the Major. "He's gone clean off his rocker. Still, it's just as well to get the crocks out of the way before the fighting starts."

Douglas went red. He looked with helpless affront at the oblivious Major, now bent over his papers. The shouting stopped. Silence. He slammed the door again, walked out across the square and entered the little gauze-covered house. Perry was lying face downwards, exactly as he had been, the unclenched hands knuckled loose on the floor. He was deeply asleep. The native orderly was back on the steps with his hand piano. The soft, brooding, tinkling melodies went on and on together with the pigeon's cooing. Douglas sat on the edge of his bed and sank into thought. His mouth was dry with loss. It seemed to him that everything he had ever wanted was being snatched from him. All his adult life he had sat in an office; now after a year's brief reprieve he was being sent back to it. He could see his future life stretching ahead, nothing unexpected, nothing new from one year's end to the next. Holidays every five years or so, retirement, death. He felt like an old man.

The year of discomfort and boredom in the Army was already arranging itself in a series of bright scenes, magical with distance. He thought of the men whom he had known all his life, been to school with, worked with, played with, now up north in "the real thing" at last. It seemed that his whole life had led without his knowing it to the climax of being with those men, his fellows, his friends, parts of himself, in real fighting, real living, real experience at last. And he was out of it. A few days before it started, he had been kicked out. A crock, he thought bitterly.

His eyes rested on Perry, sprawled out loose a couple of feet away. There was something childish about those big open fists resting on their knuckles on the floor, something appealing and childish about the closed lids fringed with sandy lashes. Tenderness, a warm protectiveness, filled him. He thought, He'll have a stiff neck lying like that. He got up, and, using all his strength, turned the big man over on his back. He was winded when he'd achieved it. He stood up, panting. His eyes were wet; he'd be out of uniform in a couple of days. Never again would he know the comradeship of men. Never. Never. He shut his eyes to steady himself. He opened them at last and looked out. It was very still out there. Thick black shadows lay stretched over the sand now. A couple of scraggy hens scratched below the steps. The orderly had dropped off to sleep, sprawled over the steps, the hand piano hanging from his fingers.

The insignificant, dreary little dorp seemed to him what he was returning to—this would be his life now. There stirred a small thought of Martha; he let it die again, and a pang of fondness for her went with it. What he felt for Martha was nothing, nothing at all compared with his year among soldiers. Rage filled him. He was filled with a need to tear, to destroy—he stood still, fists clenching and unclenching, his mind teeming images of destruction. Next morning he would be put on the plane home; he would step straight off the plane into domesticity and the office from eight until four.

A sharp pain stabbed in his stomach; he remembered he had an obligation towards himself. He went inside, and spooned out two of the cold wet eggs onto bread, and began to eat the insipid mess with disgust. He saw a pepper pot standing on the tray, and shook pepper violently all over the eggs, with a savage delight in disobeying prohibitions. Feeling slightly sick at last, he went back to the verandah, thinking he might sleep. Then he saw across the square a black-lettered sign on a small store: "Joseph's Bar."

He walked over and went in.

A fat, pale Greek youth was wiping glasses behind the bar. There was no one else in the place. Douglas asked for ginger beer and sat down. There was a single round table against the wall opposite the bar counter, with half a dozen upright wood chairs around it. In peacetime an occasional merchant or government official passed through; the bar was used by them and the local storekeepers.

Douglas took a mouthful of the prickly tepid ginger beer and let it stand. A loud offhand voice was heard just out of sight. Then Bobby came slowly past the open doorway. Her pale hair was now tidy, and bobbing up at the ends. She did not look in. Douglas called out, "Hey there, Bobby." She gave a start, but began to smile before she saw him. Douglas grinned proudly at the thought that she must have watched him enter the bar.

She came in and sat down. She was flushed with the heat. She asked for whisky, and Douglas's mouth filled unpleasantly as she began sipping it. Then she crossed her legs, blew out smoke, and fixed her pale-grey eyes attentively on him. The top buttons of her tunic were undone. Under it he could see a thin pink strap, rather grubby, loose on her shoulder. He felt a mixture of tenderness and repulsion at the sight.

"So you've had it—bad luck," she remarked in the jocular loud voice which she had decided was suitable to her role as female soldier. But she looked sympathetic.

Douglas began to talk. After a while she asked after Martha. He produced photographs. Caroline stood on two sturdy legs smiling attractively up at her father from the small card square.

"That's a fine kid," Bobby said sentimentally, and refixed her eyes on his at once. In her attitude was something touchingly devotional. She appeared to be saying that she was completely at his service.

She ordered a second whisky. His ginger beer was still nearly full. He almost succumbed, and then said, "I'd better be strong-minded, hey?"

"That's the ticket," she said. "Mucking bad luck."

It grated on him; he thought of Martha as a contrast. But the thought of Martha was not balm at all. The truth was, he had been relieved to get away from the atmosphere of bottles and napkins, and, more than this, from Martha's extraordinary tension during those months, when competent gaiety followed irritated exhaustion, and both seemed in some subtle way a criticism of him. But a more recent doubt was working in him. "Heard any news from home?" he asked her casually.

"Lazy sods, they don't write. But I got a letter from Bogie—you remember Bogie? She says she's having a wonderful time with the boys from Home."

Douglas said with a quick laugh, "Yes, they all seem to be giving it stick, all right." But his gaze still rested on her face with persistent suspicious enquiry, and she went on:

"I heard that Bella's marrying the Air Force, old Sam's breaking his heart over it."

"Pretty bad show, that."

"I heard news of Matty, come to think of it. She was at a dance at the air camp."

"Oh, yes, she told me about it," he said with an effort, frowning.

"Matty was always one for the boys. Lucky Matty, she hasn't got a figure like a sack of potatoes," she said, and laughed painfully.

"Oh, you do fine," he responded after a pause. He looked unhappily round. "I think I'll be a devil and have a drink," he said. He went over to the fat silent Greek, who polished glasses and watched these evidences of world war with an unquenchable curiosity. He fetched back two whiskies.

"Here's to the Army," he said with quiet misery. He drained his down, and sat grinning at her. "Well, I'm all right, how are you doing, are you all right?"

She drained her third quickly, and responded to the rallying call. "Oh, I'm all right, I'm fine, are you all right?"

He took the two glasses to the counter to be refilled. She watched him, smiling maternally. He came back and this time sat in the chair next to her. "Let's give it a bang. Let's give it stick."

"Oh, you're a crazy kid."

She began questioning him again about up north, with an eager determination to hear every detail, prompting him when he hesitated on the edge of something he would normally gloss over for a woman. It was as if she were taking part by proxy. She listened, her pale-pink lips slightly open in a wistful greed. At first he was gruffly disapproving, then he let it go and softened to her. Poor old Bobby, she was having a bad time stuck in this dorp, she was a nice kid.

A shadow fell over them. Perry stood at the door, stooping inwards. Behind him the sun was sending up a last wild flare of red into the soft grey sky. The dust expanse had shrunk and dimmed. A group of Africans walking through had a soft and distant look in this thin light, and their voices were high and excited: they were hurrying to get indoors before the night came down.

Perry looked at them. Douglas noted that he was rather yellow, his eyes were inflamed, but he seemed quiet enough. He looked at the whiskies and said, "That's an idea." He went to the bar, nodded at the Greek, drained his glass with slow determined thirst, handed the glass back. He leaned on his elbow watching them. He took his second glass and stood there holding it for a while untasted, while the Greek took an oil lamp off the iron hook suspended from a rafter in the middle of the room, removed the glass funnel, lit the wick, fitted back the funnel, and hung the lamp up again. It swung steadily. A drop of paraffin dropped to the brick floor, then another. The smell of paraffin was strong.

The Greek returned to the other side of the counter. Perry still leaned there considering the seated couple, as if from a long distance. He looked very handsome beside the pale, fat youth with his sad olive-coloured eyes; conventionally handsome—square-jawed, hard-mouthed, strong. He was looking now direct at Bobby, and she shifted uncomfortably under it, fiddling with her bobs of pale hair.

"Come and sit down, man, damn it," said Douglas.

Perry at once came across and sat down, as if he had needed an invitation. He gazed steadily at Bobby until she met his eyes.

"So you'll be going on up north?"

"Yes, next month."

"Following the Army?"

"That's my job."

"Nice work if you can get it."

She gave a nervous look at Douglas, who laughed and said, "Come off it, Perry man."

Perry laughed, a calculated silent heave from his chest, and fingered his glass while he looked at Bobby. She had wriggled her chair an inch nearer to Douglas, but she was looking, fascinated, over at Perry and she was flushed.

The orderly came in, addressing Perry and Douglas equally. "Baas, shall I bring your dinner here?"

"Get out," said Perry.

"It's O.K., Jim," said Douglas quickly.

The man backed and vanished into the now thick dusk.

"What've you got to eat?" said Perry loudly to the barman.

"We don't cook."

"So, you don't?"

"There's the mess. Since the war started there's been only the Army."

Perry's jaw was thrust out. Seeing it, Douglas appealed, "Couldn't you do us something? We're fed to teeth with army grub."

The Greek hesitated.

"I want roast chicken, roast potatoes, vegetables, and some jam tart," said Perry. He looked steadily over at the bar.

The Greek said, "I'll go and ask my father." He hurried out.

"Ruddy Dago," said Perry. "Bad as kaffirs." He lifted his glass. "Here's to Civvy Street."

They all drank. Douglas looked over at Bobby with a tinge of grave reproach. The thread of sympathy that had held them was snapped. She could not take her eyes off Perry. Douglas moved his chair back to the wall, and comforted his glass between both hands. He was beginning to feel the alcohol.

Bobby took a moment's alarm at being left to Perry. She drank hastily, and spilled some. Perry reached out his large paw and brushed drops off her shoulders. She shrank away.

"Well, and how's the war been treating you?" he asked, on a personal, insulting note.

"Oh, fine, fine. But it's mucking boring here, though."

"Mucking bad luck, muck everything, hey? You should meet the Ities. They've got a far wider range. You should hear their language when they get going. Shouldn't she, Douggie?"

Douglas looked away, dissociating himself.

"You mucking well should meet the bleeding Ities, then you wouldn't have to restrict yourself to bleeding mucking."

She looked at him with a helpless fascination still, and let out her short gruff laugh.

"Let up, man," said Douglas again, disgusted. "Stop it."

Perry took no notice. "Still, you've not done too badly here, there's the Major and the doctor and the sergeant."

She took his direct gaze and said, "You don't do too badly, either. There's nothing you can tell me about what the boys do away from their wives."

"But I'm not married, so that's all right. Thank God. She'd be lining the beds of the Air Force."

She forced out another laugh. He leaned forward, gripped her wrist and said, "Remember Christmas night three years ago at the Club—remember?"

"And so what?" she said, laughing.

He released her, frowned and said softly, "We had a good time then, didn't we?"

"Those were the days," said Douglas, half jocular, half wistful; they instinctively lifted their glasses to the good old days. Then Perry reached out his enormous arm over the bar, tilted the whiskey bottle standing on it, caught it as it heeled, and brought it triumphantly to the table.

The young Greek entered with a tray. Roast-beef sandwiches, mustard pickles, Marie biscuits, Cheddar cheese. He set it before them and retired silently behind the bar.

"Have some roast chicken," said Douglas cheerfully.

They ate. Perry, steadily watching Bobby over his busy knife and fork, began reminiscing about the bang they'd had this night last week. Douglas played along with him. When it came to how Perry and half a dozen Australians had wrecked the brothel, Douglas smiled uneasily, but Bobby was laughing her good-fellow laugh. Perry stopped, and said disgustedly to Douglas, "What do you think, she'd have liked to be there." He leaned over, pushed his face against hers and said, "So you'd have liked to be with us, hey?"

She pulled back her head, and said, "Oh, cut it out, Perry, you're getting me down."

"Nice girl," he remarked companionably to the roof. "Nice girl, this one."

Douglas leaned over to her, and whispered, "If you want to make your escape, then go, Bobby. He's been kicked out of the Army, that's all that's wrong with him."

She returned a small, rather offended smile. "I know, poor kid." She at once drew back towards Perry. Her lips were parted. She passed the tip of a pink tongue across them.

Perry was looking at the doctor, who had just come in. The doctor nodded at them all, and stood by the bar.

"Come and join us, Doc," said Douglas.

"Thanks, but I'm on duty." He asked for a brandy, and stood leaning by the bar, watching Perry. He said nothing, however.

"How are the boys, Doctor?" asked Bobby, one professional to another.

"Bedded them all down for the night. The plane's leaving at six tomorrow morning." He looked steadily at Perry and Douglas.

Perry ostentatiously tilted back his glass, emptied it, filled it again.

"Six o'clock," said the doctor sharply. "And anyone who's not ready can spend another three weeks here. If that tempts you."

"We'll be ready, Doc," said Douglas.

The three were set in hostile defiance against him; they were looking at him across a barrier of half-drunkenness.

"Parsons everywhere," said Perry to Bobby intimately. "Have you noticed it? Everywhere you go in this world—parsons. Hate their guts. Only to smell a parson half a mile away gives me guts-ache."

She looked apologetically but defiantly at the doctor.

"An English parson—they breed them in England." Perry jumped up, and grabbed her wrist. "Coming for a walk?"

She hesitated, then rose, brushing down her tunic. He flung down four pound notes on the table, and pulled her by the wrist after him onto the verandah. Outside there was a steady beam of moonlight.

Douglas watched Perry and Bobby walk unsteadily over to that gauze verandah opposite, heard the gauze door slam. He looked pathetically at the doctor. "Let's have a party, Doc," he said. "Come on, Doc, let's give it stick."

"Sorry. I've got a raving lunatic on my hands tonight. I don't know quite . . . If I send him down on the plane with you tomorrow—he looked, exasperated, at Douglas—"surely five of you ought to be able to look after one boy like that. He'll be under drugs."

"Oh, let him cut his ruddy throat," said Douglas cheerfully. "Who cares? Do you care? Do I care? No one cares." He reached out his arm to stop the doctor as he went past. "Come on, Doc, let's all cut our throats."

"If I were you, I'd get myself to bed," said the doctor from the doorway, with a harassed but pleasant grin. "For God's sake—you'll be in hospital if you drink like that."

"Who cares?" began Douglas again. "Do you care . . ." But the doctor had gone. Douglas turned his head carefully and focused at the Greek. "Do you care?" he asked him.

The Greek grinned unhappily.

"Come and have a drink."

The young man hesitated, then came over.

"Sit down, man, sit down."

He sat, and poured himself a drink.

"Are you married?"

"No, I've got a girl at home."

"Where's home?"

"Greece," said the Greek apologetically.

"You don't want to get married—what do you want to get married for?" Douglas laid his fist on the shoulder opposite him and thumped it. The Greek continued to grin, watching him uneasily.

"Nothing but bitches, all of them."

"I'm not married—sir." In a country where all white men are equal there are perpetual problems of etiquette.

"Call me, Douggie." He kneaded the fat young shoulder a little more, then held both hands around his glass and stared in front of him. "What's your name ?" he enquired at last, with difficulty.

"Demetrius."

"Fine name, that, very fine name." He lapsed away into a glass-eyed stare, then recovered himself. "Let me show you my wife," he said fumbling with his breast pocket. "I've the finest wife in the whole of Africa." He produced a wallet and dropped a bunch of snaps on the wet table. "Tck, tck, tck," he clicked his tongue reproachfully. "Now, now, Douggie, that's very clumsy." He fished a photograph of Martha out of a pool of whisky, and laid it before the Greek. Martha, in shorts and a sweatshirt, had the sun in her eyes and was trying to smile.

Demetrius courteously pulled out his wallet, and laid on the table a snap of a dark beauty sitting on a rock and dangling her feet in a pool. She and Martha lay side by side while the two men concentrated on them.

"You've got a fine wife, I've got a fine wife, we've both got fine wives," pronounced Douglas. He hiccupped and said, "Excuse me, I'm going to be sick." He got up, and went out to the verandah, holding on to the wall.

When he came back, the Greek was back behind the counter, and the table in the corner was wiped clean. Douglas sat, looked about, finally located him and said, "You've gone. They've all gone."

"It's getting late, sir."

"I want to have a party," said Douglas obstinately. His eyes swam, focused together on a bit of white on the floor. He bent, retrieved the snap of Martha from beside his feet, wiped it back and front on his tunic and put it into his top pocket. He remained sitting and swaying. He stared at the wall and blinked.

Demetrius wiped a few more glasses. Then he went out. In a moment he came back with himself twenty years older. The two Greeks conferred for a moment, then the father came over and said, "You'd better get to bed, sir."

"I'm staying here!" The table jumped as Douglas crashed his fist down.

"But we're closing the bar. I'll help you across to bed, sir."

"I'm staying here. I can't go to bed, because my best friend is in bed with my wife." His lower lip swelled and trembled.

The two men looked at each other, at him, and shrugged. Demetrius reached up and turned down the lamp. They went out. Douglas let his head fall forward onto his arms. His arms slipped forward until the upper half of his body lay over the table. It was now dark in the bar. A dim square of moonlight lay on the floor. It moved slowly back towards the door, slipped through the gauze and became one with the blaze of moonlight outside.

Later, Demetrius came in wearing striped pyjamas, carrying a candle. He shook Douglas twice. Then he left him, closing the gauze door with a simple hook on the inside, and sliding over a heavy door of wood.

A few minutes later Douglas sat up. It was very dark, and rather chilly. His head was clear again. He shook the wooden door in its groove, then went to the window. It was shut on the inside with a hasp and a hook. He fumbled at it a little; raised his fist and smashed it into the glass. A low tinkle came from outside. He heaved his shoulder into the pane; it flew out. He fell out with it and rolled over onto the earth four feet below. He got up unhurt under a big tree that filtered moonlight all over him. He turned himself till he faced the small gauze house, and concentrated on getting his feet to take him there. There was a small yellow glimmer coming from inside it. Overhead the moon was a great sheet of silver light. He gained the steps, climbed them, pulled open the gauze door, went in. It was light. Moonlight lay like white sand over his bed. On the one next to it he could see Perry's big body. It was in movement. He went through into the inner room.

The orderly was sitting drowsing at the table. His head was nodding and swaying over a book. Douglas focused his aching eyes to see what the book was. It was a child's reading primer, soiled and dog-eared, open at a page with a cheap coloured picture of spring lambs frisking on an English meadow and a little yellow-haired girl offering them some pink flowers. The large clear print opposite said: "Mai-sie is six. Mai-sie likes to go for a walk in the spring mea-dow. She loves the lit-tle lambs. They love her. When Mai-sie gets home, she will do her lessons. Mai-sie works hard at her les-sons. She can read. She can write. Mai-sie lives in a cot-tage on the hill near a sheep-fold. Her fa-ther is a police-man."

"Poor sod," remarked Douglas aloud, with a mixture of compassion, contempt, and a sort of twisted envy.

A small cheap alarm clock on the table said it was half past eleven. He had slept for about two hours.

He went back to the verandah. He sat on his bed. Perry was murmuring with sentimental exasperation, "Oh, come on, give us a break, kid, give us a break, kid." Bobby, invisible except for one khaki-covered arm lying across his shoulder, was quite silent. A hand, fat and very white in the moonlight, looked innocent and pathetic.

It gave Douglas vindictive pleasure that matters were not going entirely to Perry's satisfaction.

After a while he felt his head roll; he let himself fall over on the bed and was asleep at once.

He knew he was dreaming unpleasantly. There was danger in the dream. He was in the aircraft with Perry. Perry was at the controls. They were at an immense height. Looking down, he saw pretty rivers, peaceful green fields. That was England. Then he saw a tall brown purplish mountain. That was Africa. It was important to keep them separate. He saw that Perry was hunched and straining over the controls. The aircraft was slipping sideways through shrieking wind. Perry was grinning and saying, "Give us a break, give us a break, give us a break." The ground was slanting up and very near the purplish hairy mountain. Douglas woke as they crashed, immediately rising on his elbow and shaking his head clear of the dream. It was dawn. Through the gauze a clear greyish sky lay like a stretched sheet. A few yellowish streaks fanned out from the reddish hushed glow where the sun would rise. Perry was lying on his back, asleep.

Inside the room the orderly moved about, and a Primus stove hissed.

A lorry stood outside the administration building opposite. Bobby leaned beside it, apparently waiting. The white ambulance car came driving around the edge of the building and parked beside the lorry. Some native orderlies and the doctor came out and began sliding stretchers into the ambulance with rolls of blanket on them that were the casualties.

Douglas lay down again, rolling his dry and swollen tongue around his mouth. Today he would go home. He would walk into the flat and greet Martha. Tenderness for Martha and his small daughter filled him. The gay flat with its books and flowers seemed very attractive. And he would be back at his desk in Statistics in a week. They would be pleased to see him. He was a kingpin of his section, and everybody knew it. He dozed off for a moment, thinking of Martha and how that night he would be lying in bed with her. Voluptuous fantasies slid through his mind. He was asleep again; but almost at once someone shook him.

"Come on, get up, kids," said Bobby's bluff voice.

Douglas sat up. Perry was leaning on his elbow looking at Bobby, who refused to meet his eyes. She said hurriedly, "We're leaving in twenty minutes," and went down the steps with her free manly stride, pale hair bobbing on her fat white neck.

"Mucking bitch," said Perry dispassionately. He got up. Douglas was already stuffing things into his pack.

The orderly came out with boiled eggs on a tray. "Good morning, baas, good morning, baas," he said cheerfully. The reading primer was sticking up out of his breast pocket.

"Morning, Jim," said Douglas, rubbing his hands. He felt elated and optimistic.

They were eating their eggs when the doctor came over.

"How are you feeling?"

"Fine, fine."

"You don't deserve it."

"Oh, come off it, Doc."

The young English doctor smiled. "If I put the schiz onto the plane, will you keep an eye on him? He's well and truly drugged."

"The ulcers will look after the schiz," said Perry. "Leave it all to us."

"Thanks. I've got to get him out somehow. There isn't even a nurse to send with the stretcher cases. They'll be all right. They're not bad. It's only a few hours. You'll be there before lunch. This place is packing up soon, anyway."

"Bloody silly place for a hospital," said Douglas.

"It isn't a hospital. It's a transfer casualty."

"Whatever it is."

"Well, I didn't choose it," said the doctor, automatically clearing himself of responsibility like everybody else. "Could you get yourselves into the lorry, gentlemen. Please."

Douglas and Perry slung their packs on and flipped some silver to the orderly, who caught it with one hand.

"Thanks, baas, thanks, baas."

They strolled over the dust to the lorry, which was now throbbing gently all over. Bobby was already in the driver's seat.

"You can have her," said Perry to Douglas. "I don't want her."

Douglas hesitated. He did not want to drive the four miles with Bobby. But he went round to the front and climbed up beside her. She was being curt and official this morning, so he did not have to talk.

The lorry at once bounced off and away past the tin shanties into the bush. The sun was just coming up. A large red ball clung to the edges of the trees, stretched like a drop of water, then floated clear. By the time they reached the airstrip it had grown smaller, yellow, and was throwing off heat like a flame thrower. They were sweating already. Bobby drove them straight to the aircraft. The ambulance was driving away from it as they came up.

Bobby shook them all by the hand, Perry last, in an offhand, soldierly way. She at once got back into the lorry and drove off, shouting, "Give my love to the home town."

In the plane they had to wait. At the last moment a large saloon car drove up. The doctor got out, went round to the other door, and helped out the sleepy limp-looking youth. He half pushed him up the steps into Douglas's arms. Douglas and Perry hauled him in, and slumped him into the seat by Perry. He slept at once, looking very young and boyish, with his ruffle of damp fair hair on his forehead.

The doctor came in, took a last look at the stretcher cases, and said to Douglas, "Keep an eye on them, there's a good chap." He saluted and skipped thankfully down the steps and off to the car.

At once the plane swung round and began lumbering away to the end of the strip. It turned. Over the brick shack a funnel of white silk rippled out. As the aircraft roared past and up they could see a cloud of fluttering butterflies around it, like flying ants around a street lamp.

In a few minutes the bush was stretching empty beneath them. Perry was sitting beside the sick youth. He slipped sideways. Perry put his arm around him. The young flushed face was lying back on his shoulder.

Perry was watching a drift of wet cloud making rainbows in the bright sun, and humming "Roll Out the Barrel" between his teeth, the shrewed hard blue eyes narrowed and abstracted, the mouth tight, the jaw solid. He shifted himself once or twice carefully to take the weight of the boy more comfortably, then settled down himself with his eyes shut. Douglas went back to talk to the stretcher cases.

About midday the plane touched down, and the boy was lifted, still fast asleep, onto the ambulance.

4

As Douglas walked past the iron-and-brick offices at the airport, he saw a man he knew behind a table. He went in. "How's tricks?" he asked, grinning with pleasure as he watched the face clear through surprise into welcome. They slapped each other around the shoulders for a few minutes, laughing. Then Douglas said, "How about giving me a clearance to get home and see my wife?"

The friend remembered he was also authority, hesitated, then said, "I suppose it's all right—come back this afternoon."

Douglas walked out towards the gates of the airport. He could see Perry and the others nosing around the open doors of the offices to find old friends who might similarly release them. He thought he should wait for them. Then he quickly went out into the road. He stopped in surprise. Only a year ago, the tarmac had crossed an empty grass-filled vlei to the airport. Now it was bordered on both sides by new suburbs of little villas. He felt like Rip Van Winkle. He began to walk the three miles to the centre of the town. Soon a car drew up beside him, to give a lift to the soldier. A new mode of manners, this; he climbed in, and, although five minutes before he had felt like a civilian, allowed himself to be treated with the affable but rather wistful friendliness civilians offer to uniforms. They were talking all the way in of how the influx of thousands of Air Force personnel was unbalancing the country—they had practically taken it over; one could not get into cinemas, hotels, dancehalls. One said that the money they brought with them made up for it—the country was on a boom of prosperity. They might have been talking of occupation troops. Then Douglas saw the pavements full of grey-blue uniforms, and felt a stranger in his own town. It happened that the car passed the big block where his department was housed. On an impulse he asked to be set down.

He walked into the department and was greeted thankfully by his chief, who asked if he could start work next day. Warmed and flattered, Douglas mentioned the red tape that would have to be unwound before he could put on his own clothes again. His chief waved all this aside: five minutes on the telephone to the suitable person would settle all that. He settled it forthwith; the interests of the country demanded that Douglas need do no more than pay a call for form's sake at a certain office the next day. Douglas began to feel himself at home.

There was still a slight undercurrent between him and his chief:

after all, he had gone over the man's head to get into the army. At the end of an hour it had vanished. They had discussed problems of reorganization—there were precisely half the people in the office that there were in peacetime, with twice the amount of work. Then, in the deferential, rather boyish way which he used when asking for things that were his right, Douglas mentioned various personal financial matters; the chief suggested they might lunch over it. They went to the Club. In the bar were Perry and the others. This was the last chance they had of playing the part of old campaigners to older men who had been prevented from going to the wars. They took it. At three, the chief said this was all very well, but he had to get back to work. Douglas went with him. The financial situation was dealt with in half a dozen sentences on the pavement edge.

Then he turned to walk home. He was a little drunk. It occurred to him that he had been in the town five hours, and Martha might be hurt that he had not rung her. I'll give her a surprise, he thought, deciding to forget the five hours. As he neared the block of flats, he saw a young woman wheeling a child coming towards him. He thought like a soldier, Not bad, not bad at all! Then he saw it was Martha. He stopped and watched her approach with a proud and proprietary smile. She was slimmer than she had been, and rather pale. She was wearing a short, tight flowered dress, and red sandals that showed brown bare feet; and looked, in short, attractive. She was staring vaguely in front of her, and as he moved to block her way she frowned discouragingly at the soldier. Then she froze, looking at him for a long moment while she turned white, and then, suddenly, bright pink. Blinking slowly, she came to life with a stiff, nervous smile.

They embraced. For both there was something false and unpleasant in this embrace. They separated, and took refuge from the difficulties of the moment in Caroline. Douglas bounced the child up in the air a few times: he was deeply moved at the sight of this pretty little girl who was his daughter. When he set the laughing child carefully back in the push-chair, he said to Martha, "Nice work— you've made a good job of her." He was gazing proudly at her. He was thinking that this was a wife and child to be proud of. He even glanced around to see if anyone was watching. But people were hurrying by: the streets were much fuller than they had been— strangers, always strangers. He thought it would be nice to take Martha and Caroline up to the Club of an afternoon.

She smiled uncomfortably at his compliment, however, and lifted the front wheels of the push-chair around in a way which jerked Caroline so that she clutched the handrails with both hands.

"Hey, you're giving her rather a bouncing, aren't you?" he asked; but received no reply. They walked back to the flats, a couple of hundred yards away.

"Why didn't you let me know you were coming?" she asked carefully.

"Well—I thought I'd drop in." He laughed and rubbed his hands. "And then last night . . ." He launched into an account of how he and Perry and some of the lads had given it a bang last night in G——, a ghastly little dorp in the bush miles from anywhere. Bobby—she remembered Bobby—sent her love. They'd all had a hell of a party, and his mouth this morning was like a parrot's cage. Luckily he'd slept some of it off in the aircraft, but, what with one thing and another, he thought it was quicker to come home himself than to telephone. Martha listened, with a new and discouraging detachment. Douglas felt let down. She had always risen in cheerful complicity to accounts of the boys' activities.

"Will you have to stay in uniform?" was her next question.

"I saw old Keen. He wants me back as soon as he can get me. He's fixed it. I'll be back at the office tomorrow."

She turned her eyes towards him cautiously. Cautiously she enquired, "You went to the office first?"

"Well, I was passing—I wanted to have everything fixed to surprise you."

"When did you get in?"

"About three hours ago"—he softened it a little.

She said nothing. Caroline was twisting herself up on her knees in the chair, and Martha pushed her down with one hand as she wheeled. "Oh, stop it, Caroline," she said roughly.

They were in the hall of the flats. Martha undid the straps and lifted the child out. Douglas promptly caught her up on his shoulders. The family party slowly mounted the stairs.

"I've got a fine piece of news," announced Douglas. "I asked Keen what he thought of my raising money for a house—he'll fix that. He even knows of a house going for us. How's that?" he ended proudly.

She enquired, after a pause, in the manner of one wishing to give him the benefit of any doubt, "We'll be moving into a house of our own?"

"That's the ticket—yes. It's a big house, too, Matty. You know it—it's the Rellors' old house on the corner of McKechnie Street."

"But it's enormous!" exclaimed Martha. She stared at him, appalled.

"But, Matty," he said in an injured voice, "we'll have our place, we'll be buying our own place—and there'll be a garden for Caroline.

And"—here he rubbed his hands and laughed—"we'll be having another kid soon, eh?"

Her look was now steady and critical.

"I say, now—Matty!" he exclaimed, clutching at her arm. But they were at their door. She pulled her arm away, and opened it.

On the divan was seated a young man in the blue uniform, reading a newspaper. He stood up, smiling shyly but pleasantly as they entered, looking at them with very clear, very blue eyes. He was rather slight—not tall; his hair was a springy bright brown, though against the pale skin it looked dark. As Martha said hurriedly, "This is William, Douglas. My husband has suddenly pitched up, William," he held out his hand with a perfect ease and friendliness.

Martha glanced at the two hands, one white, fine, almost effeminate, the other a large red-brown paw; hairs glinted on it. She was looking at her husband's hands as she said, "If you'll excuse me, I'll make some tea." Then she saw Douglas was annoyed at finding a stranger there, and said in a way which made both men look quickly at her, "If you'd found five minutes to let me know you were coming —" She bit it off, and gave a tight smile. Then she went out, taking Caroline with her. She dropped the child into the playpen, and, as she began to protest, handed her a rusk. Caroline took it and was quiet. Martha went quickly into the little kitchen. She assembled cups on a tray, and carelessly banged the kettle onto the hotplate. She did not know what she was doing. That sudden vision of the soldier who was her husband had been a shock to her which only now began to make itself felt. She was trembling; she cracked a cup as she dropped it onto the saucer.

Douglas, in khaki with the pack on his shoulder, a red-brown man with fat knees, a good stone heavier than he had been, and reeking of beer, had seemed to her gross and commonplace. His round, rather fat red face, grinning proudly at her, had been a revelation of what he really was. She could not now remember her vision of him of even half an hour before. It was quite impossible that this man should be her husband. She was married to one of the boys; he would always, all his life, be one of the boys. At sixty he would still be a schoolboy. There was no escape from it. The condition of being a woman in wartime, she thought angrily, was that one should love not a man, but a man in relation to other men. Whether it was Douglas with the boys, or the boys of the Air Force, it was all the same—and it was precisely this thing, dangerous, and attractive, which fed the intoxication of war, heightened the pulse, and drugged them all into losing their heads. You loved not a man, but that man's idea of you in relation to his friends. But *that* had been true here, in this country, long before the war. Well, she would not; never again!

At this point, guilt, the unfailing goad, gave a warning twinge, but at far lower pressure than usual. She ignored it, and was very angry. He bounced back grinning into her life after a year without a word or a warning, and naturally went first to the boys—*she* was an afterthought. The lonely, proud, self-contained life she had made for herself was invaded just like that, by his choosing to come: thus Martha, choosing to forget that, after all, he could not help it. And now he would bounce into bed with her; the thought filled her with revulsion. That it should do so succeeded in rousing the saving guilt: she could not stand seeing herself as a bestower of sexual favours, so she hastily began to re-create that coarsened soldier into something masculine and strong and attractive.

She lifted the tea tray and marched with it into the other room. The two men were getting on famously. The sight of Douglas on the edge of the divan with his fat putteed legs sprawling filled her again with derision. He was being the administrator; he was absorbed by a description of how the airmen's sleeping huts were laid out in relation to mess halls and recreation rooms. William was making a sort of map with bits of matches on the carpet. He had a quiet, sensible way of explaining things that clearly appealed to Douglas. Martha poured tea and handed them cups, filled with an anger she could not have explained. The business of drinking tea, however, interrupted the plan of how the air camp would have been laid out if either Douglas or William had been asked to do it; and they again became aware of Martha and were silent.

"Let's have Caroline in?" suggested Douglas.

"No—she must stay in her pen for at least half an hour."

"But why?" he protested rather wistfully.

"Timetable. She'll be making a fuss soon enough as it is," she added.

Caroline was already grumbling outside; the noise was irritating Martha, they could see. William was sipping his tea with the obvious desire to leave as soon as he could. In a moment he had set down his cup and got up. "I must be getting along," he remarked. Martha and Douglas said nothing to dissuade him. He stood smiling, while his blue eyes were thoughtfully examining Martha and Douglas. "Do you want to join the group?" he asked Martha direct. "Shall we send you notices? Or perhaps you'd rather think it over now that things have changed." This last was a hasty statement in reply to her nervous silence. He gave a long diagnostic look at Douglas, then formally shook hands with him. He went out with a pleasant nod at Martha.

"What group?" asked Douglas uneasily.

"Discussion group," said Martha shortly. William had dropped in casually twice before. His manner was always friendly, but impersonal: Martha had understood that his coming was because he felt it his duty to support and encourage her towards a different view of life. She had almost decided to join the group that contemplated splitting off the old one in order—as William explained vaguely but firmly—to get down to brass tacks. The phrase appealed to Martha.

"Do you know him well?" asked Douglas jealously. She looked at him for some time in silence; her eyebrows went up. He coloured up and said firmly, "What does he mean by the group? A political group?"

She said with a sudden agressiveness, "Ever since we've been married you agreed I wasn't only to housekeep and mind babies."

They were on the edge of a quarrel about the group, since it was taboo to be jealous. "Well, I didn't say you shouldn't," he hastened to conciliate. Then, as she preserved silence: "You know, Matty, I'm in the Service, and I must be careful. You know old John lost his job because of his wife."

She flushed and said, "His wife drank, didn't she?"

"Well, but, Matty, I have to go slow."

"Since I suppose three quarters of the male population is in the Service one way and another, it seems a useful way of keeping you quiet."

"But, Matty, we have the vote."

"The vote!" she said derisively. He was puzzled. They looked at each other across a wider gulf than they knew.

"Anyway," he said, brightening, "there'll be so much work to do in the new house, you won't have time."

"Quite," said Martha. He shot her a startled, uneasy look. Martha had not, previously, been capable of saying "Quite." He smelled the influence of the British invasion. But what was particularly unsettling was her tone, calm and dismissing and fatalistic, as if she accepted a long-foreseen calamity.

"Surely," he said, in the voice of an injured boy, "surely you're pleased to have a house of your own."

Again her eyebrows rose, and she said, "There's nothing in the world I want more." Then she burst into laughter, and kissed him on the cheek, moving away immediately as he grabbed at her.

"There's Caroline," she said hastily. Caroline had in fact begun to yell with impatience. Martha went out. Silence from Caroline. Then

Douglas followed her. Martha had gone past Caroline to the bed-room. He made some hasty apologetic noises at his daughter and went into the bedroom.

Martha was arranging Caroline's night things on the bed. She glanced up, startled, as he entered; then seemed to remind herself that he had a right to. He watched her for a while, then went across and put his arms around her from behind.

"I've been missing you, Matty," he began.

She stiffened and said gaily—and it was the first time he had heard the warm, amused gaiety which was how he had thought of her in the Army—"Oh, so have I." She turned round and kissed him. After a moment she pulled away and said, "Well, I must get Caroline washed."

"Oh, damn Caroline," he said huskily. "Let's forget her for a while." She appeared not to hear him. He said in an offended voice, "Where are my civvies?"

"Packed in your trunk. If you'd let me know, I'd have got them cleaned and ready for you."

"It doesn't matter."

He found some old flannels, pulled on a sweater. "It's good to be in my own clothes again—I've put on weight," he said, rather appealingly.

She responded quickly with "Oh, it's not so bad." But the clothes were straining round him, she thought he looked gross.

"Look, Matty, how about putting Caroline in the car and running up for a drink at the Club?"

She paused and looked at him, Caroline's nightdress in her hand. He could not read her expression. "You know," she said, cautiously, "things are not as they used to be here."

He exploded in a peevish shout. "Oh, come on, don't be such a wet blanket."

The hatred between them then was so strong it frightened them both. Without comment, she reached for a jersey, slipped it on, walked out, picked up Caroline and waited at the door, all in the manner of someone obeying an order. He would have liked to slap her.

They went in silence down the stairs. In the car, he slid with satis-faction into the driver's seat and said, "It's good to be driving the old bus again."

She seemed to be very occupied with Caroline, and they drove without speaking to the Club. When they reached the turn, he stopped the car, and looked at the building, smiling twistedly. It stood unchanged in its green playing fields, the large white beautiful house, very dignified, the late-afternoon sun shining full on it. He started the car again, and drove rapidly towards it, parked hastily, jumped out, smiling with eagerness. She walked quietly beside him to the verandah.

As they went up the steps she did not look at him, but went hurriedly ahead and found a table. He stood unconsciously staring about him on the steps. His face was sagging with helpless disappointment. The long deep verandah was crowded with people, as it always had been; but they were all new faces, save for some of the girls, who smiled and waved at him. The grey-blue of the Air Force filled the place like a—well, it was wartime, after all! He came across to Martha, and sat down clumsily. Martha glanced at his face and then away. He had gone a queer yellowish colour and was breathing hard. This was the real moment of coming home; she knew it—his youth had gone up in smoke. She was very sorry for him. She did not want to be sorry, it made a guilty maternal love stir in her. She thought determinedly that the lumpish reddened face with its spoilt protruding underlip was that of a schoolboy, but longed to comfort him nevertheless. They ordered beer, and drank it quickly, while Martha kept Caroline near her. In the old days the Club babies went from table to table, lap to lap. Now there was formality and a sense of closed groups who were not willing to be disturbed. A couple of the girls came up and greeted Douglas. Every second word was Air Force slang, and it was clear they had other interests than returning crocks from up north.

Douglas watched a group of girls he had danced and played with for so many years flirting with some young officers, and then remarked, with grumbling good humour, "I begin to see there's a war on." He laughed unhappily, and she joined him in relief. The colour had come back to his face, and it wore a look of ironical acceptance.

"We ought to go," said Martha. "It's time to put Caroline to bed." He got up immediately; he was pleased to go.

As they walked down the verandah, various girls called out, "Well Douggie, and how's the war?"

"I don't know," he returned good-humouredly, "I never reached it."

When they got home, Caroline would not allow herself to be put to bed. She was delighted to have a father, her father was delighted with her. He played with her. He felt surprised respect at the little person she had become. When he laid her down, he loosened the tiny delicate arms from around his neck reluctantly. She at once climbed to her feet and rattled the bars of the crib, looking at this new man with her black alert eyes.

"We shouldn't have this crib in our bedroom now," he said, and at once he began pushing it into the other room. Martha said nothing; she felt a pang of loss at her daughter being so unceremoniously removed; then reminded herself that she had not really liked having the child in her room; she was relieved that the cause of the inexplicable tension should be removed a little further—physically at least.

"Let's go out and have a bite," suggested Douglas, having left Caroline shouting protests on the verandah.

"We can't go out and leave Caroline," said Martha promptly. It sounded almost as if she were scoring a point over him.

She was sitting on the edge of the bed, slumped forward, very still, very distant. She had changed a great deal, he decided; and tried to define the change. She felt his eyes on her and turned and looked at him defensively, flashing a guilty smile. At once he was beside her, had clasped her. "Well, Matty, it would be nice if you were a little pleased to see me."

"Of course I'm pleased to see you." But he felt she was stiff under his hands. She seemed to be listening. "Caroline's not asleep," she said warningly, meaning that she could not give her mind to love-making while the child's sounds and movements were twanging at her nerves.

He did not understand this, and said stiffly, "Oh, very well, then let's eat instead."

She quickly escaped and began to prepare a meal. He lay on his elbow on the bed reading, or rather, looking vaguely at the book while he thought in a wave of bitter longing, Up north now they're in the real thing.

Almost at once Martha produced an omelette and some stewed fruit. She seemed surprised and hurt when he suggested this was not a meal to greet a soldier with. He ate it all in a few hearty mouthfuls, and said, "Now let's eat properly."

"But what about your ulcer?"

"Oh, to hell with my ulcer."

Caroline was asleep, lying loose among her blankets, fists at the level of her head, the small face flushed.

"I'll tell the woman over the corridor," Martha said, and left him to do so. She was away inside the other flat some time; he listened to the women's voices, and it occurred to him for the first time that Martha had built up a life of her own, with obligations and responsibilities. He heard her say as she came out, "If you want to go out tomorrow, let me know."

"Who's she?" he asked her, trying to show an interest.

"Oh—she has a baby," said Martha evasively.

"She's a friend of yours?"

"A *friend?*" said Martha in surprise.

"Well—do you see much of her?"

"We don't like each other, actually. But she keeps an eye on Caroline when I'm shopping, and I look after her kid."

"Let's go to McGrath's."

"Oh, no, not McGrath's," said Martha nervously, and he flashed out again belligerently, "I said McGrath's!"

She had been wanting to save him from another disappointment; now she felt meanly pleased that it would serve him right.

At the entrance to the big marble-and-gilt lounge he paused, with a boyish, expectant look on his face. His face changed. It was, of course, filled with the R.A.F. Not a soul looked up to greet him. He moved stoically through under the gilded pillars. Then he saw a waiter he knew and greeted him like an old friend. The Indian bowed and smiled over his tray of filled glass beer mugs and said it was fine to have Mr. Knowell back again.

Douglas and Martha went into the big dining room. Uniforms . . . There was room for them at the end of a large crowded, noisy table. They ate one of those vast meals which must be among the worst offered to suffering humanity anywhere, the southern-African hotelier's contribution to the British tradition in food. Douglas ate steadily, and with great satisfaction, speaking very little.

"Well, I needed that," he announced at last, laying his spoon down after the Pears au Paris. Then: "Now let's have a drink." They moved to the lounge and drank brandy and ginger beer for an hour, while the band played gypsy music. It was a very good band now. The influx of refugees from Hitler had brought musicians who had played to very different crowds, who played now and remembered Vienna, Munich, Hamburg, Berlin.

When they got home, Caroline had hardly moved. The sight of the small white exquisite limbs loosened in sleep always gave Martha acute pleasure. She covered them reluctantly, and went to the bedroom. There Douglas was already naked: a stout young man, very white, with ruddy-brown arms and knees and face. She hung about nervously and then took her nightclothes to undress in the bathroom.

"We haven't any contraceptives," she announced defiantly as she came back.

"Well, that means you've been behaving yourself at least," he said, laughing hopefully. She got into bed beside him as if in a room full of strangers, tucking her feet in chastely with the night-gown around her ankles. "Have you, by the way?" he asked casually.

"As much or as little as you have," she said quickly, and then, as if she herself found this banner of feminism absurd, added a short un-happy laugh.

Mistakenly encouraged by the laugh, he rolled over, prodded her in the ribs and said, "Ah, come off it, Matty. Let's take a chance for tonight."

"Oh no you don't," she exclaimed involuntarily.

"Well, why not? It would be nice for Caroline to have a brother nearly her own age."

"You see no reason why I shouldn't be made pregnant on the first night you're home?" she enquired in a fine cold voice. But it sounded forlorn.

He lay on his back, arms behind his head, looking at the ceiling. On his face was an ugly, angry look; he grinned after a while with ironic appreciation. "There's no place like home," he produced at last.

At this Martha felt a confused sort of anguish, partly because she was unable to compete with the attractions of "the boys," of whom he was thinking at that moment; partly because she was behaving like the unpleasant female who gave or withheld favours; partly be-cause she thought there must be something very wrong with her not to want him. She turned out the light. There was moonlight splash-ing all over the bottom of the bed. She saw, for the first time that season, the shape of the big wheel in the window—they must have set it up that morning. She suddenly wanted to cry.

He rolled over, and she understood that he had been by no means discouraged. She set herself to be as compliant as possible; to her astonishment, even a certain pride, he was not able to distinguish the difference between this and the real thing. Afterwards, full of childish affection and a gratitude which grated on her, he said, "I was careful, Matty."

"So I should think," she said, with a sort of bright desperation. She was terrified of becoming pregnant.

The next few days, which were occupied in seeing the house, de-ciding it was satisfactory, and moving into it, going to parties, giving them, making and receiving visits, were interspersed also with love-making. She was tense with anxiety that she might have become pregnant that first night. The old trapped feeling had her again; she was sleeping badly, although for a year she had slept very well; she was again lying through the nights listening to the sad music of the fun fair, and conscious of every twinge or response of her body as if it might vouchsafe to give up its secrets if only she concentrated on it hard enough. Then she knew she was not pregnant. She was able to give her mind fully to this new task of managing a large house, four servants, Caroline and a husband.

part four

He must be a dubious hero, a man with possibilities.

c. g. jung, *On Marriage*

1

The house was in the older part of the city, at the corner of a block. From its gate one could see a mile in four directions along tree-bordered avenues. The town planners, when faced with a need for more houses, always solved the problem by laying a ruler neatly over a map which represented a patch of unused veld, causing a pattern of streets to come into existence which crossed each other regularly at right angles. Everything was straight, orderly, unproblematical; grey strips of tarmac stretched endlessly, the naked earth at either side sprouted grass and wildflowers. Above, trees: the glossy dark masses of the cedrelatoona, the sun-sculptured boughs of the jacarandas, and, between, those small stiff trees the bauhinias, with their pink-and-white blossoms perched on them like butterflies. It was October, and the jacarandas were purple and the streets were blue, as if they ran water or reflected the sky, which was unrelievedly blue and pulsing with heat.

Inside the gate was a large tree, under which Martha stood looking out. Behind her was a rough lawn, where Caroline was playing with the native girl who now attended to her. Martha turned her back on the tiring glitter of the street, and surveyed the house, which was a series of large rooms casually assembled and surrounded by a wide creeper-curtained verandah, reached by a deep flight of red cement steps. The garden was big and untidy. The garden boy squatted beside a border, gently prodding the earth with a fork while he dreamed of his own affairs. He was a young lad of about fifteen, who from time to time turned admiring eyes towards the girl. She, however, was mission-trained, and sat very neat and proper in her clean white dress, legs tucked soberly to one side, her head, outlined in a scarlet crocheted cap, bent over her knitting. She did not look at him, but occasionally called out shrilly to Caroline, who was supposed to stay in the shade. The little girl, in a brief white dress, her wisps of black hair shining iridescent in the sun, was running over the rough grass in bare feet. She stopped when she saw her mother, smiled, took two steps towards her, then turned and trotted off to the garden boy, who laid down his fork and began clapping his hands regularly to attract her.

"Caroline!" the girl called, but did not move.

Martha reflected that the boy was supposed to be digging a bed for vegetables at the back of the house, where, however, he would not see the girl; and she was supposed to be ironing at this hour. If she, Martha, were really efficient, she would at once raise her voice and put things right. But she could see no reason why they should not all stay as they were; so she left the shade of the big tree and went rapidly through the blazing sun to the house. Caroline let out a protesting wail, then lost interest, and began digging with the garden boy's fork, while he watched her, smiling proudly.

Martha gained the verandah, stood behind the creeper, and looked out. The sunlight made her eyes ache. She hastily called to the girl to take Caroline away into the shade, and turned her back on the scene of persuasion and protest that followed. As usual she was feeling uncomfortable; she hated giving orders and was always at a disadvantage with her servants. Since she could not look at Alice, the native nurse, without thinking that she ought to be married and looking after her own children, or at the garden boy without thinking that he should be at school, or at the cook in the kitchen without finding it intolerable that a grown man should be under the orders of a girl a third his age, her voice always had a tinge of guilt when she spoke to them. The houseboy, a young man of twenty bursting with health and energy, was engaged in polishing bits of furniture in the dining room. She stopped to watch him. From where she stood, greasy polish marks showed on the shining table, and she knew that it was her duty to instruct him in polishing tables. She

continued through the house to the back verandah. Here the piccanin—the small black child who was engaged, according to custom,
for odd jobs—was playing with Caroline's toys on the steps. Since
Martha pretended not to see him, he continued to roll a small green
car along the edge of a step, growling like an engine in his throat.

The kitchen was large, equipped with all kinds of modern de-
vices. The cook was putting away the vegetables and groceries
which had just been delivered from the stores. She left the kitchen
and went towards the large refrigerator which stood on the verandah. She proudly opened it; it was her secret pride that it was always
stocked with jars of sauces and mayonnaise, pastry of various kinds
folded in stiff white slabs ready for cooking, biscuit dough that
needed only to be put in the oven, jugs of iced tea and coffee, ice
cream and complicated iced puddings that had taken hours to make.
Martha told Douglas with satisfaction that she could serve a meal
for ten any time at half an hour's notice, and he was pleased with
her. But the cook, who after all existed solely to serve meals for two
adults and a child, and was delighted if half a dozen people dropped
in, suffered this organization unwillingly. Sometimes Martha told
him he might take a few hours off, and cooked what she thought of
as her own meals; and then, hurt in his pride, he retired to the back
garden, where he watched her disapprovingly. He was a very good
cook.

There was nothing to do in the refrigerator, so Martha went to
the pantry. This was a room large enough to be a room for sleeping
or working in; it was cool, with a gauze window that overlooked
the vegetable beds at the back. It had a stone floor, stone shelves,
dazzling white walls. There was a delicious cool smell of sugar and
spices, the warm fresh tang of new flour. Sacks of sugar, flour, meal,
stood along the floor. Martha dipped her fingers through the dry
glisten of the sugar, touched soft clinging flour, and gazed along
shelves where, in neat tins, were stored the groceries: tea and coffee;
the starches in all their amazing variations; corn flour and bean flour,
soya flour and the grades of oatmeals, rapoka meal and pea flour and
split peas and beans; the rices, short and long and wild and cleaned,
and ground and polished—six variations of them; the pastes from
Italy, long and thin, long and fat, and moulded into all their possible
forms, shells and buttons and letters and animals—these last for Caroline; the sagos and the tapiocas, and flour of the same; potato flour
and lentils, red and brown and grey, and samp and sugar—all the
colours and grades of it, from the fine thin white to the masses of
heavy black treacle from the West Indies. From the sugars the cans
and bottles shaded through to the exotics: dried cherries and al-

monds, coriander and ginger root and preserved and dried ginger; vanilla and candied peel, and currants and sultanas and raisins and the fine fresh crystallized fruits from the Cape. Beyond, jars of preserved peaches and apricots and plums and guavas; jams, chutneys, spiced mangoes and fruit syrups.

Martha opened one tin after another, sniffing the stored exhaling odours with keen delight, while she ran her eyes along the rows of massed and glistening bottles of fruit. This was her favourite room in the house. But she shut the door on its pleasures and went back to the verandah. A large ginger cat now sat on the steps, patting at the little car as the small black child rolled it past.

The cook came out of his kitchen and said, "Madam, what shall I cook for lunch?"

Martha consulted with him at leisure; he went back to the kitchen, and she through several rooms to the bedroom. It was large, with a pleasant high white ceiling, and windows opening on three sides into the garden. It had a conventional suite of bedroom furniture, rather ugly, and twin beds covered in green silk.

She had a choice of three rooms to sit in, but she sat on her bed, and looked at the white trumpets of the moonflowers hanging outside the window. She thought that she might very well run across the street into Mrs. Randall's for morning tea. She resisted it like a temptation, although she grumbled humorously to Douglas that these women's tea parties were driving her crazy. Gossip, gossip about their servants, she complained; and then their doctors, and how they brought up their children (she did not add, "And the dullness of their husbands"). The fact was, there was something about these daily orgies of shared complaint, for they were nothing if not that, which was beginning to attract her like a drug.

How extraordinary it was that within a month after Douglas had returned from up north she was in this large house, with all these servants, and supplied with a new circle of friends. For all the wives of Douglas's associates had come to see her, and she had gone to see them.

She was one of a set. She had been now for over a year.

They were all married couples, and the wives were pregnant, or intended to be soon, or had just had a baby. They all earned just so much a month, owned houses which they would finish paying for in about thirty years' time, and in the houses was furniture bought on hire-purchase, including refrigerators, washing machines, fine electric stoves. They all had cars, and kept between two and five servants, who cost them about two pounds a month each. They were all heavily insured.

They took holidays at the Cape once in four or five years, gave sundowner parties to each other once or twice in the month, and went dancing or to the cinema two or three times in the week. They were, in short, extremely comfortable, and faced lives in which there could never be a moment's insecurity. "Security" was the golden word written up over their doorways, security was so deeply part of them that it was never questioned or discussed: the great climax of their lives would come at fifty or fifty-five, when their houses, gardens and furniture would be their own, and the pensions and policies bore fruit.

But if there is a type of man who instinctively chooses "the Service," is there, then, a type of woman who inevitably marries him? This was the question that troubled Martha. She was uneasy because she had adapted herself so well to this life; some instinct to conform and comply had dictated that she must quell her loathing, as at entering a trap, which she had felt at the idea of being bound by a house and insurance policies until the gates of freedom opened at fifty. She was instinctively compliant, enthusiastic, and took every step into bondage with affectionate applause for Douglas. But she never felt that she really lived in this house, whose furniture had been chosen by the woman who lived in it before her, whose garden had been designed by someone else. She did not feel like Douglas's wife or Caroline's mother. She was not even bored. It was as if three parts of herself stood on one side, idle, waiting to be called into action.

She was secretly and uneasily curious as to how these other women felt, and therefore did she go to the morning tea parties, therefore did she change her dress, brush her hair, take up her handbag and make her way to the circle of women.

On the verandah of one of their houses was set a circle of grass chairs, a table with cakes and biscuits. The babies crawled around their feet, or played on the lawns outside.

The women looked sharply at each other's dresses and at the food provided, while they discussed economy. Money chimed through their talk like a regulator of a machine. For all the heavy insurances, the mortgages, the hire-purchase, the servants, were made possible because of their ingenuity with money. They could all make attractive and expensive-looking clothes for themselves, their children and even their husbands out of a few shillings' worth of stuff bought at the sales; they continually discussed recipes which might cut the grocers' bills by a fraction; they would haggle at their back doors with the native vendors over a penny like old women in a market place; they all knitted and sewed and patched and contrived like poor men's wives. There were sharp scenes between husbands and wives at every month's end; there was a continual atmosphere of contended silver shillings. They were all perpetually short of ready money, because of their god, a secure and comfortable middle age. They sighed out, "When we retire . . ." as if they were saying, "When the prison gates are opened . . ."

Martha could not ask Douglas for five shillings to last until the end of the week, without a sharp sense of failure; and, since she had caught herself using a coaxing little voice to wheedle it out of him, she had reacted sharply into a stiff pride which meant she would go without meals secretly if he did not come home for them, to save the few pence they would cost. Yet, while she resented this necessity to spend all her time on running up dresses, petticoats, shirts, and clothes for Caroline on the sewing machine; while she never ceased to be conscious of the time that went on bottling, pickling and preserving, it was all a great pride and satisfaction to her. She found that when she had nothing to do she would unpick an old dress to make it into a new one, for the sheer satisfaction of getting something for nothing; just as she would spend two hours making a pudding that looked like an illustration out of Mrs. Beeton, so that she might feel pride in the knowledge that it cost less than the rice pudding the cook would have made in its stead.

It was the time of these women which supported the whole edifice; their willingness to sink their youth in acquiring multifarious small talents, which softened the road to that great goal, comfortable middle age.

Martha had been sucked into the pattern; with part of herself she connived at it. Weeks and months would go by, and then she found herself sitting up in bed at night, sweating with fear, and she would be afraid to go asleep again: she suffered a mild repetition of that period in her childhood when she would lie awake night after night, rigid in the bed, forcing her eyes open to prevent herself slipping into a terrible dream country. Then it all passed and she became lazy and comfortable, willingly spending all her time making and mending and contriving; and she would say to herself, Yes, I shall have another baby. For that was the crux of it. If she had another baby, she would be committed to staying here; she would live in the pattern till she died. Yet that other Martha who stood idly by all this while, waiting to be used, never believed for one moment that she would stay; it was inconceivable.

Caroline was three years old. Martha knew her female self was sharply demanding that she should start the cycle of birth again. There were moods when a slow, warm, heavy longing came up, when the very sight of Caroline filled Martha with a deep physical satisfaction at her delightful little body and charming little face; and this was at the same time a desire to hold a small baby in her arms again. If she looked at one of her friends' babies in this mood, the craving was painful and insistent, and the adventure of being pregnant filled her entirely. She thought that in nine months from now, if she chose, she could hold in her arms something new and extraordinary—a new creature created from her, Martha. And what was nine months? Nothing! said Martha to herself, forgetting how the nine months of carrying Caroline had been a period out of ordinary time. Yet she did not altogether forget. And she did *not* choose to begin again.

She was looking curiously, and with a certain deep uneasiness, at the peremptory charm of that little individual, Caroline. She knew that before Caroline was born she had seen her as "a baby" merely, something felt in the deep, driving egotism of maternity as an extension of herself and dependent upon her. Yet here she was, not at all a baby, but a creature who became every day more independent, strong-willed, determined. Caroline was that hard and unalterable fact which turned Martha's life, in spite of a pleasant and helpful nursegirl, into a routine which began at five sharp every morning, when the light first showed, and ended at seven in the evening, when she went to bed. The rhythm of Caroline's needs was in sharp discord with her own; she adjusted herself, she did what was necessary, but it was her sense of duty which regulated her. Being a mother, or rather, the business of looking after a child, as distinct from carrying and giving birth to one, was not a fulfilment but a drag on herself. Yet no sooner had she looked at this fact, admitted it, than the voices of guilt made themselves heard; and they were given sanction by the mood of deep physical tenderness and longing for another baby.

It was a mood which was acknowledged in the circle of women. One of them, picking up a small baby with an eager wistfulness which told everything, would say, half humorous and half resentful, "I'm as broody as hell again, but I can't start another baby until we've finished paying for the washing machine."

But it was observable that this same young woman announced a short time later that she had started a baby, and that—with a self-conscious look—it was because she and her husband had agreed it was only fair to have a baby as soon as possible to be a companion to little George or Betty. Which deceived nobody.

This event would be succeeded, not by general discussions, for every physical phenomenon but one was discussed with the utmost frankness in the group—sex was taboo—but by a series of tête-à-têtes about that other cycle of anxiety. They were earnest, anxious discussions in the half-humorous, grumbling tone which paid loyalty to the situations they found themselves in. For if young Letty Jones could "start a baby" when, as they knew very well, she had not meant to, and simply because the sharp physical yearning for a baby had confused her out of her efficiency, then what was to prevent the same thing happening to themselves? If they could not "plan" this, as they planned everything else in their regulated lives, they felt at the mercy of what they most dreaded. They felt insecure, in short. Besides, having a baby at all, for every one of them, was a nuisance, a painful duty, which must at least be fitted into their lives in the most convenient way. The voice of their female selves was a lure whose ambiguous and double-dealing nature they understood very well—they were not supported by the book for nothing.

Once pregnant, however, there was a compulsive satisfaction in the endless discussions of the morning sickness and the indigestion and the childbeds, in the knitting and making; while what the doctor said provided unlimited material for rivalries and comparisons. Each defended her own doctor with the fervent conviction of disciples; women who shared a doctor tended towards real intimacy on account of it; while more than once sharp words about another's doctor caused periods of "not speaking" which had to be ended by the united efforts of the whole group.

Yet in spite of the grumblings, the complaints of how children tie one so, how one can never get out at night without so much fuss about arranging for the cook boy to stay, and then he gets grumpy, and nurses are more trouble than they're worth, "but I must have one or I'll be worn out, my doctor says I'm run down and must take it easy"; in spite of the half-humorous despair that one looks like a sack of potatoes, "and my stomach's like the back of an American car, and I crave for ice cream and pickles every night, isn't it funny, every night at eleven I go into the pantry and eat ice cream and pickles, and my husband says I'm mad, I'll kill him going on like this, and I get so fat when I'm pregnant, it takes me a year to lose it after and I can't get into my clothes . . ." "Oh, no, I get so thin, my husband says I'm like a broomstick, and I lose my breasts after the milk, but they say Sister Mellors downtown does massage and you can get your breasts back if you try"; in spite of the satisfaction with which the free women looked at their sister, enormous, clumsy, flushed with heat, distressed with the weight ("She doesn't carry well, does she?" "Oh, no, well, I don't either, it takes every one differently . . ." "All the same, if I looked like a cow, like she does, I'd never have a baby at all")—in spite of all this, there was something

irresistibly satisfying about the process of self-destruction, self-nar-
rowing. Which they all believed it to be.

Martha found herself looking at pregnant Mrs. du Preez, swollen
and hideous, and thinking even while she passed her hands with
secret delight over the admirable smooth lines of her own body,
How nice, that moment when your stomach pushes out, and you
put on a maternity dress. Such is the power of the voice, which was
speaking in her more and more often.

But she did not succumb. Douglas was urging her not to put it off
any longer. "It's not fair to Caroline, she'll be too old to enjoy the
kid when we do eventually have it." Recently he had said, half joking, for he was one of those who believe in the absolving power of
humour, "I'll hide that damned thing one of these nights, and that'll
make up your mind for you!" She had turned on him sharply, sick
with anger and fear, feeling her deepest self threatened. He had
coloured and stammered out, "But, Matty, it was only a joke . . ."

After a while she laughed, and even kissed him. But it had been a
moment that had the power to set a strain between them. For some
months the subject was avoided. Martha was nervously grateful that
he said nothing. She thought vaguely that soon she would have a
baby—soon, not now. She did not go so often to the women's tea
parties. She would sit on her bed, looking worriedly at an enormous
basket filled with socks and shirts she should be mending, and drift
off into an abstracted daydream that was like a drug against any
sort of action. Or she would take a fork to the back garden, where
the vegetable beds lay, and work there for hours on end, letting the
heat of the sun drug her into warm, slow well-being. It was as if she
were waiting for something.

One morning she was kneeling on an old grain sack on the wet
black soil, turning the thick rich tilth over and smoothing it ready
for the new lettuces. This being October, the air was so dry she
could feel the dampness being sucked up in damp hot waves all
around her. She was wondering why she was drawn here so often
to do work which the garden boy did so much better, for digging in
a tame vegetable bed with a little fork was the barest impostor of
"nature," which was presumably what she was in search of. And
why was it that nothing but the veld she had been brought up on, the
sere, empty, dry vleis, the scrubby little trees, the enormous burnt
windy spaces of the high veld, could satisfy her feeling for what
nature should be? Dryness, barrenness, stunted growth, the colours
that are fed from starved roots—thin browns and greys, dull greens
and sad yellows—and all under a high, dry, empty sky: these were
what she craved. The thought of a planned and comfortable country,

filled with prosperous villas in green and fruitful acres, was dismaying and distasteful. It was at this point that she heard Mrs. Quest's voice raised in command from the front garden. She sat back on her heels, felt a surge of anger rise in her; then she conscientiously set herself to fork vegetables as if nothing were happening.

Two or three times a week, Mrs. Quest drove across the few avenues which separated her house from her daughter's, and entered the establishment like a demon of constructive energy—told the cook how to clean vegetables, informed him he was a lazy thief, lectured the nursegirl for laziness, called the houseboy in from under the tree where he was cleaning shoes to confront him with dust under the sideboard, and finally cornered Martha with a list of her deficiencies as a housekeeper. She would then depart, satisfied that she had done what was right, yet conscious that the results were not what she had intended. She told her husband and her friends that Martha ruined her servants, squandered money, and neglected Caroline. She did not really mean any of it, of course. But when she discussed her daughter, these remarks came welling from some deep crack in her nature; it was almost as if she had never really made them. But they were repeated, finally they reached Martha herself, and she went to Douglas.

He was patiently amused, and urged her to take no notice. Martha, almost in tears, said that her cook was upset, the nurse in tears, the houseboy threatening to give notice.

"Oh, well, Matty, this sort of thing happens in half the houses in town. I am sure the cook understands quite well."

"I can scarcely go to the cook and tell him my mother isn't responsible for what she does!"

"He won't take any notice. Now, Matty, just pretend to listen, humour the old girl, and keep your hair on!" With this he slid an apologetic kiss onto her cheek and found something else to do. This was particularly galling to Martha because she noticed it was how the husbands of her women friends evaded their complaints about their mothers. For every one of these young married couples had one or two mothers-in-law dependent upon them for emotional satisfaction, pathetic middle-aged women left high and dry by society with nothing to do.

Tolerant humour was infuriating. Pride forbade that she should be humoured, and she had now ceased to appeal to Douglas. More, she had succeeded in preserving a tight-lipped forbearance during her mother's assaults. She kept her complaints for the circle of women, which was the one place where she was really understood.

On this particular morning, Martha was left to fork vegetables for no more than half a minute before Mrs. Quest came round the corner of the house in that rapid, forceful way of hers, her face set with determination and disapproval. So dramatic was her arrival, so urgent, that Martha instinctively rose, fork in hand, to face a calamity.

"What on earth is the matter?" she exclaimed.

Mrs. Quest stopped at six yards, and said, "My dear! Do you realize what's going on—you really should be more careful."

Martha understood that nothing had happened after all, bent to the garden bed, jabbed the fork once or twice in the earth, leaving it upright, and followed her mother as she energetically marched back to the front. As they rounded the corner, Caroline could be heard crying angrily from the verandah. She was standing in the playpen, shaking its bars with both hands. Martha went to lift her out.

"I put her in there, she's safe there," said Mrs. Quest. "Do you know, she was sitting on the garden boy's lap." A look of disgust twisted her face. "And that lazy thing Alice, or whatever her name is, was just sitting doing nothing."

Martha set Caroline down. The little girl squatted in front of Alice and began wiping the tears off her face, while Alice smiled painfully and wiped the tears off hers. The garden boy, his whole body expressing sullen hate, was forking over some nasturtiums.

Martha was as usual seething with futile anger. But she was determined to show none. She said politely to her mother, "If you'll excuse me . . ." and walked over to Alice, who saw her coming and bent her face sideways, looking at the earth while she stirred a twig round and round in the red dust. Caroline was sitting on her knees, with an arm around Alice's neck.

"It's all right, Alice," said Martha awkwardly.

Alice looked up, the whites of her eyes very clear in her round brown, pleasant face. She smiled, then dropped her eyes bashfully while some more tears splashed out. She was comforted, however.

Martha handed the child a red hibiscus flower, which she took and began to pull to pieces; and then went towards the garden boy. He kept his eyes sullenly lowered, and went on digging. Martha hesitated over various phrases, and finally brought out: "If you'd like to go to the back, Silas . . ."

He rose, shooting at her a look of such black hate that she winced.

"It's quite all right, Silas, you can play with Caroline if you like."

"I'm not a nurse for Miss Caroline," he said angrily. He walked off.

Martha went back to the house. Her mother was not to be seen, but, hearing a loud and agitated voice from the back, Martha ran through the house to the kitchen. There stood the old cook, eyes bent to the floor, holding his face expressionless, while Mrs. Quest banged open cupboards and stooped to look under the stove. Martha watched in silence. Suddenly Mrs. Quest straightened herself from a prolonged inspection of a bottom shelf, and fished out a piece of old newspaper in which were half a dozen onions and a heel of a stale loaf. "There!" she announced triumphantly. "They steal from under your nose and you take no notice."

"I gave Tobias that," said Martha quickly. But the old man would not look at her.

Mrs. Quest sniffed, then pushed the things away from her on the table. "Oh, well," she said hurriedly, "all the same, you don't lock anything up, you just leave them about, you must lose pounds' worth every day." She looked sharply around the kitchen. Her eyes fell on her daughter's cold and angry face and she flushed up.

Tobias, in a way that was meant to be noticed, tipped the piece of soiled bread into the dustbin, and put the onions on a shelf in the cupboard. Then he carefully shut all the doors which had been left open.

"There's three days' dust under the stove," said Mrs. Quest defiantly. Tobias left the kitchen in silence.

"Would you like some tea?" enquired Martha with difficulty. She was so angry that her chest and throat were constricted with it, and her throat ached. She looked in silence at her mother, who was now standing rather helplessly in the middle of the kitchen with a distressed and guilty face. She could think of nothing to say. There never was the slightest use saying anything.

"Oh, no," said Mrs. Quest quickly. "I haven't time, and there's your father, and then the Red Cross, I told Mrs. Talbot it was getting too much for me, I haven't time."

As Martha was turning to leave, taking her at her word, she said confusedly, "Oh, well, then, just a quick cup."

Martha reached out and plugged the kettle into the wall.

"Why can't Tobias get the tea?" said Mrs. Quest accusingly. "He's paid for it."

"Because I choose to do it myself," said Martha suddenly, snapping it out. She looked straight at her mother.

The small guilty blue eyes wavered and fell. "Oh, my dear," said Mrs. Quest quickly, "there's no need to speak like that, you are quite hopeless, you know!" This was with a gay little laugh. She added, "It's quite irresponsible to let Caroline be with the garden boy, he might do anything to her and . . ." She hesitated and brought out in a rush of disgust: "Filthy creatures!" Martha said nothing. She poured a stream of boiling water onto the tea leaves, and set the teapot on the tray.

"There's no need to use all that tea for just the two of us," said Mrs. Quest automatically.

Martha, carrying the tray, led the way to the living room. Mrs. Quest followed.

It was a very large room in the centre of the house. It was cool and rather dark. The stone floor had rugs scattered over it. An enormous fireplace, which stretched across half one wall, now showed a painted tub of geraniums that were like a gay parody of fire, the soft scarlet flowers splashed over trailing green.

Mrs. Quest shot a keen look around the room. She bent to tug a rug into a different position, then collapsed into a chair. She looked uncomfortable. She pulled off her hat abruptly, with a man's gesture, then patted her puffs of grey hair like a woman.

That long fine white hand, corded and knotted with work, affected Martha with pity. She looked at her mother, and thought exhaustedly that after all she could not help it. "In a different society," she concluded, falling back on her old prop, "she would be quite different." She poured tea and handed Mrs. Quest a cup, noting with irritation that she said quickly, "No sugar," although she liked sugar in her tea. Mrs. Quest's life was a complicated system of self-denials; from the antagonistic way in which this had been said, Martha deduced that giving up sugar was in some way connected with her.

"I've given up smoking for the duration of the war," said Mrs. Quest, "as a prayer for Jonathan's safety."

"Good," said Martha cautiously, after a pause.

Mrs. Quest hesitated, then brought out in a rush: "And I've given up sugar too."

As Martha did not ask why, Mrs. Quest continued, "And I've given up sugar as a prayer for you."

Martha abruptly got up and went into the bedroom. She was dry-throated with anger. Mechanically she opened her wardrobe: there hung Mrs. Quest's coat and a cardigan. She looked at her dressing table; among her brushes and trinkets lay Mrs. Quest's powder bowl. Martha understood perfectly well the force which made her mother, who had been living in her for so many years, bring her coats here and forget them, bring her personal toilet things "by accident" and forget to take them away for months, suddenly produce a nightdress, long-sleeved, tight-throated, and say, "You'd better wear this, you'll catch cold." There was never a time when half a dozen of Mrs.

Quest's personal belongings did not lie in Martha's drawers and cupboards. But while Martha had long ago understood, and with the tired pity which was the greatest degree of charity she could achieve, why it should be so, she could not prevent herself from feeling angry.

She sat on the edge of her bed, looked at the hanging trumpets of the white moonflowers, and invoked the deity society. "People like her can't help it. They've been formed in this mould." And then came, inevitably, the voice of the enemy, pride. How ridiculous, said the small jeering voice. How ridiculous you are, Martha Quest, caught in this silly, banal, *old-fashioned* situation. There's nothing new to be said about it. Martha rose from the edge of her bed, deciding that she would have a sensible talk with her mother. She returned briskly to the other room, where Mrs. Quest was sitting stirring her spoon round and round the cup as if there were sugar in it. She tautened as her daughter entered, and looked at her cautiously.

"Now, look here," began Martha with cheerful common sense, "I want to say something to you. I think I've said it before—but let's have another shot at it," she added, with rueful humour.

Mrs. Quest brightened and said in an equally jolly voice, "Well, what is it this time?"

Martha's spirits sank a little, but she said carefully, "I want you to try and remember what you would have felt if your mother had run your affairs the way you try to run mine. I don't think you'd have liked it, you know."

Feeling that this reasonable statement should be enough, she looked towards Mrs. Quest and waited. Mrs. Quest had stopped stirring, but the spoon knocked tinkling against the side of her cup—her hand was shaking. Martha noticed this with despair.

"Well, someone must keep an eye on you," said Mrs. Quest, laughing. "You're so scatterbrained, and all your servants do as they like with you—and you're ruining Caroline . . ."

Anger spurted up in Martha, she quelled it. "You brought me and my brother up the way you wanted, don't you think I should be allowed to do the same with my children?" Her voice shook. She saw that at this admission of weakness Mrs. Quest eagerly lifted her face and smiled a small triumph, as if she were conscious of an audience. "Listen to this absurd child," that smile said.

Martha's jaws were aching. She relaxed them, and said, "I'm going to ask you, I think for about the fiftieth time, to stop upsetting my servants and interfering with Caroline." This was with the desperate humour which she despised as she used it. And some demon caused her to add, in what was a cry of despair, "After all, Mother, I'm twenty-two this month."

At this Mrs. Quest produced a small amused laugh.

Martha looked through her stock of reasonable arguments, and returned to the first. "You know," she said with tired irony, "I can remember hearing you talk to my father—though I expect you've forgotten that—about your mother. You had to put your foot down, I remember your saying. She was domineering, you said." She added to herself, And you were lucky enough to leave her behind in England and took good care she didn't follow you.

"Oh, my dear!" exclaimed Mrs. Quest, distressed, "I and your father were very fond of your grandmother. How can you say such a thing?"

It occurred to Martha that she was being extremely foolish. That it had come home to her so often before, and that she apparently had no power to learn by experience, depressed her into silence.

Encouraged, Mrs. Quest said in a gay final tone, "Well, I don't mean to interfere, of course. Anyway, Caroline is my child—grandchild, I mean," she amended hastily. "And I'm not going to see her ruined."

"As a matter of interest," enquired Martha, her voice shaking, "how am I ruining Caroline?"

"Well, I mean to say—" here Mrs. Quest became confused—"well, my dear, I mean to say, she's so small for her age, and you let her go into the sun without a hat, and she's always with those black things—they're so dirty. And all that sort of thing."

"She looks remarkably well on it," brought out Martha, determinedly humorous.

"She's very pale and exhausted," said Mrs. Quest.

Suddenly Martha snapped, "Oh, shut up and get out of here. I've had enough."

She looked, astounded, at her mother, at this extraordinary phenomenon which she had after all seen so often before. Mrs. Quest, that handsome matron with her broad downright face, had collapsed into a small girl. Yes, a pathetic frightened little girl sat there, looking at Martha with small sad blue eyes which slowly filled with tears.

Pity filled Martha. She at once remembered her mother's hard and disappointing life; she said to herself that, while she, Martha, was of a generation dedicated above all to self-knowledge, Mrs. Quest knew no such obligations. She was appalled at her own cruelty. She said helplessly, "Oh, damn it *all*, Mother!" She got up, sat on the arm of Mrs. Quest's chair, and put her arm around the collapsed and shrinking shoulders. It was very unpleasant for her to touch her mother, particularly as she felt those shoulders straighten and gain strength under the contact.

Mrs. Quest turned and with an abrupt and clumsy movement of affection embraced Martha, saying inarticulately, "There, dear, I didn't really mean . . ."

Horror filled Martha. She realized that by this one moment of pity she had completely undone what she might have achieved: pity itself was contaminated, then? Not that it would have made any difference, she said to herself between set teeth. And finally, in the voice of the enemy: It's better not to fight at all, better anything than these disgusting scenes.

"Now that we are having a really frank talk," said Mrs. Quest, already herself again, "I want to tell you—it is my duty—I mean to say, everyone is saying you should have another baby."

Martha disengaged herself, got up, and moved stiffly away.

"Oh, don't be so *difficult*, Matty. Actually, that's why I've given up sugar in my tea—as a prayer to God you'll see some sense." She hesitated. "It's not fair to Douglas, it's not fair to Caroline, you're simply selfish," she concluded gaily.

"I'm not prepared to discuss it," said Martha finally, as she sat down.

"Oh, but, my dear, you must—everyone is saying . . ." She hesitated at Martha's look.

"So *everyone* is discussing whether or not I should have another baby?" enquired Martha, with extraordinary calm.

"Oh, well, you know how people talk."

"I do indeed. I'm glad I provide such a satisfactory topic for the bridge tables."

"Oh, it wasn't bridge. You know we don't play bridge so much now that the war . . . But at the Red Cross yesterday—" She coloured up and stopped. "Anyway," she recovered herself, "your father was saying to me only yesterday that you're totally and completely irresponsible, and that Douglas should put his foot down."

"My father said that?" asked Martha quickly, filled with total dismay. Then she reminded herself of previous occasions when she had taxed her father with what he was supposed to have said.

"And I took Douglas aside for a good talk yesterday. I went to his office," said Mrs. Quest, in her moment of final triumph. "He quite agrees with me."

Martha felt as if her last support had gone; but she recovered herself, and said coldly, "You've no right at all to discuss me behind my back with Douglas."

For a moment the frightened little girl appeared in Mrs. Quest, looked appealingly through her eyes—then vanished. She set down her cup, looked about her, picked up her handbag. She stood up. "Oh, dear, I'm so late."

Martha picked up, from various parts of the room, spectacles, gloves, a library book and a coat, and offered them to Mrs. Quest.

"Oh, dear," she muttered, "just put that coat in your wardrobe for the time being, I've so much to carry."

"I'll carry it to the car for you."

"Oh, no—it'll do another time."

"You already have one coat and a cardigan in my wardrobe."

"It's a very big wardrobe," said Mrs. Quest hastily.

"Not as big as all that," Martha said, and suddenly laughed irresistibly.

Mrs. Quest looked at her with suspicion, and said, "You just keep them, I'll call for them, I'm too much in a hurry, another time." She sounded flustered. The small girl was strong in her face—a little girl deprived of something she badly wanted.

Martha put the coat on a chair, and saw her mother's face brighten. She shrugged helplessly.

They went out through the various rooms to the front verandah. Alice and the garden boy and Caroline were once more seated under the tree as if nothing had happened. Caroline was lying on her back on the grass, her legs waving in the air, crooning to herself, while the boy twanged at his hand piano. A yellow butterfly hovered over the grass, and settled with fanning wings on Caroline's foot. She felt the tickle, and craned up her head to see. It was comical to see the puzzled little face watching her own motionless foot where the butterfly clung. Alice was knitting industriously.

Martha looked at Mrs. Quest to share her pleasure at the scene, but saw there only the familiar look of agonized disgust.

"Oh, Matty," said Mrs. Quest urgently, "it's so awful, you really must keep that man away from her."

Martha put her arm in her mother's, and propelled her fast down the garden path towards the car, which was parked outside the gate under a jacaranda tree. The roof of the car was scattered with loose mauve flowers. Mrs. Quest energetically whisked the flowers off, got into the driver's seat, and looked past Martha at the group under the tree. Her distress was sincere and painful.

"Matty," she began again, her voice trembling, "Mrs. Talbot told me you let that black girl sleep in Caroline's room when you go out—they have all kinds of diseases, it's awful."

"You'll be late," said Martha briskly.

"Well, you must boil the sheets afterwards." She offered Martha a small wan smile. The eyes of the two women met in pure antagonism, and immediately separated. Mrs. Quest drove off firmly down the wrong side of the street.

Martha returned indoors, past the group under the tree. Almost at once, Douglas arrived for lunch. He went first over to Caroline, offered her a small toy he had picked up for her, spoke a few cheerful words to the garden boy and the nursegirl, and came in.

As soon as the meal was served, Martha enquired abruptly, "I want to know if it's true that you and my mother have been having a nice frank talk about me behind my back."

He shot her an uncomfortable look, took a large mouthful, and swallowed it before replying: "We did have a talk, yes. She is your mother, after all," he said sentimentally.

"Quite." She said no more. She felt it as an intolerable disloyalty.

After some minutes' silence, Douglas said bluffly but uneasily, "Oh, come off it, Matty, there's no harm."

"I think there is," she said, and rang the bell for the next course. The servant came in with a complicated coloured pudding. Douglas cast an approving eye at it, and softened. The servant went out again. "Now, look here, Matty, something's got into you, and I think you should snap out of it," he said firmly.

"Just what conclusions did you and my mother come to about Caroline?"

He flushed a raw-beef colour and said hastily, "Well, she's not looking so well, is she?"

"I neglect her?"

"I didn't say that."

"What are you saying, then? You know quite well that at this time of the year all children get worn out with the heat."

"Well, perhaps you might spend more time with her."

She looked at him in amazement. "Let's get this straight. Caroline wakes at five. I have her until seven. I supervise her breakfast. I have her while Alice washes and irons. I always supervise her lunch. I have her from four until she goes to bed. I make all her clothes. She never eats a mouthful I haven't prepared myself—" But at this point she stopped; for she saw quite clearly that this was like an argument with her mother, conducted on two different levels.

"I didn't say—" he shouted, furious with her and himself. He knew he was in the wrong—he should not have succumbed to Mrs. Quest. On the other hand, he felt himself to be insulted and diminished by this cold and logical mood of Martha's.

"I should like you to say, one way or the other, if you agree with my mother that Caroline is neglected."

"Of course not," he shouted.

"Well, that's something."

"You should have another baby," he said quickly, ducking his head to his spoonful of pudding.

"So I should."

"I tell you what, Matty," he urged in a brotherly, man-to-man way. "Why not pop down to old Stern and talk it over, eh?"

"Because I am sick or Caroline is?" enquired Martha.

"Look here, Matty, let me tell you—I rang up old Stern, as a matter of fact, and made an appointment with him for this afternoon."

She digested this. "My mother said you should make me see the doctor, you rang up Dr. Stern, and asked him to talk to me for my own good."

She saw that he was on the verge of a mood which was occurring more and more often: he would suddenly turn from a sensible, masculine, responsible young man, though perhaps an angry one, into a sulky little boy, his lips quivering with self-pity. He was going to do it now. She hastily said, "I'll go and see Dr. Stern, if you like." She could not bear the sulky little boy, it made her hate him.

"That's the ticket, Matty," he said, relieved. He rose and said, "I must be getting back to the office, there's so much work. Actually, I've been thinking I won't come home to lunch. I'll take sandwiches, we're so understaffed."

She said, "Very well," casually.

He looked swiftly at her, dismayed—he seemed to feel let down. "It'll mean a long day for you," he prompted.

"I'll miss you terribly," she said at once, and he kissed her affectionately and went out.

She immediately began chiding herself for her utter dishonesty. The instinct to comply, to please, seemed to her more and more unpleasant and false. Yet she had to reassure Douglas and kiss him before he left if she was not to feel guilty and lacking as a woman.

Pushing aside this problem, she went aside to smarten herself up for Dr. Stern. But Douglas was calling her from the verandah. His voice was authoritative. She went out to him. "Look at that, Matty," he said with the sentimental note she hated. She followed his self-consciously shocked gaze, and saw Caroline asleep, sprawled on a rug under the tree, while Alice sat over her, moving a frond of leaves through the hot still air.

She looked at him, puzzled. "What's the matter?"

"She should be sleeping in her bed," he said, still in that stern, sentimental voice.

"But, Douglas, you yourself suggested that she should sleep under the tree in this weather—it's cooler than on the verandah."

He gave her a quick, rather ashamed look: the rather fattish, reddish face expressed an official indignation, however. "Why can't you have the bed moved out there?" he asked.

"But the girl stays there, Caroline isn't left," said Martha helplessly. "You know," she added humorously, "what's happening is this: You're in a mood of disapproving of me, my mother's got under your skin, and you're just looking for a stick to beat me with." She laughed uncomfortably and looked at him, waiting.

He went dark red, fidgeted; it was touch and go whether he lost his temper. He put his arms around her and said in a muffled, affectionate voice, "Oh, Matty . . ." She kissed him, feeling like a traitor to herself, and off he went to the car, beaming and happy, giving Caroline as he passed a proud and proprietory look. Alice made a kind of seated curtsy towards the master, smiling bashfully, while she continued to wave the frond of leaves over the sleeping child's face.

Martha went indoors again. She felt that some kind of crisis had been precipitated. But every instinct she had shrank away from it. To wait, that was what she would like to do—to drift on, and then something would happen, she did not know what. A rescue of some kind—someone would say something; she was listening unconsciously for the right pattern of words again. She decided to go and see her father, there was over an hour before she must be at Dr. Stern's.

When she had changed from one brief, tight bright dress into another, and painted colour into a face she thought was pale and even rather ugly, she went out to the garden with the push-chair. Caroline was now half awake, blinking up at the tree that stretched over her. Her fists were curled up beside her head—she was a baby again. Then she saw her mother, smiled, and became a little girl, scrambling energetically to her feet. Martha put her into the push-chair, and told the girl she was free until five o'clock. Alice gave her that delightful shy smile, which showed white strong teeth, and went off singing to the back garden.

Martha rapidly wheeled the chair through the patches of shade along the side of the street. Petals fell like a slow blue rain from the masses of sun-filled blossom overhead. Caroline watched them, her eyes rather strained with the midday glare. Martha thought anxiously that perhaps the child was not well after all—she was certainly pale. Perhaps she was not eating enough, perhaps she . . . Martha stopped herself, and went off along the other track of worry: what was wrong with Caroline was that she, Martha, did not feel the right way about her. Do I love her? she asked herself sternly, looking with steady criticism at the little girl. The emotion of love vanished as she examined it. At this moment she felt nothing but the bond of responsibility. Then she saw Caroline's black eyes turn towards her, and the little face opened in a warm, confiding smile. Martha's heart went soft with tenderness. At this, the other thought came driving in: It would be much better for her if I didn't. I must be careful not to be too much interested in what she does. But even as she was making these resolutions she felt her face soften in a protective smile, and she thought despairingly, Oh, Lord, there's no escaping it, she'll hate me, too. Yet the idea of her and Caroline hating each other seemed absurd.

But the child was certainly pale, Martha thought anxiously. And there was sweat on her forehead. She went faster; only another block to go. The wheels of the push-chair made two bruised tracks through the thick carpet of petals, the light dry scent of them came up all about them, a scent so faint it was like the smell of dryness itself, a ghost merely. The flowers of light, they were: she could see how the sun shaded a single flower from a light dry mauve that was almost white to a deep purple where the shade clung. She handed a blossom to the child and watched her turn it over and over in the sun; she wondered if the little brain was absorbing the same impressions that she did—then she stopped herself. Why should Caroline see what she saw? It was the blackest tyranny even to want it or think it. But here she gained the house.

Her father was asleep under a tree in a deck chair, a white handkerchief over his face. Her mother was nowhere to be seen. She hesitated; should she go into the house? But she hated it, with its tasteless furniture and its ugly pictures. But that was not the real truth. She could not see the things that had made the landscape of her childhood—a silver tray, a row of books, the pictures themselves— without sharp pain at seeing them *here*: they belonged to a ramshackle, silent house in the veld, they belonged to memory. She never entered the house unless she had to. She would spend hours with her father in the garden, but could not enter that house without a confused and painful disturbance which she did not understand.

She wheeled the push-chair as silently as she could towards her father; but as she came near, he sat up and pushed the handkerchief from his eyes, and blinked at her, his face stiff and wooden from sleep. Then it lightened into affection. He said cordially, "Hullo, old chap, nice to see you."

She put Caroline down to play, and took the deck chair beside her father. "How are you?" she asked, and waited patiently while he answered the question with preoccupied attention to detail. She gathered that on the whole he was rather better than usual.

"But you don't want to be bored with my troubles," he said hastily at the end, and asked, equally from habit, "And how are things with you?"

She hesitated. She realized she had come here to complain to him about her mother. The banality of the thing stopped her. Besides, it troubled him so, any appeal to him. She said, "Oh, I'm fine."

But he had noticed the hesitation, and was looking at her keenly. She felt uncomfortable. Nine parts of his time, Mr. Quest was safe in his inner world of memory and vague philosophical speculations; but he could come out of it abruptly, and be warm, shrewd, paternal. This, if she wanted, was one of the times. She hesitated again.

He turned his eyes away, and looked at Caroline, who was rolling over and over on the grass. "That's a nice kid," he observed, as if seeing her for the first time. Martha laughed, and again those very shrewd and knowledgeable old eyes turned towards her.

"What's the matter, old chap?" he asked.

Martha felt her lips tremble. She was shaking with dry sobs. She saw he was extremely embarrassed—he could not stand tears.

"Oh, Lord," he was saying, "don't cry, there's a good bloke." He handed her his large handkerchief, and she wiped her eyes and smiled.

"You're looking tired," he remarked, the glinting dark eyes looking right into her.

"I'm fed up," she said, in a trembling hard voice. "I'm so bored I could scream. I can't bear—anything!" she concluded defiantly, looking straight at him. She waited for his judgment.

"I've been thinking for some time things weren't right," he remarked. He fished in his pocket, pulled out the old tin where he kept his cigarettes, and offered her one, lighting it with the careful old-fashioned courtesy he never forgot. "Of course," he went on, "I've not said anything to your mother." She looked sharply at him, but saw it was the truth. "She's making various remarks," he added, embarrassed. "However . . ."

Another silence. Mr. Quest looked down at his hands in a way which was very familiar. They were large, fine, but rather limp hands. He appeared to be surprised they were his hands. He frowned worriedly at them and remarked, "I really must find my nail scissors, they've got themselves lost somewhere." Almost, he allowed himself to drift off; then he sighed, and shot her another speculative glance from under the stiff white cliffs of his eyebrows.

"What did you do it for?" he said suddenly, in a low reproachful voice. "It was so obvious it wouldn't be any good. You weren't even in love with him."

"Wasn't I?" she asked, surprised. She could not for the life of her remember what she had felt.

"You weren't in love with him, you've never been in love with anyone—anyone can tell it by looking at you," he said. That last sentence, cool, direct, the judgment of no less than an experienced man, caused her to look at him in respectful surprise. "I knew then it was a mistake—but no one can ever tell you anything. Can they, now?" he added, softening it with a sort of affectionate irritation.

"Well, so that's that," he said, directing the irritation against life itself. "Marriage, I suppose, is a necessary institution," he went on after a pause, "but for *you* to get married at nineteen . . ."

"You mean, I've made my bed and I must lie on it?" she enquired reasonably.

She was not at all prepared for what followed; she thought uncomfortably that this man not only knew her much better than she ever allowed herself to think, but seemed always to be a jump ahead of her. "You must think it all over, Matty. Whatever you do, you must do it sensibly."

He could only mean one thing. Yet never had Martha said to herself in so many words that she would leave Douglas. She felt that she would, sometime—but to say it was too frightening and definite.

"Think it over. And don't get yourself in the family way again until you're certain," said Mr. Quest firmly. They looked at each other. His eyes held an affection which made hers fill. But it was years since they had shown each other affection. "I'm very fond of you," he said in a low, embarrassed voice. "Oh, damn it all!" he exclaimed, as his cigarette fell onto his trouser leg. He brushed off the sparks, and by the time things had been restored to order the moment had passed.

He collected his thoughts carefully, and observed, "I never did like that man. I never could understand how you could marry such a—commercial traveller."

Feebly Martha said, "He's all right, you know."

"Yes, but, Matty! He's—for the Lord's sake, why couldn't you pick a man who *is* a man?" Again Martha felt herself reddening under the experienced male look. "Anyone could see with half an eye that— However, that's that," said Mr. Quest irritably.

Martha felt ashamed; at the same time she was supported. Everything would be all right, she felt.

He lit another cigarette for her, and smoked his own in silence.

"It's going to rain soon," he observed, looking at the sky. The banks of dark foliage about them hung limp and heavy. Clouds of mauve blossom seemed to dissolve into the sky in quivering light. The deep blue overhead was packed with thunderous cloud masses.

"The heat's awful," said Martha, irritated. She could feel herself hot and sticky under her dress. All the same, she liked it: the heat sang through her like the movements of her own blood. "I've got to take Caroline to the doctor," she said without moving.

"Anything wrong?" he asked politely.

"Oh, no, she's quite well."

Mr. Quest surveyed his grandchild, who was now industriously pulling lilies off their stems, and said, "The image of you at her age. Except for the eyes, of course. And the hair. Where did those eyes come from?"

"Douglas's father, I believe," said Martha. "Why?" Then, noting his look, she enquired, "What on earth do you mean?"

"Well, I've often wondered," went on Mr. Quest calmly. "After all, you don't hold with our morals; as far as I can see there's nothing to prevent Caroline being someone else's child."

Martha was extremely shocked. "You're not suggesting," she said indignantly, "that I married Douglas under false pretences?"

"I don't see what's to prevent you, if you've thrown over conventional morality. For the life of me I can't see why you married him—there must be some reason."

"There wasn't any reason," she said helplessly.

"Then you must have been in the family way."

"I was, but I didn't know it." Here she began to laugh; for some reason she could not think of it without finding it absurdly funny. "There I was pregnant, and I didn't know it, though everybody else did . . ." She laughed herself out, and sat wiping her eyes.

"I don't see the joke," he said reprovingly. "I think it's appalling. However, there's some comfort in the thought that your generation is no more competent than we were—though I don't expect you to see it."

His look at her held a familiar irritation; the moment of understanding was over; almost at once he blew out a long cloud of smoke, watched it swirl away sluggishly into the blue air, and remarked in that other, introspective voice, "Did I ever tell you about that time when I came out of hospital and I was sure I was mad?"

He knew that he had; his urgent glance nevertheless appealed that she should let him tell it again. She sat in silence for some minutes listening.

"Anyway," he concluded at a tangent, "as far as I can see, everyone is mad. Do you know, Matty, that's the only explanation for the world that I can see—everyone's as mad as hatters."

She agreed politely, and, after a decent interval, said she must leave for the doctor's. She put Caroline into the push-chair, and then kissed her father's dry papery cheek. He inclined it towards her absent-mindedly, murmuring, "Nice to see you, old chap. Drop in again soon." He looked at her—his eyes held a sly, evasive gleam. "There was something I wanted to say to you, what was it?"

She did not smile, but said seriously, "I must go now, Daddy." For that was his way of saying that if he had come out of his cloud to be her father, give her advice, support her, he did not intend to be reminded of it later. He was not going to be held responsible. There was in his smile, however, a direct mischievous quality, rather comradely, which acknowledged the situation as plainly as words. Now she smiled back, ironically.

As she wheeled the chair away, he said firmly after her, "Mad. All of us. Everyone." And with this he reached out for a book which lay face down on the grass, propped it on his knees, and began to read.

By the time she reached the doctor's rooms, she was ready to burst out angrily against the advice she expected him to give her. She could positively hear the male complacency with which Douglas had asked him to speak to her. And no doubt Dr. Stern had replied in the same tone? "Women," they might have said; "you know what women are." Somewhere from the back of her mind floated up a memory of those words, and that tone—who was speaking? Why, of course, Mr. Quest, with Mr. Van Rensberg on the farm. There was that question of masculine laughter—conspiratorial almost, but most certainly deeply offensive. Mr. Quest was one thing with men, another with his wife; Mr. Quest half an hour before, and for ten minutes, had been something different again. Martha clung tight to *that* image of a man, and, thus supported, looked over at Dr. Stern, waiting for him to put the pressure on. As she phrased it to herself.

But Dr. Stern was being as bland as he always was. He examined the child carefully, and pronounced her to be perfectly well. On Martha's insistence, he repeated, "Perfectly well—I'll issue a certificate to that effect whenever you like!" Their eyes met briefly; there was a comprehension in his which both upset and consoled her.

It appeared that he thought the interview over; but that was not what Douglas had implied. She said suddenly, "Perhaps I could see you for myself, just a moment."

He at once nodded to the nurse, yet another young woman in the glazed white overall, who took Caroline by the hand and trotted her off into the next room.

The room was full of greenish light; light slid along the polished surface of the desk; the atmosphere of hushed professional intimacy was being re-established. Dr. Stern had a card before him on his blotter. He was looking down at it, his pale flattish face without expression. He was looking very tired.

"Well, Mrs. Knowell?"

Douglas must have been telling a lie, thought Martha. Dr. Stern shot her a swift assessing glance, then pushed her card away and leaned back in his chair and yawned. "This weather makes me sleepy," he remarked conversationally. "And I was up all night with a baby. I don't know why babies are always born at night—yours was, wasn't it?" Martha waited on edge for him to add some suggestion about her having another; he did not. "At this time of the year we all feel it. You look a bit done in yourself. I should take it easy, if I were you. And Caroline—all kids get pale and fretful, and we should try to keep them as quiet as possible. I get all my mothers along in October, worrying themselves sick. Just take it easy, take things easy, I tell them."

Martha noted the recurrence of the word "all"; Dr. Stern was feeding that need in her to be absolved by being like everybody else; it was the need that sent her off to women's tea parties. There was a part of her brain which remained satirical and watchful, even amused, while it tried to analyze the process by which Dr. Stern handled her. But the watchful other person did not prevent him from playing her like a fish on a line, she thought.

"You know, Mrs. Knowell, half the women who come in to see me have nothing wrong with them, but it doesn't mean to say they don't need a doctor's advice. Now, you, as an intelligent woman, will understand that."

Martha smiled disagreeably at the "intelligent woman"; he saw the smile, but went on, "I prescribe a bottle of tonic. It does no harm. It might do some good. But I'm not going to prescribe a bottle of tonic for you. Your husband seems worried about you. You would be surprised how often I get worried telephone calls from young husbands." Here he laughed as if they shared a secret. "Perhaps it is just as well that husbands are—sometimes a little off the mark?" He waited for her to laugh.

She had frozen, however; it was too clumsy. He noted her frown, picked up his pen, and began making a series of sharp downward strokes on a scribbling pad.

Martha thought, He can't judge people deeply; what he has got is an insight into how they react. He knows I resent it, but he doesn't know what I resent. But she understood that his technique was working very well. She was feeling with him, against the world of clumsy young husbands. She reminded herself that he was not much more than thirty, not much older than herself. And then: He didn't even know I was pregnant when I came to him that time, and yet here I sit putting myself into his hands. For the first time she suspected that perhaps he *had* known she was pregnant, and understood her well enough to let her become too advanced to do anything about it. Perhaps all the women who came here were handled in the same way?

For the women of the suburbs, doctors do not make mistakes. At least, not their own doctors.

She thought of his wife. In the circle of women it was said that Mrs. Stern was not good enough for her husband. Martha had caught a glimpse of them together one Sunday afternoon in the park. Mrs. Stern was a small dark plump girl with a high-coloured face, who clung to his arm while he strolled across the grass, apparently as weary and patient as always. Martha had envied her. Being married to Dr. Stern would be something quite different from being the wife of one of the boys. She had thought that proud anxious clutching of his arm rather ridiculous; now, if she, Martha, had been married to Dr. Stern . . .

But he was speaking. "Before I got married myself I had all kinds of notions. But I've discovered that I'm not quite as clever as I thought I was. It's one thing to give advice from outside, and another to handle things yourself. I am quite sure my wife thinks me the most clumsy of fellows." He looked up and smiled. It was a pleasant and disarming smile. He shrugged, as if the whole thing was beyond him; and Martha found herself smiling with him.

"Now, look here, Mrs. Knowell," he began in a completely different tone, all his cards on the table, You would be surprised, I am sure, at the number of young married women who come here and sit where you are sitting, in just the same mood—you will forgive me for saying that I can see you are in a mood? I don't want to step in where angels fear to tread, believe me. For instance, only yesterday a patient of mine came in and she was crying her eyes out and said she couldn't stand her husband and was going to leave him. There was no other man, nothing like that, she just couldn't stand things any longer. It's the time of the year. And then, it was last week, I think, another patient I've known for years and years—" he sounded like a tolerant old man, and it occurred to Martha that he could not have known any patient for years and years, he had not been practising long enough—"well, she was in the same mood. But she was in here this morning, and she's going to have another baby, and she'd got over it. We do get over it and just jog along. When I come to think

of it, there isn't one of my women patients who doesn't come in to
me a couple of years after her marriage, wishing she was out of it all.
It's not much of a compliment to us men, I expect, but there it is,
that's life."

He again offered her his bland, tolerant smile, and she smiled back
her appreciation of this life they must all accept, since there was no
alternative. She was feeling quite remarkably relieved and consoled.
But she could not help thinking, He'll keep it up for a few minutes,
just to make sure.

And he did continue, using the words "we," "all," and "everybody"
in every sentence. She was both angrily humiliated and perversely
appreciative of the situation.

"My wife is going to have a baby quite soon, Mrs. Knowell, and,
believe me, I shall make a point of seeing she goes right away from
me and the child in about a year's time—we should all get away from
each other sometimes. I certainly shall not allow her to have a second
baby before she has been off by herself away from me for at least a
month."

The words "I certainly shall not allow" succeeded in conjuring up
such a picture of his marriage, such a complacent and uxorious
young husband, that the spell snapped. She instantly decided that he
had said to Douglas over the telephone, "Well, old chap, you know
what women are."

"I can't go for a holiday, Dr. Stern, it's out of the question." This
was flat and rather contemptuous. Dr. Stern raised those intelligent
tired eyes.

"Well, Mrs. Knowell, if you can't, you can't. Bad luck, but there
it is."

She stood up. "Well, thank you, doctor—I mustn't keep you." She
added suddenly, "I really am feeling tired—perhaps you could give
me a tonic."

He drew the prescription pad towards him and wrote. "Yes, we
none of us feel too good at this time of the year."

Caroline was brought in by the nurse. Dr. Stern escorted Martha
to the door and dismissed her with the usual invitation to drop in
whenever she liked. She went through the waiting room, which as
always was filled with women whose eyes were fixed on his door.

In the street she hesitated outside a chemist's shop, then took out
the prescription for the tonic and tore it up; she thrust the pieces
into her handbag with a really violent impulse of anger. Everything
seemed hateful. It's all so terrible, she was saying to herself. She
wheeled Caroline along the pavement, instinctively keeping in the
shade. She could not bear to think of the *everyone,* the *we* and the

all. So everyone had moods in which they ran off to the doctor, that archpriest, who gave them bottles of tonic and assured them they were exactly like everyone else? They went for a holiday, then they began another baby and were perfectly happy? All the same, she said to herself, it is the mood which is the truth, and the other a lie. She could not maintain the conviction for long. The irritable exhaustion faded at the idea of having another baby: it was so exciting to have a baby, to produce another human being out of nowhere—out of the hat, so to speak! And then it would be all settled for once and for all. No escape then! And in two or three years' time the baby would be just such another little person as Caroline was now, looking at her with judging eyes. A pang of tired fear went through her. She saw it all so very clearly. That phrase, "having a baby," which was every girl's way of thinking of a first child, was nothing but a mask to conceal the truth. One saw a flattering image of a madonnalike woman with a helpless infant in her arms; nothing could be more attractive. What one did not see, what everyone conspired to prevent one seeing, was the middle-aged woman who had done nothing but produce two or three commonplace and tedious citizens in a world that was already too full of them.

Martha was on the point of sliding off into those familiar reflections about what the women of the past had felt about it, when she was brought up short by the thought of her father. He had put the problem quite clearly; she must face it.

If she was to leave Douglas, for what way of living was she to leave? There's something so damned *vieux jeu*, she thought gloomily, in leaving like Nora, to live differently! Because we're not such fools any longer. We don't imagine that rushing off to earn one's living as a typist is going to make any difference. One is bound to fall in love with the junior partner, and the whole thing will begin all over again. The idea was so unpleasant that she swung round: Not at all; she would submit, as everyone else did.

She began daydreaming. Since there was no woman she had ever met she could model herself on, she created a brooding and female spirit in that large cool house in the avenues, surrounded by a crowd —for, while she was about it, she imagined six or seven children, not just two—a brood, then, of charming children, who fed from this source of warmth and creativeness as at a spring. A picture much more attractive than the cold and critical young woman typing letters in a business office.

One of those warm, large, delightful, maternal, humorous females she would be; undemanding, unpossessive. One never met them, but, if she put her mind to it, no doubt she could become one. She would lapse into it as into a sea and let everything go . . . And, severely suppressing the pangs of pure panic that kept rising in her every moment at the idea of abandoning the person she felt herself to be, she set herself to imagine the house, all its rooms full of children, and she in the middle like a queen ant.

She had reached a corner where she must turn off into the leafy avenues. She was dipping the wheels of the push-chair down off the pavement, when she heard a shrill whistle. There was a note in it which made her glance sharply around. On the opposite pavement stood a group of young men in the grey uniform, and they were whistling after her with mixed derision and admiration. She at once felt herself stiffen and become self-conscious. She turned her head away as the whistles rang out again, with a jeering note in them because of her aloofness, and was furious with herself because of that self-consciousness. She hastily gained the opposite pavement, and turned off into the avenue before her own so as to escape the men and her own embarrassment.

This small episode had destroyed the vision of the brooding mother with the flock of children. She could not regain it. She marched sternly up under the dropping purple jacarandas—the sun had lost its hot white glare, and was beaming out a thick yellow which shaped the jacaranda blossoms into clusters of heavy purple—and was pervaded with a disgust of herself, life, everything, so strong it was like a nausea.

She heard steps hurrying up behind her, heard her name called, and turned to see William approaching. She had not seen him since that afternoon eighteen months ago when Douglas returned.

"Were you with that—mob?" she enquired, sour but smiling.

And he grinned, returning equably, "Boys will be boys." For naturally he, the individual, had nothing to do with the group he had been part of a moment before. "Where are you going?"

"Home," said Martha, resuming her progress.

William advanced his opinion that Caroline was growing a big girl. Martha agreed. William said it was a long time since they had met. Martha said a very long time. William said he found the weather very trying. Their eyes met and they laughed.

He certainly did not look comfortable. The thick stiff cloth seemed more than ever like a variety of shell. In movement he had a quick lightness, almost grace, but the uniform was too much for him, he looked eclipsed. But from the grey carapace his pale face emerged, now rather flushed, and the very clear blue eyes—not like Douglas's eyes, which were a strong, rather muddy blue, but a deep blue, like water or sapphires—were calm and intelligent. His hair was bright rough brown, like metal in the sunshine, under a cap which he wore jauntily, at a rakish angle, as they all did—as if it was a joke that they must wear it at all.

"I'll go with you a little way—nothing better to do this fine afternoon." And he marched along beside her, hands in his pockets.

"How's the—group?" enquired Martha awkwardly.

"Oh . . . fine." But he relented and said in a friendly casual way, "We did hope you would join us. But of course it is difficult now— we see your difficulties," he amended, colouring a little.

But what did that "we" mean now?

"You've broken away from that—the old gang?'"

"Well, of course, with this sudden swing, it's easy to get things going."

"What sudden swing?"

He looked at her swiftly, frowning and incredulous. Then: "Surely it must be obvious even to the wives of prominent civil servants that there's a change in the atmosphere?"

"I haven't been reading the newspapers," she said confusedly.

He pursed up his lips a little, was silent; then he saw her apologetic face and enquired obligingly, "Why not?"

"They're all so disgusting."

"Oh granted, granted." But he again relented and said, "There are other ways of coping with it than not reading them." His air of disapproval annoyed her. She thought, He's nothing but a boy, anyway. He was about twenty, and she two years older; but she was married and had a child. She felt maternal towards him.

They had reached the house. Through the flowering hedges, beneath its sheltering trees, it looked very large, settled, permanent. The garden boy was chatting with the nursegirl under a tree, the piccanin was gathering peas in the vegetable beds, the houseboy was sweeping the deep flight of front steps.

"A delightful feudalism," he remarked pleasantly. "Truly delightful. And you the chatelaine of it all." She could not help laughing, though she was angry with him. "Oh, well, it can't be helped," he went on, casting calm blue eyes over the place. "And I'll admit that there *are* worse ways of spending one's life."

He wanted to be asked in, she could see. But she remembered Douglas: he would be angry. First, she thought confusedly, I must get this business sorted out—for once and for all!

"Give my regards to the old man," he said.

He meant Douglas. She stiffened.

"Well, so long. If you ever feel like a nice change, you've got Jasmine's telephone number." And he walked off back to town.

She was feeling mean, because she had not asked him in. Almost, she called him back. But she wheeled Caroline into the garden, and handed her over to Alice, and then went straight to the bedroom. The morning's newspaper was spread on the bedside table. She opened it and began studying it.

Since she had last looked at a newspaper, it appeared that the Russians had become heroes and magnificent fighters. They were no longer a rabble of ill-equipped moujiks fleeing before the Nazi hordes. A remarkable change—she had ceased to read the papers because she had been sickened by their gloating tone over the invasion of Russia: everyone was delighted, it was obvious, that their gallant allies were being so thoroughly beaten.

There was an epic battle going on at a place called Stalingrad which was—so some anonymous leader writer said—a turning point of the war.

The local situation had remained static. There were two leaders, written with that irritable self-satisfaction which was so familiar, about how the native population did not appreciate what the whites were sacrificing in uplifting them from their savage state, how they did not understand the dignity of labour, how they could not expect to be as civilized as the whites in under a thousand years, for this was the length of time it had required the British people to evolve from mud huts to democracy and plumbing. All this could be taken as read. In the letter columns there was a new and strident note. Two respected citizens wrote at length warning the population that there were agitators abroad who were putting ideas into the heads of the natives; "certain individuals, inspired from Moscow . . ." The Government should immediately examine these organizations, which, under cover of raising aid for Russia, were in fact spreading ideas inimical to white civilization.

This was all very interesting. The advertisement columns confirmed that all sorts of new activities were going on. As well as the usual cinema shows, dances and meetings, there were half a dozen notices of meetings run by as many organizations—Help for Our Allies, Sympathizers of Russia, and so on—on subjects like "The Constitution of the Soviet Union" and "Life on a Collective Farm in the Ukraine."

Altogether there was a feeling of movement, stir and excitement which communicated itself to Martha. But above all was she struck by the difference in tone of the paper from a year ago about the war. She rummaged in a cupboard, and found a pile of dead newspapers. Two years ago, the Russians had been dastardly and vicious criminals plotting with Hitler to dominate the world. A year ago they were unfortunate victims of unscrupulous aggression, but unluckily so demoralized that as allies they were worse than useless. Now, however, they were a race of battling giants.

While not reading the newspapers is a practice to be condemned, there are times when it can yield interesting results. For the thought which naturally presented itself to Martha was, How did the editor of this same newspaper picture his readers? There was no connection between the headlines of two years ago, a year ago, and today.

There was a knock on the door; Alice said she had brought Caroline in to be fed. Martha said that for this once she would leave the child to her. She remained sitting on the edge of the bed, trying to collect her ideas, which were in a state of extraordinary confusion.

It was quite clear that the group, however it was now constituted, were "doing something" at last. But what? Martha began to indulge in attractive day dreams of herself going among people, like a heroine from an old Russian novel. Common sense told her to desist. If Jasmine, or William, or anyone else had been going among the people, then there would have been a much stronger reaction than a couple of indignant letters to the press. The colour bar made that form of agitation impossible.

Suddenly, and without any warning, that feeling of staleness came over her, a sort of derisive boredom. She could not account for it, but the picture of a small group of people, middle-class every one of them, having meetings, running offices, even going among the people, struck her as absurd, pathetic—above all, old-fashioned. Here it was again, the enemy which made any kind of enthusiasm or idealism ridiculous.

The life she was living seemed dignified and attractive.

But no sooner had she come to this conclusion than disgust rose against it; and she thought with tender longing of these new possibilities; nothing could have seemed more heroic and admirable than Jasmine, William and the rest. Yet almost at once, and in proportion to the strength of her desire to join them at once, derision arose, that stale disgust.

She remained, tossing from one mood to the other, motionless on the edge of the bed, while the darkness came down outside and the street lights shone out.

There were steps in the middle of the house, the door opened, the lights crashed on. Douglas came in. He said in a jolly voice, "What are you doing, sitting in the dark?" But there was a cautious look on his face.

She roused herself and said, "Oh, nothing."

He looked at the mess of newspapers on the bed, and said con-

temptuously, "Oh, that rubbish!"—meaning world affairs in general—
and she saw that the self-satisfied note in his voice was of the same
quality as her own mood of gloomy fatality.

She hastily folded up the papers, with a movement as if she were
concealing something from him.

"Is Caroline in bed?"

He opened the door into the next room. Caroline was being
watched at her supper by Alice.

He returned, and said sentimentally, "Matty, surely you can give
the child her supper at least."

She shut down her anger, and remarked, "The doctor says she is
perfectly well."

"Oh—that's a good thing." He stood looking at her with a tentative
indignation.

"And I'm perfectly well, too," said Martha abruptly, smiling in a
way which she meant to be unpleasant.

"That's good." This was bluff and hearty; he turned away to hang
up his jacket in the wardrobe. "I've got some news," he began, still
in a bluff voice, which made her stiffen defensively. "Old Billy in
Y—— has got leave, and they want me to go down and take his place
for a few weeks."

"Well, are you going?"

He turned sharply, and gave her a consciously reproachful look,
biting his fat lips. "You could come, too," he said, breathing heavily.
"There's a house."

"But, Douglas, what are we to do with this one? Just shut it up?"

"Oh, well, if you feel like that . . ."

"How long are you going for?"

"Three weeks." He looked at her again, sideways. "What did old
Stern have to say?"

"Nothing much—but there really isn't any need to worry about
Caroline's well-being." Again it was a moment when the hatred
between them shocked and dismayed them both.

"Well, perhaps it's just as well we'll—have a break for a few weeks,
eh, Matty?" He came over and stood a few inches from her, smiling
in appeal.

She at once responded by rising and kissing him—but on the
cheek, for her lips, which had intended to meet his, instinctively
moved past in revulsion. This revulsion frightened her so much she
flung her arms about him and warmly embraced him.

The act of love immediately followed.

There is a type of woman—although whether she is a modern phenomenon or has always existed is not a question for novelists—who

cannot bear to be found wanting physically. In Martha's case, it worked like this: her mother had a rooted dislike for all matters sexual; therefore it was a matter of pride for Martha not only to be attractive sexually, but to be *good in bed*. There are hundreds of thousands of young women in our society who, when all else fails—they may be inefficient at their work, and bored wives and mothers—find solace in the belief that they are good in bed. Not for one moment have they ever paused in their determination to be better than their parents by flying this particular flag. But they have no hesitation in taking from their parents the romanticism which becomes the moral support not of free love—Martha came too late to believe in that; it was associated with the Twenties and thus had a stale and jaded sound to it—but of a determined hedonism, an accomplished athleticism, since "the book" lays all doubts and suspicions, above all by the variety and ingenuity of the physical attitudes it recommends. Douglas could hardly be blamed for not understanding the thoroughness of Martha's dislike for him, since that prohibition prevented her from ever expressing it in bed. The moment she did so, it would have meant the complete collapse of the romantic picture she maintained of him. A young woman of this type will expend immense energy on arranging her image of her husband into something admirable and attractive. And this as a question of principle. Such a young woman will confuse all bystanders by being charmingly devoted to her husband, angrily defending him against every word of criticism until the very moment she leaves him. After which she will not have one good word to say for him.

On this particular occasion Martha was irritable and, when she realized it, apologetic. She finally escaped with the abrupt remark, "I must go and see how Caroline is."

"Oh, but, Matty, she's got the nurse, and I'm going away for weeks."

"But she mustn't be neglected," she said, laughing in a way which told them both that the moment of reconciliation had been a failure. They ate dinner in silence, avoiding each other's eyes.

Next day, Douglas left for Y——, which was a couple of hundred miles south, a small administrative centre.

They embraced affectionately at parting. Then Douglas said sentimentally, "Do look after Caroline, Matty." He added, "You have so much to give her." He had taken to using the last phrase, half guiltily, meaning that he knew she intended that what she had to give would not all be swallowed in children and housekeeping, whereas he was determined it should be.

She said involuntarily, "Don't be so damned dishonest."

He muttered angrily, "I hope you'll be in a better temper when I come back."

After a few moments of guilt, not so much at what she had said, but because she had allowed herself to see him as clumsy and ridiculous, she went indoors, feeling deliciously alone and free.

She read a little, played with Caroline, sewed for a while, as if she had no intention of spending the three weeks of freedom in any other way. Then, without knowing until the moment she lifted down the receiver that she was going to do so, she telephoned Jasmine.

Jasmine was calm, unsurprised, and very efficient about dates and places.

Martha arranged to meet her and William the following evening, to talk things over.

2

Martha waited for that first appointment with Jasmine like a girl going to her lover. She was dressed and ready two hours before the time, and was just about to start when Jasmine telephoned to say that unluckily she had an unexpected meeting. But she would meet Martha at eight outside McGrath's so that they might both go to yet another meeting organized, by Help for Our Allies. Jasmine felt, she said in that small demure voice, that Martha would find it interesting.

Martha set herself to wait another two hours, conscious that much of her enthusiasm was ebbing. There is something in the word "meeting" which arouses an instinctive and profound distrust in the bosoms of British people at this late hour of their history. And then the name "Help for Our Allies" had a childish sound, with strong overtones of tract and even charity. Martha had lapsed back into her condition of irritated distaste long before the time appointed, and it was with an effort of will that she roused herself to go to the car. She waited outside the hotel for some twenty minutes before Jasmine and William appeared, each carrying armfuls of books and leaflets. There was between these two such a look of shared mission that Martha felt lonely and excluded as she followed them into McGrath's ballroom, which was released for this one evening from mess dinners and war charity dances.

The place was full. Seven or eight hundred people were crowded into the big ugly hall. Martha saw that they were all well-dressed and comfortable citizens, and her confusion was completed when she noticed Mr. Maynard and Mrs. Maynard seated side by side in the front row—large, imposing, black-browed, and apparently pleased to shed approval on the proceedings by being there.

She was hurried to an empty seat by Jasmine, who at once left her and pushed her way through the crowds to the platform, where she sat at a table with a group of people whom Martha did not know. Looking at her programme, however—it was beautifully printed on expensive paper—she saw that the speakers included two clergymen, two members of the Cabinet, a leader of the Social Democrat Party. These gentlemen beamed protective approval at Jasmine, a small demure figure in bright flowered silk.

Jasmine whispered for a moment to a tall, thin man, the Minister for Native Affairs, who stood up and began to speak. He spoke for about ten minutes about the glorious heroism of our Russian allies, interrupted at every moment by storms of applause. All around Martha people were sitting leaning forward, hands poised ready for the next point where they might clap approval; faces were smiling and flushed. When the tall thin man sat down, they applauded for a long time, and they began again before the next speaker could open his mouth.

Yet were these not the same citizens who had been reading and approving the *Zambesia News* in its phase of, recently, pitying these same heroes for their ragged and enslaved condition, and, not so long before that, execrating them for their barbarity?

To Martha it was quite inexplicable, and she looked for enlightenment towards the wall where William stood leaning together with a group of others. Boris and Betty were there, and some men in the uniform. Martha saw that as the applause crashed out and the speakers paused, smiling with the deprecating modesty suitable to such moments, this group tended to exchange glances under eyebrows slightly raised. When they applauded, which they did promptly, it was without that self-abandoning enthusiasm which apparently had everyone else in its grip, but in a measured way. Yet surely if there was any group of people in this room entitled to be delighted, even grateful, that the Soviet Union was being honoured in this fashion, it was this one? Their faces expressed—what was it? It was a sort of patient irony, and to Martha, who was in the first flush of adolescent longing to fling herself wholeheartedly into a cause, their look of irony was like a chill of cold water. She positively hated them for not flinging themselves away in abandoned applause, like the others. Then, turning her eyes back towards the platform, she happened to notice Mr. and Mrs. Maynard, and on their faces too was precisely that look of reserve; they too exchanged glances, with a tightening of the lips, and they clapped decently and firmly, and as if to a time limit. Martha looked more closely among the throng of eager citizens, and saw that there were several others—a couple of journalists from the *News*, a row of people near the Maynards, Colonel Brodeshaw and his wife—who were similarly doling out their applause to measured limits. From which she had to conclude that there were two groups of people in the room who were in command of themselves and their thoughts, and the look of irony which both had was in fact a rather contemptuous resignation towards the hundreds in the grip of mass emotion.

After about two hours of speeches and applause, Jasmine rose and suggested that they might ask one of the men who were "actually doing the fighting" to say a few words. William came forward and climbed on the platform. His uniform was greeted with fervour. He waited patiently for silence, his notes held ready in his hand. Then he said that of course men in the Forces were not allowed to take a part in politics, but raising money for our allies was obviously a different matter. He then, with a rapid glance downwards towards his notes, began to speak on that subject which filled Martha's thoughts. He had a quiet, easy, informal way of talking, not at all the professional manner with which they had been wooed for the last two hours, and it was noticeable that there were a few moments' chill. And there seemed to be a few people who considered that an analysis of what he called the campaign of lies about the Soviet Union was not really unpolitical. But in a short while he had the whole crowd roaring with laughter, although there was a note of discomfort in it. He had with him (or rather, Jasmine produced them obligingly from behind the table) a pile of *Zambesia News* for the past four years, and proceeded to discover and expose the contradictions and improbabilities that newspaper had offered its readers—who were now laughing delightedly, or so it seemed, at themselves. As a final feat, he took a single issue from the year before, and reduced it in a few moments to the most abject nonsense, while the crowd chuckled and the *News* reporters, who were seated at a special table to one side, took notes with expressions of calm and democratic indifference.

William then invited them to learn to read newspapers with more discrimination. He pointed out that until perhaps two months before there might have been twelve people in the whole colony—excluding the men of the Air Force, of course, he added involuntarily, causing a small chill to fall for a moment—who knew that Soviet tanks were not made of cardboard and that the Soviet people were not abject serfs. And these twelve people—he would say twelve for the sake of argument—were better informed not because they were in any way more intelligent than the ladies and gentlemen now seated before him, but because they had learned to treat the newspapers with the suspicion they deserved. As for the heroism of the Soviet people— but here the applause crashed out again, and he waited for it to stop. There were piles of books and pamphlets at the door, he concluded, and he invited them to buy them on their way out. With this he smiled, and retired from the platform by jumping lightly down from it to the floor, a feat which earned fresh handclapping and a few appreciative jeers from some men in uniform at the back. To which he responded with a half-mocking bow, and made his way to the table next the door, where he seated himself behind barricades of literature.

Jasmine got up and thanked "our young friend from the Air Force" for his contribution, and appealed for money to buy medical supplies "for our gallant allies." In a few moments the sum of over a thousand pounds had been collected; bank notes and cheques appeared everywhere, and the air was thick with the sound of chinking silver.

The meeting was over. Martha, crushed in a jam of people by a pillar, saw Mr. and Mrs. Maynard go past. Mrs. Maynard was saying, "I think one might drop a word in the right quarter."

Martha squeezed through to the table, which was now nearly empty of its books and pamphlets, and heard one of the men in uniform, a tall, dark, hollow-faced man with a satirical look, remark, "Well, what a performance—but it was the wrong audience."

"Not for collecting money," returned Jasmine with a small satisfied smile. She turned and saw Martha, who was waiting to be gathered in then and there to the bosom of this group of people where she knew she belonged. But Jasmine merely said, "Well, what did you think? Not bad, considering."

"Oh, it was marvellous!" said Martha indignantly. "Come and have some tea with me," she added hopefully.

"I can't, I have a meeting," said Jasmine at once. Then, as Martha looked disappointed, she said, "I'll ring you tomorrow."

With this Martha had to be content. She was pushing her way out in the tail of the retreating crowd, when William came after her and said, "Can't we sell you some lit?"

"What's lit?" she asked.

"We feel you should do some reading." And with this he handed her some books. "That will be twelve and sixpence."

She found the money hastily and with difficulty, reflecting that to him she was rich: he was not likely to understand the god, middle age, for whose sake she was always short of money. Then she thanked him. Her look was such that he forgot for a moment that she was a soul to be saved.

He asked intimately, "Well, did you like it?"

"Wonderful," she said again eagerly.

He smiled, and said, unexpectedly blushing, "I'll come and see you tomorrow afternoon—if you're free."

She left, feeling like a child left out of a party, because they did not at once invite her to that meeting to which they would all now go. But the way William had blushed made her feel it would not be long before she would be one of them.

At home she glanced cursorily into the nursery, where Caroline was asleep in her bed, and Alice beside her on the divan. Then she retired to her bed with the books. She read through them one after another; the dawn was coming up red behind the moonflowers when she had finished.

She had a very confused idea of what she had read; she was content to leave the mass of facts and figures until later. But behind these dull bricks of truth rose the glorious outline of a view of life she had not suspected. The emotion that gripped her was mostly rage: she was twenty-two; she had been born during that revolution, which, to say the least, had been important in the world's development, and yet this was the first time she had been told anything about it. Her rage was even greater because she had been such a willing accomplice in this process of not thinking. For there had been plenty of moments when she might have fitted a few facts together to make a truth. She had not. Her upbringing, her education, her associates, the newspapers, had all conspired to bring her to the age of twenty-two, an adult, that is, without feeling more about what was going on in the socialist sixth of the world—which happened to be the title of one of the books—than a profound reluctance to think about it at all.

Even now, as she sat there, still dressed, on the edge of her bed, she had two clear and distinct pictures of that other part of the world —one noble, creative and generous, the other ugly, savage and sordid. There was no sort of connection between the two pictures. As she looked at one, she wanted to fling herself into the struggle, to become one of the millions of people who were creating a new world; as she looked at the other, she felt staleness, futility.

What, then, was the cynicism that certainly afflicted all the people around her who thought at all? It no longer seemed even mildly attractive. With one sudden movement of her whole being she discarded it, and committed herself to the other. It was as if her eyes had been opened and her ears made to hear; it was like a rebirth. For the first time in her life she had been offered an ideal to live for.

But the immediate political emotion of anyone shaken suddenly into thinking is anger: she was filled with rage at having been cheated; she felt as if she had been lied to, led by the nose, made a fool of, all her life. She was as angry with herself as she was with the people whom she saw in this beautiful but naïve moment of awakening as an organized and cynical group who consciously devoted themselves to deceiving her and her generation out of their birthright. What she wanted, in short, was some sort of revenge: if the first political emotion of people like Martha is anger, the second is blind anarchy; if anyone had asked her in that moment to take a gun in her hand and go out to destroy those people who had been making a fool of her, she would have gone without a second thought. Luckily, however, there was no one to make any such demand.

Instead she went to the front verandah, where the day's *News* had been flung down, and opened the paper to find the report of last night's meeting. It merely said that a large sum of money had been collected for our gallant allies at a well-attended meeting. She threw it aside, and went to Caroline. She bathed her, fed her, despatched her to the garden with Alice, and waited for Jasmine to ring her. Time went past and Jasmine did not ring. Martha therefore rang Jasmine. The small quiet voice said that she could not come to see Martha, because she had a meeting. It was then ten in the morning.

In the last twelve hours, the banal and tired sound of the word "meeting" had quite vanished for Martha; and she sat and thought wistfully of those adventurous gatherings from which she was shut out. She saw Jasmine on the platform yesterday, so efficient, so self-effacing, devoted. Nothing could have appeared more glamorous than such a role.

The outward form of her day was untroubled by the violence of her impatience. She looked after Caroline and attended to the housework as usual; she felt herself to be a completely different person. Later she remembered that William was coming. She did not want to see William. She wanted Jasmine, who had, like herself, been brought up in this country, fed on the colour bar and race hatred. For William things seemed altogether too easy; he had been born, or so it seemed, with pamphlets in his hand and clear convictions in his head.

When he arrived, she offered him tea like a hostess, quite determined to say nothing to him of what she felt; besides, he was nothing but a boy. He shed packets of books and papers onto chairs, removed his jacket, flung down his cap. He would never be anything but a civilian. He was one of the thousands of British soldiers who went through the war out of intellectual conviction: it was a war against fascism and it was his duty to fight. But he never felt anything but a civilian dressed up. The difference between men like William and the passionate soldiers of the war could be seen the moment those other groups entered the colony to train as pilots—the Greeks, the Yugoslavs, the French, the Poles.

As things were, William had an afternoon off between doing clerk's work for the Air Force and addressing a meeting on Hegel, and he was prepared to take an interest in Martha.

In the camp it was said, with the mixed pride and contempt appropriate for occupation forces, that the women in the town were a pushover. His tone towards Martha was of a tentative gallantry, but Martha at once reacted against it. She felt that this commonplace flirtatiousness was nothing less than an insult to the revolution itself. She was cold and polite. He instantly became—as she put it—sensible, and she was able to like him again.

He began talking of the meeting last night—not a bad show at all, he considered; but she interrupted him. "Look, I want to know . . ." Her tone was warm and eager, startling in contrast to the coldness of only a minute before. "I've been thinking—well, if there's something going on, I want to be part of it."

"What makes you think anything is going on?" he enquired.

"Oh, don't be silly," she said crossly.

He reflected for a moment, perched on the arm of a chair, and seemed embarrassed. After a while he suggested, "You could join the committee of Help for Our Allies."

"Oh, *Lord!*" protested Martha.

"But it's very important work." Then he confirmed her instinct that there were further degrees of initiation, by remarking, "How about Sympathizers of Russia?"

She felt snubbed. "Look," she said; direct, humorous, but resentful. "You don't have to—flannel, like this. If there's a Communist group, I want to join it." She leaned forward eagerly, as if expecting to be absorbed into it that very instant.

"But there isn't one," he said.

She did not believe him. Seeing her disappointment, he said, "There really isn't. I can't go into it all now, but it's not as easy as that."

She was remembering the group of people against the wall the night before; they had the appearance of a welded whole, with their exchanged glances and shared understanding.

"Besides," he went on, in a light but uncomfortable voice, "what would the old man say?"

"Old man?" she said stiffly.

"Wives of civil servants really can't do this sort of thing."

"You talk as if he were an idiot," she said angrily. "He's progressive. He—reads the *New Statesman*," she concluded triumphantly.

But at this he let out an involuntary and delighted chuckle, and got up, with the unmistakable air of a man escaping from a situation.

"Don't go," she said quickly.

He sat down again slowly, looking at her very seriously. He had half hoped to have a casual affair with her—though without any intention of being disappointed if he did not. He was a very practical young man, and he understood quite well that this warmth, this eagerness—she was looking at him now with an earnestness that he found quite delightful—would make anything casual impossible. But he had sized up the state of affairs in the colony within a week of arriving in it, and he had no intention of getting involved in this mess of broken marriages and passionate love affairs. His plans for the future were definite, and did not include burdening himself with a spoilt colonial woman.

But she was attractive; and that eager sincerity was warming him out of common sense. He was on the point of being in love with her.

As for Martha, she had understood that he was not at all a mere boy, a child. On the contrary, compared with Douglas it was he who was the man. He was not like the immature young men that emerge from the universities, he was not like the boys of the Club. He had come from something quite different: a small, decent, upper-working-class family with roots in the labour movement. He had gone steadily and sensibly through school, and afterwards taken courses at night schools to study what he needed to know while he learned printing. The war had given him leisure, which he devoted to philosophy and physics. He was not ambitious, but he knew what he wanted. Which was to get through the war, take a few more courses, and qualify for what interested him—he wanted to be an engineer. In due course he would make a sensible marriage.

Martha asked, in that eager way which invited him to share with her the exquisite and unique experience which was his life, "Tell me, I want to know, how did you join the Communist Party?"

"I was never a member of the Party," he said at once.

She wilted away from her eagerness as if finally disillusioned. She appeared critical.

He found himself piqued; unpleasant to lose this approval so soon!

He set himself to explain. "I didn't approve of the Party's policy during the phony war. So I didn't join. I had reservations."

The way he said "the Party" struck her as comical. Not for the first time. After all, at least half the reporters, writers, civil servants, etc.—the intellectuals, in short—have at some time or another been in, around, or near the Communist Party, and ever afterwards they refer to it as "the Party," as if there could never be another, even while most passionately engaged in pretending they know nothing of it. But William might say "the Party" in that familiar, easy way; he was not in it. Her vision of him had collapsed. From being a wholehearted crusader, he had become a cautious dealer in reservations. She had been regarding the alert, intelligent young face topped by the metal-bright hair as if it had been the face of the revolution itself; now she listened to a quiet analysis of the Stalin-Hitler pact and the phony war and heard a note she knew far too well; it was this: if William had been in charge of policy during that period, it would not have been as inefficient, clumsy and inadequate as it had been with other people in charge.

Martha frowned. She was thinking uncomfortably that she was doomed to be, not attracted to—she would not admit that yet—but *with* people who administrated other people; more, people who were the dissatisfied administrators whom Fate or—and here she carefully tested the new phrase—The Logic of History did not recognize for what they were, by nature far more efficient than those whom Fate or Logic actually chose as its servants. There are people, warm-hearted and enthusiastic, but unfortunately liable because of these very qualities to a prolonged juvenescence: Martha could not bear that people tended to fall into types. It was to Douglas rather than to William that she remarked grudgingly, "Well, that may be so, but perhaps you wouldn't have done any better yourself if you'd been running the show."

He stopped himself in a long sentence which dissected the reasons why Harry Pollitt was right and not wrong in his first assessment of "the line"—he used the phrase with a sort of jaunty respect—and his look at Martha changed. That warmth and enthusiasm of hers must be met. He wavered, and fell over on the wrong side of his barrier of caution. It was in a new voice, humorous, light and intimate, that he said, "No, Matty—I would have been *much* more efficient."

She laughed at once. They looked at each other—and then away. It was too early for either of them to acknowledge that their hearts were beating fast.

He rose, and said, "I must be downtown in half an hour."

"I'll run you down in the car," she said at once.

He refused quickly—it was imperative that he should be alone to think. But he smiled intimately at her before he left, swinging his pack over his shoulder, and cramming on the little cap which made him a soldier again.

He walked rapidly off, as if really in hurry, until out of sight of the house, and then strolled comfortably under the trees. He was thinking that he had been irresponsible to encourage Martha about that Communist group she had set her heart on. The truth was that he did not know himself what was happening.

Some months ago, when Hitler attacked the Soviet Union, the left wing of the old discussion circle had suggested setting up Help for Our Allies. This was given immediate approval. Quite soon there was an organization with an office, typewriters, filing cabinets and a letterhead on which appeared the names of about fifty prominent citizens. On the committee, which was very large, were all the members of the discussion circle, from Messrs. Perr, Forester and Pyecroft down to Boris Krueger and Jasmine.

But no sooner was this running satisfactorily than the minority—Boris, Betty, Jasmine and their allies—seethed into activity with a new organization, Sympathizers of Russia. These two organizations, even to an unsophisticated eye, offered food for thought. The left wing of the Help for Our Allies formed the committee of the Sympathizers, together with a whole ferment of new people, chiefly from the Air Force, who regarded the first committee with calm contempt as cautious temporizers. For a while Jasmine had been secretary of both organizations. She was so efficient that it was a pity to waste her.

About two weeks ago, a new dissatisfaction had set in.

It had begun at the moment when Mr. Perr, in a humorous voice which nevertheless reeked of suspicion, remarked at a meeting of the Help for Our Allies Committee that the said committee had no intention of being run by a Communist faction. At this, eyes had met all around the long table, some hurt, some puzzled. No one knew of a Communist faction. As for the majority of the committee, simple people who were unpolitical on principle, they were upset, and found it all unpleasant. For they did not understand the law that people like Mr. Perr who have been called Communists in popular gossip spend nine tenths of their time proving their bona fides by attacking Communists. That committee meeting left an unpleasant taste in every mouth. As for the left wing itself, Jasmine, Betty, Boris and William, they made enquiries of each other, and concluded that Mr. Perr was suffering from the mania only to be expected of him. At this point, a certain Jackie Bolton, sergeant, administration, recently posted to the city from another down south, took them to tea at a certain café downtown, and informed them they were a lot of skulking petty bourgeois who refused to face up to their responsibilities. He, Jackie Bolton, was about to form a Communist group, and invited them to join.

But, while all their hearts leaped to this proposal, they did not at once agree. "Matters should be discussed," said Jasmine. That was three days ago.

Since then there had been a tense atmosphere in all the committees, and people tended to go off in pairs talking earnestly, looking at other couples similarly engaged with suspicious enquiry. No one knew what was going on; but they felt instinctively that Jasmine was the key to everything. Jasmine patiently cautioned them all: They must be responsible and sensible, they must not do things in a hurry. As for herself, she felt a Communist group to be premature.

Sergeant Jackie Bolton waited for twenty-four hours, and then spoke to William in the mess. "That crowd in town are all useless," was the burden of his message. He invited William to meet him at Black Ally's Café to talk it all over.

It was to this interview that William was going. He was feeling very uncomfortable about it. To a young man like William, who, as has been said, was sensible and matter-of-fact, there was something disagreeable about Jackie Bolton, who was the tall, dark, hollow-cheeked, saturnine man whom Martha had noticed exuding sarcastic disparagement at the Help for Our Allies meeting. William did not like heroics—Jackie was heroic on principle; William did not like intrigue—Jackie breathed out conspiracy with every word he spoke; he did not like drama—Jackie was dramatic. But he was going to meet him nevertheless; he could not refuse, because of that bond which, during the war, was stronger than any other, that between men wearing the same uniform.

Black Ally's was filled with aircraftsmen—it was by consent a place for the Air Force—and William entered the sordid little café with a feeling of being at home. The two men removed their caps, unbuttoned their jackets, and settled down to plates of eggs and chips.

Jackie was confidential and conspiratorial, with his large urgent black eyes, his hollow bony face, his manner of silently laughing—he would heave with laughter, without letting out a sound. He wanted to start a Communist group, led by himself, from certain men in the Air Force and a few sound types from town, excluding "all the Jasmines and Bettys and Borises," who were nothing but social democrats of the worst kind, and infected with Trotskyism to boot.

William listened in silence. He wanted to commit himself. The phrase "those types in town," was a bugle of solidarity. He was strongly bound to Jackie by the feeling of being in exile, and their good-humoured contempt for this city. He almost agreed. Then Jackie remarked that he had never been a member of the Party. He added that he considered himself a free lance of the revolution. William was chilled by that phrase. He hesitated and temporized and tried to change the subject.

He said that Matty Knowell was ripe—meaning politically; but the sergeant gave it another meaning by heaving his hollow shoulders soundlessly; and William smiled stiffly—he was on the borderline still: Matty was not yet his girl, but on the other hand he felt a strong current of sympathy for her. He frowned and said he thought Jackie was altogether too sweeping; there was Jasmine, for instance: "She's a good type."

"Better than the others," admitted Jackie. He added, laughing, "I had supper with her last night." William felt no sexual loyalty towards Jasmine, so they were able to pursue this point. They remained there for about two hours, taking the taste of the camp food out of their mouths with repeated orders of eggs and chips, drinking cup after cup of very strong tea. By that time it had been agreed that Jasmine had possibilities; Matty was to be sounded by Jackie that evening. They were both capable of education; so were all the men in uniform who had ever shown the slightest interest in politics. The male civilians, however, were all beyond hope.

They would have, they reckoned, some fifteen or twenty people as a nucleus. But still William would not commit himself. He left the sergeant with the promise that he would think it all over. He walked away uptown from the café, and already Jackie's influence was waning. He found himself distrusting the man. He decided to ring up Jasmine herself, and abide by her decision.

He rang her up from the nearest telephone. She was due at a meeting in an hour, she said, but could give him twenty minutes of her time afterwards. The calm sense of the girl's voice satisfied William that he had done right.

On the same afternoon there was another encounter, between two men who have not yet been mentioned.

The Help for Our Allies Committee was sitting. Mr. Perr was chairman. The proceedings were harmonious and orderly. But there was one item on the agenda which might cause friction. The secretary of the Sympathizers of Russia—the signature was Jasmine's—had sent a letter proposing that the two organizations should hold a joint meeting to celebrate the anniversary of the November Revolution.

Mr. Perr spoke strongly against it. Four others, all members of the old discussion circle, were equally upset at the thought that Aid for Our Allies had anything to do with politics or revolutions. The majority of the committee—housewives, clergymen and so on—could see nothing against it. The heroism of Stalingrad made even the November Revolution respectable. Besides, it had happened a long time ago.

The two men in question were both silent until the end of the discussion, though Mr. Perr repeatedly looked towards them, inviting them to speak. One was a Scotsman, a bulky bluff corporal with a broad sensible face and shrewd grey eyes; the other was Anton Hesse, a German refugee, a young man of about thirty, of middle height, very thin, very fair—he had that extreme Northern fairness, hair so blond it was almost white, very keen blue eyes of the kind which look as if there is white ice behind the iris. Anton Hesse had been on the committee since its formation. Andrew McGrew had been posted up from G——, a small southern town where he had served on the counterpart to this committee. His sensible, calm appearance inspired confidence; when he rose to speak, Mr. Perr visibly relaxed.

He said that, speaking for himself, he could see no reason why the Help for Our Allies organization should not celebrate the revolution, which after all had contributed a great deal to the defenders of Stalingrad and Leningrad; on the other hand, the function of the committee was to raise money for medical supplies, and he was quite prepared to waive his personal feelings in the interests of harmony and good feeling. With this he sat down, crossed his legs, put his pipe back in his mouth and looked—as did everyone else—towards Mr. Hesse.

Who rose, in his stiff deliberate way, and said he agreed with the last speaker. He would like to add, however, that in his personal opinion it would be better if a vote was not taken. It was clear from the discussion that the majority of the committee were in favour of joining in the celebrations; if a vote were taken it might embarrass Mr. Perr and those members who felt so strongly about it. Such embarrassments should be avoided wherever possible. He then sat down, and lit a cigarette, giving his full attention to the process.

This caused a short silence. Mr. Perr was agitated. Such was Mr. Hesse's manner that it was impossible to know whether he was being accurate and helpful or airily offensive. Mr. Perr looked uncomfortably around the table, and suggested they should pass to the next item on the agenda. Once again the unpolitical members of the committee had been made to feel that there were unpleasant undercurrents which they ought to be understanding. They all proceeded to discuss how best to produce a pamphlet, while Mr. Hesse smoked in silence, satisfied with the barb that he had left to rankle.

It was noticeable that he and Corporal McGrew watched each other for the rest of the meeting; and that afterwards they left together, apparently fortuitously. At which Mr. Perr said acidly to Mr. Forester that that damned German got under his skin—he didn't trust him an inch.

The two men walked away in silence, each waiting for the other to speak. Then the Scotsman took the initiative by remarking, "I met a friends of yours in G——. He met you in London in 1938. Barry, the name was."

"I remember Barry—the Committee for Spain."

Andrew took his pipe from his mouth and remarked, "I was on the Northern Committee during that period."

"You were?" This had a suggestion of stiff amusement.

The two pairs of eyes met frankly, and both men grinned. All the same there was a small hesitation before Andrew took the plunge: "I take it you are in the Party?"

"Since 1933," Anton said, and looked questioningly towards Andrew, who said, "I've been in since 1930."

There was a pause. Instinctively, the two men moved closer together as they walked down the pavement under the trees towards the business centre.

"I'm not quite clear as to the situation here," observed Andrew. "I only came last week."

"There's nothing here—we're the only two members that I've discovered."

"There are a couple of dozen in the camp. But as to the local situation, I would appreciate it if you would clarify my mind a little."

They both stopped. It was at a street corner. The traffic fled past noisily in two streams.

Anton narrowed his eyes, concentrated, began to speak. He spoke for about ten minutes, while the other listened. He concluded, "Taking these facts into consideration, I think it is correct to say that we have not the cadres for a party group."

Andrew nodded, but added, "I agree, more or less. But since I came I've been hearing nothing but rumours about a group. What is this group?"

"There is no group. There's a group of intellectuals—if you can call them that."

"Some of them seem quite promising."

Anton said, "I am in contact with Jasmine Cohen. She knows I am in the Party. Through her I know about the rest. They all do a lot of talking, but that doesn't do any harm."

"It's all very well," said Andrew, annoyed. "It does do harm."

"Look," said Anton. "Let's analyze the position. There are about a dozen men in the Air Force who can address envelopes and make a speech occasionally, but they aren't allowed to take part in politics. There are a handful of aliens and refugees—such as myself." He smiled with controlled bitterness. "Politics are naturally not supposed to interest us. Then there are a handful of girls who want love affairs and a bit of excitement. This is not the basis for a Communist group. Besides," he added, with finality, "the working people of this country are black."

Andrew nodded, but was thoughtful.

"What do you know about Sergeant Bolton?" went on Anton. "He keeps getting up at Help for Our Allies meetings and shouting for a revolution. He'll split the thing if he isn't stopped."

"Admittedly he's a bit—overenthusiastic." Andrew added with apologetic humour, "The feeling in the camps is rather less indirect than it is in town."

But since Anton Hesse did not feel himself part of this town, he was able to say casually, "It is bound to be."

They began walking again under the trees, which still shed their purple rain.

"It looks to me like this," observed Andrew at last. "I agree there is no basis for a group in existing conditions. But one is going to come into existence for all that. If so, we should be in on it."

Anton Hesse did not at once reply. The fair handsome face had a curious look of obstinacy, of reluctance. Andrew glanced sideways at him, but said nothing. He had heard that this man had worked in the underground against Hitler, done a spell in a concentration camp, survived torture, escaped; he respected him. But there is no law which says one Communist should like another, and he did not like him. His antipathy expressed itself thus: He's not the sort of chap I'd like to spend an evening in the pub with.

As for the German, he was conscious that his analysis of the situation had a factor in it that he ought to be ashamed of. He knew he did not want to take part in politics in this country. He had spent the last fifteen years in the political struggle in Europe, with the most sophisticated revolutionaries of his time. He had been a schoolboy when he first went to prison, and had been in and out of prison ever since. He had survived death when he had thought of himself as already dead. He had reached the backwater which he felt England to be, and had adjusted to it, only to be sent away from it to this country, where he had spent three years of such boredom and despair he had considered suicide. But Communists do not commit suicide. He loathed the empty, ill-educated, easygoing colonials; he despised the life of sundowners and goodtimers. He hated everything down to the food and the drink. Above all, the political backwardness of the place depressed him. He dreamed of that moment when the war would be over and he would be free to go back home—to Germany. But that place in his soul, Germany, was an agonizing darkness where even his loyalties were shamed. His comrades were nearly all dead. His wife was dead. He had no romantic notions left about suffering and revolutions. He had had little sympathy with the revolutionaries—"so called," as he invariably muttered to himself —of Britain, who seemed to him a pack of children. He shut himself up, shielding that raw place in himself by a shell of patience. He spent his time reading the Marxist classics and studying Russian. He was a man in cold storage for the future. To start work again here, in this half-baked country in the middle of this backward continent, and with a group of romantic amateurs—his pride revolted. There is such a thing as revolutionary snobbishness. But more than this, far deeper, was the reluctance to come out of his shell—to start *feeling* again. Yet, just as he had clung tight to that raft in the black sea of longing for death, the phrase "Communists do not commit suicide," so now he said to himself, A Communist has the duty to work in whichever country he finds himself in.

He did not know how long that silence lasted, while he walked, cold-faced and stiff, down the street beside Andrew, who strolled patiently beside him, waiting.

Then he said, "Let's go to some quiet place and talk it over."

"I've got to go to a meeting in half an hour," said Andrew. "Young William is addressing the schoolteachers on Hegel. I promised to go along and help him out."

"William Brown—on Hegel!" Anton stopped dead. "What does he know about Hegel?"

"More than the Zambesian Association of Schoolteachers, very likely," said Andrew good-humouredly. "Why don't you come along, too?"

There was a pause. "I might as well. Yes. Hegel—the Zambesian schoolteachers!"

"There are some good people among them," said Andrew with definite reproach.

The German coloured, and then said, admitting the reproof,

"You're quite right." After a pause he said, "I must find a telephone and ring up someone—I was going to dinner."

"Oh, if you've got another engagement, we can meet tomorrow."

Anton had been conducting a love affair for the last two years with an Austrian refugee, a charming woman of a silliness quite phenomenal—it was as if he took a perverse pleasure in the dullness of the relationship.

"It's not in the least important," he said, as he went towards a telephone booth.

In the meantime, William had seen Jasmine. She informed him under a bond of secrecy that there were real Communists in the town—they could do nothing without their sanction. She was prepared, however, to meet Sergeant Bolton again; he had struck her as being a valuable person.

3

About a week after these events, Mr. Maynard, who was on his way to dispense justice in the courts heard his wife's voice calling him from the drawing room. He was in the passage outside. He turned his bulk around in a half circle, took a step forward and was in the doorway.

Mrs. Maynard was giving orders to the cook for the day's menus. She stood in front of the empty fireplace, feet planted wide, arms linked behind her back. The cook—white drill, red fez, white sand shoes—was making notes in a small book.

". . . and French pancakes. I think that's all, Elijah."

He said: "Yes, madam," and retired, begging Mr. Maynard's pardon as he came past. Mr. Maynard moved a couple of inches to one side to accommodate him.

Mrs. Maynard stood silent, head slightly bent, separating her real interests from thoughts of eggs and butter.

She was wearing a greenish silk dress, loose about massive thighs and hips which, as Mr. Maynard remembered, were always encased in heavy pink brocade from waist to knee. Above was prescribed no such repression: her full low bosom rocked just above the belt, and over green folds were suspended loops of pink coral. Mr. Maynard remembered wondering what intricacies of conscience made her feel indecent without that corset even in a dressing gown, whereas to wear a brassière would have seemed to her even more indecent. Never had cloth, or even lace, confined those full, loose, empty breasts, which shook and rolled unchecked. The neat greying hair, the straight brows, seemed one with the lower half of her body—that tight mass of controlled flesh. But the upper femininity, so naïve-looking and exposed, seemed in harmony with certain moods of hers, when she was eager after an enthusiasm. Sometimes she looked almost girlish. Mr. Maynard remembered a stubborn but charming girl.

This was one of the moods. She was flushed and animated. She raised her head, let her arms fall to her sides, and began abruptly, "You remember my Coloured Committee?"

"You mentioned it."

"Well . . ." She contracted her brows, and appeared to be summoning some point which she wished to present to him. For the first time she looked at him, twisting the coral around her fingers. "It's going very well. A good response."

"I congratulate you on its composition. You seem to have got all your black sheep harnessed satisfactorily."

"I'm in a hurry," she said impatiently—meaning that she was prepared to be teased at another time. "Now, this is the point. I think some younger people would be a good thing. One might get some of the Left Group, Russian Sympathizers—whatever they call themselves."

"I think they are all fully occupied in raising money for Russia, my dear."

"A good thing, too—those poor things obviously need medical supplies." For she had taken away any unpleasantness there was in the thought of being allied to the Soviet Union by clasping the whole nation to her bosom as suitable objects for her charity. "But if they are so enthusiastic about Russia, then they can spare some time for their own unfortunates."

"I rather imagine they would ask you why you confine your sympathy to the half-castes and ignore the blacks."

"I am in a hurry," she said again. "Now, I've got Mrs. Perr and Mrs. Forester—quite reasonable woman, really. But I feel one might go further."

"What's your first step?"

"We are having a concert next week to raise money. In the Brazen Hall. By the children."

He raised his brows. "Coloured children play to white audiences?"

"It'll be a nice change for everybody. Besides, Bishop White is sponsoring it. And the Roman Catholics are being cooperative. For a change."

"And having raised the money?"

"We'll see afterwards."

"I feel that you are underestimating the idealistic enthusiasm abroad at the moment."

"Well! Surely they ought to be glad to do something for those unfortunate people!" She was genuinely indignant. Mr. Maynard was again enabled to see her as an enthusiastic girl—even as a rebel. For it is by no means an accident that people find themselves in the colonies. Mrs. Maynard, as a girl, had infuriated her family by refusing to get married at the right time. Instead, she had become a crusader for better housing in Whitechapel. She had been prevented from marrying a penniless clergyman who was similarly devoted only by the greatest effort on the part of her relations. As a revenge she had married Mr. Maynard; Africa had seemed to her both romantic and suitably exasperating to her family. She had seen herself ministering to grateful savages. And Mr. Maynard had left England because he found it insular. They had both been rebels, of a kind. Perhaps the strongest strand in their relationship was the feeling that they were rebels against tradition—even now, when their first concern was to uphold it.

For that matter, there is no white person in the colonies who has not arrived there for some similar reason: they are crusaders against tyranny to a man. Which accounts for that shrill note of protest when the world suggests that it is both stupid and old-fashioned to suppress native populations: for when these same colonials are passionately engaged in fighting against a minimum wage of one pound a month, or advocating the sjambok as a means of guidance for the uncivilized, they are always, in the bottom of their hearts, quite convinced that this too is part of their character as rebels against the tyranny and conservatism of the mother country which they left as adventurers into a free world.

Mrs. Maynard was quite genuine in her cry that these young people must feel with her in helping the unfortunate half-castes; that they should not must kill her idea of herself as a fearless and progressive person.

Mr. Maynard watched the flushed and agitated face and felt a pang of reminiscent affection. But to the matron who was his wife he remarked drily, "Well, my dear, I'll do what I can, but if my information is correct you're wasting your time. Whom do you want, particularly?"

"There's the secretary—Cohen, I think. Jewish, of course."

A brief pause while things were left unsaid.

"She seems rather efficient. And there's your friend Quest, Knowell, whatever her name is. And various girls of that kind. Also there's a batch of refugees. We should get hold of them. If I had my way they'd all be interned, anyway."

"You can't intern refugees from Hitler—they're on our side, so to speak."

She shrugged this off and said irritably, "All the same, I hear that—but it might be rumour. But after the war they'll go back to wherever they came from, and the Air Force will go, and we've our own people to think of."

"I'm late," said Mr. Maynard. "Give me the details of this concert of yours."

He left his wife in her pose before the fireplace, hands behind her back, rocking back and forth from heel to toe. The beautiful quiet room with its green-and-rose silks, its flowery carpet, was almost identical with the one in Chelsea from which he had plucked her thirty years before.

On his way downtown, he passed the Knowells' house and asked to see Martha. The cook said she was out. For some time he stood watching Caroline at play under the trees, allowing himself to dream of the daughter he had so badly wanted. Then he pulled himself away, and hurried off to the courts. At the third attempt to find Martha, he met her on the pavement outside the house, files packed under her arm, hurrying past him. He had to catch her arm to make her see him. She was looking animated and eager. He knew the look.

Having put the proposition—briefly, since she was impatient of it from the first word—he waited rather ironically.

"Let's get this straight," said Martha. "You want Jasmine Cohen and myself and Boris and Betty Krueger to come and help your wife run a concert to raise money for the Coloureds?" She sounded fully as derisive as he had expected.

He instinctively made a mental note of the names for future use, and enquired mildly, "Why not?"

"It is not," said Martha, "the nineteenth century."

"Ah."

"Charity," said Martha aggressively, "has always been an expression of the guilty consciences of a ruling class."

Thus confirmed in his diagnosis of intellectual influences not Zambesian, he enquired casually, "You know a man called Hesse?"

She looked at him suspiciously. They were standing facing each other under the tree outside her gate. She was angry and earnest. That quality of sincere enthusiasm sanctioned his own youth, and he said suddenly, "You know, my dear, I'm very fond of you."

Martha's face softened; but she was looking at a kindly old gentleman, he could see that. For one reason and another, he abruptly set himself in motion away from her.

"I'll ask them," she called after him; and he raised his hat to her with an elaborate irony that was altogether lost on her, for she had turned away before he concluded the gesture.

She mentioned to Jasmine and Anton later that day that that bunch of reactionaries wanted them to run a charity concert for the Coloured community. They smiled, briefly.

She forgot the concert. But two days later there arrived a letter from Douglas. She read it with disquiet—the letter was not from the Douglas she had been creating for herself. He was returning home in a few days. Why did she not write? And she had signed her last letter to him "Yours sincerely, Martha Quest"—what did she think she was doing? As a postscript he said he was glad to hear that she was helping the Maynards with their Coloured children; it was just up her street, he thought.

The letter conveyed a peevish and rasping complaint. Guilt, unacknowledged, began its work. She rang up Mrs. Maynard to offer her services for the concert, and felt that this gesture would be enough to convince Douglas of her goodwill. She had not clearly considered what she must do when he came back, but she held long imaginary conversations with that image of him about the future. She would make certain adjustments, he others. Her sacrifice would consist in not leaving him altogether for the group—which was not yet in existence. She saw him as a calm, sensible, brotherly young man who would fully understand what she felt.

As for William, she knew herself to be in love with him. He had kissed her one night after a meeting. That kiss had called into being a Martha she had recently forgotten—it was chalked up against Douglas that she had been able to forget, except as a question of principle, the other Martha. In short, she clamoured with every impulse for a love affair with William. But it had been agreed that a sensible talk with Douglas was the minimum concession to decency. Besides, with meetings following one another, sometimes three and four a night, there was no time for love-making. They sat on opposite sides of a room, discussing the state of affairs in Uzbekistan, while their eyes met, and neither knew whether they loved each other or the revolution. In between one meeting and another, they stood on the verandah outside the office for a moment, hands touching, while they discussed if they might arrange matters to spend half an hour folding leaflets together tomorrow. Romance can be no keener than this. Happiness flooded through them at a touch or a glance.

In the meantime, Martha was reasoning thus: her marriage with Douglas was essentially sensible—which was her euphemism for the word *modern,* too old-fashioned to be used. It had always been understood that they did not believe in jealousy or even fidelity. Besides—and this secretly justified Martha far more than these reasonable arguments—she had heard through devious routes that he was having an affair with a girl in Y——. It was obvious, then, that he should be no more than interested in the news that she intended to have a love affair with William. Everything should be honest and aboveboard—this above all. She loved William for understanding why they must wait until Douglas came back.

Two more letters came from Douglas. One complained that she had not written. But, being nothing if not dutiful, she had written twice a week since he left. The other was hysterical: Mrs. Talbot had written saying something—she could not make out what—and she, Martha, was clearly going mad. He had managed to arrange his affairs so as to be home by tomorrow morning.

Martha read these letters with fear; but instantly she revived that picture of a brotherly and understanding Douglas, and looked forward to the moment when she would tell him everything. But she had torn up the letters in a panic need to get them out of sight and thought.

At seven in the morning she was standing on the long grey platform, waiting for the train to come in. She was lighthearted and confident. The train came, black and serpentine, across the veld; vanished behind factories; appeared, enormous and black, in a rush of filthy blue smoke. She stood peering along it for Douglas. Then she saw him getting out of the carriage. The image collapsed, and she stood staring at him in incredulity and horror. It was that moment again when he had returned from up north—but then he had been in uniform, another person; now he came smiling angrily towards her, a fat and ordinary young man in a thick grey suit striped with white. She remembered her father's "commercial traveller"—that was the truth. She thought, while she looked at this stranger who was her husband, that while her father might despise clothes, he never despised them enough to wear clothes like these.

Her heart was pounding. She understood she was terrified. There was a gleam in the small blue eyes, a working of the lips, that literally terrified her. By now he had reached her, and was holding out his arms. She received his kiss on her cheek, and instantly moved away, saying, "Let's get to the car. You must be ready for breakfast."

A nervous glance showed him to be red and glaring. But they went to the car in silence. She got into the driver's seat; she needed to be doing something. Usually she moved aside to let him drive. He was looking at her with a deadly black anger which made her feel faint. But she drove fast and straight up through Indian stores and kaffir-truck shops, through the shady avenues; parked the car neatly under the tree, and walked before him through the flower beds and shrubs to the verandah. He came after her with set shoulders, reddened eyes, and a look of pursuit.

They reached the bedroom. She sat on the edge of her bed as if it were her last place of refuge, and waited for him to speak. He, however, stood threateningly near her, glowering. Suddenly she let out a short and angry laugh; at once she was dismayed, because it was the first sound either had made since they had left the station.

"Don't be so damned silly, Douglas," she said, trying to sound placatory, although her voice was embarrassed.

He shouted suddenly, his face swelling up, "Why didn't you write to me?"

"But I did write to you."

He came nearer and bent, his face working. "Why did you sign yourself like that—'Yours sincerely'?"

His face, which was so genuinely puzzled and hurt, moved her. It was the last time she was to allow herself to feel moved. "But, Douglas," she said, almost humorously. "It's not very important, is it? And I had just signed about a thousand circulars."

"You signed it 'Martha Quest'?"

"Yes." Then she added, cold and angry, "You are always talking about the danger to your career."

He straightened himself and stood blinking at her. She could see that he was finding, and then discarding, one point of attack after another.

"What did Mrs. Talbot write?" she enquired.

He turned his face aside; began to say something; changed his mind. Then: "Why are you spending all your time with this ridiculous—outfit?"

She said contemptuously, "So you're afraid of the left wing?"

At once he said in clumsy appeal, like a child, "But, Matty, you know how it is with the Service. You know I can't do as I like."

"When we got married you said you wouldn't stay in the Service," she pointed out.

He looked wounded: he felt it very unfair of her to remember things he had said then. But if she was going to take that line, he thought, it was true that he always said he hated the Service, hated the life, hated this damned second-rate country. He jerked out, "What's all this I hear about your having an affair with a corporal in the Air Force?"

"Well, what did Mrs. Talbot say?" she asked satirically.

But he flushed up again, turned his eyes aside, and began in an indignant sulky tone. "And Caroline—haven't you any sense of responsibility towards her?"

She let out a peal of angry laughter. He watched her, fascinated.

"Where is Caroline?" he urged reproachfully. "What have you done with her?"

"Caroline was playing in the garden three feet from you when you came in—as you must have seen, since you are so worried about her."

He blinked again, moving his lips. Then he turned and began hanging things up in his wardrobe. She waited for him to attack again, while she noted with calm satisfaction the thick redness of his neck, which seemed a justification of her attitude.

He turned and said, "Matty . . ." in a thick pleading voice. He came stumbling towards her, clutched her in his arms, tried to kiss her. Then, as he began fumbling with her breasts in a determined and aggressive way, she twisted herself free in a flash of such pure hate for him that her eyes went black for a moment. She allowed to raise themselves in her memory all the other times he had tried to rouse her physically when she was set against him in spirit. She moved to the dressing table, and brushed her hair, sitting with her back to him.

"What's got into you, Matty?" he shouted at last, on an aggrieved note which sounded so comically inadequate that she laughed again.

"What do you suppose can have got into me?" she enquired after a pause, calmly. She rose and faced him. She began speaking in a tone of final contempt. "I am working for the Communist Party. Though there isn't one yet, but if there is I shall join it. Also, I am attracted by a 'corporal in the Air Force.' I should have told you about it myself, there was no need to spy on me through Mrs. Talbot. And I propose to have a love affair with him. Since you've been having an affair with Mollie in Y——, I don't see why you should object."

Again he stumbled across and tried to embrace her. "Matty!" he brought out. "Matty! We're all right, aren't we? We're all right?"

This echo of the rallying cry of the Club made her laugh again, though she had no intention of laughing. He fell back from her, and this time he was grinding his teeth and glaring.

"Your breakfast is on the table," she remarked breathlessly into that glaring, working face. To her surprise, he turned and went blindly out of the room, slamming the door behind him.

She went back to the edge of her bed. She could not think. Her mind was dim, and confused, and she felt sick. For the last few weeks she had perhaps slept four hours a night; the group felt sleep to be a waste of being alive, and they had no time to eat proper meals. She felt tired, even indifferent. The ugliness of that scene seemed impossible—it was impossible that he should be so stupid and obtuse, and she so stridently self-righteous. In the space of the few minutes he was away eating breakfast, she had again succeeded in creating him as that friend with whom she could talk things over.

When he entered the room, it was cautiously, and apparently in command of himself, and she looked hopefully towards him. "Now, listen, Douglas," she began in a different voice, almost friendly, "do let's stop all this—nonsense, and be sensible."

His face was still rather swollen and red, but she was unable to make out what he was thinking. Encouraged, however, she said, "I want to suggest that I should go away for a while—two or three weeks. Let me get over it." This last phrase seemed to her as being nice to him—putting the blame for everything on herself.

"Where are you going?" he ground out.

"I don't know—anywhere."

"*Where*, I said?"

It astounded her that he thought it mattered. "I really haven't thought. Why?"

"Somewhere near an Air Force camp, I suppose."

She flushed, but let it pass.

"Which camp is the corporal in?"

"Oh, I see!" She let out another peal of laughter, and he ground his teeth again.

"You needn't think I don't know," he said. "I know—you'd go away with him."

"Well, of course," she said, surprised. "That's what I meant." She added inevitably, "You've just been in Y—— with Mollie."

He got up, and began prowling blindly about the room. He was beside himself with anger. "Mollie's a sweet kid," he said. "She's not a whore—like you."

"Oh, I don't doubt that she has preserved her virginity against all comers. But, for all that, you've been spending hours of every night in the backs of cars, doing everything but. As far as I'm concerned, it's the same thing."

He suddenly picked her brushes and hand mirror off the table and flung them crashing against the wardrobe. She remained still. She was now bitterly regretting what she had just said—she was as bad as he was. And that wasn't the point at all! She looked steadily at him,

and knew she was no longer afraid of him. She had been—very afraid.
It was because—she saw this from an inward-looking gleam in the
puffed eyes—he had slid over into that mood of self-controlled hysteria which she knew well. It was as if he were saying to invisible
onlookers, "Look how I'm treated! Look how I'm behaving!" It was
with her nerves that she understood that it was not genuine. She
waited for him to speak.

Then again he abruptly left the room. She watched him cross the
lawn to where Caroline was playing. She was amazed to see him
clutch the child to him. He was making a scene of being an
anguished father, and for her benefit. The indecency of it appalled
her. She turned away, took up some sewing, and was working at it
when he came back. She saw he was furious because she had not
been watching him.

"I think you should leave Caroline out of it," she said coldly.

He sat down again and watched her.

"Oughtn't you to go to the office?" she asked at last. He did not
reply. "Because I said I'd go down town to the Aid offices to do
some work—I could drop you if you like."

"I won't let you use the car."

"Oh, well, then, I'll walk." She put away her sewing and got up,
while he watched her with a steady, hysterical gaze.

"I'll be back for lunch," she said.

She was walking down the garden path, when she heard him
pounding up behind her. Her nerves shrunk apprehensively; then
steadied again. One glance at him reassured her. She did not understand this controlled hysteria, so self-conscious and displaying, but
she did know that in proportion to the degree he succumbed to it, she
became cold and impervious.

At the gate she turned, and was about to walk off down under the
trees, when he said sentimentally, "Why don't you get into the car
with me?"

She shrugged as if he were a madman, and climbed in beside him.
She expected him to park the car outside his office, but he said,
"Where do you want to go?"

She gave the address. He parked the car and got out with her. She
understood he was coming in with her to see whether William
would be there. She wanted to laugh again, with that fatal upwelling
of pure contempt. She said lightly, "You know, William will be working at the camp at this hour of the morning."

He did not reply. They went together up the stairs of a big block
of offices, and entered the door of the Help for Our Allies Committee. Jasmine was typing under the window. She nodded at Martha,

smiled at Douglas, and went on with her work. Douglas stood watching while Martha collected papers and arranged another typewriter for herself. Then he said, in a perfectly normal voice, for Jasmine's benefit, "Well, I'll leave you to it. See you at lunchtime." He went out again.

For a while the two women typed in silence. Then Jasmine enquired casually, "Well, how's it going?"

"Awful," said Martha briefly. Then: "Men are really quite extraordinary." She fitted paper into the machine and began on a new letter.

"Does he mind about you doing this work?"

Martha paused, thinking. She did not know what it was he really minded. For she did not believe in his jealousy for William—she had not felt jealousy herself, so she did not believe in it. More, she did not believe that Douglas *really* loved her, as she put it; really loving, now, meant the exquisite fragile relationship with William. Finally, she thought, Anyway, there's Mollie—he's got no right to be jealous. But under all these was the abiding thought, I don't see how he can complain that I am what I always said I was. For at this moment she forgot the years of feminine compliance, of charm, of conformity to what he wanted. They had all been a lie against her real nature, and therefore they had not existed.

At last she said, "I've no idea at all what he's really angry about. All I know is, he's not angry about what he thinks he's angry about." She went on with her typing, forgetting Douglas entirely in the fascination of the work.

Before they parted for lunch, Jasmine gave a small intimate grimace, and squeezed Martha's arm. "Well, good luck with the battle. All that's wrong with him," she pronounced in her maidenly and demure way, "is that his property instinct is outraged." The night before, they had been discussing the freeing of women from male tyranny in the eastern parts of the Soviet Union.

"Oh, well—obviously," agreed Martha at once.

She walked home. Douglas was not there. Her suspicion as to where he might be was confirmed when Mrs. Talbot rang her up and suggested in a murmuring, intimate voice that she might like to come and visit an old woman tomorrow morning. Martha agreed. She was again in that mood in which a woman says silently to a man, Very well, then, I will behave as you want me to—that'll put you to shame!

But it was now, as she put down the receiver, that she said for the first time, I must leave him; it's all useless. For she had a very clear picture of Douglas, who was now engaged in going from person to person to enlist sympathy. Yet she shrank from the finality of it. No, when he came back, he'd be sensible again and they could discuss it all. . . .

She spent the afternoon reading and making notes—she was to give a lecture that night.

Douglas came in rather late. One glance showed him to be in the same mood. She mentioned that Mrs. Talbot had rung her up; she expected him to be embarrassed, but he said it that sentimental voice, "Yes, Matty, do go and see her—she'll help you."

"I suppose I must expect telephone calls from—who else?"

"Oh, Matty," he murmured like a lover, while he stared at her with swollen and hate-filled eyes, "you must listen to reason, you know."

But by now he seemed to her like a madman. She finished her dinner quickly, and said, "Why don't you come with me to the meeting? There'll be at least half a dozen civil servants there, it's really quite respectable," she could not prevent herself adding.

He simply kept the glare of his eyes fixed on her. But it was a blind glare, for he was seeing himself, the object of pity and sympathy for Mrs. Talbot and—but she did not know who were the others.

"Why not come? It's very interesting, after all."

He kept silence, so she got her things and left him as he settled on a chair on the verandah with the look of a watchdog settling for the night, head on paws.

"My mother's coming in to stay," he remarked as she left. She did not reply. This did frighten her. She drove down to the meeting in a state of pure terror. It was not of Douglas, but of society. She could see her mother-in-law, her own mother, Mrs. Talbot, the Maynards, massed behind him. They were all much stronger than she was. But as soon as she walked into the room, where Jasmine nodded at her with a look of understanding, and William smiled over at her in calm support, as soon as she felt herself surrounded by people to whom "personal problems" were the unimportant background to their real responsibilities, her fear vanished.

There were about forty people in the room. This was a meeting of a subsection of the Sympathizers of Russia.

She was already reading her paper, which was about education in the Soviet Union, when she saw that Joss was seated in a corner. He was in uniform. He was on leave from up north. And in another corner sat Solly, also in uniform. She felt confused at delivering a paper in front of those young men who had been her mentors in childhood. But she kept her voice steady, and continued, not looking at either of them.

During the discussion that followed, neither of these men spoke at all. Anton Hesse controlled it, in that calm, correct way of his, which

—as she saw with dismay—caused Sergeant Bolton to smile with sarcastic forbearance. It upset her that there could be personal antagonisms inside the group itself. But she was already familiar with this atmosphere where everyone in a room was in willing respectful submission to Anton, who was able to answer any problem with two paragraphs at least (one always felt he was reading from an invisible book) of clear and grammatical prose, while they were held in sympathy with Sergeant Bolton, who leaned forward intently, holding their eyes with his, one after another, and spoke with a sort of gentle intimate persuasion. It was extraordinary, this contrast between the open sarcastic antagonism of his attitude towards Hesse and McGrew and that intimate current of sympathy he established with the neophytes. There was an intellectual pole and an emotional one.

When the meeting was over, about half the people left. The rest stood about, looking at each other. It had been decided there must be a meeting to "settle things once and for all." They were all waiting for it to start. In the meantime, no one seemed ready to take the lead. Sergeant Bolton sat lounging on his part of the bench, from time to time exchanging smiles with whoever looked his way; while Hesse and McGrew sat silent in their corner, one smoking a pipe, the other a cigarette.

Martha wondered why they did not start at once. Then she saw that people were looking towards Solly, who stood by himself against the wall, with a sarcastic smile on his face. She heard Jasmine whisper, "Damned Trotskyite," and it hurt her that Solly should be thus cast out.

She protested to Jasmine, "Oh nonsense, he's perfectly all right."

Jasmine merely smiled. She nodded towards Solly so that Martha might see what was going forward. Solly and Joss were now isolated against one wall. They were exchanging a long stare. Both were rather pale, but smiled steadily, tight-lipped. The resemblance between them was striking at that moment, though they were so dissimilar. Solly was still a tall, lanky, uncoordinated-looking youth. Joss was more solid, squat, and strong in his khaki than he had been out of it. But both faces showed a keen, hard intelligence, a grim antagonism. Then Martha saw, with a suddenly pounding heart, how Solly let his eyes waver away from Joss's stare. He looked for a moment under his brows at the others. He was still smiling, and very pale.

"Well, good luck to your—decisions," he said, blurting it out. To Martha it sounded like an appeal. Then he turned and slammed hastily out of the room.

Immediately the people in the room seemed to flow together in a long sigh of relief. It was only then that Martha understood that his staying there had been a demonstration, and it struck her as both childish and offensive. She looked towards Joss, who still remained against the wall, with an odd twisted smile, looking after his brother. Then he too sighed and looked around. At once several people went up, and one after another took him by the arm and spoke in low voices. Martha thought, I'll ask him what to do, too. But she had to wait until the others had finished. Joss nodded and listened and smiled, but seemed not altogether happy in this position.

When she at last was able to go up to him, he first smiled, remembering their childhood, and then stiffened when she began to speak. She clumsily tumbled out her problem; then she saw he was embarrassed. "I don't see why everyone comes and expects me to sort out problems," he said with an unwilling smile. "I've been back on leave two days, and every person in this room without exception has been to ask my advice."

She said, "It's the price you have to pay for being the big man from the Party down south."

He grinned, but said finally, "In the first place it's all nonsense. I have no—authority. And secondly, I've been in the Army for two years." She looked so disappointed that he said, "You should think it all out carefully, and then do what you decide to be best." He added, "It's not a small thing, breaking up a marriage."

She was indignant that Joss should offer so conventional a viewpoint.

"But if you can't stick it, then leave, of course."

She went on hastily, offering him a confused picture of quarrelling and misunderstanding—she bickered with her mother, her husband was forbidding her to work in politics: it was as if they were back in the district, and she was bringing him her problems as usual. But she saw that he was looking past her, and she turned to see that everyone was seated and engaged in making conversation so as not to hear what she was saying. She retreated in confusion to a chair, and Joss crossed the room and sat beside Hesse and McGrew. The three men sitting there inspired the deepest respect in them all. They represented the Party itself. They also inspired resentment. For everyone clamoured to start a group, and these three argued steadily against it. It was understood now that Joss, who could take an outside view of affairs, would finally decide it.

Anton Hesse glanced around, saw that everyone was looking towards him, turned to Joss, and said, "You know what the situation is. I propose to analyze the position as I see it. Afterwards the others can argue against me."

He spoke for about half an hour. For most of the people in the room, it was the first time they had heard a Marxist explaining the world. It was right over their heads. He was in fact speaking to Andrew McGrew, Boris Krueger, Joss Cohen, Sergeant Bolton. For the others, such was their innocence that they were realizing that a vague enthusiasm for the Soviet Union was not Marxism—they had imagined they were already initiates when in fact they knew nothing. They listened, watching the four intent men, with an awed respect, while Anton Hesse analyzed the world situation, considered the British Empire, dealt with the colony in which he now found himself; its class forces were thus, its potentialities so, and the stage of development it had reached was . . . The conclusion was ten minutes of facts, figures, quotations from white and blue papers, which were all neatly ranged in his head, for he had no notes.

His final sentence was, "While everyone in this room would undoubtedly agree that a Communist Party is necessary and desirable, I submit that it would be inadvisable to start one with the existing cadres."

He stopped speaking, and looked at Andrew McGrew, who took the pipe from his mouth and said, "I agree entirely. May I point out that of the twenty people in this room, fifteen will have left the colony within a few months of the end of the war?"

The five who would remain were Jasmine, Martha, Betty, her husband, Boris, and a young girl who had drifted in to join them, a delightful eager creature of about twenty, a schoolteacher recently arrived from England. These five looked towards Joss. They felt that he, one of them, brought up in the colony, would understand them, whereas these cold-minded logicians would not, for if every word Anton Hesse had said was true—and they were too ill-informed to know whether it was or not—he completely ignored the passion for service which filled them all.

But Joss said, "I would like to hear what the others have to say."

Sergeant Bolton at once began to speak. Immediately the atmosphere changed. He said that Comrades Hesse and McGrew were probably right—theoretically. But he did not set himself to be a theoretician. All he knew was, the masses of the people in the country were suffering under a yoke of oppression, and if he could set them free, that was enough theory for him. There were more people in this room than there had been, very likely and for all he knew, when Lenin met for the first time with his comrades. If they started a Communist Party, they would soon have all the decent people in the colony with them. Comrades Hesse and McGrew were defeatists and

—he felt he ought to say—unable to feel the atmosphere of the time. It was the psychologically correct moment to start a Communist Party. . . .

He was speaking, not to comrades Hesse, McGrew and Cohen, but to them, the beginners. He would turn those intense burning black eyes on theirs, hold them for a moment, then on the next person; he was leaning forward, passionate, dedicated, inspiring. He had an extraordinary power to rouse them. They would have risen at a word from him and gone into the streets to die. And yet, the very moment those potent black eyes had moved on, each felt a faint uneasiness and glanced as if for help towards the three men who sat silently watching in the corner.

When Sergeant Bolton stopped speaking—on the cry, "We should go out into the streets, we should go into the locations, we should go among the suffering masses of the country!"—something unexpected happened. For Boris Krueger began to speak. It was only then that they realized he had been very quiet, not only this evening but during any other such discussions.

He too was very pale. He was upset and angry. He said in a dead silence that he agreed entirely with Comrades Hesse and McGrew. This colony was extremely backward. (This aroused the most violent resentment in the breasts of the colonials, even though they all agreed with him.) It was correct and appropriate to further the most advanced forms of organization already in existence—such as the Sympathizers of Russia, the Help for Our Allies, and the Social Democratic Party. Also, they had the duty to educate themselves. He would like to say here and now that they were in danger of splitting what organizations there were. Sergeant Bolton's fondness for appealing for immediate revolution at committee meetings of the Help for Our Allies would succeed only in losing all their respectable sponsors—without whom no money could be collected.

At this there was a soundless heave of mirth from Sergeant Bolton, and a spontaneous groan of sympathy for him and his viewpoint from everybody but the three members of the Party. For those same respectable sponsors aroused a quite remarkable degree of contempt in Sergeant Bolton.

Anton Hesse said quietly that Boris was quite right. No one but an amateur would use the Help for Our Allies as a platform for revolution.

Sergeant Bolton turned to Anton Hesse with a sudden violent movement, and was opening his mouth for a torrent of words, when Boris intervened with a long statement which amounted to a complete denial of Sergeant Bolton's bona fides.

All the time Boris was speaking, Sergeant Bolton shook with silent derisive laughter, and he interrupted before Boris had finished. He might not be a formal member of the Party himself, he said, but he had spent the last fifteen years of his life with the real people, the real working class, and that was more, he thought, than Boris could say.

To which Boris replied stiffly that in Poland he had been a member of the Party for five years, and he thought it was correct to say there was very little he did not know about agitation and underground methods of work. But there was a time and a place for fomenting revolution, as Sergeant Bolton would know if he had not such a contempt for theory. He wanted to know why Sergeant Bolton insisted on being so conspiratorial in a country where there was no need for it—

But here Sergeant Bolton exploded in a puff of laughter and the word "Democracy!"

Boris lost his temper and said angrily that there were degrees of democracy—he did not consider it was antirevolutionary to say so.

To Martha, Jasmine, and the others, this was extremely painful. They longed only to hurl themselves "for once and for all" into complete self-abnegation; and if they were asked to spend the rest of their lives in prison, so much the better. To hear Sergeant Bolton, who aroused them in flaming sympathy, attack the Party, which was how they thought of Hesse, McGrew and Joss, checked them in their best feelings—they wanted a complete unanimity, a fused purpose "for once and for all."

But all this time Anton Hesse and Andrew McGrew and Joss sat watching the dogfight between the two men, and saying nothing.

At last Boris turned direct to them, with a clear reproach that they had been silent, and appealed, "I would like to know what Joss thinks."

Everybody looked at Joss. Boris insisted, "I suggest he sum up—let's give him the final word."

There was a cry of agreement. After a quick look around at his disciples, Sergeant Bolton also nodded.

Joss shifted his legs uncomfortably, smiled, and said, "I'm prepared to give my opinion. I have no responsibility for anything else. I'm a rank-and-file member of the Party down south, and that's all." He paused and said, "I agree with Boris. I think you should run the existing organizations, and start a discussion group on Marxist lines. You should also do a great deal of self-education. Perhaps that's of more importance than anything else." With a small smile he added, "I do not agree with Comrade Bolton that theory does not matter." A dispirited silence followed. He said quietly, "Do I have to remind you that every face in this room is white?"

"That seems to me sectarianism," said Sergeant Bolton. "We can easily recruit the Africans. There is no problem."

"Perhaps. Perhaps not."

This cautious, almost flippant remark caused Sergeant Bolton to reap a harvest of support from the eyes of the disciples. He at once cried out, "Let's take a vote on it."

Boris said angrily, "You suggest a vote on whether or not we start a Communist Party? That isn't the way to do things."

"Why not? It's the democratic method," said Sergeant Bolton triumphantly.

"Listen," said Boris, with heated calm. "The Communist Party is a world organization. You have no right to start little groups here and there as you like. You should at least enquire from a superior body— the Party down south, for instance."

"We should start one, and then inform them. You don't suppose they'd be sorry?"

At this everyone laughed, even Hesse, McGrew, and Joss.

There was a shout of "Let's take a vote." Hands shot up everywhere. They remained in the air for a very long time. Andrew McGrew's hand went up, then Anton Hesse's.

"It's decided," said Sergeant Bolton, quiet with triumph. He looked coldly towards Boris and said, "The majority is against you."

"I do not consider myself bound by such a vote," said Boris quietly. He was dead white. There was sweat on his forehead. "It's irresponsible and amateurish." He looked at Anton Hesse and Andrew McGrew and said angrily, "I'm surprised you should vote for it."

Andrew said, "Well, let's see how things work out." Anton said nothing.

Boris asked Joss, "Why didn't you vote? Does it mean you don't think there should be a party, or you don't think it's your affair?"

"I'll be back in the Army inside a week," said Joss. He looked embarrassed, however. "I've said what I think."

Sergeant Bolton said pointedly, "Half the people in the room are in uniform—not everybody finds that an excuse." But he did not pursue it; what filled him with contempt in Boris was allowed to pass in Joss.

Boris stood up, smiling a steady unhappy smile. The others were shocked to see that his eyes were filled with tears. "You can count on me with anything to do with Help for Our Allies, or the Sympathizers, or that sort of thing."

"You're simply scared of losing your job," said Sergeant Bolton, with his sarcastic smile.

There was a deep indrawn breath around the room—they were all shocked.

Boris said, "I am not afraid of losing my job. I'm not even a British national yet. But if I were I would take the same line." He looked down at the bench where his wife was still sitting. Betty was flushed; the delicate small face was wet with tears. She was unconsciously wringing her hands.

She rose suddenly, put her hand in Boris's arm, and said indignantly, "You're a lot of—children!"

Sergeant Bolton smiled steadily.

Boris again said, "I'm surprised that Comrade Hesse and Comrade McGrew should take this line—I'm surprised. . . ."

These two men, in their turn, were looking uncomfortable. But before they could say anything, Boris had gone out, supporting his wife. They could hear her crying as she went down the corridor.

"And now," said Sergeant Bolton, "let's get cracking."

Joss rose and said, "I've got to get home now."

There were cries of protest, but he simply shook his head, smiled, said, "Good night," and went out. He left behind him an impression of criticism. Authority had gone with him. They all looked towards Anton and Andrew to supply it.

"Now we've got rid of those saboteurs," said Sergeant Bolton, "let's start work."

But Andrew remarked, with humorous protest, "I want to make it quite clear that while I think Boris should have considered himself bound to stay, he's a good chap and quite sound."

"There was a vote taken—a majority vote decided there should be a Communist Party. As an old Communist, he was bound to join it."

Anton said, "I agree that he should have stayed. But I would like to protest against the word 'saboteur.'"

Sergeant Bolton let out his shoulders in his heaving silent laugh. Andrew interrupted it by saying, "We should elect a committee."

Sergeant Bolton shrugged impatiently. "A committee with a group like this?"

"Yes," said Anton, quiet but firm. "A committee."

Sergeant Bolton looked towards William, then Jasmine, then Martha. It was not until then that she realized he considered them his supporters.

At Sergeant Bolton's look Jasmine said, "I vote for Comrade Bolton." His eyes met hers and held them in a long intimate look. She blushed.

Martha hesitated, and said, "I suggest Comrade Anton." She did not look at Anton, but involuntarily at Sergeant Bolton. He was smiling with tolerant sarcasm. It was really remarkable how the man could suggest he was being betrayed. But why? One could scarcely have a committee of one. But voting at once for Anton, instead of confirming Jasmine's vote for himself, was a blow against him, those reproachful black eyes said; but he understood the world—and women too, for that matter!

She smiled apologetically; the alliances in the group were, in short, being formed even then.

There was a longish pause, which was ended by Anton's casual "I would like to suggest Comrade Andrew."

Sergeant Bolton immediately countered with "And I suggest William and Jasmine."

"Too big," said Anton Hesse immediately.

"Jasmine," insisted Sergeant Bolton.

Jasmine, whose loyalties were almost equally balanced between Anton Hesse and the sergeant, looked for confirmation towards Anton, and saw that the watchful eyes said neither one thing nor the other. "I'm not experienced enough," she said confusedly.

The young schoolteacher cried out, "I protest—why aren't there any women on the committee?"

At this all the tensions dissolved in a roar of laughter. Jasmine automatically became a member of the committee.

As the laughter subsided, Anton said, "I suggest this meeting be now closed. It's very late. The committee will discuss things and call a meeting of the whole group shortly."

They all rose. Sergeant Bolton went, smiling, over to Anton and Andrew, taking Jasmine with him. These four shortly announced they would hold a committee meeting there and then. The others had better get home to bed.

They all walked down the dark stairway in silence. There was no need to say anything. They were together, dedicated and promised, and on the pavement they wrung each other's hands, smiling at each other without speaking.

Then William came up to Martha, and said, "Is everything all right, Matty?"

She had to think before she remembered what he meant.

"Oh, yes—I expect it will sort itself out," she said hurriedly. Her mind was still on what had happened. "I don't think we should have let Boris go like that," she said.

"Oh, Jackie knows what he's doing." He was speaking out of the service loyalty, she could see. "You should see him with the lads on the camp—he's marvellous," he added.

She could imagine it. She saw Jackie Bolton, persuasive, under-standing, almost tender—she had felt the spell herself.

He said too casually, "He thinks quite a lot of you."

At first she was pleased, then she saw he was jealous because of that evening the sergeant had spent with her. She resented it.

"Shall I come up and have a talk with the old man?" he asked.

"I wish you wouldn't call him the old man," she said irritably.

"Now, don't be cross," he said persuasively, taking her hand. They were together in sympathy again. "After all—if you don't love him, that's all there is to it. You should simply tell him so. And that's that."

She laughed a little. "That isn't at all that." And now he again seemed young and inexperienced.

"Why don't you get yourself a room in town and simply leave him?"

"Oh—I don't want to hurry things."

"What's the good of dragging it out?"

"I'd better get back home quickly—it's after twelve."

She was thinking again, He really is such a baby. And he was thinking, She doesn't want to leave that comfortable life, that's all.

They parted, without even a kiss. But as she reached the car he came after her, and took her in his arms. They clung together in con-trition because they were on edge with each other.

"Why don't you simply come with me to the hotel? Then you'll have burned your boats."

"But it's so unpleasant that way."

"It's unpleasant that you have to leave him. Not how you leave him."

She was silent. He said, "Are you afraid of his divorcing you or something like that?"

"You don't understand him. He wouldn't do anything *ugly*—not really. He's just in a bad mood. He's very sensible and straightfor-ward. . . ." But here she tailed off in a sigh.

A single stroke from the bell in the church across the park fell through the air, and she said, "I really must get back."

She drove home, parked the car quietly, and then saw that the house was filled with light. On the verandah Douglas was sitting where she had left him.

"Why haven't you gone to bed?" she enquired lightly.

"Where have you been—why are you so late?"

"There were two meetings."

He ground out, "Was *he* there?"

"Well, of course," she said, on that false light note.

She went through into the bedroom, and he followed. He was grinding his teeth—she could hear the ugly sound just behind her.

"Did you sleep with him?"

She looked at him, astounded. "Of course not."

He grabbed her wrist and twisted it. "Tell me the truth."

Her wrist hurt, but pride forbade her to cry out. He dropped it, and stood looking at her with a swollen glare.

She flung her clothes off, flung on her nightgown, got into bed. "I'm going to sleep."

He stood for a moment, then abruptly went to her cupboard, and began a frantic search among her things.

She sat up. "What on earth are you doing?" She was herself dismayed by the light inappropriate tone she could not help using. But both of them were playing roles, she felt. None of this behaviour was genuine, either hers or his. She felt that something would slip into place and they would become themselves.

In the meantime he was flinging her clothes out behind him like a digging terrier. He found what he was looking for, the little box that held the contraceptives. He ground his teeth again, looking at it. Then he swiftly crossed the room and put it into a drawer of his own. "You aren't going to have it," he said.

"But I don't want it," she said, helplessly laughing.

It infuriated him. He locked the drawer and stood thinking. She could see that he was about to propel himself off into another course. Then, abruptly, he left the room. She leaned on her elbow, listening, while lights crashed on in one room after another through the dark empty house. He came back carrying Caroline, who was half awake, blinking in a sleepy smile.

Douglas aggressively presented her the child, holding her out on his two forearms. Like a tray, she thought involuntarily. He said, in the sentimental voice, "Look Matty, look at this."

She snapped out, in extreme embarrassment, "Oh, don't be revolting, Douglas."

The disgust in her voice startled him out of his own picture of himself. He stood there holding out the child, who was asleep again, on his two extended forearms, blinking at her in comical bewilderment. Then he went red with shame, and rapidly retreated again back through the rooms.

She saw the lights switch out methodically as he came back, and thought, He's not at all out of control. He might imagine that he is, but he wouldn't forget to switch the lights out if the skies were falling. It might put up the electricity bill by tuppence.

He began to undress.

Now what's going to happen next? she wondered, out of her sense of improbability—it was not possible that this was really happening.

As he was getting into his own bed, he suddenly changed direction and flumped over onto hers. He ground her shoulders, so that she felt the balls of his thumbs deep under the collarbones, and said viciously, "I'll give you another baby—that'll put an end to this nonsense."

"Oh no you don't," she remarked breathlessly. But it all seemed so much more vulgar than was probable that she looked at him with embarrassment. "You're hurting my shoulders," she pointed out reasonably. He gripped her tighter for a moment, and pushed her shoulders back. She felt an instinct to struggle, then let herself go limp and said, "It's no good trying to rape me, you know. You can't rape women unless they want to be."

The word seemed to check him. He let her go, and stood up, thinking, blinking at her. Then he went to his own bed. She put out her hand and switched out the lights. She lay in the dark, trying to breathe silently, but her heart was beating like a mine stamp.

She could hear him breathing heavily and irregularly across the space of darkness. Then she was asleep. She awoke with difficulty, hearing his voice, slow, persistent, as if he had already said it many times: "It's no use pretending to be asleep. Wake up, Matty. Tell me, Matty—did you sleep with him, did you?"

"No, I didn't."

He repeated it; she repeated it. She fell off to sleep again. Again she woke in the dark, to hear that persistent voice, this time repeating, "Did you sleep with Hesse?"

She laughed. "No, don't be absurd."

He went through a list of names—it occurred to her after a while that he had memorized a list of the names on the Help for Our Allies Committee. She preserved silence for a while; she was only half awake; tiredness kept dragging her into sleep, and then she would be awake with the pain of fingers digging into her shoulder.

She knew quite well that he knew she had not slept with William or anyone else. What, then, was this all about? He's enjoying it, flashed into her mind; and the truth of this startled her completely awake. He was thoroughly enjoying the whole thing, and particularly the idea that she might have slept with twenty men. She lay in the dark, pondering: she was being confronted for the first time in her life with that phenomenon, male jealousy when it is self-conscious, with one eye on the invisible observer; enjoyable jealousy. But she fell asleep again, and again was woken by the pain of those jabbing fingers, which pride forbade her to protest against.

Finally, towards dawn, when she was sick and dizzy with exhaustion, she said calmly, "Yes, I've slept with William, and with Anton Hesse." She then repeated, one after another, the list of the men on the committee. At once his fingers relaxed, and she heard him breathing deeply and regularly. She was wondering what he was thinking about now, when she realized he was asleep. It seemed that whatever he wanted had been given to him. She fell asleep again.

She woke to find him dressing. She looked with curiosity at this sturdy and apparently sane young man, and remarked, "Well, and how does it strike you this morning?"

But he ignored this, saying in that other voice, sentimental and pleading, "Now, don't forget you must go and see Mrs. Talbot, Matty." With this he left the room to get his breakfast.

She thought that she must immediately collect her clothes and leave him. Then she thought, No, I'll see Mrs. Talbot first.

Before he left for the office he came back, apparently normal, but with a wandering look in his eyes which told her that he was still in the grip of that hysteria. He pronounced rapidly, "I forbid you ever to see William again."

"Don't be silly," she said promptly.

This, it seemed, was what he had expected, even what he had come for, for he ground his teeth again, gazed at her in self-consciously shocked astonishment, and went out.

4

The door was opened by Mrs. Talbot herself. The door to Mr. Talbot's study was shut, and Elaine was nowhere to be seen. Mrs. Talbot was fully dressed—stiff grey silk, with white bands at throat and wrists.

Martha followed her into the drawing room and sat down. Mrs. Talbot remained standing. Her eyes were filled with tears.

"Oh, Matty," she cried out, "it can't be true, it can't. You can't be leaving such a nice boy as Douglas for that other—of course I don't know him, but . . ."

"I'm not leaving Douglas for anyone," said Martha after a pause, during which she examined this new view of the position. The words "I am leaving him to live differently" came to her tongue; she did not say them, because they sounded absurd—they should be said flippantly, in this house. Then she saw Anton Hesse in her mind's eye and brought out aggressively, "I'm going to live differently."

But Mrs. Talbot's look at her was very shrewd. "We all feel like this, you know, Matty dear."

Martha thought, She means, everyone falls in love with someone else and wants to leave their husband. But Mrs. Talbot was going on: "I remember when I was young—I was a pacifist—I quarrelled with my fiancé over the war . . . but Matty, it's all such nonsense."

This depressed Martha; but she summoned the memory of Anton Hesse again, and recovered her sense of purpose.

"You don't understand," she began. But what was she to explain to Mrs. Talbot? She was unable to go on.

"Oh, I do, I do!" Mrs. Talbot positively wrung her hands. "Oh, I was so happy thinking of you making Douggie so happy. If Elaine could be properly married, I think my last wish would be granted, and I'd die happy. How can you break it all up like this, Matty?" Now she was crying, and patting her eyes delicately with a fragment of silk.

"But, Mrs. Talbot, I'm not properly married. I'm bored, bored, bored, you can't imagine. I can't bear it. I haven't anything in common with Douglas, and I've been unhappy all the time." For this now seemed to her the simple truth.

Mrs. Talbot said in the murmuring voice, "But Matty, dear, you are such a well-suited couple, we could all see it. And he's so proud of you—and you are such a good cook, and everything like that."

Martha smiled; and Mrs. Talbot said hurriedly, "No, don't do that. . . . I can't say what I mean, let me think." She even turned her back for a moment, and looked out of the shaded windows. She appeared very beautiful to Martha then; and that was more persuasive than anything she had said. This elegant elderly woman in her pretty room had such a look of completeness, of harmony, that once again that group of people seemed absurd and graceless; everything they were, or said, rang false for a moment, beside Mrs. Talbot.

She said, "There's that nice house, you've got such a settled future, and that lovely little girl."

Martha flushed angrily. Mrs. Talbot saw it and cried out, "But he's good to you, isn't he, Matty?"

"I think he's mad," said Martha. "I hate him. I hate everything about him!" she added violently.

Another quick look from the shrewd eyes. "He's only jealous, Matty," she said placatingly.

"But there's nothing for him to be jealous about. I've always been quite faithful to him—I suppose that's what you mean. And what he means, too. And he certainly hasn't been to me," she added with the feeling that all this was irrelevant.

"Oh, Matty! They aren't like us, they really aren't, you know."

Martha interrupted with "I don't see why we should treat them like so many children." She resented having to use that "we," associating herself with Mrs. Talbot's division of humanity.

Mrs. Talbot was silent for a while. "Look, Matty," she said in a different voice, brisk and practical, "you simply must realize that everyone feels like this. Everyone."

But Martha had mechanically risen to her feet, repudiating this argument. She was picking up her handbag, about to leave.

"No, don't go yet, Matty. If you'd only tell me what you have against him?"

"But I haven't anything against him!" said Martha, laughing angrily. "I'm leaving, that's all." She looked straight at Mrs. Talbot, laughing. Suddenly she observed, without knowing she had been going to, "Besides, we don't get on sexually." She blushed, and was angry with herself.

And now Mrs. Talbot had coloured up, too, and had become animated. She turned on Martha as if this had been what she was waiting for. "Oh, Matty," she cried, "I *knew* it."

This surprised both her and Martha into silence. They turned away from each other, embarrassed. As for Martha, what she had said, the use of those words then, had had the power to set her at a distance from what everyone in their circle called their love life. Hers with Douglas slid backwards into the past, and seemed wholly abhorrent. It was finished. She had never felt anything but repulsion for him. The idea that he might ever touch her again made her shrink. Love with William shimmered ahead, a pervasive radiance which coloured the whole of life.

Mrs. Talbot was weeping again. "Oh, Matty, dear," she sobbed gently. "Oh, how I loathe this sex business!"

Martha looked at her in astonishment. She thought of the room next to this one, the large bed, and those dark suave pyjamas tumbled by Mrs. Talbot's pillow. What on earth did she mean?

She enquired, "Do you mean you don't like making love?"

At this, Mrs. Talbot gasped, and the frail enamel of her face was pink. "I can't talk about it—I'm not like you young things, you can say anything. And all your books and ideas . . ."

"Well, that isn't the point, anyway," said Martha flatly.

"But, Matty . . ." Mrs. Talbot had come quite close, and had grasped her arm; it was stiff, so she dropped it again.

"Matty, let me tell you this. The man I really loved, the one that was killed—well, sex had nothing to do with it. Nothing!"

Martha was regarding her with discomfort. Mrs. Talbot was being dishonest, she thought. "Do you mean," she asked seriously, "that sex has nothing to do with love?"

"Oh, how I hate it all!" cried out Mrs. Talbot.

She collected herself, and said quickly in a low voice, "Matty, you are making a great mistake. All that's got nothing to do with marriage—nothing at all! It never did have. If you want to have love affairs, if you feel like that—well . . . I never talk about it, *never*. But, Matty, you can have love affairs if you want—oh!" And here she finally broke down, and leaned against the back of her chair, weeping.

"Well," remarked Martha, conscientiously pointing out to herself that what Mrs. Talbot found ugly was not the fact but the talking about it. "Well, I think it's all revolting. I don't think I really understand what you're saying." Mrs. Talbot, head collapsed back against the chair, was now regarding her with an unhappy but acute gaze. "If you're in love with a man, you sleep with him. If you're not—you don't. And I'm not going to stay married to Douglas and call him a dear boy and treat him like an idiot."

"Well, I don't know," said Mrs. Talbot helplessly. "I really don't. It's all so easy, really, Matty. Everything can be arranged—if you want. There's no need for all this. And you'll only be unhappy."

"I think I'd better be going," said Martha. She went towards the door.

Mrs. Talbot came after her. "Matty," she said appealingly, "but what are you going to do? Of course, you'll probably get married, you're quite attractive." Here she blushed, at this unintended exposure of her real assessment of Martha's charm. "But, Matty, I'm sure that boy hasn't any money. He's not even an officer, is he? Of course, I know that quite nice people are in the ranks these days."

"Look," said Martha awkwardly, "I don't think you really understand any of this, you know."

"Go and see your mother and talk it over, do, Matty."

Martha stopped. It had never entered her head to do so. But it occurred to her as strange that she had not, until this moment, wondered what her parents knew.

"They're so unhappy," urged Mrs. Talbot.

"They know?" asked Martha hopelessly.

"Oh, Matty, Matty!" cried Mrs. Talbot in despair. "How could they *not* know?"

Martha kissed Mrs. Talbot's cheek, automatically inclined forward for that purpose, and offered her a hurried unhappy smile. Then she escaped.

No sooner had she reached home than there was a telephone call from Mrs. Brodeshaw, reminding her that she had promised to help with the concert that night. Would she take the car down to the Coloured area, and bring certain children to the hall at seven o'clock?

Martha said that she would. Afterwards she realized that she had committed herself to stay in the house for another day. But lethargy was setting in again. She was thinking that tonight she would have a really sensible discussion with Douglas, when the telephone rang. It was Douglas; and she listened to his sentimentally urgent voice saying that he was so glad she had stuck to her promise to help with the concert. "That's the ticket, Matty," he said. "That's the stuff."

The telephone went silent while she was still thinking of appropriate things to say. For what was this sentimental appeal about? He would surely feel about the concert exactly as she did; yet he was making it a personal triumph for himself that she should go. But if he was indulging in unreal emotions, what was she doing? One thing answered another, always: she looked from outside, for one shocked moment, at that frozen obstinacy she called pride, and hastily averted her eyes from it. For if she ceased to maintain it, even for a moment, she would be lost; she could positively feel, rising inside her, a satisfied self-pity—which was the emotion that would well up from the cracked surface of that "pride." But she would not let it crack. She must behave like this, there was nothing else she could do. She would go to that concert, and then—wait and see. Something would happen, something she did not understand was working itself out.

She was very tired—she had not slept; she was hungry—she could not remember when she had eaten properly. She hurriedly ate some stale cake she found in the pantry, and set off for the offices downtown. They were empty. She spent the rest of her day addressing piles of envelopes in solitude. She did not leave the offices until it was time to fetch the children for the concert. She walked home to get the car; Douglas had left it there for this purpose, and gone off somewhere on his own.

She drove off downtown. She felt, as usual, that she was entering a new world when she turned into the squalid little street she was looking for. Extreme poverty lay a hundred yards from wealth—as, indeed, it tends to do, but in this case it coincided with a physical ghetto. Five parallel streets, each about half a mile long, held the Coloured community. This was still the nineteenth century. She, Martha, could expect to live to a ripe old age; and if she bore a child, it did not enter her head it might not live. Here people would die in early middle age, and babies died like flies in their first year. She, Martha, had never had anything more urgent to worry about than whether her emotional life was or was not satisfactory. Here were debt and anxiety and dirt and an atmosphere of a doom which might strike at any moment through illness or death. This was the other world—or rather, how nine tenths of the people of the world lived— and all she could feel about it was that everything that could be said about poverty had already been said; poverty was boring; there was no need for it to exist, and therefore she felt as if it already did not exist. It had, as Anton might say, been bypassed by history. But Anton would certainly not approve of this feeling of almost exasperated boredom: it occurred to her that joining the Communist Party did not make one a Communist. She was feeling, as she drove through these squalid streets, exactly as she always did: she had not been issued, as she had vaguely expected, with a completely new set of emotions.

She left the car in the street, while the usual swarm of ragged urchins gathered about it. She entered the building where she would find the children she must drive to the hall. It was built in three sides around a courtyard. A gutter ran dirty water down the middle, washing flapped over her head. All around the verandah which opened off the court stood dark-skinned men and women and children, watching her curiously. She felt like an intruder. She asked to be directed, and found a door standing open in a corner. It was a small room. Evidently a family lived here, for it had two large broken-down beds, a wooden table on which lay a loaf of bread in a bit of newspaper, some wooden chairs, and a wood stove. It seemed full of people. Two little girls detached themselves from the mass, and came shyly forward, while a large fat Coloured woman chivvied at them to be good with the kind lady.

It was all false and unpleasant, the high subservient voice of the woman, the thin little girls with their dirty hair and their ragged frocks, the smell of poverty, sharp and sour. The only honest thing in the place was a young man lounging against a wall, lounging of set purpose, radiating a calculated insolence and resentment. But no one else seemed to resent her. She went rapidly from room to room, and assembled another five little girls, all as ragged and as dirty as the first two. As she left, a whole group of women stood calling admonishments and threats after their children, in order to impress her with their respectability and their willingness to oblige.

She took the children to the car, and helped them in. None of them had been in a car before, she realized. The little girl sitting next to her was trembling and shrinking away. Martha understood she was afraid of her and asked her name. A small high voice piped, "Flora!"

At once the others offered their names—a chorus of Sandra, Marie and Anne. Then they began a high nervous giggle which upset Martha. She understood that the firm kind patronage of a Mrs. Maynard would at once set these children at their ease. She asked shyly what they were to do at the concert, and they burst out singing, "Three little girls from school are we . . ."

"No, Sand'a, not girls, Miss Pattren sez maids."

"Meds," corrected the small sharp-eyed imp who was Sandra. And they began again cheerfully, "Three little meds from school are we . . ."

They kept it up until they reached the hall, where Martha parked the car and helped them out. They stood uncertainly, hands devoutly folded in front of them in a way which suggested the influence of the Church, and watched her with bright curious eyes. She led them to a room at the back of the hall, and ushered them into a scene of crowded confusion.

Mrs. Maynard, in a black lace dinner frock, was helping Mrs. Anderson strip half a dozen brown infants naked and clothe them in neat white dresses. Martha saw that among the white women were Stella, Stella's mother, Mrs. Talbot, Mrs. Lowe-Island, and Mrs. Brodeshaw. A rotund priest stood beaming in one corner.

She retired to the hall itself. It was a barn of a place, with a plain board floor, and walls stained a sad mustard colour, but strings of little coloured bulbs were festooned everywhere, and someone had tied bunches of red balloons over the doors. The place was full, since it was the first time people of colour had entertained a white audience. The *News* had made a point of it that morning. There was a feeling of expectant curiosity, made benevolent by those names on the programme: Mrs. Maynard, Mrs. Player, Mrs. Brodeshaw.

After a long wait, the curtain, a heavy piece of dark-green serge, jerked slowly to one side on its brass hooks, and there stood Miss Pattern, a representative for this occasion of the Roman Catholic Church. She was wearing thick linen of electric blue, over which a faded little face peered with a mixture of encouragement and apology. She raised her hand nervously, silence fell, and she began to speak.

She had been asked by the committee—of which she was proud to be a member—to introduce this concert, which, she felt sure everyone would agree, was a novel and enterprising attempt to introduce one section of the community to another. Perhaps some people might feel that it was not altogether—how should she put it?—advisable to let our less fortunate brothers, to whom we stood in the position of parents and guides, start running before they could walk, but children have to begin sometime, don't they? And many people, among whom she was happy to say were some of great prestige and influence, felt that art was the greatest of the barrier-breakers, and she was sure that everyone present would be proud to attend at the first occasion when people of colour, or, as they preferred to be called (she emphasized this), the Coloured community, entertained a white audience. It was a landmark in the cultural life of their city. A happy event. (Here she blushed, stopped, then courageously continued.) She would like to make a few more points, if the distinguished audience would indulge her. The more enlightened members of the community, among whom she felt sure were all the members of this audience, could feel that a new wind was blowing. Times were changing. Ideas were abroad. It was natural that their fellow citizens . . . (she paused, looked at them firmly, and repeated) fellow-citizens should want to be in the stream of change. It was much better that such movements, or perhaps she should say tendencies, should be guided and encouraged by people of experience and common sense, than left to be prey of those agitators and trouble makers who unfortunately were always ready to exploit discontent.

She paused again, seemed about to go on, then leafed through her notes, shifting one piece of paper behind another. "I think that's all I have to say, ladies and gentlemen." She bowed forward from her waist, with a nervous smile, and retired backstage.

There was some perfunctory applause. Then, since it was observed that Mrs. Player and Mrs. Brodeshaw and Mrs. Maynard were clapping loud and firm from the front seats, the audience took it up again. The sound died in a ragged volley as a small girl smiling a stretched, fixed smile appeared where Miss Pattern had stood. Martha recognized her with difficulty as one of those she had brought from the slum. She was now shiningly clean; her pigtails stood stiffly out to each side of her head, tied with large pink bows; her dress was starched white. She stood for some moments stretching her head hopefully to one side, as if listening, before they realized she had forgotten her lines. Then she proceeded to repeat, phrase for phrase, in a high tense shriek, a speech whispered to her from behind a fold of green serge. Unfortunately, it was impossible to understand a word of it. She retired, in confusion, to a storm of clapping, and shouts of "Shame!" from some rowdies at the back, who had come under the impression that the concert was the work of the Sympathizers of Russia—apparently Miss Pattern's speech had confirmed their worst suspicions. But they were hushed sternly by the loyalists.

A gramophone began playing very loudly "The Blue Danube."

About fifty children flocked onto the stage, jigging and prancing, every face stretched in a prescribed smile. There was no attempt to follow the rhythm. After five minutes or so, the gramophone abruptly stopped again. Some continued to jig wildly, others stopped. Confusion. The gramophone set off in the middle of a bar, and then the green serge folds on either side shook violently. The music stopped finally with a loud squawk, and the children dived in all directions off the stage.

There was loud derisive laughter from the back. But Mrs. Maynard turned and delivered a frowning stare at them.

There followed a short sketch between a little girl in a poke bonnet and crinolines and a little boy in blue knee pants. Neither wore shoes. It was a proposal of marriage, which evoked cries of "How sweet!" from the front rows, and more raucous insinuating laughter from the back. After a pause, during which the stage remained empty, the same two children walked down the stage as bride and bridegroom—white butter muslin and black casement cloth—while all the other children flung confetti at them.

Then came three little girls against a bevy of other little girls: "Three Little Maids from School Are We"; but, as Martha had hoped, they had forgotten "maids," and sang "girls."

Then a long, long pause. The audience fidgeted, and the stage remained empty. A hitch, obviously. Miss Pattern emerged and, smiling with complicity towards the audience, proceeded to play some Chopin waltzes. Her eyes were fixed anxiously on some point off stage. Suddenly she sharpened her pace, brought the waltz to a galloping end, and rose, hastily gathering her music. She almost ran off, as a little boy of about twelve was propelled on by an invisible push from someone. He was wearing a child's Red Indian headdress, white shirt, white shorts, no shoes. He came very slowly and reluctantly to the front of the stage, sweating with teror, and, with wandering eyes and long intervals of silence, proceeded to recite selected portions from *Hiawatha*. Suddenly he stopped in the middle of a line; his mouth remained open for a while, then he bolted off the stage. Tumultuous applause.

And now it was the interval.

Martha worked her way to the back, and was delighted to find that groups of earnest and enraged Zambesians were forming a committee to protest to "the Prime Minister himself if need be" because of this insult to white civilization.

She returned to her seat, hoping for the worst.

It appeared that protests had already been received during the interval, for the second half of the programme began with a speech by Mrs. Maynard herself. She delivered it with great firmness, eyes and rings flashing, her black lace swaying, looking at the back rows. They must move with the times, she informed them decisively. Did they realize that the Coloured community lived in conditions which would disgrace pigs? (Ironical cheers from the back.) The whole area was a breeding ground for disease, which, as anybody with a haporth of sense would realize, was no respecter of persons or colour bars. If this concert did nothing else, it might make the white community realize what a danger spot it tolerated in its midst."

There were a couple more cheers, rather enfeebled, apparently by the processes of thought. Mrs. Maynard stood, subduing them all by her presence, for a few silent moments, then retired to her seat.

The programme resumed without incident. The Southern Sambos did an Irish jig with great spirit. A chorus sang "Tipperary." There was a vivacious rendering of that inevitable song "Hold Him Down, the Zulu Warrior." Then another pause. It was prolonged. The barrackers at the back plucked up courage and began booing. Mrs. Maynard stood up in the front row, and glared at them over the intervening rows. Then something unexpected happened. Towards the middle of the hall a solid mass of grey-blue indicated the presence of the Air Force; half a hundred aircraftsmen, tired of the cinema, had come in search of entertainment. Now they began shouting, "Up with Uncle Joe!" and "Progress, that's what we want!" One yelled, "Down with the colour bar!"

Some of the more solid citizens were observed leaving their seats and slipping out of the side doors.

Then Miss Pattern came slowly onto the stage. She was very nervous. She apologized for the delay, but the committee had been wondering whether to allow the next item in view of the—response of the audience. She had to make it quite clear that the committee took no responsibility for the next item. The leaders of the Coloured community had suggested it. It had been agreed to because . . . She hesitated some moments, and then remarked firmly, "Anyway, it shows the sort of thing we've got to contend with. The sketch was written by a Coloured boy, a South African Cape Coloured, now in England." Another pause. "There is talent among them—real talent. It should be directed. It *must* be directed," she cried out, on the verge of tears, and ran off the stage.

And now the audience leaned forward intently. The stage was completely dark.

Then a white patch gleamed in the darkness and a high, shrill voice said, "I am Asia. I am the teeming millions of Asia. I am . . ." There was a sudden chorus of boos from the back.

Another white patch appeared, and a second voice shouted desperately, "I am India . . ." But the rest of this was lost in tumult.

The white patches were agitatedly swaying in the darkness on the stage, and shrill isolated voices could be heard: Hunger, Poverty, Misery.

The audience was standing up. Someone was singing "The Red Flag." The lights came on to show three small urchins draped in white sheets, shouting above the din from the hall. "I am Africa," yelled one determinedly. Miss Pattern appeared on the edge of the stage, waving her hands. Africa, India and Asia rushed off the stage, tripping over their sheets, while Miss Pattern smiled appealingly at the audience. The back rows were now singing "Sarie Marais," while the delighted aircraftsmen in the middle were sitting with arms linked, swaying from side to side, and singing, "The people's flag is deepest red . . ."

Mrs. Maynard rose to her feet, climbed up the wooden steps that led to the stage, and stood waiting for silence. At last she got it. She said it was a disgraceful exhibition and she was appalled at their irresponsibility.

The khaki rows at the back hissed; and were at once answered from the Air Force blue with satirical cheers.

"You will kindly have the goodness to stand up for the last item," Mrs. Maynard said, and stood aside while the stage filled with the children waving Union Jacks. She lifted her hand—the rings flashed and glittered—and brought it down on the first chord of the National Anthem. The audience sang it boisterously through to the end, with undercurrents of "Sarie Marais" and "The Red Flag."

Afterwards, the place seethed as if stirred by a vast stick. People hastily left; isolated groups of Air Force and the khaki-clad—some uniforms, some not—looked at each other and meditated whether it was worth while to fight. A couple of halfhearted dogfights were developing as Martha squeezed out, and saw Douglas waiting for her, smiling mistily, as if from emotion.

"Wait," she said, "wait." She ran around to the back door, while he followed. She wanted to know what was going on behind the scenes. She found a dozen matrons energetically divesting the children of their stage clothes, while they congratulated each other on their courage: "It's time they woke up!" "Yes, I think we've broken the ice."

But it was not a united committee any longer. Mrs. Lowe-Island, upright and sturdy in mauve chiffon, was whispering to Mrs. Anderson that the Communists had introduced that disgraceful last item onto the programme, the whole town was full of Communists, they were everywhere. Miss Pattern leaned against a wall, half laughing and half crying, while Mrs. Maynard gruffly urged her to pull herself together and the fat priest hovered by making sympathetic tut-tutting noises.

And now arrived six of the other committee, all fine open-necked sun-burnt young Zambesians, all angry, but earnestly reproachful. Martha heard the note she had heard so often recently from Douglas, and looked at him involuntarily to see if he recognized it. It was that sentimental appeal, the note of goodness betrayed.

Mrs. Maynard confronted them, calm and majestic, and proceeded to point out that the art of good government was to make use of dissatisfaction for social ends. This being too abstract—it was countered with an indignant "But we can't have the kaffirs doing as they like!"—she translated it thus: "My dear young man, they will get out of hand unless you give them rope."

They looked at each other rather doubtfully, and Mrs. Lowe-Island came in to support. With her hands on her hips, eyes burning, she said that people like them encouraged the Communists. Of course Communist influence had caused that last item on the programme, but why did they behave like that, the way to treat Communists was to take no notice of them, all they wanted to do was to make trouble. . . .

Mrs. Lowe-Island's speech and personality being more understandable to them, violent discussion continued, while Mrs. Maynard stood on one side, watching thoughtfully, with no more than the faintest smile on her face. Finally, when her lieutenant ran out of breath, she stepped forward and invited all six of them up to her house for a discussion next afternoon "at six o'clock, mind, because I have to be at Government House for dinner."

They retired, prepared to control their indignation until they had heard the other side, like true democrats. Only then did Mrs. Maynard allow herself to look exasperated. "And I'm so busy!" she was heard to exclaim. Unfortunately nine tenths of the time of any political leader must be spent not on defeating his opponents, but on manipulating the stupidities of his own side.

Martha's charges were soon delivered into her hands, in their faded rags and bare feet. She was thanked profusely by Mrs. Brodeshaw for her kind cooperation, while Douglas grinned a bashful boy's smile just behind her.

She took the children to the car. Douglas came with her.

"Well, Matty?" he enquired eagerly. It really seemed that he expected her to show enthusiasm.

"Everything that happens in this place is like a caricature—it simply isn't possible that it should happen at all."

She heard his breathing change. She said hastily, "Were you there? Did you see it?"

"I saw the last part. But, Matty—it's a beginning. It would have been impossible to have Coloured people entertaining the whites even a year ago."

"The beginning of what?" she enquired reasonably. She noted with dismay how amusement and indignation, any emotion she might have been feeling, vanished instantly under the calm cold anger that rose in her the moment she heard him begin to breathe deep, saw his face redden and swell. "Don't let's start again until we've dropped the children," she said quickly.

The house in the slum was in darkness. Martha shepherded the children over the rough court, under the bits of washing. A slit of yellow showed under a door. It opened slowly. From the light of a stub of candle stuck in a bottle, she saw a room full of sleeping breathing bodies. The large woman, still dressed, came forward and received the children, who began bolting along the verandah this way and that like so many rabbits into their doors. The woman began curtseying and bobbing, while she took her child to her skirts. "Thenk-you, missus, thenk-you, missus."

Martha said good night, and went back to the car.

Douglas said: "My mother's come."

"Oh—well, that's good," she said flatly.

"Now, do let her talk to you, Matty," he implored in that lover's tone.

Mrs. Knowell was sitting in the drawing room, reading. She rose at the sight of Martha, smiling uncertainly. Martha also hesitated. Then she realized they were both bothered by a problem of etiquette: Was it suitable for a young woman on the verge of leaving her husband to kiss that husband's mother? She went forward and kissed Mrs. Knowell on the cheek. The older woman grasped Martha to her in a quick anxious embrace, and then released her.

"Matty," she said urgently, "Matty . . ."

They looked around. Douglas had gone into the next room, leaving the door open. He called out in a loud, hearty voice, "You two girls would like to have a nice chat!"

Martha glanced towards Mrs. Knowell, embarrassed. That lady, as tired, bony and yellow as ever, looked indignant, and then involun-

tarily smiled and sighed. Both women flushed guiltily, and became
solemn, conscious that they were disliking each other.

"I've come to stay a few days," began Mrs. Knowell quickly. "I
hope you don't mind, Matty." She glanced towards the open door.

"Of course not," said Martha politely. She smiled again; she realized that she wanted to burst into hysterical laughter. She noted that
upwelling of hysteria with terror. She controlled herself and said
coldly, "Well, this is a mixup, isn't it?"

"Oh, it is, Matty—it is. Awful," agreed the elder lady sullenly. She
was about to say something else; then Martha could see that she was
thinking, I must not interfere. She settled back in her chair, and said,
"You must be tired."

Martha at once said she was. She looked nervously away; she
wanted to escape.

Then Mrs. Knowell scrambled up, came close, and said in a low,
angry voice, "Matty—must you? Must you, Matty?"

"Yes, I must," said Martha at once.

Mrs. Knowell's face twitched, then she smiled a cold, disapproving
appeal, and said, "You must do what you think is best."

Martha was deeply touched. She impulsively embraced the old
lady again, suppressing the distaste she felt at touching the emaci-
ated body. The skin felt cold and clammy. And Mrs. Knowell was
trembling with emotion. Martha could not stand the emotion. She
gave the elder lady a quick apologetic smile and went to the bedroom.

Douglas immediately followed. "I think you might have spared her
a little more time," he began.

"Douglas," she suddenly wailed, "do for God's sake shut up."

She saw a look of satisfaction come onto his face at that despairing
wail. He began firmly, "Matty, I must talk to you." His eyes were
stern and calm, his voice steady. This, in fact, was that sensible and
brotherly young man. "We must get this thing sorted out. Tonight."

She felt fear rising in her. "You don't think we should have a jury
of Mrs. Talbot and your mother and my mother?" she asked sarcastically.

The moment was over—his eyes reddened, his lips shook.

"I'm going to bed—to sleep," she said. She was in bed in a few
moments. She turned away from him and thought, I must sleep, I'll
go mad if I don't sleep. She was drifting off when—as she put it—it
began again.

That night was a repetition of the last. Again he worked himself
up into a rage of misery, cross-questioning her about every man she
might have casually met during the last four years. And again she

was astounded and appalled—it was like listening to a madman talking. Towards dawn she did what she had done the night before. She recited a list of about forty names, enthusiastically admitting guilt with all of them. And at once he was satisfied and went to sleep.

It was all impossible—but it was happening.

Several days went by. She went to meetings, worked at the office, spent as little time as possible in the house. She returned at night to sleep broken every five minutes by a tug at the elbow and that stupid, maudlin questioning.

But why did she not leave? All she had to do was to take a suitcase, put a few clothes into it, and go. But she could not. She still felt that something must happen: someone would say something, and she would be released.

She was now in a condition of tense heightened exhaustion. Her brain ticked over steadily, with a clear, cold analysis. She was watching the situation from outside, as if she were not implicated in it, and even with absorbed fascination.

She was considering such questions as, What did the state of self-displaying hysteria Douglas was in have in common with the shrill, maudlin self-pity of a leader in the *Zambesia News* when it was complaining that the outside world did not understand the sacrifices the white population made in developing the blacks? For there was a connection, she felt. Not in her own experience, nor in any book, had she found the state Douglas was now in. Yet precisely that same note was struck in every issue of the local newspapers—goodness betrayed, self-righteousness on exhibition, heartless enemies discovered everywhere.

But *she* was being heartless; she was as cold as a stone; and had to be.

She would even begin making such dispassionate comparisons to her mother-in-law, who would watch her, disquieted and disapproving, and murmur, "But, Matty, men are like this, you know."

"Nonsense."

"All you young people," she cried, in her sad yellow voice, "you have such awful ideas." And then: "Life is so terrible, Matty, it's so sad, and you make it worse."

"It isn't," snapped Martha, frightened.

She made resolutions not to talk thus to the old lady. It was cruel and stupid. But at the bottom of it, she knew, was a vengeance against Douglas: You drag your mother into this, so that I can talk to her—well, then, I shall! She was playing that female role to its limit.

And all the time it was as if it were happening to somebody else.

She was surprised that all the women of the set had come to her, one after another, in secret, to say that they admired her courage, and wished they could do the same. They saw it simply as escaping from an unsatisfactory marriage: the political side of it did not exist. They were not political, and besides, at this particular point in history, Communism was respectable. All of them, however, began telling stories of their intimate lives which she had never suspected as possible. With what low-voiced and eager relish did they divulge these secrets! Then it occurred to her that what unpleasant things had not happened it was necessary to invent—precisely because they wanted her, Martha, to share with them the enjoyable crises that were taking place in her life.

She made one discovery. It was this. That her feeling that she was being moved along a process which had its own laws was justified. When a woman left her husband, or threatened to leave him—that is, a woman of her type, who insisted on her rights to behave as a man would—then the husband went through certain actions like an automaton, beginning with confiscating the contraceptives, threatening to make her forcibly pregnant, accusing her of multifarious infidelities, and ending in self-abasing weeping appeals that she should change her mind and stay. The thought that Douglas might weep and appeal horrified Martha. She felt she could not withstand it. But even more frightening, because it was so humiliating, was the idea that what she did and what Douglas did was inevitable, they were involved in a pattern of behaviour which they could not alter.

To Mrs. Knowell she remarked: "I'm beginning to see how the whole thing works. When a woman leaves her husband she is forgiven on one condition: that she complain shrilly about how badly he treats her. Then certain women will champion her. They are the women who themselves would like to leave and don't. It is these women who will re-establish her, provided she marries another suitable man. But it all depends on whether she complains and arouses sympathy. They won't forgive me, because I have no intention of complaining. It's disgusting," she said firmly and shrilly. Then she hated herself for that shrillness. For that group of women, in their secret interviews with her, were such a bunch of self-righteous and outraged feminists—and there was nothing she hated more!

"Oh, but, Matty," said the old lady apprehensively, "surely my Douggie doesn't ill-treat you."

"No, of course he doesn't," said Martha angrily. Then she felt overwhelmed with guilt because she was making the old woman so unhappy.

If only Martha would weep! If only she would drop her voice and nervously complain of small unhappinesses! With what delicacy and kindness then would the old lady comfort her, and approach Douglas; how gently she would have brought the young couple together again; and then, having fulfilled her function as an old lady who was allowed no other, with what pride and tact would she have effaced herself! But, instead, here was this set-faced, cold-eyed, satirical young woman who never, not for a moment, allowed herself to weep or to soften.

The old lady lay awake at night, thinking of her life, and particularly of those children she had borne and lost. Inside her, even now, there were spaces of dark pain because of those children; even now her arms ached with emptiness when she remembered them. Whatever loneliness and disappointment she had felt had flowed long ago into those small lives, cut off so soon. She had never allowed herself to say, I was lonely, I am unhappy. She wept for the dead children who ought now to be a group of tall and strong young men and women around her. Small Caroline was so like the daughter who had died of malaria that swampy hot rainy season. And Martha was prepared to leave Caroline, leave everything—for what? Mrs. Knowell lay awake night after night, looking into the darkness, crying steadily, tears soaking down a set, unmoving face; she felt betrayed by Martha. Her own life was made to look null and meaningless because Martha would not submit to what women always had submitted to. She longed for that moment when Martha would fling herself into her arms and cry out that Douglas could not understand her, but she would stay with him, that she was unhappy, but would make the best of it.

As for Martha, it had occurred to her that this compulsive process of analysis and comparison was nothing but an excuse for doing nothing. She was retiring to that bed each night for the sheer fascination of seeing what would follow, and because she was able to think contemptuously of Douglas, Aren't you ashamed to behave like a self-pitying child—look at yourself!

She was so disturbed by this thought that she set off to see Jasmine, having first made an appointment, since she would otherwise be at a meeting.

Until this moment Jasmine had appeared only in her public guise —a secretary on a platform, a girl never without files and papers. She was now revealed to be the daughter of a prosperous Jewish family. It was a large house, very comfortable, and secluded from the street in a well-kept garden. Inside this house Jasmine had a suite of rooms, filled with books, files and typewriters.

She was calm and sympathetic. She listened without comment

while Martha made a long self-critical speech about how intellectuals were doomed to futility because they always thought about
things instead of doing them. For one of the advantages of living in
the suburbs of the world is that commonplaces which are too tedious
for repetition anywhere else come as overwhelming discoveries.
From the fact that the working people are destined to deliver the
world follow certain other conclusions as night follows the day.
Martha had discovered, rather to her surprise, that she must be an
intellectual. Therefore: Was it, then, the case, she enquired, that intellectuals were bound to be useless to the revolution because their
behaviour would always inspire such disgust in the onlookers that
no one would take them seriously? She was developing this with all
the fervour of someone on the track of a completely new idea,
when she saw that there was a look of patient irony on the small,
sedate face.

"Now, Matty," said Jasmine reproachfully, "why don't you just
leave him and be done with it?"

Martha was checked.

"We simply can't understand," said Jasmine firmly, "why you don't
just leave. You really look awful, Matty."

"Well, I don't get much sleep," admitted Martha.

"Naturally not. And it's not doing you any good. You're quite
useless at meetings—you talk the most dreadful nonsense, you know.
We are all very sympathetic, but we do wish you'd get it over with."
And then, the calm, demure little face changing not at all: "Besides,
there might be a revolutionary situation at any moment—and here
you are wasting time on personal matters!"

Martha promised that she would take herself in hand at once. She
went downtown and engaged a room, told the landlady that she
would move in tomorrow, and then returned home.

She was now bound to leave tomorrow. She still felt like a fly
caught in the web of her incapacity to move. She set off to see her
parents.

She came near the house and saw her father in his chair under the
tree. A newspaper was slanted up over his face, half concealing it.
She stopped. He was surely looking at her? She waved, and hurried
in through the flowering bushes of the crowded garden. By the time
she had reached him, the paper had slid over his face, and his hands
were folded over his chest. She stood looking around. The house was
warmly glowing off sunlight from its red brick, the leaves glittered,
across the street the acres of the park stretched in lawns and ordered
flower beds and calm unmoving trees. There was no wind. A servant
was chopping wood at the back of the house. There was no sign of

Mrs. Quest. She pulled up a chair and sat close to him, waiting. She could see his closed eyes just over the edge of the paper. The sun shone warm over the lines and creases of his face. A little mesh of lines at the corner of his eye quivered. This time, she thought, I'll stay here till you wake. You aren't going to escape from it.

A couple of birds dropped from a tree into the bird bath, and dipped and swooped over it in flashes of yellow and black. They fought in a ball of flying feathers, bounced apart, and then, with a flurry of chitterings, rose together into the tree. Mr. Quest opened his eyes cautiously in the direction of the noise. Seeing his daughter in the corner of his vision, he let out a groan, and let his head fall back again.

"Daddy!" said Martha indignantly.

He remained with his eyes shut for a few moments, then opened them, and slowly woke up, blinking. He coughed, and enquired as if he had just seen her, "Well, old chap?" But his eyes were evasive. "Lord, that was a deep sleep," he observed. "Those birds are making a row." They were fighting again; drops of water flew sparkling from the bird bath as they skimmed shrilly over it.

"Oh, very well," said Martha crossly, getting up.

"Just going in to see your mother?" enquired Mr. Quest hopefully. "Well, that's a good thing. I'm not feeling very well this morning." He pulled his paper upright and began to read.

Perhaps he didn't see me after all? she wondered. Then she saw in his eyes that sly, triumphant gleam she knew so well. She smiled, intending that he should see it. But he would not look. She walked off dispiritedly to the house.

Mrs. Quest was cutting out on the back verandah. Piles of white material lay everywhere.

Martha had been planning a quiet, reasonable discussion with her mother, who would first be upset, and then understand her point of view. This consoling fantasy had even included a warm embrace, and tears shed together. It was only when she actually arrived in her mother's presence that she understood this was absurd.

"Oh, is that you, Matty?" Mrs. Quest said, and went on cutting. She had a look of withdrawn, sullen disapproval. Martha thought that her mother was rather like Douglas just then, there was that swollen reddened look about the face, the accusing eyes. But she went straight into battle, with the abrupt announcement, heart pounding, knees trembling: "Mother, I am going to leave Douglas."

Mrs. Quest went on cutting for a moment, the big scissors flashing. Her hands were shaking. The scissors fumbled and slipped. She turned on Martha, hands lifted in fists. "Mrs. Talbot told me. I always knew you'd come to this," she cried dramatically.

Martha had not expected the torrent of abuse that then followed. She realized that all the arguments she had come armed with were irrelevant. She must listen to this until its end, crossing off one after another, as it were, the threats and accusations which were supplied to Mrs. Quest—by what? She sounded like a vituperative kitchen-maid. Martha had no idea that this elderly and proper matron knew such language. Mrs. Quest said that Martha was killing her father; Martha said briskly, "Nonsense." Mrs. Quest said she was ruining Caroline; to which Martha replied that she could not see, even at the very worst, that Caroline would turn out any worse or more neurotic than the children of ordinary marriages. Mrs. Quest said she would never speak to Martha again, and that she must immediately marry that corporal, or whatever he was, and go to England to save her, Mrs. Quest, from this disgrace. Finally, she wrung her hands and said it was a woman's role to sacrifice herself, as she had done, for the sake of her children.

Martha reflected that Mrs. Quest did not really believe in any of this, she was simply playing a role laid down for her.

Just as, in early middle age, she had written letters to be opened after her death, which she felt was imminent, to her husband choosing his future wife, to her children exhorting them to forget her immediately and not to wear mourning—behaviour which, as Martha had discovered from enquiries among her friends was common to all their mothers at a certain stage in life—so now did she feel she must refuse ever to see Martha again, must exclaim over and over again that Martha was killing her father.

But at last she cried out in complete despair, from the heart, "And what will people say?" For this was the kernel of the matter.

Martha went home with the feeling that she had accomplished another stage in that curious process which would set her free.

And now it was that the thought of parting with Caroline became real. She took the child into the garden. Caroline played with her toys on a rug, while Martha talked to her. She felt as if the child understood perfectly what she was saying—more, that there was only one person who really understood her, and that was Caroline. She felt a deep bond between them, of sympathy and understanding. When Caroline lifted her arms to be picked up, Martha took her on her lap, and for the last time touched the small round knees, the perfect dimpled arms, and was pleased because Caroline would never stay quiet in her arms: she was at once striving to be up, twisting herself to reach over her mother's shoulder for some leaves, or bending for a feathery head of grass. Martha held the energetic and vibrant little creature tight for a moment, and whispered in a flush of pure tenderness, "You'll be perfectly free, Caroline. I'm setting you free."

Then she gave the child to Mrs. Knowell, and went indoors. She packed her clothes and her books. These belonged to her. She would not touch any of the things that she had brought into the ménage: nothing that had been given to the marriage, rather than to herself. She left the wardrobe empty, save for her mother's coats and wraps.

Then she waited for Douglas to come. He did not until very late that night. He had been with Mrs. Quest.

He looked savagely at her and said, "I'm going to make you have another baby." He did not believe it, but he said it, gripping her shoulders and twisting them. The door was open into the next room, where Mrs. Knowell sat knitting.

"You ought to shut the door first, at least," said Martha with a grunt of nervous laughter.

He started back, looked vaguely around, and went to shut it. She wondered what was coming next. He took a few steps towards her, then turned and went to a cupboard and pulled out a revolver. It was the revolver he had insisted on leaving with her when he went up north with the Army.

"I shall shoot you and Caroline," he said to her. He started rummaging for bullets. He stood up, fitting in the greasy plugs of steel. He was crying, she saw with discomfort. The tears were springing from under his swollen lids and splashing onto his shirt. She thought, Well, he might shoot us. But she was unable to believe in it.

He finished arranging the revolver, and stood pointing it vaguely in her direction, his face working. He thought for a while, then said in a voice choked but full of satisfaction, "I shall shoot Caroline first and you afterwards." He went into the nursery. Martha followed him to the door, her heart pounding with fear. He was bending over the bed, shaking with sobs, the hand holding the revolver hanging loose at his side. But his eyes were rolling around in her direction to see if she was watching him.

She went into the drawing room and said to his mother, "Douglas says he's going to shoot Caroline and me." She laughed, and again noted the hysteria in her voice. She steadied herself and said in a flat steady voice, "I don't think for a moment that he will, but he says so."

Mrs. Knowell did not look at Martha. She laid aside her knitting, with tight sad lips, and came into the bedroom. Now Douglas was standing in the middle of the room, the revolver dangling loose from his hand. He was saying, "I shall shoot myself. I have nothing to live for."

His mother went to him and took him in her arms, and murmured, "There, there, my baby. She won't leave you, she won't."

Martha said nothing. Douglas staggered a few steps, and collapsed, heaving with sobs, on the bed. Mrs. Knowell was saying, "It's all right, dear. She couldn't leave you—could you, Matty?" Now she looked with peremptory anger at Martha, the yellowing eyes exhausted, but not frightened. Martha obeyed her. She came and sat down on the other side of Douglas, but was unable to touch him. She saw that what his mother wanted was for her to put her arms around Douglas, and promise in a maternal murmur that she would not leave him. This was what Douglas was waiting for.

She saw the revolver still dangling limp in his fingers. She took it from him, rose, and went to the dressing table. With her back to the couple sitting on the edge of the bed, she clumsily slid the chamber around and let the bullets fall out. She had never handled the thing before.

Then she stood looking helplessly at them. Mrs. Knowell was still murmuring in that dry tired voice: "It's all right, it's all right." And Douglas was seated, his thighs apart, looking at her with insistent reddened eyes.

Suddenly she lifted the empty revolver and handed it to him—she did not know why. He took it, then bounced up, letting out a yell of affronted rage. "Matty!" he yelled. "Matty!"

Mrs. Knowell rose, and said drily, "I think you'd both better get to bed and have some sleep." She went out.

Douglas stood, his face working, doubtful of what he would do next. Then he said, "I shall go out and shoot myself." He repeated it, waiting for her to appeal to him.

"Oh, do stop it, Douglas," she said, exasperated.

He held his shoulders straight, then whirled around and marched out with the revolver into the moonlight. There was a bright moon that night.

She sat for a while thinking, Perhaps I ought to go after him. Then, in a small flush of panic: Perhaps he managed to put a bullet in the chamber after all. But she knew he had not.

After all, she thought, people do shoot themselves. They do it constantly, she added, unable to stop herself salting in the humour. It was no good: not for a moment was she able to believe he would shoot himself. She rolled over on the bed and was asleep immediately.

When she woke, everything was very quiet, and Douglas was standing at the foot of the bed looking at her with his steady reproach. "You've been asleep," he ground out.

"You haven't let me have half an hour's consecutive sleep in weeks," she pointed out.

He carefully put the revolver away in his drawer, collected the bullets from the dressing table, and fitted them into their box. Then he turned towards her. His face was quite different, set and murderous. She thought, Those women said there was a point where they started knocking you about. She remembered the satisfaction in their voices and thought, Oh, no, not for me. She quickly stood up beside the bed, warily facing him, every sense alert. He was leaning forward now, about to spring.

"Douglas!" she cried out. But it was too late. He jumped, brought her down, and began pulling out handfuls of her hair. She thought, I simply will not—I won't! She struggled a little, then, as he was shifting his hands for a better grip, rolled free sideways along the floor and got to her feet. He was coming after her. She walked straight out of the room, into the garden, and out into the street. Moonlight was pouring down. It was long after midnight; the houses were all dark.

She was going to her mother. I'll stay with her until morning, she thought, and then come and get my things.

She walked steadily down the middle of the street, which glared white with the moon, banked by the heavy dark trees. He was following her. It was about ten minutes' walk to the other house. She was numb, her knees shook, but she made herself walk quietly, although she could feel fear crinkling up and down her back in cold waves at the thought that he was coming after her. But as soon as she glanced over her shoulder and saw him, she was not afraid. He came striding along, head down, like someone training for a walking match, she thought disgustedly.

It seemed a very long way. She had time to think of many things: she had forgotten to pack her sponge; she must tell Alice about Caroline's lunch tomorrow—Caroline did not like carrots, it was absurd that Alice kept cooking them, children should not be made to eat what they did not like; she must remember to tell the cook to whip the ice cream in good time . . .

As she neared the gate, which gleamed dead white, she heard him running. She began to run, in an impulse of pure panic. They reached the verandah together. He reached out to grab her shoulder; she twisted it under his hand and fled to a window, where she banged hard on the glass.

Now he stood behind her, breathing heavily.

The window opened inwards; her mother stood there, blinking with sleep.

"I want to speak to you," said Martha quickly.

"Wait a minute," said Mrs. Quest nervously.

She vanished, and Martha ran to the door off the verandah. Douglas followed. Mrs. Quest stood in the doorway, and Martha said, "Mother, I want to come in."

Mrs. Quest looked at Martha and at Douglas with a sullen, disapproving face.

"Mother," said Martha desperately, "I must come in, let me in."

Douglas had gripped both her arms from behind and was wrenching them methodically.

"Mother!" she yelled out.

Mrs. Quest looked away and said evasively, "But it's late, what are you doing here?"

"Mother!" wailed Martha. Her arms were almost being wrenched out of their sockets. It had never entered her head that her mother would not let her in. Now she saw that it was obvious she would not. Mrs. Quest observed them furtively, and onto her face came a look of satisfaction and pleasure.

"He's hurting me," said Martha, keeping her voice steady now, out of pride.

"Be quiet, you'll wake your father, he's not well."

"Mother, you aren't going to let him bully me?"

"Well, you deserve it," said Mrs. Quest. "He's quite right. Now go back to bed," she added quickly, in a vaguely admonishing way.

Douglas, apparently as surprised as Martha, had let go her arms. She stood rubbing them, looking at her mother. Then she shrugged and laughed. For Mrs. Quest was retreating hurriedly indoors.

"Go back to him," she was saying, "it serves you right." The door shut in Martha's face.

That cold dark door shut in her face made Martha go sick inside for a moment. Then she said in a bright angry voice, "Well, so much for that." She turned to Douglas and said, "And now let's go home." She set off walking, not caring whether he followed or not. She no longer cared about him one way or the other.

He came up level with her. "Lord, what a performance," she remarked, laughing angrily. "What's it all about? You don't believe in it, I don't believe in it—what do we do it for, then?"

"I suppose you arranged that so as to have a witness?" he asked suddenly.

"What do you mean?" She had no idea what he was talking about.

They walked the distance in silence. She was not at all afraid of him now. He was not there, for her.

When they reached the bedroom, she said at once, "And now I'm going to sleep." She fell on the bed fully dressed, and added casually, "I shall leave you tomorrow morning."

She saw a look of satisfied misery on his face. He let out a calculated groan, collapsed on the bed face down. But he was asleep at once.

In the morning he was quite changed. He looked almost obsequious. "I'll help you to pack," he said.

"I think that's taking it too far," she said. "Besides, I am packed."

"Well, you'd better take the car for your things."

"Oh—I don't need it."

"I suppose *he* will come and fetch them."

The truth was that she had almost forgotten William.

"I'll tell you one thing," he said, in a firm organizing voice, "I shan't give you a divorce."

"I haven't asked for one," she pointed out. Then she added spitefully, "I suppose it hasn't entered your head that I could divorce you for what happened in Y——?"

His face changed. Far from not having thought of it, she saw, he had worked it all out, and had already probably taken legal advice. He had a crafty considering look, and was blinking his eyes, framing a noncommittal answer which would not give him away, when she said with a sort of gay contempt, "My poor Douglas, my poor, poor Douglas."

She picked up her suitcase and looked about. She had forgotten nothing.

"Do take the car, Matty," he pleaded sentimentally.

"Oh, well, I give up," she said. "Good, I'll be delighted to use it. I'll bring it back in half an hour."

He carried her case to the car. When they reached it, they saw Mrs. Talbot and Elaine coming towards them under the trees, which were lit with early-morning sunlight. They wore pale summer dresses and large straw hats. It was about nine in the morning.

Martha thought, What can have happened to get Mrs. Talbot out of bed so early? Then Douglas went forward to welcome them. He had slumped into a pose of weary suffering. His smile at Mrs. Talbot was the quivering smile of a child. He shook Elaine's hand wordlessly. Martha stood dumb. An idea had come into her mind: Obviously Elaine would marry Douglas. Nothing could be more satisfactory. All the same, she felt a pang at the thought of Elaine in her place, Elaine with Caroline. Almost, almost, she gave in and went back.

The three of them, Mrs.Talbot, Elaine, Douglas, were standing in a group beside the car, waiting for her to get in.

Suddenly Douglas's face worked again. "Matty, you haven't said goodbye to Caroline—surely you'll see her before you go?"

That was for the benefit of Mrs. Talbot and Elaine. She saw them exchange the briefest of shocked, comprehending smiles.

She got into the car, which was filled with books at the back. Her two suitcases were beside her. Her eyes were half blinded with tears. But she blinked them clear, and drove away.

As she reached the corner of the street she saw Mr. Maynard come strolling down under the trees on his way to the courts. He raised his hand, and she stopped.

"Deserting?" he enquired.

"Quite so."

"You look extraordinarily pleased about it." It was true, she was now so elated she felt as light as an air bubble. "Well, what are you going to do now?"

She misunderstood him and said, "I'm going to drop my things in my room, look for a job, and then—there are five hundred envelopes to be addressed before tomorrow morning." She said it as if describing the height of human bliss.

"Well, well, well," he commented.

She slowly let out the clutch.

"I suppose with the French Revolution for a father and the Russian Revolution for a mother, you can very well dispense with a family," he observed.

She pushed in the clutch again and looked at him from behind that veil which was between her and the rest of the world. After a while she conceded, "That is really a very intelligent remark."

"Not at all."

"I really am in a hurry, Mr. Maynard."

"So I can see. I'm not going to forgive you for leaving my god-daughter," he said, smiling painfully.

"I haven't asked you to," she said coldly, wincing. She shrugged herself up in the driver's seat as if chilly, and her face looked pinched and bleak.

"Well, good luck, at any rate," he said suddenly, rather gruff.

Her smile at him was painful. She was going to cry, he could see. He hastily raised his hat, and walked off in one direction, while the car slid off in another.